Praise for the Riddle-Master Trilogy

"It is a rare thing that Patricia McKillip has done, to write a fantasy trilogy good enough to be compared to Tolkien, and yet to have very little that is Tolkienesque about it. Her 'Riddle-Master' books are, in fact, very close to true originals and can be compared to *The Lord of the Rings* only in the broadest sense that they are both set in a magical, created world that is made very real to the reader."

—*A Reader's Guide to Fantasy*, by Baird Searles,
Beth Meacham, and Michael Franklin

"McKillip has created powerful images of a haunting silence, a universe full of secret purposes and terrible possibilities."

— *The National Observer*

"An intricate plot accented by distinctive writing and evocative imagery."

—*ALA Booklist*

"Patricia A. McKillip has created a world populated by mysterious harpists, riddle-masters who preserve the ancient wisdoms in Gaelic triad-like questions/strictures, land-heirs magically tied to their native soil, and overseeing it all, an intriguing entity known only as the High One, who may be many things. I couldn't put it down."

— Katherine Kurtz,
author of *The Chronicles of Deryni*

"Patricia McKillip is far and away the best of the younger fantasy writers. She is a storytelling sorceress, just now coming into her full power."

— Peter S. Beagle,
author of *The Last Unicorn*

Ace Books by Patricia A. McKillip

THE FORGOTTEN BEASTS OF ELD
THE SORCERESS AND THE CYGNET
THE CYGNET AND THE FIREBIRD
THE BOOK OF ATRIX WOLFE
WINTER ROSE
SONG FOR THE BASILISK
RIDDLE-MASTER: THE COMPLETE TRILOGY
THE TOWER AT STONY WOOD
OMBRIA IN SHADOW
IN THE FORESTS OF SERRE
ALPHABET OF THORN
OD MAGIC
HARROWING THE DRAGON
SOLSTICE WOOD
THE BELL AT SEALEY HEAD

Collected Works

CYGNET

Riddle-Master

The Complete Trilogy

PATRICIA A. MCKILLIP

THE BERKLEY PUBLISHING GROUP
Published by the Penguin Group
Penguin Group (USA) Inc.
375 Hudson Street, New York, New York 10014, USA
Penguin Group (Canada), 90 Eglinton Avenue East, Suite 700, Toronto, Ontario M4P 2Y3, Canada
(a division of Pearson Penguin Canada Inc.)
Penguin Books Ltd., 80 Strand, London WC2R 0RL, England
Penguin Group Ireland, 25 St. Stephen's Green, Dublin 2, Ireland (a division of Penguin Books Ltd.)
Penguin Group (Australia), 250 Camberwell Road, Camberwell, Victoria 3124, Australia
(a division of Pearson Australia Group Pty. Ltd.)
Penguin Books India Pvt. Ltd., 11 Community Centre, Panchsheel Park, New Delhi—110 017, India
Penguin Group (NZ), Cnr Airborne and Rosedale Roads, Albany, Auckland 1310, New Zealand
(a division of Pearson New Zealand Ltd.)
Penguin Books (South Africa) (Pty.) Ltd., 24 Sturdee Avenue, Rosebank, Johannesburg 2196, South Africa

Penguin Books Ltd., Registered Offices: 80 Strand, London WC2R 0RL, England

RIDDLE-MASTER

Cover art by Kinuko Y. Craft.

PRINTING HISTORY
The Riddle-Master of Hed, Del Rey edition published 1976
Heir of Sea and Fire, Del Rey edition published 1977
Harpist in the Wind, Del Rey edition published 1979
Ace trade paperback omnibus edition / March 1999

Ace trade paperback ISBN: 0-441-00596-9

Visit our website at
www.penguin.com

PRINTED IN THE UNITED STATES OF AMERICA

30 29 28 27 26

Introduction

LONG AGO, WHEN I was very young, and the science fiction and fantasy section of the typical bookstore was about the same length as from my nose to my thumb, I discovered Tolkien's *Lord of the Rings* trilogy. Even now, just typing those words onto my computer screen makes a magic spell across time. I remember traveling in those distant lands in the company of hobbits and heroes, the way you remember a journey to a foreign country when you were a child. Then the world was entirely new; there were no comparisons between then and now, between what might have been and what is. Everything was possible; everything was unfamiliar; everything seemed powerful in its strangeness, its potential, its past, its language. *I want to write that,* I thought, as passionately as anyone else my age and of my generation who had been scribbling fairy tales and Ruritanian romances for years, and who had read everything from *Hamlet* to *The City and the Pillar*, and who had never run across anything like that trilogy in her reading life. I only knew that I wanted to go back to the place where I had been in those books, to that land, that richness, that mystery, that story.

Some twelve years, thousands of pages and many versions later, I finished the *Riddle-Master* trilogy. Even after so many years, I can find small jewels of inspiration mined from Tolkien's novels: the riddling, the underground waters and caves, the sense of destiny, prophecy inherent in the myth of the return of the king. Of course those little tinkerings with mallet and pick led me, through those twelve years, to some major mining projects, much shoveling and boring into myths and early poetry, epics and eddas, into the fascinating fool's gold of *The White Goddess,* into the rich and strangely unmined possibilities for female heroes, which glittered with color and a wealth of tales for the taking. What I found in Tolkien inspired me to learn; what I learned I put into *The Riddle-Master of Hed, Heir of Sea and Fire,* and *Harpist in the Wind.*

I can't say, though I've been asked, that the *Riddle-Master* trilogy was the work I've cherished most, or that it is closest to my heart. It certainly was then; but this is not then, this is now. It is, and will always be, closest to my childhood's heart, the heart of whoever that young woman was who wrote those novels. She taught me magic, and the love of storytelling, which are two things that do not die unless you let them. Beyond that, I won't speak for her. She chose this story, which I could not write now any more than I could wear her improbable clothes. But now and then I still catch glimpses of that land that once she traveled, across hundreds of miles of binder paper, and I think, as if it were a true country: I have been there. I remember.

The Riddle-Master of Hed

For Carol
the first eleven chapters

Harpist in the Wind

For all who waited, and especially
for Steve Donaldson,
who always called at the right time

for Gail,
who reminded me of the difference
between logic and grace

and for Kathy,
who waited the longest.

Map by Kathy McKillip

Notes on people and places may be found on page 573

Riddle-Master

The Complete Trilogy

The Riddle-Master of Hed

1

MORGON OF HED met the High One's harpist one autumn day when the trade-ships docked at Tol for the season's exchange of goods. A small boy caught sight of the round-hulled ships with their billowing sails striped red and blue and green, picking their way among the tiny fishing boats in the distance, and ran up the coast from Tol to Akren, the house of Morgon, Prince of Hed. There he disrupted an argument, gave his message, and sat down at the long, nearly deserted tables to forage whatever was left of breakfast. The Prince of Hed, who was recovering slowly from the effects of loading two carts of beer for trading the evening before, ran a reddened eye over the tables and shouted for his sister.

"But, Morgon," said Harl Stone, one of his farmers, who had a shock of hair grey as a grindstone and a body like a sack of grain. "What about the white bull from An you said you wanted? The wine can wait—"

"What," Morgon said, "about the grain still in Wyndon Amory's storage barn in east Hed? Someone has to bring it to Tol for the traders. Why doesn't anything ever get done around here?"

"We loaded the beer," his brother Eliard, clear-eyed and malicious reminded him.

"Thank you. Where is Tristan? Tristan!"

"What!" Tristan of Hed said irritably behind him, holding the ends of her dark, unfinished braids in her fists.

"Get the wine now and the bull next spring," Cannon Master, who had grown up with Morgon, suggested briskly. "We're sadly low on Herun wine; we've barely enough to make it through winter."

Eliard broke in, gazing at Tristan. "I wish I had nothing better to do than sit around all morning braiding my hair and washing my face in buttermilk."

"At least I wash. You smell like beer. You all do. And who tracked mud all over the floor?"

They looked down at their feet. A year ago Tristan had been a thin, brown reed of a girl, prone to walking field walls barefoot and whistling through her front teeth. Now she spent much of her time scowling at her face in mirrors and at anyone in range beyond them. She transferred her scowl from Eliard to Morgon.

"What were you bellowing at me for?"

The Prince of Hed closed his eyes. "I'm sorry. I didn't mean to bellow. I simply want you to clear the tables, lay the cloths, reset them, fill pitchers of milk and wine, have them fix platters of meat, cheese, fruit and vegetables in the kitchen, braid your hair, put your shoes on and get the mud off the floor. The traders are coming."

"Oh, Morgon . . ." Tristan wailed. Morgon turned to Eliard.

"And you ride to east Hed and tell Wyndon to get his grain to Tol."

"Oh, Morgon. That's a day's ride!"

"I know. So go."

They stood unmoving, their faces flushed, while Morgon's farmers looked on in unabashed amusement. They were not alike, the three children of Athol of Hed and Spring Oakland. Tristan, with her flighty black hair and small, triangular face, favored their mother. Eliard, two years younger than Morgon, had Athol's broad shoulders and big bones, and his fair, feathery hair. Morgon, with his hair and eyes the color of light beer, bore the stamp of their grandmother, whom the old men remembered as a slender, proud woman from south Hed: Lathe Wold's daughter. She had had a trick of looking at people the way Morgon was gazing at Eliard, remotely, like a fox glancing up from a pile of chicken feathers. Eliard puffed his cheeks like a bellows and sighed.

"If I had a horse from An, I could be there and back again by supper."

"I'll go," said Cannon Master. There was a touch of color in his face.

"I'll go," Eliard said.

"No, I want . . . I haven't seen Arin Amory for a while. I'll go." He glanced at Morgon.

"I don't care," Morgon said. "Just don't forget why you're going. Eliard, you help with the loading at Tol. Grim, I'll need you with me to barter—the last time I did it alone, I nearly traded three plow horses for a harp with no strings."

"If you get a harp," Eliard interrupted, "I want a horse from An."

"And I have to have some cloth from Herun," Tristan said. "Morgon, I have to have it. Orange cloth. Also I need thin needles and a pair of shoes from Isig, and some silver buttons, and—"

"What," Morgon demanded, "do you think grows in our fields?"

"I know what grows in our fields. I also know what I've been sweeping around under your bed for six months. I think you should either wear it or sell it. The dust is so thick on it you can't even see the colors of the jewels."

There was silence, brief and unexpected, in the hall. Tristan stood with her arms folded, the ends of her braids coming undone. Her chin was raised challengingly, but there was a hint of uncertainty in her eyes as she faced Morgon. Eliard's mouth was open. He closed it with a click of teeth.

"What jewels?"

"It's a crown," Tristan said. "I saw one in a picture in a book of Morgon's. Kings wear them."

"I know what a crown is." He looked at Morgon, awed. "What on earth did you trade for that? Half of Hed?"

"I never knew you wanted a crown," Cannon Master said wonderingly. "Your father never had one. Your grandfather never had one. Your—"

"Cannon," Morgon said. He raised his hands, dropped the heels of them over his eyes. The blood was high in his face. "Kern had one."

"Who?"

"Kern of Hed. He would be our great-great-great-great-great-great-great-great-grandfather. No. One more great. It was made of silver, with a green jewel in it shaped like a cabbage. He traded it one day for twenty barrels of Herun wine, thereby instigating—"

"Don't change the subject," Eliard said sharply. "Where did you get it? Did you trade for it? Or did you . . ." He stopped. Morgon lifted his hands from his eyes.

"Did I what?"

"Nothing. Stop looking at me like that. You're trying to change the subject again. You traded for it, or you stole it, or you murdered someone for it—"

"Now, then—" Grim Oakland, Morgon's portly overseer, said placatingly.

"Or you just found it lying in the corncrib one day, like a dead rat. Which?"

"I did not murder anyone!" Morgon shouted. The clink of pots from the kitchen stopped abruptly. He lowered his voice, went on tartly, "What are you accusing me of?"

"I didn't—"

"I did not harm anyone to get that crown; I did not trade anything that doesn't belong to me for it; I did not steal it—"

"I wasn't—"

"It belongs to me by right. What right, you have not touched on yet. You asked a riddle and tried to answer it; you are wrong four times. If I bumbled through riddles like that, I wouldn't be here talking to you now. I am going down to welcome the traders at Tol. When you decide to do some work this morning, you might join me."

He turned. He got as far as the front steps when Eliard, the blood mounting to his face, broke away from the transfixed group, moved across the room with a speed belied by his size, threw his arms around Morgon and brought him off the steps face down in the dirt.

The chickens and geese scattered, squawking indignantly. The farmers, the small boy from Tol, the woman who cooked, and the girl who washed pots jammed the door at once, clucking.

Morgon, groping for the breath the smack of the earth had knocked out of him, lay still while Eliard said between his teeth, "Can't you answer a simple question? What do you mean you wouldn't be talking to me now? Morgon, what did you do for that crown? Where did you get it? What did you do? I swear I'll—"

Morgon lifted his head dizzily. "I got it in a tower." He twisted suddenly, throwing Eliard off balance into one of Tristan's rosebushes.

The battle was brief and engrossing. Morgon's farmers, who until the previous spring had been under Athol's placid, efficient rule, stared half-shocked, half-grinning as the Prince of Hed was sent rolling across a mud puddle, staggered to his feet, and, head lowered like a bull, launched himself at his brother. Eliard shook himself free and countered with a swing of his fist that, connecting, sounded in the still air like the distant thunk of ax into wood. Morgon dropped like a sack of grain.

Then Eliard fell to his knees beside the prone body and said, aghast, "I'm sorry. I'm sorry. Morgon, did I hurt you?"

And Tristan, mute and furious, dumped a bucket of milk over their heads.

There was an odd explosion of whimpering from the porch as Cannon Master sat down on a step and buried his face in his knees. Eliard looked down at his muddy, sodden tunic. He brushed futilely at it.

"Now look what you did," he said plaintively. "Morgon?"

"You squashed my rosebush," Tristan said. "Look what you did to Morgon in front of everybody." She sat down beside Morgon on the wet ground. Her face had lost its habitual scowl. She wiped Morgon's face with her apron. Morgon blinked dazedly, his eyelashes beaded with milk. Eliard sat back on his haunches.

"Morgon, I'm sorry. But don't think you can evade the issue this way."

Morgon moved a hand cautiously after a moment, touched his mouth. "What's—? What was the issue?" he asked huskily.

"Never mind," Tristan said. "It's hardly something to brawl about."

"What is this all over me?"

"Milk."

"I'm sorry," Eliard said again. He put a coaxing hand under Morgon's shoulder, but Morgon shook his head.

"Just let me lie here for a moment. Why did you hit me like that? First you accuse me of murder and then you hit me and pour milk all over me. It's sour. Sour milk. You poured sour milk all over—"

"I did," Tristan said. "It was milk for the pigs. You threw Eliard into my rosebush." She touched Morgon's mouth again with her apron. "In front of everyone. I'm so humiliated."

"What did I do?" Morgon said. Eliard sighed, nursing a tender spot over his ribs.

"You made me lose my temper, speaking to me like that. You're slippery as a fish, but I grasped one thing. Last spring you got a crown you shouldn't have. You said that if you answered riddles as badly as I do, you wouldn't be here now. I want to know why. Why?"

Morgon was silent. He sat up after a moment, drawing his knees up, and dropped his head against them.

"Tristan, why did you pick today of all days to bring that up?"

"Go ahead, blame me," Tristan said without rancor. "Here I am running around with patches at my elbows, and you with pearls and jewels under your bed."

"You wouldn't have patches if you'd tell Narly Stone to make you some clothes that fit. You're growing, that's all—"

"Will you stop changing the subject!"

Morgon lifted his head. "Stop shouting." He glanced over Eliard's shoulder at the row of motionless, fascinated figures, and sighed. He slid his hands over his face, up through his hair. "I won that crown in a riddle-game I played in An with a ghost."

"Oh." Eliard's voice rose again sharply. "A what?"

"The wraith of Peven, Lord of Aum. That crown under my bed is the crown of the Kings of Aum. They were conquered by Oen of An six hundred years ago. Peven is five hundred years old. He lives bound in his tower by Oen and the Kings of An."

"What did he look like?" Tristan asked. Her voice was hushed. Morgon shrugged slightly; his eyes were hidden from them.

"An old man. An old lord with the answers to a thousand riddles in his eyes. He had a standing wager going that no one could win a riddle-game with him. So I sailed over with the traders and challenged him. He said great lords of Aum, An and Hel—the three portions of An—and even riddle-masters from Caithnard had challenged him to a game, but never a farmer from Hed. I told him I read a lot. Then we played the game. And I won. So I brought the crown home and put it under my bed until I could decide what to do with it. Now, was that worth all the shouting?"

"He forfeited his crown to you when he lost," Eliard said evenly. "What would you have forfeited if you had lost?"

Morgon felt his split mouth gingerly. His eyes strayed to the fields beyond Eliard's back. "Well," he said finally. "You see, I had to win."

Eliard stood up abruptly. He took two strides away from Morgon, his hands clenched. Then he turned around and came back and squatted down again.

"You fool."

"Don't start another fight," Tristan begged.

"I'm not a fool," Morgon said. "I won the game, didn't I?" His face was still, his eyes distant, steady on Eliard's face. "Kern of Hed, the Prince with the cabbage on his crown—"

"Don't change—"

"I'm not. Kern of Hed, in addition to being the only Prince of Hed besides me to own a crown, had the dubious fortune of being pursued one day by a Thing without a name. Perhaps it was the effects of Herun wine. The Thing called his name over and over. He ran from it, going into his house of seven rooms and seven doors, and locking each door behind him until he came to the inmost chamber, where he could run no farther. And he heard the sound of one door after another being torn open, and his name called each time. He counted six doors opened, his name called six times. Then, outside the seventh door, his name was called again, but the Thing did not touch the door. He waited in despair for it to enter, but it did not. Then he grew impatient, longing for it to enter, but it did not. Finally he reached out, opened the door himself. The Thing was gone. And he was left to wonder, all the days of his life, what it was that had called out to him."

He stopped. Eliard said in spite of himself, "Well, what was it?"

"Kern didn't open the door. That is the only riddle to come out of Hed. The stricture, according to the Riddle-Masters at Caithnard is this: Answer the unanswered riddle. So I do."

"It's not your business! Your business is farming, not risking your life in a stupid riddle-game with a ghost for a crown that's worthless because you keep it hidden under your bed. Did you think of us, then? Did you go before or after they died? Before or after?"

"After," Tristan said.

Eliard's fist splashed down in a pool of milk. "I knew it."

"I came back."

"Suppose you hadn't?"

"I came back! Why can't you try to understand, instead of thinking as though your brains are made of oak. Athol's son, with his hair and eyes and vision—"

"No!" Tristan said sharply. Eliard's fist, raised and knotted, halted in midair. Morgon dropped his face again against his knees. Eliard shut his eyes.

"Why do you think I'm so angry?" he whispered.

"I know."

"Do you? Even—even after six months, I still expect to hear her voice unexpectedly, or see him coming out of the barn, or in from the fields at dusk. And you? How will I know, now, that when you leave Hed, you'll come back? You could have died in that tower for the sake of a stupid crown and left us watching for the ghost of you, too. Swear you'll never do anything like that again."

"I can't."

"You can."

Morgon raised his head, looked at Eliard. "How can I make one promise to you and another to myself? But I swear this: I will always come back."

"How can you—"

"I swear it."

Eliard stared down at the mud. "It's because he let you go to that college. That's where your priorities were confused."

"I suppose so," Morgon said wearily. He glanced up at the sun. "Half the morning gone, and here we sit in the muck with sour milk drying on our hair. Why did you wait so long to ask me about the crown?" he asked Tristan. "That's not like you."

She shrugged a little, her face averted. "I saw your face, the day you came back with it. What are you going to do with it?"

He moved a strand of hair out of her eyes. "I don't know. I suppose I should do something with it."

"Well, I have a few suggestions."

"I thought you might." He stood up stiffly and caught sight of Cannon sitting on the porch. "I thought you were going to east Hed," he said pointedly.

"I'm going. I'm going." Cannon said cheerfully. "Wyndon Amory would never have forgiven me if I hadn't seen the end of this. Have you still got all your teeth?"

"I think so." The group at the doorway began shifting, breaking up under his gaze. He reached down, pulled Eliard to his feet. "What's the matter?"

"Nothing that isn't ordinarily the matter when you roll over a rosebush. I don't know if I have a clean tunic."

"You do," Tristan said. "I washed your clothes yesterday. The house is a mess; you—we're a mess, and the traders are coming, which means all the women will be coming over to look at their wares in our dirty hall. I'll die of shame."

"You never used to care," Eliard commented. "Now you're always complaining. You used to run around with mud on your feet and dog hair all over your skirt."

"That," Tristan said icily, "was when there was someone to take care of the house. Now there isn't. I do try." She whirled away, the hens fluttering out of her path. Eliard felt at his stiff hair, sighing.

"My brains are made of oak. If you pump for me, I'll pump for you."

They stripped and washed behind the house. Then Eliard went to Grim Oakland's farm to help load the grain in his storage barn onto carts, and Morgon walked through the stubbled fields to the shore road that led to Tol.

The three trade-ships, their sails furled, had just docked. A ramp boomed down from one of them as Morgon stepped onto the wharf; he watched a horse being led down by a sailor, a beautiful, long-legged mare bred in An, jet black, with a bridle that flashed minute flecks of jewels in the sun. Then traders hailed him from the prow of a ship, and he went to meet them as they disembarked.

They were a vivid group, some dressed in the long, thin, orange and red coats from Herun, others in full robes from An, or the close-fitting, lavishly embroidered tunics from Ymris. They wore rings and chains from Isig, fur-lined caps from Osterland, which they gave away, together with bone-handled knives and copper brooches, to the children clustering shyly to watch. The ships carried, among other things, iron from Isig and Herun wine.

Grim Oakland came a few minutes later, as Morgon was inspecting the wine.

"I'd need a drink, too, after that," he commented. Morgon started to smile and changed his mind.

"Is the grain loaded?"

"Nearly. Harl Stone is bringing the wool and skins down from your barn. You'd be wise to take all the metal they carry."

Morgon nodded, his eyes straying again to the black horse tethered to the dock rail. A sailor lugged a saddle down from the ship, balanced it on the rail next to the horse. Morgon gestured with his cup.

"Who owns that mare? It looks like someone came with the traders. Or else Eliard traded Akren for her secretly."

"I don't know," Grim said, his red-grey brows peaked. "Lad, it's none of my business, but you shouldn't let your private inclinations interfere with the duty you were born to."

Morgon sipped wine. "They don't interfere."

"It would be a grave interference if you were dead."

He shrugged. "There's Eliard."

Grim heaved a sigh. "I told your father not to send you to that school. It addled your thinking. But no. He wouldn't listen. I told him it was wrong to let you go away from Hed so long; it's never been done, no good would come of it. And I was right. No good has come. You running off to a strange land, playing riddle-games with—with a man who should have the decency to stay put once he's dead and buried in the earth. It's not good. It's not—it's not the way a land-ruler of Hed should want to behave. It's not done."

Morgon held the cool metal of the cup against his cracked mouth. "Peven couldn't help wandering around after he was dead. He killed seven of his sons with misused wizardry, and then himself out of sorrow and shame. He couldn't rest in the ground. He told me that after so many years he had a hard time remembering all his sons' names. That worried him. I learned their names at Caithnard, so I could tell him. It cheered him up."

Grim's face was red as a turkey wattle. "It's indecent," he snapped. He moved away, lifted the lid on a chest full of bars of iron, and slammed it shut again. A trader spoke at Morgon's elbow.

"You are pleased with the wine, Lord?"

Morgon turned, nodding. The trader ported a thin, leaf-green coat from Herun, a cap of white mink, and a harp of black wood slung by a strap of white leather over one shoulder. Morgon said, "Whose horse? Where did you get that harp?"

The trader grinned, sliding it from his shoulder. "Remembering how your lordship likes harps, I found this one for you in An. It was the harp of the harpist of Lord Col of Hel. It is quite old, but see how beautifully preserved."

Morgon slid his hands down the fine, carved pieces. He brushed the strings with his fingers, then plucked one softly. "What would I do with all those strings?" he murmured. "There must be over thirty."

"Do you like it? Keep it with you awhile; play it."

"I can't possibly . . ."

The trader silenced him with a flick of hand. "How can you set a value to such a harp? Take it, become acquainted with it; there is no need to make a decision now." He slipped the strap over Morgon's head. "If you like it, no doubt we can come to a satisfactory arrangement . . ."

"No doubt." He caught Grim Oakland's eye and blushed.

He carried the harp with him to the trade-hall at Tol, where the traders inspected his beer, grain and wool, ate cheese and fruit, and bartered for an hour with him while Grim Oakland stood watchfully at his elbow. Empty carts were brought to the dock then, to load metal, casks of wine, and blocks of salt from the beds above Caithnard. Plow horses to be taken to Herun and An were penned near the dock for loading; the traders began to tally the grain sacks and kegs of beer. Wyndon Amory's carts lumbered down the coast road, unexpectedly, near noon.

Cannon Master, riding in the back of one, leaped down and said to Morgon, "Wyndon sent them out yesterday; one of them lost a wheel so the drivers fixed it at Sil Wold's farm and stayed the night. I met them coming. Did they talk you into the harp?"

"Almost. Listen to it."

"Morgon, you know I'm as musical as a tin bucket. Your mouth looks like a squashed plum."

"Don't make me laugh," Morgon pleaded. "Will you and Eliard take the traders to Akren? They're about finished here."

"What are you going to do?"

"Buy a horse. And a pair of shoes."

Cannon's brows rose. "And a harp?"

"Maybe. Yes."

He chuckled. "Good. I'll take Eliard away for you."

Morgon wandered down into the belly of a ship where half a dozen horses from An were stabled for the journey. He studied them while men stacked sacks of grain beyond him in the shadowy hold. A trader found him there; they talked awhile, Morgon running his fingers down the sleek neck of a stallion the color of polished wood. He emerged finally, drawing deep breaths of clean air. Most of the carts were gone; the sailors were drifting toward the trade-hall to eat. The sea nuzzled the ships, swirled white around the massive trunks of pine supporting the docks. He went to the end of the pier and sat down. In the distance, the fishing boats from Tol rose and dipped like ducks in the water; far beyond them, a dark thread along the horizon, lay the vast, sprawling mainland, the realm of the High One.

He set the harp on one knee and played a harvest-song whose brisk, even rhythm kept time to the sweep of a scythe. A fragment of a Ymris ballad teased his memory; he was picking it out haltingly from the strings when a shadow fell over his hands. He looked up.

A man he had never seen before, neither trader nor sailor, stood beside him. He was quietly dressed; the fine cloth and color of his blue-black tunic, the heavy chain of linked, stamped squares of silver on his breast were bewildering. His face was lean, fine-boned, neither young nor old; his hair was a loose cap of silver.

"Morgon of Hed?"

"Yes."

"I am Deth, the High One's harpist."

Morgon swallowed. He shifted to rise, but the harpist forestalled him, squatting down to look at the harp.

"Uon," he said, showing Morgon a name half-hidden in a whorl of design. "He was a harpmaker in Hel three centuries ago. There are only five of his harps in existence."

"The trader said it belonged to the harpist of Lord Col. Did you come—? You must have come with them. Is that your horse? Why didn't you tell me before that you were here?"

"You were busy; I preferred to wait. The High One instructed me last spring to come to Hed, to express his sorrow over the deaths of Athol and Spring. But I was trapped in Isig by a stubborn winter, delayed in Ymris by a seige of Caerweddin, and requested, just as I was about to embark from Caithnard, in an urgent message from Mathom of An, to get to Anuin. I'm sorry to have come so late."

"I remember your name," Morgon said slowly. "My father used to say Deth played at his wedding." He stopped, listening to his words; a shudder weltered out of him unexpectedly. "I'm sorry. He thought it was funny. He loved your harping. I would like to hear you play."

The harpist settled himself on the pier and picked up Uon's harp. "What would you like to hear?"

Morgon felt his mouth pulled awry in spite of himself by a smile. "Play . . . let me think. Would you play what I was trying to play?"

"'The Lament for Belu and Bilo.'" Deth tuned a string softly and began the ancient ballad.

Belu so fair was born with the dark
Bilo, the dark; death bound them also.
Mourn Belu, fine ladies,
Mourn Bilo.

His fingers drew the tale faultlessly from the flashing, close-set strings. Morgon listened motionlessly, his eyes on the smooth, detached face. The skilled hands, the fine voice worn to precision, traced the path of Bilo, helpless in its turbulence, the death he left in his wake, the death that trailed him, that rode behind Belu on his horse, ran at his horse's side like a hound.

Belu so fair followed the dark
Bilo; death followed them so;
Death cried to Bilo out of Belu's voice,
to Belu, out of Bilo . . .

The long, surfeited sigh of the tide broke the silence of their deaths. Morgon stirred. He put his hand on the dark, carved face of the harp.

"If I could make that sound come out of that harp, I would sell my name for it and go nameless."

Deth smiled. "That's too high a price to pay even for one of Uon's harps. What are the traders asking for it?"

He shrugged. "They'll take what I'm offering for it."

"You want it that badly?"

Morgon looked at him. "I would sell my name for it, but not the grain my farmers have scorched their backs harvesting, or the horses they have raised and gentled. What I will offer belongs only to me."

"There's no need to justify yourself to me," the harpist said mildly. Morgon's mouth crooked; he touched it absently.

"I'm sorry. I spent half the morning justifying myself."

"For what?"

His eyes dropped to the rough, iron-bound planks of the pier; he answered the quiet, skilled stranger impulsively. "Do you know how my parents died?"

"Yes."

"My mother wanted to see Caithnard. My father had come two or three times to visit me while I was at the College of Riddle-Masters at Caithnard. That sounds simple, but it was a very courageous thing for him to do: leave Hed, go to a great strange city. The Princes of Hed are rooted to Hed. When I came home a year ago, after spending three years there, I found my father full of stories about what he had seen—the trade-shops, the people from different lands—and when he mentioned a shop with bolts of cloth and furs and dyes from five kingdoms, my mother couldn't resist going. She loved the feel and colors of fine cloth. So last spring they sailed over with the traders when the spring trading was done. And they never came back. The return ship was lost. They never came back." He touched a nailhead, traced a circle around it. "There was something I had been wanting to do for a long time. I did it, then. My brother Eliard found out about it this morning. I didn't tell him at the time because I knew he would be upset. I just told him that I was going to west Hed for a few days, not that I was going across the sea to An."

"To An? Why did you—" He stopped. His voice went suddenly thin as a lath. "Morgon of Hed, did you win Peven's crown?"

Morgon's head rose sharply. He said after a moment, "Yes. How—? Yes."

"You didn't tell the King of An—"

"I didn't tell anyone. I didn't want to talk about it."

"Auber of Aum, one of the descendents of Peven, went to that tower to try to win back the crown of Aum from the dead lord and found the crown gone and Peven pleading to be set free to leave the tower. Auber demanded in vain the name of the man who had taken the crown; Peven said only that he would answer no more riddles. Auber told Mathom, and Mathom, faced with the news that someone had slipped quietly into his land, won a riddle-game men have lost their lives over for centuries, and left as quietly, summoned me from Caithnard and asked me to find that crown. Hed is the last place I expected it to be."

"It's been under my bed," Morgon said blankly. "The only private place in Akren. I don't understand. Does Mathom want it back? I don't need it. I haven't even looked at it since I brought it home. But I thought Mathom of all people would understand—"

"The crown is yours by right. Mathom would be the last to contest that." He paused; there was an expression in his eyes that puzzled Morgon. He added gently, "And yours, if you choose, is Mathom's daughter, Raederle."

Morgon swallowed. He found himself on his feet, looking down at the harpist, and he knelt down, seeing suddenly, instead of the harpist, a pale, high-boned face full of unexpected expressions, shaking itself free of a long, fine mass of red hair.

He whispered, "Raederle. I know her. Mathom's son Rood was at the college with me; we were good friends. She used to visit him there. . . . I don't understand."

"The King made a vow at her birth to give her only to the man who took the crown of Aum from Peven."

"He made a . . . What a stupid thing for him to do, promising Raederle to any man with enough brains to outwit Peven. He could have been anyone—" He stopped, the blood receding a little beneath his tan. "It was me."

"Yes."

"But I can't . . . She can't marry a farmer. Mathom will never consent."

"Mathom follows his own inclinations. I suggest you ask him."

Morgon gazed at him. "You mean cross the sea to Anuin, to the king's court, walk into his great hall in cold blood and ask him?"

"You walked into Peven's tower."

"That was different. I didn't have lords from the three portions of An watching me, then."

"Morgon, Mathom bound himself to his vow with his own name, and the lords of An, who have lost ancestors, brothers, even sons in that tower, will give you nothing less than honor for your courage and wit. The only question you have to consider at this moment is: Do you want to marry Raederle?"

He stood up again, desperate with uncertainty, ran his hands through his hair, and the wind, roused from the sea, whipped it straight back from his face. "Raederle." A pattern of stars high above one brow flamed vividly against his skin. He saw her face again, at a distance, turned back to look at him. "Raederle."

He saw the harpist's face go suddenly still, as if the wind had snatched in passing its expression and breath. The uncertainty ended in him like a song's ending.

"Yes."

HE SAT ON a keg of beer on the deck of a trade-ship the next morning, watching the wake widen and measure Hed like a compass. At the foot of the keg lay a pack of clothes Tristan had put together for him, talking all the while so that neither of them was sure what was in it besides the crown. It bulged oddly, as though she had put everything she touched into it, talking. Eliard had said very little. He had left Morgon's room after a while; Morgon had found him in the shed, pounding out a horseshoe.

He had said, remembering, "I was going to get you a chestnut stallion from An with the crown."

And Eliard threw the tongs and heated shoe into the water, and, gripping Morgon's shoulders, had borne him back against the wall, saying, "Don't think you can bribe me with a horse," which made no sense to Morgon, or, after a moment, to Eliard. He let go of Morgon, his face falling into easier, perplexed lines.

"I'm sorry. It just frightens me when you leave, now. Will she like it here?"

"I wish I knew."

Tristan, following him with his cloak over her arm as he prepared to leave, stopped in the middle of the hall, her face strange to him in its sudden vulnerability. She looked around at the plain, polished walls, pulled a chair straight at a table. "Morgon, I hope she can laugh," she whispered.

The ship scuttled before the wind; Hed grew small, blurred in the distance. The High One's harpist had come to stand at the railing; his grey cloak snapped behind him like a banner. Morgon's eyes wandered to his face, unlined, untouched by the sun. A sense of incongruity nudged his mind, of a riddle shaping the silver-white hair, the fine curve of bone.

The harpist turned his head, met Morgon's eyes.

Morgon asked curiously, "What land are you from?"

"No land. I was born in Lungold."

"The wizards' city? Who taught you to harp?"

"Many people. I took my name from the Morgol Cron's harpist Tirunedeth, who taught me the songs of Herun. I asked him for it before he died."

"Cron," Morgon said. "Ylcorcronlth?"

"Yes."

"He ruled Herun six hundred years ago."

"I was born," the harpist said tranquilly, "not long after the founding of Lungold, a thousand years ago."

Morgon was motionless save for the sway of his body to the sea's rhythm. Little threads of light wove and broke on the sea beyond the sunlit, detached face. He whispered, "No wonder you harp like that. You've had a thousand years to learn the harp-songs of the High One's realm. You don't look old. My father looked older when he died. Are you a wizard's son?" He looked down at his hands then, linked around his knees, and said apologetically, "Forgive me. It's none of my business. I was just—"

"Curious?" The harpist smiled. "You have an inordinate curiosity for a Prince of Hed."

"I know. That's why my father finally sent me to Caithnard—I kept asking questions. He didn't know how to account for it. But, being a wise, gentle man, he let me go." He stopped again, rather abruptly, his mouth twitching slightly.

The harpist, his eyes on the approaching land said, "I never knew my own father. I was born without a name in the back streets of Lungold at a time when wizards, kings, even the High One himself passed through the city. Since I have no land-instinct and no gifts for wizardry, I gave up long ago trying to guess who my father was."

Morgon's head lifted again. He said speculatively, "Danan Isig was ancient as a tree even then, and Har of Osterland. No one knows when the wizards were born, but if you're a wizard's son, there's no one to claim you now."

"It's not important. The wizards are gone; I owe nothing to any living ruler but the High One. In his service I have a name, a place, a freedom of movement and judgment. I am responsible only to him; he values me for my harping and my discretion, both of which are improved by age." He bent to pick up his harp, slid it over his shoulder. "We'll dock in a few moments."

Morgon joined him at the rail. The trade-city Caithnard, with its port, inns and shops, sprawled in a crescent of land between two lands. Ships, their sails bellying the orange and gold colors of Herun traders, were flocking from the north to its docks like birds. On a thrust of cliff forming one horn of the moon-shaped bay stood a dark block of a building whose stone walls and small chambers Morgon knew well. An image of the spare, mocking face of Raederle's brother rose in his mind; his hands tightened on the rail.

"Rood. I'll have to tell him. I wonder if he's at the college. I haven't seen him for a year."

"I talked with him two nights ago when I stayed at the college before crossing to Hed. He had just taken the Gold Robe of Intermediate Mastery."

"Perhaps he's gone home for a while, then." The ship took the last roll and wash of wave as it entered the harbor, then slackened speed, the sailors shouting to one another as they took in sail. Morgon's voice thinned. "I wonder what he'll say . . ."

The sea birds above the still water wove like shuttles in the wind. The docks sliding past them were littered with goods being loaded, unloaded: bolts of cloth, chests, timber, wine, fur, animals. The sailors hailed friends on the dock; traders called to one another.

"Lyle Orn's ship will leave for Anuin with the tide this evening," a trader told Deth and Morgon before they disembarked. "You'll know it by its red and yellow sails. Do you want your horse, Lord?"

"I'll walk," Deth said. He added to Morgon, as the gangplank slid down before them. "There is an unanswered riddle on the lists of the Masters at the college: Who won the riddle-game with Peven of Aum?"

Morgon slung his pack to his shoulder. He nodded. "I'll tell them. Are you going up to the college?"

"In a while."

"At evening-tide, then, Lords," the trader reminded them as they descended. They separated on the cobbled street facing the dock, and Morgon, turning left, retraced a path he had known for years. The narrow streets of the city were crowded in the high noon with traders, sailors ashore from different lands, wandering musicians, trappers, students in the bright, voluminous robes of their ranks, richly dressed men and women from An, Ymris, Herun. Morgon, his pack over one shoulder, moved through them without seeing them, oblivious to noise and jostling. The back streets quieted; the road he took wound out of the city, left tavern and trade-shop behind, rose upward above the brilliant sea.

Occasional students passed him, going toward the city, their voices, wrestling with riddles, cheerful, assured. The road angled sharply, then at the end the ground levelled, and the ancient college, built of rough dark stones, massive as a piece of broken cliff itself, stood placidly among the tall, wind-twisted trees.

He knocked at the familiar double doors of thick oak. The porter, a freckled young man in the White Robe of Beginning Mastery opened them, cast a glance over Morgon and his pack, and said portentiously, "Ask and it shall be answered here. If you have come seeking knowledge, you shall be received. The Masters are examining a candidate for the Red of Apprenticeship, and they must not be disturbed except by death or doom. Abandon your name to me."

"Morgon, Prince of Hed."

"Oh." The porter dabbed at the top of his head and smiled. "Come in. I'll get Master Tel."

"No, don't interrupt them." He stepped in. "Is Rood of An here?"

"Yes; he's on the third floor, across from the library. I'll take you."

"I know the way."

The darkness of the low arched corridors was broken at each end only by wide leaded windows set in walls of stone a foot thick. Rows of closed doors ran down each side of the hall. Morgon found Rood's name on one, on a wood slat, a crow delicately etched beneath it. He knocked, received an unintelligible answer, and opened the door.

Rood's bed, taking up a quarter of the small stone room, was piled with clothes, books, and the prince of An. He sat cross-legged in a cloud of newly acquired gold robe, reading a letter, a cup of fragile dyed glass in one hand half-full of wine. He looked up, and at the abrupt, arrogant lift of his head, Morgon felt suddenly, stepping across the threshold, as though he had stepped backward into a memory.

"Morgon." Rood heaved himself up, walked off the bed, trailing a wake of books behind him. He hugged Morgon, the cup in one hand, the letter in the other. "Join me. I'm celebrating. You are a stranger without your robe. But I forget: you're a farmer now. Is that why you're in Caithnard? Did you come over with your grain or wine or something?"

"Beer. We can't make good wine."

"How sad." He gazed at Morgon like a curious crow, his eyes red-rimmed, blurred. "I heard about your parents. The traders were full of it. It made me angry."

"Why?"

"Because it trapped you in Hed, made a farmer out of you, full of thoughts of eggs and pigs, beer and weather. You'll never come back here, and I miss you."

Morgon shifted his pack to the floor. The crown lay hidden in it like a guilty deed. He said softly, "I came . . . I have something to tell you, and I don't know how to tell you."

Rood loosed Morgon abruptly, turned away. "I don't want to hear it." He poured a second cup for Morgon and refilled his own. "I took the Gold two days ago."

"I know. Congratulations. How long have you been celebrating?"

"I don't remember." He held out the cup to Morgon, wine splashing down over his fingers. "I'm one of Mathom's children, descended from Kale and Oen by way of the witch Madir. Only one man has ever taken the Gold in less time than I have. And he went home to farm."

"Rood—"

"Have you forgotten everything you learned by now? You used to open riddles like nuts. You should have become a Master. You have a brother, you could have let him take the land-rule."

"Rood," Morgon said patiently. "You know that's impossible. And you know I didn't come here to take the Black. I never wanted it. What would I have done with it? Prune trees in it?" Rood's voice snapped back at him with a violence that startled him.

"Answer riddles! You had the gift for it; you had the eyes! You said once you wanted to win that game. Why didn't you keep your word? You went home to make beer instead, and some man without a name or a face won the two great treasures of An." He crumpled the letter, held it locked in his fist like a heart. "Who knows what she's waiting for? A man like Raith of Hel with a face beaten out of gold and a heart like a rotten tooth? Or Thistin of Aum, who's soft as a baby and too old to climb into bed without help? If she is forced to marry a man like that, I'll never forgive you or my father. Him because he made such a vow in the first place, and you because you made a promise in this room you did not keep. Ever since you left this place, I made a vow to myself to win that game with Peven, to free Raederle from that fate my father set for her. But I had no chance. I never had even a chance."

Morgon sat down on a chair beside Rood's desk. "Stop shouting. Please. Listen—"

"Listen to what? You could not even be faithful to the one rule you held true above all others." He dropped the letter, reached out abruptly, drew the hair back from Morgon's brow. "Answer the unanswered riddle."

Morgon pulled away from him. "Rood! Will you stop babbling and listen to me? It's hard enough for me to tell you this without you squawking like a drunk crow. Do you think Raederle will mind living on a farm? I have to know."

"Don't profane crows; some of my ancestors were crows. Of course Raederle can't live on a farm. She is the second most beautiful woman in the three portions of An; she can't live among pigs and—" He stopped abruptly, still in the middle of the room, his shadow motionless across the stones. Under the weight of his lightless gaze a word jumped in the back of Morgon's throat. Rood whispered, "Why?"

Morgon bent to his pack, his fingers shaking faintly on the ties. As he drew out the crown, the great center stone, colorless itself, groping wildly at all the colors in the room, snared the gold of Rood's robe and blazed like a sun. Transfixed in its liquid glare, Rood caught his breath sharply and shouted.

Morgon dropped the crown. He put his face against his knees, his hands over his ears. The wine glass on the desk snapped; the flagon on a tiny table shattered, spilling wine onto the stones. The iron lock on a massive book sprang open; the chamber door slammed shut with a boom.

Cries of outrage down the long corridors followed like an echo. Morgon, the blood pounding in his head, straightened. He whispered, his fingers sliding over his eyes, "It wasn't necessary to shout. You take the crown to Mathom. I'm going home." He stood up, and Rood caught his wrist in a grip that drove to the bone.

"You."

He stopped. Rood's hold eased; he reached behind Morgon and turned the key in the door against the indignant pounding on it. His face looked strange, as though the shout had cleared his mind of all but an essential wonder.

He said, his voice catching a little, "Sit down. I can't. Morgon, why didn't . . . why didn't you tell me you were going to challenge Peven?"

"I did. I told you two years ago when we had sat up all night asking each other riddles, studying for the Blue of Partial Beginning."

"But what did you do—leave Hed without telling anyone, leave Caithnard without telling me, move unobtrusively as a doom through my father's land to face death in that dark tower that stinks in an east wind? You didn't even tell me that you had won. You could have done that. Any lord of An would have brought it to Anuin with a flourish of shouts and trumpets."

"I didn't mean to worry Raederle. I simply didn't know about your father's vow. You never told me."

"Well, what did you expect me to do? I have seen great lords leave Anuin to go to that tower for her sake and never return. Do you think I wanted to give you that kind of incentive? Why did you do it, if not for her, or for the honor of walking into the court at Anuin with that crown? It couldn't have been pride in your knowledge—you didn't even tell the Masters."

Morgon picked up the crown, turned it in his hands. The center stone faced him, striped with the dust and green of his tunic. "Because I had to do it. For no other reason than that. And I didn't tell anyone simply because it was such a private thing . . . and because I didn't know, coming alive out of that tower at dawn, if I were a great riddle-master or a very great fool." He looked at Rood. "What will Raederle say?"

The corner of Rood's mouth crooked up suddenly. "I have no idea. Morgon, you caused an uproar in An the like of which has not been experienced since Madir stole the pigherds of Hel and set them loose in the cornfields of Aum. Raederle wrote to me that Raith of Hel promised to abduct her and marry her secretly at her word; that Duac, who has always been as close to our father as his shadow, is furious about the vow and has scarcely spoken three words to him all summer; that the lords of the three portions are angry with him, insisting he break his vow. But it is easier to change the wind with your breath than our father's incomprehensible mind. Raederle said she has been having terrible dreams about some huge, faceless, nameless stranger riding to Anuin with the crown of Aum on his head, claiming her and taking her away to some rich, loveless land inside some mountain or beneath the sea. My father has sent men all over An searching for the man who took that crown; he sent messengers here to the college; he has asked the traders to ask wherever in the High One's realm they go. He didn't think of asking in Hed. I didn't either. I should have. I should have known it would not be some powerful, nightmarish figure—it would be something even more unexpected. We have been expecting anyone but you."

Morgon traced a pearl, milky as a child's tooth, with one finger. "I'll love her," he said. "Will that matter?"

"What do you think?"

Morgon reached for his pack restlessly. "I don't know, and neither do you. I am terrified of the look that will be on her face when she sees the crown of Aum carried into Anuin by me. She'll have to live at Akren. She'll have to . . . she'll have to get used to my pigherder, Snog Nutt. He comes for breakfast every morning. Rood, she won't like it. She was born to the wealth of An, and she'll be horrified. So will your father."

"I doubt it," Rood said calmly. "The lords of An may be, but it would take the doom of the world to horrify my father. For all I know, he saw you seventeen years ago when he made that vow. He has a mind like a morass, no one, not even Duac, knows how deep it is. I don't know what Raederle will think. I only know that I would not miss seeing this if my death were waiting for me at Anuin. I'm going home for a while; my father is sending a ship for me. Come with me."

"I'm expected on a trade-ship sailing this evening; I'll have to tell them. Deth is with me."

Rood quirked a brow. "He found you. That man could find a pinhole in a mist." There was a pound at his door; he raised his voice irritably. "Go away! Whatever I broke, I'm sorry!"

"Rood!" It was the frail voice of the Master Tel, raised in unaccustomed severity. "You have broken the locks to Nun's books of wizardry!"

Rood rose with a sigh and flung open the door. A crowd of angry students behind the old Master raised voices like a cacophony of crows at the sight of him. Rood's voice battered against them helplessly.

"I know the Great Shout is forbidden, but it's a thing of impulse rather than premeditation, and I was overwhelmed by impulse. Please shut up!"

They shut up abruptly. Morgon, coming to stand beside Rood with the crown of Aum in his hands, its center stone black as the robe Master Tel wore, met the gaze of the Master without speaking.

Master Tel, the annoyance in his sparse, parchment-colored face melting into astonishment, gathered his voice again, set a riddle to the strain of silence, "Who won the riddle-game with Peven of Aum?"

"I did," said Morgon.

He told them the tale sitting in the Masters' library, with its vast ancient collection of books running the length and breadth of the walls. The eight Masters listened quietly, Rood in his gold robe making a brilliant splash among their black robes. No one spoke until he finished, and then Master Tel shifted in his chair and murmured wonderingly, "Kern of Hed."

"How did you know?" Rood said. "How did you know to ask that one riddle?"

"I didn't," Morgon said. "I just asked it once when I was so tired I couldn't think of anything else to ask. I thought everyone knew that riddle. But when Peven shouted 'There are no riddles of Hed!' I knew I had won the game. It wasn't a Great Shout, but I will hear it in my mind until I die."

"Kern." Rood's mouth twisted into a thin smile. "Since spring the lords of An have been asking two questions only: who is Raederle to marry, and what was the one riddle Peven couldn't answer? Hagis King of An, my father's grandfather, died in Peven's tower for lack of that riddle. The lords of An should have paid more attention to that small island. They will now."

"Indeed," Master Ohm, a lean, quiet man whose even voice never changed, said thoughtfully. "Perhaps in the history of the realm too little attention has been paid to Hed. There is still a riddle without an answer. If Peven of Aum had asked you that, with all your great knowledge you might not be here today."

Morgon met his eyes. They were mist-colored, calm as his voice. He said, "Without an answer and a stricture, it would have been disqualified."

"And if Peven had held the answer?"

"How could he? Master Ohm, you helped us search a whole winter the first year I came here for an answer to that riddle. Peven took his knowledge from books of wizardry that had belonged to Madir, and before that to the Lungold wizards. And in all their writings, which you have here, no mention is made of three stars. I don't know where to look for an answer. And I don't . . . it's far from my mind these days."

Rood stirred. "And this is the man who put his life in the balance with his knowledge. Beware the unanswered riddle."

"It is that: unanswered, and for all I know it may not need an answer."

Rood's hand cut the air, his sleeve fluttering. "Every riddle has an answer. Hide behind the closed doors in your mind, you stubborn farmer. A hundred years from now students in the White of Beginning Mastery will be scratching their heads trying to remember the name of an obscure Prince of Hed who, like another obscure Prince of Hed, ignored the first and last rule of riddle-mastery. I thought you had more sense."

"All I want," Morgon said succinctly, "is to go to Anuin, marry

Raederle, and then go home and plant grain and make beer and read books. Is that so hard to understand?"

"Yes! Why are you being so obtuse? You of all people?"

"Rood," Master Tel said in his gentle voice, "you know an answer to the stars on his face was sought and never found. What more do you suggest he do?"

"I suggest," Rood said, "he ask the High One."

There was a little silence. The Master Ohm broke it with a rustle of cloth as he shifted. "The High One would indeed know. However I suspect you will have to provide Morgon with more incentive than pure knowledge before he would make such a long, harsh journey away from his land."

"I don't have to. Sooner or later, he'll be driven there."

Morgon sighed. "I wish you would be reasonable. I want to go to Anuin, not Erlenstar Mountain. I don't want to ask any more riddles; spending a night from twilight to dawn in a tower rotten with cloth and bone, racking my brain for every riddle I ever learned, gave me a distaste for riddle-games."

Rood leaned forward, every trace of mockery gone from his face. "You will take honor from this place, and Master Tel has said you will take the Black today for doing what even the Master Laern died attempting. You will go to Anuin, and the lords of An, and my father and Raederle will give you at least the respect due to you for your knowledge and your courage. But if you accept the Black, it will be a lie; and if you offer the peace of Hed to Raederle, that also will be a lie, a promise you will not keep because there is a question you will not answer, and you will find, like Peven, that it is the one riddle you do not know, not the thousand you do know, that will destroy you."

"Rood!" Morgon checked, his mouth tight, his hands tight on the arms of his chair. "What are you trying to make of me? What is it you are trying to make of me?"

"A Master—for your own sake. How can you be so blind? How can you so stubbornly, so flagrantly, ignore everything you know is true? How can you let them call you a Master? How can you accept from them the Black of Mastery while you turn a blind eye at truth?"

Morgon felt the blood well into his face. He said tautly, Rood's face suddenly the only face in the still room, "I never wanted the Black. But

I do claim some choice in my life. What those stars on my face are, I do not know; and I don't want to know. Is that what you want me to admit? You take the eyes that your father, and Madir, and the shape-changer Ylon gave you and probe your own cold, fearless way into truth, and when you take the Black, I will come and celebrate with you. But all I want is peace."

"Peace," Master Tel said mildly, "was never one of your habits, Rood. We can only judge Morgon according to our standards, and by those he has earned the Black. How else can we honor him?"

Rood stood up. He undid his robe, let it slide to the floor, stood half-naked in the startled gaze of the Masters. "If you give him the Black, I will never wear any robe of Mastery again."

A muscle in Morgon's rigid face jumped. He leaned back in his chair, his stiff fingers opening, and said icily, "Put your clothes back on, Rood. I have said I didn't want the Black, and I won't take it. It's not the business of a farmer of Hed to master riddles. Besides, what honor would it give me to wear the same robe Laern wore and lost in that tower, and that Peven wears now?"

Rood gathered his robe in one hand, walked to Morgon's chair. He leaned over it, his hands on the arms. His face loomed above Morgon's, spare, bloodless. He whispered, "Please. Think."

He held Morgon's eyes, held the silence in the room with the motionless, taut set of his body until he moved, turned to leave. Then Morgon's own body loosened as though the black gaze had drained out of it. He heard the door close and dropped his face in one hand.

"I'm sorry," he whispered. "I didn't mean to say that about Laern. I lost my temper."

"Truth," the Master Ohm murmured, "needs no apology." His mist-colored eyes, unwavering on Morgon's face, held a gleam of curiosity. "Not even a Master assumes he knows everything—except in rare cases, such as Laern's. Will you accept the Black? You surely deserve it, and as Tel says, it is all we have to honor you."

Morgon shook his head. "I want it. I do want it. But Rood wants it more than I do; he'll make better use of it than I will, and I would rather he take it. I'm sorry we argued here—I don't know how it got started."

"I'll talk to him," Tel promised. "He was being rather unreasonable, and unnecessarily harsh."

"He has his father's vision," Ohm said. Morgon's eyes moved to him after a moment.

"You think he was right?"

"In essence. So do you, although you have chosen not to act—as is, according to your rather confused standards, your right. But I suspect a journey to the High One will not be as useless as you think."

"But I want to get married. And why should I trouble whatever destiny Rood thinks I have until it troubles me? I'm not going out hunting a destiny like a strayed cow."

The corner of Master Ohm's lean mouth twitched. "Who was Ilon of Yrye?"

Morgon sighed noiselessly. "Ilon was a harpist at the court of Har of Osterland, who offended Har with a song so terribly that he fled from Har out of fear of death. He went alone to the mountains, taking nothing but his harp, and lived quietly, far from all men, farming and playing his harp. So great was his harping in his loneliness, that it became his voice, and it spoke as he could not, to the animals living around him. Word of it spread from creature to creature until it came one day to the ears of the Wolf of Osterland, Har, as he prowled in that shape through his land. He was drawn by curiosity to the far reaches of his kingdom, and there he found Ilon, playing at the edge of the world. The wolf sat and listened. And Ilon, finishing his song and raising his eyes, found the terror he had run from standing on his threshold."

"And the stricture?"

"The man running from death must run first from himself. But I don't see what that has to do with me. I'm not running: I'm simply not interested."

The Master's elusive smile deepened faintly. "Then I wish you the peace of your disinterest, Morgon of Hed," he said softly.

Morgon did not see Rood again, though he searched through the grounds and the cliff above the sea half the afternoon for him. He took supper with the Masters, and found, wandering outside afterward into the dead wind of twilight, the High One's harpist coming up the road.

Deth, stopping, said, "You look troubled."

"I can't find Rood. He must have gone down to Caithnard." He ran a hand through his hair in a rare, preoccupied gesture, and set his shoulders against the broadside of an oak. Three stars gleamed below his hairline, muted in the evening. "We had an argument; I'm not even sure now what it was about. I want him with me at Anuin, but it's getting late, and I don't know now if he'll come."

"We should board."

"I know. If we miss the tide, they'll sail without us. He's probably drunk in some tavern, wearing nothing but his boots. Maybe he would rather see me take a long journey to the High One than marry Raederle. Maybe he's right. She doesn't belong in Hed, and that's what upset him. Maybe I should go down and get drunk with him and go home. I don't know." He caught the harpist's patient, vaguely mystified expression and sighed. "I'll get my pack."

"I must speak to Master Ohm briefly before we leave. Surely Rood, of all people, would have told you the truth about how he feels toward the marriage."

Morgon shrugged himself away from the tree. "I suppose so," he said moodily. "But I don't see why he has to upset me at a time like this."

He retrieved his pack from the chaos of Rood's room and bade the Masters farewell. The sky darkened slowly as he and the harpist took the long road back to the city; on the rough horns of the bay the warning fires had been lit; tiny lights from homes and taverns made random stars against the well of darkness. The tide boomed and slapped against the cliffs, and an evening wind stirred, strengthened, blowing the scent of salt and night. The trade-ship stirred restlessly in the deep water as they boarded; a loosed sail cupped the wind, taut and ghostly under the moon. Morgon, standing at the stern, watched the lights of the harbor ripple across the water and vanish.

"We'll reach Anuin in the afternoon, the wind willing," an affable, red-bearded trader with a weal down the side of his face said to him. "Sleep above or below as it pleases you. With the horses we carry, you may be happier up here in the air. There are plenty of skins from your own sheep to keep you warm."

"Thank you," Morgon said. Sitting on a great spool of cable, his arms resting on the rail, he watched the white wake furl to the turn of the silent helmsman's tiller. His thoughts slid to Rood; he traced the threads of their argument to its roots, puzzled over it, retraced it again. The wind carried voices of the handful of sailors manning the ship, a snatch of traders' discussion of the goods they carried. The masts groaned with the weight of wind; the ship, heavy with cargo, neatly balanced, cut with an easy roll from bow to stern through the waves. Morgon, the east wind numbing his cheek, lulled by the creak and dip of the vessel, put his head on his arms and closed his eyes. He was asleep when the ship shuddered as though the twelve winds had seized it at once, and, startling awake, he heard the furious, unchecked thump of the tiller.

He stood up, a call dying in his throat, for the deck behind him was empty. The ship, its sails full-blown to the harsh wind, reeled, throwing him back against the rail. He caught his balance desperately. The chart-house, where the traders had been lamp-lit as they pored over their papers, was dark. The wind, whimpering, drove hard into the sails, and the ship rolled, giving Morgon a sudden glimpse of white froth. He straightened slowly with it, his teeth set hard, feeling the prick of sweat on his back even in the cold spray.

He saw the hatch to the hold open reluctantly against the wind, recognized the web-colored hair in the moonlight. He made his way toward it in a lull of wind, clinging to whatever stay and spare corner he passed. He had to shout twice to make himself heard.

"What are they doing down there?"

"There's no one in the hold," Deth said. Morgon, staring at him, made no sense of the words.

"What?"

Deth, sitting in the open hatchway, put a hand on Morgon's arm. At the touch, and his quick, silent glance across the decks, Morgon felt his throat suddenly constrict.

"Deth—"

"Yes." The harpist shifted the harp slightly on his shoulder. His brows were drawn hard.

"Deth, where are the traders and sailors? They can't have just—just vanished like pieces of foam. They . . . Where are they? Did they fall overboard?"

"If they did, they put up enough sail before they left to take us with them."

"We can take it down."

"I think," Deth said, "we won't have time." The ship flung them both, as he spoke, backward in a strange, rigid movement. The animals screamed in terror; the deck itself seemed to strain beneath them, as though it were being pulled apart. A rope snapped above Morgon's head, slashing across the deck; wood groaned and buckled around them. He felt his voice tear out of him.

"We're not moving! In open sea, we're not moving!"

There was a rush of water beneath him, bubbling through the open hold; the ship sagged on its side. Deth caught Morgon as he slid helplessly across the deck; a wave breaking against the low side drenched them both, and he gagged on the cold, bitter water. He managed to stand, clinging with one hand to Deth's wrist, and flung his arms around the mast, tangling his fingers in the rigging. His face close to the harpist's, his feet sliding to the tilt of the deck, he shouted hoarsely, "Who were they?"

If the harpist gave him an answer, he did not hear it. Deth's figure blurred in the sweep of a wave; the mast snapped with a jar Morgon felt to his bones, and the striped canvas weighted with rigging and yard slapped him loose from his hold and swept him into the sea.

HE WOKE, FLUNG like a rag amid a harvest of dry kelp, his face in the sand, his mouth full of sand. He lifted his face; a bone-white beach strewn with seaweed and bleached driftwood blurred under one eye; his other eye was blind. He dropped his head, his eye closing again, and someone on his blind side touched him.

He started. Hands tugged at him, rolled him onto his back. He stared into a wild white cat's ice-blue eyes. Its ears were flattened. A voice said warningly, "Xel."

Morgon tried to speak, but made only the strange, harsh noise that a crow might make.

The voice said, "Who are you? What happened to you?"

He tried to answer. His voice would not shape the words. He realized, as he struggled with it, that there were no words in him anywhere to shape answers.

"Who are you?"

He closed his eyes. A silence spun like a vortex in his head, drawing him deeper and deeper into darkness.

He woke again tasting cool water. He reached for it blindly, drank until the crust of salt in his mouth dissolved, then lay back, the empty cup rolling from his hands. He opened his good eye again a moment later.

A young man with lank white hair and white eyes knelt beside him on the dirt floor of a small house. The threads of the voluminous, richly embroidered robe he wore were picked and frayed; the skin was stretched taut, hollow across his strange, proud face.

He said as Morgon blinked up at him, "Who are you? Can you speak now?"

Morgon opened his mouth. Like a small wave receding, something he had once known slipped quietly, silently away from him. The breath exploded out of him suddenly, violently; he dug the heels of his hands into his eyes.

"Be careful." The man pulled his hands from his face. "It looks as though you hit your head on something; blood and sand are caked over your eye." He washed it gently. "So you can't remember your name. Did you fall off a ship in that storm last night? Are you of Ymris? Of Anuin? Of Isig? Are you a trader? Are you of Hed? Of Lungold? Are you a fisher from Loor?" He shook his head in puzzlement at Morgon's silence. "You are mute and inexplicable as the hollow gold balls I dig up on Wind Plain. Can you see now?" Morgon nodded, and the man sat back on his haunches, frowning down at Morgon's face as though it held a name in it somewhere. His frown deepened suddenly; he reached out and brushed at the hair plastered dry with salt against Morgon's forehead. His voice caught. "Three stars."

Morgon lifted his hand to touch them. The man said softly, incredulously, "You don't remember even that. You came out of the sea with three stars on your face, with no name and no voice, like a portent out of the past. . . ." He stopped as Morgon's hand fell to his wrist, gripped it, and Morgon made the grunt of a question. "Oh. I am Astrin Ymris." Then he added formally, almost bitterly, "I am the brother and land-heir of Heureu, King of Ymris." He slid an arm under Morgon's shoulders. "If you'll sit, I'll give you some dry clothes."

He pulled the torn, wet tunic off Morgon, washed the drying sand from his body, and helped him into a long, hooded robe of rich dark cloth. He fetched wood, stirred up the embers under a cauldron of soup; by the time it had heated, Morgon had fallen asleep.

He woke at dusk. The tiny house was empty; he sat up, looking around him. It had little furniture: a bench, a large table cluttered with odd objects, a high stool, the pallet Morgon had slept on. Tools leaned against the doorway: a pick, a hammer, a chisel, a brush; dirt clung to them. Morgon rose, went to the open door. Across the threshold a great, wind-blown plain swept westward as far as he could see. Not far from the house, dark, shapeless stoneworks rose, blurred in the fading light. To the south lay, like a boundary line between lands, the dark line of a vast forest. The wind, running in from the sea, spoke a hollow, restless language. It smelled of salt and night, and for a moment, listening to it, some memory reeled into his mind of darkness, water, cold, wild wind, and he gripped the door posts to keep from falling. But it passed, and he found no word for it.

He turned. Strange things lay on Astrin's broad table. He touched them curiously. There were pieces of broken, beautifully dyed glass, of gold, shards of finely painted pottery, a few links of heavy copper chain, a broken flute of wood and gold. A color caught his eye; he reached for it. It was a cut jewel the size of his palm, and through it flowed, as he turned it, all the colors of the sea.

He heard a step and looked up. Astrin, Xel at his side, came in, dropped a heavy, stained bag by the hearth.

He said, stirring the fire, "It's beautiful, isn't it. I found that at the foot of Wind Tower. No trader I showed it to could give me the name for that stone, so I took it to Isig, to Danan Isig himself. He said that never in his mountain had he seen such a jewel, nor did he know anyone beside himself and his son, who could have cut it so flawlessly. He gave me Xel out of friendship. I had nothing to give him, but he said I had given him a mystery, which is sometimes a precious thing." He checked the pot above the flames, then reached for the bag and a knife hanging by the fire. "Xel caught two hare; I'll cook them for supper . . ." He looked up as Morgon touched his arm. He let Morgon take the knife from him. "Can you skin them?" Morgon nodded. "You know you can do that. Can you remember anything else about yourself? Think. Try to—" He stopped at the helpless, tormented expression on Morgon's face, gripped Morgon's arm briefly. "Never mind. It will come back to you."

They ate supper by firelight, the door closed against a sudden drenching rain. Astrin ate quietly, the white huntress Xel curled at his feet; he seemed to have settled back into a habit of silence, his thoughts indrawn, until he finished. Then he opened the door a moment to the driving rain, closed it, and the cat lifted its head with a yowl. Astrin's movements became restless as he touched books and did not open them, set shards of glass together that did not fit and dropped them, his face expressionless as though he were listening to something beyond the rain. Morgon, seated at the hearth, his head aching and the cut over his eye pressed against cool stones, watched him. Astrin's prowling brought him finally in front of Morgon; he gazed down at Morgon out of his white, secret eyes until Morgon looked away.

Astrin sat down with a sigh beside him. He said abruptly, "You are as secret as Wind Tower. I've been here five years in exile from Caerweddin. I speak to Xel, to an old man I buy fish from in Loor, to occasional traders, and to Rork, High Lord of Umber, who visits me every few months. By day I go digging out of curiosity in the great ruined city of the Earth-Masters on Wind Plain. By night, I dig in other directions, sometimes in books of wizardry I've learned to open, sometimes out there in the darkness above Loor, by the sea. I take Xel with me, and we watch something that is building on the shores of Ymris under night cover, something for which there is no name. . . . But I can't go tonight; the tide will be rough in this wind, and Xel hates the rain." He paused a moment. "Your eyes look at me as though you understand everything I'm saying. I wish I knew your name. I wish . . ." His voice trailed away; his eyes stayed, speculative, on Morgon's face.

He rose as suddenly as he had sat down, and took from his shelves a heavy book with a name on it stamped in gold: Aloil. It was locked with two apparently seamless bindings of iron. He touched them, murmuring a word, and they opened. Morgon went to his side; he looked up. "Do you know who Aloil was?" Morgon shook his head. Then his eyes widened a little as he remembered, but Astrin continued, "Most people have forgotten. He was the wizard in service to the Kings of Ymris for nine hundred years before he went to Lungold, then vanished along with the entire school of wizards seven hundred years ago. I bought the book from a trader; it took me two years to learn the word to open it. Part of the poetry Aloil wrote was to the wizard Nun, in service to Hel. I tried her name to open the book, but that didn't work. Then I remembered the name of her favorite pig out of all the pig herds of Hel: the speaking pig, Hegdis-Noon—and that name opened the book." He set the heavy book on the table and pored over it.

"Somewhere in here is the spell that made the stone talk on King's Mouth Plain. Do you know that tale? Aloil was furious with Galil Ymris because the king refused to follow Aloil's advice during a siege of Caerweddin, and as a result Aloil's tower was burned. So Aloil made a stone in the plain above Caerweddin speak for eight days and nights in such a loud voice that men as far as Umber and Meremont heard it, and the stone recited all Galil's secret, very bad attempts at writing poetry. From that the plain got its name." He glanced up to see Morgon's smile. He straightened. "I haven't talked so much in a month. Xel can't laugh. You make me remember I'm human. I forget that sometimes, except when Rork Umber is here, and then I remember, all too well, who I am." He looked down, turned a page. "Here it is. Now if I can read his handwriting. . . ." He was silent a few moments, while Morgon read over his shoulder and the candlelight spattered over the page. Astrin turned to him finally. He held Morgon gently by the arms and said slowly, "I think if this spell can make a stone speak, it may make you speak. I haven't done much mind-work; I've gone into Xel's mind, and once into Rork's, with his permission. If you are afraid, I won't do this. But perhaps if I go deep enough, I can find your name. Do you want me to try?"

Morgon's hands touched his mouth. He nodded, his eyes holding Astrin's, and Astrin drew a breath. "All right. Sit down. Sit quietly. The first step is to become as the stone. . . ."

Morgon sat down on the stool. Astrin, standing across from him, grew still, a dark shape in the flickering light. Morgon felt an odd shifting in the room, as if another vision of the same room had superimposed itself over his own, and refocused slightly. Odd pieces of thought rose in his mind: the plain he had looked at, Xel's face, the skins he had hung to dry. Then there was nothing but a long darkness and a withdrawal.

Astrin moved, the fire reflected strangely in his eyes. He whispered, "There was nothing. It is as though you have no name. I couldn't reach the place where you have your name and your past hidden from yourself. It's deep, deep. . . ." He stopped as Morgon rose. His hands closed tight on Astrin's arms; he shook Astrin a little, imperatively, and

Astrin said, "I'll try. But I've never met a man so hidden from himself. There must be other spells; I'll look. But I don't know why you care so much. It must be the essence of peace, having no name, no memory. . . . All right. I'll keep looking. Be patient."

Morgon heard him stirring at sunrise the next day and got up. The rain had stopped; the clouds hung broken above Wind Plain. They ate a breakfast of cold hare, wine and bread, then, carrying Astrin's tools, Xel following, they walked across the plain to the ancient, ruined city.

It was a maze of broken columns, fallen walls, rooms without roofs, steps leading nowhere, arches shaken to the ground, all built of smooth, massive squares of brilliant stone all shades of red, green, gold, blue, grey, black, streaked and glittering with other colors melting through them. A wide street of gold-white stone, grass thrusting up between its sections, began at the eastern edge of the city, parted it, and stopped at the foot of the one whole building in the city: a tower whose levels spiraled upward from a sprawling black base to a small, round, deep-blue chamber high at the top. Morgon, walking down the center street at Astrin's side, stopped abruptly to stare at it.

Astrin said, "Wind Tower. No man has ever been to the top of it—no wizard either. Aloil tried; he walked up its stairs for seven days and seven nights and never reached the end of them. I've tried, many times. I think at the top of that tower there must lie the answer to questions so old we've forgotten to ask them. Who were the Earth-Masters? What terrible thing happened to them that destroyed them and their cities? I play like a child among the bones of it, finding a fine stone here, a broken plate there, hoping that one day I'll find a key to the mystery of it, the beginning of an answer. . . . I took a chip off these great stones also to Danan Isig; he said he knew of no place in the High One's realm where they quarried such stone." He touched Morgon briefly, to get his eyes. "I'll be there, in that chamber without a roof. Join me when you wish."

Morgon, left to his own in the hollow, singing city, wandered through the roofless halls and wall-less chambers, between piles of broken stones rooted deep to the earth by long grass. The winds sped past like wild horses, pouring through empty rooms, thundering down the street to spiral the tower and moan through its secret chamber. Morgon, following them, drawn to the huge, bright structure, put one hand flat on its blue-black wall, one foot on its first step. The gold steps curved away from him; the winds pushed him like children, tumbled past him. He turned away after a moment, went to find Astrin.

He worked all day at Astrin's side, digging quietly in a little room whose floor was sunk beneath the earth, crumbling the earth in his hands, searching it for bits of metal, glass, pottery. Once, his hands full of the moist black earth, he caught the strong, good smell of it, and something leaped in him, longing, responding. He made a sound without knowing it. Astrin looked up.

"What is it? Did you find something?"

He dropped the earth and shook his head, feeling tears behind his throat and not knowing why.

Walking home at dusk, their finds carefully wrapped in old cloth, Astrin said to him, "You are so patient here. Perhaps you belong here, working among these forgotten things, in silence. And you accept my strange ways so unquestioningly, as though you can't remember how men do live with one another. . . ." He paused a moment, then went on slowly, as if remembering himself, "I haven't always been alone. I grew up in Caerweddin, with Heureu, and the sons of our father's High Lords, in the beautiful, noisey house Galil Ymris made out of the Earth-Master's stones. Heureu and I were close then, like shadows of each other. That was before we quarrelled." He shrugged the words away as Morgon looked at him. "It makes no difference here. I'll never go back to Caerweddin, and Heureu will never come here. I had just forgotten that once I wasn't alone. You forget easily."

He left Morgon that night after supper. Morgon, brushing dirt off pieces of pottery they had found, waited patiently. The wind rose hours after sunset; he grew uneasy, feeling them pull at the joints of the small house, heave at it as if to uproot it. He opened the door aimlessly once to look for Astrin; the wind tore it from his grip, sent it crashing back and fought with him, face-to-face, as he edged it closed.

When the wind died finally, a silence dropped like thin fingers of moonlight across Wind Plain. The tower rose out of broken stone, whole and solitary, yielding nothing to the moon's eye. Morgon added wood to the fire, made a torch of an oak branch, and went outside. He heard heavy breathing suddenly from the side of the house, an odd, dragging step. He turned and saw Astrin hunched against the wall of the house.

He said, as Morgon put out his torch underfoot and went to help him, "I'm all right." His face was mist-colored in the light from the window; he flung an arm around Morgon heavily, and together they stumbled across the threshold, Astrin sat down on the pallet. His hands were scratched raw; his hair was tangled with sea spray. He held his right hand against his side and would not move it, until Morgon, watching the dark stain bloom under his fingers, made a harsh noise of protest. Astrin's head dropped back on the pallet; his hand slid down. He whispered as Morgon ripped a seam open, "Don't. I'm short of clothes. He saw me first, but I killed him. Then he fell in the sea, and I had to dive for him among the rocks and tide, or they would have found him. I buried him in the sand. They won't find him there. He was made . . . He was shaped out of seaweed and foam and wet pearl, and the sword was of darkness and silver water. It bit me and flew away like a bird. If Xel hadn't warned me, I would be dead. If I hadn't turned . . ." He flinched as Morgon touched his side with a wet cloth. Then he was silent, his teeth locked, his eyes closed, while Morgon washed the shallow wound gently, closed it and bound it with strips from his dry robe. He heated wine; Astrin drank it and his shivering stopped. He lay back again. "Thank you. Xel—thank you. If Xel comes back, let her in."

He slept motionless, exhausted, waking only once near dawn, when Xel came whining to the door, and Morgon sleepless by the fire, rose to open it for the wet, bedraggled huntress.

Astrin said little of the incident the next day. He moved stiffly, with a tight, sour expression that eased only when his eyes fell on Morgon's mute, worried face. They spent the day indoors, Astrin prowling through wizards' books like an animal scenting, and Morgon trying to wash and mend Astrin's robe while questions he could not ask struggled like trapped birds in the back of his throat.

Astrin came out of his grim thoughts, finally, near sunset. He closed a book with a sigh, its iron bonds locking automatically, and said, staring out at the plain, "I should tell Heureu." Then his hand snapped down flat on the book and closed. He whispered, "No. Let him see with his own eyes. The land is his business. Let him put his own name to this.

He drove me out of Caerweddin five years ago for speaking the truth; why should I go back?"

Morgon, watching from the hearth as he struggled with needle and seam, made a questioning sound. Astrin, a hand to his side, turned to add wood to the fire for their evening meal. He paused a moment, to drop one hand on Morgon's shoulder. "I am glad you were here last night. If there is anything I can possibly do for you, I will do it."

He did not go out again at night for a while. Morgon worked at his side during the days, digging in the city; in the long, quiet evenings he would try to piece together shards of pottery, of glass, while Astrin searched through his books. Sometimes they hunted with Xel in the wild oak forest just south of them, which stretched from the sea far west beyond the limits of Ymris.

Once Astrin said, as they walked through the gentle, constant fall of dead oak leaves, "I should take you to Caithnard. It's just a day's journey south of these woods. Perhaps someone knows you there." But Morgon only looked at him blankly, as if Caithnard lay in some strange land at the bottom of the sea, and Astrin did not mention it again.

Morgon found a few days later a cache of lovely red and purple glass in a corner of the chamber they were working in. He took the fragments to Astrin's house, brushed off the dirt and puzzled over them. It rained heavily the next day; they could not go out. The small house smelled damp, and the fire smoked. Xel prowled restlessly, wailing complaints every now and then to Astrin, who sat murmuring over a spell-book he could not open. Morgon, some rough paste Astrin had made in front of him, began to fit together, piece by piece, the shards of glass.

He looked up as Astrin said irritably, "Xel, be quiet. I've run out of words. Yrth was the most powerful of the wizards after the Founder, and he locked his books too well."

Morgon opened his mouth, made a small sound, a puzzled look on his face. He turned abruptly, found a half-burned twig in the fire and blew it out. He wrote on the tabletop in ash, "You need his harp."

Astrin, watching, slid rather abruptly off the stool. He stood looking over Morgon's shoulder. "I need his what? Your handwriting is as difficult as Aloil's. Oh. Harp." His hand closed on Morgon's shoulder. "Yes. Perhaps you're right. Perhaps he did lock the book with a series of notes from the harp he made—or with the one low string that is said to shatter weapons. But where would I find it? Do you know where it is?"

Morgon shook his head. Then he dropped the twig, staring down at it as if it had been writing of its own volition. He turned his head after a moment, met Astrin's eyes. Astrin opened one of Aloil's spell-books abruptly, pushed a quill into Morgon's hand. "Who paid for his shape with the scars on his hands and to whom?"

Morgon began to write slowly down the margins of one of Aloil's spells. When he had finished the answer to the ancient Osterland riddle and begun the stricture, Astrin's voice broke from him in a little hiss.

"You studied at Caithnard. No man without a voice studies at that college—I know; I spent a year there myself. Can you remember it? Can you remember anything of it?"

Morgon stared back at him. He rose as if to go at once, the bench overturning behind him; Astrin caught him as he reached the door.

"Wait. It's nearly dusk. I'll go with you to Caithnard tomorrow, if you'll wait. There are some questions I want to ask the Masters myself."

They rose before dawn the next morning, to the soft drizzle of rain batting against the roof. It cleared before sunrise; they left Xel sleeping beside the fire and headed south across the wet, grassy plain toward the border of Ymris. The sun rose behind rain clouds drifting like ships above the grey sea. The wind shivered through the trees, plucked the last few wet leaves as they entered the woods, heading for the great traders' road that ran the length of Ymris and beyond, connecting the ancient city of Lungold to Caithnard.

"We should reach the road by noon," Astrin said. Morgon, the hem of his long robe drenched with dew, his eyes on the numberless trees as though he could see through them to a city he did not know, made an absent, answering noise. Crows flicked black through the distant branches; their harsh voices echoed back at him, mocking. He heard voices; a couple of traders, laughing, startled a tree full of birds as they rode through the early morning, their packs bulging. They came abreast of Morgon and Astrin; one of them stopped, bowing his head courteously.

"Lord Astrin. You're a ways from home." He turned, slipping his pack-strings loose. "I have a message from Mathom of An to Heureu

Ymris concerning—I believe—the man who won Peven's crown. As a matter of fact, I have messages for half the land-rulers of the realm. I was going to stop by your house and put it into your care."

Astrin's white brows closed. "You know I haven't seen Heureu for five years," he said rather coldly. The trader, a big, red-haired man with a scar down the side of his face, lifted a brow.

"Oh? You see, the difficulty is I'm taking ship from Meremont, so I will not be going to Caerweddin." He reached into his pack. "I would ask you to take him this message."

The silver of a blade soared in an arc out of the pack, flashed with a whistle down at Astrin. The trader's horse startled, and the sword blade, skimming past Astrin's face, shirred the sleeve of Morgon's outflung arm. He leaped forward after the first stunned, incredulous moment, caught the trader's wrist before it could lift again; the second trader, whirling his mount behind Morgon, brought the edge of his own blade down, high under Morgon's uplifted arm.

The blade tangled a little in the dark, heavy cloth. Morgon, the breath and sound knocked out of him by the blow, heard Astrin groan, then, for a moment, heard nothing. An odd quietness rose in his mind, a sense of something green, familiar, that smelled not unlike the wet, crushed grass; it faded away before he could name it, but not before he knew it held his name. Then he found himself swaying on his knees, breathing heavily, his lips caught between his teeth, blinking away something he thought was blood but was only the rain beginning again.

A horse, bare backed, galloped away into the trees; Astrin, a bloodstained sword in one hand, was unbuckling the saddle from the other. He wrenched it off, led the horse by the bit over to Morgon. There was a smear of blood across his face; the traders lay sprawling beside their packs and saddles.

He said, his own breath fast, "Can you stand? Where are you hurt?" He saw the black stain spreading down under Morgon's arm and winced. "Let me see."

Morgon shook his head, holding the arm clamped to his side with his hand. He struggled to his feet, swallowing sound after sound that would have set the crows mocking; Astrin got a firm grip on his good arm. His face, always colorless, seemed grey in the rain.

"Can you make it back to the house?"

He nodded and managed to make it as far as the edge of the plain.

He woke again as Astrin, dismounting behind him, pulled him gently down from the horse and into the house. He kicked the door shut with his foot as Xel, scenting them at the door, streaked out. Morgon collapsed on the pallet; Astrin, taking a skinning knife to the robe, managed despite Morgon's mute argument, to find the wound that began in the soft skin of the armpit and slanted down to lay three ribs bare.

Astrin made a sound in his throat. There was a knock on the door then; he whirled, reaching in a single, skilled movement for the sword by the pallet, and rising. He flung the door open; the point of the bloody sword came to rest on the breastbone of a trader who said, "Lord . . ." and then became uncharacteristically inarticulate.

"What?"

The trader, a broad man in a flowing Herun coat, black-bearded, kindly-faced, backed a step. "I have a message from . . ." He stopped again as the sword, shivering in Astrin's grip, rose from his breast to his throat. He finished in a whisper, "Rork Umber. Lord, you know me—"

"I know." Morgon, lifting his head with an effort, saw the skin stretched waxen across Astrin's face. "That's why if you turn now, and go very quickly, I might let you leave this place alive."

"But, Lord . . ." His eyes broke from Astrin's face in helpless curiosity, met Morgon's, and Morgon saw the flash of his own name in the dark, astonished eyes. He made an eager, questioning noise; the trader drew a breath. "That's what happened to him? He can't talk—"

"Go!" The harsh, desperate edge in Astrin's voice startled even Morgon. The trader, his face white under his beard, held his ground stubbornly.

"But the High One's harpist is in Caerweddin, looking—"

"I have just killed two traders, and by the High One's name, I swear I will kill a third if you don't get off my doorstep!"

The trader disappeared from the doorway; Astrin watched until the sound of hooves died. Then, his hands shaking, he leaned the sword against the doorpost and knelt beside Morgon again.

"All right," he whispered. "Lie still. I'll do what I can."

He was forced to leave Morgon at the end of two days, to get help from an old fisherman's wife at Loor, who picked the herbs for him he needed and watched Morgon while he slept and hunted. After five days, the old woman went back home with chips of the Earth-Masters' gold in her hand; and Morgon, too weak to walk, could at least sit up and drink hot soup.

Astrin, worn himself with short nights and worry, said, after half a day of silence, as though he had resolved something in his own mind, "All right. You can't stay here; I don't dare take you to Caithnard or Caerweddin. I'll take you to Umber, and Rork can send for Deth. I need help."

He did not leave Morgon alone after that. As Morgon became stronger, they spent hours painstakingly piecing together the fragments of red and purple glass that Morgon had found; it began to take the shape of a fragile bowl, beautifully dyed, the red streaks becoming figures moving around the sides in the pattern of some ancient tale. Excited by it, Morgon, his pen scratching across Aloil's spells, talked Astrin into searching for the remaining pieces. They spent a day in the ruined city, found three more pieces and returned to meet the fisherman's wife on Astrin's doorstep. She had brought them a basket of fresh fish; she harried Morgon back into bed, scolded Astrin, and cooked supper for them.

The next morning they finished the bowl. Astrin placed the final pieces carefully, Morgon hovering at his shoulder, scarcely breathing. The red figures became whole, moving through the misty purple in some strange action. Astrin, trying to decipher it without touching the bowl as the paste dried, gave an impatient murmur as someone knocked on the door. Then his face tightened. He reached for the sword, held it loosely as he opened the door. He said, "Rork!" and then nothing more.

Three men came past Astrin into the house. They wore silver-white mail under their long, heavy, beautifully embroidered coats; swords were slung on jewelled belts at their hips.

The black-bearded trader whom Astrin had driven from his door said, looking at Morgon, "There he is. The Prince of Hed. Look at him. He's hurt, he can't speak. He doesn't even know me, and I bought grain and sheep from him five weeks ago; I knew his father."

Morgon stood up slowly. Other men entered: a tall, richly dressed, red-haired man with a harried expression on his face; another guard; a pale-haired harpist. Morgon looked for Astrin's face in the confusion of faces, found in it the same incredulous horror he saw in the strangers' eyes.

Astrin breathed, "Rork, it's not possible. I found him tossed up by the sea—he couldn't speak, he couldn't . . ."

The eyes of the High Lord of Umber met the harpist's, received affirmation; he said wearily, "He's the Prince of Hed." He ran a hand through his bright hair, sighing. "You had him. Deth has been looking for him for five weeks, and this trader finally brought some tale to the King at Caerweddin that you had gone mad and killed two traders, wounded the Prince of Hed, kept him imprisoned, somehow—through a spell, I suppose—stole his voice. Can you imagine what Heureu thinks? There's a strange rebellion building in Meremont and Tor, among the coastal lords, that not even the High Lords can account for. We're bidden to arms for the second time in a year, and on top of that the land-heir of Ymris is accused of murder and imprisoning a land-ruler. The King sent armed men to take you if you resist; the High One sent his harpist to place you under the doom if you try to escape, and I came . . . I came to listen to you."

Astrin put a hand over his eyes. Morgon, his eyes moving bewilderedly from one face to another, hearing a name that belonged to him yet had no meaning, made another sound. The trader sucked a breath.

"Listen to him. Five weeks ago he could talk. When I saw him, he was lying there making noises, with the blood pouring out of his side, and Lord Astrin standing at the door with blood on his sword, threatening to kill me. It's all right," he added soothingly to Morgon. "You're safe now."

Morgon drew a breath. The sound he wanted to make was cut short before it came; instead he lifted the bowl they had put together so patiently and smashed it against the table. He had their attention then, but as they stared at him, startled, he could not speak. He sat down again, his hands sliding over his mouth.

Astrin took a step toward him, stopped. He said to Rork, "He can't ride all that way to Caerweddin; his wound is barely healed. Rork surely you don't believe—I found him washed up on the beach, nameless, voiceless—you can't believe I would harm him."

"I don't," Rork said. "But how did he get hurt?"

"I was taking him to Caithnard, to see if the Masters recognized him. We met two traders who tried to kill us both. So I killed them. And then this one came, knocking on my door when I had just brought the Prince of Hed in, hardly knowing if he were dead or alive. Can you blame me for being something less than hospitable?"

The trader took off his cap and passed a hand through his hair. "No," he admitted. "But Lord, you might have listened to me. Who were these traders? There hasn't been a renegade trader in fifty years. We see to that. It's bad for business."

"I have no idea who they were. I left the bodies in the woods, not far from the edge, as you would go straight south from here to reach the trade-road."

Rork nodded briefly to the guards. "Find them. Take the trader with you." He added, as they left, "You'd better pack. I brought two mounts and a packhorse from Umber."

"Rork." The white eyes were pleading. "Is it necessary? I've told you what happened; the Prince of Hed can't speak, but he can write, and he'll bear witness for me before you and the High One's harpist. I have no wish to see Heureu; I have nothing to answer for."

Rork sighed. "I will have, if I don't bring you back with me. Half the High Lords of Ymris gathered at Caerweddin heard this tale, and they want an answer to it. You have white hair and white eyes, you meddle with ancient stones and books of wizardry; no one has seen you at Caerweddin in five years, and for all anyone knows it's entirely possible that you have gone mad and done exactly what the trader said you did."

"They'll believe you."

"Not necessarily."

"They'll believe the High One's harpist."

Rork sat down on the stool, rubbed his eyes with his fingers. "Astrin. Please. Go back to Caerweddin."

"For what?"

Rork's shoulders slumped. The High One's harpist said then, his voice quiet, even, "It's not that simple. You are under the doom of the High One, and if you choose not to answer to Heureu Ymris, you will answer to the High One."

Astrin's hands went down flat on the table among the glass shards.

"For what?" He held the harpist's eyes. "The High One must have known the Prince of Hed was here. What can he possibly hold me accountable for?"

"I cannot answer for the High One. I can only give you that warning, as I have been instructed. The doom for disobedience is death."

Astrin looked down at the splinters of glass between his hands. He sat down slowly. Then he reached out, touched Morgon. "Your name is Morgon. No one told you." He added wearily to Rork, "I'll have to pack my books; will you help me?"

The guards and the trader returned an hour later. The trader, an odd expression on his face, replied only vaguely to Rork's questions.

"Did you recognize them?"

"One of them, yes. I think. But . . ."

"Do you know his name? Can you attest to his character?"

"Well. Yes. I think. But . . ." He shook his head, his face strained. He had not dismounted, as though he wanted to stay no longer than necessary in the lonely, wild corner of Ymris. Rork turned, seized with the same impatience.

"Let's go. We have to reach Umber by nightfall. And—" He glanced up as a stray tear of rain caught his eyes, "It's going to be a weary ride to Caerweddin."

Xel, too wild to live at Caerweddin, sat on the doorstep as they left, watching them curiously. They rode eastward across the plain, while the clouds darkened behind the ancient, ruined city, and wind passed like some lost, invisible army across the grass. The rain held miraculously until early evening, when they crossed a river at the northern edge of the plain and caught a road that led through the rough hills and green woods of Umber to Rork's house.

They spent the night there, in the great house built of red and brown stones from the hills, in whose vast hall all the lesser lords of Umber seemed to be gathered at once. Morgon, knowing only the silence of Astrin's house, was uneasy among the men whose voices rumbled like the sea with talk of war, the women who treated him with a fine, bewildering courtesy and spoke to him of a land he did not know. Only Astrin's face, closed and aloof to the strangeness, reassured him; and the harpist, playing at the supper's end, wove a sound within the dark, fire-washed stones that was like the wind-haunted peace Morgon remembered. At night, alone in a chamber big as Astrin's house, he lay awake listening to the hollow wind, groping blindly for his name.

They left Umber at dawn, rode through a morning mist that coiled and pearled on black, bare orchards. The mist resolved into a rain that stayed with them all the way up the long road from Umber to Caerweddin. Morgon, riding hunched against it, felt the damp collect in his bones, like a mildew. He bore it absently, vaguely aware of Astrin's concern, something drawing his thoughts forward, an odd pull out of the darkness of his ignorance. Finally, racked by a nagging cough as he rode, he felt the half-healed wound in his side scored as with fire, and he reined sharply. The High One's harpist put a hand on his shoulder. Looking at the still, austere face, Morgon drew a sudden breath, but the moment's strange recognition wavered and passed. Astrin, riding back to them, his face taut, unapproachable, said briefly, "We're almost there."

The ancient house of the Ymris Kings stood near the sea on the mouth of the Thul River, which ran eastward across Ymris from one of the seven Lungold Lakes. Trade ships were anchored in its deep waters; a fleet of ships with the scarlet and gold sails of Ymris were docked at the mouth of the river like colorful birds. As they rode across the bridge, a messenger, sighting them, turned hurriedly into the open gates of a sprawling stone wall. Beyond it, on a hill, stood the house that Galil Ymris had built, its proud face and wings and towers alive with beautiful patterns of color formed by the brilliant stones of the Earth-Masters.

They rode through the gates, up the gentle incline of a cobbled road. Thick oak doors in the mouth of a second wall were opened for them: they entered a courtyard where serving men took their horses as they dismounted and flung heavy fur cloaks over their shoulders. They went in silence across the wide yard, the rain gusting against their faces.

The King's hall, built of smooth, dark, glittering stones, held a fire that ran half the length of the inner wall. They were drawn to the fire like moths, shuddering and dripping, unaware of the men falling silent, motionless around them. A quick step on the stones made them turn.

Heureu Ymris, lean, big boned, his dark hair speckled with rain, bent his head courteously to Morgon and said, "You are welcome to my house. I met your father not too long ago. Rork, Deth, I am in your debt. Astrin—" He stopped then, as though the word he had spoken was strange or bitter to his mouth. Astrin's face was closed as surely as one of Yrth's books; his white eyes were expressionless. He looked placeless in the rich hall, with his colorless face and worn robe. Morgon, suddenly possessed of a father he did not know, wished futilely, desperately, that he and Astrin were back where they belonged, in the small house by the sea fitting pieces of glass shard together. He glanced around at the silent, watching strangers in the hall. Something snagged his eye then, down the long hall, something that flamed across the distance, turning his face toward it like a touch.

A sound came out of him. In the shifting torchlight, a great harp stood on a table. It was of beautiful, ancient design, with gold twisted into pale, polished wood inlaid with moons and quarter moons of ivory or bone. Down the face of it, among full moons, inset in gold, were three flawless blood-red stars.

Morgon went toward them, feeling as though his voice and name and thoughts had been stripped from him a second time. There was nothing in the room but those flaming stars and his movement toward them. He reached them, touched them. His fingers moved from them to trace the fine network of gold buried deep in the wood. He ran his hand across the strings, and at the rich, sweet sounds that followed, a love of that harp filled him, overpowering all care, all memory of the past, dark weeks. He turned, looked back at the silent group behind him. The harpist's quiet face rippled a little in the firelight. Morgon took a step toward him.

"Deth."

4

NO ONE MOVED. Morgon, feeling a world slip easily, familiarly into place as though he were waking from a dream, gave a second look at the massive, ancient walls of the house, at the strangers watching him, jewelled, double-linked chains of rank flashing on their breasts. His eyes went back to the harpist. "Eliard . . ."

"I went to Hed to tell him—somehow—that you might have drowned; he said you must be still alive since the land-rule had not passed to him. So I searched for you from Caithnard to Caerweddin."

"How did you—?" He stopped, remembering the empty ship sagging on its side, the screaming horses. "How did we both survive?"

"Survive what?" Astrin said. Morgon gazed at him without seeing him.

"We were sailing to An at night. I was taking the crown of Peven of Aum to Anuin. The crew just vanished. We went down in a storm."

"The crew did what?" Rork demanded.

"They vanished. The sailors, the traders, in open sea . . . In the middle of a storm, the ship just stopped and sank, with all its grain and animals." He stopped again, feeling the whip of the wet, mad winds, remembering someone who was himself and yet not himself lying half-drowned on the sand, nameless, voiceless. He reached out to touch the harp. Then, staring down at the stars burning under his hand like the stars on his face, he said sharply, amazed, "Where in the world did this come from?"

"Some fisherman found it last spring," Heureu Ymris said, "not far from where you and Astrin were staying. It had washed up on the beach. He brought it here because he thought it was bewitched. No one could play it."

"No one?"

"No one. The strings were mute until you touched them."

Morgon moved his hand away from it. He saw the awed expression in Heureu's eyes repeating itself in Astrin's as they looked at him, and he felt again, for a moment, a stranger to himself. He turned away from the harp, walked back to the fire. He stopped in front of Astrin; their eyes met in a little, familiar silence. Morgon said softly, "Thank you."

Astrin smiled for the first time since Morgon had met him. Then he looked over Morgon's shoulder at Heureu. "Is that sufficient? Or do you still intend to bring me to judgment for trying to murder a land-ruler?"

Heureu drew a breath. "Yes." His face, set with the same stubbornness, was a dark reflection of Astrin's. "I will, if you try to walk out of this hall without giving me any explanations of why you killed two traders, and threatened to kill a third when he saw the Prince of Hed wounded in your house. There have been enough unfounded rumors spreading through Ymris about you; I will not have something like this added to them."

"Why should I explain? Will you believe me? Ask the Prince of Hed. What would you have done with me if he hadn't found his voice?"

Heureu's own voice rose in exasperation. "What do you think I would have done? While you've been at the other end of Ymris digging up potshards, Meroc Tor has been arming half the coastal lands of Ymris. He attacked Meremont yesterday. You would be dead by now if I hadn't sent Rork and Deth to get you out of that hut you've been clinging to like a barnacle."

"You sent—?"

"What do you think I am? Do you think I believe every tale I hear about you—including the one that you go out in animal-shape every night and scare cattle?"

"I do what?"

"You are the land-heir of Ymris, and you are my brother whom I grew up with. I'm tired of sending messengers to Umber every three months to find out from Rork if you are alive or dead. I have a war on my hands that I don't understand and I need you. I need your skill and your mind. And I need to know this: who were those traders that tried to kill you and the Prince of Hed? Were they men of Ymris?"

Astrin shook his head. He looked dazed. "I have no idea. We were . . . I was taking him to Caithnard to see if the Masters knew him when we were attacked. He was wounded; I killed the traders. I don't believe they were traders."

"They weren't," the trader who had come with them said glumly; and Morgon said, suddenly, "Wait. I remember. The red-haired man—the one who spoke to us. He was on the ship."

Heureu looked at them bewilderedly. "I don't understand." Astrin turned to the trader.

"You knew him."

The trader nodded. His face was white, unhappy in the firelight. "I knew him. I've looked at that face I saw in the woods night and day, tried to tell myself that the death in it was playing tricks on me. But I can't. There was the same front tooth gone, the same scar he got when a loading cable snapped and hit him in the face—it was Jarl Aker, from Osterland."

"Why would he attack the Prince of Hed?" Heureu asked.

"He wouldn't. He didn't. He's been dead for two years."

Heureu said sharply, "That's not possible."

"It's possible," Astrin said grimly. He was silent, struggling a little with himself while Heureu watched. "Meroc Tor's rebels aren't the only men arming themselves in Ymris."

"What do you mean?"

Astrin glanced at the curious, expectant faces of the gathering in the hall. "I would rather tell you privately. That way if you don't—" He stopped abruptly. A woman had joined Heureu quietly; her dark, shy eyes, flicking over the group, lingered a little on Morgon's face, then moved to Astrin's.

She said, her brows crooked, her voice soft in the murmurings of the fire, "Astrin, I'm glad you've come back. Will you stay now?"

Astrin's hands closed at his sides, his eyes going to Heureu's face.

There was a mute, brittle struggle between them; the Ymris King, without moving, seemed to shift closer to the woman.

He said to Morgon, "This is my wife, Eriel."

"You don't favor your father," she commented interestedly. Then the blood burned into her face. "I'm sorry—I wasn't thinking."

"It's all right," Morgon said gently. The firelight brushed like soft wings over her face, her dark hair. Her brows crooked again, troubled. "You don't look well. Heureu—"

The Ymris King stirred. "I'm sorry. You could all do with some dry clothes and food; you've had a rough ride. Astrin, will you stay? The only thing I ask is that if you ever speak of that matter that came between us five years ago, you give me unshakable, absolute proof. You've been away from Caerweddin long enough; there's no one I need more now."

Astrin's head bowed. His hands in his frayed sleeves were still closed. He said softly, "Yes."

An hour later, Morgon, washed, shorn of five weeks' growth of hair, the edge taken off his hunger, surveyed the fur-covered bed in his chamber and lay down without undressing. There was a knock on his door in what seemed only a moment later; he sat up, blinking. The room, except for a low fire, was dark. The stone walls seemed to move and settle around him as he rose; he could not find the door. He considered the problem, murmured the stricture of an ancient riddle from An:

"See with your heart what your eyes cannot, and you will find the door that is not."

The door opened abruptly in front of him, light flaring in from the hall. "Morgon."

The harpist's face and silver hair were oddly blurred with torchlight. Morgon said with an odd sense of relief, "Deth. I couldn't find the door. For a moment I thought I was in Peven's tower. Or the tower Oen of An built to trap Madir. I just remembered that I promised Snog Nutt I would fix his roof before the rains start. He's so addled he won't think of telling Eliard; he'll sit there all winter with the rain dripping down his neck."

The harpist put a hand on his arm. His brows were drawn. "Are you ill?"

"I don't think so, no. Grim Oakland thinks I should get another pigherder, but Snog would die of uselessness if I took his pigs away from him. I'd better go home and fix his roof." He started as a shadow loomed across the threshold.

Astrin, unfamiliar in a short, close-fitting coat, his hair neatly trimmed, said brusquely to Deth, "I have to talk to you. Both of you. Please." He took a torch from the hall; the shadows flitted away in the room, sat hunched in corners, behind furniture.

Astrin closed the door behind them, turned to Morgon, "You have got to leave this house."

Morgon sat down on the clothes chest. "I know. I was just telling Deth." He found himself shivering suddenly, uncontrollably, and moved to the fire that Deth was rousing.

Astrin, prowling through the room like Xel, demanded of Deth, "Did Heureu tell you why we quarrelled five years ago?"

"No. Astrin—"

"Please. Listen to me. I know you can't act, you can't help me, but at least you can listen. I left Caerweddin the day Heureu married Eriel."

An image of the shy, fragile face, richly colored with firelight, rose in Morgon's mind. He said sympathetically, "Were you in love with her, too?"

"Eriel Meremont died five years ago on King's Mouth Plain."

Morgon closed his eyes. The harpist, kneeling with his hands full of wood, was so still not even the light trembled on the chain across his breast. He said, his voice changeless as ever, "Do you have proof?"

"Of course not. If I had proof, would that woman who calls herself Eriel Meremont still be married to Heureu?"

"Then who is married to Heureu?"

"I don't know." He sat down finally beside the fire. "The day before the wedding, I rode with Eriel to King's Mouth Plain. She was tired of the preparations and wanted a few moments of peace, and she asked me to go with her. We were close; we had known each other since we were children, but there was nothing more than deep friendship between us. We rode to the ruined city of the plain and separated. She went to sit on one of the broken walls to watch the sea, and I just walked through the city, wondering as always what force had scattered the stones like leaves on the grass. At one moment, as I walked, everything grew suddenly very quiet: the sea, the wind. I looked up. I saw a white bird flying above me against the blue sky. It was very beautiful, and I remember thinking that the silence must be like the still eye of a maelstrom. Then I heard a wave break, and the wind rise. I heard a strange cry; I thought the bird had made it. Then I saw Eriel ride past me without looking back or speaking. I called to her to wait, but she didn't look back. I went to get my horse, and when I passed the rock she had been sitting on, I saw a white bird lying dead on it. It was still warm, still bleeding. I held it in my hands, and felt sorrow and terror overwhelm me as I remembered the silence, and the cry of the bird and Eriel riding away from me without looking back. I buried the bird there among the ancient stones above the sea. That night I told Heureu what I had seen. We ended up shouting at each other, and I swore as long as he was married to that woman I would never return to Caerweddin. I think Rork Umber is the only man to whom Heureu told the truth about why I left. He never told Eriel, but she must know. I only began to realize what she must be as I watched the army being gathered, ships built, arms unloaded at night from Isig and Aniun. . . . I've seen, late at night, what Meroc Tor has not: that part of this army he has formed is not human. And that woman is of this nameless, powerful people." He paused, his eyes moved from Deth's face to Morgon's. "I decided to stay at Caerweddin for one reason only: to find proof of what she is. I don't know what you are, Morgon. They gave you a name in my house, but I've never heard of a Prince of Hed winning a riddle-game with death, playing an ancient harp made only for him by someone, sometime, who put the touch of a destiny on that harp's face."

Morgon leaned back in his chair. He said wearily, "I can't use a harp to fix Snog Nutt's roof."

"What?"

"I've never heard that a destiny is of any use at all to a Prince of Hed. I'm sorry Heureu married the wrong woman, but that's his business. She's beautiful, and he loves her, so I don't see why you're upset. I was on my way to Anuin to get married myself when I nearly got killed. Logically it would seem that someone wants to kill me, but that's their business; I don't want to be bothered trying to figure out why. I'm not stupid; once I start asking questions—even one question: What are three stars—I'll begin a riddle-game I don't think I'll want to finish. I don't want to know. I want to go home, fix Snog Nutt's roof, and go to bed."

Astrin gazed at him a moment, then turned to Deth. "Who is Snog Nutt?"

"His pigherder."

Astrin reached out, touched Morgon's face. "You may as well have died in that woods for all the good four days' riding in the rain has done you. I'd row you back to Hed and patch your pigherder's roof myself if I thought you could even walk out of this room and stay alive. I'm afraid for your life in this house, especially now since you found that harp so conveniently here, under the eyes of Eriel Ymris. Deth, you nearly lost your own life because of those people; who does the High One say they are?"

"The High One, beyond saving my life and doubtlessly Morgon's, for his own reasons, has said absolutely nothing to me. I had to find out for myself whether Morgon was alive, and where he was. It was unexpected, but the High One follows his own inclinations." He settled a log on the fire and stood up. Lines had formed, faint, taut, down the sides of his mouth. He added, "You know I can do nothing without his instructions. I cannot in any way offend the King of Ymris, since I act in the High One's name."

"I know. You'll notice I haven't asked you if you believe me or not. But do you have any suggestions?"

Deth glanced at Morgon. "I suggest you send for the King's physician."

"Deth—"

"There is nothing either one of us can do but wait. And watch. As ill as Morgon is, he should not be left alone."

Something eased in the lean, colorless face. He rose abruptly. "I'll get Rork to help us watch. He may not believe me, but he knows me well enough to be uneasy about this."

The King's physician, the Lady Anoth, an elderly, comforting, dry-voiced woman took one look at Morgon, and, ignoring his arguments, gave him something that whirled him into a drugged sleep. He woke hours later, light-headed, restless. Astrin, who had stayed to keep watch over him, had fallen asleep by the fire, exhausted. Morgon eyed him a moment, wanting to talk, then decided to let him sleep. His thoughts strayed to the harp in the hall; he heard again the light, rich voice of it, felt the taut, perfectly tuned strings under his fingers. A thought occurred to him then, a question underlying the agelessness, the magic behind the harp. He rose a little unsteadily, wrapped himself in fur from the bed, and left the room soundlessly. The hallway was empty, quiet; the torchlight flared over the private faces of closed doors. With an odd certainty, he found his way down a stairway that led to the great hall.

The stars gleamed like eyes in the shadows. He touched the harp, picked it up, feeling the unexpected lightness of it in spite of its size. The fine, ancient scroll and web of gold burned under his fingers. He touched a string, and at the lovely, solitary sound, he smiled. Then a fit of coughing shook him, tearing painfully at his side; he dropped his face in the fur to still the sound.

A startled voice said behind him, "Morgon."

He straightened after a moment, white, exhausted. Eriel Ymris came down the stairs, followed by a girl with a torch. He watched her come to him quietly through the long hall, her unbound hair making her look very young. He said curiously, "Astrin told me you were dead."

She stopped. He could not read the expression in her eyes. Then she said composedly, "No. You are."

His hands shifted position slightly on the harp. Somewhere, too distant to trouble him, something in him was crying out a warning. He shook his head. "Not yet. Who are you? Are you Madir? No, she's dead. And she didn't kill birds. Are you Nun?"

"Nun is dead, too." She was watching him without blinking, her eyes fire-flecked. "You don't go back far enough, Lord. Go back as far as your mind will take you, to the earliest riddle that was asked, and I am older than that."

He threw his mind back to his studies, touched riddle after riddle but found her nowhere. He said incredulously, "You don't exist in the books of the Masters—not even in the books of wizardry that have been opened. Who are you?"

"The wise man can give a name to his enemy."

"The wise man knows he has enemies," he said a little bitterly. "What is it? Is it the stars? Would it help to tell you that the last thing

I want to do is fight you; I simply want to be left alone to rule Hed in peace."

"Then you shouldn't have left your land to begin weaving riddles at Caithnard. The wise man knows his own name. You don't know my name; you don't know your own. It's better for me if you die that way, in ignorance."

"But why?" he said bewilderedly, and she took a step toward him. At her side, the young girl turned suddenly into a big, red-haired trader with a weal across his face, who wielded instead of a torch a sword of lean, ash-colored metal. Morgon moved back, felt the wall behind him. He watched the sword rise in a dreamlike slowness. It burned the skin of his throat, and he started.

"Why?" The blade had drained the sound from his voice. "At least tell me why."

"Beware the unanswered riddle." She looked away from him, nodded at the trader.

Morgon closed his eyes. He said, "Never underestimate another riddler," and plucked the lowest string of the harp.

The sword shattered in midair, and he heard a cry like a faint bird cry. Then all around him came a terrible cacophony of sound as ancient shields lining the far wall burst with hollow, metallic ringing, and their split pieces drummed on the floor. Morgon felt himself drop from a great distance, fall like a shield to the floor, and he buried the noise of his falling in the fur. Voices followed the din and hum of metal, flurried, indistinct.

Someone tugged at him. "Morgon, get up. Can you get up?" He lifted his head; Rork Umber, dressed in little more than a cloak and a knife belt, helped him up.

Heureu, staring down at them from the stairs, with Eriel behind him, demanded amazedly, "What is going on? It sounds like a battlefield in here."

"I'm sorry," Morgon said. "I broke your shields."

"You did. How in Aloil's name did you do that?"

"Like this." He plucked the string again, and the knife in Rork's belt, and the pikes of the guards in the doorways snapped. Heureu drew a breath, stunned.

"Yrth's harp."

"Yes," Morgon said. "I thought it might be." His eyes moved to Eriel's face as she stood behind Heureu, her hands against her mouth. "I thought—I dreamed you were here with me."

Her head gave a little, startled shake. "No. I was with Heureu."

He nodded. "It was a dream, then."

"You're bleeding," Rork said suddenly. He turned Morgon toward the light. "How did you get that cut on your throat?"

Morgon touched it. He began to shake then, and he saw, above Eriel, Astrin's haggard, bloodless face.

Drugged again, he dreamed of ships tossing in a wild, black sea, decks empty, sails ripped to ribbons; of a beautiful, black-haired woman who tried to kill him by playing the lowest string on a starred harp, and who wept when he shouted at her; of a riddle-game weaving through his dreams that never ended, with a man whose face he never saw, who asked riddle after riddle, demanding answers, yet never answered any himself. Snog Nutt appeared from somewhere, waiting patiently, with rainwater falling down his neck, for the game to end, but it was interminable. Finally the strange riddler turned into Tristan, who told him to go home. He found himself in Hed, walking through the wet fields at dusk, smelling the earth. Just as he reached the open doors of his house, he woke.

The room with its beautiful patterned walls of blue and black stone was filled with a grey afternoon light. Someone sitting by the fire bent over to settle a falling log. Morgon recognized the lean, outstretched hand, the loose, silver hair.

He said, "Deth."

The harpist rose. His face was hollowed, faintly lined with weariness; his voice, calm as always, held no trace of it. "How do you feel?"

"Alive." He stirred and said reluctantly, "Deth, I have a problem. I may have been dreaming, but I think Heureu's wife tried to kill me."

Deth was silent. In a rich, dark, full-sleeved robe he looked a little like a Caithnard Master, his face honed from years of study. Then he touched his eyes briefly with his fingers and sat down on the edge of the bed.

"Tell me."

Morgon told him. The rain he had heard now and again in his dreaming began to tap softly against the wide windows; he listened to it a moment when he had finished, then added, "I can't figure out who she might be. She has no place in the tales and riddles of the kingdom . . . just as the stars have no place. I can't accuse her; I have no proof, and she would just look at me out of her shy eyes and not know what on earth I was talking about. So I think I should leave this place quickly."

"Morgon, you have been lying ill for two days since you were found in that hall. Assuming you have the strength to leave this room, what would you do?"

Morgon's mouth crooked. "I'm going to go home. The wise man does not shake a hornet's nest to see what's buzzing in it. I've left Hed without a land-ruler for six weeks; I want to see Eliard and Tristan again. I'm accountable to the High One for the name I was born with in Hed, not for some strange identity I seem to have beyond Hed." He paused; the rain changed, began battering hard at the glass. His eyes strayed to it. "I am curious," he admitted. "But this is one riddle-game I have sense enough to stay out of. The High One can play it."

"The High One is not the one being challenged."

"It's his realm; I'm not responsible for the power games in Ymris."

"You may be if the stars on your face set them in motion."

Morgon looked at him. His mouth drew taut; he turned restlessly, wincing a little, the shadows of pain and exhaustion in his face deepening. Deth dropped a hand on his arm. "Rest," he said gently. "If you choose, when you're well enough to leave, to go back to Hed, unless the High One gives me other instructions, I'll travel with you. If you disappear again between Hed and Ymris, I would only have to search for you."

"Thank you. I don't understand, though, why the High One left you ignorant of where I was. Did you ask him?"

"I'm a harpist, not a wizard to throw my mind from here to Erlenstar Mountain. He comes into my mind at will; I cannot go into his."

"Well, he must have known you were searching for me. Why didn't he tell you?"

"I can only guess. The High One's mind is the great web of the minds of those in his realm. He weaves to his own ends, threading back and forth between action and action to make a pattern, which is why his reactions to events are often unexpected. Five years ago, Heureu Ymris married, and Astrin Ymris left Caerweddin carrying a fact like a stone in him. Perhaps the High One used you to bring Astrin and his fact back to Caerweddin to face Heureu."

"If that's true, then he knows what she is." He stopped. "No. He could have acted when Heureu married, that would have been simpler. Her children will be the land-heirs of Ymris; if she were that powerful, that lawless, surely the High One would have acted then. Astrin must be wrong. I must have been dreaming, that night. And yet . . ." He shook his head, his hand sliding over his eyes. "I don't know. I'm glad all this is none of my business."

The King's physician checked him, forbade him to set one foot on the floor, and gave him a hot, heady mixture of wine and herbs at evening that slid him into a dreamless sleep. He woke only once, sometime in the middle of the night, to find Rork Umber reading by the fire. The High Lord's bright hair blurred against the flames as Morgon's eyes closed and he slept again.

Heureu and Eriel came to see him the next afternoon. Astrin, who had relieved Rork, stood at the broad windows, overlooking the city; Morgon saw the eyes of the king and his land-heir meet a moment, expressionlessly. Then Heureu pulled chairs to the bedside and sat down.

He said tiredly, "Morgon, Anoth ordered me not to disturb you, but I must. Meroc Tor has laid siege to the High Lord of Meremont; I am leaving in two days with a force from Ruhn, Caerweddin and Umber to break it. I have had word that there is a fleet of warships on the coasts of Meremont ready to set sail for Caerweddin if Meremont falls. If those ships succeed in reaching Caerweddin, you're liable to be trapped here indefinitely. For your own safety, I think you should be moved north, to the house of the High Lord of Marcher."

Morgon did not answer for a moment. He said slowly, "Heureu, I am grateful for the care you've given me, and for your kindness. But I would rather not go any farther from Hed than I am now. Can you spare a ship to send me home?"

The dark, troubled face eased a little. "I can. But I thought you might object to going home by sea. I can send you in one of my own trade-ships, under guard. I know my own traders well; I've sailed with them."

"You have?"

"To Anuin, Caithnard, even Kraal . . ." He smiled reminiscently. "That was when I was younger, and my father was still alive. Astrin went to Caithnard to study, but I chose to learn about the world beyond Ymris in a different way. I loved it, but since I took the land-rule, I have rarely left Ymris."

"Is that when you met my father? On one of your journeys?"

Heureu shook his head. "I met your parents last spring, when Eriel and I visited Caithnard."

"Last spring." He drew a breath. "You saw them then. I had no idea."

"You couldn't have," Eriel said softly, and Astrin, at the window, turned. Her soft brows were crooked a little anxiously, but she continued, "We met when—when Heureu bumped into your mother, Spring, on a crowded street and broke a glass bowl she was carrying. She started crying. I think she was frightened of all the people and the noise. And your father tried to get her to stop—we all tried—but she wouldn't come out from behind her hands. So we just talked for a while. We told each other our names, and your father began to tell us about you, how you went to college there. He was very proud of you. And, of course, your mother came out then, because we were talking about her child." She smiled quickly at the memory; then her brows drew together again, and her eyes dropped from his gaze. "We had supper together and talked into the night. Your mother . . . I had—I had a child that died a few months before that, and I was never able to speak about it to anyone until that night, to her. So when we returned to Caerweddin and heard what happened to them, I felt . . . I was deeply grieved."

Morgon's lips parted as he watched her. His eyes flicked once to Astrin, but the white eyes were unreadable. Heureu's hand touched hers, closed over it. He said gently, "Morgon, your father said something that I remembered suddenly last night. He told me he had bought a harp for you, a very beautiful, odd-looking harp he thought you'd like. He had paid almost nothing for it, to some wandering Lungold trader because it was cursed, it didn't play. He said no sensible man believed in curses. I asked him how you would be able to play it, then, and he just smiled and said he thought you could. He didn't show it to me because it was packed on the ship. I realized last night that your father must have known you could play that harp because it had your stars on its face."

Morgon tried to speak; his voice would not come. He rose suddenly, unsteadily, stood staring into the fire, oblivious to everything but one terrible thought. "Is that what happened? Someone saw those stars and made a death-ship for them, whose crew vanished, left them alone, helpless, with the ship tearing apart around them, not knowing, not understanding why? Is that how they died? Is that—" He turned abruptly saw the wine in its glass flagon by the fire, the cups of glass and gold, and he swept them in a single, furious movement off the table to smash against the stones. The broken shards beaded with red wine on the floor brought him back to himself. He said, his face bloodless, drawn, "I'm sorry . . . I didn't . . . I keep breaking things."

Heureu had risen. He gripped Morgon firmly; his voice sounded distant, then returned, full. "I should have thought a little—I should have thought. Lie down before you hurt yourself. I'll get Anoth."

Morgon, scarcely hearing them leave, pushed his face tightly against the crook of his arm, felt tears burn like seawater in his eyes.

He woke later, slowly, to the sound of low intense voices: Astrin's and Heureu's. The muted anger in the King's voice broke the web of his dark dreaming like a cold wind.

"Do you think I'm witless, Astrin? I don't have to ask where to find you or Rork Umber, or even the High One's harpist, even at midnight. What Deth does is the High One's business, but if you and Rork spent as much time concerning yourself with the problems at hand as you do exhausting yourselves guarding against an illusion in this room, I would feel easier about the fate of Caerweddin."

Astrin's voice came back at him, cold, edged. "There are more illusions in this land than the woman you married. Anyone could come in here wearing a face so familiar none of us would think to see beneath it—"

"What do you want me to do? Mistrust every man and woman in my house? Is that what moved you to the far corner of Ymris—such terrible mistrust? I've seen the way you look at her, talk to her. What is it? Is it her unborn children you are jealous of? Do you want the land-rule that badly? I've heard that rumor too, but I've never come close to believing it before."

Astrin stared at him, silent, motionless, his colorless face like a mask. Then something broke in it; he turned away. He whispered, "I can take anything from you but that. I'm going back to Wind Plain. That woman nearly killed the Prince of Hed in your hall three nights ago; I'm not staying to watch her succeed. You watch; you married her."

He left Heureu gazing at the open, empty doorway. Morgon saw the first, faint uncertainty in his eyes before he followed.

Morgon shifted restlessly. The irresolvable quarrel, the hopeless questioning, the black, heavy thought of his parents' deaths loomed like a growth in his mind. He tried to get up, yielded, and fell back into a half-sleep. He woke with a startled murmur as the door opened again. Astrin came to his side.

Morgon said huskily, "I keep dreaming of that bowl I broke: the figures are moving around it in some strange pattern, a riddle I am on the verge of answering when it shatters, and with it all the answers to all the riddles in the world shatter. Why did you come back? I wouldn't blame you if you had left."

Astrin did not answer. Instead, with brief, methodical movements, he pulled the furs off Morgon, bundled them in his arms, and pushed them with all his strength against Morgon's face.

The fur in Morgon's face stifled his startled cry. The heavy weight of it melted around him, forced into his dry mouth, his eyes. He gripped the hands that held it down, struggled to pull them apart to move from the bed while the blood snapped and sang in his ears, and the darkness seemed to eddy him in huge, ponderous circles.

Then he found air again, a clean edge of it, and knelt on the floor, his voice sobbing, rattling like pebbles as he breathed. Next to the fire, Heureu, his hands twisted in the shoulders of Astrin's robe, had the man against the wall, while Rork Umber's sword lay like a lick of flame against his breast.

Morgon pulled himself up. Heureu and Rork were gazing incredulously at the mute, white-eyed figure. Rork was whispering, as if he had no breath for speech, "I don't believe it. I don't believe—"

A movement in the doorway caught Morgon's eye. He tried to speak; his voice, bruised, trapped, made for one last time a harsh, desperate bird-cry that turned their uncomprehending faces towards him.

"Heureu."

The King whirled. Astrin stood in the doorway. For a moment neither he nor Heureu moved; then expression came into Heureu's eyes. He said, "Be careful. I haven't got your gift for seeing. If I get you confused, I'll never understand this."

Rork said sharply, "Heureu!"

The figure beneath his sword was fading. It drifted like smoke beyond their eyes into the air, until suddenly it was gone and a white bird shot through the air towards Astrin.

He flung up his arms as it struck his face. They cried out together, he and the bird; he stumbled and fell, his hands over his eyes. Morgon reached him first, held him, and saw the blood trickling between the taut fingers covering one eye. There was a crash behind them; wind moaned into the room through the colored, jagged spears of window glass the bird left in its passing.

Heureu went to Astrin. Murmuring gently, incoherently, he moved Astrin's fingers from his eye. He drew a sharp breath, and snapped to a white-faced page staring at them in the hall.

"Get Anoth."

Astrin, his head in the crook of Morgon's shoulder, his eyes closed, said raggedly, "I was going to leave, but I couldn't. I came back to Morgon's room to see if you were still there, and as I came down the hall, I saw . . . I saw myself go into the room ahead of me. So I did something I've never been able to do before. I threw a call to you through the stones, into your mind—the wizard's call. I wait—I waited. That was hard to do, but you wanted proof."

"I know. Lie still. You've done—" He stopped. For a moment nothing of him moved, his breath, his hands, his eyes, while the blood drained slowly from his face. He whispered, "So long ago. That white bird." He stopped, kneeling hunched over Astrin, and they were silent. He rose abruptly; Rork gripped his shoulder.

"Heureu."

The King pulled away from him, strode down the long, empty hallway. Morgon closed his eyes. The Lady Anoth came, grim and breathless, to bandage Astrin's eye. Rork helped him up. Relieved of his burden, Morgon stood alone for the moment. He went to the window, touched the broken glass. He saw then, beyond Caerweddin, the stones of the ruined city on King's Mouth Plain, scattered like the bones of some gigantic, nameless man.

He dressed, went downstairs to the great hall. Firelight coiled deep in the stars on the face of the harp. He picked it up, slung it by its jewelled strap over his shoulder. He heard a step behind him and turned. The High One's harpist, his hair web-colored in the hearthlight, reached out, touched the stars.

He said softly, "I was there when Yrth made this harp. I heard the first song it ever played . . ."

His hand moved, closed gently on Morgon's shoulder, and Morgon's trembling eased. He said, "I want to leave."

"I'll ask the king to put a ship and guards at your disposal. You should be well enough to travel to Hed, if you're careful."

"I'm not going to Hed. I am going to Erlenstar Mountain." The stars, as he looked down on them, seemed like a reflection of his own face. "I can ignore the threats to my own life. I can deny my curiosity. I can deny that there is in me, somewhere, a man whose name I do not know. But I can't deny that these stars on my face may be deadly to those I love. So I am going to Erlenstar Mountain to ask the High One why."

The harpist was silent; Morgon could not read the expression in his eyes. "Are you going by sea?"

"No. I want to get there alive."

"It's late in the year for travelling north. It will be a long, lonely, dangerous journey; you'll be away from Hed for months."

"Are you trying to dissuade me?" Morgon asked, surprised.

The hand at his shoulder tightened faintly. "I haven't been to Erlenstar Mountain for three years, and, barring instructions from the High One, I would like to go home. May I travel with you?"

Morgon bowed his head, touched the harp, and stray strings sounded gently, haltingly, as though he were feeling for the beginning of some great song. "Thank you. But will you mind travelling with a man tracked by death?"

"Not when that man is carrying the harp of the Harpist of Lungold."

They left at dawn the next morning, so quietly only Heureu and the half-blind Ymris land-heir knew they had gone. They rode northward through King's Mouth Plain, their long morning shadows splaying across the massive, patternless stones. A gull, wheeling in the cool air, gave one cry above them, like a challenge, then winged, bright in the clear morning, southward over the line of lean, blue-sailed warships taking the slow tide of the Thul toward the sea.

5

THEY JOURNEYED SLOWLY through Ymris, as Morgon fought the last stages of his illness, avoiding the great houses of the Ymris lords, taking shelter after an easy day's riding in small villages that blossomed at the crux of a patchwork of field, or in the curve of a river. Deth paid for their shelter with his harping. Morgon, nursing a cold in miserable silence, sipping hot broth the women made for him, watched weary farmers and unruly children settle quietly to the sound of Deth's beautiful, intricate harping, his fine, skilled voice. They were given without hesitation any song, ballad, dance they asked for; and occasionally someone would bring out his own harp, a harp that had been passed down for generations, and recite a curious history of it, or play a variation of a song that Deth could invariably repeat after listening once. Morgon, his eyes on the ageless face bent slightly above the polished oak harp, felt the familiar nudge of a question in the back of his mind.

In the rocky fields and low border hills of Marcher, where villages and farms were rare on the rough land, they found themselves camping for the first time in the open. They stopped beside a narrow stream under a stand of three oaks. The late sun in the clear, dark-blue sky glanced off the red faces of rocks pushing up in the soil, and turned the hill grass gold. Morgon, coaxing a young fire, paused a moment and looked around him. The rough, undulating land flowed toward old, worn hills that seemed in their bald, smooth lines like old men sleeping. He said wonderingly, "I've never seen such lonely land."

Deth, unpacking their store of bread, cheese, wine and the apples and nuts one villager had given them, smiled. "Wait until you reach Isig Pass. This is gentle country."

"It's immense. If I had travelled this long in a straight line across Hed, I would have been walking on the ocean bottom a week ago." He added a branch to the fire, watched the flames eat across the dry leaves. The dull ache and weariness of fever had dropped away from him finally, leaving him clear-headed and curious, enjoying the cool wind and the colors. Deth handed him the wineskin; he took a mouthful. The fire, rousing, shimmered in the clean air like some rich, strange cloth; Morgon, catching a reflection of it in his memories, said slowly, "I should write to Raederle."

He had not spoken her name since they had left Caithnard. The colors of the memory resolved into long, flighty, fiery hair, hands flashing with gold and amber, amber-colored eyes. He tossed another branch on the fire and felt the harpist's eyes on his face. He sat back against a tree, reached for the wine again.

"And Eliard. The traders will probably tell him enough to worry him grey-haired before any letter of mine reaches him. If I get killed on this journey, he'll never forgive me."

"If we skirt Herun, you may not be able to send letters until we reach Osterland."

"I should have thought of writing before." He passed the wineskin to the harpist and sliced a wedge of cheese; his eyes strayed again to the fire. "After our father died, we grew so close that sometimes we dream the same dreams. . . . I was that close to my father as his land-heir. I felt him die. I didn't know how or why or where; I simply knew, at that moment, that he was dying. And then that he was dead, and the land-rule had passed to me. For a moment I saw every leaf, every new-planted seed, every root in Hed . . . I was every leaf, every new-planted seed. . . ." He leaned forward, reached for the bread. "I don't know why I'm talking about that. You must have heard it a hundred times."

"The passage of the land-rule? No. From what little I have heard, though, the passing isn't so gentle in other lands. Mathom of An told me some of the various bindings that demand constant attention from the land-rulers of An: the binding of the spell-books of Madir, the binding of the ancient, rebellious lords of Hel in their graves, the binding of Peven in his tower."

"Rood told me that. I wonder if Mathom has set Peven free now that I have the crown. Or rather," he added ruefully, "now that Peven's crown is at the bottom of the sea."

"I doubt it. The kings' bindings are not broken lightly. Nor are their vows."

Morgon, tearing a chunk of bread from the loaf, felt a light flush burn his face. He looked at the harpist, said a little shyly, "I believe that. But I could never ask Raederle to marry me if she had no other reason than Mathom's vow to accept me. It's her choice, not Mathom's, and she may not choose to live in Hed. But if there's a chance, then I just want to write and tell her that I will come, eventually, in case—if she wants to wait." He took a bite of bread and cheese, asked rather abruptly, "How long will it take us to get to Erlenstar Mountain?"

"If we reach Isig Mountain before winter, it will take perhaps six weeks. If the snow gets to Isig before us, we may have to stay there until spring."

"Would it be faster to go around Herun to the west and up through the wilderness lands to Erlenstar without going through the Pass?"

"Through the back door of Erlenstar? You would have to be part wolf to survive the backlands in this season. I've taken that way only a few times in my life, and never this late in the year."

Morgon tilted his head back against the tree. "It occurred to me a couple of days ago," he said, "when I started to think again, that if you weren't with me, I would not have the slightest idea what direction to go next. You move through this land as though you've been across it a thousand times."

"I may have. I've lost count." He fed the fire, the eager flames flicking in his quiet eyes. The sun had gone down; the grey wind set the dry leaves chattering above them in some unknown tongue.

Morgon asked suddenly, "How long have you been in the High One's service?"

"When Tirunedeth died, I left Herun, and the High One called me to Erlenstar Mountain."

"Six hundred years. . . . What did you do before that?"

"Harped, travelled. . . ." He fell silent, his eyes on the fire; then he added almost reluctantly, "I studied awhile at Caithnard. But I didn't want to teach, so I left after taking the Black."

Morgon, raising the wineskin to his mouth, lowered it without drinking. "I had no idea you were a Master. What was your name, then?" As the question left his tongue, he felt the blood burn again in his face, and he said quickly, "Forgive me. I forget that some things I want to know are none of my business."

"Morgon—" He stopped. They ate in silence awhile, then Deth reached for his harp, uncased it. He ran a thumb softly across the strings. "Have you tried to play that harp of yours yet?"

Morgon smiled. "No. I'm afraid of it."

"Try."

Morgon took the harp out of the soft leather case Heureu had given him for it. The burning net of gold, the bone-white moons and polished wood held him wordless a moment with their beauty. Deth plucked the high string on his harp; Morgon echoed it softly, his own string perfectly pitched. Deth took him slowly down the gleaming run of strings, and he found note after note precisely tuned. Only twice the sounds jarred slightly, and each time Deth stopped to tune his own harp.

He said, as Morgon's fingers moved to the low note, "I don't have a string to tune that to."

Morgon moved his hand quickly. The sky was black above them; the wind had stilled. The firelight traced the groins and arches of the dark, twisted branches sheltering them. He said wonderingly, "How can it still be in tune after all these years, even after it was washed up from the sea?"

"Yrth bound the pitch into those strings with his voice. There is no harp more beautiful in the High One's realm."

"And neither you nor I can play it." His eyes moved to Deth's harp, its pale, carved pieces burnished in the firelight. It was adorned with neither metal nor jewels, but the oak pieces were finely scrolled on all sides with delicate carving. "Did you make your harp?"

Deth smiled, surprised. "Yes." He traced a line of carving, and something in his face opened unexpectedly. "I made it when I was young, by my standards, after years of playing on various harps. I shaped its pieces out of Ymris oak beside night fires in far, lonely places where I heard no man's voice but my own. I carved on each piece the shapes of leaves, flowers, birds I saw in my wanderings. In An, I searched three months for strings for it. I found them finally; sold my horse for them. They were strung to the broken harp of Ustin of Aum, who died of sorrow over the conquering of Aum. Its strings were tuned to his sorrow, and its wood was split like his heart. I strung my harp with them, matching note for note in the restringing. And then I returned them to my joy."

Morgon drew a breath. His head bowed suddenly, his face hidden from the harpist. He was silent for a long time, while Deth waited, stirring the fire now and then, the sparks shooting upward like stars. He lifted his head finally.

"Why did Yrth put the stars on this harp?"

"He made it for you."

Morgon's head gave a swift, single shake. "No one could have known of me. No one."

"Perhaps," Deth said quietly. "But when I saw you in Hed, I thought of that harp; and the stars on it and the stars on your face fit together like a riddle and its answer."

"Then who . . ." He stopped again, his voice unsteady. He leaned back, his face blurring in the shadows. "I can't ignore all this and I can't understand it, though I've been trying very hard to do both. I'm a riddle-master. Why am I so terribly ignorant? Why did Yrth never mention the stars in his works? Who is behind me, trailing me in the dark, and where does she come from? If these stars signalled such a reaction from such strange, powerful people, why were the wizards themselves ignorant of both the stars and the people? I spent one entire winter with Master Ohm at Caithnard, looking for a reference to the stars in the history, poetry, legends and songs of the realm. Yrth himself, writing about the making of that harp at Isig, never mentioned the stars. Yet my parents are dead, Astrin lost an eye, and I've been nearly killed three times because of them. There's so little sense to this, sometimes I think I'm trying to understand a dream, except that no dream could be so deadly. Deth, I am afraid even to begin to untangle this."

Deth put a branch on the fire, and a wave of light etched Morgon's face out of the shadows. "Who was Sol of Isig and why did he die?"

Morgon turned his face away. "Sol was the son of Danan Isig. He was pursued through the mines of Isig Mountain one day by traders who wanted to steal from him a priceless jewel. He came to the stone door at the bottom of Isig, beyond which lay dread and sorrow older even than Isig. He could not bring himself to open that door, which no man had ever opened, for fear of what might lie in the darkness beyond it. So his enemies found him in his indecision, and there he died."

"And the stricture?"

"Turn forward into the unknown, rather than backward toward death." He was silent again, his eyes hidden. He righted the harp; his fingers moved over the strings, picked out the melody of a gentle ballad of Hed.

Deth, listening, said, "'The Love of Hover and Bird' . . . Can you sing it?"

"All eighteen verses. But I can't play it on this—"

"Watch." He positioned his own harp. "When you open your mind and hands and heart to the knowing of a thing, there is no room in you for fear."

He taught Morgon chords and key changes on the great harp; they played late into the night, sending harp-notes like flurries of birds into the darkness.

They spent one more night in Ymris, then crossed the worn hills and turned eastward, skirting the low mountains, beyond which lay the plains and tors of Herun. The autumn rains began again, monotonous, persistent, and they rode silently through the wilderness between the lands, hunched into voluminous, hooded cloaks, their harps trussed in leather, tucked beneath them. They slept in what dry places they could find in shallow caves of rock, beneath thick groves of trees, their fires wavering reluctantly in wind and rain. Deth, when the rains slackened, played songs Morgon had never heard before, from Isig, Herun, Osterland, from the court of the High One. He would try to follow Deth's playing on his own harp, his notes lagging, faltering, then suddenly meeting Deth's, matching them, and the voices of the two harps would meld for a moment, tuned and beautiful, until he lost himself again and stopped, frustrated, bringing a smile to Deth's face. And somehow the sound of their harping reached the ears of the Morgol at the court deep in Herun.

They rode long one day through wet, rocky land. They camped late in the evening, too tired to do more than build a small fire when the rain drizzled to a stop, eat, and stretch out in their damp bedrolls to sleep. Morgon, restless on the rough ground, woke every now and then to grope at a stone beneath him. He dreamed of mile upon mile of lonely land, the rain drumming on it unceasingly and he heard beneath the drumming the slower beat of hooves. Shifting, he felt the hard nudge of a rock underneath him, and opened his eyes. In the faint, orange wash of embers, he saw a face looming over Deth, a spearhead stopped above his heart.

Morgon, his mouth dry, reached for a stone the size of his fist, raised himself abruptly and threw it. He heard a thump and a gasp, and the face vanished. Deth woke with a start. He sat up, looking at Morgon, but before he could speak, a rock shot with fine accuracy out of the darkness, smacked against the arm Morgon was leaning on, and he dropped.

A voice said irritably, "Do we have to throw rocks at each other like children?"

Deth said, "Lyra."

Morgon raised his head. A girl of fourteen or fifteen stepped to their fire, stirred the embers until they caught, and tossed a handful of twigs on it. Her heavy, loose coat was the color of flame; her dark hair was drawn back from her face, coiled in a thick braid on the crown of her head. Finished, she straightened, holding one arm as though it pained her. In the other hand she held a light spear of ash and silver. Morgon sat up. Her eyes flicked to his face and the spear shifted swiftly to him.

"Are you done?"

Morgon demanded, "Who are you?"

"I am Lyraluthuin, daughter of the Morgol of Herun. You are Morgon, Prince of Hed. We are instructed to bring you to the Morgol."

"In the middle of the night?" Then he said, "We?"

She lifted an arm suddenly, and like a ring of color out of the darkness other young women in long, bright, richly woven coats surrounded their camp, spearpoints forming a jagged, glittering circle. Morgon, rubbing his arm, eyed them darkly. His eyes flicked to Deth in a sudden, urgent question. Deth shook his head.

"No. If this were a trap set by Eriel, you would be dead by now."

"I don't know who Eriel is," Lyra said. Her voice had lost its annoyance; it was light, assured. "And this is not a trap. It's a request."

"You have a strange way of making a request," Morgon commented. "I would like the honor of meeting the Morgol of Herun, but I dare not take the time now. We must reach Isig Mountain before the snow starts."

"I see. Would you like to ride into Crown City as befits a ruler, or would you rather ride slung over your saddle like a sack of grain?"

Morgon stared at her. "What kind of a welcome is that? If the Morgol ever came to Hed, she would never be welcomed with—"

"Rocks? You attacked me first."

"You were standing over Deth with a spear in your hand! Should I have stopped to ask why?"

"You should have known I wouldn't touch the High One's harpist. Please rise and saddle your horse."

Morgon lay back, folding his arms. "I'm not going anywhere," he said firmly, "except back to sleep."

"It's not the middle of the night," Lyra said calmly. "It's nearly dawn." In a swift movement, she thrust her spear across him and picked up his harp by the strap. He caught at it rising; the spearhead swooped away from him with its burden. She tilted the spear, let the harp slide down it to her shoulder. "The Morgol warned me of that harp. You could have broken our spears if you had been thinking. Now that you've gotten up, please saddle your horse."

Morgon drew an outraged breath, then saw somewhere in the clear look she gave him, a suppressed smile that reminded him oddly of Tristan. The anger left his face, but he sat down again on the bare ground and said, "No. I haven't time to go to Herun."

"Then you will be—"

"And if you take me bound into the City of Circles, the traders will have the tale all over the realm by spring, and I will complain first to the Morgol, and then to the High One."

She was silent for a breath; then her chin went up. "I am of the chosen guard of the Morgol, and I have a duty to perform. You will come, one way or another."

"No."

"Lyra," Deth said. There was an overtone of amusement in his voice, and his words seemed almost perfunctory. "We must go to Isig before winter. We have no time for delay."

She bowed her head respectfully. "I do not seek to delay you. I didn't even want to wake you. But the Morgol requires the Prince of Hed."

"The Prince of Hed requires the High One."

"I have a duty—"

"Your duty does not preclude the respectful treatment of land-rulers."

"Respectful or not," Morgon said, "I'm not going. Why are you discussing the matter with her? Tell her. She'll listen to you. She's a child, and we can't be bothered with children's games."

Lyra surveyed him composedly. "No one who knows me calls me that. I said you would come one way or another. The Morgol has questions she would like to ask you about the stars on your face and that harp. She has seen it before. I would have told you sooner, but I lost my temper when you threw that rock."

Morgon looked up at her. "Where?" he said. "Where did she see it?"

"She'll tell you. There is also a riddle I am to give you when we have crossed the mountains and the marshes, and Crown City is in our sight. She says it holds your name."

In the wash of the single flame, the blood ran suddenly out of Morgon's face. He rose. "I'll come."

Riding from dawn to sunset, they followed Lyra through a little-travelled pass in the low, ancient mountains, and camped on the other side of them the next night. Morgon, wrapped in his cloak by the fire, sat watching the chill, misty breath of the marshes ease toward them up the mountain. Deth, his hands seemingly inured to the cold, played a lovely, wordless song that danced into Morgon's thoughts, drawing him out of them until he yielded and listened.

He said when it ended, "What was that? It was beautiful."

Deth smiled. "I never gave it a name." He sat a moment in silence, then reached for the harp case. Lyra, appearing without a sound in their circle of fire-light, begged, "Don't stop. Everyone is listening. That was the song you composed for the Morgol."

Morgon looked at the harpist, amazed. Deth said, "Yes," his fingers moving lightly down the strings, sliding into a new weave. Lyra took Morgon's harp from her shoulder and set it down beside him.

"I meant to give you this earlier." She sat down, held out her hands to the fire. The light gave her young face rich, rounded shadings; Morgon's eyes were drawn to it. He said abruptly, "Do you always wait outside the borders of Herun to abduct land-rulers passing by?"

"I didn't abduct you," she said imperturbably. "You chose to come. And—" she went on as he drew breath to expostulate, "I usually lead traders through the marshes. Visitors from other lands are rare, and when they come, sometimes they don't know enough to wait for me, and they fall in the marshes or get lost. Also, I protect the Morgol when she travels beyond Herun, and carry out whatever other duties she gives me. I'm skilled with a knife, a bow, and a spear; and the last man who underestimated my skill is dead."

"You killed him?"

"He forced me to. He was going to rob traders under my protection, and when I warned him to stop he ignored me, which was not wise. He was going to kill one of the traders, so I killed him."

"Why does the Morgol let you travel unattended, if such things happen to you?"

"I am her guard, and I am expected to take care of myself. And you: why are you travelling unarmed as a child through the High One's realm?"

"I have the harp," he reminded her stiffly, but she shook her head.

"It's no use to you in its case. There are other enemies besides me in the out-lands: wild men who prey on traders beyond the boundaries of king's laws, exiles—you should arm yourself."

"I'm a farmer, not a warrior."

"There's not a man in the High One's realm who would dare touch Deth. But you—"

"I can take care of myself. Thank you."

Her brows flicked up. She said kindly, "I'm only trying to give you the benefit of my experience. No doubt Deth can take care of you if there's trouble."

Deth's voice trailed into his harping. "The Prince of Hed is remarkably adept at surviving. . . . Hed is a land renowned for its peace, a concept often difficult to understand."

"The Prince of Hed," Lyra said, "is no longer in Hed."

Morgon looked at her distantly across the fire. "An animal doesn't change its skin or its instincts because it travels out of one land into another."

She disregarded his argument and said helpfully, "I could teach you to throw a spear. It's simple. It might be useful to you. You had good aim with that rock."

"That's a good enough weapon for me. I might kill someone with a spear."

"That's what it's for."

He sighed. "Think of it from a farmer's point of view. You don't uproot cornstalks, do you, before the corn is ripe? Or cut down a tree full of young green pears? So why should you cut short a man's life in the mist of his actions, his mind's work—"

"Traders," Lyra said, "don't get killed by pear trees."

"That's not the point. If you take a man's life, he has nothing. You can strip him of his land, his rank, his thoughts, his name, but if you take his life, he has nothing. Not even hope."

She listened quietly, the light moving in her dark eyes. "And if there is a choice between your life and his, which one would you choose?"

"My life, of course." Then he thought about it and winced a little. "I think."

She loosed a breath. "It's unreasonable."

He smiled in spite of himself. "I suppose so. But if I ever killed anyone, how would I tell Eliard? Or Grim Oakland?"

"Who is Eliard? Who is Grim Oakland?"

"Grim is my overseer. Eliard is my brother, my land-heir."

"Oh, you have a brother? I always wanted one. But I have no one except cousins, and the guard, which is like a family of sisters. Do you have a sister?"

"Yes. Tristan."

"What is she like?"

"Oh, a little younger than you. Dark, like you. A little like you except that she doesn't annoy me as much."

To his surprise, she laughed. "I did, didn't I? I wondered when you would stop being angry with me." She got to her feet in a single, lithe movement. "I think the Morgol may not be very pleased with me either, but I'm not generally polite to people who surprise me, as you did."

"How will the Morgol know?"

"She knows." She bent her dark head to them. "Thank you for your playing, Deth. Good night. We will ride at dawn."

She stepped out of the firelight, faded into the night so quietly they could not hear a single footstep. Morgon reached for his bedroll. The mist from the marshes had come upon them and the night was damp and chill as a knife's edge. He put another branch on the fire and lay close to it. A thought struck him as he watched the flames, and he gave a short, mirthless laugh.

"If I were skilled in arms, I might have thrown a spear at her this morning instead of a rock. And she wants to teach me."

The next morning, he saw Herun, a small land ringed with mountains, fill like a bowl with dawn. Morning mists fell as they reached the flat lands, and great peaks of rock rose through them like curious faces. Low plains of grass, wind-twisted trees, and ground that sucked at their horse's hooves appeared and disappeared in the whorls of mist. Now and then Lyra stopped until the shifting mists revealed some landmark that showed her the path.

Morgon, accustomed to land that was predictable underfoot, rode unconcerned until Lyra, stopping a moment for him to catch up to her, said, "These are the great Herun marshes. Crown City lies on the other side of them. The path through them is a gift from the Morgol, which few people know. So if you must enter or leave Herun quickly, go north across the mountains rather than this way. Many people in a hurry have vanished here without a trace."

Morgon looked with sudden interest at the ground his horse walked on. "I'm glad you told me."

The mists rolled away eventually, baring a blue sky without a cloud, vibrant against the wet green plains. Stone houses, small villages rose on the crests of the undulating plain, huddled at the feet of stone peaks that rose without preface from the ground. In the distance, a road stroked the plain white here and there in its twistings. A smudge detached itself from the horizon smoky with mountains, and began to take shape. A pattern of stonework gleamed against the earth: a vast circle of red, upright stones like flaming sentinels around a black oval house. As they neared, a river spilling from the northern mountains rose to their view, split blue through the plain and ran into the heart of the stonework.

"Crown City," Lyra said. "It is also known as the City of Circles." She stopped her horse; and the guard behind her stopped.

Morgon said, his eyes on the distant stones, "I've heard of that city. What are the seven circles of Herun and who built them? Rhu, the fourth Morgol, structured the city, planning a circle for each of eight riddles his curiosity set to him and he answered. His journey to answer the eighth riddle killed him. What that riddle was no one knows."

"The Morgol knows," Lyra said. Her voice drew Morgon's eyes from the city. He felt something jump deep within him. She went on, holding his eyes. "The riddle that killed Rhu is the one I am to give you now from the Morgol: Who is the Star-Bearer, and what will he loose that is bound?"

Morgon's breath stopped. He shook his head once, his mouth shaping a word without sound. Then he shouted it at her, startling her: "No!"

He wrenched his horse around, kicked it, and it leaped forward. The grassy plain blurred beneath him. He bent low in the saddle, heading toward the marshlands innocently smooth under the sun, and the low mountains beyond. He did not hear the hooves behind him until a flick of color drew his eyes sideways. His face set, rigid, he urged his horse forward, the earth pounding beneath him, but the black horse stayed with him like a shadow, neither slowing nor speeding while he raced toward the line where the earth locked with the sky. He felt his horse falter suddenly, its speed slacken, and then Deth reached across for his reins, brought him jolting to a stop.

He said, his breathing quick, "Morgon—"

Morgon jerked his reins free from Deth's hold and backed his horse a step. He said, his voice shaking, "I'm going home. I don't have to go any farther with this. I have a choice."

Deth's hand went out toward him quickly, as though to soothe a frightened animal. "Yes. You have a choice. But you will never reach Hed riding blind through the Herun marshes. If you want to go back to Hed, I'll take you. But Morgon, think a little first. You are trained to think. I can lead you through the marshes, but then what will you do? Will you go back through Ymris? Or by the sea from Osterland?"

"I'll skirt Ymris and go to Lungold—I'll take the trade road to Caithnard—I'll disguise myself as a trader—"

"And if you reach Hed by some thread of chance, then what? You will be bound nameless on that island for the rest of your life."

"You don't understand!" His eyes were startled, like an animal's at bay. "My life has been shaped before me—shaped for me by something—someone who has seen my actions before I even see a reason for them. How could Yrth have seen me hundreds of years ago to make this harp for me? Who saw me two thousand years ago to set the riddle to my life that killed the Morgol Rhu? I am being forced into some pattern of action I can't see, I can't control—given a name I do not want—I have the right of choice! I was born to rule Hed, and that is where I belong—that is my name and my place."

"Morgon, you may see yourself as the Prince of Hed, but there are others seeking answers to those same questions you ask, and they will give you this name: Star-Bearer, and there will be no peace for them until you are dead. They will never let you live peacefully in Hed. They will follow you there. Will you open the doors of Hed to Eriel? To those that killed Athol, and tried to kill you? What mercy will they have for your farmers, for your toothless pigherder? If you go back to Hed now, death will ride behind you, beside you, and you will find it waiting for you beyond the open doors of your house."

"Then I won't go to Hed." His face struggled against itself; he turned it away from Deth. "I'll go to Caithnard, to take the Black, and teach—"

"Teach what? The riddles that are no truth to you, nothing more than ancient tales spun at twilight—"

"That's not true!"

"What of Astrin? Heureu? They are bound also in the riddle of your life; they need your clear vision, your courage—"

"I have none! Not for this! Death at least I have seen; I can look at it and give it a name, but this—this path that is building before me—I can't even see! I don't know who I am, what I was born to do. In Hed, at least I have a name!"

Deth's voice quieted. He had crossed the distance Morgon held between them; his hand gripped Morgon's forearm gently. "There is a name for you beyond Hed. Morgon, what use are the riddles and strictures of Caithnard, if not for this? You are Sol of Isig, caught up by fear between death and a door that has been closed for thousands of years. If you have no faith in yourself, then have faith in the things you call truth. You know what must be done. You may not have courage or trust or understanding or the will to do it, but you know what must be done. You can't turn back. There is no answer behind you. You fear what you cannot name. So look at it and find a name for it. Turn your face forward and learn. Do what must be done."

The winds breathed down the long plain, broke against them, turning the grass silver. Behind them, like a cluster of bright flowers, the guard of the Morgol waited.

Morgon's fingers crushed his reins and loosed them. He lifted his head slowly, "It's not your business, as the High One's harpist, to give me such advice. Or do you speak to me as one who can wear by right the Black of Mastery? No riddle-master at Caithnard ever gave me that name, Star-Bearer; they never knew it existed. Yet you accept it as though you expected it. What hope that no one else but you has ever seen, what riddle, are you seeing in me?" The harpist, his eyes falling suddenly from Morgon's, did not answer. Morgon's voice rose, "I ask you this: Who was Ingris of Osterland and why did he die?"

Deth shifted his hand on Morgon's arm. There was an odd expression on his face. He said after a moment, "Ingris of Osterland angered Har, the King of Osterland one night when he appeared as an old man at Ingris's door, and Ingris refused to take him in. So the wolf-King put this curse on him: That if the next stranger who came to Ingris's house did not give his name, then Ingris would die. And the first stranger who came after Har left was—a certain harpist. That harpist gave Ingris everything he asked for: songs, tales, the loan of his harp, the history of his travellings—everything but the name Ingris wanted to hear, though Ingris demanded it in despair. But the harpist could give him only one word, each time Ingris asked for his name, and that word, as Ingris heard it, was Death. So in fear of Har, and in despair of the curse, he felt his heart stop and he died." He paused.

Morgon, his face growing quiet as he listened, said haltingly, "I never thought . . . You could have given Ingris your name. Your true name. The stricture is: Give what others require of you for their lives."

"Morgon, there were things I could not give Ingris, and things I cannot give you now. But I swear this: If you finish this harsh journey to Erlenstar Mountain, I will give you anything you ask of me. I will give you my life."

"Why?" he whispered.

"Because you bear three stars."

Morgon was silent. Then he shook his head a little. "I will never have the right to ask that."

"The choice will be mine. Have you thought that the stricture also applies to you? You must give what others require of you."

"And if I can't?"

"Then, like Ingris, you will die."

Morgon's eyes dropped. He sat motionless but for the winds that thrummed like harp notes about him, plucked at his hair, his cloak. He turned his horse finally, rode slowly back to the guard, who, accepting his return in silence, proceeded to the City of Circles.

THE MORGOL OF Herun welcomed them into her courtyard. She was a tall woman with blue-black hair drawn back from her face, falling without a ripple against her loose robe of leaf-green cloth. Her house was a vast oval of black stone. Water from the river flowing beneath it fanned over stone fountains in her yard, formed tiny streams and pools where fish slipped like red and green and gold flames beneath the tracery of shadows from the trees. The Morgol went to Deth's side as he dismounted, smiling at him. They were of a similar height, and her eyes were luminous gold.

"I didn't mean for Lyra to disturb you," she said. "I hope you are not inconvenienced."

An answering smile tugged at his mouth. There was a tone in his voice Morgon had never heard before. "El, you knew I would go where the Prince of Hed chose to go."

"Now, how could I have known that? Your path has always been your own. But I'm glad you chose to come. I dream of your harping."

She walked with him to Morgon, as silent women took their horses out of the yard, and others carried their gear into the house. Her strange eyes melted over him. She held out her hand to him. "I am Elrhiarhodan, the Morgol of Herun. You may call me El. I am very glad you've come."

He bent his head to her, aware suddenly of his travel-stained clothes and unkempt hair. "You gave me no choice."

"No," she said gently, "I did not. You look very tired. For some reason I expected you to be older, or I would have waited to tell you that riddle myself, instead of frightening you with it like that." She turned her head to greet Lyra. "Thank you for bringing the Prince of Hed to me. But was it necessary to throw a rock at him?"

A smile touched Lyra's eyes at Morgon's amazement. She said gravely, "Mother, the Prince of Hed threw a rock at me first, and I lost my temper. Also, I said things which were—not entirely diplomatic. But I don't think he's angry with me any more. He doesn't seem to be any kind of a warrior."

"No, but he had good aim, and if he had been armed, you would be dead, which I would not like at all. The people of Hed do not, as a habit, take arms against others, a laudable restraint. It was perhaps not wise to enter their camp in the dark; you must learn to avoid misunderstandings. But you brought them here safely, and for that I thank you. Now get some food, my child, and some sleep." Lyra left them, and the Morgol tucked her fingers into the crook of Deth's arm. "She has grown since you saw her last. But then you have not come to Herun in some time. Come in."

She led them into her house, through its doors of silver and pale wood. Within, the arched corridors wandered, seemingly without plan, from one room to another; the rooms, with delicate cloth tapestries, strange plants, rich woods and finely wrought metals, followed one another like treasure boxes. The Morgol stopped finally in a room warm with hangings of orange and gold, and bade them rest on soft, enormous cushions covered with white wool. She left them.

Morgon, drowning muscle by weary muscle in sheepskin, closed his eyes and whispered, "I can't remember the last time I touched a bed. . . . Does she go into our minds?"

"The Morgol has the gift of sight. Herun is a small, very rich land; the morgols have developed their sight since the Years of Settlement, when an army from north Ymris attacked Herun with an eye to its mines. Herun is ringed with mountains; the Morgols learned to see through them. I thought you knew that."

"I didn't realize their sight was that good. She startled me." Then he fell asleep, not even waking when, moments later, servants entered with trays of food and wine and all their gear.

He woke hours later to find Deth gone. He washed and dressed himself in the light, loose robe of orange and gold cloth the Morgol had left for him. She had given him also a knife of milky metal sheathed in bone, which he let lie. A servant led him to a broad room, white from floor to ceiling. The guards in their bright robes chattered at one end of it on cushions around a firebed, with trays of steaming dishes on low tables before them. Deth, Lyra and the Morgol sat at a table of polished white stone, the silver cups and plate in front of them sparkling with amethyst. The Morgol, in a robe of silver and white, her hair braided and bound, beckoned to Morgon, smiling. Lyra shifted to give him a place beside her. She served him from dishes of hot spiced meats, seasoned fruits and vegetables, cheeses and wines. Deth, to one side of the Morgol, sat harping softly. He drew a song to a close, then, very lightly, played a phrase from the song he had composed for her.

Her face turned toward him as though he had spoken her name; she smiled and said, "I have made you harp long enough. Sit beside me and eat."

Deth put his harp down and joined her. He was dressed in a coat silver-white as his hair; a chain of silver and tiny, fire-white stones hung on his breast.

Morgon, watching their close faces as the Morgol served him, was drawn out of his preoccupation by Lyra, who said, "Your food is getting cold. He didn't tell you then?"

"What? No." He took a bite of seasoned mushrooms. "At least not in words. I guessed from that song. I don't know why I'm surprised. No wonder he allowed you to take us into Herun."

She nodded. "He wanted to come, but of course the choice was yours."

"Was it? How did the Morgol know the one thing that would have brought me into Herun?"

Lyra smiled. "You are a riddle-master. She said you would answer to a riddle like a hound to scent."

"How did she know that?"

"When Mathom of An was searching for the man who had taken Peven's crown, his messengers came even to Herun with the tale. So, being curious, she made it her business to find out who had it."

"But so few people knew—Deth, Rood of An, the Masters—"

"And the traders who took you from Hed to Caithnard. The Morgol has a talent for finding things out."

"Yes." He moved his cup an inch on the table, frowned down at it a moment. Then he turned to the Morgol, waiting while she spoke with Deth until she paused, and he said, "El." Her coin-colored eyes came to his face. He drew a breath. "How did you know that riddle you gave me? It is listed nowhere in the books of the Masters, and it should have been."

"Should it, Morgon? It seems to be such a dangerous riddle, that only one man should try to answer it. What would the Masters have done with it?"

"They would have searched for the answer. That's their business. Riddles are often dangerous, but an unanswered riddle may be deadly."

"True, as Dhairrhuwyth found—which seems the more reason for keeping it private."

"No," he said, "ignorance is deadly. Please. Where did you find it? I have—I have had to come to Herun to find my name. Why?"

Her eyes dropped, hidden from his a moment. She said slowly, "I found the riddle years ago in an ancient book the Morgol Rhu left as the record of his travellings. The book had been word-locked by the wizard Iff of the Unpronounceable Name, who was in the service to Herun at the time. I had a little difficulty opening the book. Iff had bound it with his name."

"And you pronounced it?"

"Yes. A wise old scholar at my court suggested that perhaps Iff's name should be sung as well as pronounced, and he spent many long hours with me trying to find the notes that belonged with the syllables of Iff's name. Finally, by sheer accident, I sang the name on the right tones, pronouncing it correctly, and unlocked the book. The last entry the Morgol had made in it was the riddle that he left Herun to answer: the riddle of the Star-Bearer. He wrote that he was going to Erlenstar Mountain. Danan found his body and sent it home from Isig. The scholar who helped me is dead, and I—with little more reason than instinct—kept the riddle to myself."

"Why?"

"Oh . . . because it is dangerous; because I had heard from the traders of a child growing up with three stars on his face in Hed; and because I asked a Master at Caithnard what he knew of three stars and he said he had never heard anything about them, and that Master's name was Ohm."

"Master Ohm?" he said startled. "He taught me. Why did his name stop you?"

"It was a small thing, but it set my mind on a train of thought . . . I took his name to be a shortening of a Herun name. Ghisteslwchlohm."

Morgon stared at her. His face lost color. "Ghisteslwchlohm. Who was the Founder of Lungold, and what are the nine strictures of his teachings? But he died. Seven hundred years ago when the wizards disappeared from Lungold."

"Perhaps," she said. "But I wonder . . ." She stirred herself out of her thoughts, touched his wrist. "I'm disturbing your supper with my idle conjectures. But you know, a strange thing happened that I have always wondered about. I have good vision; I can see through anything I choose, though I don't generally choose to see through the people I'm talking to: it tends to be distracting. But while I was with Ohm in the Masters' Library, at one point he had turned to look for a book on his shelves, and as he put his hand on it, I looked through him automatically to see the title. But I couldn't see through him. I could see through the walls of the college, through the cliff and into the sea—but my vision could not pass through Ohm."

Morgon swallowed a tasteless mouthful. "Are you saying—?" His voice caught. "What are you saying?"

"Well, it took me months to put pieces together, since, like you, I would rather have complete faith in the integrity of the Masters of Caithnard. But now, especially since you have come and I can put that riddle to a name and a face, I tend to think that perhaps the Master Ohm is Ghisteslwchlohm, the Founder of the School of Wizards at Lungold, and that he destroyed Lungold."

Morgon made an inarticulate sound in the back of his throat. Lyra protested weakly, "Mother, it's very hard to eat when you say things like that. Why would he have destroyed Lungold after going through all the trouble to found it?"

"Why did he found the College a thousand years ago?"

Lyra shrugged a little. "To teach the wizards. He was the most powerful wizard in the High One's realm, and the other wizards were half-wild, undisciplined; they were unable to use their powers to the full extent. So why would Ohm have tried to teach them to be more powerful if all he wanted to do was destroy their power?"

"Did he gather them there to teach them?" the Morgol said, "or to control them?"

Morgon found his voice again. He said softly, his hands gripping the rough edge of the stone table, "What evidence? On what evidence do you base your conclusions?"

The Morgol drew a breath. The food was growing cold in front of them all. Deth sat quietly listening, his head bent; Morgon could not see his face. Laughter drifted toward them occasionally from the lower tables; the fire in the bed probed to the heart of a log with soft, silken rustlings. "On evidence of an ignorance I do not like," she said. She held his eyes. "Why could the Masters tell you nothing of the stars on your face?"

"Because in their studies no mention was made of them."

"Why?"

"Because—the tales of the kingdoms, their songs and poetry have never mentioned them. The wizards' books that the Masters took from Lungold, which form the basis of their knowledge, say nothing of them."

"Why?"

He was silent, groping for a plausible answer. Then his face changed. He whispered, "Iff, at least, knew what riddle Rhu was trying to answer. He must have known. He talks about Rhu and his searchings in the books the Masters have opened at Caithnard; he listed every riddle Rhu went to answer except that one—"

"Why?"

"I don't . . . I don't know why. Are you saying that Ohm—Ghisteslwchlohm—brought them together to control their knowledge, to teach them only what he wanted them to know? That matters concerning the stars are things he kept them ignorant of—or perhaps even took from their minds?"

"I think it is possible. I think from what I have learned about you from Deth today, that it's quite probable."

"But why? For what possible purpose would he have done that?"

"I don't know. Yet." She continued softly, "Suppose you were a wizard restless with power, drawn to Lungold by the powers of Ohm and his promises of great skill and knowledge. You placed your name in his mind; with your trust in his skill, your absolute faith in his teachings, you did without question whatever he asked of you, and in return he channelled your own energies into powers you scarcely dreamed you had. And then suppose, one day, somehow, you realized that this wizard, whose mind could control yours so skillfully, was false to his teachings, false to you, false to every man, king, scholar, farmer, that he had ever served. What would you do if you found that he had dangerous plans and terrible purposes that you could not even guess at, and that the very foundations of his teachings were a lie? What would you do?"

Morgon was silent. He looked down, watched his hands close on the table into fists, as though they belonged to someone else. He whispered, "Ohm." Then his head gave a quick shake and he said, "I would run. I would run until no one, man or wizard, could find me. And then I would begin to think."

"I would kill him," Lyra said simply. Morgon's hands opened.

"Would you? With what? He would vanish like a mist before your spear touched him. You can't solve riddles by killing people."

"Then if this Master Ohm is Ghisteslwchlohm, what are you going to do about him? You'll have to do something."

"Why me? The High One can deal with him—and the fact that he hasn't is a good proof that Master Ohm is not the Founder of Lungold."

Deth raised his head. "I recall you used that same argument at Caerweddin."

Morgon sighed. He said reluctantly, "It fits, I suppose, but I can't believe it. I can't believe that either Ohm or Ghisteslwchlohm is evil, although that might explain the strange, sudden disappearance of the wizards and the tales of the violence of their leaving. But Ohm—I lived with him for three years. He never . . . he treated me with great kindness. It makes no sense."

The Morgol looked at him thoughtfully. "It doesn't, no. All this reminds me of a riddle from An, I believe. Re of Aum."

"Who was Re of Aum?" Lyra asked, and the Morgol, at Morgon's silence, answered imperturbably, "Re of Aum offended the Lord of Hel once and became so frightened that he had a great wall built around his house in fear of revenge. He hired a stranger to build it, who promised him a wall no man could destroy or climb, either by force or wizardry. The wall was built; the stranger took his pay; and Re at last felt secure. One day, when he decided that the Lord of Hel had realized the futility of revenge, he decided to venture out of his lands. And then he travelled around his wall three times but found no gate to let him out. And slowly he realized that the Lord of Hel himself had built that wall." She paused. "I've forgotten the stricture."

"Never let a stranger build walls around you," Lyra guessed. "Then Ghisteslwchlohm built his wall of ignorance in Caithnard as well as Lungold, which is why Morgon does not know who he is. It's very complicated. I prefer problems I can throw spears at."

"What about Eriel?" Morgon said abruptly. "Has Deth told you about her?"

"Yes," the Morgol said. "But that, I think, is a completely different problem. If Ohm wanted you dead, he could easily have killed you while you were a student. He didn't react to the stars on your face the way those—those nameless people do."

"That woman," Morgon said, "has a name."

"Do you know it?"

"No. I have never heard of anyone like her. And I'm more frightened of her hidden name than I am of a man whose name I know."

"Perhaps Ohm hid her name, too," Lyra said. She shifted uneasily. "Morgon, I think you should let me teach you to defend yourself. Deth, tell him."

"It's not my business to argue with the Prince of Hed," Deth said mildly.

"You argued with him this afternoon."

"I didn't argue. I simply pointed out the illogic of his arguments."

"Oh. Well, why doesn't the High One do something. It's his business. There is a strange people on his coasts, trying to kill the Prince of Hed—we could fight them. Ymris has an army; the people of An bear arms, from Kraal to Anuin, the High One could gather an army. I don't understand why he doesn't."

"Osterland could arm itself," Morgon said; "Ymris, Anuin, even Caithnard, but those people could wash over Hed like a seawave, and it would be barren in a day. There must be a better way to fight them."

"Arm Hed."

Morgon's cup came down with a little clink on the table. "Hed?"

"Why not? I think you should at least warn them."

"How? The fishermen of Tol go out every morning, and the only thing they have ever found in the sea is fish. I'm not even sure the farmers of Hed believe anything exists beyond Hed, and the High One. Of all the six kingdoms, Hed is the only one the wizards never sought service in—there wasn't anything for them to do. The wizard Talies visited it once and said it was uninhabitable: it was without history, without poetry, and utterly without interest. The peace of Hed is passed like the land-rule, from ruler to ruler; it is bound into the earth of Hed, and it is the High One's business, not mine, to break that peace."

"But—" Lyra said stubbornly.

"If I ever carried a weapon into Hed and told the people of Hed to arm themselves, they would look at me as though I were a stranger—and that is what I would be: a stranger in my own land, the weapon like a disease that would wither all the living roots of Hed. And if I did it without the High One's sanction, he could take the land-rule from me."

Lyra's dark brows crooked above her eyes. "I don't understand," she said again. "Ymris is always fighting within itself; An and Aum and Hel have had terrible wars in the past. The old lords of Herun have battled each other; why is Hed so different? Why should the High One care if it's armed or not?"

"It just evolved that way. It made its own laws in the Years of Settlement, and the laws grew to bind the Princes of Hed. It had nothing anyone would have fought for: no wealth, no great stretches of land, no seat of power or mystery, just good farmland and good weather, in a land so small not even the Kings of An in their years of conquering, were tempted by it. Men found the rulers they wanted to keep the peace, and their instinct for peace drove deep into the land like a seed. It's in my blood. To change that in me, I would have to change my name . . ."

Lyra was silent, her dark eyes on Morgon's face as he drank. He felt, as he put his cup down again, the light touch of her hand on his shoulder. "Well, then, since you won't protect yourself, I'll come with you and guard you," she said. "There's no one in the Morgol's guard who could do that better than I could—no one in all Herun." She looked across him to El. "May I have your permission?"

"No," Morgon said.

"Do you doubt my skill?" She picked up her knife, poised the blade between finger and thumb. "Do you see that rope at the far end of the room holding the torch?"

"Lyra, please do not set the room on fire," the Morgol murmured.

"Mother, I'm trying to show him—"

"I believe you," Morgon said. He turned to take the hand holding the knife in his hands. Her fingers were lean and warm, stirring a little, like a bird in his hold, and something he had half-forgotten in the long, rough weeks touched him unexpectedly. He kept his voice steady, gentle with an effort. "Thank you. But if you were hurt or killed trying to defend me, I would never forgive myself as long as I lived. My only hope is travelling as quickly and quietly as possible; doing that, I will be safe."

He saw the doubt in her eyes, but she said only, putting the knife down, "Well, in this house I will guard you. And even you can't argue with that."

Deth played for the Morgol after they finished supper—sweet, wordless songs from the ancient court of An, ballads from Ymris and Osterland. The room was hushed when he finished, empty but for the four of them; the candles were burned low in their holders. The Morgol rose reluctantly.

"It's late," she said. "I'll replenish your supplies so that you won't have to stop in Osterland, if you'll tell me what you need in the morning."

"Thank you," Deth said, slipping the harp strap over his shoulder. He looked at her a moment in silence, and she smiled. He added softly, "I want to stay. I will come back."

"I know."

She led them back through the wandering maze of corridors to their room. Water and wine, soft blankets had been left for them; the fire burned steadily, sending out a clean, elusive scent.

Morgon said before El turned to go, "May I leave some letters with you for the traders? My brother has no idea where I am."

"Of course. I'll have paper and ink brought to you. And may I ask something of you? May I see your harp?"

He took it out of the case for her. She turned it in her hands, touching the stars and the fine tracery of gold, the white moons. "Yes," she said softly. "I thought I recognized it. Deth told me some time ago about Yrth's harp, and when a trader brought this harp into my house last year, I was sure Yrth must have made it—it was a spell-bound harp, with its mute strings. I wanted so badly to buy it, but it was not for sale. The trader said it was promised to a man in Caithnard."

"What man?"

"He didn't say. Why? Morgon, what did I say to trouble you?"

He drew a breath. "Well, you see, my father—I think my father bought it in Caithnard for me last spring, before he died. So if you could remember what the trader looked like, or find out his name—"

"I see." Her hand closed gently on his arm. "I see. Yes, I will get his name for you. Good night."

Lyra, in a short, dark tunic, took her place at the doorway as the Morgol left, her straight back to them, her spear motionless, upright in her hand. A servant brought paper, pens, ink and wax; Morgon sat down in front of the fire. He stared into it, the ink drying on his pen, for a long time; he murmured once, "What am I going to say to her?" And slowly he began to write.

Finished finally with Raederle's letter, he wrote a brief note to Eliard, sealed it, and lay back against the cushions, watching the flames meld and separate, half-aware of Deth's quiet movements as he sorted and checked their gear. He lifted his head finally, looked at the harpist.

"Deth . . . did you know Ghisteslwchlohm?"

Deth's hands stilled. They moved again after a moment, loosening a knot in a bedroll. He said without looking up, "I spoke to him only twice, very briefly. He was a distant, awesome figure in Lungold, then, in the years before the wizards' disappearance."

"Did it ever occur to you that Master Ohm might be the Founder of Lungold?"

"There was no evidence of it that would have made such a thought occur to me."

Morgon reached out to add wood to the fire; shadows falling in webs and tapestries from the ceiling, shifted and settled. He murmured, "I wonder why the Morgol couldn't see through Ohm. I don't know what land he's from; it may be that he was born, like Rood, with some witchery in his blood. . . . I never thought to ask where he was born. He was simply Master Ohm, and it seemed he had been at Caithnard forever. If El told him she thought he was Ghisteslwchlohm, he would probably laugh . . . except I've never seen him laugh. It happened so long ago, the destruction of Lungold; the wizards have been silent as death since then. None of them could possibly be alive." His voice trailed away. He turned on his side, his eyes closing. A little while later he heard Deth begin to harp gently, dreamily, and he drifted asleep to the sound.

He woke to the song of a different harpist. The harping wove through him like a net, the slow, deep beat measured to the sluggish, jarring beat of his blood, the swift, wild high notes ripping at the fabric of his thoughts like tiny, panicked birds. He tried to move but something weighed on his hands, his chest. He opened his mouth to call for Deth; the sound that came out of him was again the squawk of the black crow.

He opened his eyes and found he had dreamed them open. He opened them again and saw nothing but the dark behind his eyelids. A terror rose in his throat, sending the birds in his mind into a frenzy. He reached out of himself as though he were swimming through deep, heavy swells of darkness and sleep, straining himself toward awareness. And finally he heard the harpist's voice and saw between his lashes the faint, fiery eyes of embers.

The voice was husky, rich, and word by word it bound him with a nightmare.

Withering your voice, as the
roots of your land are withering.
Slow your heart's-blood
slow as the dragging waters,
the rivers of Hed.
Tangling are your thoughts
as the yellow vines are tangling,
drying, snapping underfoot.
Withering the life of you
as the late corn is withering . . .

Morgon opened his eyes. The darkness and the red, panting embers whirled around him until the darkness rose about his face like a tide, and the fire seemed tiny, far away. In the well of night he saw Hed drifting like a broken ship in the sea; he heard the vine leaves whispering drily, felt in his veins the rivers slowing, thickening, draining dry, their beds cracking to the harpist's weave. He made a harsh, incredulous noise, and saw the harpist finally, beyond the fire, his harp made of strange bones and polished shell, his face lost in shadows. The face seemed to lift a little at Morgon's voice; he caught a flick of fire-scorched gold.

Dry, dust dry, the earth
the earth of you, land-ruler
lord of the dying. Parching the fields
of your body, moaning the wind
of your last word
across the waste of them,
the wasteland of Hed.

A tide seemed to be draining back from the dark, broken land, drawing the last of the river waters with it, drawing the stream-waters out of Hed, leaving the coasts bare, leaving a wasteland of shell and sand around Hed as it drained back to the black edges of the world. Morgon, feeling the dry, cold earth, the life of Hed draining away with the sea, fading away from him, drew a breath. He shouted with his last strength a protest that was no word but a bird cry against the impossibility of the harp song. The squawk brought him back to himself, as though his body, fraying into darkness, had pulled itself together again. He got to his feet, shaking, so weak he tripped over the hem of his long robe and fell near the fire. He picked up, before he rose again, handfuls of hot ash, chips of dead wood and flung them at the harpist. The harpist, his face jerking away from them, rose. His eyes in the dim light were pale, flecked with gold. He laughed, and the heel of his hand slammed upward against Morgon's chin. Morgon's head snapped back; he fell to his knees, dizzy, choking, at the harpist's feet. His fingers slid through harp strings sending a faint cacophony of sound into the darkness. The harpist's own harp, whistling down, brushed past Morgon's head as he moved and broke into pieces against his collarbone.

He cried out at the sharp, sickening snap of bone. Through the sweat and haze in his eyes, he saw Lyra standing motionless in the doorway, her back to him as if he were silent as a dream behind her. The hurt, unreasoning anger in him cleared his head a little. Still kneeling, he threw himself against the harpist, lunging with his good shoulder, knocking him off-balance against the heavy cushions. Then, his fingers tangled in the harp strap, he flung the harp in his hand out, arching toward the harpist. It crashed with a spattering of notes, and Morgon heard a faint, involuntary gasp.

He flung himself onto the shadowed figure. The harpist struggled beneath him; in the faint light from the hall Morgon saw blood streaking down his face. A knife seemingly made from air blurred towards Morgon; he caught desperately at the harpist's wrist; the harpist's other hand closed with a hawk's grip on Morgon's broken shoulder.

He groaned, the blood drained out of his face, the harpist darkening in his sight. And then he felt the shifting shape of the man he held, the fraying of form beneath him. His teeth clenched, he held onto the figure with his good hand as though he were holding onto his name.

He lost count of the brief, desperately struggling shapes he gripped. He smelled wood, the musk of animal fur, felt feathers beat against his hand, a marsh-slime ooze ponderously through his hold. He held the great, shaggy hoof of a horse whose effort to rear pulled him to his knees; a salmon slick and panicked, who nearly flipped out of his hold; a mountain cat who whirled in fury to slash at him. He held animals so old they had no names; he recognized them with wonder from their descriptions in ancient books. He held a great stone from one of the Earth-Masters' cities that almost crushed his hand; he held a butterfly so beautiful he nearly let it free rather than harm its wings. He held a harp string whose sound pierced his ears until he became the sound itself. And the sound he held turned into a sword.

He held the blade of it, silver-white, half as long as himself; strange whorls of design wound down the blade, delicately etched, snagging the light from the scattered embers. The hilt was of copper and gold. Set in gold, fire sparkling in their cores, were three stars.

His grip loosened. The dry, whistling breath in his throat stopped until there was no sound in the room. Then, with a sudden, furious cry, he flung the sword away from him, across the floor, where it spun on the stones of the doorway, startling Lyra.

She picked it up and whirled, but it came alive in her grasp and she dropped it again, backing away from it into the hall. She gave a shout; there was a flurry of voices down the hall. The sword vanished; in its place stood the master of the shapes.

He moved swiftly, turning toward Morgon; Lyra's spear, thrown a fraction of a second late, skimmed past him and ripped through one of the cushions beside Morgon. Morgon, still on his knees, watched the figure breaking through the web of shadows, the hair weaving into darkness, the face sparse, shell-colored, the eyes heavy-lidded, blue-green, gleaming with their own light. The body was fluid, blurred, the colors of foam, the colors of the sea; he moved without noise, his strange garments shifting lights the colors of wet seaweed, of wet shell. As he came, inexorable as tide, Morgon sensed an enormous, undefined power, restless and unfathomed like the sea, impersonal as the light behind the eyes fixed on his face.

Lyra's cry jarred him as if out of a dream. "The spear! Morgon! The spear by your hand. Throw it!"

He reached for it.

There was a movement in the sea-colored eyes like a distant, faint flick of a smile. Morgon rose, backed slowly, holding the spear with both hands between them. He heard Lyra's desperate cry, "Morgon!" His hands began to shake; the smile deepened in the strange eyes. With the sob of a rare Ymris curse that tore out of him, Morgon drew back his arm and threw.

"I'M GOING HOME," Morgon said.

"I don't understand you," said Lyra. She was sitting beside him at the fire, a light, crimson coat over her guard's tunic, her face smudged with sleeplessness. Her spear lay loosely under one hand at her side. Two other guards stood at the doorway facing opposite directions, their spearheads, in the fragile morning sunlight, forming a gleaming apex of light. "He would have killed you if you hadn't killed him. It's that simple. There is no law in Hed that forbids you to kill in self-defense, is there?"

"No."

"Then why?" She sighed, her eyes on his face as he stared into the flames. His shoulder was set and bound; his face was set, as accessible as a word-locked book. "Are you angry because you were not well-guarded in the Morgol's house? Morgon, I asked the Morgol this morning to be relieved of my place in the guard because of that, but she refused."

She had his attention, then. "There was no reason for you to do that."

Her chin rose slightly. "There was reason. Not only did I stand there doing nothing while you were fighting for your life, when I finally did try to kill the shape-changer, I missed. I never miss."

"He created an illusion of silence; it wasn't your fault that you heard nothing."

"I failed to guard you. That's simple, too."

"Nothing is simple."

He leaned back against the cushions, wincing a little; his brows pinched together again. He was silent; she waited, asked tentatively, "Well, then are you angry with Deth because he was with the Morgol when you were attacked?"

"Deth?" He looked at her blankly. "Of course not."

"Then what are you angry about?"

He looked down at the silver cup and the wine she had poured for him, touched it. Finally, the words dredged slowly, painfully from him as out of some shameful place, "You saw the sword."

She nodded. "Yes." The perplexed line between her brows deepened. "Morgon, I'm trying to understand."

"It's hardly difficult. Somewhere in this realm there is a starred sword waiting for the Star-Bearer to claim it. And I refuse to claim it. I'm going home where I belong."

"But Morgon, it's only a sword. You don't even have to use it if you don't want to. Besides, you might need it."

"I will need it." His fingers were rigid on the circle of silver. "That would be inevitable. The shape-changer knew. He knew. He was laughing at me when I killed him. He knew exactly what I was thinking when no one except the High One himself could have known."

"What were you thinking?"

"That no man could accept the name the stars on that sword gave him and still keep the land-rule of Hed."

Lyra was silent. The uneasy sunlight faded, leaving the room grey with shadows; leaves, wind-tossed, tapped like fingers against the window. She said finally, her hands clasped tightly around her knees, "You can't just turn your back on this and go home."

"I can."

"But you—you're a riddle-master, too—you can't just stop answering riddles."

He looked at her. "I can. I can do anything I must to keep the name I was born with."

"If you go back to Hed, they'll kill you there. You don't even have guards in Hed."

"At least I will die in my own land, be buried in my own fields."

"How can it matter so much? How can you face death in Hed that you can't face in Herun?"

"Because it's not death I'm afraid of—it's losing everything I love for a name and a sword and a destiny I did not choose and will not accept. I would rather die than lose the land-rule."

She said wistfully, "What about us? What about Eliard?"

"Eliard?"

"If they kill you in Hed, they'll still be there and so will Eliard. And we'll be alive, asking questions without you to answer them."

"The High One will protect you," he said grimly. "That's his business. I can't do it. I'm not going to follow the path of some fate dreamed up for me thousands of years ago, like a sheep going to be fleeced." He took a sip of the wine finally, saw her uncertain, anxious face. He said more gently, "You are the land-heir of Herun. Some day you will rule it, and your eyes will turn as gold as the Morgol's. This is your home; you would die to defend it; your place is here. At what price would you give up Herun, turn your face from it forever?"

She was silent; one shoulder gave a little shrug. "Where else could I go? I don't belong anywhere else. But it's different for you," she added, as he opened his mouth. "You do have another name, another place. You are the Star-Bearer."

"I would rather be a pigherder in Hel," he said tartly. He dropped his head back wearily, one hand massaging his shoulder. Rain began then, thin, tentative; the plants in the Morgol's garden bowed under it. He closed his eyes, smelled, unexpectedly, the autumn rains falling over three-quarters of Hed. There was a sound of fresh wood falling on the fire, and the eager snap of flame. The voices of the flames tangled together, turned familiar after a while; he heard Tristan and Eliard arguing comfortably, pointlessly, beside the hearth at Akren, with Snog Nutt, a handful of bones and cobweb, snoring like rain in the background. He half-listened to the argument woven into the soft whispers of the fire, until the voices began to fade and he had to strain to hear them; they finally died away, and he opened his eyes to the cold, grey rain of Herun.

Deth was sitting opposite him, speaking softly to the Morgol, uncoiling broken strings from his harp. Their faces turned as Morgon straightened. El, her long hair unbound, brushing her tired face, said, "I sent Lyra to bed. I have set guards at every crack and crevice of this house, but it's difficult to suspect the ground-mist, or the spider wandering in from the rain. How do you feel?"

"All right." Then, his eyes on Deth's harp, he whispered, "I remember. I heard strings break, when I struck the shape-changer. That was your harp."

"Only five strings," Deth said. "A small price to pay Corrig for your life. El gave me strings from Tirunedeth's harp to match them." He put the harp down.

"Corrig." Morgon drew breath; the Morgol was gazing at Deth wonderingly. "Deth, how of all things do you know that shape-changer's name."

"I harped with him once, years ago. I met him even before I entered the High One's service."

"Where?" the Morgol asked.

"I was riding alone down the northern coast from Isig, in the far reaches belonging neither to Isig nor Osterland. I camped one night on the beach, sat late in the night beside my fire, harping . . . and out of the darkness came an answering harping, beautiful, wild, flawless. . . . He came into the circle of my firelight, glistening with tide, his harp of shell and bone and mother of pearl, and demanded songs of me. I played as well for him as for the kings I had played to; I dared not do less. He gave me songs in return; he stayed with me until dawn, until the sun rose, and his song as the red northern sun flamed across the sea burned in my heart for days after I heard it. He melted like mist into the morning sea-mist, but first he gave me his name. He asked for mine. I told him, and he laughed."

"He laughed at me last night," Morgon whispered.

"He played for you, too, from what you told us, then."

"He played my death. The death of Hed." His eyes lifted from the core of the fire. "What kind of power could do that? Was it truth? Or illusion?"

"Did it matter?"

He shook his head. "No. He was a very great harpist. . . . Does the High One know what he was."

"The High One said nothing to me, beyond instructing me to leave Herun with you as quickly as possible."

Morgon was silent. He got to his feet awkwardly, went to the window. Through the glistening air, as though he had the Morgol's vision, he could see the wide, wet plains of Caithnard where trade-ships were setting sail for An, Isig, Hed. He said softly, "Deth, tomorrow, if I can ride, I am going east to the trade-port Hlurle, to take a ship home. I should be safe; no one will expect that. But even if they find me again at sea, I would rather die a land-ruler returning home than a nameless, placeless man being forced into a life I can't understand or control."

There was no answer but the rain pounding with impersonal fury against the glass. Then, as the sound tapered away, he heard the harpist rise, felt a hand on his shoulder, turning him. He met the dark, dispassionate gaze silently; the harpist said softly, "It's more than the killing of Corrig. Will you tell me what is troubling you?"

"No."

"Do you want me to accompany you to Hed?"

"No. There's no reason for you to risk your life again."

"How will you reconcile turning back with what you held true at Caithnard?"

"I have made a choice," Morgon said steadily, and the hand fell from his shoulder. He felt the tooth of an odd sorrow bite into him, the sorrow of an ending, and he added, "I'll miss you."

Something came into the harpist's face, breaking through the calm agelessness of it until Morgon sensed for the first time the concern, the uncertainty, the endless experience that ran through his mind like water beneath ice. Deth did not answer; his head bent slightly as to a king or an inevitability.

Morgon left the city of circles before dawn two days later. He wore against the thin, icy mists a heavy, richly lined coat the Morgol had given him. A hunting bow that Lyra had made for him hung with his saddlebags. He had left the packhorse with Deth, since Hlurle lay scarcely three days away, a small port the traders used to unload goods bound for Herun. Deth had given Morgon what money he had had left in case he had to wait, for in late autumn, in the heavy seas, ships grew scarce on the northern coast.

Morgon's harp lay at his back, encased against the damp air; his horse's hooves made soft rhythmic whispers through the long grass of the pastures. The sky was clear before dawn; the stars, huge, cold, gave him light. In the distance tiny lights from farmhouses winked alive, golden eyes in the darkness. The fields of the city gave way to a plain where huge stones rose origin-less as wizards around him. He felt their shadows as he rode beneath them. Mists fell then, rolling down from the hills; following Lyra's advice he stopped, found shelter under a rare tree, and waited.

He spent the first night at the foot of the eastern hills. That night, among the silent trees, alone for the first time in many weeks, he watched the smoke-colored dusk fade gently into night, and, in the light of his small, solitary fire, he took out the starred harp and began to play. The sound was rich and true under his fingers, made for a delicate, expert skill. After an hour his playing slowed. He sat examining the harp as he had never done before, tracing every curve of gold, marvelling at the white moons untarnished by age, sea, use. He touched the stars softly, as though he were touching flame.

The next day he spent picking a path through the low, empty hills. He found a stream lancing between them and followed it, winding through groves of pale ash and oak trees with their beautiful, endless weavings of dark, bare branches. The stream, quickening, bouncing over tree roots and green rocks, led him out of the trees to the bald, whistling eastern slopes where he could see unexpectedly, the flat no-man's-land of the eastern coast running between Ymris and Osterland, the faint white heads of mountains rising in the farthest point of the High One's realm, and the broad, endless eastern sea.

The stream joined a wide river that had curled around north Herun; struggling with a mental map, he realized it was the Cwill that took its roaring white waters from White Lady Lake, the enormous lake deep in the wastelands that fed also the seven Lungold Lakes. Hlurle, he remembered, lay just north of its mouth. He camped that night on the joint of land between the stream and the river, his thoughts lulled by their two voices: one deep, secret, swift; the other light, high, hospitable. He lay quietly by the fire, his head resting on his saddle, reaching out now and then to add a branch or a pinecone to the flames. Gently as small birds landing in his mind came questions he no longer had to answer; he looked at each one curiously, as though it had never occurred to him before, dispassionately, as though the answers had nothing to do with him, or with the white-haired, half-blind Ymris land-heir, or with the King of Ymris struggling with a strange war growing on his coasts, or with the Morgol, the peace of her house shattered by a hint of power that had no origins, no definition. He saw in his mind's eye the stars on his face, the stars on the harp, the stars on the sword. He looked at himself as though he were a figure in some ancient tale: a Prince of Hed reared to harvest bare-backed in the sun, to puzzle over the varied diseases of trees and animals, to read the weather from the color of a cloud, or a tension in a breathless afternoon, to the simple, hard-headed, uncurious life of Hed. He saw that same figure in the voluminous robe of a Caithnard student poring late at night over ancient books, his lips shaping, soundlessly, riddle, answer, stricture, riddle, answer, stricture; walking, from pure choice, one morning into a cold tower in Aum, finding himself, in the face of death, with no name, no way of life, no birthright to save him but his mind. He saw a Prince of Hed with three stars on his face leave his land, find a starred harp in Ymris, a sword, a name, and a hint of doom in Herun. And those two figures out of the ancient tale: the Prince of Hed and the Star-Bearer, stood apart from each other; he could find nothing that reconciled them.

He broke a branch, fed it to the fire; his thoughts turned to the High One whose home lay in the heart of one of the distant mountains to the north. The High One, from the beginning, had left men free to find their own destinies. His sole law was land-law, the law that passed like a breath of life from land-heir to land-heir; if the High One died, or withdrew his immense and intricate power, he could turn his realm into a wasteland. The evidences of his powers were subtle and unexpected; he was thought of, when at all, with both awe and trust; his dealings with rulers, generally through his harpist, were invariably courteous. His one concern was the land; his one law, the law instilled deeper than thought, deeper than dreaming, in his land-rulers. Morgon thought of the terrible tale of Awn of An, who, trying to discourage an army from Hel, had set fire to An, sending flames billowing over half the land, burning harvests, orchards, shearing the hillsides and riverbanks. Safe at last, he had awakened out of a sleep of exhaustion to realize he had lost the wordless, gentle awareness of things beyond eyesight that had been with him, like a hidden eye, since the death of his father. His land-heir, running grief-stricken into the room, had stopped, astonished, to find him still alive. . . .

The fire sank low, like a beast curling to sleep. Morgon tossed a handful of twigs and dry acorns on it, and it started awake. Awn had killed himself. The wizard Talies, methodical and sharp-tongued, who had hated Awn's warring, recorded the incident with relish, mentioned it to a passing trader, and within three months, precarious as trading was in those years of turmoil, all battling had ceased abruptly in the High One's realm. Peace did not last long; the battles over boundary and kingship had not ended yet, but they grew less frequent, and less devastating. Then the ports and the great cities had begun to grow: Anuin, Caithnard, Caerweddin, Kraal, Kyrth. . . .

And now, some strange, dark power, unsuspected by most lands, unchecked by the High One, was building along the coasts. Not since the wizards lived had there been people of such power; the wizards, themselves skilled, restless and arbitrary, would never have dreamed of trying to kill a land-ruler. There had been scarcely a hint of their existence in the tales and histories of the land until breaking a silence of centuries, they had roused to meet the Star-Bearer at Caithnard. A face floated into the fire before Morgon's eyes: foam-white, blurred, eyes luminous like wet kelp, wet shell . . . they held a smile, knowing what he was thinking, knowing. . . .

He touched the heart of the questioning; his lips moved, whispering it, "Why?"

A little cold breeze moved across the river; his fire shivered under it. He realized then how tiny that fire was against the enormous darkness. A fear prickled over him; he froze, straining to hear above the water the soft breaking of a twig, the stirring of leaves around him. But the chattering stream distorted sounds, and the wind rose, tuneless in the bare branches. He lay back. His fire sank into itself; the stars clinging to the black oak limbs seemed to shake and sway in the winds. A few drops of rain fell, hard as acorns, to the earth. As though the wind carried an echo of the vast emptiness about him, his fear died away. He turned on his side, slept without dreaming.

The next day, following the Cwill, he reached the sea. Hlurle, little more than a dock, a scattering of warehouses, inns, and small, worn houses, lay hunched under a mist of rain beating in from the sea. There were two ships moored among the fishing boats, their furled sails were blue. There seemed to be no one around. He rode, drenched and shivering, down the wharf, hearing beneath the rain, the rattle of chain, the musing creak of timber, the occasional nudge of a boat against the dock. Ahead of him, light from a small tavern spilled into the wet air. He stopped there, dismounted under its broad eaves.

Inside, the rough tables and benches, lit by smokey torches and an enormous fire, were full of sailors, traders with jewels on their hands, in their caps, disgruntled fishermen who had come in with the rain. Morgon, enduring a brief, casual scrutiny as he walked dripping to the fire, unbuttoned his coat with numb fingers and hung it to dry. He sat down on the bench in front of the fire; the tavern keeper paused at his elbow.

"Lord?" he said questioningly, and then, with a glance at the coat, "You are far from home."

Morgon nodded tiredly. "Beer," he said. "And what is that I smell?"

"A fine, thick stew, with tender lamb, mushrooms, and wine—I'll bring you a bowl."

He ate and drank in weary silence, the smoke and heat and tangle of voices lulling as the river's voice. He sat sipping his beer, which he realized probably came from Hed, when the smell of wet wool and a chill of rain and wind disturbed him. A trader, the fur trim on his cloak beaded with water, sat down beside him. Morgon felt eyes on his face.

The man rose after a moment, divested himself of his cloak with a sprinkle of rain, and said apologetically, "Your pardon, Lord. You're wet enough without my help."

He was richly dressed in black leather and velvet, his hair and his eyes in a rough, kindly face as dark as blackbird's wings. Morgon, drowsy in the warmth, stirred himself and put his mind to practical matters. There was no way of knowing whether he spoke to a man or the illusion of a man; he accepted the risk and said, "Do you know where those ships are going?"

"Yes. They are bound back to Kraal, to go into dry dock for the winter." He paused, his shrewd eyes on Morgon's face. "You don't want to go north? What do you need?"

"Passage to Caithnard. I'm supposed to be at the college."

The man shook his head, his brow wrinkling. "It's late in the season. . . . Let me think. We just came from Anuin, stopping at Caithnard, Tol, and Caerweddin."

"Tol," Morgon said involuntarily. "For what?"

"To take Rood of An from Caithnard to Hed." He caught the tavern maid's attention and got wine. Morgon settled back against the bench, his brows drawn, hoping Rood had contented himself with going only as far as Hed in search of him. The trader took a long swallow of wine, sat back himself. He said moodily, "It was a depressing journey. There was a storm around Hed that blew us down the coast, and we were in living fear of losing both the ship and Rood of An. . . . He's got a sharp tongue when he's seasick," he added thoughtfully, and Morgon almost laughed. "At Tol, there was Eliard of Hed, and the young one—Tristan—pleading for news of their brother. All I could tell them was that he'd been seen in Caerweddin, but I couldn't tell them what he was doing there. We lost sail in that storm, but we found we couldn't land in Meremont; there were king's warships in the harbor there, so we limped to Caerweddin. I heard then, for the first time, that his young wife had vanished, and his brother was home again, half-blind. No one knows what to make of it." He sipped wine. Morgon, his eyes on the fire, felt his mind fill with faces: Astrin's, white-eyed, twisted with pain; the Lady Eriel's, shy, beautiful, merciless; Heureu's face, realizing slowly what kind of woman he had married. . . . He shivered. The trader glanced at him.

"You're wet through. That was a long ride from Herun. I wonder if I know your father."

Morgan smiled at the hint. "Probably. But he's got a name so long even I can't pronounce it for you."

"Ah." There was an answering smile in the dark eyes. "Your pardon. I wouldn't pry for the world. But I need some idle chatter to warm my bones. I've got a wife waiting for me in Kraal, if we make it there, and two little sons I haven't seen for two months. Passage to Caithnard. . . . The only ships would be coming down from Kraal, and I can't remember who's up there. Wait." He turned, shouted into the din behind them. "Joss! Who's left in Kraal?"

"Three of Rustin Kor's ships, waiting for a cargo of timber from Isig," a voice boomed back in answer. "We didn't pass them; they must be still up there. Why?"

"The Herun lordling needs to get back to the College. Will they stop here, do you think?"

"Rustin Kor has half a warehouse full of Herun wine here; he'll pay winter storage fees if he doesn't stop."

"He'll stop," the trader said, turning back to Morgon. "I remember. It's Mathom of An who wants the wine. Do you like riddling, then? Do you know who's a great riddler? The wolf of Osterland. I was in his court last summer at Yrye, trying to interest him in a pair of amber cups, when a man came in from Lungold to challenge him to a game. Har has a standing wager that any man who wins a game with him can have the first thing he asks for when the game is done. It's a tricky prize: there's a tale of one man, long ago, who won the game after a day and a night, and he was so dry the first thing he asked for was a cup of water. I don't know if that's true. Anyway, this man—he was a little, wizened, arrogant one, looked as if he'd been sucked dry by riddles—kept Har at it two days, and the old wolf loved it. Everyone got drunk listening, and I sold more cloth and jewels there than I had all year. It was wonderful. Finally the wolf-king asked a riddle the little man couldn't answer—he'd never heard of it. He got angry and challenged the riddle. Har told him to go take the riddle to the Masters at Caithnard, and then he asked ten riddles in a row the man couldn't answer, one right after another—I thought the little one was going to burst with choler. But Har soothed him and said he hadn't played such a great game in years."

"What was the first riddle the man couldn't answer?" Morgon asked curiously.

"Oh—let me think. What will one star call out of dark. . . . No. What will one star call out of silence, one star out of darkness, and one star out of death?"

Morgon's breath caught sharply. He straightened, his face rigid, white, his eyes narrowed, searching the trader's. For a moment the dark face wavered before him in the flames, elusive, expressionless as a mask; and then he realized that the trader was staring at him in utter astonishment.

"Lord, what did I say?" Then his face changed, and his hand went out abruptly toward Morgon. "Oh," he whispered, "I think you are no Herun lordling."

"Who are you?"

"Lord, my name is Ash Strag from Kraal; I have a wife and two children, and I would sooner cut off my hand than hurt you. But do you realize how they've been looking for you?"

Morgon's hands eased open. He said after a moment, his eyes unwavering on the anxious face, "I know."

"You're going home, now? From Anuin to Caerweddin, I heard always the same question: Have you news of the Prince of Hed? What is it? Are you in trouble? Can I help you?" He paused. "You don't trust me."

"I'm sorry—"

"No. I heard. I heard a tale from Tobec Rye, the trader who found you with Lord Astrin in Ymris. He gave me some mad story that you and the High One's harpist had been nearly drowned on a trade-ship whose crew vanished, and that one of the traders on it had been Jarl Acker. I saw Jarl Acker die, two years ago during a run from Caerweddin to Caithnard. He caught a fever, and he asked to be buried in the sea. So we—so we did that." His voice dropped again, hushed. "Someone stole his shape back out of the sea?"

Morgon dropped against the bench back. His blood was still jumping sickly. "You didn't—you didn't tell that to my brother."

"Of course not." He was silent again, studying Morgon, his dark brows winging together. "It was true, about the vanishing traders? Someone wants to kill you? That's why you're afraid of me. But you weren't afraid until I mentioned the stars. Those stars. Lord, is someone trying to kill you because of the stars on your face?"

"Yes."

"But why? Who in the world could benefit, killing a Prince of Hed? It's irrational."

Morgon drew a breath. The familiar din was unchanged behind him; there was no one near enough to hear them, or who even looked curious. All knew that if anything of interest were gleaned from

Morgon's presence, it would be promptly shared in his absence. He rubbed his face with his hands. "Yes. Did Har answer the riddle about the stars?"

"No."

"How are Eliard and Tristan?"

"Worried sick. They asked if you were on your way home from Caerweddin, and I said as tactfully as possible that perhaps you were pursuing a circuitous route because no one knew where you were. I never expected to see you as far north as Hlurle."

"I've been in Herun."

Ash Strag shook his head. "It's unheard of." He sipped wine, brooding. "I don't like it. People of strange power impersonating traders—are they wizards?"

"No. I suspect they're even more powerful."

"And they're pursuing you? Lord, I'd go straight to the High One."

"They've tried to kill me four times," Morgon said wearily, "and I'm only as far as Herun."

"Four times, once at sea—"

"Twice at Ymris, and once again in Herun."

"Caerweddin." The sharp eyes flicked to him. "You went to Caerweddin, and now the King's wife is vanished, and Astrin Ymris, who came with you, is blind in one eye. What happened while you were there? Where is Eriel Yrmis?"

"Ask Heureu."

The drawn breath hissed away into the sound of rain. "I don't like it," the trader whispered. "I've heard tales I wouldn't repeat to my own brother, met men who had hearts made of the leavings of animals, but I've never heard anything like this. I've never heard of anything that could strike at the land-rulers before, so quietly, so powerfully. And it's all because of your stars?"

Morgon winced. "I'm going home," he said, almost to himself. The trader, holding their cups up in the air to get the tavern maid's attention, got them filled, pushed Morgon's back to him. He said carefully, "Lord, is it wise to go by sea?"

"I can't go back through Ymris. I've got to risk it."

"Why? You're halfway to Isig—more than halfway. Lord, come with us to Kraal—" He sensed Morgon's faint withdrawal, and said gently, "I know. I know. I don't blame your mistrust. But I know myself, and there's not a man in this room I mistrust. It would be better for you to risk going north with us than to take a strange ship to Hed. If you wait here too long, your enemies may find you."

"I'm going home."

"But, Lord, they'll kill you in Hed!" His voice had risen; he checked, glancing around him. "How do you expect your farmers to protect you? Go to the High One. How can you find answers to anything in Hed?"

Morgon, staring at him, began to laugh suddenly. He covered his eyes with his fingers; felt the trader's hand on his shoulder. He whispered, "I'm sorry, but I've never had a trader hand me the heart of a maze of riddles so aptly before."

"Lord . . ."

He dropped his hands, his face quieting. "I will not go with you. Let the High One answer a few riddles; I'm doing no good. The realm is his business; Hed is mine."

The hand at his shoulder shook him lightly, as if to wake him. "Hed is doing well as it is, Lord," the trader said softly. "It's the rest of us, the world outside of Hed you've troubled in your passing, that I'm worried about."

The ships sailed with the evening tide. Morgon watched them leave in an eerie, beautiful band of lavender-white twilight stretching across the sea beneath the rain clouds. He had stabled his horse, taken a room in the tavern to wait for Rustin Kor's ships; the rain-streaked window gave him a view of the quiet docks, the wild sea, and the two ships, taking the sullen waves with the grace of sea birds. He watched them until the light faded and their sails darkened. Then he lay on the bed, something nagging at the back of his mind, something he could not touch, though he wove strand after strand of thought trying to trace it. Raederle's face slipped unexpectedly into his mind, and he was startled at the joylessness he felt in himself at the thought of her.

He had raced her up the hill to the College once, years ago, she in a long, green dress she had hiked to her knees to run in. He had let her win, and, at the top, happy, panting, she had mocked his courtesy. Rood came behind with a handful of jewelled pins that had fallen out of her hair; he tossed them to her; they caught light like a swarm of strange, glittering insects, scarlet, green, amber, purple. Too tired to catch them, she had let them fall around her, laughing, her red hair massed like a mane in the wind. And Morgon had watched her, forgetting to laugh, forgetting even to move, until he saw Rood's black eyes on his face, quizzical, for once almost gentle. And, remembering back, he heard Rood's voice, harsh, stripped of pity on the last day they had met: *If you offer the peace of Hed to Raederle, that will be a lie.*

He sat up on the bed, knowing now what bothered him. Rood had known from the beginning. He could not go to Anuin taking honor for winning a game of riddles in a tower in Aum when all round him riddles were forming, deadly and imperative, for a game he refused to play. He could turn his back on other kingdoms, close the doors of the peace of Hed about himself, but to reach out to her would be to reach out to the strangeness, the uncertainty of his other name, for he could offer her nothing less than himself.

He rose, sat on the window ledge a long time, watching the wet world grow dark before him. An impossible web of riddles was being woven about his name; he had wrenched himself from it once; he had only to lift his hand to touch it, become ensnared in it again. He had a choice, for the moment: to return to Hed, live quietly without Raederle, asking no questions, waiting for the day when the storm brewing, growing on the coasts and the mainland would unleash its full fury at Hed—that day, he knew, would come soon. Or to set his mind to a riddle-game he had no hope of winning, and whose prize, if he did win, was a name that might cut every tie that bound him to Hed.

He moved after a while, realized the room was black. He got up, felt for a candle in the dark, lit it. The flame etched his face in the window, startling him. The flame itself was a star in his hand.

He dropped the candle to the floor, ground the flame underfoot, and lay back down on the bed. Late that night, after the rain had stopped and the wind's voice had dropped to a murmur, he fell asleep. He woke again at dawn, went downstairs to buy food and a skin of wine from the tavern keeper. Then he saddled his horse, left Hlurle without looking back, heading north to Yrye, to ask the King of Osterland a riddle.

8

TWO WEEKS AFTER he left Hlurle, the winter snow began to fall. He had felt its coming, tasted it in the air, heard it coming in the voices of wild, restless winds. He had gone up the coast to the mouth of the Ose, the great river whose roots lay in the heart of Erlenstar Mountain. The river ran through Isig Pass, past the doorstep of Isig Mountain, to form the southern boundary of Osterland on its way to the sea. Morgon followed it upriver patiently, through unclaimed land, forgotten forests that only traders sailing down from Isig ever saw, rough, rocky country where herds of deer, elk, mountain sheep ranged, their coats thick against the winter. Once he thought he saw moving through a far stretch of forest a herd of vesta, their legendary horns thin slivers of gold among the trees. But against the white, empty sky, they could have been a drift of mist, and he was uncertain.

He moved as quickly as possible through the wild country, feeling the snow at his heels, hunting sporadically, wondering in the back of his mind if the wilderness would ever end, or if there were any men left in the High One's realm, or if the river he followed were perhaps not the Ose but some unmapped water that wound westward into the vast, uninhabited backlands of the realm. That thought woke him more than once at night, to wonder what he was doing in the middle of nowhere,

where a broken bone, a frightened animal, a sudden storm could kill him as easily as his enemies. The constant fears ran like a current in his mind. Yet there was an odd peace he sometimes felt when at night there were no colors but the fire and the black sky, and no sounds in the world but his harp. At those moments he belonged to the night; he felt nameless, bodiless, as though he could take root and become a tree, drift apart and become the night.

Finally, he began to see farms in the distance, herds of sheep, cattle grazing by the river, and knew somewhere he had crossed into Osterland. Partly from caution, partly out of a habit of silence that had grown with him the past weeks, he avoided the farms and small towns along the river. He stopped only once to buy bread, cheese and wine, and to get directions to Yrye. The curious glances made him uneasy; he realized how strange he must seem, neither trader nor trapper, coming out of the backlands of Osterland with a bright, worn, Herun coat and hair like an ancient hermit's.

Yrye, the wolf-king's home, lay north, in the arms of Grim Mountain, the central peak in a range of low, border mountains; there was a road leading to it out of one of the villages. Morgon, riding out of the town, camped for the night in a woods nearby. The winds whined like wolves through the pine; he woke near dawn chilled to the bone, made a fire that fluttered like a helpless bird. The winds moved about him as he rode that day, speaking to one another in some rough, deep language. At evening they quieted; the sky was a smooth fleece of cloud beyond which the sun wandered and set unnoticed. In the night the snow began to fall; he woke beneath a coat of white.

The fall was gentle, the cold winds were still; he rode through the day in a dreamlike silence of white broken only by the flick of a blackbird's wing, a brown hare's scuttle to shelter. He fashioned a tent, when he stopped at evening, out of the tanned skin he had been sleeping on, and found a snarled patch of dry bramble for kindling. His thoughts turned, as he ate, to the strange, ancient king who in his riddle-gatherings had chanced upon another the Masters at Caithnard had never learned. Har, the wolf-king, had been born even before most of the wizards; he had ruled Osterland since the years of Settlement. Tales of him were numerous and awesome. He could change shape. He had been tutored by the wizard Suth, during Suth's wildest years. He bore scars on his hands the shape of vesta horns, and he riddled like a Master. Morgon leaned back against a boulder, sipped hot wine slowly, wondering where the king had got his knowledge. He felt again the faint stirrings of curiosity that had been dulled for weeks, of a longing to return to the world of men. He finished his wine, reached out to pack the cup. And then he saw, beyond the circle of his fire, eyes watching him.

He froze. His bow lay on the other side of the fire; his knife was stuck upright on the wedge of cheese. He began to reach for it slowly. The eyes blinked. There was a gathering, a soft stirring; then a vesta walked into his firelight.

Something jumped in the back of Morgon's throat. It was huge, broad as a farmhorse, with a deer's delicate, triangular face. Its pelt was blazing white; its hooves and crescents of horn were the color of beaten gold. It eyed him fathomlessly out of eyes of liquid purple, then reached up above his head to nibble at a pine bough. Morgon, his breath still as though he were reaching toward a forbidden thing, lifted one hand to the white, glowing fur. The vesta did not seem to notice the gentle touch. After a moment Morgon reached for his bread, tore a piece. The vesta's head lowered curiously at the scent, nuzzled at the bread. Morgon touched the narrow bone of its face; it jerked beneath his hand, and the purple eyes rose again, huge and dimensionless, to his face. Then the vesta lowered its head, continued eating, while he gently scratched the space between its horns. It finished the piece, sniffed his hand for more. He fed it the rest, piece by piece, until there was no more. It searched his empty hands, his coat a moment, then turned, faded with scarcely a sound back into the night.

Morgon drew a full breath. The vesta, he had heard, were shy as children. It was a rare pelt seen in tradeshops, for they were wary of men, and the weight of Har's wrath lay on any man, trader or trapper, caught killing vesta. They followed snow, wandering farther and farther into the mountains during the summer. Morgon, with a sudden touch of unease, wondered what it had smelled in the air that night that had brought it so far from the mountains.

Before morning he found out. A wind, wailing like a bee swarm, wrenched the tent loose over his head and spun it into the river. Huddled beside his horse, his eyes stinging with snow, he waited for a dawn that it seemed would never come. When it did come finally, it only turned the blankness of night into a milky chaos through which Morgon could not even see the river running ten steps away from him.

A helpless, terrible despair rose in him. Chilled even beneath the thick hooded coat, the winds snarling like wolves around him, he lost sense of the river's position, felt the whole world a blind, patternless turmoil. He forced himself to remember. He rose stiffly, feeling his horse trembling with cold under the blanket he had thrown over it. He murmured something to it out of numb lips; heard it thrashing nervously to stand as he turned. Head bent against the snow, he walked almost blindly to where he thought the river was. It loomed out of the blizzard at him unexpectedly, swift, eddied with snow; he nearly stepped headlong into it. He turned back to get his horse, bent to retrace his footsteps. When he reached the end of them, he found his horse gone.

He stood still and called to it; the wind pushed the words back into his mouth. He took a step toward a shadow in the snow, and it melted away before his eyes into whiteness. When he turned again, he could not see in the drift of snow, either his pack or his harp.

He went forward blindly, dug in the snow with his hands, beneath boulders and trees that melted out of the blizzard. He tried to see; the wind spat flakes huge as coins into his eyes. He searched desperately, furiously, losing what fragile sense of direction he had gained, moving patternlessly, dazed by the incessant, whining winds.

He found the harp finally, already half-buried; as he held it in his hands, he began to think again. It lay where he had left it, beneath the boulder he had slept beside; the river, he knew, was to his left. His pack, and saddle were somewhere in the mist in front of him; he did not dare lose sense of the river again to look for them. He hung his harp over his shoulder and slowly, carefully, found his way back to the river.

His trek upriver was painfully slow. He stayed dangerously close to the water in order to see the faint, slate-grey glints of it; sometimes when everything melted before his eyes into one monotonous white blur, he would stop short, wondering if he had been threading his way along an illusion. His face and hands grew numb; the hair outside of his hood was icy. He lost all sense of time, not knowing if moments or hours had passed since he had started walking, not knowing whether it was noon or evening. He dreaded the coming of night.

He walked headlong into a tree once, instead of moving around it; he stood where he had stopped, his face resting against the cold, rough bark. He wondered absently how long he could continue, what would happen when he could not move another step, when night fell and he could no longer follow the river. The tree, swaying rhythmically in the wind, was soothing. He knew he should move, but his arms refused to loose the trunk. Unexpectedly, for his thoughts were formless as the blizzard, he saw Eliard's face in his mind, angry, troubled, and he heard his own voice out of some long-lost past. *I swear this: I will come back.*

His grip on the tree loosened reluctantly. He remembered the belief in Eliard's eyes. If Eliard had not believed him, he could root himself like a tree in the middle of the Osterland blizzard; but Eliard, stubborn, literal, would expect him to keep his vow. He opened his eyes again; the colorless world was still there, just beyond his eyelids, and he wanted to weep with the weariness of it.

Imperceptibly, the world began to darken. He did not notice at first, intent on the water, and then he realized that the river itself was melting into the wind. He stumbled frequently over roots, icy rocks, found it more and more tiring to fling an arm out to catch his balance. Once a rock slid into the water under his foot; only a wild grab at a branch saved him from following it. He found his footing again, gripped the tree, shivering uncontrollably like a dog. Looking up to keep himself awake, he was appalled at the color of the wind.

He set his face hard against the bark, tried to think. Night he could not outwit. He could find shelter—a cave, a hollow tree—try to build a fire; the chances of doing either were minute. He could not follow the river in the dark, yet if he left it, he would probably wander aimlessly for a short time, then simply stop and disappear into the snow and wind, become, in his vanishing, another curiosity of Hed, like Kern, for the Masters to put on their lists. He considered the problem stubbornly, staring at the whorls of bark to keep his eyes open. Shelter, a fire, impossible as they seemed, were his only hope. He straightened stiffly, realized that the tree, not his body, had been supporting him. An odd, moist warmth, frightening him more than anything else that day, touched his face; he startled, turning. The head of a vesta loomed over him out of the snow.

He did not know how long he stared into the purple eyes. The vesta was motionless, the wind rippling through its fur. His hands began to move of their own accord, brushing over the face, the neck; he murmured things almost to soothe himself more than it. He inched away from the tree, his hands following the arch of its neck, its back, until he stood at its side, his numb hands curled into the thick hair on its back. It moved finally, reaching for a pinecone on the tree. Poised, his lips tight between his teeth, he leaped for its back.

He was unprepared for the sudden, incredible explosion of speed that shot him like an arrow into the heart of the storm. He gripped the horns, his teeth clenched, his eyes closed, the harp crushed against his ribs; he was almost unable to breathe from the winds slamming against his face. A sound came out of him; as if in answer to it, the wild sprint of panic melted slowly into a slower, steadier pace that was effortless and faster than any horse he had ever ridden. He clung close to the creature's warmth, not wondering where it was going, nor how long it would permit him to stay on its back, simply concentrating on the single thought of staying with it until it could run no more.

He fell into a light sleep, feeling beneath his sleep the effortless, rhythmic movement. His hands, cramped around the horns, loosened; he lost his balance and fell, hitting the earth hard. The sky was black, blazing overhead; silence lay above the light snow like an element. He got to his feet, gazing at star after star blurring together into light, curving down to meet the white horizon. He saw the vesta looking back at him, motionless, white against the snow. He went towards it. For a moment it simply watched him as though he were a curious animal. Then, its steps delicate, barely breaking the snow, it walked to meet him. He lifted himself onto its back, his arms shaking with the effort. It began to run again toward the stars.

He woke to the curious touch of snow on his face. The vesta walked sedately through the empty, snow-covered streets of a city. Beautiful, brightly painted wood houses and shops lined the streets, their doors and shutters closed in the early dawn. Morgon straightened with an effort, breaking a crust of snow on his coat. The vesta turned a corner; ahead of him Morgon saw a great unwalled house, its weathered walls patterned with wood gathered from distant corners of the realm; oak, pale birch, red-toned cedar, dark, rich timber; the eaves, window frames and double doors were traced with endless whorls of pure gold.

The vesta walked fearlessly into the yard and stopped. The dark house sat dreaming in the snow. Morgon stared at it senselessly a moment; the vesta made a little restless movement beneath him, as though it had finished a task and were anxious to leave. Morgon slid off its back. His muscles refused to hold him; he fell sharply to his knees, the harp jerked down beside him. Under the deep, curious gaze of the vesta, he tried to get up, fell back helplessly, trembling with exhaustion. The vesta nudged at him, its warm breath in his ear. He slid his arm around its neck, his face dropping against its face. It was still for a moment in his hold. Then it broke free with a sudden movement, its head jerking back; and as the circle of gold horn lifted like the rim of the sun against the white sky, the vesta faded, and a man stood in its place.

He was tall, lithe, white-haired, half-naked in the snow. His eyes in his lean, lined face were ice-blue; his hands, reaching down to Morgon, were scarred with the white imprint of vesta-horns.

Morgon whispered, "Har." A little smile flared like a flame behind the light eyes. The wolf-king slid a powerful arm under Morgon's arm, lifted him to his feet.

"Welcome." He helped Morgon patiently up the steps, flung open the wide doors to a hall the size of the barn at Akren, with a firebed running almost the length of it. Har's voice rose, shearing the silence; a couple of crows squawked, startled, on the ledge of a long window. "Is this house hibernating for the winter? I want food, wine, dry clothes, and I will not wait for them until my bones snap like ice with old age and my teeth drop out. Aia!"

Servants scurried blearily into the hall; dogs, springing up, swarmed eagerly about their legs. Half a tree trunk was thrown on the drowsing fire; sparks shot up toward the roof. A mantle of white wool was put over Har's shoulders; Morgon's clothes were stripped from him with unexpected thoroughness on the threshold. A long woolen tunic was pulled over his head, and a mantle of many colored furs thrown over his shoulders. Trays of food were brought in, placed by the fire; Morgon caught the smell of hot bread and hot, spiced meat. He sagged in Har's grip; wine, cold, dry, was forced into his mouth. He swallowed it and choked, felt the blood begin to move again in him, sluggishly, painfully.

A woman came into the hall as they sat down at last and began to eat. She had a strong, lovely old face, hair the color of old ivory braided to her knees. She came to the fire, tightening a belt as she walked, her eyes moving from Har's face to Morgon's.

She dropped a gentle kiss on Har's cheek and said placidly, "Welcome home. Whom did you bring this time?"

"The Prince of Hed."

Morgon's head turned sharply. His eyes caught Har's, held them in an unspoken question. The little perpetual smile deepened in the wolf-king's eyes. He said, "I have a gift for naming. I'll teach it to you. This is my wife, Aia. I found him wandering on foot in a blizzard beside the Ose," he added to her. "I have been shot at, in vesta form; a trapper threw a weighted net over me once in the hills behind Grim Mountain before he realized who I was; but I have never been fed a loaf of bread by a man half the traders in the realm have been trying to find." He turned again to Morgon, who had stopped eating. He said, his voice gentle in the snapping fire, "You and I are riddle-masters; I will play no games with you. I know a little about you, but not enough. I don't know what is driving you to Erlenstar Mountain, or who you are hiding from. I want to know. I will give you whatever you ask of me in knowledge or skills in return for one thing. If you had not come into my land I would have gone to yours eventually, in one form or another: an old crow, an old trader at your door selling buttons in exchange for knowledge. I would have come."

Morgon put his plate down. Strength was coming back into his body and a strength, a sense of purpose was waking, at Har's words, in his mind. He said haltingly, "If you hadn't found me by the river, I would have died. I will give you whatever help you need."

"That's a dangerous thing to promise blindly in my house," Har commented.

"I know. I've heard a little of you, too. I will give you what help you need."

Har smiled. His hand came to rest a moment, lightly, on Morgon's shoulder. "You made your way inch by inch up the Ose, against the wind in a raging blizzard, clinging to that harp like your life. I tend to believe you. The farmers of Hed are known for their stubbornness."

"Perhaps." He leaned back, his eyes closing in the hot drift of the fire. "But I left Deth in Herun to go back to Hed. I came here instead."

"Why did you change your mind?"

"You sent a riddle out of Osterland to find me. . . ." His voice trailed silent. He heard Har say something from the heart of the fire, he saw the blizzard again, formless, whirling, darkening, darkening. . . .

He woke in a small rich room, dark with evening. He lay without thought, his arm over his eyes, until a scrape of metal by the hearth made him turn his head. Someone was probing the fire; at the sudden lift of a white head, Morgon said, startled, "Deth!"

The head turned. "No. It's me. Har said I am to serve you." A boy rose from the fireside, lit the torch beside Morgon's bed. He was a few years younger than Morgon, big-boned, his hair milky-white. His face was impassive, but Morgon sensed a shyness, a wildness beneath it. His eyes in the torchlight were a lustrous familiar purple. Under Morgon's puzzled gaze, his voice went on, breaking a little now and then as though it were not frequently used. "He said . . . Har said I am to give you my name. I am Hugin. Suth's son."

Morgon's blood shocked through him. "Suth is dead."

"No."

"All the wizards are dead."

"No. Har knows Suth. Har found . . . he found me three years ago, running among the vesta. He looked into my mind and saw Suth."

Morgon stared up at him wordlessly. He gathered the tangled, aching knot of his muscles and bones, and rolled upright. "Where are my clothes? I have got to talk to Har."

"He knows," Hugin said. "He is waiting for you."

Washed, dressed, Morgon followed the boy to Har's great hall. It was filled with people, rich men and women from the city, traders, trappers, musicians, a handful of simply dressed farmers, drinking hot wine by the fire, talking, playing chess, reading. The informality reminded Morgon of Akren. Har, Aia beside him scratching the dog at her knee, sat in his chair by the fire, listening to a harpist. As Morgon made his way through the crowd, the king's eyes lifted, met his, smiling.

Morgon sat down on a bench beside them. The dog left Aia to scent him curiously, and he realized then with a slight shock, that it was a wolf. Other animals lay curled by the fire: a red fox, a squat badger, a grey squirrel, a pair of weasels white as snow in the rushes.

Aia said tranquilly as he scratched the wolf's ears gingerly, "They come in from the winter, Har's friends. Sometimes they spend a season here, sometimes they come bringing news of both men and animals in Osterland. Sometimes our children send them when they can't come to visit us—that white falcon sleeping high on the rafters, our daughter sent."

"Can you speak to them?" Morgon asked. She shook her head smiling.

"I can only go into Har's mind, and then when he is in his own shape. It's better that way; otherwise I would have worried much more about him when I was younger and he wandered away, prowling his kingdom."

The harp song came to an end; the harpist, a lean, dark man with a dour smile, rose to get wine. The wolf moved to Har as the king reached for his own cup. The king poured Morgon wine, sent a servant for food. Then he said, his voice soft in the weave of sounds about them, "You offered me your help. If you were any other man, I would not hold you to that, but you are a Prince of Hed, the most unimaginative of lands. What I ask will be very difficult, but it will be valuable. I want you to find Suth."

"Suth? Har, how can he be alive? How, after seven hundred years?"

"Morgon, I knew Suth." The voice was still soft, but there was an edge to it as to a chill wind. "We were young together, so long ago. We hungered for knowledge, not caring how it was got, how we used ourselves, one another. We played riddle-games even before Caithnard existed, games that lasted years as we were forced to search for answers. He lost an eye during those wild years; he himself scarred my hands with the vesta-horns, teaching me how to change shape. When he vanished with the school of wizards, I thought he must be dead. Yet three years ago, when a young vesta changed shape to a boy in front of my eyes, and when I looked into the thoughts and memories of his mind, I saw the man he knew as his father, and I knew that face as I know my heart. Suth. He is alive. He has been running, hiding for seven hundred years. Hiding. When I asked him once how he lost his eye, he laughed and said only that there was nothing that may not be looked upon. Yet he has seen something, turned his back to it and run, vanished like a snowfall in a land of snow. He did well to hide. He knows me. I have been at his heels like a wolf for three years, and I will find him."

Patterns were shattering, shifting in Morgon's mind, leaving him groping, blind. "The Morgol of Herun suggested that Ghisteslwchlohm, the Founder of Lungold, is also alive. But that was pure conjecture, there is no evidence. What is he running from?"

"What is driving you to Erlenstar Mountain?"

Morgon put his cup down. He slid his fingers through his hair, drawing it back from his face so that the stars shone blood-red against his pallor. "That."

Har's hands shifted slightly, his rings flashing. Aia sat motionless, listening, her eyes hooded with thought. "So," the king said, "the movement of this great game of power revolves upon Hed. When did you first realize that?"

He thought back. "In Ymris. I found a harp with three stars matching the stars on my face, which no one else could play. I met the woman married to Heureu Ymris, who tried to kill me, for no other reason than those stars, who said she was older than the first riddle ever asked—"

"How did you come to be in Ymris?"

"I was taking the crown of Aum to Anuin."

"Ymris," Har pointed out, "is in the opposite direction."

"Har, you must know what happened. Even if all the traders in the realm had gone to the bottom of the sea with the crown of Aum, you would still probably know, somehow."

"I know what happened," Har said imperturbably. "But I do not know you. Be patient with me, an old man, and begin at the beginning."

Morgon began. By the time he finished the tale of his travellings, the hall was empty but for the king, Aia, the harpist playing softly, listening, and Hugin, who had come in to sit at Har's feet with his head against the king's knees. The torches burned low; the animals were sighing, dreaming in their sleep. His voice ran dry finally. Har got up, stood looking into the fire. He was silent a long time; Morgon saw his hands close at his sides.

"Suth . . ."

Hugin's face flashed toward him at the name. Morgon said tiredly, "Why would he know anything? The Morgol thinks that knowledge of the stars must have been stripped from the wizards' minds."

Har's hands eased open. He turned to look at Morgon, weighing a thought. He said, as though he had not heard Morgon's question, "You dislike killing. There are other methods of defense. I could teach you to look into a man's mind, to see beyond illusion, to close the doors of your own mind against entrance. You are vulnerable as an animal without its winter pelt. I could teach you to outwit winter itself . . ."

Morgon gazed back at him. Something moved in his mind, the glint of a half-surfaced thought. He said, "I don't understand," though he had begun to.

"I told you," Har said, "you should never promise a thing blindly in my house. I believe Suth is running with the vesta behind Grim Mountain. I will teach you to take the vesta-shape; you will move among them freely through the winter as a vesta, yet not a vesta. Your body and instincts will be the vesta's, but your mind will be your own; Suth may hide from the High One himself, but he will reveal himself to you."

Morgon's body shifted a little. "Har, I have no gift for shape-changing."

"How do you know?"

"I'm not . . . No man of Hed was ever born with gifts like that." He shifted again, feeling himself with four powerful legs honed to speed, a head heavy with gold horn, no hands for touching, no voice for speaking.

Hugin said hesitantly, unexpectedly, "It's a thing to love—being the vesta. Har knows."

Morgon saw Grim Oakland's face, Eliard's face, staring at him uncomprehendingly, baffled: You can do what? Why would you want to do that? He felt Har watching him, and he said softly, reluctantly, "I will try, because I promised you. But I doubt if it will work; all my instincts go against it."

"Your instincts." The king's eyes reflected fire suddenly like an animal's, startling Morgon. "You are stubborn. With your face toward Erlenstar Mountain, a thousand miles farther than any Prince of Hed has ever gone beyond his land, a harp and a name in your possession, you still cling to your past like a nestling. What do you know about your instincts? What do you know about yourself? Will you doom us all with your own refusal to look at yourself and give a name to what you see?"

Morgon's hands closed on the edge of the bench. He said evenly, struggling to keep his voice from shaking, "I am a land-ruler, a riddle-master and a star-bearer, in that order—"

"No. You are the Star-Bearer. You have no other name but that, no other future. You have gifts no land-ruler of Hed was ever born with; you have eyes that see, a mind that weaves. Your instincts took you out of Hed before you even realized why; out of Hed to Caithnard, to Aum, to Herun, to Osterland, whose king had no pity for those who run from truth."

"I was born—"

"You were born the Star-Bearer. The wise man knows his own name. You are no fool; you can sense as well as I can what chaos is stirring beneath the surface of our existence. Loose your grip on your past; it is meaningless. You can live without the land-rule if you must; it's not essential—"

Morgon found himself on his feet before he even realized he had moved. "No—"

"You have a very capable land-heir, who stays home and farms instead of answering obscure riddles. Your land can exist without you; but if you run from your own destiny, you are liable to destroy us all."

He stopped. A sound had come out of Morgon, involuntarily, a harsh, indrawn sob without tears. Aia's face, Hugin's face, seemed etched of white stone in the light; only the king's face moved in the shifting fire, alien, neither man's nor animal's. Morgon put his hands over his mouth to still the sound and whispered, "What price do you put on landlaw? What incentive will you offer me to forsake it? What price will you pay me for all the things I have ever loved?"

The light, glittering eyes were unmoved, unwavering on his face. "Five riddles," Har said. "Coin for the man who has nothing. Who is the Star-Bearer and what will he loose that is bound? What will one star call out of silence, one star out of darkness, and one star out of death? Who will come in the time's ending and what will he bring? Who will sound the earth's harp, silent since the Beginning? Who will bear stars of fire and ice to the Ending of the Age?"

Morgon's hand slid slowly away from his mouth. The hall was soundless. He felt tears run like sweat down his face. "What ending?" The wolf-king did not answer. "What ending?"

"Answering riddles is your business. Suth gave me those riddles one day, like a man giving his heart to a friend for safekeeping. I have carried them unanswered since his disappearance."

"Where did he learn them?"

"He knows."

"Then I will ask him." His face was bloodless, streaked with fire; his eyes, the color of charred wood, held Har's, seemed to draw from them, in that moment, something of their pitilessness. "I will answer those riddles for you. And I think, when I have done that, you will wish to the last breath of your life that I had never set foot beyond Hed."

He sat the next morning in a round stone shed behind Har's house, waiting for the fire Hugin had built to bring some relief of warmth to the icy floor. He wore a light, short linen tunic; his feet were bare. There were pitchers of watered wine in a corner, cups, but nothing else, neither food nor bedding. The door was closed; there were no windows, only the hole in the roof through which the smoke billowed out, flurries of snow burning, melting, in it. Har sat opposite him, his face shaping and reshaping in the flames. Hugin, cross-legged behind him, was motionless as though he did not breathe.

"I am going into your mind," the face beyond the fire said. "I will see things you keep there privately. Do not try to fight my prying. If you wish to elude me, simply let the thoughts drain out of you like water, become formless, invisible as wind."

Morgon felt a light touch sorting his thoughts. Isolated moments, past events, rose unbidden in his mind: Rood, studying with him late at night, a candle hunched between them; the Lady Eriel speaking softly to him in a dark hall as his fingers slid toward the last, low string of a harp; Tristan, her feet muddy, watering her rose bushes; Lyra, picking up a sword that came alive in her hands, changing shape. He let the strange knowledge of another mind, the sense of other untrapped thoughts stay in his mind without struggling until unexpectedly out of the darkness of his thoughts he saw a man's body whirl away from him, the spear in his chest holding the fluid, shifting, sea-colored lines of him still until his face became clear for one moment before he fell. Morgon started, murmuring. Har's eyes gazed at him from the flames, unblinking.

"There is nothing that may not be faced, nothing that may not be looked upon. Again."

The memories of his life ran behind his eyes in a current of slowly changing scenes, some of which Har seemed to linger over in his curiosity. As the hours passed, unmeasured except by the ashes of dying wood, Morgon accepted the probing patiently, learned to yield without flinching to memories buried deep in him. Then, wearied, he began to ease away from the incessant searching, let his thoughts slip away from him, become shapeless, like a mist through which the groping mind moved without finding a resting place. Finally, abruptly, he found himself on his feet, pacing back and forth in the tiny room, thinking of nothing but the hunger worrying at him like an animal, the cold that burned his feet as he walked, the cry of his body, like the incessant, unbearable cry of a child for sleep. He prowled the small hut, not hearing Har when he spoke, not seeing Hugin staring up at him, not noticing the door open to deep night when Hugin left to get more wood. Then he felt something forming in his mind that Har had not touched yet, the most private moment of his life: an uneasiness, a growing terror, the beginning of a grief so terrible that any moment he might drown in it. He tried to elude the probing, pitiless mind, felt the grief welling, blooming, struggled furiously against it, against Har without success, until he saw again in the firelight the unmoved, curious eyes, and he took the only escape left to him, slipping out of his own thoughts beyond the surface of another mind.

It was as though he had stepped into another world. He saw the shed from Har's eyes, saw himself standing, surprised in the shadows. He tapped hesitantly the continuous spring of memory deep in Har's mind. He saw a young woman with sun-colored hair he knew was Aia, watching the soaking and bending of the wood that would pattern the walls of her new home. He saw a wizard with wild white hair and grey-gold eyes standing barefoot in snow, laughing before he melted into a lank wolf's form. He saw the private world of Osterland: a fox's den in the warm earth under the snow swarming with red pups, a white owl's nest in the hollow of a high tree, a herd of starving deer in the sparse, cold backlands, a farmer's simple house, the plain walls gleaming with tools, his children rolling like puppies in front of the fire. He followed Har's path through his kingdom, sometimes in animal form, sometimes as a slightly wealthy, slightly foolish old man, his sharp mind gleaning knowledge beneath his sleepy eyes. He realized as he began to recognize places Har had travelled, that he had not confined his wanderings to Osterland. A familiar house rose in Har's mind: with a shock of surprise that threw Morgon back into himself, he recognized the threshold of his own home.

He said, "When? . . ." His voice grated as though he had wakened from sleep.

"I went to Hed to meet Kern. I was curious about a tale I heard of him and a Thing without a name. I had forgotten about that. You did well."

Morgon sat down again on the stones. The demands of his body seemed vague, impersonal, as though they came from his shadow. The fire in the hearth died, flared again, dwindled, flared. The stones grew warm. Morgon went into Hugin's mind, discovered his wordless language, shared with him a complaint of hunger that surprised a smile into the vesta eyes. Then Har held Morgon's mind, probing constantly, teaching him to thrust past the barriers of a locked mind, to defend his own barriers, attacking and parrying again and again until Morgon, ready to explode with a rage of weariness, cleared his mind beyond possibility to try again. Har loosed him; he felt the sweat dripping down his face, his back, felt himself trembling even in the heat.

"How long . . . how long have we? . . ." His throat was parched.

"What is that to either of us? Hugin, get wine."

Hugin knelt next to Morgon with a cup. The boy's face was drawn, the skin beneath his eyes was dark with weariness. But his still face gave back to Morgon something of a smile. The small shed was dim with smoke. Morgon could not tell whether it was day or night beyond the smoke hole in the roof. Hugin opened the doors a moment; winds, blade-sharp, leaped in, scattering snow. The world was black beyond. The sweat froze on Morgon's arms. He began to shiver, and Hugin closed the door.

"Again," Har said softly, and slipped into Morgon's mind like a cat, while Morgon groped, surprised, for the memory of his teachings. The long hours began again, Morgon struggling either to keep his mind free from Har's probing, or to find a path through Har's closed mind. Hugin sat shadow-still beside him. Sometimes Morgon saw him sleeping, stretched on the stones. Sometimes when he pulled away from Har, exhausted, the purple eyes turned to him, and he saw through them an image of the vesta. Then he began to see a vesta where Hugin sat, and was unsure afterward if Hugin had put the thought into his mind, or if the boy's shape were shifting back and forth. Once he looked across the fire and saw not Har but a lean grey wolf with yellow, smiling eyes.

He rubbed his eyes with the heels of his hands, and Har returned saying, "Again."

"No," he whispered, feeling his mind and body slip away from him. "No."

"Then leave."

"No."

The smoke engulfed him like a wind. He seemed to look down at himself from a distance, as though the man half-blind, too weak to move had nothing to do with him. Hugin and Har seemed formed of smoke, now king and wizard's boy, now wolf and vesta, watching, waiting. The wolf began to move closer to him, closer, circling him, fire in its eyes, until it stood next to him. Morgon felt his hands opened, a pattern traced with ash on his palms.

Then the wolf said, "Now."

The pain brought him abruptly back to himself. He opened his eyes, blinking at the salt tears of sweat that ran into them, and the purple eyes of the vesta gazed deep into his. A blade flashed in the corner of his eye; a sound split through his dry throat. Turning, fleeing away from the smoke, the agony of his weariness, the sear of the knife, he stumbled into the world beyond the vesta-eyes.

The stone walls melted away into the single flat line of winter horizon. He stood alone in a privacy of snow and sky, listening to the winds, untangling the scents in them. Somewhere within him, behind him, he sensed a struggling, a turmoil of thought; he avoided it, groping away from it, searching more deeply into the easy silence he had discovered. The winds snapped out of the sharp blue of the sky, carrying shades and tones of smell he could suddenly give names to: water, hare, wolf, pine, vesta. He heard the high, whirling voices of the winds, knew their strength, but felt them only vaguely. The chaotic, fearful voices he fled from weakened, mingled with the wind's meaningless wail. He drew a long, clean breath of the winter, felt the voice fade. The wind traced its passage through him, molded the sinews of his heart, flowed through his veins, honed his muscles to its unfaltering strength and speed. He felt it urge against him, challenging him; and the hard, restless muscles of his body locked suddenly for a race with the wind.

The stones rose out of the unknown. He moved bewilderedly, seeking escape, aware of strange, silent figures watching him. The fire snapped at him; he backed away from it and turned. His horns scraped against the stones. Then, with a panic exploding through him, he realized that he had horns. He found himself in his own shape, trembling, staring at Har, his hands throbbing again, sticky with blood.

Hugin opened the door. A weak midday light stained the snow on the threshold. Har rose, his own hands trembling slightly. He said nothing, and Morgon, as familiar with the mind of the King as he was with his own, felt the panic die away, a stillness take its place. He went to the door, his steps halting, and leaned on the frame, breathing the wind, his limp hands staining his tunic. He felt an odd sorrow, as though he had turned away from something nameless in him. Har put a hand on his shoulder.

"Rest, now. Rest. Hugin—"

"I know. I will take him."

"Bind his hands. Stay with him. Both of you: rest."

9

As MORGON'S HANDS healed, Har continued the training; Morgon learned to take the vesta-shape for long periods of time. Hugin guided him around Yrye; they ate pine in the forest fringing Yrye, climbed the steep crags and forests of Grim Mountain, rising behind Yrye. The vesta-instincts confused Morgon at first; he struggled against them as against deep water, and would find himself standing half-naked in deep winter, with Hugin nuzzling at him, his mind-voice running into Morgon's.

Morgon, let's run. You like vesta-running; you are not afraid of that. Morgon, come out of the cold.

And they would run for miles in the snow without tiring, their hooves barely skimming the snow, the great hearts and muscles of their bodies fine-tuned to the effortless movement. They would return to Yrye in the evenings, sometimes late at night, bringing back within them the silence of the still winter night. Har would be waiting for them in the hall, talking to Aia or listening to his harpist play softly beside the hearth. Morgon spoke little to Har during this time, as though something in his mind were healing along with his hands. Har waited, watched, silent himself. Finally one night Morgon and Hugin returned late, and the unexpected sound of their laughter, curtailed sharply as they entered, made Aia smile. Morgon went to Har unhesitantly, sat down beside him, while Hugin went to get food. He looked down at the palms of his hands, the bone-white imprint of vesta-horns on them.

Har said, "It's not such a terrible thing to be, a vesta, is it?"

He smiled. "No. I love it. I love the silence of it. But how will I explain to Eliard?"

"That," Har said a little drily, "is liable to be the least of your worries. Other men have come to me through the years begging me to teach them the mind-work, shape-changing; very, very few have ever left that room with the vesta-scars on their hands. You have great gifts. Hed was far too small a world for you."

"It's unprecedented. How will I explain that to the High One?"

"Why must you justify your abilities?"

Morgon looked at him. He said peacefully, "Har, you know, in spite of the arguments you used with me, that I am still answerable to the High One as the land-ruler of Hed, no matter how many deadly harpists out of the sea call me Star-Bearer. I would like to keep it that way, if possible."

The smile deepened in Har's eyes. "Then perhaps the High One will justify yourself to you. Are you ready to look for Suth?"

"Yes. I have some questions to ask him."

"Good. I believe he may be in the lake-lands north of Grim Mountain, on the fringe of the great northern wastes. There is a large herd of vesta on the other side of the mountain; I rarely join them. I've searched the rest of my kingdom and have found no sign of him. Hugin will take you there."

"Come with us."

"I can't. He would only run from me, as he has done for seven hundred years." He paused. Morgon saw his thoughts drift back into some memory, his eyes narrow.

He said, "I know. That's the blade that harrows the brain: Why? You knew Suth: what would he have run from?"

"I thought he would have died rather than run from anything. Are you sure you are ready? It may take months."

"I'm ready."

"Then leave at dawn, quietly, with Hugin. Look beyond Grim; if you cannot find Suth there, look along the Ose—but watch for trappers. Let the vesta know you. They will sense you are also a man, and Suth will hear of you if he is in contact with them. If there is even a hint of danger, return to Yrye at once."

"I will," Morgon said absently. He saw suddenly, in his mind's eye, long, quiet weeks beyond the snow-covered mountain, in the backlands of the world, where he would move to a rhythm of night and day, wind, snow and silence he had come to love. Har's eyes, insistent on his face, brought him out of his dreaming. There was a wry edge of warning in them.

"If you die in vesta-shape on my lands, I will have that imperturbable harpist on my doorstep asking why. So be careful."

They left at dawn, both in vesta-shape. Hugin led Morgon up the slopes of Grim Mountain, through high rocky passes where mountain goats stared at them curiously and hawks wheeled on the wind, searching for food. They slept that night among the rocks, then descended the next day into the lake-land beyond Grim, where no one but a few trappers lived, collecting skins for traders on the edge of the northern wastes. Herds of vesta passed like mist through the land, untouched, untroubled. Morgon and Hugin joined them quietly, unchallenged by the leaders of the herds who accepted them as they accepted Har, as strange but not threatening. They moved with the herds, ranging through the lake-lands, feeding on pine. They slept in the open at night, the winds scarcely penetrating their long fur. Wolves circled them occasionally, hungry yet wary; Morgon heard their distant howling in his dreams. He responded to them without fear, yet aware of their power if they came upon a young or aged vesta strayed from the herd. When he and Hugin had searched one herd for images of the one-eyed Suth, they moved to find another in the deep forests, or beside frozen, moon-colored lakes. Finally, Morgon found a pattern of images repeating itself in the minds of one herd: the image of a vesta with one eye purple, the other white as web.

He stayed with that herd, eating, sleeping with it, waiting in hope that the half-blind vesta would join it. Hugin, troubled by the same image, ranged away from the herd among the lakes and hills, searching. The moon grew round above them, dwindled and began to grow again, and Morgon grew restless himself. He began to roam in curiosity, searching the low hills of the northern boundaries. One day he went over them and looked across at the flat, empty wastes. The winds lifted snow, swept it like sand across the plains, honed into a single, unbroken line the bounds of the world. No life seemed hidden beneath the snow; the sky itself was empty, colorless. In the far west, he saw the great head of Erlenstar Mountain, and the flat, white lands behind it. He turned, oddly cold, and went back into Osterland.

Coming back down from the hills, he saw a vesta, grey-white with age, with its horns oddly trapped by something beneath the snow. Its head lowered, shoulders and haunches straining against the hold on its horns, it could not see the grey slink of wolves gathering behind it. Morgon caught a scent of them, thick, acrid in the wind. He found himself suddenly racing towards them, making a sound he had never heard from himself before.

The wolves scattered, whining, among the rocks. One of them, mad with hunger, snapped at Morgon's face then turned to leap at the trapped vesta. An odd rage surged through Morgon. He reared, striking. His sharp hooves caught the wolf's head, crushed it, spattering blood on the snow. The cloying smell welled over him; a sudden confusion of instinct thrust him out of the vesta-shape. He found himself barefoot in the snow, struggling with a wrench of nausea.

He moved upwind, knelt before the vesta. He groped in the snow beneath its horns, feeling the hidden branch that had trapped it. He reached up to soothe the vesta with one hand, and found himself looking into a blind eye.

He sat back on his heels. The wind searched the threads of his light tunic, racking his body, but he did not notice. He let his thoughts drift curiously beyond the blind eye, and the swift, skillful withdrawal of thought told him what he wanted to know.

"Suth?" The vesta eyed him, motionless. "I've been looking for you."

A darkness welled over his mind. He struggled with it desperately, not knowing how to avoid the single, insistent command that beat over and over in his mind like the single beat of water in a soundless cave. He felt his hands slip into the snow, wrench at the hidden branch. Then the impulse ceased abruptly. He felt his thoughts searched and did not move until the strange mind withdrew and he heard the command again: *Free me.*

He heaved the branch loose. The vesta straightened, flinging back its head. Then it vanished. A man stood before Morgon, lean, powerful, his white hair fraying in the wind, his single eye grey-gold.

His hand brushed across Morgon's face, seeking the stars; he lifted Morgon's hand, turned it palm-upward, traced the scar on it, and something like a smile flashed in his eye.

Then he put his hands on Morgon's shoulders, as though feeling the humanness of him, and said incredulously, "Hed?"

"Morgon of Hed."

"The hope I saw a thousand years ago and before is a Prince of Hed?" His voice was deep, like a wind's voice; long-disused. "You have met Har; he left his mark on you. Good. You'll need every bone of help you can get."

"I need your help."

The wizard's thin mouth twisted. "I can give you nothing. Har should have known better than to send you for me. He has two good eyes; he should have seen."

"I don't understand." He was beginning to feel the cold. "You gave Har riddles; I need answers to them. Why did you leave Lungold? Why have you hidden even from Har?"

"Why would anyone hide from the tooth of his own heart?" The lean hands shook him a little. "Can you not see? Not even you? I am trapped. I am dead, speaking to you."

Morgon was silent, staring at him. Behind the flame of laughter like Har's in his single eye, there was an emptiness vaster than the northern wastes. He said, "I don't understand. You have a son; Har cares for him."

The wizard's eyes closed. He drew a deep breath. "So. I hoped Har might find him. I am so tired, so tired of this. . . . Tell Har to teach you to guard against compulsion. What are you of all people doing with three stars on your face in this game of death?"

"I don't know," Morgon said tautly. "I can't escape them."

"I want to see the end of this; I want to see it—you are so impossible, you might win this game."

"What game? Suth, what has been happening for seven hundred years? What keeps you trapped here living like an animal? What can I do to help you?"

"Nothing. I am dead."

"Then do something for me! I need help! The third stricture of Ghisteslwchlohm is this: The wizard who hearing a cry for help turns away, the wizard who watching an evil does not speak, the wizard who searching for truth looks away from it: these are the wizards of false power. I understand running, but not when there is no place left to run to."

Something stirred deep in the emptiness of the gold eye. Suth smiled, again with the wry twist of mouth that reminded Morgon of Har.

He said with an odd gentleness, "I place my life in your hands, Star-Bearer. Ask."

"Why did you run from Lungold?"

"I ran from Lungold because—" His voice stopped. He reached suddenly to Morgon, his breath coming in sharp, white flashes. Morgon caught at him, felt himself pulled down in the grip and sag of the wizard.

"Suth!"

Suth's hands twisted the cloth at his throat, forced him closer to the open, straining mouth that gave him one final word formed with the husk of its breath.

"Ohm . . ."

He carried the dead wizard on his back to Yrye. Hugin walked beside him, sometimes in vesta shape, sometimes, for a mile or so, in his own shape, a tall, silent boy with one hand holding Suth balanced on the vesta beside him. As they travelled over the mountain, Morgon felt in some deep place an impatience with the vesta-form, as though he had worn it too long. The land stretched before them, white to the white sky under the mold of winter. Yrye itself lay half-hidden in drifts of snow. When they reached it at last, Har was on the threshold to meet them.

He said nothing, took the body from Morgon's back and watched him turn at last into himself, with two months' growth of hair and the scars puckered on his hands. Morgon opened his mouth to say something; he could not speak. Har said softly, "He has been dead for seven hundred years. I'll take him. Go in."

"No," Hugin said. Har, bent over Suth's body, looked up at him.

"Then help me."

They carried him together around the back of the house. Morgon went inside. Someone threw fur over his shoulders as he passed; he drew it around him absently, scarcely feeling it, scarcely seeing the handful of curious faces turned toward him, watching. He sat down by the fire, poured himself wine. Aia sat down on the bench beside him. She put a hand on his arm, gripped it gently.

"I'm glad you're safe, you and Hugin, my children. Don't grieve for Suth."

He found his voice. "How did you know?"

"I know Har's mind. He'll bury his sorrow like a man burying silver in the night. Don't let him."

Morgon looked down into his cup. Then he put it on the table, pushed the heels of his hands against his eyes. "I should have known," he whispered. "I should have thought. One wizard, alive after seven centuries, and I forced him out of hiding so he could die in my arms . . ." He heard Har and Hugin come in, dropped his hands. Har sat down in his chair. Hugin sat at his feet, his white head resting against Har's knee. His eyes closed. Har's hand rested a moment in his hair. His eyes went to Morgon's face.

"Tell me."

"Take it from me," Morgon said wearily. "You knew him. You tell me." He sat passively while memories of the days and long white nights passed through his mind, culminated in the wolf killing, in the last few moments of the wizard's life. Finished, Har loosed him, sat quietly, his eyes impassive.

"Who is Ohm?"

Morgon stirred. "Ghisteslwchlohm, I think—the founder of the School of Wizards of Lungold."

"The Founder is still alive?"

"I don't know who else it could be." His voice caught.

"What troubles you? What have you not told me?"

"Ohm—Har, one of the . . . one of the Masters at Caithnard was named Ohm. He . . . I studied with him. I respected him greatly. The Morgol of Herun suggested that he might be the Founder." Har's hands closed suddenly on the arms of his chair. "There was no evidence—"

"The Morgol of Herun would not say something like that without evidence."

"It was scant—just his name, and the fact that she couldn't . . . she couldn't see through him—"

"The Founder of Lungold is at Caithnard? Still controlling whatever wizards may be alive?"

"It's conjecture. It's only that. Why would he have kept his own name for all the world to guess—"

"Who would guess, after seven centuries? And who would be powerful enough to control him?"

"The High One—"

"The High One." Har rose abruptly; Hugin started. The wolf-king moved to the fire. "His silence is almost more mysterious than Suth's. He has never been one to meddle greatly in our affairs, but this much restraint is incredible."

"He let Suth die."

"Suth wanted to die," Har said impatiently, and Morgon's voice snapped away from him furiously.

"He was alive! Until I found him!"

"Stop blaming yourself. He was dead. The man you spoke to was not Suth but a husk that had no name."

"That's not true—"

"What do you call life? Would you call me living if I turned in fear away from you, refused to give you something that would save your life? Would you call me Har?"

"Yes." His voice softened. "Corn bears its name in the seed in the ground, in the green stalk, in the yellow dried stalk whose leaves whisper riddles to the wind. So Suth bore his name, giving me a riddle in the last breath of his life. So I blame myself because there is no longer anywhere in this world the man that bore his name. He took the vesta-form; he had a son among them; there were things that somewhere beneath his fear and helplessness, he remembered how to love."

Hugin's head dropped forward against his knees. Har's eyes closed. He stood at the fire without speaking, without moving, while lines of weariness and pain worked themselves through the mask of his face.

Morgon twisted on the bench, dropped his face in his arms on the table behind him. He whispered, "If Master Ohm is Ghisteslwchlohm, the High One will know. I'll ask him."

"And then?"

"And then . . . I don't know. There are so many pieces that don't fit. . . . It's like the shards I tried to fit together once in Ymris, not having all the pieces, not even knowing if the pieces belonged together at all."

"You can't travel alone to the High One."

"Yes, I can. You've taught me how. Har, nothing alive could stop me from finishing this journey now. If I had to, I'd drag my own bones out of a grave to the High One. I must have answers."

He felt Har's hands on his shoulders, unexpectedly gentle, and raised his head.

Har said softly, "Finish your journey; there's nothing any of us can do without answers. But go no farther than that alone. There are kings from Anuin to Isig who will help you, and a harpist at Erlenstar Mountain who is skilled at more things than harping. Will you give me this promise? That if Master Ohm is Ghisteslwchlohm, you will not rush blindly back to Caithnard to tell him you know?"

Morgon shrugged a little, wearily. "I don't believe he is. I can't. But I promise."

"And come back to Yrye, rather than going straight to Hed. You will be far more dangerous when you are less ignorant, and I think the forces gathering against you will move swiftly then."

Morgon was silent; a pain touched his heart and withdrew. He whispered, "I won't go home. . . . Ohm, the shape-changers, even the High One—they seem to be balanced in a false peace, waiting for some kind of signal to act. . . . When they finally do, I don't want to give them any reason to be near Hed." He stirred, his face turning to Har's. Their eyes met a moment in an unspoken knowledge of one another. Morgon's head bowed. "Tomorrow, I will go to Isig."

"I'll take you as far as Kyrth. Hugin can ride with us, carry your harp. In vesta-shape, it should take only two days."

Morgon nodded. "All right. Thank you." He paused, looking again at Har; his hands moved a little, helplessly, as though groping for a word.

"Thank you."

They left Yrye at dawn. Morgon and the wolf-king were in vesta-form; Hugin rode Har, carrying the harp and some clothes Aia had packed for Morgon. They ran westward through the quiet day, across farmland buried in a crust of unbroken snow, skirting towns whose chimney smoke wove into an ash-white sky. They ran far into the night, through the moonlit forests, up the low rocky foothills until they reached the Ose, winding down northward from Isig. They fed there, slept awhile, then rose before dawn to continue up the Ose, across the foothills into the shadow of Isig Mountain. The white head of the mountain, blind with snow, loomed over them as they ran, its depths secret, inexhaustible with minerals, metals, bright, precious jewels. The trade-city Kyrth sprawled at its roots; the Ose wandered through it on its long journey toward the sea. West of Kyrth, rocky peaks and hills jutted like a rough sea, parting between waves to form the winding pass that led to Erlenstar Mountain.

They stopped just before they reached the city. Morgon took his own shape, put the heavy, furred cloak Hugin had carried for him over his shoulders, slid the harp and pack straps around his neck. He stood, waiting for the great vesta beside him to take Har's shape once again, but it only watched him out of eyes that seemed to glint in the fading afternoon, with a familiar, elusive smile. So he slid an arm around its neck, pushed his face a moment against the white, cold fur. He turned to Hugin, embraced him; the boy said softly, "Find what killed Suth. And then come back. Come back."

"I will."

He left them without looking back. He followed the river into Kyrth, found the main road through the city crowded even in mid-winter with traders, trappers, craftsmen, miners. The road wound up the mountain above the city, the snow on it broken and scarred by cartwheels. It grew quiet in the twilight; the trees began to blur together. In the distance, obscured sometimes by the jut of mountain, Morgon saw the dark walls of Danan Isig's house, the jagged lines of its walls shaped as though the wind and weather and restless earth had formed them. After a while, out of the corner of his eye, he saw a man who walked beside him quietly as a shadow.

Morgon stopped abruptly. The man was big, thewed like a tree, with hair and beard grey-gold against the white fur of his hood. His eyes were the color of pine. He said quickly, "I mean no harm. I am curious. Are you a harpist?"

Morgon hesitated. The green eyes were gentle, mild on his face; he said finally, his voice still a little rough from the long months away from men, "No. I'm travelling. I wanted to ask Danan Isig for shelter for the night, but I don't know—does he keep his house open to strangers?"

"In midwinter, any traveller is welcome. Did you come from Osterland?"

"Yes. From Yryr."

"The wolf-king's lair . . . I'm going to Harte now myself. May I walk with you?"

Morgon nodded. They walked a little in silence, the hard, broken snow crunching underfoot. The man drew a deep breath of pine-scented air, let it mist away. He said placidly, "I met Har once. He came to Isig disguised as a trader selling furs and amber. He told me privately he was trying to find a trapper who had been selling vesta-pelts to the traders, which was true, but I think he also came out of curiosity, to see Isig Mountain."

"Did he find the trapper?"

"I believe so. He also walked the veins and roots of Isig before he left. Is he well?"

"Yes."

"I'm glad to hear it. He must be an aged wolf now, as I am an ancient tree." He stopped. "Listen. You can hear where we stand the waters running deep below us through Isig."

Morgon listened. The murmur and hiss of water endlessly falling wound deep below the wind's voice. Cliffs bare of snow reared above them, melting into grey-white mists. Kyrth looked small below them, sheltered in a single curve of mountain.

"I would like to see the inside of Isig," he said suddenly.

"Would you? I'll show it to you. I know that mountain better than I know my own mind."

Morgon looked at him. The aged, broad face crinkled a little under his gaze. He said softly, "Who are you? Are you Danan Isig? Is that why I didn't hear you? Because you had just come out of your own shape-changing?"

"Was I a tree? Sometimes I stand so long in the snow watching the trees wrapped in their private thoughts that I forget myself, become one of them. They are as old as I am, old as Isig . . ." He paused, his eyes running over Morgon's untrimmed hair, his harp, and added, "I heard something from the traders about a Prince of Hed travelling to Erlenstar Mountain, but that may only have been rumor; you know how they gossip . . ."

Morgon smiled. The pine-colored eyes smiled back at him. They started walking again; snow began to drift down, catching in the fur on their hoods, in their hair. The road swung wide around a jut of hillside to reveal again the rough black walls and pine-shaped towers of Harte. Its windows, patterned and stained with color, were already blazing with torchlight. The road ran into its mouth.

"The doorway into Isig," Danan Isig said. "No one goes in or out of the mountain without my knowledge. The greatest craftsmen of the realm come to train in my home, work with the metals and jewels of Isig. My son Ash teaches them, as Sol used to before he was killed. It was Sol who cut the stars that Yrth set in your harp."

Morgon touched the harp strap. A sense of age, of roots, of beginnings was waking in him at Danan's words. "Why did Yrth put stars on the harp?"

"I don't know. I didn't wonder, then. . . . Yrth worked months on that harp, carving it, cutting the designs for the inlay; he had my craftsmen cut the ivory and set the silver and stones in it. And then he went up into the highest room in the oldest tower of Harte to tune the harp. He stayed seven days and nights, while I closed the forges in the yard so that the pounding wouldn't bother him. Finally, he came down and played it for us. There was no more beautiful harp in the world. He said he had taken its voices from the waters and winds of Isig. It held us breathless, the harping and the harpist. . . . When he had finished playing, he stood still a moment, looking down at it. Then he passed the flat of his hand over the strings, and they went mute. When we protested, he laughed and said the harp would choose its own harpist. The next day he left, taking it with him. When he returned to my service a year later, he never mentioned the harp. It was as though we had all dreamed the making of it."

Morgon stopped. His hand twisted in the harp strap while he stared at the distant, darkening trees as though somehow he could shape the wizard out of the twilight. "I wonder—"

Danan said, "What is it?"

"Nothing. I would like to speak to him."

"So would I. He was in my service almost from the Years of Settlement. He came to me from some strange place west of the realm I had never heard of; he would leave Isig for years at a time, exploring other lands, meeting other wizards, other kings . . . every time he returned, he would be a little more powerful, gentler. He had a curiosity like a trader's and a laugh that boomed down into the lower mines. It was he who discovered the cave of the Lost Ones. That was the only time I ever saw him completely serious. He told me I had built my home over a shadow, and that I would be wise to forbid the waking of that shadow. So my miners have been careful never to disturb it, especially since they found Sol dead at its doorway. . . ." He was silent a little, then added, as though he had heard Morgon's unspoken question, "Yrth took me to it once to show me. I don't know who made the door to the cave; it was there before I came, green and black marble. The inner cave was incredibly rich and beautiful, but—there was nothing in it that I could see."

"Nothing."

"Just stones, silence, and a terrible sense of something lying just beyond eyesight, like a dread in the bottom of your heart. I asked Yrth what it was, but he never told me. Something happened there before the settlement of Isig, long before the coming of men to the realm of the High One."

"Perhaps during the wars of the Earth-Masters."

"I think there may be a connection. But what, I don't know; and the High One, if he knows what happened, has never said."

Morgon thought of the beautiful, ruined city on Wind Plain, of the glass shards he had uncovered like a hint of an answer in one of the empty, roofless rooms. And suddenly, thinking of it, the terrible dread of a simple answer struck him, and he stopped again in the still, icy dusk, the mountain polished smooth and white as a bone in front of him. He whispered, "Beware the unanswered riddle."

"What?"

"No one knows what destroyed the Earth-Masters. Who could

have been more powerful than they were, and what shape that power has taken . . ."

"It was thousands of years ago," Danan said. "What could that have to do with us?"

"Nothing. Perhaps. But we've been assuming just that for thousands of years, and the wise man assumes nothing. . . ."

The mountain-king said wonderingly, "What is it you see ahead of us in the darkness that no one else can?"

"I don't know. Something without a name. . . ."

They reached the dark arch of the gates of Harte just as the snow began to fall again. The yard, with its many forges and workshops, was nearly empty; here and there a red-gold light shown through a half-opened door; the shadow of some craftsman at his work spilled across the threshold. Danan led Morgon across the yard into a hall whose rough walls were filigreed with flickering colors of jewels still embedded in the stone. A stream cut a curved path through the floor; a great firebed suspended above it warmed the stones, fire dancing over the dark water. Miners, craftsmen dressed simply in the colors of the mountain, traders in their rich garb, trappers in fur and leather glanced up as Danan entered, and Morgon shifted instinctively to a line of shadow beyond the torch's reach.

Danan said gently, "There's a quiet room in the east tower where you can wash and rest; come down later when it's not so crowded. Most of these men will return to Kyrth after supper; they only work here." He led through a side door out of the hall, up a stairway winding through the core of a wide tower. He added, "This is the tower Yrth stayed in. Talies used to visit him here, and Suth, a couple of times. Suth was a wild one, hair white as snow even when he was young. He frightened the miners, but I saw him once changing into shape after shape to amuse my children." He stopped on a landing, drew back heavy hangings of white fur in a doorway. "I'll send someone to make up your fire." He paused, said a little hesitantly, "If it isn't asking too much of you, I would love to hear that harp again."

Morgon smiled. "No. It's not asking too much. Thank you. I'm grateful for your kindness."

He went into the room, sliding the straps from his shoulder. The walls were hung with fur and tapestry, but the hearth was swept clean and the room was cold. Morgon sat down in a chair beside the hearth. The stones formed a circle of silence about him. He could hear nothing, no laughter from the hall, no wind outside. A loneliness unlike even the loneliness of his path through the unclaimed lands touched him. He closed his eyes, felt weariness deeper than sleep sucking at the core of him. He rose restlessly, pulling away from it. Men came in then, bringing wood, water, wine, food; he watched them build the fire, light torches, set water to heat. When they were gone, he stood for a long time at the fire, staring into it. The water began to hiss; he undressed slowly, washed. He ate something he could not taste, poured wine, sat without drinking it while the night locked like a fist around the tower and the strange dread eddied like a tide deep in his heart.

His eyes closed again. For a while he ran with the vesta on the surface of his dreams, until he found himself floundering in the snow in his own shape as they melted away in the distance. Then, the loneliness poignant, unbearable, he traversed space and time with a wizard's skill, found himself at Akren. Eliard and Grim Oakland were talking in front of the fire; he went towards them eagerly, said Eliard's name. Eliard turned, and at the blankness in his eyes Morgon saw himself suddenly, his hair lank, his face drawn, the vesta scars vivid on his hands. He said his name. Eliard, shaking his head, said bewilderedly, *You must be mistaken. Morgon isn't a vesta.* Morgon turned to Tristan, who was holding some pointless, rambling discussion with Snog Nutt. She smiled at him eagerly, hopefully, but the hope died quickly and an uneasiness came into her eyes. Snog Nutt said sorrowfully, *He said he would fix my leaking roof, before the rain, but he went away and he never did, and he hasn't come.* He found himself abruptly at Caithnard, pounding on a door; Rood, flinging it open with a whirl of black sleeve, said irritably, *You're too late. Anyway, she's the second most beautiful woman in An; she can't marry a vesta.* Turning, Morgon saw one of the Masters walking down the hall. He ran to catch up. The bowed, hooded head lifted finally at his pleadings; Master Ohm's eyes met his, grave, reproachful, and he stopped, appalled. The Master walked away from him without speaking; he said over and over without response, *I'm sorry, I'm sorry, I'm sorry.*

He found himself on Wind Plain. It was dark; the sea lay heaving, blue-green with unearthly lights on a moonless night. Isig Mountain seemed so close that he could see the light from Danan's house. Something was gathering itself in the darkness; he could not tell whether it was the wind or the sea; he only knew that an enormity was building itself, huge, nameless, inexorable, sucking into itself all strength, all laws and patterns, all songs, riddles, histories, to explode them into chaos on Wind Plain. He began to run desperately for shelter while the winds howled and the sea half a mile away raised waves so high the spray lashed across his face. He headed for the light of Danan's house. He realized slowly, as he ran, that Harte was broken, empty as an Earth-Masters' city, and that the bone-white light came from deep within Isig. He stopped. A voice split through the mountain out of a cave whose green marble door had not been opened for centuries, cut through the growling, bickering of wind and sea, and said his name.

"Star-Bearer."

10

HE WOKE WITH a start, his heart pounding, listening for the echo of the voice that had wakened him; it seemed to linger, a strange voice, neither man's nor woman's, among the stones. Someone was gripping him, saying his name, someone so familiar that Morgon asked unsurprised, "Did you call me?" Then his hands rose, locked on the harpist's arms.

"Deth."

"You were dreaming."

"Yes." The tower walls, the fire, the silence were forming around him again. His hands loosened slowly, dropped. The harpist, a dust of snow on his shoulders and hair, slid the harp from his shoulder, leaned it against the wall.

"I chose to wait for you quietly in Kyrth rather than at Harte; Danan wasn't sure if I was still there, so he didn't tell you." The even, undisturbed voice was soothing. "You took much longer than I expected."

"I got caught in a blizzard." He straightened, running his hands over his face. "Then I met Har . . ." His head lifted abruptly; he stared at the harpist. "You were waiting for me? You expected—Deth, how long have you been here?"

"Two months." He took his coat off; snow spattered into the fire. "I left Herun the day after you did, travelled up the Ose, without stopping, to Kyrth. I asked Danan to keep watch for you, told him where to reach me in Kyrth, and then—waited." He paused a moment. "I was worried."

Morgon watched his face. He whispered, "I had every intention of returning to Hed. You knew that. You couldn't have known I would come here, not after two months, not in dead winter."

"I chose to trust that you would come."

"Why?"

"Because if you had turned your back on your name, on the riddles you must answer—if you had gone back to Hed alone, unprotected, to accept the death you knew must come—then it wouldn't have mattered where I went, whether to Erlenstar Mountain or the bottom of the sea. I have lived for a thousand years, and I can recognize the smell of doom."

Morgon closed his eyes. The word, hanging in the air like a harp note between them, seemed to ease something out of him; his shoulders slumped. "Doom. You see it, too. Deth, I touched the bone of it in Osterland. I killed Suth."

He heard the harpist's voice untuned for the first time. "You did what?"

He opened his eyes. "I'm sorry. I mean that he died because of me. Har saved my life in that blizzard, so I gave him a promise, ignoring the fact that it is unwise to promise things blindly to the wolf-king." He turned a palm upward; the scar shone like a withered moon in the firelight. "I learned the vesta-shape. I ran with the vesta for two months with Suth's son Hugin, who has white hair and purple eyes. I found Suth behind Grim Mountain, an old vesta with one blind eye that he had lost, riddling. He died there."

"How?"

Morgon's hands closed suddenly on the chair arms. "I asked him why he had run from Lungold—I quoted the third stricture of the Founder to him, demanding help when he knew—he knew. . . . He made a choice; he tried to answer me, but he died trying. He pulled me down with him, there at the end of the world where there was nothing but snow and wind and vesta, he died, he was killed, the only wizard seen by men for seven centuries; I was left holding him, holding the last word he ever spoke like a riddle too terrible to answer—"

"What word?"

"Ohm. Ghisteslwchlohm. The Founder of Lungold killed Suth."

Morgon heard the soft, swift draw of the harpist's breath. His eyes were hidden, his face oddly still. He said, "I knew Suth."

"You knew Master Ohm. You knew Ghisteslwchlohm." His grip was rigid on the wood. "Deth, is Master Ohm the Founder of Lungold?"

"I will take you to Erlenstar Mountain. Then, with permission from the High One, if he does not answer that question for you, I will."

Morgon nodded. He said more calmly, "I'm wondering how many other wizards are still alive under Ghisteslwchlohm's power. I'm also wondering why the High One has never acted."

"Perhaps because his business is the land, not the school of wizards of Lungold. Perhaps he has already begun to act in ways you do not recognize."

"I hope so." He took a cup Deth poured for him, swallowed wine. He added after a moment, "Deth, Har gave me five riddles Suth had given him. He suggested I answer them since I had nothing better to do with my life. One of them is: Who will come in the time's ending and what will he bring? I assume that the Star-Bearer is the one who will come; I have come; I don't know what it is I will bring; but what troubles me most is not who, or what, but when. The time's ending. Walking to Harte with Danan I remembered the ruined cities on Wind Plain, on King's Mouth Plain, and how no one really knows what destroyed the Earth-Masters. It happened long before the Years of Settlement; we assumed because the stones had fallen, the weeds grew between them, that a great, terrible war had come and gone, and nothing more of it existed but the empty stones. We also assumed that the wizards were dead. The one thing I know that could destroy us all is the death of the High One. I'm afraid that whatever destroyed the Earth-Masters before the realm was even formed, has been waiting ever since to challenge the last of the Earth-Masters."

"I think it's quite probable," Deth said quietly. He leaned forward, his face etched with fire, and roused the half-log on the hearth. A flurry of sparks burned in the air like fiery snow.

"Has the High One ever explained the destruction of the cities?"

"Not as far as I know. One of the Masters at Caithnard when I was there said he had made a journey to ask the High One that, since it was one of the unanswered riddles on their lists; the High One simply said that the cities were ancient, empty before he mastered the land-law of the realm."

"Which is saying either that he doesn't know, or that he doesn't choose to tell."

"It's unlikely that he doesn't know."

"Then why—" He stopped. "Only the High One could explain the High One. So I will have to ask him."

Deth looked at him. "I have a question of my own," he said slowly. "I asked it in Herun; you chose not to answer it. But now you wear vesta-scars on your hands, you have spoken your own name, and you are putting your mind to this mystery like a Master. I would like to ask it again."

Morgon, thinking back, said, "Oh. That."

"What was it that made you leave Herun to return home?"

"Something Corrig changed into. And the laughter in his eyes when I killed him." He rose restlessly, went to a window, gazed out at the unrelieved blackness that enclosed Isig.

The harpist said behind him, "What shape?"

"A sword. With three stars on its hilt." He turned abruptly at the silence. "I have thought about it, and the conclusion I have come to is that no one, not even the High One himself, can force me to claim it."

"That's true." Deth's voice was changeless, but there was a faint line between his brows. "Did it occur to you to ask yourself where Corrig might have seen it?"

"No. I'm not interested."

"Morgon. The shape-changers know it belongs to you, that inevitably you will find it, as you found the harp, even though you may not claim it. And when you do, they will be there, waiting."

In the silence, a pitch-laden branch wailed softly. Morgon moved a little at the sound. He said, "I'm nearly at Erlenstar Mountain—that sword could be anywhere . . ."

"Perhaps. But Danan told me once that Yrth made a sword he showed to no one, centuries before he made the harp. Where he put it, no one knows; only one thing is certain: he said he had buried it beneath the place where he forged it."

"Where did—" He stopped. He saw the sword again, recognized the master touch in the flawless designs on its blade, the sure, purposeful shaping of the stars. He put a hand to his eyes, asked, though he already knew the answer, "Where was it forged?"

"Here. In Isig Mountain."

Morgon went down with Deth then, the harp over his shoulder, to talk to Danan. The mountain-king, sitting beside the fire with his children and grandchildren in the quiet hall, looked up with a smile as they entered.

"Come, sit down. Deth, I wasn't sure if you were still in Kyrth or if you had lost hope and chanced the Pass when I sent for you today. You've been so silent. Morgon, this is my daughter Vert, my son Ash, and these—" he paused to lift a small girl tugging herself onto his knee, "—are their children. They all wanted to hear your harping."

Morgon sat down, a little dazed. A tall, fair man with Danan's eyes, a slender woman with hair the color of pine bark, and a dozen children of varying shapes were looking at him curiously.

The woman, Vert, said despairingly to him, "I'm sorry, but Bere wanted to come, so all of mine had to come, and where my children go, Ash's go, so—I hope you don't mind them." She put her hand on the shoulder of a young boy with blunt, black hair and her grey eyes. "This is Bere."

Another black head appeared suddenly at Morgon's knee: a little girl hardly big enough to walk. She stared up at him, then, going unsteady on her feet, clutched at him drunkenly. She grinned toothlessly at him as he slid his hand down her back to steady her, and his mouth twitched. Ash said, "That one belongs to Vert: Suny. My wife is in Caithnard, and Vert's husband, who is a trader, is making a winter run to Anuin, so we put them all together for the time being. I don't know how we'll ever get them sorted out again."

Morgon, his fingers rubbing up and down between Suny's shoulder blades as she gripped his knee, looked up suddenly. "You all came to hear me play?"

Ash nodded. "Please. If you don't mind. That harp and the making of it are legends in Isig. When I heard you were here with it, I couldn't believe it. I wanted to bring all the craftsmen in Kyrth with me to see it, but my father restrained me."

Morgon untied the harp case. Suny tugged the case strings curiously out of his fingers; Bere whispered, "Suny—" She ignored him; he stepped to Morgon's side, lifted her up patiently and held her. Morgon, aware of the curious, expectant faces watching him, said futiley, "I haven't played in two months." No one answered. The stars, as he uncovered the harp, pulled it free of the case, caught fire; the white moons seemed rimmed with it as the flame's reflection travelled a liquid path down the silver inlay. He touched a string; the note sounded in the silence, pure, sweet, hesitant as a question; he heard someone loose a breath.

Ash's hand moved involuntarily toward the stars, dropped. He breathed, "Who did the inlay?"

"Zec of Hicon, in Herun—I can't remember his full name," Danan said. "He was trained by Sol. Yrth designed the patterns."

"And Sol cut those stars. May I see them?" he pleaded, and Morgon passed the harp to him. Something small, formless had bloomed in the back of his mind at Ash's words; he could not trace it. Bere peered over Ash's head, his lips parted as Ash studied the harp; Suny, reaching wildly for a gleaming harp string, startled him and he straightened, shifting his hold of her.

Vert begged, "Ash, stop counting the facets on the stones; I want to hear it."

Ash handed it reluctantly back to Morgon. Morgon took it as reluctantly, and Vert, her eyes softening with sudden understanding, said, "Play something you love. Play something from Hed."

Morgon righted the harp on his knee. His fingers strayed over the strings aimlessly a moment, then wandered into the gentle, sad chords of a ballad. The rich, beautiful tones only he could sound reassured him; even the simple love-ballad he had heard a hundred times took on an ancient dignity. As he played, he began to smell oak burning in the fire before him, saw the light around him wash over the walls of Akren. The song woke a peace in him that he knew instinctively was in Hed that night: a stillness of land dormant under snow, of animals dreaming placidly in warm places. The peace touched his face, easing, for the moment, the tension and weariness out of it. Then two things pieced together in the back of his mind, effortlessly, inarguably, and he stopped, his fingers motionless on the harp strings.

There was a small, inarticulate protest. Then he heard Deth's voice out of the shadows where he had seated himself, away from the children, "What is it?"

"Sol. He wasn't killed by traders because he was too frightened to hide from them in the Cave of the Lost Ones. He was killed—as my parents were killed, as the Morgol Dhairrhuwyth was killed—by shape-changers. He had gone into the cave and come out again to die on the threshold because of what he had seen. And what he saw in there was Yrth's starred sword."

They were still, even the children, their faces turned to him, unblinking. Then Vert shivered as though a cold wind had touched her, and Ash, all the joy of the harp faded from his face said, "What sword?"

Morgon looked at Danan. The king's lips were parted; he seemed struggling back toward a memory. "That sword . . . I remember. Yrth forged it in secret; he said he had buried it. I never saw it; no one did. That was so long ago, before Sol was born, when we were just opening the upper mines. I never thought about it. But how could you possibly know where it is? Or what it looks like? Or that Sol was killed because of it?"

Morgon's fingers moved from the strings to clasp the wood; his eyes fell to it as though the neat sweep of strings ordered his thoughts. "I know a sword exists with three stars on it, exactly like the stars on this harp; I know the shape-changers have seen it, too. My parents were drowned crossing from Caithnard to Hed bringing this harp to me. The Morgol Dhairrhuwyth was killed travelling through Isig Pass to answer a riddle about three stars. The wizard Suth was killed in Osterland a week ago because he knew too much about those stars and tried to tell me—" Ash's hand reached out to stop him.

"Suth was killed—Suth?"

"Yes."

"But how? Who killed him? I thought he was dead."

Morgon's hands shifted a little. His eyes met Deth's briefly. "That is something I will ask the High One. I think Yrth hid that sword there in the cave of the Lost Ones because he knew it was one place no one would go. And I think Sol was killed not by traders but by either the shape-changers, or—by whoever killed Suth, because he knew too much about those stars. I don't know your mountain, Danan, but I know that a man trying to escape death doesn't run toward it."

There was silence, except for the weave and rustle of flames and a sigh from one of the children asleep on the floor. It was broken unexpectedly by Vert.

"That's what always puzzled me," she said slowly. "Why Sol did run down that way when he knew the mountain so well he could vanish like a dream in passageways no one else could see. You remember, Ash, when we were small—"

"There's one way to find out," Ash said abruptly. He was on his feet; Danan's swift, immediate, "No!" overran Morgon's.

The mountain-king said succinctly, "That, I forbid. I will not lose another land-heir." Ash faced him a moment without moving, his mouth set; then the stubbornness went out of his face. He sat down; Danan added wearily, "Besides, what good would that do us?"

"The sword, if it's there, belongs to Morgon. He'll want it—"

"I don't want it," Morgon said.

"But if it belongs to you . . ." Ash said, "if Yrth made it for you—"

"I don't recall being asked if I wanted a sword. Or a destiny. All I want is to get to Erlenstar Mountain without being killed—which is another reason I'm not interested in going down to that cave. And, being, incidently, the Prince of Hed, I don't want to go armed before the High One."

Ash opened his mouth, and closed it. Danan whispered, "Suth . . ." A baby began to wail, a thin, sad sound; Vert started.

"Under your chair," Ash said. "Kes." He glanced around at the uneasy, uncomprehending faces. "We'd better put them to bed." He retrieved a blinking, bewildered baby from the thick fur at his feet, heaved it like a sack to his shoulder.

Danan said as he rose, "Ash."

Their eyes met again. Ash said gently, "You have my promise. But I think it's time that cave was opened. I didn't know there was a deathtrap in the heart of Isig." He added to Morgon before he turned to go, "Thank you for playing."

Morgon watched him leave, a child in each arm. The group faded away beyond the light. He looked down at the harp; a twist of bitterness rose in his throat. He stirred, slid the harp mechanically back into the case.

A soft conversation between Deth and Danan checked as he rose; the mountain-king said, "Morgon, Sol—no matter who killed him—has been dead three hundred years. Is there any way I can help you? If you want that sword, I have a small army of miners."

"No." His face was taut, white in the firelight. "Let me argue with my fate a little longer. I have been protesting from Caithnard to Isig, though, and it hasn't done much good."

"I would drain the gold from the veins of Isig to help you."

"I know."

"When I walked with you this afternoon, I didn't realize you bore the vesta-scars. That's a rare thing to see on any man, above all a man of Hed. It must be a marvellous thing to run with the vesta."

"It is." His voice loosened a little at the memory of the calm, endless snow, the silence lying always beneath the wind. Then he saw Suth's face, felt the hands pulling at him as he knelt in the snow, and his face turned sharply; the memories faded.

Danan said gently, "Is that how you plan to get through the Pass?"

"I planned it that way, thinking I would be alone. Now—" He glanced questioningly at Deth.

The harpist said, "It will be difficult for me, but not impossible."

"Can we leave tomorrow?"

"If you wish. But Morgon, I think you should rest here a day or two. Travelling through Isig Pass in mid-winter will be tiring even for a vesta, and I suspect you ran your strength dry in Osterland."

"No. I can't wait. I can't."

"Then we'll leave. But get some sleep."

He nodded, then said, his head bowed, to Danan, "I'm sorry."

"For what, Morgon? For stirring my centuries-old grief?"

"That, too. But I'm sorry I couldn't play this harp for you the way it cries out to be played."

"You will."

Morgon took the tower steps slowly, feeling the harp whose weight he had never noticed, dragging at his back. He wondered, as he rounded the final curve, if Yrth had walked up the stairs every night to the top of the tower, or if he had practiced the enviable art of displacement, moving from point to point in the wink of an eye. He reached the landing, drew back the hangings, and found someone standing in front of his fire.

It was Vert's son, Bere. He said without preamble as Morgon jumped, "I'll take you to the cave of the Lost Ones."

Morgon eyed him without answering. The boy was young, perhaps ten or eleven, with broad shoulders and a grave, placid face. He was unembarrassed by Morgon's scrutiny; Morgon stepped in finally, letting the hangings fall closed behind them. He shrugged the harp from his shoulder, set it down.

"Don't tell me you've been there."

"I know where it is. I got lost once, exploring. I kept going deeper and deeper into the mountain, partly because I kept taking the wrong turnings and partly because I decided as long as I really was lost I might as well see what was down there."

"Weren't you afraid?"

"No. I was hungry. I knew Danan or Ash would find me. I can see in the dark; that's from my mother. So we could go very quietly without light—except in the cave, you'll need one there."

"Why are you so anxious to go there?"

The boy took a step toward him, his brows crooked slightly. "I want to see that sword. I've never seen anything like that harp. Elieu of Hel, the brother of Raith, Lord of Hel, came here two years ago; he is beginning to do work a little like that—the inlay, the designs—but I've never seen anything as beautiful as the work on that harp. I want to see what kind of work Yrth did with the sword. Danan makes swords for lords and kings in An and Ymris, they're very beautiful. I'm training with Ash and Elieu; and Ash says I will be a master craftsman some day. So I have to learn everything I can."

Morgon sat down. He smiled suddenly at the square-shouldered, peaceful artist. "It sounds very reasonable. But you heard what I told Danan about Sol."

"Yes. But I know everyone in this house; no one would try to kill you. And if we went very quietly, no one would even know. You wouldn't have to take the sword—you could just wait at the door for me. Inside, I mean, because—" His mouth set wryly. "I am a little afraid to go in there alone. And you're the only other person I know who would go with me."

The smile faded from Morgon's eyes; he rose abruptly, restlessly. "No. You're wrong. I won't go with you. I gave my reasons to Danan, and you heard them."

Bere was silent a moment, his eyes searching Morgon's face. "I heard them. But, Morgon, this is—this is important. Please. We could just go, quickly, and then just come back—"

"Like Sol came back?"

Bere's shoulders twitched a little. "That was a long time ago—"

"No." He saw the sudden despair in the boy's eyes. "Please. Listen. I have been half a step ahead of death since I left Hed. The people trying to kill me are shape-changers; they may be the miners or the traders who ate with you at Danan's table tonight. They may be here waiting, thinking I will do just that: claim Yrth's sword, and if you and I are caught in the cave by them, they will kill us both. I have too much regard for both my intelligence and my life to be trapped like that."

Bere shook his head, as if shaking Morgon's words away. He took another step forward; the firelight left his face shadowed, pleading. "It's not right just leaving it there, just ignoring it. It belongs to you, it's yours by right, and if it's anything like the harp, no other lord in the realm will have a more beautiful sword."

"I hate swords."

"It's not the sword," Bere said patiently. "It's the craft. It's the art. I'll keep it if you don't want it."

"Bere—"

"It's not right that I can't see it." He paused. "Then I'll have to go alone."

Morgon reached the boy with one quick step, gripped the square, implacable shoulders. "I can't stop you," he said softly. "But I will ask you to wait until I've left Isig, because when they find you dead in that cave, I don't want to see Danan's face."

Bere's head bowed, his shoulders slumped under Morgon's hold; he turned away. "I thought you'd understand," he said, his back to Morgon. "I thought you'd understand what it is to have to do something."

He left. Morgon turned after a moment, wearily. He added wood to the fire and lay down. For a long time, watching the flames, feeling the exhaustion settling into his bones, he could not sleep. Finally he drifted into a darkness where odd images began to form and break like deep slow bubbles from a cauldron.

He saw the high, dark walls of inner Isig, veined with torchlight: silver, gold, iron black; saw, in the secret parts of the mountain, uncut jewels, crystals of fire and ice, mid-night-blue, smokey-yellow cracking through their husks of stone. Arched trails, high passageways wandered through webs of shadow. Rocks thrust downward from ceilings vaulted and lost in blackness, formed by the slow sculpture of forgotten ages. He stood in a silence that had its own voice. He followed like a breath of wind the slow, imperceptible movements of dark streams, thin as glass, that deepened, then hewed through hidden chasms and spilled into vast, measureless lakes, where tiny nameless things lived in a colorless world. At the end of one river he found himself in a chamber of milk-white blue-veined stone. Three steps led upward out of a pool of water to a dais on which two long cases of beaten gold and white jewels stood glittering beneath a torch. A sadness touched him for the dead of Isig: Sol, and Grania, Danan's wife; he stepped into the pool, reached out to a casket. It opened unexpectedly, from within. A face, blurred, unrecognizable, neither man's nor woman's, looked up at him and said his name: *Star-Bearer*.

He found himself in an abrupt shift back in his own chamber, dressing again, while a voice murmuring out of the corridors of Isig called to him, low and insistent as a child's call in the night. He turned to go, then checked, slid the harp over his shoulder. He moved without sound down the empty tower stairs, through the hall where the vast fire had dwindled. He found without faltering the doors of the stone archway beyond the hall that opened into the mountain itself, to the wet, cool shaft that led downward into the mines. Instinctively, without question, he found his way through the main corridors, down passages and stairways, into the mine shaft below. He took a torch from the wall there. A split in the solid rock at the end of the shaft loomed before him; the call trailed out of it and he followed without question. The path beyond was unlit, worn with age. The half-formed heads of growing rock thrust upward underfoot, slippery with the endless drip of water.

The ceiling loomed down at him so suddenly he was forced to bend beneath it, then shot upward into impossible heights while the walls nudged against him and he carried the torch high over his head to ease himself through. The silence hung ponderous as the swell of rock overhead; he smelled, in his dream, the faint, clean, acrid scent of liquid stone.

He had no sense of time, of weariness, of cold; only the vague drift of shadows, the endless, complex pattern of passages he followed with an odd certainty. He wound deeper and deeper into the mountain, his torch burning steadily, untouched by wind; sometimes he could see the reflection of it in a pool far beneath the thin ledge he walked. The trails began to level finally; the stones closed about him, edging down from the ceiling, together at the sides. The stones were broken around him, as from some ancient inner turmoil. He had to step over some of them that had shaken free like great teeth from the ceiling. The trail stopped abruptly at a closed door.

He stood looking at it, his shadow splayed behind him on the wall. Someone said his name; he reached out to open it. Then, as though he had reached through the surface of his dream, he shuddered and woke himself. He was standing in front of the door to the cave of the Lost Ones.

He blinked senselessly at it, recognizing the polished green stone teared with black, shot with fire from his torch. Then, as the chill he had not felt in his dream began to seep through his clothes, and he realized the enormous mass of rock, silence, darkness sitting above his head, he took a step backward, a sound beginning to build in his throat. He whirled abruptly; found a darkness that his torch, beating a minute, jagged circle of light about him, could not begin to unravel. His breath hissed out of him; he ran a few steps forward, stumbled over a broken rock and brought himself up short against the wet wall of rock. He remembered then the endless, chaotic path he had taken in his dream. He swallowed drily, his blood panicked through him, the sound still building in his throat.

Then he heard the voice of his dream, the voice that had led him out of Danan's house, down through the maze of the mountain:

"Star-Bearer."

It came from behind the door, a strange voice, clean, timbreless.

The sound stilled the panic in him; he saw clearly as though with a third eye the implications of danger beyond the door, and the implications of a knowledge beyond hope. He stood for a long time, shivering every once in a while from the cold, his eyes on the door, weighing probability against possibility. Thousands of years old, unweathered, originless, the door yielded no answer to his waiting. Finally, he laid one hand flat on the smooth stone. The door swung at his gentle touch to a crack of darkness. He eased forward, torchlight flaring off walls massed with undiscovered beds and veins of jewels. Someone stepped into the light, and he stopped.

He drew a soft, shaking breath. A hand, the bones of it blurred, tapered, touched him, as Suth had done, feeling the reality of him. He whispered, his eyes on the still, molded face, "You are a child."

The pale head lifted, the eyes star-white, met his. "We are the children." The voice was the same, a child's clear, dreaming voice.

"The children?"

"We are all the children. The children of the Earth-Masters."

His lips moved, forming a word without shape. Something that was no longer panic began to grow heavy, unwieldy, in his throat and chest. A vague, gleaming boy's face moved a little under his eyes. He reached out to it suddenly, found it unyielding to his touch.

"We have become stone in the stone. Earth mastered us."

He lifted the torch. Around him, light, vague figures of children were rising out of the shadows, gazing at him curiously, without fear, as though he were something they had dreamed. Faces the light traced were as delicate, molded stone.

"How long—how long have you been here?"

"Since the war."

"The war?"

"Before the Settlement. We have been waiting for you. You woke us."

"You woke me. I didn't know . . . I didn't know—"

"You woke us, and we called. You have the stars." The lean hand moved, touching them. "Three to life, three to the winds, and three to—" He lifted the sword he carried, offered the starred hilt of it to Morgon, "death. That was promised us."

He swallowed the word like a bitterness in his mouth; his fingers closed around the blade. "Who promised it to you?"

"Earth. Wind. The great war destroyed us. So we were promised a man of peace."

"I see." His voice shook. "I see." He stooped, bringing himself to the boy's level. "What is your name?"

The boy was silent a moment, as though he could not answer. The still lines of his face shifted again; he said haltingly, "I was . . . I was Tirnon. My father was Tir, Master of Earth and Wind."

"I was Ilona," a small girl said suddenly. She came to Morgon trustingly, her hair curving like a fall of ice down her shoulders. "My mother was . . . my mother was . . ."

"Trist," a boy behind her said. His eyes held Morgon's as though he read his own name there. "I was Trist. I could take any shape of earth, bird, tree, flower—I knew them. I could shape the vesta, too."

"I was Elore," a slender girl said eagerly. "My mother was Rena—she could speak every language of the earth. She was teaching me the language of the crickets—"

"I was Kara—"

They crowded around him, oblivious of the fire, their voices painless, dreaming. He let them talk, watching incredulously the delicate, lifeless faces; then he said abruptly, his voice cutting into theirs, "What happened? Why are you here?"

There was a silence. Tirnon said simply, "They destroyed us."

"Who?"

"Those from the sea. Edolen. Sec. They destroyed us so that we could not live on earth anymore; we could not master it. My father gave us protection to come here, hidden from the war. We found a dying-place."

Morgon was still. He let the torch drop slowly; shadows eased again over the circle of children. He whispered, "I see. What can I do for you?"

"Free the winds."

"Yes. How?"

"One star will call out of silence the Master of the Winds; one star out of darkness the Master of Darkness; one star out of death the children of the Masters of the Earth. You have called; they have answered."

"Who is—"

"The war is not finished, only silenced for the regathering. You will bear stars of fire and ice to the Ending of the Age of the High One—"

"But we cannot live without the High One—"

"This we have been promised. This will be." The boy seemed no longer to hear his voice, but a voice out of the memory of an age. "You are the Star-Bearer, and you will loose from their order the—"

He stopped abruptly. Morgon broke the silence. "Go on."

Tirnon's head bent. He gripped Morgon's wrist suddenly, his voice taut with anguish, "No."

Morgon lifted his torch. Beyond the fragile planes of faces, the curve of bone, the shape of slender body, the light caught at a shadow that would not yield. In the rags of darkness a dark head lifted; a woman, her face beautiful, quiet, shy, looked at him and smiled.

He rose, the stars leaping fiery about him. Tirnon's head fell on his bent knees; Morgon saw the lines of his body begin to melt together. He turned quickly, pushing through the stone door; it flung him outward and he saw, coming toward him down the trail, carrying lights in the palms of their hands, men of the color and movement of the sea.

He had a moment of utter panic, until he saw out of the corner of his eye, an opening, a slender side path beside him. He flung the torch as far away from him as possible; it blazed like a star towards his pursuers. Then, feeling for the opening, he slipped blind into an unknown path that at every breath and movement rose against him. He felt his way, his hands sliding over wet, smooth skulls of rock, his face and shoulders beaten against the unexpected outcroppings that formed at every twist. Darkness fashioned the trail, fashioned the mold of stones beneath his hands. Behind him the blackness lay unbroken; ahead it pressed against his eyes. He stopped once, appalled at his blindness, and heard above his harsh breathing the relentless silence of Isig. He blundered on, his hands flayed from scraping across unseen rock, blood from a cut on his face catching like tears in his eyelashes, until the stone gave way beneath his feet and he fell into blackness, his cry drowned in water.

He pulled himself back on the raw slab of shore, still clinging without realizing it to the sword, and lay hearing nothing but his breathing like little whimpering sobs. Then, as he began to quiet, he heard a footstep near his face, another's breathing. His breath stopped. Someone touched him.

He rolled to his feet abruptly, backed; a voice whispered, "Morgon, watch out. The water—"

He stopped, his lips caught hard between his teeth, straining to see the pale shadow of a face, but the dark was absolute. Then he recognized the voice.

"Morgon. It's me, Bere. I'm coming toward you. Don't move, or you'll fall in the water again. I'm coming . . ."

It took, as he felt the blood pounding in the back of his throat, all the courage he possessed to stay still, let the darkness come to him. A hand touched him again. Then he felt the sword move in his grip and made a sound.

"It was there. You were right. I knew it. I knew he would have etched the blade. It's . . . I can't see that well; I need—" His voice stopped briefly. "What did you do? You cut your hand, carrying it like that."

"Bere. I can't see you. I can't see anything. There are shapechangers trying to find me—"

"Is that what they are? I saw them. I hid in the rocks, and you ran past me. Do you want me to leave you here and get—"

"No. Can you help me find a way back?"

"I think so. I think if we follow the water it leads toward one of the lower mines. Morgon, I'm glad you came for the sword, but what made you go without telling Danan? And how did you find your way down here? Everyone is looking for you. I went up to talk to you later to see if you'd changed your mind, but you were gone. So I went to Deth's room, to see if you were there, but you weren't, and he heard me and woke up. I told him you were gone, and he dressed and woke Danan, and Danan woke the miners. They're all looking for you. I came ahead. I don't understand—"

"If we get back to Danan's house alive, I'll explain it to you. I'll explain anything—"

"All right. Let me carry the sword for you." The hand at his wrist tugged him forward. "Be careful: there's a low overhang to your left. Bend your head."

They moved quickly through the darkness, silent but for Bere's murmured warnings. Morgon, his body tense against unexpected blows, strained to see one faint brush of stone or glimmer of water, but his eyes found no place to rest. He closed them finally, let his body flow after Bere's. They began to climb; the path wound endlessly upward. The walls moved like living things under his hands, now narrowing, closing until he eased between them sideways, now flowing wide, stretching beyond his reach, then leaping back together again. Finally Bere stopped at some isolated piece of darkness.

"There are steps here. They lead to the mine shaft. Do you want to rest?"

"No. Go on."

The steps were steep, endless. Morgon, shivering with cold, feeling the blood well and drip over his fingers, began to see shades and flares of color behind his closed eyes. He heard Bere's sturdy, tired breathing; the boy said finally with a sigh, "All right. We're at the top." He stopped so suddenly that Morgon bumped into him. "There's light in the shaft. It must be Danan! Come on—"

Morgon opened his eyes. Bere went in front of him through an arch of stones whose walls rippled unexpectedly with wavering light. Bere called softly, "Danan?" And then he pushed back, stumbling against Morgon, the breath hissing sharply out of his throat. A blade, grey-green, raked across the light, struck his head and he fell, the sword ringing beneath him.

Morgon stared down at his limp, motionless body, looking oddly small on the harsh stones. Something unwieldy, uncontrollable, shook through him, welled to an explosion of fury behind his eyes. He ducked a sword thrust that bit at him like a silver snake, pulled the harp strap over his neck and dropped it, then reached for the sword beneath Bere. He plunged through the archway, eluding by a hairsbreadth two blades that whistled through the air behind him, caught a third on its way down, brought it up, high upward to a dull ring and blaze of sparks, then loosed it abruptly and slashed sideways. Blood burst like a sun across one shell-colored face. A blaze of fire ripping down his arm, caught his attention; he whirled. A blade drove toward him; he sent it spinning almost contemptuously across the floor with a single, two-handed stroke; then reversed the ponderous circle of the blade's sweep and the shape-changer, coughing, hunched himself over the line of blood slashing from shoulder to hip. Yet another blade descended at him like a thread of silver that would have split him; he jerked back from it. He brought his sword down like an ax against a stump in a field, and the shape-changer, catching the blade in his shoulder, pulled it out of Morgon's hands as he fell.

The silence settled ponderously about him. He stared down at the stars, shaken slightly with the last breath of the shape-changer; the hilt was webbed with blood. One of the strange lights, fallen and still burning, lay just beyond the shape-changer's outstretched hand. Morgon, looking at it, shuddered suddenly, violently. He turned, extinguishing the light with a step, walked forward until he could go no further and pushed his face against the solid black wall of stone.

THE SLASH DOWN his arm took two weeks to heal, and he had scars striped across the vesta-horns on his left hand from the sword blade. He said nothing when Danan's miners, their torchlight flaring into the cave, found him, the dead shape-changers, and the great sword with its stars winking like blood-red eyes. He had said nothing, though something moved behind his eyes, when Bere, one hand on his head, a line of blood down his face, stumbled blinking into the light. Walking up through the mines, he had heard Danan's questions, but did not answer them. He had not walked long when the darkness of the mountain plummetted down at him, the torches growing small, going blue, and cold, and then black.

He broke the silence finally, lying in his chamber with his arm bound from shoulder to wrist, watching Bere, his square face intent, absolutely content, making sketches of the engravings on the sword. Bere, in response to his request, got Deth and Danan. Morgon told them flatly, precisely, what they wanted to know.

"Children . . ." Danan whispered. "When Yrth took me there, I saw only stones. How did he know what they were?"

"I'll ask him."

"Yrth? You think he is still alive?"

"If he is alive, I'll find him." He paused briefly, his eyes, indrawn, inaccessible. "There is someone else involved in this game beyond the Founder, the shape-changers, the strange names I was given—Edolen, Sec; someone they called the Master of the Winds. Perhaps they meant the High One." He looked at Deth. "The High One is also a Wind-Master?"

"Yes."

"And there is a Master of Darkness, who will no doubt reveal himself when he's ready. The age of the High One is drawing to an end—"

"But how can that be?" Danan protested. "Our lands will die without the High One."

"I don't know how it can be. But I touched the face of the son of a Wind-Master while he spoke to me, and it was of stone. I think if that is possible, anything is possible, including the destruction of the realm. This is not our war—we didn't begin it, we can't end it, we can't avoid it. There is no choice."

Danan drew a breath to speak, but said nothing. Bere's pen had stopped, his face was turned toward them. Danan's breath went out of him slowly. "The ending of the age. . . . How can anyone put an end to a mountain? Morgon, you may be wrong. Those who began this war thousands of years ago did not know they would have to reckon with men who will fight for what they love. These shape-changers can be destroyed; you have proved that."

"Yes. I have. But they don't have to fight us. If they destroy the High One, we are doomed."

"Then why are they trying to kill you? Why have they been attacking you instead of the High One? It makes no sense."

"It does. Every riddle has an answer. When I begin to piece together all the answers to the questions I must ask, then I will have the beginnings of an answer to your question."

Danan shook his head. "How can you do it? Not even the wizards could."

"I'll do it. I have no choice."

Deth said little; when they left, taking Bere with them, Morgon rose painfully, went to one of the windows. It was dusk; the flanks of the mountain were blue-white, motionless with the coming night. He stood watching the great trees weave into shadows. Nothing moved, not an animal or a snow-weighted branch, while the white head of Isig gradually blurred into the black, starless sky.

He heard steps on the stairs; the hangings slid apart, and he said without turning, "When should we leave for Erlenstar Mountain?"

"Morgon—"

He turned then. "That's a note I rarely hear in your voice: protest. We're on the threshold of Erlenstar Mountain, and there are a thousand questions I need answers to—"

"Erlenstar Mountain is Erlenstar Mountain," Deth said quietly, "a place where you may or may not find the answers you want. Be patient. The winds that blow down from the northern wastes through Isig Pass are merciless in deep winter."

"I've stood in those winds before and not even felt them."

"I know. But if you step into that winter before you are strong enough to bear it, you will not live two days beyond Kyrth."

"I'll survive," Morgon said savagely. "That's what I'm best at—surviving by any means, any method. I have great gifts, unusual in a Prince of Hed. Did you see the miners' faces when they walked into that cave and found us all? With all the traders in this house, how long will it be, do you think, before that tale reaches Hed? Not only am I adept at killing, I have a sword with my name on it to do it with, given to me by a stone-faced child, given to him by a wizard who forged it assuming that the man whose name it bore would accept his own destiny. I am trapped. If there is nothing I can do but what I am meant to do, then I will do it, now, as quickly as possible. There is not a breath of wind. If I leave tonight, I could reach Erlenstar Mountain in three days."

"Five," Deth said. "Even the vesta sleep." He moved to the fire, reached for wood. His face, lit as the flames leaped up, revealed hollows and hair-thin lines that had not been there before. "How far could you run with a crippled leg?"

"Do you suggest I wait here to be killed?"

"The shape-changers moved against you here and lost. With Danan's house guarded, the sword taken, the answers the stone-faced children gave you inaccessible, they may prefer to wait for your move."

"And if I don't move?"

"You will. You know that."

"I know," he whispered. He whirled abruptly away from the window. "How can you be so calm? You are never afraid; you are never surprised. You have lived for a thousand years, and you took the Black of Mastery—how much of all this did you come to expect? You were the one to give me my name in Herun." He saw the startled, almost imperceptible wariness in the harpist's eyes, and he felt his mind turn on the question awkwardly, like an old mill groaning into movement. "What did you expect from me? That having put my mind to this game, I would leave anything or anyone unquestioned? You knew Suth—did he give you the riddles he learned of those stars? You knew Yrth; you said you were in Isig when he made my harp. Did he tell you what he had seen in the cave of the Lost Ones? You were born in Lungold: were you there when the School of Wizards was abandoned? Did you study there yourself?"

Deth straightened, meeting Morgon's eyes. "I am not a Lungold wizard. I have never served any man but the High One. I studied awhile at the School of Wizards because I found myself growing old without aging, and I thought perhaps my father had been a wizard. I had no great gifts for wizardry so I left—that is the extent of my acquaintance with the Lungold wizards. I searched for you five weeks in Ymris; I waited two months for you in Kyrth without touching my harp, in case someone realized who I was and who I must be waiting for; I searched Isig Mountain with Danan's miners for you: I saw your face when they found you. Do you think that if there is something I could do for you, I would not do it?"

"Yes." There was a sharp, brittle silence before either of them moved. Morgon reached methodically for the sword Bere had been sketching by the fire, swung it in a wide, blazing half-circle, smashed it in a snap of blue sparks against the stone wall. It gave a deep, flawless, bell-like protest before he dropped it, and he said bitterly, hunched over his stinging hands, "You could answer my questions."

He broke his seclusion in the tower finally, went out into the craftsmen's yard a few days later. His arm was nearly healed; a half-forgotten strength was returning to him. He stood in the broken snow smelling the metal-smiths' fires. The world seemed becalmed under a still, grey-white sky. Danan spoke his name; he turned. The mountain-king, enveloped in fur, put a gentle hand on his shoulder.

"I'm glad to see you better."

He nodded. "It's good to be out. Where is Deth?"

"He rode into Kyrth this morning with Ash. They'll be back at sundown. Morgon, I have been thinking . . . I wanted to give you something that might help you; I racked my brains trying to think what, when it occurred to me that there are times in your journey that you might simply want to disappear from enemies, from friends, from the world, to rest awhile, to think. . . . There's nothing less obvious than a tree in a forest."

"A tree." Something in his mind quickened. "Danan, can you teach me that?"

"You have the gift for shape-changing. Shaping a tree is much easier than shaping the vesta. You must simply learn to be still. You know what kind of stillness is in a stone, or a handful of earth."

"I knew once."

"You know, deep in you." Danan looked up at the sky, then glanced at the bustling, preoccupied workers around him. "It's easy to be still on a day like this. Come. No one will miss us for a while."

Morgon followed him out of Harte, down the winding, quiet road, then into the forests high above Kyrth. Their footprints broke deep into the powdery snow; they brushed pine branches heavy with it, shook soft snow flurries loose that bared webs of wet, dark fir. They walked silently until, turning, they could not see the road, or Kyrth below it, or Harte, only the dark, motionless trees. They stood there listening. The clouds, softly shaped by the wind, rested on the silence; trees were molded to a stillness that formed the whorls of their bark, curve of branch, the heavy, downward sweep of their needles and pinnacle of tip. A hawk floated in the silence, barely rippling it, dove deep into it and vanished. Morgon, after a long while, turned to Danan, feeling suddenly alone, and found beside him a great pine, still and dreaming above Isig.

He did not move. The chill from his motionlessness began to trouble him, then passed as the silence became a tangible thing measuring his breath, his heartbeat, seeping into his thoughts, his bones until he felt hollowed, a shell of winter stillness. The trees circling him seemed to enclose a warmth like the stone houses at Kyrth, against the winter. Listening, he heard suddenly the hum of their veins, drawing life from deep beneath the snow, beneath the hard earth. He felt himself rooted, locked into the rhythms of the mountain; his own rhythms drained away from him, lost beyond memory in the silence that shaped him. Wordless knowledge moved through him, of slow measureless age, of fierce winds borne beyond breaking point, of seasons beginning, ending, of a patient, unhurried waiting for something that lay deeper than roots, that lay sleeping in the earth deeper than the core of Isig, something on the verge of waking . . .

The stillness passed. He moved, felt an odd stiffness as though his face were being formed out of bark, his fingers dwindling from fingers of twig. His breath, which he had not noticed for a while, went out of him in a quick, white flash.

Danan said, his voice measured to the unhurried rhythm of the silence, "When you have a moment, practice so you can fade in a thought from man to tree. Sometimes I forget to change back. I watch the mountains fade into twilight and the stars push through the darkness like jewels pushing through stone, and forget myself until Bere comes calling for me, or I hear the movements of Isig beneath me and remember who I am. It's a restful, comfortable thing to be. When I'm too tired to live any longer, I will walk as far as I can up Isig, then stop and become a tree. If this path you take becomes unbearable, you can simply disappear for a while, and no wizard or shape-changer on earth will find you until you are ready."

"Thank you." His voice startled him as though he had forgotten he possessed one.

"You have great power. You took to that as easily as one of my own children."

"It was simple. So simple it seems strange that I never tried it before." He walked beside Danan, following their broken trail back to the road, still feeling the placid winter stillness. Danan's voice, with its own inner peace, scarcely disturbed it.

"I remember once when I was young spending an entire winter as a tree, to see what it was like. I scarcely felt the time passing. Grania sent the miners looking for me; she came herself, too, but I never noticed her, any more than she noticed me. You can survive terrible storms in that shape, if you need to, on your way to Erlenstar Mountain; even the vesta tire, after a while, running against the wind."

"I'll survive. But what about Deth? Is he a shape-changer?"

"I don't know. I've never asked him." His face wrinkled a little in thought. "I've always suspected he has greater gifts than harping and tact, and yet I can't imagine seeing him turn into a tree. It doesn't sound like something he would do."

Morgon looked at him. "What gifts do you suspect?"

"Nothing in particular; I just wouldn't be very surprised by anything he could do. There is a silence in him that as often as I have talked with him, he has never broken. You probably know him better than anyone."

"No. I know that silence. . . . Sometimes I think it's simply a silence of living, then at other times, it changes into a silence of waiting."

Danan nodded. "Yes. But waiting for what?"

"I don't know," Morgon said softly. "I want to know."

They reached the road. A cart rattled over it filled with skins from trappers in Kyrth. The driver, recognizing them, slowed his horses, and they hoisted themselves onto the tail. Danan said, leaning back against the skins, "I've been curious about Deth since the day he walked into my court one winter, seven hundred years ago, and asked to be taught the ancient songs of Isig in exchange for his harping. He looked much the same as he does now, and his harping . . . even then, it was unearthly."

Morgon turned his head slowly. "Seven hundred years ago?"

"Yes. I remember it was just a few years after I heard about the wizards' disappearance."

"I thought—" He stopped. A cartwheel jogged over a hidden stone in the dark rutted snow. "Then he wasn't in Isig when Yrth made my harp?"

"No," Danan said surprisedly. "How could he have been? Yrth made the harp about a hundred years before the founding of Lungold, and Lungold is where Deth was born."

Morgon swallowed something in the back of his throat. Snow began to fall again lightly, aimlessly; he looked up at the blank sky with a sudden, desperate impatience. "It's beginning all over again!"

"No. Couldn't you feel it, deep in the earth? The ending . . ."

Morgon sat alone in his chamber that evening without moving, his eyes on the fire. The circle of stones, the circle of the night surrounded him with a familiar implacable silence. He held the harp in his hands but he did not play it; his fingers traced slowly, endlessly, the angles and facets of the stars. He heard Deth's step finally; the shift of the hangings, and he lifted his head, caught the harpist's eyes as he entered, sent the swift, tentative probe of thought past the blurring, fathomless eyes.

He felt a brief sensation of surprise, as though, opening the door of some strange, solitary tower, he had stepped into his own house. Then something snapped back into his own mind like a blaze of white fire; shocked, blinded, he stumbled to his feet, the harp clattering on the floor. He heard nothing for a moment, saw nothing, and then, as the brilliant haze receded behind his eyes, he heard Deth's voice.

"Morgon—I'm sorry. Sit down."

Morgon lifted his head from his hands finally, blinking; flecks of color swam across the room. He took a step, bumped into the wine table; Deth eased him back to his chair.

He whispered, "What was that?"

"A variation of the Great Shout. Morgon, I had forgotten the mind-work you learned from Har; you startled me." He poured wine, held it out. Morgon, his hands closed, rigid, the vibrations of the shout moving like a tide in his head, opened one hand stiffly to take it. He stood up again unsteadily, sent the cup flying across the room, wine splashing out of it, to crack against the wall.

He faced the harpist, asked reasonably, "Why did you lie to me about being in Isig when Yrth made his harp? Danan said it was made before you were born."

There was no surprise, just a flash of understanding in the harpist's eyes. His head bent slightly; he poured more wine and took a sip. He sat down, cradling the cup in his hands.

"Do you think I lied to you?"

Morgon was silent. He said almost surprised, "No. Are you a wizard?"

"No. I am the High One's harpist."

"Then will you explain why you said you were in Isig a hundred years before you were born?"

"Do you want a half-truth or truth?"

"Truth."

"Then you will have to trust me." His voice was suddenly softer than the fire sounds, melting into the silence within the stones. "Beyond logic, beyond reason, beyond hope. Trust me."

Morgon closed his eyes. He sat down, leaned his aching head back. "Did you learn that at Lungold?"

"It was one of the few things I could learn. I was caught accidentally in a mind-shout of the wizard Talies once, when he lost his temper. He taught it to me, in apology."

"Will you teach it to me?"

"Now?"

"No. I can barely think now, let alone shout. Do you use it often?"

"No. It can be dangerous. I simply felt another mind entering mine and reacted. There are simpler ways to disengage; if I had realized it was you, I would never have hurt you." He paused. "I came in to tell you that the High One has set his name into every rock and tree in Isig Pass; the lands beyond Isig are his, and he can feel every footfall like a heartbeat. He will allow no one but us through. Danan suggests we leave when the ice on the Ose begins to break. That should be soon; the weather is turning."

"I know. I felt it. Danan taught me the tree-shape this afternoon." He rose to pick up his wine cup from across the room. He added, pouring wine, "I trust you, with my name and my life. But my life has been torn out of my control, shaped to the answering of riddles. You have given me one tonight; I will answer it."

"That," the harpist said simply, "is why I gave it to you."

A few days later, going up Isig alone to practice shape-changing, Morgon caught again the current of stillness and found in it an unexpected tap of warmth rising deep from the earth, spreading through vein and joint of branch until, himself again, he felt it still in the tips of his fingers, the roots of his hair. A wind breathed across Isig; he looked into it and smelled the earth of Hed.

He found Deth with Danan, talking to one of the craftsmen in the yard. Danan, glancing up as he came to them, smiled and reached into an inner pocket in his cloak. "Morgon, one of the traders came in from Kraal today—they start coming like birds at the beginning of spring. He brought a letter for you."

"From Hed?"

"No. He said he's been carrying it for four months, from Anuin."

"Anuin . . ." Morgon whispered. He pulled his gloves off, broke the seal quickly. He read silently; the men watched him. The soft south wind that had touched him in the mountains rustled the paper in his hands. He did not look up immediately when he was finished; he was trying to remember a face that time and distance had worn into a lovely blur of colors. He raised his head finally.

"She wants to see me." The faces in front of him were, for a moment, indistinguishable. "She told me to stay off ships, coming home. She said to come home."

He heard the boom and crack of the Ose that night in his dreams and woke to the sound. By morning, webs of broken ice had formed on it like filigree; two days later the river, dark and swollen with melting snow, spun wedges of ice huge as carts past Kyrth, heading eastward toward the sea. The traders began packing their wares at Harte, bound for Kraal and the sea. Danan gave Morgon a packhorse and a sweet-tempered, shaggy-hooved mare bred in Herun. He gave Deth a chain of gold and emerald for his playing during the long, quiet evenings. At dawn one morning, the mountain-king, his two children, and Bere came out to bid farewell to Morgon and Deth. As the sun rose in a blaze of blue, cloudless sky above Isig, they rode through Kyrth, down the little-travelled road that led through Isig Pass to Erlenstar Mountain.

Bare granite peaks glittered around them as the rising sun pushed slabs of light inch by inch down the mountainsides. The road, kept clear three seasons of the year by men who worked for the High One, was rough with fallen stones, trees snapped by wind and snow. It wound beside a river, rose upward to the rim and edge of mountains. Great falls unlocked by the gentle, persistent south wind, murmured in hidden places among the trees, or glittered in frozen silver outpourings high between the peaks. In the silence, the sound of hoof on bare rock snapped in the air like iron.

They spent the first night camped beside the river. Above them the sky, deep flaming blue during the day, began to stain with night. Their fire flickered back at the huge stars like a reflection. The river lazed beside them, deep and slow; they were silent until Morgon, washing a pot and cups in the river, heard out of the immense darkness a blaze of harp song that ran quick and fiery as the sunlit waters of a falls. He listened, crouched by the river until he felt his hands burn with cold. He went back to the fire. Deth softened the song to match the river's murmur, his face and the polished lines of the harp drawn clear by the fire. Morgon added wood to the fire. The harping stopped; he made a sound of protest.

"My hands are cold," Deth said. "I'm sorry." He reached for the harp case. Morgon, leaning back against a fallen log, gazed back at the cold, aloof faces of stars caught in the webs of pine needles.

"How long will it take us?"

"In good weather it takes ten days. If this weather holds, it shouldn't take us much longer."

"It's beautiful. It's more beautiful than any land I've seen in my life." His eyes moved to the harpist's face, half-hidden under his arm as he lay beside the fire. The quiet mystery of him began to nag at Morgon again. He put aside his questions with an effort and said instead, "You were going to teach me the mind-shout. Can you teach me the Great Shout, too?"

Deth lifted his arm, slid it beneath his head. His face looked open, for once, peaceful. "The Great Shout of the body is unteachable; you simply have to be inspired." He paused, added thoughtfully, "The last time I heard it was at the marriage between Mathom of An and Cyone, Raederle's mother. Cyone shouted a shout that harvested an entire crop of half-ripe nuts and snapped all the harp strings in the hall. Luckily I heard it from a mile away; I was the only harpist able to play that day."

Morgon gave a grunt of laughter. "What was she shouting about?"

"Mathom never told anyone."

"I wonder if Raederle could do that."

"Probably. It was a formidable shout. The body-shout is uncontrollable and very personal; the mind-shout will be more useful to you. It's a gathering in one quick moment all the energy in your mind, concentrated into one sound. Wizards used it to call one another in different kingdoms, if they had to. Both shouts may be used in defense, although the body-shout is unwieldy. If you are unusually moved, however, it is very effective. The mind-shout is generally the more dangerous: if you shout with full force into the mind of a man sitting close to you, he may lose consciousness. So be very careful with it. Try it. Call my name."

"I'm afraid to."

"I'll stop you if it's too strong. It takes time to learn to gather force. Concentrate."

Morgon stilled his mind. The fire smudged before his eyes, thinning into the darkness. The face opposite him became nameless as a tree or a stone. Then he slid past the shell of the face and let his thoughts blaze suddenly with Deth's name. His concentration shattered, he saw the face and the fire and the ghosts of trees form again before him.

Deth said patiently, "Morgon, you sounded as though you were on the other side of a mountain. Try again."

"I don't know what I'm doing—"

"Say my name, as you would naturally, using your mind-voice. Then shout it."

He tried again. This time, forgetting Har's teaching, thrown back against himself, he heard the shout futile in his own mind. He cleared his mind, tried again, and produced a full concentration of inner sound, which seemed to build and explode like a bubble in a cauldron. He winced.

"I'm sorry—did I hurt you?"

Deth smiled. "That was a little better. Try again."

He tried again. By the time the moon rose, he had exhausted his ability to concentrate. Deth sat up, reached for wood.

"You are trying to produce an illusion of sound without sound. It's not easy, but if you can exchange thoughts with a man, you should be able to shout at him."

"What am I doing wrong?"

"Perhaps you're being too cautious. Think of the Great Shouters of An: Cyone of An; Lord Col of Hel and the witch Madir, whose shouting-feud over the land-right to an oak forest their pigs fed in is legendary; Kale, first King of An, who scattered an enormous army from Aum by his shout of despair over its numbers. Forget you are Morgon of Hed and that I am a harpist named Deth. Somewhere deep in you is a wealth of power you are not using. Tap it, and you might make the beginnings of a mind-shout that doesn't sound as if it's coming out of the bottom of a well."

Morgon sighed. He tried to clear his mind, but like leaves there came drifting through it the bright images of Col and Madir throwing shouts at each other that cracked in the blue sky of An like lightning; of Cyone, dressed in purple and gold on her wedding day shouting an immense, mysterious shout of legendary result; of Kale, his face lost in the shadows of faded centuries, shouting with utter despair the hopelessness of his first battle. And Morgon, moved oddly by the tale, shouted Kale's shout and felt it snap away from him clean as an arrow into the eye of a beast.

Deth's face drifted before him again, frozen still above the fire.

Morgon said, feeling oddly peaceful, "Was it better?"

Deth did not answer for a moment. Then he said cautiously, "Yes."

Morgon straightened. "Did I hurt you?"

"A little."

"You should have—why didn't you stop me?"

"I was too surprised." He drew a deep breath. "Yes. That was much better."

The next day the river dropped away from them as they rode, the path rising high above it, tracing the mountainside, the white slope melting downward to halt at the blue-white water. For a while they lost sight of it, riding through the trees. Morgon, watching the slow procession of ancient trees, thought of Danan, and the mountain-king's face seemed to look back at him out of aged, wrinkled bark. Midafternoon brought them back to the cliff edge, where they saw again the brilliant, impatient river and the mountains shrugging off their coats of winter snow.

The packhorse, straying aside, sent a rock below them, bouncing into the river; Morgon turned to tug it back. The bright sun glanced off the peak above them; fingers of light flicked along a row of icicles on the cliff. Morgon glanced up at the slope above their heads, and the bone-white blaze of mountain burned in his eyes.

He looked away, and said to Deth, "If I wanted to harvest a crop of nuts in Hed with the Great Shout, how would I do it?"

Deth, brought out of his own thoughts, said absently, "Provided that the crop of nuts is in a secluded place away from your animals, who would scatter to the twelve winds at a shout like that, you would draw on the same source of energy you used last night. The difficulty lies in producing a sound without considering physical limitations. It requires both sufficient impulse and great abandon, which is why you would do better to wait for a good wind."

Morgon considered. The gentle, rhythmic clop of hooves and the distant voice of the river sounded frail against the silence, which seemed impervious to any shout. He thought back to the previous night, trying to find again the source of inexhaustible energy, private and undefined, that had overwhelmed him to produce the silent shout. The sun, leaping from behind a bend in the road, suddenly showered his path with stars. The unbroken blue of the sky quivered with a great, soundless note. He drew a breath of the hidden sound and loosed a shout.

There was an answering shout from the mountains. For a second he listened to it without surprise. Then he saw Deth stop ahead of him; his face turned back in surprise. He dismounted, wrenched at the pack-horse's reins, and Morgon, suddenly placing the sound, slid off his horse and drew it to the wall of the cliff. He crouched flat beside it as the hiss and rattle of stones swept towards them, bounced onto the road and down the slope.

The rumble shook through bare peaks and hidden forests. A boulder half the size of a horse struck the cliff edge above their heads, sailed lightly over them and flung itself down the slope towards the river, crushing a tree as it passed. Then the silence, regathered and locked into place, strained at their ears in triumph.

Morgon, flat against the cliff as though he were holding it up, turned his head cautiously. Deth's eyes met his, expressionless. Then expression came back into them.

He said, "Morgon—"

He stopped. He eased the trembling horses away from the cliff. Morgon soothed his own horse, brought it back on the road. He stood beside it, suddenly too tired to mount, sweat pricking his face in the chill air.

He said after a moment, blankly, "That was stupid."

Deth dropped his face against his horse. Morgon, who had never heard him laugh before, stood amazed in the snow, listening. The sound flung itself back at them from the high crevices until the laughter of stone and man tangled into an unhuman sound that jarred Morgon's ears. He took a step forward, disturbed. As Deth sensed the movement, he quieted. His hands were twisted, locked in his horse's mane; his shoulders were rigid.

Morgon said softly, "Deth—"

The harpist's head lifted. He reached for the reins, mounted slowly without looking at Morgon. Down the slope a great tree, half uprooted, its trunk snapped like a bone, laid its face against the snow. Morgon, staring down at it, swallowed drily. "I'm sorry. I had no business practicing the Great Shout on a mountain of melting snow. I could have killed us both."

"Yes." The harpist checked briefly, as though feeling for his voice. "The Pass seems to be proof against shape-changers, but not against you."

"Is that why you were laughing like that?"

"I don't know what else to do." He looked at Morgon finally. "Are you ready to go on?"

Morgon drew himself on his own horse wearily. The late sun, drifting towards Erlenstar Mountain, was drawing a wake of light down the Pass.

Deth said, "The road descends down to the river in a couple of miles; we can camp then."

Morgon nodded. He added, soothing the neck of his trembling mare, "It didn't sound that loud."

"No. It was a gentle shout. But it was effective. If ever you shout the Great Shout in truth, I think the world will crack."

In eight days they tracked the river to its source: the melting slopes and high snowbound peak of the mountain that overlooked the kingdoms of the High One. They saw the end of the road on the morning of the ninth day; it crossed the Ose and ran into the mouth of Erlenstar. Morgon reined, catching his first glimpse of the threshold of the High One. Lines of huge, ancient trees marked the road, which, cleared of snow across the river, glittered like the inner walls of Harte. The outer door was a crack in the stone face of the mountain, smoothed and molded to an arch. A man walked out of the arch as he watched, came down the fiery road to wait at the bridge.

"Seric," Deth said. "The High One's Watcher. He was trained by the wizards at Lungold. Come."

But he did not move himself. Morgon, a mixture of fear and

excitement beginning to gnaw at him, glanced at Deth, waiting. The harpist sat still, his face quiet as always, looking at the door into Erlenstar. Then his head turned. His eyes on Morgon's face held an odd expression, half-searching, half-questioning, as though he were weighing a riddle and an answer in his mind. Then, without resolving one to the other, he moved forward. Morgon followed him down the final length of road, across the bridge where Seric, his long, loose robe seemingly woven from all the colors under the sun, stopped them.

"This is Morgon, Prince of Hed," Deth said, as he dismounted. Seric smiled.

"So Hed has come at last to the High One. You are welcome. He expects you. I'll take your horses."

Morgon walked beside Deth down the flickering path, alive with worn, uncut jewels. The mouth of Erlenstar opened to a wide sweep of inner hallway, a great fire ring in the middle of it. Seric took their horses down one side of it. Deth led Morgon towards arched double doors. They opened softly. Men in the same light, beautiful robes bent their heads to Morgon, closed the doors again behind them.

Light pricked endlessly through the shadows, drawn by the play of fire on jewelled floor, walls, arched dome of rock, as though the High One's house were the center of a star. Deth, his hand light on Morgon's arm, led him forward towards a dais at the other side of the round room. On the third step a high-backed throne carved of a single yellow crystal sat between two torches. Morgon stopped at the bottom of the steps. Deth left his side, went to stand beside the throne. The High One, his robe sun-gold, his white hair drawn back from his brow to free the simple, austere lines of it, lifted his hands from the arms of the throne and brought the tips of his fingers together.

"Morgon of Hed. You are very welcome," he said softly. "How may I help you?"

Morgon's blood shocked through him, then slowed unbearably with the dull pound of his heart. The jewelled walls pulsed around him in silent, flickering beats of light. He looked at Deth. The harpist stood quietly, the midnight eyes watching him dispassionately. He looked back at the High One, but the face remained undisguised by richness: the face of a Master of Caithnard he had known for three years and never known.

His voice became heavy, ragged. "Master Ohm—"

"I am Ohm of Caithnard. I am Ghisteslwchlohm, the Founder of Lungold, and—as you have guessed—its destroyer. I am the High One."

Morgon shook his head, a weight growing behind his throat, his eyes. He turned again to Deth, who blurred suddenly in his gaze, yet, blurred, stood with a silence undisturbed and insurmountable as the silence sitting heavy as ice above Isig Pass. "And you—" he whispered.

"I am his harpist."

"No," he whispered. "Oh, no." Then he felt the word well up from some terrible source, tear out of him, and the barred doors of the High One's house split from top to bottom with the force of that shout.

Heir of Sea and Fire

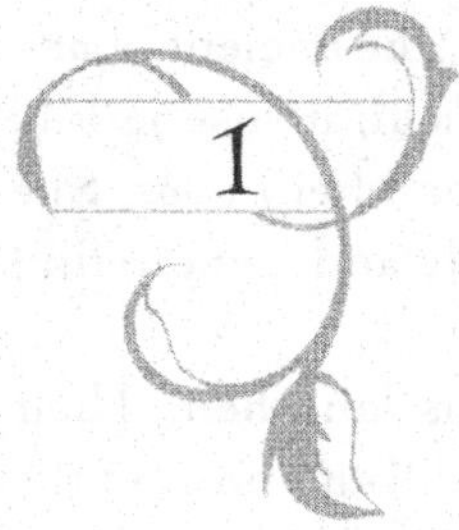

IN SPRING, THREE things came invariably to the house of the King of An: the year's first shipment of Herun wine, the lords of the Three Portions for the spring council, and an argument.

The spring of the year following the strange disappearance of the Prince of Hed, who had, with the High One's harpist, vanished like a mist in Isig Pass, the great house with its seven gates and seven white towers seemed to be cracking like a seed pod out of a long, bitter winter of silence and grief. The season dusted the air with green, set patterns of light like inlay on the cold stone floors, and roused restlessness like sap in the deep heart of An, until Raederle of An, standing in Cyone's garden, which no one had entered for the six months since her death, felt that even the dead of An, their bones plaited with grass roots, must be drumming their fingers in their graves.

She stirred after a while, left the tangle of weeds and withered things that had not survived the winter, and went back into the King's hall, whose doors were flung wide to the light. Servants under the eye of Mathom's steward, were shaking the folds out of the lords' banners, hanging them precariously from the high beams. The lords were due any day, and the house was in a turmoil preparing to receive them. Already their gifts had been arriving for her: a milk-white falcon bred in the wild peaks of Osterland from the Lord of Hel; a brooch like a gold wafer from Map Hwillion, who was too poor to afford such things; a flute of polished wood inlaid with silver, which bore no name, and worried Raederle, since whoever had sent it had known what she would love. She watched the banner of Hel unrolling, the ancient boar's head with tusks like black moons on an oak-green field; it rose jerkily on its hangings to survey the broad hall out of its small fiery eyes. She gazed back at it, her arms folded, then turned suddenly and went to find her father.

She found him in his chambers arguing with his land-heir. Their voices were low, and they stopped when she entered, but she saw the faint flush on Duac's cheekbones. In the pale slashes of his brows and his sea-colored eyes, he bore the stamp of Ylon's wild blood, but his patience with Mathom when everyone else had exhausted theirs was considered phenomenal. She wondered what Mathom had said to upset him.

The King turned a dour crow's eye to her; she said politely, for his mood in the mornings was unpredictable, "I would like to visit Mara Croeg in Aum for a couple of weeks, with your permission. I could pack and leave tomorrow. I've been in Anuin all winter, and I feel—I need to get away."

There was not a flicker of change in his eyes. He said simply, "No," and turned to pick up his wine cup.

She stared at his back, annoyed, and discarded courtesy like an old shoe. "Well, I'm not going to stay here and be argued over like a prize cow out of Aum. Do you know who sent me a gift? Map Hwillion. Only yesterday he was laughing at me for falling out of a pear tree, and now he's got his first beard and an eight-hundred-year-old house with a leaky roof, and he thinks he wants to marry me. You're the one who promised me to the Prince of Hed; can't you put a stop to all this? I'd rather listen to the pig herds of Hel during a thunderstorm than another spring council arguing with you about what to do with me."

"So would I," Duac murmured. Mathom eyed them both. His hair had turned iron-grey seemingly overnight; his sorrow over Cyone's death had limned his face to the bone, but it had neither tempered nor bittered his disposition.

"What do you want me to tell them," he asked, "other than what I have told them for nineteen years? I have made a vow, binding beyond life, to marry you to the man winning Peven's game. If you want to run away and live with Map Hwillion under his leaky roof, I can't stop you—they know that."

"I don't want to marry Map Hwillion," she said, exasperated. "I would like to marry the Prince of Hed. Except that I don't know any more who he is, and no one else knows where he is. I am tired of waiting; I am tired of this house; I am tired of listening to the Lord of Hel tell me that I am being ignored and insulted by the Prince of Hed; I want to visit Mara Croeg in Aum, and I don't understand how you can refuse such a simple, reasonable request."

There was a short silence, during which Mathom considered the wine in his cup. An indefinable expression came into his face; he set the cup down and said, "If you like, you can go to Caithnard."

Her lips parted in surprise. "I can? To visit Rood? Is there a ship—" And then Duac brought his hand down flat on the wine table, rattling cups.

"No."

She stared at him, astonished, and he closed his hand. His eyes were narrowed slightly as he gazed back at Mathom. "He's asked me to go, but I've already refused. He wants Rood home."

"Rood? I don't understand."

Mathom moved away from the window suddenly with an irritated whirl of sleeve. "I might as well have the entire council in here babbling at me at once. I want Rood to take a leave from his studies, come back to Anuin for a while; he'll take that fact best from either Duac or you."

"You tell him," Duac said inflexibly. Under the King's eye he yielded, sat down, gripping the arms of his chair as though he were holding fast to his patience. "Then will you explain so I can understand? Rood has just taken the Red of Apprenticeship; if he stays he'll take the Black at a younger age than any living Master. He's done fine work there; he deserves the chance to stay."

"There are more riddles in the world than those in the locked books behind the walls of that College in Caithnard."

"Yes. I've never studied riddle-mastery, but I have an idea that you can't answer them all at once. He's doing the best he can. What do you want him to do? Go lose himself at Erlenstar Mountain like the Prince of Hed?"

"No. I want him here."

"For what, in Hel's name? Are you planning to die or something?"

"Duac," Raederle breathed, but he waited stubbornly for the King to answer. She felt, like a live thing beneath the irritation and obstinacy in them both, the binding between them beyond all definition. Then Duac heaved himself to his feet at Mathom's silence and snapped before he slammed the door behind him so hard the stones seemed to rattle, "By Madir's bones, I wish I could see into that peatbog you call a mind!"

Raederle sighed. She looked at Mathom, who seemed in spite of the rich robe he wore, black and impervious as a wizard's curse in the sunlight. "I'm beginning to hate spring. I won't ask you to explain the world to me, just why I can't go visit Mara Croeg while Cyn Croeg is here at the council."

"Who was Thanet Ross and why did he play a harp without strings?"

She stood a moment, dredging the answer out of interminable, half-forgotten hours of riddlery. Then she turned; she heard his voice again, just before the door slammed once more, "And stay out of Hel."

She found Duac in the library, staring out the window. She joined him, leaning against the window, looking down at the city that sloped gently away from the King's house to spill around the rim of the harbor. Trade-ships were drifting in with the midmorning tide, their colored sails deflating in the wind like weary sighs. She saw the white and green of Danan Isig's ships bringing the marvellous crafts from Isig Mountain; and a hope stirred in her that the northern Kingdom had sent news more valuable than all its beautiful cargo. Duac stirred beside her, as the peace of the ancient library with its smell of hide, wax and the iron of old shields returned the composure to his face. He said softly, "He is the most pig-headed, arbitrary and exasperating man in the Three Portions of An."

"I know."

"Something's going on in his head; something's bubbling behind his eyes like a bad spell . . . It worries me. Because if it came to a choice between a blind step into a bottomless pit with him and a walk across the apple orchards with the Lords of An at their finest, I would shut my eyes and step. But what is he thinking?"

"I don't know." She dropped her chin in her palms. "I don't know why he wants us all home now. I don't understand him. I asked him why I couldn't leave, and he asked me why Thanet Ross played a harp with no strings."

"Who?" Duac looked at her. "How could . . . Why did he play a harp with no strings?"

"For the same reason he walked backward and shaved his head instead of his beard. For no reason except that there was no reason. He was a sad man and died backward."

"Oh."

"He was walking backward for no reason and fell in a river. Nobody ever saw him again, but they assumed he died since there was no reason—"

"All right," Duac protested mildly. "You could spin that one into yarn."

She smiled. "See what education you missed, not being destined to marry a riddle-master." Then her smile faded; she bowed her head, traced a crack in the old mortar. "I feel as though I'm waiting for a legend to come down from the north, breaking out of winter with the spring water . . . Then I remember the farmer's son who used to put shells to my ears so I could hear the sea, and, Duac, that's when I become afraid for him. He has been gone so long; there has not been one word from him for a year, and no one in the realm has heard so much as a harp-note from the High One's harpist. Surely the High One would never keep Morgon so long from his land. I think something must have happened to them in Isig Pass."

"As far as anyone knows, the land-rule hasn't passed from Morgon," Duac said comfortingly, but she only shifted restlessly.

"Then where is he? At least he could get a message to his own land. The traders say that every time they stop at Tol, Tristan and Eliard are there at the dock waiting, hoping for news. Even at Isig, with all they say happened to him, he managed to write. They say he has scars on his hands like vesta-horns, and he can take the shape of trees . . ."

Duac glanced down at his own hands as if he expected to see the withered moons of white horns in them. "I know . . . The simplest thing to do would be to go to Erlenstar Mountain and ask the High One where he is. It's spring; the Pass should be clearing. Eliard might do it."

"Leave Hed? He's Morgon's land-heir; they'd never let him leave."

"Maybe. But they say there's a streak of stubbornness long as a witch's nose in the people of Hed. He might." He leaned over the ledge suddenly; his head turned towards a distant, double-column of riders making their way across the meadows. "Here they come. In full plumage."

"Who is it?"

"I can't . . . blue. Blue and black retinue; that would be Cyn Croeg. He appears to have met someone green . . ."

"Hel."

"No. Green and cream; very small following."

She sighed. "Map Hwillion."

She stood by the window after Duac left to tell Mathom, watching the riders veer around the nut orchards, flickering in and out of the lacework of black, bare branches. They appeared again at a corner of the old city wall, to take the main road through the city, which led twisting and curving through the market and old high houses and shops whose windows would be wide open like eyes, full of watchers. By the time they disappeared through the gates of the city, she had decided what to do.

Three days later, she sat beside the pig-woman of the Lord of Hel under an oak tree, weaving grass blades into a net. From all around her in the placid afternoon came the vast snort and grumble of the great pig herds of Hel as they stirred through the tangled roots and shadows of oak. The pig-woman, whom no one had ever bothered to name, was smoking a meditative pipe. She was a tall, bony, nervous woman, with long, dishevelled grey hair and dark grey eyes; she had tended the pigs as long as anyone could remember. They were related, she and Raederle, through the witch Madir, in some obscure way they were trying to figure out. The pig-woman's great gift was with pigs; she was abrupt and shy with people, but the beautiful, fiery Cyone had inherited Madir's interest in pigs and had become friends with the taciturn pig-woman. But not even Cyone had discovered what Raederle knew: the odd store of knowledge that the pig-woman had also inherited from Madir.

Raederle picked another tough stem of grass, sent it snaking in and out of the small, square weave. "Am I doing this right?"

The pig-woman touched the tight strands and nodded. "You could carry water in that," she said, in her plain, rugged voice. "Now, then, I think King Oen had a pigherder whom Madir might have been fond of, in Anuin."

"I thought she might have been fond of Oen."

The pig-woman looked surprised. "After he built the tower to trap her? You told me that. Besides, he had a wife." She waved the words and her pipe smoke away at once with her hand. "I'm not thinking."

"No king I ever heard of married Madir," Raederle said wryly. "Yet somehow the blood got into the king's line. Let's see: she lived nearly two hundred years, and there were seven kings. I believe we can forget Fenel; he was too busy fighting almost to father a land-heir, let alone a bastard. I don't even know if he kept pigs. It is possible," she added, struck, "that you are a descendant of a child of Madir and one of the Kings."

The pig-woman gave a rare chuckle. "Oh, I doubt it. Me with my bare feet. Madir liked pigherders as much as she liked kings."

"That's true." She finished with the grass blade and pushed the stems close, frowning down at them absently. "It is also possible that Oen might have grown fond of Madir after he realized she wasn't his enemy, but that seems a little scandalous, since it was through him that Ylon's blood came into the Kings' line. Oen was furious enough about that."

"Ylon."

"You know that tale."

The pig-woman shook her head. "I know the name, but no one ever told me the tale."

"Well." She sat back against the tree trunk, the sun shimmering in and out of her eyes. Her own shoes were off; her hair was loose; and there was a small spider making a bewildered foray up one strand. She brushed it off without noticing. "It's the first riddle I ever learned. Oen's land-heir was not his own son, but the son of some strange sea-lord, who came into Oen's bed disguised as the king. Nine months afterward, Oen's wife bore Ylon, with skin like foam and eyes like green seaweed. So Oen in his anger built a tower by the sea for this sea-child, with orders that he should never come out of it. One night, fifteen years after his birth, Ylon heard a strange harping from the sea, and such was his love of it, and desire to find its source, that he broke the bars on his window with his hands and leaped into the sea and vanished. Ten years later Oen died, and to his other sons' surprise, the land-rule passed to Ylon. Ylon was driven by his own nature back to claim his heritage. He reigned only long enough to marry and beget a son who was as dark and practical as Oen, and then he went back to the tower Oen had built for him and leaped to his death on the rocks below." She touched the tiny net, squared a corner. "It's a sad tale." A frown strayed into her eyes, absent, puzzled, as if she had almost remembered something, but not quite. "Anyway, Ylon's face appears once or twice a century, and sometimes his wildness, but never his terrible torment, because no one with his nature has ever again inherited the land-rule. Which is fortunate."

"That's true." The pig-woman looked down at the pipe in her hand, which had gone out during her listening. She tapped it absently against the tree root. Raederle watched an enormous black sow nudge her way through the clearing in front of them to loll panting in the shade.

"It's almost Dis's time."

The pig-woman nodded. "They'll all be black as pots, too, sired by Dark Noon."

Raederle spotted the boar responsible, the great descendant of Hegdis-Noon, rooting among the old leaves. "Maybe she'll bear one who can talk."

"Maybe. I keep hoping, but the magic, I think, has gone out of the blood and they are born silent."

"I wish a few of the Lords of An had been born silent."

The pig-woman's brows flicked up in sudden comprehension. "That's it, then."

"What?"

She shifted, shy again. "The spring council. It's nothing of my business, but I didn't think you had ridden for three days to find out if we were first or third cousins."

Raederle smiled. "No. I ran away from home."

"You . . . . Does your father know where you are?"

"I always assume he knows everything." She reached for another stem of grass. The odd, tentative frown moved again into her face; she looked up suddenly to meet the pig-woman's eyes. For a moment, the direct, grey gaze seemed a stranger's look, curious, measuring, with the same question in it that she had barely put words to. Then the pig-woman's head bowed; she reached down to pick an acorn out of an angle of root and tossed it to the black sow. Raederle said softly, "Ylon . . ."

"He's why you can do these small things I teach you so well. He and Madir. And your father with his mind."

"Maybe. But—" She shook the thought away and leaned back again to breathe the tranquil air. "My father could see a shadow in a barrow, but I wish he didn't have a mouth like a clam. It's good to be away from that house. It grew so quiet last winter I thought whatever words we spoke would freeze solid in the air. I thought that winter would never end . . ."

"It was a bad one. The Lord had to send for feed from Aum and pay double because Aum itself was growing short of corn. We lost some of the herd; one of the great boars, Aloil—"

"Aloil?"

The pig-woman looked suddenly a little flustered. "Well, Rood mentioned him once, and I thought—I liked the name."

"You named a boar after a wizard?"

"Was he? I didn't . . . Rood didn't say. Anyway, he died in spite of all I could do for him, and the Lord himself even came to help with his own hands."

Raederle's face softened slightly. "Yes. That's one thing Raith is good with."

"It's in his blood. But he was upset about—about Aloil." She glanced at Raederle's handiwork. "You might want to make it a little wider, but you'll need to leave a fringe to hold it after you throw it."

Raederle stared down at the tiny net, watching it grow big then small again in her mind's eye. She reached for more grass, and felt, as her hand touched the earth, the steady drum of hoofbeats. She glanced, startled, toward the trees. "Who is that? Hasn't Raith left for Anuin yet?"

"No, he's still here. Didn't you—" She stopped as Raederle rose, cursing succinctly, and the Lord of Hel and his retinue came into the clearing, scattering pigs.

Raith brought his mount to a halt in front of Raederle; his men, in pale green and black, drew to a surprised, disorderly stop. He stared down at her, his gold brows pulling quickly into a disapproving frown, and opened his mouth; she said, "You're going to be late for the council."

"I had to wait for Elieu. Why in Hel's name are you running around in your stockinged feet in my pig herds? Where is your escort? Where—"

"Elieu!" Raederle cried to a brown-bearded stranger dismounting from his horse, and his happy smile, as she ran to hug him, made him once again familiar.

"Did you get the flute I sent to you?" he asked, as she gripped his arms; she nodded, laughing.

"You sent it? Did you make it? It was so beautiful it frightened me."

"I wanted to surprise you, not—"

"I didn't recognize you in that beard. You haven't been out of Isig for three years; it's about time you—" She checked suddenly, her hold tightening. "Elieu, did you bring any news of the Prince of Hed?"

"I'm sorry," he said gently. "No one has seen him. I sailed down from Kraal on a trade-ship; it stopped five times along the way, and I lost count long ago of how many people I had to tell that to. There is one thing, though, that I came to tell your father." He smiled again, touched her face. "You are always so beautiful. Like An itself. But what are you doing alone in Raith's pig herds?"

"I came to talk to his pig-woman, who is a very wise and interesting woman."

"She is?" Elieu looked at the pig-woman, who looked down at her feet.

Raith said grimly, "I would have thought you had outgrown such things. It was foolish of you to ride alone from Anuin; I'm amazed that your father—he does know where you are?"

"He has probably made a fairly accurate guess."

"You mean you—"

"Oh, Raith, if I want to make a fool of myself that's my business."

"Well, look at you! Your hair looks as though birds have been nesting in it."

Her hand rose impulsively to smooth it, then dropped. "That," she said frostily, "is also my business."

"It's beneath your dignity to consort with my pig-woman like some—like some—"

"Well, Raith, we are related. For all I know she has as much right in the court at Anuin as I have."

"I didn't know you were related," Elieu said interestedly. "How?"

"Madir. She was a busy woman."

Raith drew a long breath through his nose. "You," he said ponderously, "need a husband." He jerked his reins, turning his mount; at his straight, powerful back and rigorous movements something desperate, uneasy, touched Raederle. She felt Elieu's hand on her shoulder.

"Never mind," he said soothingly. "Will you ride back with us? I would love to hear you play that flute."

"All right." Her shoulders slumped a little. "All right. If you're there. But first tell me what news you have to tell my father that brought you all the way down from Isig."

"Oh." She heard the sudden awe in his voice. "It's about the Prince—about the Star-Bearer."

Raederle swallowed. As if the pigs themselves had recognized the name, there was a lull in their vigorous snortings. The pig-woman looked up from her feet. "Well, what?"

"It was something Bere, Danan's grandson, told me. You must have heard the tale about Morgon, about the night he took the sword from the secret places of Isig, the night he killed three shape-changers with it, saving himself and Bere. Bere and I were working together, and Bere asked me what the Earth-Masters were. I told him as much as I knew, and asked him why. And he told me then that he had heard Morgon telling Danan and Deth that in the Cave of the Lost Ones, where no one had ever gone but Yrth, Morgon found his starred sword, and it had been given to him by the dead children of the Earth-Masters."

The pig-woman dropped her pipe. She rose in a swift, blurred movement that startled Raederle. The vagueness dropped from her face like a mask, revealing a strength and sorrow worn into it by a knowledge of far more than Raith's pigs. She drew a breath and shouted, "What?"

The shout cracked like lightning out of the placid sky. Raederle, flinging her arms futilely over her ears, heard above her own cry the shrill, terrified cries of rearing horses, and the breathless, gasping voices of men struggling to control them. Then came a sound as unexpected and terrible as the pig-woman's shout: the agonized, outraged protest of the entire pig herd of Hel.

Raederle opened her eyes. The pig-woman had vanished, as though she had been blown away by her shout. The unwieldy, enormous pig herd, squealing with pain and astonishment, was heaving to its feet, turning blindly, massing like a great wave, panic rippling to the far edges of the herd in the distance. She saw the great boars wheeling, their eyes closed, the young pigs half-buried in the heave of bristled backs, the sows, huge with their unborn, swaying to their feet. The horses, appalled by the strange clamor and the pigs jostling against them, were wrenching out of control. One of them stepped back onto a small pig, and the double screech of terror from both animals sounded across the clearing like a battle horn. Hooves pounding, voices shrilling and snorting, the pride of Hel for nine centuries surged forward, dragging men and horses helplessly with them. Raederle, taking prompt, undignified shelter up the oak tree, saw Raith trying desperately to turn his horse and reach her. But he was swept away with his retinue, Elieu, whooping with laughter, bringing up the rear. The herd ebbed away and vanished into the distant trees. Raederle, straddling a bough, her head beginning to ache with the aftermath of the shout, thought of the pigs running along with the Lord of Hel all the way into the King's council hall in Anuin, and she laughed until she cried.

She found, riding wearily back into her father's courtyard at twilight three days later, that some of the pigs had gotten there before her. The inner walls were blazoned with the banners of the lords who had arrived; beneath the banner of Hel, limp in the evening air, were penned seven exhausted boars. She had to stop and laugh again, but the laughter was more subdued as she realized that she had to face Mathom. She wondered, as a groom ran to take her horse, why, with all the people in the house, it was so quiet. She went up the steps, into the open doors of the hall; amid the long lines of empty tables and the sprawl of chairs, there were only three people: Elieu, Duac and the King.

She said a little hesitantly as they turned at her step, "Where is everyone?"

"Out," Mathom said succinctly. "Looking for you."

"Your whole council?"

"My whole council. They left five days ago; they are probably scattered, like Raith's pigs, all over the Three Portions of An. Raith himself was last seen trying to herd his pigs together in Aum." His voice was testy, but there was no anger in his eyes, only a hiddenness, as if he were contemplating an entirely different train of thought. "Did it occur to you that anyone might be worried?"

"If you ask me," Duac murmured into his wine cup, "it seemed more like a hunting party than a search party, to see who would bring home the prize." Something in his face told Raederle that he and Mathom had been arguing again. He lifted his head. "You let them go like a cageful of freed birds. You can control your own lords better than that. I've never seen such shambles made of a council in my life, and you wanted it so. Why?"

Raederle sat down next to Elieu, who gave her a cup of wine and a smile. Mathom was standing; he made a rare, impatient gesture at Duac's words. "Does it occur to you that I might have been worried?"

"You weren't surprised when you heard she was gone. You didn't tell me to go after her, did you? No. You're more interested in sending me to Caithnard. While you do what?"

"Duac!" Mathom snapped, exasperated, and Duac shifted in his chair. The King turned a dour eye to Raederle. "And I told you to stay out of Hel. You had a remarkable effect on both Raith's pigs and my council."

"I'm sorry. But I told you I needed to get out of this house."

"That badly? Riding precipitously off into Hel and back without an escort?"

"Yes."

She heard him sigh.

"How can I command obedience from my land when I cannot even rule my own household?" The question was rhetorical, for he exacted over his land and his house what he chose.

Duac said with dogged, weary patience, "If you would try explaining yourself for once in your life, it would make a difference. Even I will obey you. Try telling me in simple language why you think it is so imperative for me to bring Rood home. Just tell me. And I'll go."

"Are you still arguing about that?" Raederle said. She looked curiously at their father. "Why do you want Duac to bring Rood home? Why did you want me to stay out of Hel, when you know I am as safe on Raith's lands as in my garden?"

"Either," Mathom said tersely, "you, Duac, bring Rood home from Caithnard, or I will send a ship and a simple command to him. Which do you think he would prefer?"

"But why—"

"Let him puzzle his own brain about it. He's trained to answer riddles, and it will give him something to do."

Duac brought his hands together, linked them tightly. "All right," he said tautly. "All right. But I'm no riddler and I like things explained to me. Until you explain to me precisely why you want the one who will become my land-heir if you die back here with me, I swear by Madir's bones that I'll see the wraiths of Hel ride across this threshold before I call Rood back to Anuin."

There was a chilling leap of pure anger in Mathom's face that startled Raederle. Duac's face lost nothing of its resolve, but she saw him swallow. Then his hands pulled apart, lowered to grip the table edge. He whispered, "You're leaving An."

In the silence, Raederle heard the far, faint bickering of sea gulls. She felt something hard, a word left in her from the long winter, melt away. It brought the tears for a moment into her eyes so that Mathom blurred to a shadow when she looked at him. "You're going to Erlenstar Mountain. To ask about the Prince of Hed. Please. I would like to come with you."

"No." But the voice of the shadow was gentle.

Elieu's head was moving slowly from side to side. He breathed, "Mathom, you can't. Anyone with even half a mind to reason with must realize—"

"That what he is contemplating," Duac interrupted, "is hardly a simple journey to Erlenstar Mountain and back." He rose, his chair protesting against the stones. "Is it?"

"Duac, at a time when the air itself is an ear, I do not intend to babble my business to the world."

"I am not the world. I am your land-heir. You've never been surprised once in your life, not when Morgon won that game with Peven, not even at Elieu's news of the waking of the children of the Earth-Masters. Your thoughts are calculated like a play on a chess-board, but I don't think even you know exactly who you are playing against. If all you want to do is to go to Erlenstar Mountain, you would not be sending for Rood. You don't know where you are going, do you? Or what you will find, or when you will get back? And you knew that if the Lords of the Three Portions were here listening to this, there would be an uproar that would shake the stones loose in the ceiling. You'll leave me to face the uproar, and you'll sacrifice the peace of your land for something that is not your concern but the business of Hed and the High One."

"The High One." Something harsh, unpleasant in the King's voice made the name almost unfamiliar. "Morgon's own people scarcely know a world exists beyond Hed, and except for one incident, I would wonder if the High One knows that Morgon exists."

"It's not your concern! You are liable to the High One for the rule of An, and if you let loose of the bindings in the Three Portions—"

"I don't need to be reminded of my responsibilities!"

"You can stand there plotting to leave An indefinitely and tell me that!"

"Is it possible that you can trust me when I weigh two things in the balance and find one looming more heavily than a momentary confusion in An?"

"Momentary confusion!" Duac breathed. "If you leave An too long, stray too far away from it, you will throw this land into chaos. If your hold on the things you bind in the Three Portions loosens, you'll find the dead kings of Hel and Aum laying siege to Anuin, and Peven himself wandering into this hall looking for his crown. If you return at all. And if you vanish, as Morgon did, for some long, wearisome length of time, this land will find itself in a maelstrom of terror."

"It's possible," Mathom said. "So far in its long history An has had nothing more challenging to fight than itself. It can survive itself."

"What worse can happen to it than such a chaos of living and dead?" He raised his voice, battering in anger and desperation against the King's implacability. "How can you think of doing this to your land? You don't have the right! And if you're not careful, you'll no longer have the land-rule."

Elieu leaned forward, gripped his arm. Raederle stood up, groping for words to quiet them. Then she caught sight of a stranger entering the hall, who had stopped abruptly at Duac's shout. He was young, plainly dressed in sheepskin and rough wool. He glanced in wonder at the beautiful hall, then stared a little at Raederle without realizing it. The numb, terrible sorrow in his eyes made her heart stop. She took a step towards him, feeling as though she were stepping irrevocably out of the predictable world. Something in her face had stopped the quarrel. Mathom turned. The stranger shifted uneasily and cleared his throat.

"I'm—my name is Cannon Master. I farm the lands of the Prince of Hed. I have a message for the King of An from—from the Prince of Hed."

"I am Mathom of An."

Raederle took another step forward. "And I am Raederle," she whispered, while something fluttered, trapped like a bird, in the back of her throat. "Is Morgon . . . Who is the Prince of Hed?"

She heard a sound from Mathom. Cannon Master looked at her mutely a moment. Then he said very gently, "Eliard."

Into their incredulous silence, the King dropped one word like a stone. "How?"

"No one—no one knows exactly." He stopped to swallow. "All Eliard knows is that Morgon died five days ago. We don't know how, or where, only that it was under very strange and terrible circumstances. Eliard knows that much because he has been dreaming about Morgon the past year, feeling something—some nameless power weighing into Morgon's mind. He couldn't—he couldn't seem to free himself from it. He didn't even seem to know himself at the end. We can't begin to guess what it was. Five days ago, the land-rule passed to Eliard. We remembered the reason why Morgon had left Hed in the first place, and we—Eliard decided . . ." He paused; a faint flush of color came into his weary face. He said diffidently to Raederle, "I don't know if you would have chosen to come to Hed. You would have been—you would have been most welcome. But we thought it right that you should be told. I had been once to Caithnard, so I said I'd come."

"I see." She tried to clear the trembling in her throat. "Tell him—tell him I would have come. I would have come."

His head bowed. "Thank you for that."

"A year," Duac whispered. "You knew what was happening to him. You knew. Why didn't you tell someone? Why didn't you let us know sooner?"

Cannon Master's hands clenched. He said painfully, "It's what—it's what we ask ourselves now. We—we just kept hoping. No one of Hed has ever asked outside of Hed for help."

"Has there been any word from the High One?" Elieu asked.

"No. Nothing. But no doubt the High One's harpist will show up eventually to express the High One's sorrow over the death of—" He stopped, swallowing the bitterness from his voice. "I'm sorry. We can't—we can't even bury him in his own land. I'm ignorant as a sheep outside of Hed; I hardly know, stepping out of your house, which direction to turn to go home. So I have to ask you if, beyond Hed, such things happen to land-rulers so frequently that not even the High One is moved by it."

Duac stirred, but Mathom spoke before he could. "Never," he said flatly. Cannon, drawn by something smoldering in his eyes, took a step toward the King, his voice breaking.

"Then what was it? Who killed him? Where, if the High One himself doesn't care, can we go for an answer?"

The King of An looked as though he were swallowing a shout that might have blown the windows out of the room. He said succinctly, "I swear by the bones of the unconquered Kings of An, that if I have to bring it back from the dead I will find you an answer."

Duac dropped his face in one hand. "You've done it now." Then he shouted, while Cannon stared at him, amazed, "And if you go wandering through this realm like a peddlar and that darkness that killed Morgon snatches you out of time and place, don't bother troubling me with your dreams because I won't look for you!"

"Then look to my land," Mathom said softly. "Duac, there is a thing in this realm that eats the minds of land-rulers, that is heaving restlessly under the earth with more hatred in it than even in the bones of the dead of Hel. And when it rouses at last, there will not be a blade of grass in this land untouched by it."

He vanished so quickly that Duac started. He stood staring at the air where Mathom had gone out like a dark, windblown flame. Cannon said, appalled, "I'm sorry—I'm sorry—I never dreamed—"

"It wasn't your fault," Elieu said gently. His face was bloodless. He put a hand on Raederle's wrist; she looked at him blindly. He added to Duac, "I'll stay in Hel. I'll do what I can."

Duac ran his hands up his face, up through his hair. "Thank you." He turned to Cannon. "You can believe him. He'll find out who killed Morgon and why, and he'll tell you if he has to drag himself out of a grave to do it. He has sworn that, and he is bound beyond life."

Cannon shuddered. "Things are much simpler in Hed. Things die when they're dead."

"I wish they did in An."

Raederle, staring out at the darkening sky beyond the windows, touched his arm suddenly. "Duac . . ."

An old crow swung over the garden on a drift of wind, then flapped northward over the rooftops of Anuin. Duac's eyes followed it as though something in him were bound to the deliberate, unhurried flight. He said wearily, "I hope he doesn't get himself shot and cooked for dinner."

Cannon looked at him, startled. Raederle, watching the black wings shirr the blue-grey twilight, said, "Someone should go to Caithnard to tell Rood. I'll go." Then she put her hands over her mouth and began to cry for a young student in the White of Beginning Mastery who had once put a shell to her ear so she could hear the sea.

2

SHE REACHED CAITHNARD four days later, the sea, green and white as Ylon's memory, rolled her father's ship into the harbor with an exuberant twist of froth, and she disembarked, after it anchored, with relief. She stood watching sailors unload sacks of seed, plowhorses, sheepskins and wool from the ship next to them; and, farther down, from a ship trimmed in orange and gold, strong, shaggy-hooved horses and gilded chests. Her own horse was brought to her; her father's ship-master, Bri Corbett, came down finally, issuing reminders to the crew all the way down the ramp, to escort her to the College. He swivelled an eye bleak as an oyster at a sailor who was gaping at Raederle from under a grain sack, and the sailor shut his mouth. Then he took the reins of their mounts, began threading a slow path through the crowded docks.

"There's Joss Merle, down from Osterland, I'll wager," he said, and pointed out to Raederle a low, wide-bellied ship with pine-colored sails. "Packed to the boom with furs. Why he doesn't spin circles in that tub, I'll never know. And there's Halster Tull, there, on the other side of the orange ship. Your pardon, Lady. To a man who was once a trader, being at Caithnard in spring is like being in your father's wine cellar with an empty cup; you don't know where to look first."

She smiled a little and realized, from the stiffness of her face, how long it had been since she had last done it. "I like hearing about them," she said politely, knowing her silence during the past days had worried him. A cluster of young women were chattering at the ramp of the orange and yellow ship in front of them. Their long, elegant robes wove, glinting, with the air; they seemed to be pointing every conceivable direction, their faces bright with excitement as they talked, and her smile deepened slightly. "Whose is the orange ship?"

The ship-master opened his mouth. Then he closed it again, frowning. "I've never seen it before. But I would swear . . . No. It couldn't be."

"What?"

"The Morgol's guards. She so rarely leaves Herun."

"Who are?"

"Those young women. Pretty as flowers, but show one of them the wrong side of your hand and you'd wind up in the water halfway to Hed." He cleared his throat uncomfortably. "Your pardon."

"Don't talk about crows, either."

"No." Then he shook his head slowly. "A crow. And I would have sailed him with my own hands, if need be, clear up the Ose to Erlenstar Mountain."

She stepped around a precarious stack of wine kegs. Her eyes slid suddenly to his face. "Could you? Take my father's ship all the way up the Ose?"

"Well. No. There's not a ship in the world that could take the Pass, with all its rapids and falls. But I would have tried, if he'd asked me."

"How far could he have gone by ship?"

"To Kraal, by sea, then up the Winter River to join with the Ose near Isig. But it's a slow journey upriver, especially in spring when the snow waters are making for the sea. And you'd need a shorter keel than your father's ship has."

"Oh."

"It's a broad, placid river, the Winter, to the eye, but it can shift ground so much in a year you'd swear you were sailing a different river. It's like your father; you never quite know what it's going to do next." He flushed deeply, but she only nodded, watching the forest of genially bobbing masts.

"Devious."

They mounted when they reached the street and rode through the bustling city, up the road that wound above the white beaches to the ancient College. There were a few students sprawled on the ground, reading with their chins on their fists; they did not bother to look up until the ship-master made the rare gesture of knocking. A student in the Red with a harried expression on his face swung open the door and inquired rather abruptly of his business.

"We have come to see Rood of An."

"If I were you, I would try a tavern. The Lost Sailor, by the wharf, is a good bet, or the King's Oyster—" He saw Raederle, then, mounted behind the ship-master, and took a step toward her. "I'm sorry, Raederle. Will you come in and wait?"

She put a name finally to the lean, red-haired riddler. "Tes. I remember. You taught me how to whistle."

His face broke into a pleased smile. "Yes. I was in the Blue of Partial Beginning, and you were—you . . . Anyway," he added at the ship-master's expression, "the Masters' library is empty, if you would care to wait."

"No, thank you," she said. "I know where the Lost Sailor is, but where is the King's Oyster?"

"On Cutters Street. You remember it; it used to be the Sea-Witch's Eye."

"Who," Bri Corbett barked, "in Hel's name do you think you're talking to? How would she know the name or whereabouts of any inn or tavern in any city anywhere in this realm?"

"I know," Raederle said with some asperity, "because every time I come here Rood either has his nose in a book or a cup. I was hoping this time it would be a book." She stopped, then, uneasy, crumpling the reins in her hands. "Has he—have you heard the news out of Hed?"

"Yes." His head bowed; he repeated softly, "Yes. A trader brought the news last night. The College is in a turmoil. I haven't seen Rood since then, and I've been up all night with the Masters." She sighed, and his head came up. "I would help you look, but I'm due down at the docks to escort the Morgol to the College."

"It's all right. We'll find him."

"I'll find him," Bri Corbett said with emphasis. "Please, Lady, the Caithnard taverns are no place for you."

She turned her horse. "Having a father flying around in the shape of a crow gives you a certain disregard for appearances. Besides, I know which ones are his favorites."

They looked in them all without success. By the time they had asked a half a dozen of them, they had an eager following of young students who knew Rood, and who went through each tavern with methodical and startling thoroughness. Raederle, watching them through a window as they checked under the tables, murmured in amazement, "When does he find time to study?"

Bri Corbett took off his hat, fanned his sweating face with it. "I don't know. Let me take you back to the ship."

"No."

"You're tired. And you must be hungry. And your father will trim my sails for me if he ever hears of this. I'll find Rood and bring him to the ship."

"I want to find him. I want to talk to him."

The students jostled without their quarry back out of the inn. One of them called to her, "The Heart's Hope Inn on Fish-Market Street. We'll try that."

"Fish-Market Street?"

"The south horn of the harbor. You might," he added thoughtfully, "want to wait for us here."

"I'll come," she said.

The street, under the hot eye of the afternoon sun, seemed to shimmer with the smell of fish lying gutted and glassy-eyed in the market stalls. The ship-master groaned softly. Raederle, thinking of the journey they had made from the contemplative peace of the College through the maze of Caithnard to the most noisome street in the city, littered with assorted fishheads, backbones and spitting cats, began to laugh weakly.

"Heart's Hope Inn . . ."

"There it is," Bri Corbett said heavily as the students disappeared into it. He seemed almost beyond speech. The inn was small, tired, settling on its hindquarters with age, but beyond its dirty, mullioned windows there seemed to be an unwarranted, very colorful collage of activity. The ship-master put his hand on the neck of Raederle's mount. He looked at her. "No more. I'll take you back now."

She stared wearily at the worn stone threshold of the inn. "I don't know where else to look. Maybe the beaches. I want to find him, though. Sometimes there's one thing worse than knowing precisely what Rood is thinking, and that's not knowing what he's thinking."

"I'll find him, I swear it. You—" The inn door opened abruptly, and he turned his head. One of the students who had been helping them was precipitated bodily to the cobble-stones under the nose of Bri Corbett's horse. He staggered to his feet and panted, "He's there."

"Rood?" Raederle exclaimed.

"Rood." He touched a corner of his bleeding mouth with the tip of his tongue and added, "You should see it. It's awesome."

He flung the door wide and plunged back into a turmoil of color, a maelstrom of blue, white and gold that whirled and collided against a flaming core of red. The ship-master stared at it almost wistfully. Raederle dropped her face in her hands. Then she slid tiredly off her horse. A robe of Intermediate Mastery, minus its wearer, shot out over her head, drifted to a gold puddle on the stones. She went to the door, the noise in the tavern drowning the ship-master's sudden, gargled protest. Rood was surfacing in his bright, torn robe from the heaving tangle of bodies.

His face looked meditative, austere, in spite of the split on one cheekbone, as if he were quietly studying instead of dodging fists in a tavern brawl. She watched, fascinated, as a goose, plucked and headless, flapped across the air above his head and thumped into a wall. Then she called to him. He did not hear her, one of his knees occupying the small of a student's back while he shook another, a little wiry student in the White, off his arm onto the outraged innkeeper. A powerful student in the Gold, with a relentless expression on his face, caught Rood from behind by the neck and one wrist, and said politely, "Lord, will you stop before I take you apart and count your bones?" Rood, blinking a little at the grip on his neck, moved abruptly; the student loosed him and sat down slowly on the wet floor, bent over himself and gasping. There was a general attack then, from the small group of students who had come with Raederle. Raederle, wincing, lost sight of Rood again; he rose finally near her, breathing deeply, his hands full of a brawny fisherman who looked as massive and impervious as the great White Bull of Aum. Rood's fist, catching him somewhere under his ribs, barely troubled him. Raederle watched while he gathered the throat of Rood's robe in one great hand, clenched the other and drew it back, and then she lifted a wine flagon in her hand, one that she could not remember picking up, and brought it down on the head of the bull.

He let go of Rood and sat down blinking in a shower of wine and glass. She stared down at him, appalled. Then she looked at Rood, who was staring at her.

His stillness spread through the inn until only private, fierce struggles in corners still flared. He was, she saw with surprise, sober as a stone. Faces, blurred, battle-drunk, were turning towards her all over the room; the innkeeper, holding two heads he was about to bang together, was gazing at her, open-mouthed, and she thought of the dead, surprised fish in the stalls. She dropped the neck of the flagon; the clink of it breaking sounded frail in the silence. She flushed hotly and said to the statue that was Rood, "I'm sorry. I didn't mean to interrupt. But I've been looking all over Caithnard for you, and I didn't want him to hit you before I could talk to you."

He moved finally, to her relief. He turned, lost his balance briefly, caught it, and said to the innkeeper, "Send the bill to my father."

He stepped off the porch with a jar he must have felt to his teeth, reached for Raederle's horse and clung to it, his face against the saddlecloth a moment before he spoke to her. Then he lifted his head, blinked at her. "You're still here. I didn't think I'd been drinking. What in Hel's name are you doing standing in all those fishbones?"

"What in Hel's name do you think I'm doing here?" she demanded. Her voice, strained, low, let free finally all the grief, confusion and fear she felt. "I need you."

He straightened, slid an arm around her shoulders, held her tightly, and said to the ship-master, who had dropped his head in his hands and was shaking it, "Thank you. Will you send someone to take my things out of the College?"

Bri Corbett's head came up. "Everything, Lord?"

"Everything. Every dead word and dry wine stain in that room. Everything."

He took Raederle to a quiet inn in the heart of the city. Seated with a flagon of wine in front of them, he watched her drink in silence, his hands linked over his own cup. He said finally, softly, "I don't believe he is dead."

"Then what do you believe? That he was simply driven mad and lost the land-rule? That's a comforting thought. Is that why you were tearing that inn apart?"

He shifted, his eyes falling. "No." He reached out, put his hand on her wrist, and her fingers, molding the metal of her cup, loosened and came to rest on the table. She whispered, "Rood, that's the terrible thing I can't get out of my mind. That while I was waiting, while we were all waiting, safe and secure, thinking he was with the High One, he was alone with someone who was picking his mind apart as you would pick apart the petals of a closed flower. And the High One did nothing."

"I know. One of the traders brought the news up to the College yesterday. The Masters were stunned. Morgon unearthed such a vipers' nest of riddles, and then so inconveniently died without answering them. Which put the entire problem at their door, since the College exists to answer the answerable. The Masters are set face-to-face with their own strictures. This riddle is literally deadly, and they began wondering exactly how interested they are in truth." He took a sip of his wine, looked at her again. "Do you know what happened?"

"What?"

"Eight old Masters and nine Apprentices argued all night about who would travel to Erlenstar Mountain to speak to the High One. Every one of them wanted to go."

She touched the torn sleeve of his robe. "You're an Apprentice."

"No. I told Master Tel yesterday I was leaving. Then I—then I went to the beach and sat up all night, not doing anything, not even thinking. I came into Caithnard finally and stopped at that inn for something to eat, and while—while I was eating, I remembered an argument I had with Morgon before he left about not facing his own destiny, not living up to his own standards when all he wanted to do was make beer and read books. So he went and found his destiny in some remote corner of the realm, driven, by the sound of it, mad as Peven. So. I decided to take the inn apart. Nail by nail. And then go and answer the riddles he couldn't answer."

She gave a little, unsurprised nod. "I thought you might. Well, that's another piece of news I have to give you."

He touched his cup again, said warily, "What?"

"Our father left An five days ago to do just that. He—" She winced as his hands went down sharply on the table, causing a trader at the next table to choke on his beer.

"He left An? For how long?"

"He didn't . . . He swore by the ancient Kings to find what it was that killed Morgon. That long. Rood, don't shout."

He swallowed it, rendered himself momentarily wordless. "The old crow."

"Yes . . . He left Duac at Anuin to explain to the lords. Our father was going to send for you to help Duac, but he wouldn't say why, and Duac was furious that he wanted you to abandon your studies."

"Did Duac send you to bring me home?"

She shook her head. "He didn't even want me to tell you. He swore that he wouldn't send for you until the wraiths of Hel crossed the threshold at Anuin."

"He did that?" Rood said with disgusted wonder. "He's getting as irrational as our father. He would have let me sit in Caithnard studying for a rank that suddenly has very little meaning while he tries to keep order among the living and dead of An. I'd rather go home and play riddle-games with the dead kings."

"Will you?"

"What?"

"Go home? It's a—it's a smaller thing to ask of you than going to Erlenstar Mountain, but Duac will need you. And our father—"

"Is a very capable and subtle old crow . . ." He was silent, frowning, his thumbnail picking at a flaw in his cup. He leaned back in his chair finally and sighed. "All right. I can't let Duac face that alone. At least I can be there to tell him which dead king is which, if nothing else. There's nothing I could do in Erlenstar Mountain that our father wouldn't do, and probably do better. I would give the Black of Mastery to see the world out of his eyes. But if he gets into trouble, I don't promise not to look for him."

"Good. Because that's another thing Duac said he wouldn't do."

His mouth crooked. "Duac seems to have lost his temper. I can't say that I blame him."

"Rood . . . Have you ever known our father to be wrong?"

"A hundred times."

"No. Not irritating, frustrating, annoying, incomprehensible and exasperating. Just wrong."

"Why?"

She shrugged slightly. "When he heard about Morgon—that's the first time in my life I can remember seeing him surprised. He—"

"What are you thinking about?" He leaned forward abruptly. "That vow he made to marry you to Morgon?"

"Yes. I always wondered a little, if it might have been foreknowledge. I thought maybe that's why he was so surprised."

She heard him swallow; his eyes, speculative, indrawn, reminded her of Mathom. "I don't know. I wonder. If so—"

"Then Morgon must be alive."

"But where? In what circumstances? And why in the name of the roots of the world won't the High One help him? That's the greatest riddle of them all: the miasma of silence coming out of that mountain."

"Well, if our father goes there, it won't be so silent." She shook her head wearily. "I don't know. I don't know which to hope for. If he is alive, can you imagine what a stranger he must be even to himself? And he must—he must wonder why none of us who loved him tried to help him."

Rood opened his mouth, but the answer he would have given her seemed to wither on his tongue. He brought the heels of his hands up to his eyes. "Yes. I'm tired. If he is alive—"

"Our father will find him. You said you would help Duac."

"All right. But . . . All right." He dropped his hands, stared into his wine. Then he pushed his chair back slowly. "We'd better go; I have books to pack."

She followed him again into the bright, noisy street. It seemed, for a moment, to be flowing past her in a marvellous, incomprehensible pattern of color, and she stopped, blinking. Rood put a hand on her arm. She realized then that she had nearly stepped in front of a small, elegant procession. A woman led it. She sat tall and beautiful on a black mount, her dark hair braided and jewelled like a crown on her head, her light, shapeless green coat of some cloth that seemed to flow like a mist into the wind. Six young women whom Raederle had seen at the dock followed her in two lines, their robes, saddlecloths and reins of rich, vivid colors, their spears of ash inlaid with silver. One of them, riding close behind the Morgol, had the same black hair and fine, clean cast of face. Behind the guard came eight men on foot carrying two chests painted and banded with copper and gold; they were followed by eight students from the College, riding according to their ranks and the color of their robes: scarlet, gold, blue and white. The woman, riding as serenely through the press as through a meadow, glanced down suddenly as she passed the inn; at the brief, vague touch of the gold eyes, Raederle felt the odd shock, unfamiliar and deep within her, of a recognition of power.

Rood breathed beside her, "The Morgol of Herun . . ."

He moved so quickly after the procession passed, gripping her wrist and pulling her, that she nearly lost her balance. She protested, "Rood!" as he ran to catch up with it, tugging her past amazed spectators, but he was shouting himself.

"Tes! Tes!" He caught up finally, Raederle flushed and irritated behind him, with the red-robed scholar. Tes stared down at him.

"What did you do? Fall face first in an empty wine bottle?"

"Tes, let me take your place. Please." He caught at the reins, but Tes flicked them out of reach.

"Stop that. Do you want us to get out of pace? Rood, are you drunk?"

"No. I swear it. I'm sober as a dead man. She's bringing Iff's books; you can see them any time, but I'm going home tonight—"

"You're what?"

"I have to leave. Please."

"Rood," Tess said helplessly. "I would, but do you realize what you look like?"

"Change with me. Tes. Please. Please."

Tes sighed. He pulled up sharply, tangling the line of horsemen behind him, slid off his horse and pulled wildly at the buttons on his robe. Rood tore his own robe over his head and thrust himself into Tes's, while the riders behind them made caustic remarks about his assertion of sobriety. He leaped onto Tes's horse and reached down for Raederle.

"Rood, my horse—"

"Tes can ride it back up. It's the chestnut back there at the inn; the saddlecloth has her initials on it. Come up—" She put her foot on his in the stirrup and he pulled her urgently into the saddle in front of him, urging the horse into a quick trot to catch up with the second, receding line of scholars. He shouted back, "Tes, thank you!"

Raederle, clenching her teeth against the jog of cobblestones, refrained from comment until he had brought the small line of riders behind him back into the sedately moving procession. Then she said, shifting down from the hard edge of the saddle, "Do you have any idea of how ridiculous that must have looked?"

"Do you know what we're about to see? Private books of the wizard Iff, opened. The Morgol opened them herself. She's donating them to the College; the Masters have been talking of nothing else for weeks. Besides, I've always been curious about her. They say all information passes eventually through the Morgol's house and that the High One's harpist loves her."

"Deth?" She mulled over the thought curiously. "Then I wonder if she knows where he is. No one else seems to."

"If anyone does, she does."

Raederle was silent, remembering the strange insight she had glimpsed in the Morgol's eyes, and her own unexpected recognition of it. They left the noisy, crowded streets behind them gradually; the road widened, rising toward the high cliff and the dark, wind-battered college. The Morgol, glancing back, set a slower pace uphill for the men carrying the chests. Raederle, looping out over the ocean, saw Hed partly misted under a blue-grey spring storm. She wondered suddenly, intensely, as she had never wondered before, what lay at the heart of the small, simple island that it had produced out of its life and history the Star-Bearer. And then, briefly, it seemed she could see beneath the rain mists on the island to where a young man colored and thewed like an oak, was crossing the yard from a barn to a house, his yellow head bent under the rain.

She moved abruptly, murmuring; Rood put a hand up to steady her. "What's the matter?"

"Nothing. I don't know. Rood—"

"What?"

"Nothing."

One of the guards detached herself then from the line, rode back towards them. She turned her horse again to ride beside them in a single, flowing movement of mount and rider that seemed at once controlled and instinctive. She said politely, appraising them, "The Morgol, who was introduced to the students at the docks, is interested in knowing who joined her escort in the place of Tes."

"I am Rood of An," Rood said. "This is my sister, Raederle. And I am—or I was until last night—an Apprentice at the College."

"Thank you." She paused a little, looking at Raederle; something young, oddly surprised, broke through the dark, preoccupied expression in her eyes. She added unexpectedly, "I am Lyraluthuin. The daughter of the Morgol."

She cantered back to the head of the procession. Rood, his eyes on the tall, lithe figure, gave a soft whistle.

"I wonder if the Morgol needs an escort back to Herun."

"You're going to Anuin."

"I could go to Anuin by way of Herun . . . She's coming back."

"The Morgol," Lyra said, rejoining them, "would like very much to speak with you."

Rood pulled out of line, following her up the hill. Raederle, sitting half-on and half-off the saddlebow, clinging to Rood and the horse's mane as she jounced, felt slightly silly. But the Morgol, her face lighting with a smile, seemed only pleased to see them.

"So you are Mathom's children," she said. "I have always wanted to meet your father. You joined my escort rather precipitously, and I did not expect at all to find in it the second most beautiful woman of An."

"I came to Caithnard to give Rood some news," Raederle said simply. The Morgol's smile faded; she nodded.

"I see. We heard the news only this morning, when we docked. It was unexpected." She looked at Rood. "Lyra tells me that you are no longer an Apprentice at the College. Have you lost faith in riddle-mastery?"

"No. Only my patience." His voice sounded husky; Raederle, glancing at him, found that he was blushing, as far as she knew, for the first time in his life.

The Morgol said softly, "Yes. So have I. I have brought seven of Iff's books and twenty others that have been collected in the library at the City of Circles through the centuries to give to the College, and a piece of news that, like the news from Hed, should stir even the dust in the Masters' library."

"Seven," Rood breathed. "You opened seven of Iff's books?"

"No. Only two. The wizard himself, the day that we left for Caithnard, opened the other five."

Rood wrenched at his reins; Raederle swayed against him. The guard behind him broke their lines abruptly to avoid bumping into him; the men bearing the chests came to a quick halt, and the students, who had not been paying attention, reined into one another, cursing. The Morgol stopped.

"Iff is alive?" He seemed oblivious of the mild chaos in his wake.

"Yes. He had hidden himself in my guard. He had been in the Herun court, in one guise or another, for seven centuries, for he said it was, even in its earlier days, a place of scholarship. He said—" Her voice caught; they heard, when she continued, the rare touch of wonder in it. "He said he had been the old scholar who helped me to open those two books. When the scholar died, he became my falconer, and then a guard. But that he didn't care for. He took his own shape on the day they say Morgon died."

"Who freed him?" Rood whispered.

"He didn't know."

Raederle put her hands to her mouth, suddenly no longer seeing the Morgol's face, but the ancient, strong-boned face of the pig-woman of Hel, with the aftermath of a great and terrible darkness in her eyes.

"Rood," she whispered. "Raith's pig-woman. She heard some news Elieu brought from Isig about the Star-Bearer, and she shouted a shout that scattered the pig herds of Hel like thistledown. Then she disappeared. She named . . . she named one boar Aloil."

She heard the draw of his breath. "Nun?"

"Maybe the High One freed them."

"The High One." Something in the Morgol's tone, thoughtful as it was, reminded Raederle of Mathom. "I don't know why he would have helped the wizards and not the Star-Bearer, but I am sure, if that is the case, that he had his reasons." She glanced down the road, saw the lines in order and resumed her pace. They had nearly reached the top of the hill; the grounds, shadowed and gilded with oak leaves, stretched beyond the road's end.

Rood glanced at the Morgol, asked with unusual hesitancy, "May I ask you something?"

"Of course, Rood."

"Do you know where the High One's harpist is?"

The Morgol did not answer for a moment, her eyes on the bulky, rough-hewn building whose windows and doors were brilliant with color as the students crowded to watch her arrival. Then she looked down at her hands. "No. I have had no word from him."

The Masters came out, black as crows among the swirl of red and gold, to meet the Morgol. The chests were carried up to the library, the books examined lovingly by the Masters as they listened with wonder to the Morgol's tale of how she had opened the two. Raederle glanced at one set on the broad stand made for it. The black writing looked pinched and ascetic, but she found unexpectedly, turning a page, precise, delicate drawings of wild flowers down the margin. It made her think again of the pig-woman, smoking her pipe with her bare feet among the oak roots, and she smiled a little, wonderingly. Then the one still figure in the room caught her eye: Lyra, standing by the door in a habitual stance, her back straight, her feet apart, as if she were keeping watch over the room. But her eyes were smudged with a blackness, and she was seeing nothing.

The room fell silent as the Morgol told the Masters of the reappearance of the wizard Iff. She asked Raederle to repeat the tale of the pig-woman, and Raederle complied, giving them also the startling news that had brought Elieu down from Isig. That, no one had heard, not even the Morgol, and there was an outburst of amazement after she finished. They asked questions in their kind voices she could not answer; they asked questions among themselves no one could answer. Then the Morgol spoke again. What she said Raederle did not hear, only the silence that was passed like a tangible thing from Master to Master, from group to group in the room until there was not a sound in the room except one very old Master's breathing. The Morgol's expression had not changed; only her eyes had grown watchful.

"Master Ohm" said a frail, gentle Master whose name was Tel, "was with us at all times until last spring, when he journeyed to Lungold for a year of peaceful study and contemplation. He could have gone anywhere he wished; he chose the ancient city of the wizards. His letters to us have been carried by the traders from Lungold." He paused, his passionless, experienced eyes on her face. "El, you are as known and respected for your intelligence and integrity as is this College; if there is any criticism you would make of it, don't hesitate to tell us."

"It is the integrity of the College that I question, Master Tel," the Morgol said softly, "in the person of Master Ohm, who I doubt you will ever see within these walls again. And I question the intelligence of us all, myself included. Shortly before I left Herun, I had a visit from the King of Osterland, who came very simply and privately. He wondered if I had news of Morgon of Hed. He said he had gone to Isig, but not to Erlenstar Mountain, for the mists and storms were terrible through the Pass, too terrible even for a vesta. While he was with me, he told me something that reinforced suspicions that I have had since my last visit here. He said that Morgon had told him that the last word the wizard Suth had spoken as he lay dying in Morgon's arms, was Ohm's name. Ohm. Ghisteslwchlohm. The Founder of Lungold, Suth accused with his last breath." She paused, her eyes moving from face to motionless face. "I asked Har if he had taken the question to the College, and he laughed and said that the Masters of Knowledge could recognize neither the Star-Bearer nor the Founder of Lungold."

She paused again, but there was no protest, no excuse from the men listening. Her head bowed slightly. "Master Ohm has been in Lungold since spring. The High One's harpist has not been seen since then, and from all accounts, the High One himself has been silent since then. The death of the Prince of Hed freed the wizards from the power held over them. I suggest that the Founder of Lungold freed the wizards because in killing the Star-Bearer, he no longer needed to fear their power or interference. I also suggest that if this College is to continue to justify its existence, it should examine, very carefully and very quickly, the heart of this impossible, imperative tangle of riddles."

There was a sound like a sigh through the room; it was the sea wind, searching the walls, like a bird, to get free. Lyra turned abruptly; the door had closed behind her before anyone realized she had moved. The Morgol's eyes flicked to the door, then back to the Masters, who had begun to speak again, their voices murmuring, hushed. They began to group themselves around the Morgol. Rood stood with his hands flat on one of the desks, leaning over a book, but his face was bloodless, his shoulders rigid, and Raederle knew he was not seeing it. Raederle took a step towards him. Then she turned, eased through the Masters to the door and went out.

She passed students in the hall waiting, eager and curious, for a glimpse of the books; she scarcely heard their voices. She barely felt the wind, grown cool and restless in the early spring dusk, pulling at her as she walked through the grounds. She saw Lyra standing beneath a tree at the cliff's edge, her back to the College. Something in the taut set of her shoulders, her bowed head, drew Raederle towards her. As she crossed the grounds, Lyra's spear lifted, spun a circle of light in the air, and plunged point down into the earth.

She turned at a rustle of leaf she heard under the rustle of wind-tossed trees. Raederle stopped. They looked at one another silently. Then Lyra, giving shape to the grief and anger in her eyes, said almost challengingly, "I would have gone with him. I would have protected him with my life."

Raederle's eyes moved away from her to the sea . . . the sea far below them, the half-moon of harbor it had hollowed, the jut of land to the north beyond which lay other lands, other harbors. Her hands closed. "My father's ship is here at Caithnard. I can take it as far as Kraal. I want to go to Erlenstar Mountain. Will you help me?"

Lyra's lips parted. Raederle saw a brief flash of surprise and uncertainty in her face. Then she gripped her spear, pulled it again out of the earth and gave a little emphatic nod. "I'll come."

WHEN LYRA TOOK the Morgol's guards into Caithnard later that evening to look for lodgings, Raederle followed them. She had left, in front of Rood's horse in the College stable, a small tangle of bright gold thread she had loosened from her cuff. Within the tangle, in her mind, she had placed her name and an image of Rood stepping on it, or his horse, and then riding without thought every curve and twist of thread through the streets of Caithnard until, reaching the end, he would blink free of the spell and find that neither the ship nor the tide had waited for him. He would suspect her, she knew, but there would be nothing he could do but ride back to Anuin, while Bri Corbett, under the urgings of the Morgol's guard, sailed north.

The guard had not been told. She heard fragments of their conversation, their laughter under the hollow, restless boom of the sea as she rode behind them down the hill. It was nearly dark; the wind dulled her horse's steps, but still she kept, as Lyra had advised, a distance between her and the guard. She felt, all the way into Caithnard, the touch of the Morgol's eyes at her back.

She caught up with the guard at a quiet side street near the docks. They were looking a little bewildered; one girl said, "Lyra, there's nothing but warehouses here." Lyra, without answering, turned her head and saw Raederle. Raederle met her brief, searching gaze, then Lyra looked at the guard. Something in her face quieted them. Her hand tightened and loosened on her spear. Then she lifted her chin.

"I am leaving tonight for Erlenstar Mountain with Raederle of An. I am doing this without permission from the Morgol; I am deserting the guard. I couldn't protect the Prince of Hed while he was alive; all I can do now is find out from the High One who killed him and where that one is. We're sailing to Kraal in her father's ship. The ship-master has not yet been informed. I can't . . . Wait a minute. I can't ask you to help me. I can't hope that you would do such a shameful, disgraceful thing as leaving the Morgol alone, unguarded in a strange city. I don't know how I can do it. But what I do know is that we can't steal a ship by ourselves."

There was a silence when she stopped, but for a door rattling back and forth somewhere in the wind. The guards' faces were expressionless. Then one of them, a girl with a silky blond braid and a sweet, sunburned face, said fiercely, "Lyra, are you out of your mind?" She looked at Raederle. "Are you both out of your minds?"

"No," Raederle said. "There's not a trader in the realm who would take us, but my father's ship-master has already half an inclination to go. He could never be persuaded, but he could be forced. He respects you, and once he grasps the situation, I don't think he'll argue much."

"But what will the Morgol say? What will your own people say?"

"I don't know. I don't care."

The girl shook her head, speechless. "Lyra—"

"Imer, you have three choices. You can leave us here and go back to the College and inform the Morgol. You can take us by force back to the College, which would greatly exceed your duty and would offend the people of An, not to mention me. You can come with us. The Morgol has twenty guards waiting in Hlurle to escort her back to Crown City; all she has to do is send word to them, and they'll join her at Caithnard. She'll be safe. What she will say to you, however, if she finds that you have let me go off by myself to Erlenstar Mountain, I would not like to hear."

Another girl, with a dark, plain face, and the rough timbre of the Herun hill towns in her voice, said reasonably, "She'll think we've all deserted."

"Goh, I'll tell her it was my responsibility."

"You can hardly tell her you coerced us all. Lyra, stop being a fool and go back to the College," Imer said.

"No. And if you touch me, I will resign immediately from the guard. You'll have no right to use force against the land-heir of Herun." She paused, her eyes moving from face to face. Someone sighed.

"How far do you think you'll get, with the Morgol's ship half a day behind you? She'll see you."

"Then what have you got to worry about? You know you can't let me go to Erlenstar Mountain by myself."

"Lyra. We are the chosen guard of the Morgol. We are not thieves. We are not kidnappers."

"Then go back to the College." The contempt in her voice held them motionless. "You have the choice. Go back to Herun with the Morgol. You know as much as anyone what the Star-Bearer was. You know how he died, while the world went about minding its own business. If no one demands answers from the High One about the wizard who killed him, about the shape-changers, then I think one day much too soon a hundred guards at Crown City will not be enough to protect the Morgol from disaster. If I have to walk to Erlenstar Mountain, I'll do it. Will you help me or not?"

They were silent again, lined against her, Raederle saw, like warriors in a field, their faces shadowed, unreadable. Then a small, black-haired girl with delicate, slanting brows said resignedly, "Well, if we can't force you to stay, maybe the ship-master will bring you to your senses. How do you propose to steal his ship?"

She told them. There was grumbling, argument over the method, but it lacked fire; their voices died away finally. They sat waiting resignedly. Lyra turned her horse. "All right, then."

They fell into casual position behind her. Raederle, riding beside her, saw in a wash of inn-light, that Lyra's hands were shaking on the reins. She frowned down at her own reins a moment, then reached across to touch Lyra. The dark head lifted; Lyra said, "This is the easy part, stealing a ship."

"It's hardly stealing. It's my father's ship, and he's in no position to quibble. I don't—there's no one in An who will judge me, but you have your own kind of honor."

"It's all right. It's just that I've trained for seven years in the Morgol's guard, and in Herun I have thirty guards under my command. It goes against all my training to leave the Morgol like this, taking her guard with me. It's unheard of."

"She'll be safe at the College."

"I know. But what will she think of me?" She slowed her horse as they came to the end of the street and saw the King's ship in the moonlight, pulling restlessly at its anchor. There was a light in the charthouse. They heard a thud from the deck, and someone said, panting, "That's the last of Rood's books. If we all don't find ourselves, along with them, at the bottom of the sea, I'll eat one, iron bindings and all. I'm going for a quick cup before we sail."

Lyra glanced behind her; two of the guards dismounted, went soundlessly after him as he strode whistling down the dock. The others followed her and Raederle to the ramp of the ship. Raederle, hearing only the slough of water, the rattle of chain and her own quiet steps, glanced behind once to make sure they were still there. She felt, at their eerie silence, as though she were followed by ghosts. One slipped away at the top of the ramp to check the deck of the ship; the other two went with Lyra to the hold. Raederle waited a few moments for them to do their work beneath the deck. Then she entered the chart house, where Bri Corbett was exchanging gossip and a cup of wine with a trader. He glanced up, surprised.

"You didn't ride down alone, did you? Did Rood bring the horses up?"

"No. He's not coming."

"He's not coming? Then what does he want done with all his things?" He eyed her suspiciously. "He's not going off somewhere on his own like his father, is he?"

"No." She swallowed the dryness from her mouth. "I am. I'm going to Erlenstar Mountain; you will take me as far as Kraal. If you don't, the Morgol's ship-master, I'm sure, can be persuaded to take over the ship."

"What?" Bri Corbett rose, his grey brows lifting to his hairline. The trader was grinning. "Someone else sail your father's ship? Over my dead and buried bones, maybe. You're distraught, child, come and sit—" Lyra, spear in hand, slid like a wraith into the light, and he stopped. Raederle could hear his breathing. The trader stopped grinning. Lyra said, "Most of the crew was below. Imer and Goh have them under guard. They weren't taken seriously at first, until one man got pinned to a ladder with an arrow in his sleeve and his pant leg—he's not hurt—and Goh shot the cork out of one of the wine kegs with another. They're pleading for someone to put the cork back in."

"That's their ration of wine for the journey," Bri Corbett breathed. "Good Herun wine." The trader had edged to his feet. Lyra's eyes moved to him and he stilled.

Raederle said, "Two guards followed the man who left the ship; they will be finding the rest of your crew. Bri, you wanted to go to Erlenstar Mountain anyway. You said so."

"You were—you weren't taking me seriously!"

"You might not be serious. I am."

"But your father! He'll curse the teeth out of my head when he finds out I'm taking his daughter and the land-heir of Herun on some misbegotten journey. The Morgol will have Herun up in arms."

"If you don't want to captain the ship, we'll find someone who will. There are plenty of men in the taverns, on the docks, who could be paid to take your place. If you want, we'll leave you tied somewhere along with this trader, to assure everyone of your complete innocence."

"Roust me from my own ship!" His voice cracked.

"Listen to me, Bri Corbett," she said evenly. "I lost a friend I loved and a man I might have married somewhere between Isig Pass and Erlenstar Mountain. Will you tell me what I have to go home for? More endless silence and waiting at Anuin? The Lords of the Three Portions bickering over me while the world cracks apart like Morgon's mind? Raith of Hel?"

"I know." His hand went out to her. "I understand. But you can't—"

"You said you would sail this ship to the High One's doorstep if my father had asked. Did you ever think that my father might find himself in the same danger Morgon was in? Do you want to sail comfortably back to Anuin and leave him there? If you force us by some chance off this ship, we'll go by other means. Will you want to go to Anuin and give Duac that news, on top of everything else? I have questions. I want answers to them. I am going to Erlenstar Mountain. Do you want to sail this ship for us, or shall I find someone else to do it?"

Bri Corbett brought his clenched fist down on the table. He stared at it a moment, red, wordless. Then his head lifted again slowly; he gazed at Raederle as if she had just come in the door and he had forgotten why. "You'll need another ship at Kraal. I told you that."

"I know." Her voice shook slightly at the look in his eyes.

"I can find you one at Kraal. You'll let me take it up the Winter?"

"I'd rather . . . I'd rather have you than anyone."

"We don't have supplies enough for Kraal. We'll have to stop at Caerweddin, maybe, or Hlurle."

"I've never seen Caerweddin."

"It's a beautiful city; Kraal at Isig—lovely places. I haven't seen them since . . . We'll need more wine. The crew's a good one, the best I've ever sailed with, but they worry about essentials."

"I have some money, and some jewels. I thought I might need them."

"You did." He drew a long breath. "You remind me of someone. Someone devious." The trader made an inarticulate protest, and Bri's eyes went to Lyra. "What," he inquired respectfully, "would you like to do with that one? You let him go, and he'll be pounding at the College door before we get out of the harbor."

Lyra considered him. "We could tie him, leave him on the docks. They'll find him in the morning."

"I won't say a word," the trader said, and Bri laughed.

Raederle said quickly, "Bri, he is the one witness to the fact that you aren't responsible for this; will you remember your own reputation?"

"Lady, either I'm going because half a dozen half-grown women took over my ship, or because I'm mad enough to want to take Mathom's daughter and the Morgol's land-heir up to the high point of the world by themselves. Either way, I'm not left with much in the way of a reputation. You'd better let me see if my crew's all here; we should get underway."

They found part of the crew arriving, escorted up the ramp by two of the Morgol's guards. The men, at the sight of Bri Corbett, broke into bewildered explanations; Bri said calmly, "We're being kidnapped. You'll be getting extra pay for the privilege. We're heading north. See who is missing, and ask the rest of the men in the hold if they would kindly come up and do their jobs. Tell them to cork the wine; we'll get more in Ymris, and that they'll get no sympathy from me if they lay a finger on the Morgol's guards."

The two guards looked questioningly at Lyra, who nodded. "One of you stand at the hatch; the other watch the docks. I want this ship under guard until it clears the harbor." She added to Bri Corbett, "I trust you. But I don't know you, and I'm trained to be careful. So I'll watch you work. And remember: I've spent more nights than I can count under the open sky, and I know which stars point north."

"And I," Bri said, "have seen the Morgol's guards in training. You'll get no argument from me."

The crew appeared, disgusted and puzzled, to be dispatched to their duties under the watchful eyes of the guard. One last sailor came up the ramp singing. He eyed the guards with aplomb, winked at Lyra, and reached down to Imer, who was kneeling and tying the trader's wrists, lifted her chin in his hand and kissed her.

She pushed him away, losing her balance, and the trader, pulling the rope off his hands, caught her under the chin with his head as he rose. She sat down heavily on the deck. The trader, tripping a sailor in his way, dove for the ramp. Something he scarcely saw, glistening faintly, fell in front of him as he ran down the ramp. He ignored an arrow that cut into the wood a second before his foot hit it. The sailors crowded curiously to the rail beside the guards as they shot. Bri Corbett, shouldering between Lyra and Raederle, cursed.

"I suppose you shouldn't hit him," he said wistfully. Lyra, signalling a halt to the shooting, did not answer. There was a sudden cry and a splash; they leaned forward out over the rail. "What ails the man? Is he hurt?" They heard him cursing as he splashed in the water, then the drag of a mooring chain as he pulled himself back up. His step sounded again, quick, steady, and then there was another splash. "Madir's bones," Bri breathed. "He can't even see straight. He's coming back toward us. He must be drunk. He could tell the world I have the Morgol, the King of An and fourteen wizards aboard, for all anyone would believe his tale. Is he going in again?" There was a muffled thud. "No; he fell in a rowboat." He glanced at Raederle, who had begun to laugh weakly.

"I forgot about the water. Poor man."

Lyra's eyes slid uncertainly to her face. "What . . . Did you do something? What exactly did you do?"

She showed them her frayed cuff. "Just a little thing the pig-woman taught me to do with a tangled piece of thread . . ."

The ship got underway finally, slipping like a dream out of the dark harbor, leaving the scattering of city lights and the beacons flaring on the black horns of the land. Lyra, relaxing her guard when the ship turned unerringly northward and the west wind hit their cheeks, joined Raederle at the side. They did not speak for a while; the handful of lights vanished as the cliffs rose under the stars to block them. The jagged rim of unknown land running like a black thread against the sky was the only thing to be seen. Then Raederle, shivering a little in the cool night wind, her hands tightening on the rail, said softly, "It's what I've been wanting to do for two years, since he lost that crown somewhere around here in the bottom of the sea. But I couldn't have done it alone. I've never been farther than Caithnard in my life, and the realm seems enormous." She paused, her eyes on a moonlit swirl and dip of froth; she added with simple pain, "I only wish I had done it sooner."

Lyra's body made a rare, restive movement against the side. "How could any one of us have known to go? He was the Star-Bearer; he had a destiny. Men with destinies have their own protection. And he was travelling to the High One escorted by the High One's harpist. How could we have known that not even the High One would help him? Or help even his own harpist?"

Raederle looked at her shadowed profile. "Deth? Does the Morgol think he is dead?"

"She doesn't know. She— that was one reason she came here, to see if the Masters had any knowledge of what might have happened to him."

"Why didn't she go to Erlenstar Mountain?"

"I asked her. She said because the last land-ruler who had gone to see the High One was never seen nor heard of again."

Raederle was silent. Something that was not the wind sent a chill rippling through her. "I always thought Erlenstar Mountain must be the safest, the most beautiful place in the world."

"So did I." Lyra turned as the small, dark-haired guard spoke her name. "What, Kia?"

"The ship-master is giving us quarters in the king's cabin; he says it's the only one big enough for us all. Do you want a guard during the night?"

Lyra looked at Raederle. It was too dark to see her face, but Raederle could sense the question on it. She said slowly, "I would trust him. But why even tempt him to turn back? Can you stay awake?"

"In shifts." She turned to Kia again. "One guard at the helm in two hour shifts until dawn. I'll take the first watch."

"I'll join you," Raederle said.

She spent most of the two hours trying to teach Lyra the simple spell she had worked on the trader. They used a piece of twine the intrigued helmsman gave them. Lyra, frowning down at it for some minutes, threw it in the path of a sailor who walked over it and went serenely about his business.

The helmsman protested. "You'll have us all overboard," but she shook her head.

"I can't do it. I stare and stare at it, but it's only a piece of old twine. There's no magic in my blood."

"Yes, there is," Raederle said. "I felt it. In the Morgol."

Lyra looked at her curiously. "I've never felt it. One day, I'll have her power of sight. But it's a practical thing, nothing like this. This I don't understand."

"Look at it, in your mind, until it's not twine anymore but a path, looped and wound and twisted around itself, that will bind the one who touches it to its turnings . . . See it. Then put your name to it."

"How?"

"Know that you are yourself, and the thing is itself; that's the binding between you, that knowledge."

Lyra bent over the twine again. She was silent a long time, while Raederle and the helmsman watched, then Bri Corbett came out of the charthouse and Lyra tossed the twine under his boot.

"Where," he demanded of the helmsman, "in Hel's name are you taking us? Prow first into the Ymris coast?" He stepped unswervingly to the wheel and straightened their course. Lyra got to her feet with a sigh.

"I am myself, and it's an old piece of twine. That's as far as I can get. What else can you do?"

"Only a few things. Make a net out of grass, make a bramble stem seem like an impossible thorn patch, find my way out of Madir's Woods, where the trees seem to shift from place to place. . . . Little things. I inherited the powers from the wizard Madir, and someone—someone named Ylon. For some reason neither of my brothers could do such things, either. The pig-woman said magic finds its own outlet. It used to frustrate them, though, when we were children, and I could always find my way out of Madir's Woods and they never could."

"An must be a strange land. In Herun, there's very little magic, except what the wizards brought, long ago."

"In An, the land is restless with it. That's why it's such a grave thing that my father left his land indefinitely. Without his control, the magic works itself loose, and all the dead stir awake with their memories."

"What do they do?" Her voice was hushed.

"They remember old feuds, ancient hatreds, battles, and get impulses to revive them. War between the Three Portions in early times was a passionate, tumultuous thing; the old kings and lords died jealous and angry, many of them, so the land-instinct in kings grew to bind even the dead, and the spellbooks of those who played with sorcery, like Madir and Peven . . ."

"And Ylon? Who was he?"

Raederle reached down to pick up the twine. She wound it around her fingers, her brows drawn slightly as she felt the tangle run deceptively smooth and even in her hands. "A riddle."

Imer came then to relieve Lyra, and she and Raederle went gratefully to bed. The easy roll of the ship in the peaceful sea sent Raederle quickly to sleep. She woke again at dawn, before the sun rose. She dressed and went on deck. The sea, the wind, the long line of the Ymris coast were grey under the dawn sky; the mists along the vast, empty eastern horizon were beginning to whiten under the groping sunlight. The last of the guards, looking bleary at her post, glanced at the sky and headed for bed. Raederle went to the side feeling disoriented in the colorless world. She saw a tiny fishing village, a handful of houses against the bone-colored cliffs, nameless on the strange land; its minute fleet of boats was inching out of the dock into open sea. A flock of gulls wheeled crying overhead, grey and white in the morning, then scattered away southward. She wondered if they were flying to An. She felt chilly and purposeless and wondered if she had left her name behind with all her possessions at Anuin.

The sound of someone being sick over the rail made her turn. She stared mutely at the unexpected face, afraid for a moment that she had stolen out of the harbor a ship full of shape-changers. But no shape-changer, she decided, would have changed deliberately into such a miserable young girl. She waited considerately until the girl wiped her mouth and sat down in a pallid heap on the deck. Her eyes closed. Raederle, remembering Rood's agonies when he sailed, went to find the water bucket. She half-expected, returning with the dipper, that the apparition would have vanished, but it was still there, small and inconspicuous, like a bundle of old clothes in a corner.

She knelt down, and the girl lifted her head. She looked, opening her eyes, vaguely outraged, as though the sea and ship had conspired against her. Her hand shook as she took the dipper. It was a lean hand, Raederle saw, strong, brown and calloused, too big, yet, for her slender body. She emptied the dipper, leaned back against the side again.

"Thank you," she whispered. She closed her eyes. "I have never, in my entire life, felt so utterly horrible."

"It will pass. Who are you? How did you get aboard this ship?"

"I came—I came last night. I hid in one of the rowboats, under the canvas, until—until I couldn't stand it anymore. The ship was swaying one way, and the boat was swaying another. I thought I was going to die . . ." She swallowed convulsively, opened her eyes and shut them again quickly. The few freckles on her face stood out sharply. Something in the lines of her face, in the graceful determined bones of it, made Raederle's own throat close suddenly. The girl, taking a gulp of wind, continued, "I was looking for a place to stay last night when I heard you talking by the warehouses. So I just—I just followed you on board, because you were going where I want to go."

"Who are you?" Raederle whispered.

"Tristan of Hed."

Raederle sat back on her heels. A memory, brief and poignant, of

Morgon's face, clearer than she had seen it for years, imposed itself over Tristan's; she felt a sharp, familiar ache in the back of her throat. Tristan looked at her with an oddly wistful expression; then turned her face quickly, huddling a little closer into her plain, shapeless cloak. She moaned as the ship lurched and said between clenched teeth, "I think I'm going to die. I heard what the Morgol's land-heir said. You stole the ship; you didn't tell anyone in your own lands. I heard the sailors talking last night, about how the guards forced them to go north, and that—that they were better off pretending they wanted to go in the first place, rather than making themselves the laughing-stock of the realm by protesting. Then they talked about the High One, and their voices went softer; I couldn't hear."

"Tristan—"

"If you put me ashore, I'll walk. You said that yourself, that you'd walk. I had to listen to Eliard crying in his sleep when he dreamed about Morgon; I would have to go wake him. He said one night—one night he saw Morgon's face in his dream, and he cou . . . he couldn't recognize him. He wanted to go then, to Erlenstar Mountain, but it was dead winter, the worst in Hed for seventy years, old Tor Oakland said, and they persuaded him to wait."

"He couldn't have gotten through the Pass."

"That's what Grim Oakland told him. He almost went anyway. But Cannon Master promised he would go, too, in spring. So spring came . . ." Her voice stopped; she sat absolutely still a moment, looking down at her hands. "Spring came and Morgon died. And all I could see in Eliard's eyes, no matter what he was doing, was one question: Why? So I'm going to Erlenstar Mountain to find out."

Raederle sighed. The sun had broken through the mists finally, patterning the deck through the criss-cross of stays with a web of light. Tristan, under its warm touch, seemed a shade less waxen; she even straightened a little without wincing. She added, "There's nothing you can say that will make me change my mind."

"It's not me, it's Bri Corbett."

"He took you and Lyra—"

"He knows me, and it's difficult to argue with the Morgol's guards. But he might balk at taking the land-heir of Hed, especially if no one knows where in the world you are. He might turn the ship around and head straight for Caithnard."

"I wrote Eliard a note. Anyway, the guards could stop him from turning."

"No. Not in open sea, when there's no one else we could get to sail the ship."

Tristan glanced painfully at the rowboat slung beside her. "I could hide again. No one's seen me."

"No. Wait." She paused, thinking. "My cabin. You could stay there. I'll bring you food."

Tristan blanched. "I don't think I'm planning to eat for a while."

"Can you walk?"

She nodded with an effort. Raederle helped her to her feet, with a swift glance around the deck, and led her down the steps to her own small chamber. She gave Tristan a little wine, and when Tristan reeled to the bed at a sudden welter of the ship, covered her with her cloak. She lay limp, to the eye scarcely visible or breathing, but Raederle heard her voice hollow as a voice out of a barrow as she closed the door, "Thank you . . ."

She found Lyra wrapped in a dark, voluminous cloak at the stern, watching the sun rise. She greeted Raederle with a rare, impulsive smile as Raederle joined her.

Raederle said softly, so that the helmsman would not hear, "We have a problem."

"Bri?"

"No. Tristan of Hed."

Lyra stared at her incredulously. She listened silently, her brows knit, as Raederle explained.

She gave a quick glance at Raederle's cabin, as though she could see through the walls to the inert form on the bed, then she said decisively, "We can't take her."

"I know."

"The people of Hed have already suffered so much over Morgon's absence; she's the land-heir of Hed, and she must be . . . How old is she?"

"Thirteen, maybe. She left them a note." She rubbed her eyes with her fingers. "If we turn back to Caithnard now, we could talk to Bri until spiders spun webs on him, and he would never agree to take us north again."

"If we turn back," Lyra said, "we may find ourselves face-to-face with the Morgol's ship. But Tristan has got to go back to Hed. Did you tell her that?"

"No. I wanted time to think. Bri said we would have to stop for supplies. We could find a trade-ship to take her back."

"Would she go?"

"She isn't in any condition to argue at the moment. She's never been out of Hed in her life; I doubt if she has any idea of where Erlenstar Mountain is. She's probably never even seen a mountain in her life. But she has—she has all of Morgon's stubbornness. If we can get her off one ship and onto another while she's still seasick, then she might not realize what direction she's going until she winds up back on her own doorstep. It sounds heartless, but if she—if anything happened to her on the way to Erlenstar Mountain, I don't think anyone, in or out of Hed, could bear hearing of it. The traders will help us."

"Should we tell Bri Corbett?"

"He would turn back."

"We should turn back," Lyra said objectively, her eyes on the white scrollwork of waves on the Ymris coast. She turned her head, looked at Raederle. "It would be hard for me to face the Morgol."

"I am not going back to Anuin," Raederle said softly. "Tristan may never forgive us, but she'll have her answers, I swear by the bones of the dead of An. I swear by the name of the Star-Bearer."

Lyra's head gave a quick, pleading shake. "Don't," she breathed. "It sounds so final, as if that is the only thing you will do with your life."

Tristan slept most of the day. In the evening, Raederle brought her some hot soup; she roused herself to eat a little, then vanished back under her cloak when the night winds, coming out of the west pungent with the smell of turned earth, gave the ship an energetic roll. She moaned despairingly, but Bri Corbett, in the chart house, was pleased.

"We'll make it to Caerweddin by midmorning if this wind holds," he told Raederle when she went to bid him good-night. "It's a marvellous wind. We'll take two hours there for supplies and still outrun anyone who might be following."

"You'd think," Raederle commented to Lyra when she went to borrow a blanket, since Tristan was sleeping on top of hers, "all this was his idea in the first place." She made herself an unsatisfying bed on the floor and woke, after a night of sketchy sleeping, feeling stiff and slightly sick herself. She stumbled into the sunlight, taking deep breaths of the mellow air, and found Bri Corbett talking to himself at the bow.

"They're not out of Kraal, they're not Ymris trade-ships, too low and sleek," he murmured, leaning out over the rail. Raederle, trying to keep her hair from being whipped to a wild froth in the wind, blinked at the half-dozen ships bearing down at them. They were low, lean, single-masted ships; their billowing sails were deep blue, edged with a thin silver scallop. Bri brought one hand down on the rail with a sharp exclamation. "Madir's bones. I haven't seen one of those in ten years, not since I've been in your father's service. But I didn't hear a word of it at Caithnard."

"What?"

"War. Those are Ymris war-ships."

Raederle, suddenly awake, stared at the light, swift fleet. "They just ended a war," she protested softly to no one. "Hardly a year ago."

"We must have missed trouble by a cat's breath. It's another coastal war; they must be watching for shiploads of arms."

"Will they stop us?"

"Why should they? Do we look like a trade-ship?" He stopped then; they stared at one another, shaken by the same realization.

"No," Raederle said. "We look like the private ship of the King of An, and we're about as conspicuous as a pig in a tree. Suppose they want to give us an escort to Caerweddin? How are you going to explain the presence of the Morgol's guards on—"

"How am I going to explain? Me? Did I hear any complaint about the color of my sails when you overran my ship and demanded I take you north?"

"How was I to know Ymris would start a war? You were the one gossiping with that trader; he didn't mention it? You didn't have to keep so close to the land; if you had kept more distance between us and Ymris, we wouldn't be running into the Ymris King's ships. Or did you know about them? Were you hoping we'd be stopped?"

"Hagis's beard!" Bri snapped indignantly. "If I wanted to turn around, there's not a guard trained yet who could stop me, especially not these—the only thing they would shoot to harm aboard this ship are knotholes and corks, I know that. I'm sailing north because I want to—and who in Hel's name is that?"

He was staring, his face a deep, veined purple, at Tristan, who had staggered out to throw up over the rail. Bri, watching, swallowed words, making little, incredulous noises in his throat. He found his voice again as Tristan straightened, mist-colored and sweating.

"Who is that?"

"She's just a—a stowaway," Raederle said futilely. "Bri, there's no need to be upset. She'll get off at Caerweddin—"

"I won't, either," Tristan said slowly but distinctly. "I'm Tristan of Hed, and I'm not getting off until we reach Erlenstar Mountain."

Bri's lips moved without sound. He seemed to billow with air like a sail; Raederle, wincing, waited to bear the brunt of it, but instead he turned and exploded across the deck to the helmsman, who jumped as if a mast had snapped behind him, "That's enough! Turn this ship around. I want her prow in the harbor at Tol so fast she leaves her reflection in the Ymris water."

The ship wheeled. Tristan clung with tight-lipped misery to the rail. Lyra, taking the last few steps to Raederle's side at a slide, saw Tristan and asked resignedly, "What happened?"

Raederle shook her head helplessly. The fierce blue of the Ymris sails came between them and the sun then; she groped for her voice. "Bri."

One of the war-ships, cutting so close she could taste the fine, sheer edge of its spray, seemed to be bearing to a single point in their path. "Bri!" She caught his attention finally as he bellowed at the sailors. "Bri! The war-ships! They think we're running from them!"

"What?" He gave the ship that was tacking to cut them off an incredulous glare and issued an order so abruptly his voice cracked. There was another lurch; the ship lost speed, slowed, and as the Ymris ship matched its pace they could see the silver mesh and sword hilts of the men aboard. Their own ship stopped and sat wallowing. Another war-ship eased to the windward side; a third guarded the stern. Bri dropped his head in his hands. A voice floated over the water; Raederle turned her head, catching only a few crisp words from a white-haired man.

Bri, shouting back an acquiescence, said briefly, heavily, "All right. Head her north again. We've got a royal escort to Caerweddin."

"Who?"

"Astrin Ymris."

THEY ENTERED THE harbor at Caerweddin with a war-ship at either side of them. The mouth of the river itself was guarded; there were only a few trade-ships entering, and these were stopped and searched before they were allowed farther up the broad, slow river to the docks. Raederle, Tristan, Lyra and the guards stood at the rail watching the city slide past them. Houses and shops and winding cobbled streets spilled far beyond its ancient walls and towers. The King's own house, on a rise in the center of the city, seemed a strong and forceful seat of power, with its massive blocked design and angular towers; but the carefully chosen colors in the stone made it oddly beautiful. Raederle thought of the King's house at Anuin, built to some kind of dream after the wars had ceased, of shell-white walls and high, slender towers; it would have been fragile against the forces that contended against the Ymris King. Tristan, standing beside her, reviving on the placid waters, was staring with her mouth open, and Raederle blinked away another memory of a small, quiet, oak hall, with placid, rain-drenched fields beyond it.

Lyra, frowning at the city, said softly to Raederle, as Bri Corbett gave glum orders behind them, "This is humiliating. They had no right to take us like this."

"They asked Bri if he were heading for Caerweddin; he had to say yes. He was spinning around in the water so much that he must have looked suspicious. They probably thought," she added, "when he ran, that he might have stolen the ship. Now they are probably getting ready to welcome my father to Caerweddin. They are going to be surprised."

"Where are we?" Tristan asked. It was the first word she had spoken in an hour. "Are we anywhere near Erlenstar Mountain?"

Lyra looked at her incredulously. "Haven't you even seen a map of the realm?"

"No. I never needed to."

"We are so far from Erlenstar Mountain we might as well be in Caithnard. Which is where we will be in two days' time anyway—"

"No," Raederle said abruptly. "I'm not going back."

"I'm not either," Tristan said. Lyra met Raederle's eyes above her head.

"All right. But do you have any suggestions?"

"I'm thinking."

The ship docked alongside of one of the warships; the other, waiting, in a gesture at once courteous and prudent, until Bri sank anchor into the deep water, then turned and made its way back toward the sea. The splash of iron, the long rattle and thump of the anchor chain sounded in the air like the final word of an argument. They saw, as the ramp slid down, a small group of men arrive on horseback, richly dressed and armed. Bri Corbett went down to meet them. A man in blue livery carried a blue and silver banner. Raederle, realizing what it was, felt the blood pound suddenly into her face.

"One of them must be the King," she whispered, and Tristan gave her an appalled look.

"I'm not going down there. Look at my skirt."

"Tristan, you are the land-heir of Hed, and once they learn that, we could be dressed in leaves and berries for all they'll realize what we're wearing."

"Should we carry our spears down?" Imer asked puzzledly. "We would if the Morgol were with us."

Lyra considered the matter blankly. Her mouth crooked a little. "I believe I have deserted. A spear in the hand of a dishonored guard isn't an emblem but a challenge. However, since this is my responsibility, you're free to make your own decision."

Imer sighed. "You know, we could have locked you in the cabin and told Bri Corbett to turn around. We talked about it that first night, when you took the watch. That was one mistake you made. We made our own decision, then."

"Imer, it's different for me! The Morgol will have to forgive me eventually, but what will all of you go home to?"

"If we do get home, bringing you with us," Imer said calmly, "the Morgol will probably be a lot more reasonable than you are. I think she would rather have us with you than not. The King," she added a little nervously, looking over Lyra's shoulder, "is coming on board."

Raederle, turning to face him, felt Tristan grip her wrist. The King looked formidable at first glance, dark, powerful and grim, with body armor like the delicate, silvery scales of fish, beneath a blue-black surcoat whorled with endless silver embroidery. The white-haired man of the war-ship came with him, with his single white eye; his other eye was sealed shut against something he had seen. As they stood together, she felt the binding between them, like the binding between Duac and Mathom, and recognized, with a slight shock, the eccentric land-heir of the Ymris King. His good eye went suddenly to her face, as though he had sensed her recognition. The King surveyed them silently a moment. Then he said with simple, unexpected kindliness, "I am Heureu Ymris. This is my land-heir, my brother Astrin. Your ship-master told me who you are, and that you are travelling together under peculiar circumstances. He requested a guard for you past the Ymris coast, since we are at war, and he wanted no harm to come to such valuable passengers. I have seven war-ships preparing to leave at dawn for Meremont. They will give you an escort south. Meanwhile, you are very welcome to my land and my house."

He paused, waiting. Lyra said abruptly, a slight flush on her face, "Did Bri Corbett tell you that we took his ship? That we—that I—that none of the Morgol's guard are acting with her knowledge? I want you to understand who you will welcome into your house."

There was a flick of surprise in his eyes, followed by another kind of recognition. He said gently, "Don't you think you were trying to do exactly what many of us this past year have only thought of doing? You will honor my house."

They followed him and his land-heir down the ramp; he introduced them to the High Lords of Marcher and Tor, the red-haired High Lord of Umber, while their horses were unloaded. They mounted, made a weary, slightly bedraggled procession behind the King. Lyra, riding abreast of Raederle, her eyes on Heureu Ymris's back, whispered, "Seven war-ships. He's taking no chances with us. What if you threw a piece of gold thread in the water in front of them?"

"I'm thinking," Raederle murmured.

In the King's house, they were given small, light, richly furnished chambers where they could wash and rest in private. Raederle, concerned for Tristan in the great, strange house, watched her ignore servants and riches, and crawl thankfully into a bed that did not move. In her own chamber, she washed the sea spray out of her hair, and, feeling clean for the first time in days, stood by the open window combing her hair dry and looking out over the unfamiliar land. Her eyes wandered down past the busy maze of streets, picked out the old city wall, broken here and there by gates and arches above the streets. The city scattered eventually into farmland and forest, orchards that were soft mists of color in the distance. Then, her eyes moving east again to the sea, she saw something that made her put her comb down, lean out the open casement.

There was a stonework, enormous and puzzling, on a cliff not far from the city. It stood like some half-forgotten memory, or the fragments on a torn page of ancient, incomplete riddles. The stones she recognized, beautiful, massive, vivid with color. The structure itself, bigger than anything any man would have needed, had been shaken to the ground seemingly with as much ease as she would have shaken ripe apples out of a tree. She swallowed drily, remembering tales her father had made her learn, remembering something Morgon had mentioned briefly in one of his letters, remembering, above all, the news Elieu had brought from Isig about the waking, in the soundless deep of the Mountain, of the children of the Earth-Masters. Then something beyond all comprehension, a longing, a loneliness, an understanding played in the dark rim of her mind, bewildering her with its sorrow and recognition, frightening her with its intensity, until she could neither bear to look at the nameless city, nor turn away from it.

A knock sounded softly at her door; she realized then that she was standing blind, with tears running down her face. The world, with a physical effort, as if two great stones locked massively, ponderously into position, shifted back into familiarity. The knock came again; she wiped her face with the back of her hand and went to open it.

The Ymris land-heir, standing in the doorway, with his alien face and single white eye startled her for some reason. Then she saw its youngness, the lines worn in it of pain and patience. He said quickly, gently, "What is it? I came to talk with you a little, about the—about Morgon. I can come back."

She shook her head. "No. Please come in. I was just—I—" She stopped helplessly, wondering if he could understand the words she had to use. Some instinct made her reach out to him, grip him as though to keep her balance; she said, half-blind again, "People used to say you lived among the ruins of another time, that you knew unearthly things. There are things—there are things I need to ask."

He stepped into the room, closed the door behind him. "Sit down," he said, and she sat in one of the chairs by the cold hearth. He brought her a cup of wine, then took a chair beside her. He looked, still wearing mail and the King's dark livery of war, like a warrior, but the slight perplexity in his face was of no such simple mind.

"You have power," he said abruptly. "Did you know that?"

"I know—I have a little. But now, I think, there may be things in me I never—I never knew." She took a swallow of wine; her voice grew calmer. "Do you know the riddle of Oen and Ylon?"

"Yes." Something moved in his good eye. He said, "Yes," again, softly. "Ylon was a shape-changer."

She moved slightly, as away from a pain. "His blood runs in the family of the Kings of An. For centuries he was little more than a sad tale. But now, I want—I have to know. He came out of the sea, like the shape-changer Lyra saw, the one who nearly killed Morgon—he was of that color and wildness. Whatever—whatever power I have comes from Madir. And from Ylon."

He was silent for a long time, contemplating the riddle she had given him while she sipped wine, the cup in her hands shaking slightly. He said finally, groping, "What made you cry?"

"That dead city. It—something in me reached out and knew . . . and knew what it had been."

His good eye moved to her face; his voice caught. "What was it?"

"I was—I stood in the way. It was like someone else's memory in me. It frightened me. I thought, when I saw you, that you might understand."

"I don't understand either you or Morgon. Maybe you, like him, are an integral piece in some great puzzle as old and complex as that city on King's Mouth Plain. All I know of the cities is the broken things I find, hardly a trace of the Earth-Masters' passage. Morgon had to grope for his own power, as you will; what he is now, after—"

"Wait." Her voice shook again, uncontrollably. "Wait."

He leaned forward, took the unsteady cup from her and set it on the floor. Then he took her hands in his own lean, tense hands. "Surely you don't believe he is dead."

"Well, what alternative do I have? What's the dark side to that tossed coin—whether he's alive or dead, whether he's dead or his mind is broken under that terrible power—"

"Who broke whose power? For the first time in seven centuries the wizards are freed—"

"Because the Star-Bearer is dead! Because the one who killed him no longer needs to fear their power."

"Do you believe that? That's what Heureu says, and Rork Umber. The wizard Aloil had been a tree on King's Mouth Plain for seven centuries, until I watched him turn into himself, bewildered with his freedom. He spoke only briefly to me; he didn't know why he had been freed; he had never heard of the Star-Bearer. He had dead white hair and eyes that had watched his own destruction. I asked where he would go, and he only laughed and vanished. Then, a few days later, traders brought the terrible tale out of Hed of Morgon's torment, of the passing of the land-rule, on the day Aloil had been freed. I have never believed that Morgon is dead."

"What . . . Then what is left of him? He has lost everything he loved, he has lost his own name. When Awn—when Awn of An lost his own land-rule while he was living, he killed himself. He couldn't—"

"I lived with Morgon when he was nameless once before. He found his name again in the stars that he bears. I will not believe he is dead."

"Why?"

"Because that isn't the answer he was looking for."

She stared at him incredulously. "You don't think he had a choice in the matter?"

"No. He is the Star-Bearer. I think he was destined to live."

"You make that sound more like a doom," she whispered. He loosed her hands and rose, went to stand at the window where she had been gazing out at the nameless city.

"Perhaps. But I would never underestimate that farmer from Hed." He turned suddenly. "Will you ride with me to King's Mouth Plain, to see the ancient city?"

"Now? I thought you had a war to fight."

His unexpected smile warmed his lean face. "I did, until we saw your ship. You gave me a respite until dawn, when I lead you and your escort out of Caerweddin. It's not a safe place, that plain. Heureu's wife was killed there. No one goes there now but me, and even I am wary. But you might find something—a stone, a broken artifact—that will speak to you."

She rode with him through Caerweddin, up the steep, rocky slope onto the plain above the sea. The sea winds sang hollowly across it, trailing between the huge, still stones that had rooted deep into the earth through countless centuries. Raederle, dismounting, laid her hand on one impulsively; it was clear, smooth under her palm, shot through with veins of emerald green.

"It's so beautiful. . . ." She looked at Astrin suddenly. "That's where the stones of your house came from."

"Yes. Whatever pattern these stones made has been hopelessly disturbed. The stones were nearly impossible to move, but the King who took them, Galil Ymris, was a persistent man." He bent down abruptly, searched the long grass and earth in the crook of two stones and rose again with something in his hand. He brushed it off: it winked star-blue in the sunlight. She looked at it as it lay in his palm.

"What is it?"

"I don't know. A piece of cut glass, a stone. . . . It's hard to tell sometimes exactly what things are here." He dropped it into her own hand, closed her fingers around it lightly. "You keep it."

She turned it curiously, watched it sparkle. "You love these great stones, in spite of all their danger."

"Yes. That makes me strange, in Ymris. I would rather putter among forgotten things like an old hermit-scholar than take seven war-ships into battle. But war on the south coasts is an old sore that festers constantly and never seems to heal. So Heureu needs me there, even though I try to tell him I can taste and smell and feel some vital answer in this place. And you. What do you feel from it?"

She lifted her eyes from the small stone, looked down the long scattering of stones. The plain was empty but for the stones, the silver-edged grass and a single stand of oak, gnarled and twisted by the sea wind. The cloudless sky curved away from it, building to an immensity of nothingness. She wondered what force could ever draw the stones again up into it, straining out of the ground, pulled one onto another, building to some immense, half-comprehensible purpose that would shine from a distance with power, beauty and a freedom like the wind's freedom. But they lay still, gripped to the earth, dormant. She whispered, "Silence," and the wind died.

She felt, in that moment, as if the world had stopped. The grass was motionless in the sunlight; the shadows of the stones seemed measured and blocked on the ground. Even the breakers booming at the cliff's foot were still. Her own breath lay indrawn in her mouth. Then Astrin touched her, and she heard the unexpected hiss of his sword from the scabbard. He pulled her against him, holding her tightly. She felt, under the cold mesh of armor, the hard pound of his heart.

There was a sigh out of the core of the world. A wave that seemed as if it would never stop gathering shook the cliff as it broke and withdrew. Astrin's arm dropped. She saw his face as she stepped back; the drawn, hollow look frightened her. A gull cried, hovering at the cliff's edge, then disappeared; she saw him shudder. He said briefly, "I'm terrified. I can't think. Let's go."

They were both silent as they rode down the slope again towards the lower fields and the busy north road into the city. As they cut across a field full of sheep bawling with the indignity of being shorn, the white, private horror eased away from Astrin's face. Raederle, glancing at him, felt him accessible again; she said softly, "What was it? Everything seemed to stop."

"I don't know. The last time—the last time I felt it, Eriel Ymris died. I was afraid for you."

"Me?"

"For five years after she died, the King lived with a shape-changer as his wife."

Raederle closed her eyes. She felt something build in her suddenly, like a shout she wanted to loose at him that would drown even the voices of the sheep. She clenched her hands, controlling it; she did not realize she had stopped until he spoke her name. Then she opened her eyes and said, "At least he had no land-heir to lock away in a tower by the sea. Astrin, I think there is something sleeping inside of me, and if I wake it, I will regret it until the world's end. I have a shape-changer's blood in me, and something of his power. That's an awkward thing to have."

His good eye, quiet again, seemed to probe with detachment to the heart of her riddle. "Trust yourself," he suggested, and she drew a deep breath.

"That's like stepping with my eyes shut onto one of my own tangled threads. You have a comforting outlook on things."

He gripped her wrist lightly before they started to ride again. She found, her hand easing open, the mark of the small stone she held ridged deeply into her palm.

Lyra came to talk to her when she returned to the King's house. Raederle was sitting at the window, looking down at something that sparkled like a drop of water in her hand. "Have you thought of a plan yet?" Lyra said.

Raederle, lifting her head, sensed the restlessness and frustration in her tight, controlled movements, like the movements of some animal trapped and tempered into civility. She gathered her thoughts with an effort.

"I think Bri Corbett could be persuaded to turn us north after we leave the river, if we can get Tristan on her way home. But Lyra, I don't know what would persuade Astrin Ymris to let us go."

"The decision is ours; it has nothing to do with Ymris."

"It would be hard to convince either Astrin or Heureu of that."

Lyra turned abruptly away from the window, paced to the empty grate and back. "We could find another ship. No. They'd only search us, going out of the harbor." She looked as close as she would ever come to throwing something that was not a weapon. Then, glancing down at Raederle, she said unexpectedly, "What's the matter? You look troubled."

"I am," Raederle said, surprised. Her head bent; her hand closed again over the stone. "Astrin—Astrin told me he thinks Morgon is alive."

She heard a word catch in Lyra's throat. Lyra sat down suddenly next to her, gripping the stone ledge with her hands. Her face was white; she found her voice again, pleaded, "What—what makes him think so?"

"He said Morgon was looking for answers, and death wasn't one of them. He said—"

"That would mean he lost the land-rule. That was his greatest fear. But no one—no one can take away that instinct but the High One. No one—" She stopped. Raederle heard the sudden clench of her teeth. She leaned back wearily, the stone shining like a tear in her palm. Lyra's voice came again, unfamiliar, stripped bare of all passion, "I will kill him for that."

"Who?"

"Ghisteslwchlohm."

Raederle's lips parted and closed. She waited for the chill that the strange voice had roused in her to subside, then she said carefully, "You'll have to find him first. That may be difficult."

"I'll find him. Morgon will know where he is."

"Lyra—" Lyra's face turned toward her, and the words of prudence caught in Raederle's throat. She looked down. "First we have to get out of Caerweddin."

The dark, unfamiliar thing eased out of Lyra. She said anxiously, "Don't tell Tristan what you told me. It's too uncertain."

"I won't."

"Isn't there something you can do for us? We can't turn back now. Not now. Make a wind blow the war-ships away, make them see an illusion of us going south—"

"What do you think I am? A wizard? I don't think even Madir could do those things." A bead of sunlight caught in the strange stone; she straightened suddenly. "Wait." She held it up between forefinger and thumb, catching the sun's rays. Lyra blinked as the light slid over her eyes.

"What? What is that?"

"It's a stone Astrin found on King's Mouth Plain, in the city of the Earth-Masters. He gave it to me."

"What are you going to do with it?" Her eyes narrowed again as the bright light touched them, and Raederle lowered it.

"It flashes like a mirror . . . All I learned from the pig-woman is concerned with illusion, small things out of proportion: the handful of water seeming a pool, the twig a great fallen log, the single bramble stem an impassible tangle. If I could—if I could blind the war-ships with this, make it blaze like a sun in their eyes, they couldn't see us turn north, they wouldn't be able to outrun us."

"What that? It's no bigger than a thumbnail. Besides," she added uneasily, "how do you know what it is? You know a handful of water is a handful of water. But you don't know what this was meant for, so how will you know exactly what it might become?"

"If you don't want me to try it, I won't. It's a decision that will affect us all. It's also the only thing I can think of."

"You're the one who has to work with it. How do you know what name the Earth-Masters might have put to it? I'm not afraid for us or the ship, but it's your mind—"

"Did I," Raederle interrupted, "offer you advice?"

"No," Lyra said reluctantly. "But I know what I'm doing."

"Yes. You're going to get killed by a wizard. Am I arguing?"

"No. But—" She sighed. "All right. Now all we have to do is tell Bri Corbett where he's going so that he'll know to get supplies. And we have to send Tristan home. Can you think of any possible way to do that?"

They both thought. An hour later, Lyra slipped unostensibly out of the King's house, went down to the docks to inform Bri that he was heading north again, and Raederle went to the King's hall to talk to Heureu Ymris.

She found him in the midst of his lords, discussing the situation in Meremont. When he saw her hesitating at the doorway of the great hall, he came to her. Meeting his clear, direct gaze, she knew that she and Lyra had been right: he would be less difficult to deceive than Astrin, and she was relieved that Astrin was not with him. He said, "Is there something you need? Something I can help you with?"

She nodded. "Could I talk to you a moment?"

"Of course."

"Could you—is it possible for you to spare one of your war-ships to take Tristan home? Bri Corbett will have to stop at Caithnard to let Lyra off and pick up my brother. Tristan is unreasonably determined to get to Erlenstar Mountain, and if she can find a way to get off Bri's ship at Caithnard, she'll do it. She'll head north, either on a trade-ship or on foot, and either way she is liable to find herself in the middle of your war."

His dark brows knit. "She sounds stubborn. Like Morgon."

"Yes. And if she—if anything happened to her, too, it would be devastating to the people of Hed. Bri could take her to Hed before he brings us to Caithnard, but in those waters he must pass over, Athol and Spring of Hed were drowned, and Morgon was nearly killed. I would feel easier if she had a little more protection than a few guards and sailors."

He drew a quick, silent breath. "I hadn't thought of that. Only five of the war-ships are carrying a great many arms and men; two are more lightly manned patrols watching for shiploads of arms. I can spare one to take her back. If I could, I would send those war-ships with you all the way to Caithnard. I have never seen such a valuable assortment of people on such a misguided, ill-considered journey in my life."

She flushed a little. "I know. It was wrong of us to take Tristan even this far."

"Tristan! What about you and the Morgol's land-heir?"

"That's different—"

"How, in Yrth's name?"

"We at least know there's a world between Hed and the High One."

"Yes," he said grimly. "And it's no place for any of you, these days. I made sure your ship-master understood that, too. I don't know what possessed him to leave the Caithnard harbor with you."

"It wasn't his fault. We didn't give him any choice."

"How much duress could you possibly have put him under? The Morgol's guards are skilled, but hardly unreasonable. And you might as easily have met worse than my war-ships off the Ymris coast. There are times when I believe I am fighting only my own rebels, but at other times, the entire war seems to change shape under my eyes, and I realize that I am not even sure myself how far it will extend, or if I can contain it. Small as it is yet, it has terrifying potential. Bri Corbett could not have chosen a worse time to sail with you so close to Meremont."

"He didn't know about the war—"

"If he had been carrying your father on that ship, he would have made it his business to know. I reminded him of that, also. As for Astrin taking you today to King's Mouth Plain—that was utter stupidity." He stopped. She saw the light glance white off his cheekbones before he lifted his hands to his eyes, held them there a moment. She looked down, swallowing.

"I suppose you told him that."

"Yes. He seemed to agree with me. This is no time for people of intelligence, like Astrin, you and Bri Corbett, to forget how to think." He put a hand on her shoulder then, and his voice softened. "I understand what you were trying to do. I understand why. But leave it for those who are more capable."

She checked an answer and bent her head, yielding him tacitly the last word. She said with real gratitude, "Thank you for the ship. Will you tell Tristan in the morning?"

"I'll escort her personally on board."

Raederle saw Lyra again later in the hall as they were going to supper. Lyra said softly, "Bri argued, but I swore to him on what's left of my honor that he would not have to try to outrun the war-ships. He didn't like it, but he remembered what you did with that piece of thread. He said whatever you do tomorrow had better be effective, because he won't dare face Heureu Ymris again if it isn't."

Raederle felt her face burn slightly at a memory. "Neither will I," she murmured. Tristan came out of her room then, bewildered and a little frightened, as if she had just wakened. Her face eased at the sight of them; at the trust in her eyes, Raederle felt a pang of guilt. She said, "Are you hungry? We're going down to the King's hall to eat."

"In front of people?" She brushed hopelessly at her wrinkled skirt. Then she stopped, looked around her at the beautifully patterned walls glistening with torchlight, the old shields of bronze and silver hung on them, the ancient, jewelled weapons. She whispered, "Morgon was in this house," and her shoulders straightened as she followed them to the hall.

• • • • •

They were wakened before dawn the next morning. Bundled in rich, warm cloaks Heureu gave them, they rode with him, Astrin, the High Lords of Umber and Tor and three hundred armed men through the quiet streets of Caerweddin. They saw windows opening here and there, or the spill of light from a door as a face peered out at the quick, silent march of warriors. At the docks, the dark masts loomed out of a pearl-colored mist over the water; the voices, the footsteps in the dawn seemed muted, disembodied. The men broke out of their lines, began to board. Bri Corbett, coming down the ramp, gave Raederle one grim, harassed glance before he took her horse up. The Morgol's guards followed him up with their horses.

Raederle waited a moment, to hear Heureu say to Tristan, "I'm sending you home with Astrin in one of the warships. You'll be safe with him, well-protected by the men with him. It's a fast ship; you'll be home quickly."

Raederle, watching, could not tell for a moment who looked more surprised, Tristan or Astrin. Then Tristan, her mouth opening to protest, saw Raederle listening and an indignant realization leaped into her eyes. Astrin said before she could speak, "That's over two days there and a day back to Meremont—you'll need that ship to watch the coast."

"I can spare it that long. If the rebels have sent for arms, they'll come down most likely from the north, and I can try to stop them at Caerweddin."

"Arms," Astrin argued, "are not all we're watching for." Then his eyes moved slowly from Heureu's face to Raederle's. "Who requested that ship?"

"I made the decision," Heureu said crisply, and at his tone, Tristan, who had opened her mouth again, closed it abruptly.

Astrin gazed at Raederle, his brows puckered in suspicion and perplexity. He said briefly to Heureu, "All right. I'll send you word from Meremont when I return."

"Thank you." His fingers closed a moment on Astrin's arm. "Be careful."

Raederle boarded. She went to the stern, heard Bri's voice giving oddly colorless orders behind her. The first of the war-ships began to drift like some dark bird to the middle of the river; as it moved the mist began to swirl and fray over the quiet grey water, and the first sunlight broke on the high walls of the King's house.

Lyra came to stand beside Raederle. Neither of them spoke. The ship bearing Tristan slid alongside them, and Raederle saw Astrin's face, with its spare lines and ghostly coloring, as he watched the rest of the war-ships ease into position behind him. Bri Corbett, with his slower, heavier vessel, went last, in the wake of the staggered line. In their own wake came the sun.

It burned the froth behind them. Bri said softly to the helmsman, "Be ready to turn her at half a word. If those ships slow and close around us in open sea, we might as well take off our boots and wade to Kraal. And that's what I intend to do if they give chase and stop us. Astrin Ymris would singe one ear off me with his tongue and Heureu the other, and I could carry what's left of my reputation back to Anuin with me in a boot with a hole in it."

"Don't worry," Raederle murmured. The stone flashed like a king's jewel in her hand. "Bri, I'll need to float this behind us or it will blind us all. Do you have a piece of wood or something?"

"I'll find one." The placid sigh of the morning tide caught their ears; he turned his head. The first ship was already slipping into the open sea. He said again, nervously as the salt wind teased at their sails, "I'll find one. You do whatever it is you're doing."

Raederle bent her head, looked down at the stone. It dazzled like a piece of sun-shot ice, light leaping from plane to plane of its intricately cut sides. She wondered what it had been, saw it in her mind's eye as a jewel in a ring, the center eye of a crown, the pommel of a knife, perhaps, that darkened in times of danger. But did the Earth-Masters ever use such things? Had it belonged to them or to some fine lady in the Ymris court who dropped it as she rode or to some trader who bought it in Isig, then lost it, flickering out of his pack as he crossed King's Mouth Plain? If it could blaze like a tiny star in her hand at the sun's touch, she knew the illusion of it would ignite the sea, and no ship would see to pass through it, even if it dared. But what was it?

The light played gently in her mind, dispersing old night-shadows, pettinesses, the little, nagging memories of dreams. Her thoughts strayed to the great plain where it had been found, the massive stones on it like monuments to a field of ancient dead. She saw the morning sunlight sparkle in the veins of color on one stone, gather in a tiny fleck of silver in a corner of it. She watched that minute light in her mind, kindled it slowly with the sunlight caught in the stone she held. It began to glow softly in her palm. She fed the light in her mind; it spilled across the ageless stones, dispersing their shadows; she felt the warmth of the light in her hand, on her face. The light began to engulf the stones in her mind, arch across the clear sky until it dazzled white; she heard as from another time, a soft exclamation from Bri Corbett. The twin lights drew from one another: the light in her hand, the light in her mind. There was a flurry of words, cries, faint and meaningless behind her. The ship reeled, jolting her; she reached out to catch her balance, and the light at her face burned her eyes.

"All right," Bri said breathlessly. "All right. You've got it. Put it down—it'll float on this." His own eyes were nearly shut, wincing against it.

She let him guide her hand, heard the stone clink into the small wooden bowl he held. Sailors let it over the side in a net as if they were lowering the sun into the sea. The gentle waves danced it away. She followed it with her mind, watching the white light shape into facet after facet in her mind, harden with lines and surfaces, until her whole mind seemed a single jewel, and looking into it, she began to sense its purpose.

She saw someone stand, as she stood, holding the jewel. He was in the middle of a plain in some land, in some age, and as the stone winked in his palm all movement around him, beyond the rim of her mind, began to flow towards its center. She had never seen him before, but she felt suddenly that his next gesture, a line of bone in his face if he turned, would give her his name. She waited curiously for that moment, watching him as he watched the stone, lost in the timeless movement of his existence. And then she felt a stranger's mind in her own, waiting with her.

Its curiosity was desperate, dangerous. She tried to pull away from it, frightened, but the startling, unfamiliar awareness of someone else's mind would not leave her. She sensed its attention on the nameless stranger whose next movement, the bend of his head, the spread of his fingers, would give her his identity. A terror, helpless and irrational, grew in her at the thought of that recognition, of yielding whatever name he held to the dark, powerful mind bent on discovering it. She struggled to disperse the image in her mind before he moved. But the strange power held her; she could neither change the image nor dispel it, as though her mind's eye were gazing, lidless, into the core of an incomprehensible mystery. Then a hand whipped, swift, hard, across her face; she pulled back, flinching against a strong grip.

The ship, scudding in the wind, boomed across a wave, and she blinked the spray out of her eyes. Lyra, holding her tightly, whispered, "I'm sorry. I'm sorry. But you were screaming." The light had gone; the King's war-ships were circling one another bewilderedly far behind them. Bri, his face colorless as he looked at her, breathed, "Shall I take you back? Say the word, and I'll turn back."

"No. It's all right." Lyra loosed her slowly; Raederle said again, the back of her hand over her mouth, "It's all right, now, Bri."

"What was it?" Lyra said. "What was that stone?"

"I don't know." She felt the aftermath of the strange mind again, demanding, insistent; she shuddered. "I almost knew something—"

"What?"

"I don't know! Something important to someone. But I don't know what, I don't know why—" She shook her head hopelessly. "It was like a dream, so important then, and now it's—it makes no sense. All I know is that there were twelve."

"Twelve what?"

"Twelve sides to that stone. Like a compass." She saw Bri Corbett's bewildered expression. "I know. It makes no sense."

"But what in Hel's name made you scream like that?" he demanded.

She remembered the powerful, relentless mind that had trapped her own in its curiosity, and knew that though he would turn back to face even the war-ships again if she told him of it, there would be no place in the realm where she could be truly safe from it. She said softly, "It was something of power, that stone. I should have used a simpler thing. I'm going to rest awhile."

She did not come out of her cabin again until evening. She went to the side, then, stood watching stars burn like distant reflections of her mind-work. Something made her turn her head suddenly. She saw, swaying comfortably to the ship's motion, Tristan of Hed, standing like a figurehead at the prow.

5

TRISTAN WOULD NOT speak to anyone for two days. Bri Corbett, torn between taking her back and avoiding at all costs the hoodwinked escort and the one-eyed Ymris prince, spent a day cursing, then yielded to Tristan's mute, reproachful determination and sailed north on his own indecision. They left, at the end of those two days, the Ymris coastline behind them. The unsettled forests, the long stretch of barren hills between Herun and the sea were all they saw for a while, and gradually they began to relax. The wind was brisk; Bri Corbett, his face cheerful and ruddy under the constant sun, kept the sailors jumping. The guards, unused to idleness, practiced knife throwing at a target on the wall of the chart house. When a sudden roll of the ship caused a wild throw that nearly sliced a cable in two, Bri put a halt to that. They took up fishing instead, with long lines trailing from the stern. Sailors, watching as they bent over the rail, remembered the dead thwick of knife blade into the chart house wall and approached with caution.

Raederle, after futile attempts to soothe Tristan, who stood aloof and quiet, looking northward like a dark reminder of their purpose, gave up and left her alone. She stayed quiet herself, reading Rood's books or playing the flute she had brought from Anuin, that Elieu of Hel had made for her. One afternoon she sat on the deck with it and played songs and court dances of An and plaintive ballads that Cyone had taught her years before. She wandered into a sad, simple air she could not recall the name of and found, when she finished, that Tristan had turned away from the rail and was watching her.

"That was from Hed," she said abruptly. Raederle rested the flute on her knees, remembering.

"Deth taught it to me."

Tristan, wavering, moved away from the rail finally, sat down beside her on the warm deck. Her face was expressionless; she did not speak.

Raederle, her eyes on the flute, said softly, "Please try to understand. When the news of Morgon's death came, it was not only Hed that suffered a loss, but people all over the realm who had helped him, who loved him and worried about him. Lyra and Bri and I were simply trying to spare the realm, your own people especially, more fear and worry about you. Hed seems a very special and vulnerable place these days. We didn't mean to hurt you, but we didn't want, if anything happened to you, to be hurt again ourselves."

Tristan was silent. She lifted her head slowly, leaned back against the side. "Nothing's going to happen to me." She looked at Raederle a moment, asked a little shyly, "Would you have married Morgon?"

Raederle's mouth crooked. "I waited two years for him to come to Anuin and ask me."

"I wish he had. He never was very sensible." She gathered her knees up, rested her chin on them, brooding. "I heard the traders say he could change shape into an animal. That frightened Eliard. Can you do that?"

"Change shape? No." Her hands tightened slightly on the flute. "No."

"And then they said—they said last spring he had found a starred sword and killed with it. That didn't sound like him."

"No."

"But Grim Oakland said if someone were trying to kill him, he couldn't just stand there and let them. I can understand that; it's reasonable, but . . . after that, with someone else making a harp and a sword for him that were his because of the stars on his face, he didn't seem to belong to Hed any more. It seemed he couldn't come back and do the simple things he had always done—feed the pigs, argue with Eliard, make beer in the cellar. It seemed he had already left us forever, because we didn't really know him any more."

"I know," Raederle whispered. "I felt that way, too."

"So—in that way—it wasn't so hard when he died. What was hard was knowing . . . was knowing what he was going through before he died and not being able to—not—" Her voice shook; she pressed her mouth tightly against one arm. Raederle tilted her head back against the side, her eyes on the shadow the boom cut across the deck.

"Tristan. In An, the passage of the land-rule is a complex and startling thing, they say, like suddenly growing an extra eye to see in the dark or an ear to hear things beneath the earth . . . Is it that way in Hed?"

"It didn't seem that way." Her voice steadied as she mulled over the question. "Eliard was out in the fields when it happened. He just said he felt that suddenly everything—the leaves and animals, the rivers, the seedlings—everything suddenly made sense. He knew what they were and why they did what they did. He tried to explain it to me. I said everything must have made sense before, most things do anyway, but he said it was different. He could see everything very clearly, and what he couldn't see he felt. He couldn't explain it very well."

"Did he feel Morgon die?"

"No. He—" Her voice stopped. Her hands shifted, tightened on her knees; she went on in a whisper, "Eliard said Morgon must have forgotten even who he was when he died, because of that."

Raederle winced. She put her hand on Tristan's taut arm. "I'm sorry. I wasn't trying to be cruel; I was just—"

"Curious. Like Morgon."

"No!" The pain in her own voice made Tristan lift her head, look at her surprisedly.

She was silent again, studying Raederle almost as though she had never seen her before. She said, "There's something I've always wondered, in the back of my mind, from the first time I heard about you."

"What?"

"Who is the most beautiful woman in An?" She flushed a little at

Raederle's sudden smile, but there was a shy, answering smile in her eyes. "I was always curious."

"The most beautiful woman in An is Map Hwillion's sister, Mara, who married the lord Cyn Croeg of Aum. She is called the Flower of An."

"What are you called?"

"Just the second most beautiful woman."

"I've never seen anyone more beautiful than you. When Morgon first told us about you, I was frightened. I didn't think you could live in Hed, in our house. But now . . . I don't know. I wish—I wish things had turned out differently."

"So do I," Raederle said softly. "And now, will you tell me something? How in the world did you manage to get off that war-ship and onto this one without anyone, Astrin, Heureu, Bri or all those warriors seeing you?"

Tristan smiled. "I just followed the King onto the war-ship and then followed him off again. Nobody expected to see me where I wasn't supposed to be, and so they didn't. It was simple."

They passed Hlurle at night. Bri Corbett, with thought of another cask of Herun wine, suggested a brief stop there until Lyra reminded him of the twenty guards waiting at Hurle to escort the Morgol back to Herun. He abandoned the idea hastily and stopped instead farther up the coast, at the mouth of the turbulent Ose, where they took a quick, welcome respite from the sea. The town there was small, full of fishermen and trappers who brought their furs twice a year from the wilderness to sell to the traders. Bri bought wine, all the fresh eggs he could find and replenished their water supply. Lyra, Raederle and Tristan left letters for the traders to take south. No one recognized them, but they departed in a wake of curiosity that the letters, astonishingly addressed, did nothing to abate.

Three days later, at midmorning, they reached Kraal.

The city straddling Winter River was rough-hewn out of the stones and timber of Osterland. Beyond it, they caught their first close glimpse of the wild land, shaggy with pine, and of the distant blue-white mist of mountains. The harbor was full of trade-ships, barges with their gleaming upright lines of oars, riverboats making their slow way up the deep, green waters.

Bri, maneuvering carefully through the crowd, seemed to be calculating every shiver of wood under his feet, every wrinkle that appeared in the sails. He took the wheel from the helmsman once; Raederle heard him say, "That current must be dragging the barnacles off the hull. I've never seen the water so high. It must have been a terrible winter through the Pass . . ."

He found a berth unexpectedly in the crowded docks; the sight of the blue and purple sails of the King of An and the ship's incongruous passengers caused brisk and audible speculation among the shrewd-eyed traders. The women were all recognized as they stood at the rails, before the ship was fully secured to the moorings. Tristan's mouth dropped as she heard her own name, coupled with an unflattering query of the state of Bri Corbett's mind, shouted across the water from a neighboring ship.

Bri ignored it, but the burn on his face seemed to deepen. He said to Raederle as the ramp slid down, "You'll get no peace in this city, but at least you've got a good escort if you want to leave the ship. I'll try to get a barge and oarsmen; it'll be slow, and it will cost. But if we wait for the snow water to abate and a halfway decent wind to sail up, we may find the Morgol herself joining us. And that would really give these calk-brained, rattle-jawed gossip-peddlars, who are about to lose their teeth, something to talk about."

He managed with an energy that came, Raederle suspected, from a dread of glimpsing among the river traffic that taut, brilliant sail of an Ymris war-ship, to secure by evening a barge, a crew and supplies. She, Lyra, Tristan and the guards returned after a hectic afternoon among curious traders, trappers and Osterland farmers, to find their horses and gear being transferred onto the barge. They boarded the flat, inelegant vessel, found room almost on top of one another to sleep. The barge, lifting to the shift of the tide at some black hour of the morning, left Kraal behind as they slept.

The trip upriver was long, tedious and grim. The waters had flooded villages and farms as they spilled down from the Ose. They were withdrawing slowly, leaving in their wake gnarled, sodden, uprooted trees, dead animals, fields of silt and mud. Bri had to stop frequently, cursing, to loosen snags of roots, branches and broken furniture that got in their way. Once, an oarsman, pushing them away from a dark, tangled mound, freed something that stared at the sun out of a dead-white, shapeless face a moment before the current whirled it away. Raederle, her throat closing, heard Tristan's gasp. The waters themselves in the constant flickering shadows of trees, seemed lifeless, grey as they flowed down from the High One's threshold. After a week of glimpsing, between the trees, men clearing pieces of barn and carcasses of farm animals out of their fields, and watching nameless things lift to eye level out of the deep water at the stir of an oar, even the guards began to look haggard. Lyra whispered once to Raederle, "Did it come like this down from Erlenstar Mountain? This frightens me."

At the fork, where the Winter River broke away from the Ose, the waters cleared finally with the brisk, blue-white current. Bri anchored at the fork, for the barge could go no farther, unloaded their gear and sent the barge back down the silent, shadowed river.

Tristan, watching it disappear into the trees murmured, "I don't care if I have to walk home; I am not going on that river again." Then she turned, lifting her head to see the green face of Isig Mountain rising like a sentinel before the Pass. They seemed to be surrounded by mountains, the great mountain at whose roots the Osterland King lived, and the cold, distant peaks beyond the dead northern wastes. The morning sun was blazing above the head of Erlenstar Mountain, still glittering with unmelted snow. The light seemed to fashion the shadows, valleys, granite peaks that formed the Pass into the walls of some beautiful house lying open to the world.

Bri, his tongue full of names and tales he had not spoken for years, led them on horseback up the final stretch of river before the Pass. The bright, warm winds coming out of the backlands of the realm drove to the back of their memories the grey, dragging river behind them, and the secret, unexpected things dredged from its depths.

They found lodgings for a night in a tiny town that lay under the shadow of Isig. The next afternoon, they reached Kyrth, and saw at last the granite pillars honed by the Ose that were the threshold of Isig Pass. The sunlight seemed to leap goatlike from peak to peak; the air crackled white with the smell of melting ice. They had paused at a curve of road that led on one hand to Kyrth, on the other across a bridge to Isig. Raederle lifted her head. The ancient trees about them rose endlessly, face merging into face up the mountain, until they blurred together against the sky. Nearly hidden in them was a house with dark, rough walls and towers, windows that seemed faceted like jewels with color. Ribbons of smoke were coming up from within the walls; on the road a cart wheeled in and out of the trees toward it. The arch of its gates, massive and formidable as the gateway into the Pass, opened to the heart of the mountain.

"You'll need supplies," Bri Corbett said, and Raederle brought her thoughts out of the trees with an effort.

"For what?" she asked a little wearily. His saddle creaked as he turned to gesture towards the Pass. Lyra nodded.

"He's right. We can hunt and fish along the way, but we need some food, more blankets, a horse for Tristan." Her voice sounded tired, too, oddly timbreless in the hush of the mountains. "There will be no place for us to stay until we reach Erlenstar Mountain."

"Does the High One know we're coming?" Tristan asked abruptly, and they all glanced involuntarily at the Pass.

"I suppose so," Raederle said after a moment. "He must. I hadn't thought about it."

Bri, looking a little nervous, cleared his throat. "You're going just like that through the Pass."

"We can't sail and we can't fly; have you got any better suggestions?"

"I do. I suggest you tell someone your intentions before you ride headlong into what was a death trap for the Prince of Hed. You might inform Danan Isig you're in his land and about to go through the Pass. If we don't come back out, at least someone in the realm will know where we vanished."

Raederle looked again up at the enormous house of the King, ageless and placid under the vibrant sky. "I don't intend to vanish," she murmured. "I can't believe we're here. That's the great tomb of the Earth-Master's children, the place where the stars were shaped and set into a destiny older than the realm itself . . ." She felt Tristan stir behind her; saw, in her shadow on the ground, the mute shake of her head.

"This couldn't have anything to do with Morgon!" she burst out, startling them. "He never knew anything about land like this. You could drop Hed like a button in it and never see it. How could—how could something have reached that far, across mountains and rivers and the sea, to Hed, to put those stars on his face?"

"No one knows that," Lyra said with unexpected gentleness. "That's why we're here. To ask the High One." She looked at Raederle, her brows raised questioningly. "Should we tell Danan?"

"He might argue. I'm in no mood to argue. That's a house with only one door, and none of us knows what Danan Isig is like. Why should we trouble him with things he can't do anything about anyway?" She heard Bri's sigh and added, "You could stay in Kyrth while we go through the Pass. Then, if we don't return, at least you'll know." His answer was brief and pithy; she raised her brows. "Well, if that's the way you feel about it . . ."

Lyra turned her horse toward Kyrth. "We'll send a message to Danan."

Bri tossed his objections into the air with his hands. "A message," he said morosely. "With this town crammed to the high beams with traders, the gossip will reach him before any message does."

Reaching the small city, they found his estimations of the traders' skills well-founded. The city curved to one side of the Ose, its harbor full of river-boats and barges heavily laden with furs, metals, weapons, fine plate, cups, jewels from Danan's house, straining against their moorings to follow the flood waters. Lyra dispatched three of the guards to find a horse for Tristan, and the others to buy what food and cooking pots they might need. She found in a smelly tanners' street, hides for them to sleep on, and in a cloth shop, fur-lined blankets. Contrary to Bri's expectations, they were rarely recognized, but in a city whose merchants, traders and craftsmen had been immobilized through a long, harsh winter into boredom, their faces caused much cheerful comment. Bri, growling ineffectually, was recognized himself, and crossed the street while Raederle paid for the blankets, to speak to a friend in a tavern doorway. They lingered a little in the cloth shop examining the beautiful furs and strange, thick wools. Tristan hovered wistfully near a bolt of pale green wool until a grim, wild expression appeared suddenly on her face and she bought enough for three skirts. Then, laden to the chin with bundles, they stepped back into the street and looked for Bri Corbett.

"He must have gone in the tavern," Raederle said, and added a little irritably, for her feet hurt and she could have used a cup of wine. "He might have waited for us." She saw then, above the small tavern, the dark, endless rise of granite cliff and the Pass, itself, blazing with a glacial light as the last rays of the sun struck peak after icy peak. She took a breath of the lucent air, touched with a chill of fear at the awesome sight, and wondered for the first time since she had left An, if she had the courage to come face-to-face with the High One.

The light faded as they watched; shadows slipped after it, patching the Pass with purple and grey. Only one mountain, far in the distance, still burned white in some angle of light. The sun passed finally beyond the limits of the world, and the great flanks and peaks of the mountain turned to a smooth, barren whiteness, like the moon. Then Lyra moved slightly, and Raederle remembered she was there.

"Was that Erlenstar?" Lyra whispered.

"I don't know." She saw Bri Corbett come out of the tavern, then cross the street. His face looked oddly somber; he seemed as he reached them and stood looking at them, at a loss for words. His face was sweating a little in the cool air; he took his cap off, ran his fingers through his hair, and replaced it.

Then he said for some reason to Tristan, "We're going to Isig Mountain, now, to talk to Danan Isig."

"Bri, what's wrong?" Raederle asked quickly. "Is there—is it something in the Pass?"

"You're not going through the Pass. You're going home."

"What?"

"I'm taking you home tomorrow; there's a keel-boat going down the Ose—"

"Bri," Lyra said levelly. "You are not taking anyone as far as the end of the street without an explanation."

"You'll get enough of one, I think, from Danan." He bent unexpectedly, put his hands on Tristan's shoulders, and the familiar, stubborn expression on her face wavered slightly. He lifted one hand, groped for his hat again, and knocked it into the street. He said softly, "Tristan . . ." and Raederle's hand slid suddenly over her mouth.

Tristan said warily, "What?"

"I don't . . . I don't know how to tell you."

The blood blanched out of her face. She stared back at Bri and whispered, "Just tell me. Is it Eliard?"

"No. Oh, no. It's Morgon. He's been seen in Isig, and, three days ago, in the King's court in Osterland. He's alive."

Lyra's fingers locked in a rigid, painful grip above Raederle's elbow. Tristan's head bent, her hair brushing over her face. She stood so quietly they did not realize she was crying until her breath caught with a terrible sound in her throat, and Bri put his arms around her.

Raederle whispered, "Bri?" and his face turned to her.

"Danan Isig himself gave word to the traders. He can tell you. The trader I spoke to said—other things. You should hear them from Danan."

"All right," she said numbly. "All right." She took Tristan's cloth from her as Bri led them toward the horses. But she turned to see the dark, startled expression in Lyra's eyes and, beyond her, the darkness moving down the Pass in the wake of the silvery Ose.

They found two of the guards before they left the city. Lyra asked them briefly to find lodgings in Kyrth; they accepted the situation without comment, but their faces were puzzled. The four followed the road across the bridge up the face of the mountain, which had settled into a shadowy, inward silence that the beat of their horse's hooves on the dead pine needles never penetrated. The road's end ran beneath the stone archway into Danan's courtyard. The many workshops, kilns and forges all seemed quiet, but as they rode through the darkened yard, one of the workshop doors opened suddenly. Torchlight flared out of it; a young boy, gazing at the metalwork in his hands, stepped under the nose of Bri's horse.

Bri reined sharply as the horse startled; the boy, glancing up in surprise, put an apologetic hand on the horse's neck and it quieted. He blinked at them, a broad-shouldered boy with black, blunt hair and placid eyes. "Everyone's eating," he said. "May I tell Danan who has come, and will you eat with us?"

"You wouldn't be Rawl Ilet's son, would you?" Bri asked a little gruffly. "With that hair?"

The boy nodded. "I'm Bere."

"I am Bri Corbett, ship-master of Mathom of An. I used to sail with your father, when I was a trader. This is Mathom's daughter, Raederle of An; the Morgol's land-heir, Lyra; and this is Tristan of Hed."

Bere's eyes moved slowly from face to face. He made a sudden, uncharacteristic movement, as though he had quelled an impulse to run shouting for Danan. Instead he said, "He's just in the hall. I'll get him—" He stopped speaking abruptly, a jump of excitement in his voice, and went to Tristan's side. He held her stirrup carefully for her; she gazed down at his bent head in amazement a moment before she dismounted. Then he yielded and ran across the dark yard, flung the hall doors open to a blare of light and noise, and they heard his voice ringing above it: "Danan! Danan!" Bri, seeing the puzzled look on Tristan's face, explained softly, "Your brother saved his life."

The King of Isig followed Bere out. He was a big, broad man whose ash-colored hair glinted with traces of gold. His face was brown and scarred like tree bark, touched with an imperturbable calm that seemed on the verge of being troubled as he looked at them.

"You are most welcome to Isig," he said. "Bere, take their horses. I'm amazed that the three of you travelled so far together, and yet I've heard not a word of your coming."

"We were on our way to Erlenstar Mountain," Raederle said. "We didn't give anyone word of our leaving. We were buying supplies in Kyrth when Bri—when Bri gave us a piece of news that we could scarcely believe. So we came here to ask you about it. About Morgon."

She felt the King's eyes study her face in the shadows a moment, and she remembered then that he could see in the dark. He said, "Come in," and they followed him into the vast inner hall. A weave of fire and darkness hung like shifting tapestries on the walls of solid stone. The cheerful voices of miners and craftsmen seemed fragmented, muted in the sheer silence of stone. Water wound in flaming, curved sluices cut through the floor, trailed lightly into darkness; torchlight spattered across raw jewels thrusting out of the walls. Danan stopped only to give a murmured instruction to a servant, then led them up a side staircase that spiralled through the core of a stone tower. He stopped at a doorway, drew back hangings of pure white fur.

"Sit down," he urged them, as they entered. They found places on the chairs and cushions covered with fur and skins. "You look worn and hungry; food will be brought up, and I'll tell you while you eat what I can."

Tristan, her face quiet again, bewildered with wonder, said suddenly to Danan, "You were the one who taught him how to turn into a tree."

He smiled. "Yes."

"That sounded so strange in Hed. Eliard couldn't understand how Morgon did it. He used to stop and stare up at the apple trees; he said he didn't know what Morgon did with—with his hair, and how could he breathe—Eliard." Her hands tightened on the arms of her chair; they saw the flash of joy in her eyes that was constantly tempered by a wariness. "Is he all right? Is Morgon all right?"

"He seemed so."

"But I don't understand," she said almost pleadingly. "He lost the land-rule. How can he be alive? And if he's alive, how can he be all right?"

Danan opened his mouth, closed it again as servants entered with great trays of food and wine, bowls of water. He waited while the fire was laid against the cool mountain evening, and they had washed and begun to eat a little. Then he said gently, as though he were telling a story to one of his grandchildren, "A week ago, walking across my empty yard at twilight, I found someone coming towards me, someone who seemed to shape himself, as he moved, out of the twilight, the ember smoke, the night shadows, someone I never again thought to see in this world. . . . When I first recognized Morgon, I felt for a moment as though he had just left my house and come back, he looked that familiar. Then, when I brought him into the light, I saw how he was worn to the bone, as if he had been burned from within by some thought, and how his hair was touched, here and there, with white. He talked to me far into the night, telling me many things, and yet it seemed that there was always some dark core of memory he would not open to me. He said that he knew he had lost the land-rule and asked for news of Hed, but I could tell him almost nothing. He asked me to give word to the traders that he was alive, so that you would know."

"Is he coming home?" Tristan asked abruptly. Danan nodded.

"Eventually, but . . . he told me he was using every shade of power he had learned just to stay alive—"

Lyra leaned forward. "What do you mean 'learned'? Ghisteslwchlohm taught him things?"

"Well, in a way. Inadvertently." Then his brows pulled together. "Now, how did you know that? Who it was that had trapped Morgon?"

"My mother guessed. Ghisteslwchlohm had also been one of the Masters at Caithnard when Morgon studied there."

"Yes. He told me that." They saw something harden in the peaceful eyes. "You see, apparently the Founder of Lungold was looking for something in Morgon's mind, some piece of knowledge, and in probing every memory, every thought, burning away at the deep, private places of it, he opened his own mind and Morgon saw his vast reserves of power. That's how he broke free of Ghisteslwchlohm at last, by drawing from the wizard's mind the knowledge of his strengths and weaknesses, using his own power against him. He said, near the end, at times he did not know which mind belonged to whom, especially after the wizard stripped out of him all instinct for the land-rule. But at the moment he attacked finally, he remembered his name, and knew that in the long, black, terrible year he had grown stronger than even the Founder of Lungold . . ."

"What about the High One?" Raederle said. Something had happened in the room, she felt; the solid stones circling the firelight, the mountains surrounding the tower and the house seemed oddly fragile; the light itself a whim of the darkness crouched at the rim of the world. Tristan's head was bent, her face hidden behind her hair; Raederle knew she was crying soundlessly. She felt something beginning to break in her own throat, and she clenched her hands against it. "What . . . Why didn't the High One help him?"

Danan drew a deep breath. "Morgon didn't tell me, but from things he did say, I think I know."

"And Deth? The High One's harpist?" Lyra whispered. "Did Ghisteslwchlohm kill him?"

"No," Danan said, and at the tone in his voice even Tristan lifted her head. "As far as I know he's alive. That was one thing Morgon said he wanted to do before he went back to Hed. Deth betrayed Morgon, led him straight into Ghisteslwchlohm's hands, and Morgon intends to kill him."

Tristan put her hands over her mouth. Lyra broke a silence brittle as glass, rising, stumbling into her chair as she turned. She walked straight across the room until a window intruded itself in her path, and she lifted both hands, laid them flat against it. Bri Corbett breathed something inaudible. Raederle felt the tears break loose in spite of the tight grip of her hands; she said, struggling at least to control her voice, "That doesn't sound like either one of them."

"No," Danan Isig said, and again she heard the hardness in his voice. "The stars on Morgon's face were of some thought born in this mountain, the stars on his sword and his harp cut here a thousand years before he was born. We're touching the edge of doom, and it may be that the most we can hope for is an understanding of it. I have chosen to place whatever hope I have in those stars and in that Star-Bearer from Hed. For that reason I have complied with his request that I no longer welcome the High One's harpist into my house or allow him to set foot across the boundaries of my land. I have given this warning to my own people and to the traders to spread."

Lyra turned. Her face was bloodless, tearless. "Where is he? Morgon?"

"He told me he was going to Yrye, to talk to Har. He is being tracked by shape-changers; he moves painstakingly from place to place, taking shape after shape out of fear. As soon as he left my doorstep at midnight he was gone—a brush of ash, a small night animal—I don't know what he became." He was silent a moment, then added wearily, "I told him to forget about Deth, that the wizards would kill him eventually, that he had greater powers in the world to contend with; but he told me that sometimes, as he lay sleepless in that place, his mind drained, exhausted from Ghisteslwchlohm's probing, clinging to despair like a hard rock because that was the only thing he knew belonged to him, he could hear Deth piecing together new songs on his harp. . . . Ghisteslwchlohm, the shape-changers, he can in some measure understand, but Deth he cannot. He has been hurt deeply, he is very bitter . . ."

"I thought you said he was all right," Tristan whispered. She lifted her head. "Which way is Yrye?"

"Oh, no," Bri Corbett said emphatically. "No. Besides, he's left Yrye, by now, surely. Not one step farther north are any of you going.

We're sailing straight back down the Winter to the sea, and then home. All of you. Something in this smells like a hold full of rotten fish."

There was a short silence. Tristan's eyes were hidden, but Raederle saw the set, stubborn line of her jaw. Lyra's back was an inflexible, unspoken argument. Bri took his own sounding of the silence and looked satisfied.

Raederle said quickly before anyone could disillusion him, "Danan, my father left An over a month ago in the shape of a crow, to find out who killed the Star-Bearer. Have you seen or heard anything of him? I think he was heading for Erlenstar Mountain; he might have passed this way."

"A crow."

"Well, he—he is something of a shape-changer."

Danan's brows pulled together. "No. I'm sorry. Did he go directly there?"

"I don't know. It's always been difficult to know what he's going to do. But why? Surely Ghisteslwchlohm wouldn't be anywhere near the Pass, now." A memory came to her then, of the silent grey waters of the Winter coming down from the Pass, churning faceless, shapeless forms of death up from its shadows. Something caught at her voice; she whispered, "Danan, I don't understand. If Deth has been with Ghisteslwchlohm all this year, why didn't the High One warn us, himself, about him? If I told you that we intended to leave tomorrow, go through the Pass to Erlenstar Mountain to talk to the High One, what advice would you give us?"

She saw his hand lift in a little, quieting gesture. "Go home," he said gently. But he would not meet her eyes. "Let Bri Corbett take you home."

She sat late that night, thinking, after they had finished talking, and Danan's daughter, Vert, had taken them to small, quiet rooms in the tower to sleep in. The thick stones were chilly; the mountain had not fully emerged into spring, and she had lit a small fire laid in the hearth. She gazed into the restless flames, her arms around her knees. The fire flickered like thoughts in her eyes. Out of it rose fragments of knowledge she had; she wove them back and forth into one shapelessness after another. Somewhere far beneath her, she knew, hardened forever into memory, were the dead children of the Earth-Masters; the fire shivering over her hands might have drawn their faces out of their private blackness, but never warmed them. The stars that had grown in that same darkness, that had been brought to light and given their own pattern in Danan's house, would have burned like questions in the flame, but of their own place in a greater pattern they offered little answer. The thought of them lit her mind like the blue-white stone Astrin had given her; she saw again the strange face always on the verge of turning towards her, moving into identity. Another face shifted into her mind: the private, austere face of a harpist who had placed her uncertain fingers on her first flute, who had, with his flawless harping and vigilant mind, been the emissary of the High One for centuries. The face had been a mask; the friend who had led Morgon out of Hed, down the last steps to near-destruction, had been for centuries a stranger.

She shifted; the flames broke apart and rejoined. Things did not match, nothing seemed logical. Ylon leaped in her mind, at the sea's harping; the sea he came out of had given her and Mathom gifts of power; it had nearly given Morgon his death. Something in her had wept with a memory at the sight of the ruined city at King's Mouth Plain; something in her had wrenched at her mind for the dangerous knowledge in the core of the small blue stone. Morgon had ridden towards the High One's house, and the High One's harpist had twisted his path into horror. A wizard had ripped from his mind the right he had been born with; the land-law, which no one but the High One could alter, and the High One had done nothing. She closed her eyes, feeling the prick of sweat at her hairline. Deth had acted in the High One's name for five centuries; he had been given nothing less, in those centuries, than absolute trust. Following some private pattern of his own, in an unprecedented, inconceivable act, he had conspired to destroy a land-ruler. The High One had occasionally, in early days, dispensed doom for the simple intention. Why had he not acted against this man who had betrayed him as well as the Star-Bearer? Why had the High One not acted against Ghisteslwchlohm? Why . . . She opened her eyes, the fire flaring painfully at her widened pupils, and she blinked, seeing the room washed in flame. Why had Ghisteslwchlohm, who had the whole of the backlands of the realm to hide in, and who should have felt the need to hide, kept Morgon so close to Erlenstar Mountain? Why, when Deth had harped to himself that long year while

Morgon clung to the despair that was his life, had the High One never heard that harping? Or had he?

She stumbled to her feet, away from the hot flames, away from an answer, impossible, appalling, on the verge of language in her mind. The hangings moved aside so quietly in the doorway that their movement seemed almost an illusion of the fire. She thought, barely seeing a dark-haired woman in the half-light, that it was Lyra. Then, staring into the dark, quiet eyes of the woman, something settled into place deep within her, like a stone falling to a ponderous silence on the ground floor of Isig Mountain.

She whispered, scarcely realizing she spoke, "I thought so."

SHE FELT HER mind invaded, probed skillfully. This time, when the image in the stone reappeared, drawn out of memory, with the elusive, unfamiliar face, she did not struggle. She waited as the woman was waiting, for the movement, the turn of the head towards her that would name that face, put a name also to its irrevocable doom. But he seemed frozen in her last glimpse of him; the invisible rush towards him was caught, stilled in motion. The image faded finally; the woman drew out other memories, bright, random scenes from Raederle's past. She saw herself as a child again, talking to the pigs while Cyone talked to the pig-woman; running through Madir's woods effortlessly recognizing tree and the illusion of tree while Duac and Rood shouted in frustration behind her; arguing with Mathom over the endless riddles he had her learn while the summer sun lay on the stones at her feet like an immutable golden disc. The woman lingered long over her relationship with the pig-woman, the small magic things the pig-woman taught her; Mathom's marriage plans for her seemed to intrigue the woman also, as well as his imperturbable stubbornness against the opposition he faced from the lords of An, from Duac, from Cyone, from Raederle herself when she understood at last what he had done. A dark, weary tower in Aum rose unbidden in her mind, an isolated shadow in an oak wood; the woman loosed her at that point, and Raederle felt that for the first time, she was surprised.

"You went there. To Peven's tower."

Raederle nodded. The fire had coiled down into the embers; she was trembling as much from weariness as from the chill. The woman seemed to hover, mothlike, on the edge of the faint light. She glanced at the fire, and it sprang alive, lean and white, etching the quiet, delicate face again out of the darkness.

"I had to. I had to know what price my father had set to my name before I was ever born. So I went there. I couldn't go in, though. It was a long time ago; I was afraid . . ." She shook her head slightly, bringing her own thoughts back from the memory. She faced the woman again across the strange fire; the white flame twisted and burned in the depths of the still eyes. "Who are you? Something in me knows you."

"Ylon." The flame curved into something of a smile. "We are kinswomen, you and I."

"I know." Her voice sounded dry, hollow; her heart was beating its own hollow place within her. "You have had many kinsmen in the line of the Kings of An. But what are you?"

The woman sat beside the hearth; she lifted one hand to the flame in a gesture at once beautiful and childlike, then said, "I am a shape-changer. I killed Eriel Ymris and took her shape; I half-blinded Astrin Ymris; I came very close to killing the Star-Bearer, although it was not his death I was interested in. Then. I am not interested in yours, if you are wondering."

"I was," Raederle whispered. "What—what is it you are interested in?"

"The answer to a riddle."

"What riddle?"

"You'll see it yourself, soon enough." She was silent, her eyes on the fire, her hands still in her lap, until Raederle's own eyes went to the flame, and she groped for the chair behind her. "It's a riddle old as the crevices of old tree roots, as the silence molding the groins of inner Isig, as the stone faces of the dead children. It is essential, as wind or fire. Time means nothing to me, only the long moment between the asking of that riddle and its answer. You nearly gave it to me, on that ship, but you broke the binding between you and the stone in spite of me. That surprised me."

"I didn't—I couldn't break it. I remember. Lyra hit me. You. That was you in my mind. And the riddle: You need to put a name to that face?"

"Yes."

"And then—and then what? What will happen?"

"You are something of a riddler. Why should I play your game for you?"

"It's not a game! You are playing with our lives!"

"Your lives mean nothing to me," the woman said dispassionately. "The Star-Bearer and I are looking for answers to the same questions: he kills when he needs to; our methods are no different. I need to find the Star-Bearer. He has grown very powerful and very elusive. I thought of using you or Tristan as bait to trap him, but I will let him make his own path awhile. I think I can see where it's leading him."

"He wants to kill Deth," Raederle said numbly.

"It won't be the first great harpist he has killed. But he dare not turn his attention from Ghisteslwchlohm too long, either. Morgon or the wizards must kill the Founder. The wizards themselves, from the way they are secretly moving towards Lungold, have a revenge of their own to satisfy. They will no doubt destroy one another, which will not matter; they've scarcely been alive for seven centuries." She caught the expression on Raederle's face, the words she swallowed, and smiled. "Nun? I watched her at Lungold, the powerful, the beautiful. She would hardly call herding pigs and making grass nets living."

"What would you call what you're doing?"

"Waiting." She was silent a moment, her imperturbed eyes on Raederle's face. "Are you curious about yourself? Of the extent of your own powers? They are considerable."

"No."

"I have been honest with you."

Raederle's hands loosened on the arms of her chair. Her head bowed; she felt again, at the woman's words, the odd sense of kinship, if not trust, an inescapable understanding. She said softly, the despair settling through her again, "Ylon's blood has been in my family for generations; no one, however troubled by it, ever realized that he was anything more than the son of a sea legend, just another inexplicable shape of the magic of An. Now I know what his father was. One of you. That gives me some kinship with you. But nothing else, nothing of your compassionlessness, your destructiveness—"

"Only our power." She shifted forward slightly. "Ylon's father and I tried to do the same thing: to disturb the land-rule of An and Ymris by giving their kings heirs of mixed blood and twisted instinct. It was for a purpose, and it failed. The land saw to its own. Only Ylon bore the torment of land-rule; his power dissipated in his descendants, grew unused, dormant. Except in you. One day, perhaps, you could put a name to that power, and that name would surprise you. But you will not live that long. You only know of Ylon's sadness. But have you ever wondered, if we are so terrible, what made him break out of his prison to return to us?"

"No," Raederle whispered.

"Not compassion, but passion . . ." Something in her voice opened then, like a flick of light in the deep of Isig opening a vein of unexpected richness to view, and she stopped. She reached down, touched the white fire with one hand, drew it softly into a glistening spider's web, a polished bone, a scattering of stars, a moon-white chambered shell, shape weaving into shape, falling from her hand, a handful of blazing flowers, a net knotted and glinting as with seawater, a harp with thin, glistening strings. Raederle, watching, felt a hunger stir in her, a longing to possess the knowledge of the fire, the fire itself. The woman's face had grown oblivious of her, intent on her work; it seemed touched with wonder itself at each fiery, beautiful shape. She let the fire fall at last like drops of water or tears back into the bed. "I take my power, as you take yours, from the heart of things, in a recognition of each thing. From the inward curve of a grass blade, from the pearl troubling as a secret deed in the oyster shell, from the scent of trees. Is that so unfamiliar to you?"

"No." Her voice seemed to come from a distance, somewhere beyond the small room, the shadowed stones.

The woman continued softly, "You can know it: the essence of fire. You have the power. To recognize it, to hold it, shape it, even to become fire, to melt into its great beauty, bound to no man's laws. You are skilled with illusion; you have played with a dream of the sun's fire. Now work with fire itself. See it. Understand it. Not with your eyes or your mind, but with the power in you to know and accept, without fear, without question, the thing as itself. Lift your hand. Hold it out. Touch the fire."

Raederle's hand moved slowly. For a moment the shifting, bone-white, lawless thing before her that she had known all her life yet never known, seemed, as it wove in and out of the darkness, a child's riddle. She reached out to it tentatively, curiously. Then she realized that, in reaching towards it, she was turning away from her own name—the familiar heritage of An that had defined her from her birth—towards a heritage that held no peace, a name that no one knew. Her hand, curved to the flame, closed abruptly. She felt the heat, the fire's barrier, then, and drew back from it quickly. Her voice broke from her.

"No."

"You can, when you choose. When you lose your fear of the source of your power."

"And then what?" She brought her eyes away from her hand with an effort. "Why are you telling me that? Why do you care?"

Something moved minutely in the planes of the face, as though far away, in the darkness, the door of a thought had closed. "For no reason. I was curious. About you, about your father's vow binding you to the Star-Bearer. Was that foreknowledge?"

"I don't know."

"The Star-Bearer, I expected, but not you. Will you tell him, or will you let him guess, if you ever see him again, that you are kin to those trying to destroy him? If you ever bear him children, will you tell him whose blood they carry?"

Raederle swallowed. Her throat felt dry, her skin stretched taut and dry as parchment across her face. She had to swallow again before her voice would come. "He is a riddle-master. He won't need to be told." She found herself on her feet then, with the hollow in her growing deep, unbearable. She turned blindly away from the woman. "So he'll win me with one riddle and lose me with another," she added, hardly realizing what she was saying. "Is that any of your business?"

"Why else am I here? You are afraid to touch Ylon's power; then remember his longing."

The hopeless sorrow struck like a tide, welled through Raederle until she saw nothing, heard nothing, felt nothing but the grief and longing that had filled her at the sight of King's Mouth Plain. But she could not escape from it; her own sorrow was woven to it. She smelled then the bitter smell of the sea, dried kelp, iron rusted with the incessant spray that Ylon must have smelled; heard the hollow boom of the tide against the foundation stones of his tower, the suck of it bearing back from the green, pointed teeth of rocks below him. She heard the lament of sea birds wheeling aimlessly to the wind. Then she heard out of a world beyond eyesight, a world beyond hope, a harping tuned to her grief, playing back, in sympathy, her own lament. It was a fragile harping, almost lost in the brush of rain over the sea, on the flow and ebb of the tide. She found herself straining to hear it, moving towards it, straining, until her hands touched cold glass, as Ylon's hands would have touched the iron bars over his window. She blinked away the harping, the sea; it receded slowly. The woman's voices receded with it.

"We are all tuned to that harping. Morgon killed the harpist, Ylon's father. So where, in a world of such unexpected shape, will you put your certainty?"

The silence at her leaving was like the full, charged silence before a storm. Raederle, still standing at the window, took one step towards the doorway. But Lyra could give her no help, perhaps not even understanding. She heard a sound break out of her, shiver across the silence, and she held it back with her hands. A face slipped into her thoughts: a stranger's face now, worn, bitter, troubled, itself. Morgon could not help her, either, but he had weathered truth, and he could face, with her, one more thing. Her hands had begun to move before she realized it, emptying the clothes from her pack, scattering the fruit, nuts and sweetmeats on the wine table into it, pushing on top of them a soft skin lying across one of the chairs, buckling the pack again. She threw her cloak over her shoulders and went silently out of the room, leaving behind her like a message the white, twisting flame.

She could not find the stables in the dark, so she walked out of the King's yard, down the mountain road in the thin moonlight to the Ose. She remembered from Bri's maps, how the Ose ran southward a little, curving around the foothills behind Isig; she could follow it until it began to turn east. Morgon would be heading south, down from Osterland, carrying his tale to Herun, she guessed; or was he, like the wizards, on his way to Lungold? It did not matter; he would have to go south, and with his wizard's mind alert to danger, perhaps he would sense her travelling alone and on foot in the backlands and investigate.

She found an old cart trail, rutted and overgrown, running along the side of the river, and she followed it. At first, fleeing the King's house, her grieving had seemed to make her invisible, impervious to weariness, cold, fear. But the swift, insistent voice of the Ose brought her out of her thoughts, shivering into the dark. The moon patched the road with shadows, the voice of the river hid other voices, sounds she was not certain she heard, rustling that may or may not have come from behind her. The ancient pines with their calm, wrinkled faces, Danan's face, gave her comfort. She heard the crash and snarl of animals once, near her, and stopped short, then realized that she did not really care what might happen to her, and probably, neither did they. The river dragged the sound of their quarrel away. She walked on until the cart road ended abruptly in a clump of brambles, and the moon began to set. She unpacked the skin, lay down and covered herself. She slept, exhausted and heard in her dreams a harping above the constant movement of the Ose.

She woke at sunrise; her eyes burned at the touch of the sun. She splashed water from the river on her face and drank it, then ate a little food from her pack. Her bones ached; her muscles protested at every movement until she began to walk again and forgot about them. Making her own path down the river did not seem difficult; she skirted bramble patches, climbed over rocks when the banks rose steeply above it, gathered her torn skirts to wade when the bank was impassible, washed her bruised, scratched hands in the river and felt the sun beat down on her face. She ignored the time passing, intent on nothing but her own movement until it came to her, slowly and forcibly, that she was being followed.

She stopped then. All the weariness and ache of her body caught up with her, draining through her until she swayed, balanced on a rock in the river. She bent, drank water, and looked behind her again. Nothing moved through the lazy hot noon hour, and yet she sensed movement, her name in someone's mind. She drank again, wiped her mouth on her sleeve, and began to work out of it a piece of silver thread.

She left several of them in her trail, intricately wound and tangled. She drew long grass blades together and knotted them; they looked fragile to the eye, but to a man or a horse tripping over them, they would seem strong as taut rope. She poised wayward stems of brambles over her path, seeing, in her mind's eye, the formidable prickly clumps they would seem to anyone else. In one place she dug a fist-sized hole, lined it with leaves, and then filled it with water she carried in her hands. It stared back at the blue sky like an eye, a round unobtrusive pool that could stretch like a dream into a wide, impassible lake.

The nagging following began to be less urgent; she guessed that it had met with some of her traps. She slowed a little herself, then. It was late afternoon; the sun hovered above the tips of the pine. A little wind shivered through them, the cool evening wind, rousing. It carried a loneliness in its wake, the loneliness of the backlands. She glimpsed then the long succession of days and nights ahead of her, the lonely trek through the unsettled lands, nearly impossible for one weaponless, on foot. But behind her lay Isig Pass with its dark secret; in An there was no one, not even her father, to give her a measure of understanding. She could only hope that her blind need would stumble onto its own source of comfort. She shivered a little, not at the wind, but at the empty rustle of its passing, and went on. The sun set, drawing fingers of light through the trees; the twilight lay in an unearthly silence over the world. Still she moved, without thinking, without stopping to eat, without realizing that she walked on the thin line of exhaustion. The moon rose; her constant tripping over things she could not see in the dark began to slow her. She fell once, seemingly for no reason, and was surprised when she found it difficult to rise. She fell again, a few paces later, with the same surprise. She felt blood trickle down her knee and put her hand in a patch of nettles as she rose. She stood nursing her hand under one arm, wondering why her body was shaking, for the night was not very cold. Then she saw, like a dream of hope, the warm, slender dance of flame within the trees. She went towards it with one name in her mind. Reaching it finally, she found in the circle of its light the High One's harpist.

For a moment, standing at the edge of the light, she saw only that it was not Morgon. He was sitting back against a rock beside the fire, his face bent; she saw only his silver-white hair. Then he turned his head and looked at her.

She heard his breath catch. "Raederle?"

She took a step backward, and he moved abruptly, as if to rise and stop her before she vanished again into the darkness. Then he checked himself, leaned back deliberately against the rock. There was an expression on his face she had never seen before, that kept her lingering at the light. He gestured to the fire, the hare spitted over it.

"You look tired; sit down awhile." He turned the spit; a breath of hot meat came to her. His hair was ragged; his face looked worn, lined, oddly open. His voice, musical and edged with irony, had not changed.

She whispered, "Morgon said that you—that you harped while he lay half-dead in Ghisteslwchlohm's power."

She saw the muscles in his face tighten. He reached out, edged a broken branch into the fire. "It's true. I will reap my reward for that harping. But meanwhile, will you have some supper? I am doomed; you are hungry. One has very little to do with the other, so there is no reason for you not to eat with me."

She took another step, this time towards him. Though he watched her, his expression did not change, and she took another. He took a cup from his pack, filled it with wine from a skin. She came close finally, held out her hands to the blaze. They hurt her; she turned and saw the cuts on them from brambles, the white blisters from the nettles. His voice came again. "I have water . . ." It faded. She glanced down at him, watched him pour water from another skin into a bowl. His fingers shook slightly as he corked the skin; he did not speak again. She sat finally, washed the dirt and dried blood from her hands. He passed her wine, bread and meat in the same silence, sipped wine slowly while she ate.

Then he said, his voice sliding so evenly into the silence that it did not startle her, "Morgon, I expected to find in the night at my fire's edge, or any one of five wizards, but hardly the second most beautiful woman of the Three Portions of An."

She glanced down at herself absently. "I don't think I'm that any more." A pang of sorrow caught at her throat as she swallowed; she put the food down and whispered, "Even I have changed shape. Even you."

"I have always been myself."

She looked at the fine, elusive face, with its unfamiliar shadow of mockery. She asked then, for both the question and the answer seemed impersonal, remote, "And the High One? Whom have you harped to for so many centuries?"

He leaned forward almost abruptly to stir the lagging fire. "You know to ask the question; you know the answer. The past is the past. I have no future."

Her throat burned. "Why? Why did you betray the Star-Bearer?"

"Is it a riddle-game? I'll give answer for answer."

"No. No games."

They were silent again. She sipped her wine, felt, coming alive all through her, little aches and throbbings from cuts, pulled muscles, bruises. He filled her cup again when she finished. She broke the silence, easy in his presence for some reason, as though they sat together in the same black hollow of sorrow. "He already killed one harpist."

"What?"

"Morgon." She moved a little, shifting away from the longing the name gave her. "Ylon's father. Morgon killed Ylon's father."

"Ylon," he said tonelessly, and she lifted her head, met his eyes. Then he laughed, his hands linked hard around his cup. "So. That sent you into the night. And you think, in the midst of this chaos, that it matters?"

"It matters! I have inherited a shape-changer's power—I can feel it! If I reached out and touched the fire, I could hold it in the palm of my hand. Look . . ." Something: the wine, his indifference, her hopelessness, made her reckless. She stretched out her hand, held it curved in a motionless caress to the heat and curve of a flame. The reflection of it flickered in Deth's eyes; its light lay cradled in the lines and hollows of the stone he leaned against, traced the roots of ancient trees into untangling. She let the reflection ease through her thoughts, followed every shift of color and movement, every fade and mysterious renewal out of nothingness. It was of an alien fabric that ate darkness and never died. Its language was older than men. It was a shape-changer; it groped for the shape of her mind as she watched it, filled her eyes so that she saw a single leaf fall in a liquid, burning tear through the darkness to the ground. And deep within her, rousing out of a dormant, lawless heritage came the fiery, answering leap of understanding. The lucent, wordless knowledge of fire filled her; the soft rustlings became a language, the incessant weave a purpose, its color the color of the world, of her mind. She touched a flame then, let it lay in her hand like a flower. "Look," she said breathlessly, and closed her hand over it, extinguishing it, before the wonder in her broke the binding between them, separating them, and it hurt her. The night fell around her again, as the tiny flame died. She saw Deth's face, motionless, unreadable, his lips parted.

"Another riddle," he whispered.

She rubbed her palm against her knee, for in spite of her care it hurt a little. A breath of reason, like the cool air off the northern peaks brushed her mind; she shivered, and said slowly, remembering, "She wanted me to hold the fire, her fire . . ."

"Who?"

"The woman. The dark woman who had been Eriel Ymris for five years. She came to me to tell me we were kin, which I had already guessed."

"Mathom trained you well," he commented, "to be a riddle-master's wife."

"You were a Master. You told him that once. Am I so good with riddles? What do they lead to but betrayal and sorrow? Look at you. You not only betrayed Morgon, but my father and everyone in this realm who trusted you. And look at me. What lord of An would bother to draw enough breath to ask for me, if he knew who claimed kinship with me?"

"You are running from yourself, and I am running from death. So much for the tenets of riddle-mastery. Only a man with a brain and heart implacable as the jewels in Isig could bear adhering to them. I made my decision five centuries ago about the values of riddles, when Ghisteslwchlohm asked me to Erlenstar Mountain. I thought nothing in the realm could break his power. But I was wrong. He broke himself against the rigid tenets of the Star-Bearer's life and fled, leaving me alone, unprotected, harpless—"

"Where is your harp?" she asked, surprised.

"I don't know. Still in Erlenstar Mountain, I assume. I don't dare harp now. That was the only other thing Morgon heard, besides Ghisteslwchlohm's voice, for a year."

She flinched, wanting to run from him then, but her body would not move. She cried out at him, "Your harping was a gift to Kings!" He did not answer; his cup rose, flashed again in the firelight. When he spoke finally, his voice seemed shaded, like the fire's voice.

"I've played and lost to a Master; he'll take his vengeance. But I regret the loss of my harp."

"As Morgon must regret the loss of his land-rule?" Her own voice shook. "I'm curious about that. How could Ghisteslwchlohm rip that from him—the instinct for the land-law that is known only to Morgon and the High One? What piece of knowledge did the Founder expect to find beneath the knowledge of when the barley would begin to sprout or what trees in his orchard had a disease eating secretly at their hearts?"

"It's done. Can you let—"

"How can I? Did you think you were betraying only Morgon? You taught me 'The Love of Hover and Bird' on the flute when I was nine. You stood behind me and held my fingers down on the right notes while I played. But that hardly matters, compared to what the land-rulers of the realm will feel when they realize what honor they have given to the harpist of the Founder of Lungold. You hurt Lyra badly enough, but what will the Morgol, herself, think when Morgon's tale reaches her? You—" She stopped. He had not moved; he was sitting as she had first seen him, with his head bent, one hand on his bent knee, the cup cradled in it. Something had happened to her, in her anger. She lifted her head, smelled the fine, chill, pine-scented air off Isig, felt the night that lay over her like its shadow. She sat at a tiny fire, lost in that vast blackness, her dress torn, her hair tangled and dirty, her face scratched, probably so haggard no Lord of An would recognize her. She had just put her hand in the fire and held it; something of its clarity seemed to burn in her mind. She whispered, "Say my name."

"Raederle."

Her own head bent. She sat quietly awhile, feeling the name in her like a heartbeat. She drew breath at last, loosed it. "Yes. That woman nearly made me forget. I ran from Isig in the middle of the night to look for Morgon somewhere in the backlands. It seems unlikely, doesn't it, that I'll find him that way."

"A little."

"And no one in Danan's house knows if I am alive or dead. That seems inconsiderate. I forgot that, having Ylon's power, I still have my own name. That's a very great power, that alone. The power to see . . ."

"Yes." He lifted his head finally, lifted the cup to drink again, but instead put it down with a curious care on the ground. He sat back, his face thrown clear in the light; the mockery in it had gone. She drew her knees together, huddling against herself, and he said, "You're cold. Take my cloak."

"No."

His mouth crooked slightly, but he said only, "What is Lyra doing in Isig Mountain?"

"We came to ask the High One questions—Lyra, Tristan of Hed, and I—but Danan told us that Morgon was alive, and he advised against going through the Pass. It took me hours to think why. And it has taken this long—a day and two nights—to think of another question. But there's no one to ask, except Morgon, and you."

"You would trust me with a question?"

She nodded a little wearily. "I don't understand you anymore; your face changes shape every time I look at you, now a stranger, now the face of a memory . . . But whoever you are, you still know as much, if not more, as anyone else about what is happening in the realm. If Ghisteslwçhlohm took the High One's place at Erlenstar Mountain, then where is the High One? Someone still holds order in the realm."

"True." He was silent, an odd tautness to his mouth. "I asked Ghisteslwchlohm that five centuries ago. He couldn't answer me. So I lost interest. Now, with my own death inevitable, I am still not very interested, any more than the High One, where he is, seems remotely interested in any problems in the realm beyond land-law."

"Perhaps he never existed. Perhaps he's a legend spun out of the mystery of the ruined cities, passed through the ages until Ghisteslwchlohm took the shape of it . . ."

"A legend like Ylon? Legends have a grim way of twisting into truth."

"Then why did he never stop you from harping in his name? He must have known."

"I don't know. No doubt he has reasons. Whether he or Morgon dooms me, it makes little difference; the result will be the same."

"There's nowhere you can go?" she asked, surprising both herself and him. He shook his head.

"Morgon will close the realm to me. Even Herun. I will not go there, in any event. I was already driven out of Osterland, three nights ago, crossing the Ose. The wolf-king spoke to his wolves . . . A pack found me camping on his land, a remote corner of it. They did not touch me, but they let me know I was not welcome. When word reaches Ymris, it will be the same. And An . . . The Star-Bearer will drive me where he wants me. I saw the hollow he made of the High One's house when he finally broke free—it seemed as if Erlenstar Mountain itself was too small to hold him. He paused, in passing, to wrench the strings out of my harp. His judgment of me I don't contest, but . . . that was one thing in my life I did well."

"No," she whispered. "You did many things well. Dangerously well. There wasn't a man, woman or child in the realm who didn't trust you: you did that well. So well that I am still sitting beside you, talking to you, even though you hurt someone I love past bearing. I don't know why."

"Don't you? It's simply that, alone in the backlands under a sky black as the pit of a dead king's eye, we have nothing left but our honesty. And our names. There is great richness in yours," he added almost lightly, "but not even hope in mine."

She fell asleep soon afterwards beside his fire, while he sat quietly drinking wine and feeding the fire. When she woke in the morning, he was gone. She heard rustlings in the brush, voices; she shifted painfully, freeing an arm to push back the covering over her. Then she checked. She sat up abruptly, staring down at her hand, in which the fire had burned like an extension of herself the night before. On her palm, scored white, were the twelve sides and delicate inner lines of the stone Astrin had given her on King's Mouth Plain.

LYRA, TRISTAN AND the guards rode out of the trees, then, into the tiny clearing where Raederle sat, Lyra reined sharply at the sight of her, dismounted without a word. She looked dishevelled herself, worn and tired. She went to Raederle, knelt beside her. She opened her mouth to say something, but words failed her. She opened her hand instead, dropped between them three tangled, dirty pieces of thread.

Raederle stared down at them, touched them. "That was you behind me," she whispered. She straightened, pushing hair out of her eyes. The guards were dismounting. Tristan, still on her horse, was staring at Raederle, wide-eyed and frightened. She slid to the ground abruptly, came to Raederle's side.

"Are you all right?" Her voice was sharp with worry. "Are you all right?" She brushed pieces of pine needle and bark out of Raederle's hair gently. "Did anyone hurt you?"

"Who were you running from?" Lyra asked. "Was it a shape-changer?"

"Yes."

"What happened? I was just across the hall; I couldn't sleep. I didn't even hear you leave. I didn't hear—" She stopped abruptly, as at a memory. Raederle pushed wearily at the cloak that had been covering her; it was hot, heavy in the bright morning. She drew her knees up, dropping her face against them, feeling a complaint from every bone at the simple movements.

The others were silent; she could feel their waiting, so she said haltingly after a moment, "It was—one of the shape-changers came to my room, spoke to me. After she left, I wanted—I wanted to find Morgon very badly, to talk to him. I was not thinking very clearly. I left Danan's house, walked in the night until the moon set. Then I slept awhile and walked again, until—until I came here. I'm sorry about the traps."

"What did she say? What could she have said to make you run like that?"

Raederle lifted her head. "Lyra, I can't talk about it now," she whispered. "I want to tell you, but not now."

"All right." She swallowed. "It's all right. Can you get up?"

"Yes." Lyra helped her stand; Tristan reached for the cloak, bundled it in her arms, gazing anxiously over it.

Raederle glanced around. There seemed to be no trace of Deth; he had passed in and out of the night like a dream, but one of the guards, Goh, casting about with a methodical eye, said, "There was a horseman here." She gazed southward as if she were watching his passage. "He went that way. The horse might have been bred in An, from the size of the hoof. It's no plow horse, or Ymris war horse."

"Was it your father?" Lyra asked a little incredulously. Raederle shook her head. Then she seemed to see for the first time the heavy, rich, blue-black cloak in Tristan's arms. Her teeth clenched; she took the cloak from Tristan, flung it into the ashes of the fire bed, seeing across from it as she did so, the harpist's face changing to every shift of firelight. Her hands locked on her arms; she said, her voice steady again, "It was Deth."

"Deth," Lyra breathed, and Raederle saw the touch of longing in her face. "He was here? Did you speak to him?"

"Yes. He fed me. I don't understand him. He told me that everything Morgon said about him is true. Everything. I don't understand him. He left his cloak for me while I was sleeping."

Lyra turned abruptly, bent to check the trail Goh had found. She stood again, looking southward. "How long ago did he leave?"

"Lyra," Imer said quietly, and Lyra turned to face her. "If you intend to track that harpist through the backlands of the realm, you'll go alone. It's time for us all to return to Herun. If we leave quickly enough, we can reach it before Morgon does, and you can ask him your questions. The tale itself will reach Herun before any of us do, I think, and the Morgol will need you."

"For what? To guard the borders of Herun against Deth?"

"It might be," Goh said soothingly, "that he has some explanation to give only to the Morgol."

"No," Raederle said. "He said he would not go to Herun."

They were silent. The wind roused, sweet-smelling, empty, stalking southward like a hunter. Lyra stared down at the cloak in the ashes. She said blankly, "I can believe he betrayed the Star-Bearer if I must, but how can I believe he would betray the Morgol? He loved her."

"Let's go," Kia urged softly. "Let's go back to Herun. None of us knows any more what to do. This place is wild and dangerous; we don't belong here."

"I'm going to Herun," Tristan said abruptly, startling them with her decisiveness. "Wherever that is. If that's where Morgon is going."

"If we sail," Raederle said, "we might get there before he does. Is Bri— Where is Bri Corbett? He let you come after me alone?"

"We didn't exactly stop to ask his permission," Lyra said. The guards were beginning to mount again. "I brought your horse. The last time I saw Bri Corbett, he was searching the mines with Danan and the miners."

Raederle took her reins, mounted stiffly. "For me? Why did they think I would have gone into the mines?"

"Because Morgon did," Tristan said, "when he was there." She pulled herself easily onto the small, shaggy pony the guards had brought for her. Her face was still pinched with worry; she viewed even the genial profile of Isig with a disapproving eye. "That's what Danan said. I got up near morning to talk to you, because I had a bad dream. And you were gone. There was only that fire, white as a turnip. It frightened me, so I woke Lyra. And she woke the King. Danan told us to stay in the house while he searched the mines. He was also afraid you had been kidnapped. But Lyra said you weren't."

"How did you know?" Raederle asked, surprised.

The guards had formed a loose, watchful circle around them as they rode back through the trees. Lyra said simply, "Why would you have taken your pack and all the food in the room if you had been kidnapped? It didn't make sense. So while Danan searched his house, I went into town and found the guards. I left a message for Danan, telling him where we were going. Finding your trail wasn't difficult; the ground is still soft, and you left pieces of cloth from your skirt on brambles beside the river. But then your horse stepped on one of the threads you dropped and pulled out of Goh's hold; we spent an hour chasing it. And after we caught it finally, Kia rode over another thread and went off into the brush before anyone saw her. So we spent more time tracking her. After that, I watched for your threads. But it took me awhile to realize why our horses kept stumbling over things that weren't there, and why there were mountains of brambles along the river that your footprints seemed to disappear into. And then we came to that lake . . ." She paused, giving the memory a moment of fulminous silence. The blood was easing back into Raederle's face as she listened.

"I'm sorry it was you. Was—Did it work?"

"It worked. We spent half an afternoon trying to round one shore of it. It was impossible. It simply didn't look that big. It just stretched. Finally Goh noticed that there were no signs that you had walked around it, and I realized what it might be. I was so hot and tired I got off my horse and walked straight into it; I didn't care if I got wet or not. And it vanished. I looked behind me, and saw all the dry ground we had been skirting, making a path around nothing."

"She stood in the middle of the water and cursed," Imer said, with a rare grin. "It looked funny. Then, when we reached the river again, to pick up your trail, and saw that tiny pool, no bigger than a fist, we all cursed. I didn't know anyone but a wizard could do that with water."

Raederle's hand closed suddenly over its secret. "I've never done it before." The words sounded unconvincing to her ears. She felt oddly ashamed, as though, like Deth, she held a stranger's face to the world. The calm, ancient face of Isig rose over them, friendly in the morning light, its raw peaks gentled. She said with sudden surprise, "I didn't get very far, did I?"

"You came far enough," Lyra said.

They reached Isig again at noon the next day. Bri Corbett, grim and voluble with relief, took one look at Raederle, stayed long enough to hear Lyra's tale, then departed to find a boat at Kyrth. Raederle said very little, either to Danan or Bri; she was grateful that the mountain-king refrained from questioning her. He only said gently, with a perception that startled her, "Isig is my home; the home of my mind, and still, after so many years, it is capable of surprising me. Whatever you are gripping to yourself in secret, remember this: Isig holds great beauty and great sorrow, and I could not desire anything less for it, than that it yields always, unsparingly, the truth of itself."

Bri returned that evening, having wheedled places for them all, their horses and gear, on two keelboats packed and readied to leave for Kraal at dawn. The thought of another journey down the Winter made them all uneasy, but it was, when they finally got underway, not so terrible as before. The floodwaters had abated; the fresh, blue waters of the upper Ose pushed down it, clearing the silt and untangling the snags. The boats ran quickly on the crest of the high water; they could see, as the banks flowed past them, the Osterland farmers pounding the walls of their barns and pens back together again. The piquant air skimmed above the water, rippling it like the touch of birds' wings; the warm sun glinted off the metal hinges of the cargo chests, burned in flecks of spray on the ropes.

Raederle, scarcely seeing at all as she stood day after day at the rail, was unaware of her own disturbing silence. The evening before they were due to reach Kraal, she stood in the shadowy twilight under the lacework of many trees, and realized, only after the leaves had blurred into darkness, that Lyra was standing beside her. She started slightly.

Lyra, the weak light from the chart house rippling over her face, said softly, "If Morgon has already passed through Crown City when we get there, what will you do?"

"I don't know. Follow him."

"Will you go home?"

"No." There was a finality in her voice that surprised her. Lyra frowned down at the dark water, her proud, clean-lined face like a lovely profile on a coin. Raederle, looking at her, realized with helpless longing, the assuredness in it, the absolute certainty of place.

"How can you say that?" Lyra asked. "How can you not go home? That's where you belong, the one place."

"For you, maybe. You could never belong anywhere but in Herun."

"But you are of An! You are almost a legend of An, even in Herun. Where else could you go? You are of the magic of An, of the line of its kings; where . . . What did the woman say to you that is terrible enough to keep you away from your own home?"

Raederle was silent, her hands tightening on the rail. Lyra waited; when Raederle did not answer, she went on, "You have scarcely spoken to anyone since we found you in the forest. You have been holding something in your left hand since then. Something—that hurts you. I probably wouldn't understand it. I'm not good with incomprehensible things, like magic and riddling. But if there is something I can fight for you, I will fight it. If there is something I can do for you, I will do it. I swear that, on my honor—" Raederle's face turned abruptly toward her at the word, and she stopped.

Raederle whispered, "I've never thought about honor in my life. Perhaps it's because no one has ever questioned it in me, or in any of my family. But I wonder if that's what's bothering me. I would have little of it left to me in An."

"Why?" Lyra breathed incredulously. Raederle's hand slid away from the rail, turned upward, open to the light.

Lyra stared down at the small, angular pattern on her palm. "What is that?"

"It's the mark of that stone. The one I blinded the warships with. It came out when I held the fire—"

"You—she forced you to put your hand in the fire?"

"No. No one forced me. I simply reached out and gathered it in my hand. I knew I could do it, so I did it."

"You have that power?" Her voice was small with wonder. "It's like a wizard's power. But why are you so troubled? Is it something that the mark on your hand means?"

"No. I hardly know what that means. But I do know where the power has come from, and it's not from any witch of An or any Lungold wizard. It's from Ylon, who was once King of An, a son of a queen of An and shape-changer. His blood runs in the family of An. I have his power. His father was the harpist who tried to kill Morgon in your house."

Lyra gazed at her, wordless. The chart house light flicked out suddenly, leaving their faces in darkness; someone lit the lamps at the bow. Raederle, her face turning back to the water, heard Lyra start to say something and then stop. A few minutes later, still leaning against the rail at Raederle's side, she started again and stopped. Raederle waited for her to leave, but she did not move. Half an hour later, when they were both beginning to shiver in the nightbreeze, Lyra drew another breath and found words finally.

"I don't care," she said softly, fiercely. "You are who you are, and I know you. What I said still stands; I have sworn it, the same promise I would have given to Morgon if he hadn't been so stubborn. It's your own honor, not the lack of it, that is keeping you out of An. And if I don't care, why should Morgon? Remember who the source of half his power is. Now let's go below before we freeze."

They reached Kraal almost before the morning mists had lifted above the sea. The boats docked; their passengers disembarked with relief, stood watching the cargo being unloaded while Bri went to find Mathom's ship and sailors to load their gear again. Kia murmured wearily to no one, "If I never set foot on a ship again in my life, I will be happy. If I never see a body of water larger than the Morgol's fish pools . . ."

Bri came back with the sailors and led them to the long, regal ship swaying in its berth. After the barge and keelboats, it looked expansive and comfortable; they boarded gratefully. Bri, with one eye to the tide, barked orders contentedly from the bow, as the sailors secured what supplies they needed, stabled the horses, brought the gear from the keelboats and loaded it all again. Finally the long anchor chain came rattling out of the sea; the ship was loosed from its moorings, and the stately blue and purple sails of An billowed proudly above the river traffic.

Ten days later they docked at Hlurle. The Morgol's guards were there to meet them.

Lyra, coming down the ramp with the five guards behind her, stopped at the sight of the quiet, armed gathering on the dock. One of the guards, a tall, grey-eyed girl, said softly, "Lyra—"

Lyra shook her head. She lifted her spear, held it out in her open hands, quiescent and unthreatening, like an offering. Raederle, following, heard her say simply, "Will you carry my spear through Herun for me, Trika, and give it for me to the Morgol? I will resign when I get to Crown City."

"I can't."

Lyra looked at her silently, at the still faces of the fourteen guards behind Trika. She shifted slightly. "Why? Did the Morgol give you other orders? What does she want of me?"

Trika's hand rose, touched the spear briefly and fell. Behind Lyra, the five guards were lined, motionless, across the ramp, listening. "Lyra." She paused, choosing words carefully. "You have twenty witnesses to the fact that you were willing, for the sake of the honor of the Morgol's guards, to ride unarmed into Herun. However, I think you had better keep your spear awhile. The Morgol is not in Herun."

"Where is she? Surely she isn't still at Caithnard?"

"No. She came back from Caithnard over a month ago, took six of us with her back to Crown City, and told the rest of us to wait for you here. Yesterday, Feya came back with the news that she had—that she was no longer in Herun."

"Well, if she isn't in Herun, where did she go?"

"No one knows. She just left."

Lyra brought her spear down to rest with a little thump at her side. She lifted her head, picked out a lithe, red-haired guard with her eyes. "Feya, what do you mean she left?"

"She left, Lyra. One night she was there having supper with us, and the next morning she was gone."

"She must have told someone where she was going. She never does things like that. Did she take servants, baggage, any guards at all?"

"She took her horse."

"Her horse? That's all?"

"We spent the day questioning everyone in the house. That's all she took. Not even a packhorse."

"Why didn't anyone see her leave? What were you all guarding, anyway?"

"Well, Lyra," someone said reasonably, "she knows the changes of our watch as well as any of us, and no one would ever question her movements in her own house."

Lyra was silent. She moved off the ramp, out of the way of the curious sailors beginning to unload their gear. Raederle, watching her, thought of the calm, beautiful face of the Morgol as she rode up the hill to the College, the gold eyes turning watchful as the Masters gathered around her. A question slid into her mind; Lyra, her brows crooking together, asked it abruptly, "Has Morgon of Hed spoken to her?"

Feya nodded. "He came so quietly no one saw him but the Morgol; he left just as quietly, except—except that—nothing was very peaceful in Herun after his leaving."

"She gave orders?" Her voice was level. Beside Raederle, Tristan sat down heavily at the foot of the ramp, dropped her face into her hands. Feya nodded again, swallowing.

"She gave orders that the northern and western borders were to be guarded against the High One's harpist, that no one in Herun should give him lodgings or aid of any kind, and that anyone seeing him in Herun should tell either the guards or the Morgol. And she told us why. She sent messengers to all parts of Herun to tell people. And then she left."

Lyra's gaze moved from her, past the worn, grey clutter of warehouse roofs lining the docks, to the border hills touched to a transient, delicate green under the late spring sun. She whispered, "Deth."

Trika cleared her throat. "We thought she might have gone to look for him. Lyra, I don't—none of us understand how he could have done the terrible thing the Star-Bearer accused him of; how he could have lied to the Morgol. It doesn't seem possible. How could—how could he not love the Morgol?"

"Maybe he does," Lyra said slowly. She caught Raederle's quick glance and added defensively, "She judged him like Danan, like Har: without even listening to him, without giving him the right to self-defense that she would give to the simplest man from the Herun marsh towns."

"I don't understand him either," Raederle said steadily. "But he admitted his guilt when I talked to him. And he offered no defense. He had none."

"It doesn't seem to have occurred to anyone, even Morgon, that perhaps Ghisteslwchlohm held Deth in his power, as he held the wizards, and forced him to bring Morgon to him instead of to the High One."

"Lyra, Ghisteslwchlohm is—" She stopped, felt the sluice of the sea wind between them like an impossible distance. She sensed their waiting, and finished wearily, "You're saying that the Founder is more powerful than the High One, forcing his harpist against his will. And if there is one thing I believe about Deth, it is that no one, maybe not even the High One, could force him to do something he did not choose to do."

"Then you've condemned him, too," Lyra said flatly.

"He condemned himself! Do you think I want to believe it, either? He lied to everyone, he betrayed the Star-Bearer, the Morgol and the High One. And he put his cloak over me so that I wouldn't be cold while I slept, that night in the backlands. That's all I know." She met Lyra's dark, brooding gaze helplessly. "Ask him. That's what you want, isn't it? Find him and ask him. You know where he is: in the backlands, heading toward Lungold. And you know that must be where the Morgol is going."

Lyra was silent. She dropped down on the ramp beside Tristan, yielding to a weary, vulnerable uncertainty.

Goh said simply after a moment, "We have no instructions from the Morgol to stay in Herun. No one should travel in the backlands alone."

"I wonder if she looked beyond Herun and saw him alone . . ." She took a breath impulsively, as though to give an order, then closed her mouth abruptly.

Trika said soberly, "Lyra, none of us knows what to do; we have no orders. It would be a relief to us all if you postponed resigning for a while."

"All right. Saddle your horses and let's go to Crown City. No matter how secretly she rode out of Herun, even the Morgol must have left some kind of trail."

The guards dispersed. Raederle sat down beside Lyra. They were silent as a sailor tramped down the ramp, leading Lyra's horse and whistling softly.

Lyra, her spear slanted on her knees, said suddenly to Raederle, "Do you think I'm right in following her?"

Raederle nodded. She remembered the worn, familiar face of the harpist, etched in the firelight with an unfamiliar mockery as he drank, the light irony in his voice that had never been there before. She whispered, "Yes. She'll need you."

"What will you do? Will you come?"

"No. I'll sail back to Caithnard with Bri. If Morgon is heading south, he might go there."

Lyra glanced at her. "He'll go to An."

"Maybe."

"And then where will he go? Lungold?"

"I don't know. Wherever Deth is, I suppose."

On the other side of Lyra, Tristan lifted her head. "Do you think," she said with unexpected bitterness, "that he'll come to Hed before that? Or is he planning to kill Deth and then go home and tell everyone about it?"

They looked at her. Her eyes were heavy with unshed tears; her mouth was pinched taut. She added after a moment, staring down at the bolt heads in the planks, "If he wouldn't move so fast, if I could just catch up with him, maybe I could persuade him to come home. But how can I do that if he won't stay still?"

"He'll go home eventually," Raederle said. "I can't believe he's changed so much he doesn't care about Hed anymore."

"He's changed. Once he was the land-ruler of Hed, and he would rather have killed himself than someone else. Now—"

"Tristan, he has been hurt, probably more deeply than any of us could know . . ."

She nodded a little jerkily. "I can understand that with my head. People have killed other people in Hed, out of anger or jealousy, but not—not like that. Not tracking someone like a hunter, driving him to one certain place to be killed. It's—what someone else would do. But not Morgon. And if—if it happens, and afterwards he goes back to Hed, how will we recognize each other any more?"

They were silent. A sailor carrying a keg of wine across his shoulders shook the ramp with his slow, heavy, persistent steps. Behind them, Bri Corbett shouted something, lost like a sea gull's cry in the wind. Raederle stirred.

"He'll know that," she said softly. "Deep in him. That he has every justification to do this except one. That the only man who might condemn him for it would be himself. Maybe you should trust him a little. Go home and wait and trust him."

There was another step behind them. Bri Corbett said, looking down at them, "That is the most rational thing I've heard this entire journey. Who's for home?"

"Caithnard," Raederle said, and he sighed.

"Well, it's close enough for a start. Maybe I can look for work there, if your father decides he doesn't want to see my face in An after this. But if I can just get you and this ship together back into the harbor at Anuin, he can curse the hair off my head and I'll still be content."

Lyra stood up. She hugged Bri suddenly, upsetting his hat with her spearhead. "Thank you. Tell Mathom it was my fault."

He straightened his hat, his face flushed, smiling. "I doubt if he'd be impressed."

"Have you heard any news of him here?" Raederle asked. "Is he back home?"

"No one seems to know. But—" He stopped, his brows tugging together, and she nodded.

"It's been nearly two months. He doesn't have a vow to fulfill anymore, since Morgon is alive, and he won't have a house to return to if he doesn't get himself back to An before it rouses." The guards rounded the dock side, in two straight lines. Kia, holding Lyra's horse, brought it over to her. Raederle and Tristan stood up, and Lyra gave them her quick, taut embrace.

"Good-bye. Go home." She held Raederle's eyes a moment before she loosed her and repeated softly, "Go home."

She turned, mounted, and gave them a spear-bearer's salute, her spear flaring upward like a silver torch. Then she wheeled her horse, took her place beside Trika at the head of the lines, and led the guards out of the Hlurle docks without looking back. Raederle watched her until the last guard disappeared behind the warehouses. Then she turned almost aimlessly and saw the empty ramp before her. She went up slowly, found Bri and Tristan watching the flicker of spears in the distance. Bri sighed.

"It's going to be a quiet journey without someone using the boom for target practice. We'll finish getting supplies here and sail a straight run past Ymris to Caithnard. Making," he added grimly, "the widest possible detour around Ymris. I would rather see the King of An himself off my bowsprit than Astrin Ymris."

They saw neither on the long journey to Caithnard, only an occasional trade-ship making its own prudent path around the troubled Ymris coast. Sometimes the ships drew near to exchange news, for tales of the errant ship out of An had spread from one end of the realm to the other. The news was always the same: war in Ymris had spread up into Tor and east Umber; no one knew where Morgon was; no one had heard anything of Mathom of An; and one startling piece of news from Caithnard: the ancient College of Riddle-Masters had sent away its students and closed its doors.

The long journey ended finally as the weary ship took the lolling afternoon tide into the Caithnard harbor. There were cheers and various remarks from the dockside as the dark sails wrinkled and slumped on the mast and Bri eased the ship into its berth. Bri ignored the noise with patience tempered by experience, and said to Raederle, "We're taking in a little water; she'll need repairs and supplies before we continue to Anuin. It will be a day or two, maybe. Do you want me to find you lodgings in the city?"

"It doesn't matter." She gathered her thoughts with an effort. "Yes. Please. I'll need my horse."

"All right."

Tristan cleared her throat. "And I'll need mine."

"You will." He eyed her. "For what? Riding across the water to Hed?"

"I'm not going to Hed, I've decided." She bore up steadily under his flat gaze. "I'm going to that city—the wizards' city. Lungold. I know where it is; I've looked on your maps. The road leads straight out of—"

"Hegdis-Noon's curved eyeteeth, girl, have you got a sensible bone anywhere in you?" Bri exploded. "That's a six-weeks journey through no-man's land. It's only because I have a hold weeping bilge water that I didn't take you straight to Tol. Lungold! With Deth and Morgon headed there, the Founder and who knows how many wizards coming like wraiths out of the barrows of Hel, that city is going to fall apart like a worm-eaten hull."

"I don't care. I—"

"You—"

They both stopped, as Tristan, her eyes moving past Bri, took a step backward. Raederle turned. A young man with a dark, tired, vaguely familiar face had come up the ramp. Something in his plain dress, his hesitant entry onto Bri's ship, stirred a memory in her mind. His eyes went to her face as she moved, and then, beyond her, to Tristan.

He stopped, closing his eyes, and sighed. Then he said, "Tristan, will you please come home before Eliard leaves Hed to look for you."

Something of the mutinous, trapped expression in her eyes faded. "He wouldn't."

"He would. He will. A trader coming down from Kraal spotted this ship at Hlurle and said you were coming south. Eliard was ready to leave then, but we—I won a wrestling match with him, and he said if I came back without you, he'd leave Hed. He's worn to the bone with worry, and his temper is short as a hen's nose. There's no living on the same island with him, drunk or sober."

"Cannon, I want to come home, but—"

Cannon Master shifted his stance on the deck. "Let me put it this way. I have asked you politely, and I will ask you again. The third time, I won't ask."

Tristan gazed at him, her chin lifted. Bri Corbett allowed a slow smile of pure contentment to spread over his face. Tristan opened her mouth to retort; then, under the weight of Cannon's implacable, harassed gaze, changed tactics visibly.

"Cannon, I know where Morgon is, or where he's going to be. If you'll just wait, just tell Eliard to wait—"

"Tell him. I told him it was a fine morning once and he threw a bucket of slops at me. Face one thing, Tristan: when Morgon wants to come home, he'll come. Without help from any of us. Just as he managed to survive. I'm sure, by now, he appreciates the fact that you cared enough to try to find out what happened to him."

"You could come with me—"

"It takes all my courage just to stand here with that bottomless water between me and Hed. If you want him to come home, then go back yourself. In the High One's name, give him something he loves to come home to."

Tristan was silent, while the water murmured against the hull and the lean black shadow of the mast lay like a bar at her feet. She said finally, "All right," and took a step forward. She stopped. "I'll go home and tell Eliard I'm all right. But I don't promise to stay. I don't promise that." She took another step, then turned to Raederle and held her tightly. "Be careful," she said softly. "And if you see Morgon, tell him . . . Just tell him that. And tell him to come home."

She loosed Raederle, went slowly to Cannon's side. He dropped a hand down her hair, drew her against him, and after a moment she slid an arm around his waist. Raederle watched them go down the ramp, make their way through the hectic, disorderly docks. A longing for Anuin wrenched at her, for Duac, and Elieu of Hel, for Rood with his crow-sharp eyes, for the sounds and smells of An, sun-spiced oak and the whisper, deep in the earth, of the endless fabric of history.

Bri Corbett said gently behind her, "Don't be sad. You'll smell the wind of your own home in a week."

"Will I?" She looked down and saw the white brand on her palm that had nothing to do with An. Then sensing the worry in him, she added more lightly, "I need to get off this ship, I think. Will you ask them to bring my horse up?"

"If you'll wait, I'll escort you."

She put a hand on his shoulder. "I'll be all right. I want to be alone for a while."

She rode through the docks, down the busy merchants' streets of the city, and if anyone troubled her, she did not notice. The fading afternoon drew a net of shadows across her path as she turned onto the silent road that led up to the College. She realized she had seen no students that day, with their bright robes and restless minds, anywhere in Caithnard. There were none on the road. She took the final wind to the top and saw the empty sweep of the College grounds.

She stopped. The dark, ancient stones with their blank windows seemed to house a hollowness, a betrayal of truth as bitter and terrible as the betrayal at Erlenstar Mountain. The shadow of that mountain had swept across the realm into the hearts of the Masters, until they found the greatest deceit within their own walls. They could send the students away, but she knew that though they might question themselves, they would never question the constant, essential weave and patterning of Riddle-Mastery.

She dismounted at the door and knocked. No one came, so she opened it. The narrow hall was empty, dark. She walked down it slowly, glimpsing through the long line of open doors each small chamber that had once held bed, books and endless games over guttering candles. There was no one downstairs. She took the broad stone stairs to the second floor and found more lines of open doors, the rooms holding no more in them than an expressionless block of sky. She came finally to the door of the Masters' library. It was closed.

She opened it. Eight Masters and a King, interrupting their quiet discussion, turned to her, startled. The King's eyes, ancient, ice-blue, burned as he looked at her with sudden curiosity.

One of the Masters rose. He said gently, "Raederle of An. Is there some way we can help you?"

"I hope so," she whispered, "because I have no place else to go."

SHE TOLD THEM, sitting in their gentle, impartial silence, of the shape-changer, who had come to her in Danan's house, and of her flight out of Isig Mountain. She told them of the stone Astrin had found on King's Mouth Plain and showed them the mark of it on her palm. She told them how she had held fire in the empty hollow of night in the backlands, while the wine cup of the High One's harpist flashed and fell in its light. She told them, knowing they knew it, but telling them by right of sorrow and heritage, the tale of Ylon, born out of An and the formless sea, and she saw in their eyes the gathering of the threads of riddlery. When she finished, dusk had crept in to the room, blurring the silent, dark-robed figures, old parchment and priceless, gold-hinged manuscripts. One of the Masters lit a candle. The flame gave her the patient, weary working of lines on his face, and beyond him, the spare, ungentle face of the Osterland King. The Master said simply, "We are all questioning ourselves these days."

"I know. I know how imperatively. You have not closed your doors only because you accepted the Founder of Lungold as a Master here. I know who was there to meet Morgon when Deth brought him to Erlenstar Mountain."

The taper the Master held dipped toward a wick and halted. "You know that, too."

"I guessed. And later, Deth—Deth told me it was so."

"He seems to have spared you very little," Har said. His voice sounded dry, impersonal, but she saw in his face a hint of the anger and confusion the harpist had loosed into the realm.

"I was not asking to be spared. I wanted truth. I want it now, so I came here. It's a place to start from. I can't go back to An with this. If my father were there, maybe I could. But I can't go back and pretend to Duac and Rood and the Lords of An that I belong to An as surely as the roots of trees and the old barrows of Kings. I have power, and I am afraid of it. I don't know—I don't know what I might loose in myself without meaning to. I don't know, any more, where I belong. I don't know what to do."

"Ignorance," the wolf-king murmured, "is deadly."

Master Tel shifted, his worn robe rustling in the hush. "You both came for answers; we have few to give you. Sometimes, however, the turn of a question becomes an answer; and we do have many questions. Above all: one regarding the shape-changers. They appeared almost without warning at the moment the Star-Bearer began realizing his destiny. They knew his name before he did; they knew of the sword bearing his stars deep in the grave of the Earth-Masters' children at Isig. They are old, older than the first weave of history and riddlery, originless, unnamed. They must be named. Only then will you know the origins of your own power."

"What else do I need to know about them, except that they have tried to destroy the King's lines in An and Ymris, that they blinded Astrin, they almost killed Morgon, they have no mercy, no pity, no love. They gave Ylon his life, then drove him to his death. They have no compassion even for their own—" She stopped, then, remembering the voice of the shape-changer striking its unexpected, puzzling timbre of richness.

One of the Masters said softly, "You have touched an incongruity?"

"Not compassion, but passion . . ." she whispered. "The shape-changer answered me with that. And then she wove her fire into such beauty that I hungered for her power. And she asked me what had driven Ylon back to them, if they were so terrible. She made me hear the harping Ylon heard, made me understand his longing. Then she told me Morgon had killed the harpist." She paused in their silence, the practiced stillness of old men, the heart of patience. "She handed me that riddle." Her voice was toneless. "That incongruity. Like Deth's kindness, which maybe was only habit, and . . . maybe not. I don't know. Nothing—the High One, this College, good or evil—seems to keep its own shape any more. That's why I wanted Morgon, then, so badly. At least he knows his own name. And a man who can name himself can see to name other things."

Their faces under the restless candlelight seemed molded out of shadow and memory, they sat so quietly when her voice faded.

At last Master Tel said gently, "Things are themselves. We twist the shapes of them. Your own name lies within you still, a riddle. The High One, whoever he is, is still the High One, though Ghisteslwchlohm has worn his name like a mask."

"And the High One's harpist is what?" Har asked. Master Tel was silent a moment, withdrawing into a memory.

"He studied here, also, centuries ago . . . I would not have believed a man who took the Black could have so betrayed the disciplines of riddle-mastery."

"Morgon intends to kill him," Har said brusquely, and the Master's eyes lifted again, startled.

"I had not heard . . ."

"Is that a betrayal of riddle-mastery? The wise man does not pursue his own shadow. There are no instincts of his own land-law in him to stay his hand; there is not one land-ruler, including the Morgol, who will not comply with his wishes. We give him understanding; we bar the gates to our kingdoms as he requests. And we wait for his final betrayal: self-betrayal." His implacable gaze moved from face to face like a challenge. "The Master is master of himself. Morgon has absolute freedom of this realm. He has no longer the restraints of land-law. The High One is nowhere in evidence except in the evidence of his existence. Morgon has bound himself, so far, to his destiny by the tenets of riddle-mastery. He also has enormous, untested power. Is there a riddle on the master lists that permits the wise man to revenge?"

"Judgment," one of the Masters murmured, but his eyes were troubled. "Who else is permitted to judge and condemn this man who has betrayed the entire realm for centuries?"

"The High One."

"In lieu of the High One—"

"The Star-Bearer?" He twisted their silence like a harp string, then broke it. "The man who wrested his power from Ghisteslwchlohm because no one, not even the High One, gave him any help? He is bitter, self-sufficient, and by his actions he is questioning even the elusive restraints of riddle-mastery. But I doubt if he sees even that in himself, because wherever he looks there is Deth. His destiny is to answer riddles. Not destroy them."

Something eased in Raederle's mind. She said softly, "Did you tell him that?"

"I tried."

"You complied with his wishes. Deth said he was driven out of Osterland by your wolves."

"I had no desire to find even the shape of Deth's footprint in my land." He paused; his voice lost its harshness. "When I saw the Star-Bearer, I would have given him the scars off my hands. He said very little about Deth or even about Ghisteslwchlohm, but he said . . . enough. Later, as I began to realize what he was doing, how far from himself he seemed to have grown, the implications of his actions haunted me. He was always so stubborn . . ."

"Is he coming to Caithnard?"

"No. He asked me to take his tale and his riddles to the Masters, who in their wisdom would decide whether or not the realm could bear the truth about the one we have called the High One for so long."

"That's why you shut your doors," she said suddenly to Master Tel, and he nodded, with the first trace of weariness she had ever seen in him.

"How can we call ourselves Masters?" he asked simply. "We have withdrawn into ourselves not out of horror, but out of a need to reconstruct the patterns we have called truth. In the very fabric of the realm, its settlement, histories, tales, wars, poetry, its riddles—if there is an answer there, a shape of truth that holds to itself, we will find it. If the tenets of riddle-mastery themselves are invalid, we will find that, too. The Master of Hed, in his actions, will tell us that."

"He found his way out of that dark tower in Aum . . ." she murmured. Har shifted.

"Do you think he can find his way out of another tower, another deadly game? This time, he has what he always wanted: choice. The power to make his own rules for the game."

She thought of the cold, sagging tower in Aum, rising like a solitary riddle itself among the gold-green oak, and saw a young man, simply dressed, stand in front of the worm-eaten door in the sunlight a long time before he moved. Then he lifted a hand, pushed the door open, and disappeared, leaving the soft air and the sunlight behind him. She looked at Har, feeling as though he had asked her a riddle and something vital hung balanced on her simple answer. She said, "Yes," and knew that the answer had come from someplace beyond all uncertainty and confusion, beyond logic.

He was silent a moment, studying her. Then he said, his voice gentle as the mill of snow through the still, misty air of his land, "Morgon told me once that he sat alone in an old inn at Hlurle, midway on his journey to Erlenstar Mountain, and waited for a ship to take him back to Hed. That was one point when he felt he had a choice about the matter of his destiny. But one thing stopped him from going home: the knowledge that he could never ask you to come to Hed if he could not give you the truth of his own name, of himself. So he finished his journey. When I saw him come into my house not long ago, as simply as any traveller seeking shelter in my house from the night, I did not at first see the Star-Bearer. I saw only the terrible, relentless patience in a man's eyes: the patience born out of absolute loneliness. He went into a dark tower of truth for you. Do you have the courage to give him your own name?"

Her hands closed tightly, one clenched over the pattern of angles on her palm. She felt something in her that had been knotted like a fist ease open slowly. She nodded, not trusting her voice, and her hand opened, glinting with secret knowledge in the candlelight. "Yes," she said then. "Whatever I have of Ylon's power, I swear by my name, I will twist it beyond possibility into something of value. Where is he?"

"Coming through Ymris, undoubtedly, on his way to Anuin, and then to Lungold, since that seems where he is forcing Deth to go."

"And then where? After that, where? He will not be able to go back to Hed."

"No. Not if he kills the harpist. There would be no peace for him in Hed. I don't know. Where does a man go to escape from himself? I'll ask him that when I see him in Lungold."

"You're going there—"

He nodded. "I thought he might need one friend in Lungold."

"Please, I want to come with you."

She saw the unspoken protest in the Masters' faces. The wolf-king flicked a thin brow. "How far will you go to escape from yourself? Lungold? And then where? How far can a tree escape from its roots?"

"I'm not trying to—" She stopped then, not looking at him.

He said softly, "Go home."

"Har," Master Tel said somberly, "that is advice you might well give yourself. That city is no place even for you. The wizards will seek Ghisteslwchlohm there; the Star-Bearer will seek Deth; and if the shape-changers gather there also, not a living thing in that city will be safe."

"I know," Har said, and the smile deepened faintly in his eyes. "There were traders in Kraal when I passed through it, who asked me where I thought the wizards had gone when they vanished. They were men who used both eyes to see out of, and they could look across half the realm to wonder if they wanted to risk their lives trading in a doomed city. Traders, like animals, have an instinct for danger."

"So do you," Master Tel said, with some severity, "but without the instinct to avoid it."

"Where do you suggest we go to be safe in a doomed realm? And when, in the void between a riddle and its answer, was there ever anything but danger?"

Master Tel shook his head. He yielded the argument finally when he realized it had become one-sided. They rose then for supper, cooked for them by a handful of students who had no other family but the Masters, no home but the College. They spent the rest of the evening in the library, while Raederle and the wolf-king listened, discussing the possible origins of the shape-changers, the implications of the stone found on King's Mouth Plain, and the strange face within it.

"The High One?" Master Tel suggested at one point, and Raederle's throat closed in a nameless fear. "Is it possible they could be so interested in finding him?"

"Why should they be any more interested in the High One than he is in them?"

"Perhaps the High One is hiding from them," someone else

suggested. Har, sitting so quietly in the shadows Raederle had almost forgotten him, lifted his head suddenly, but he said nothing. One of the other Masters picked up the weave of the thought.

"If the High One lived in fear of them, why wouldn't Ghisteslwchlohm? The law of the High One in the realm has been untroubled; he seems oblivious of them, rather than frightened. And yet . . . he is an Earth-Master; Morgon's stars are inextricably bound to the earlier doom of the Earth-Masters and their children; it seems incredible that he has made no response to this threat to his realm."

"What precisely is the threat? What are the extent of their powers? What are their origins? Who are they? What do they want? What does Ghisteslwchlohm want? Where is the High One?"

The questions spun into a haze like torch smoke in the room; massive books were drawn from the shelves, pored over, left lying with wax from the candles pooling in their margins. Raederle saw the various unlockings of wizards' books, heard the names or phrases that opened the seamless bindings of iron or brass or gold; saw the black, hurried writing that never faded, the blank pages that revealed their writings like an eye slowly opening to the touch of water, or fire, or a line of irrelevant poetry. Finally the broad tables were hidden beneath books, dusty rolls of parchment, and guttered candles; and unanswered riddles seemed to be burning on the wicks, lying in the shadows of the chair-backs and bookshelves. The Masters fell silent. Raederle, struggling with weariness, thought she could still hear their voices of their thoughts converging and separating, questioning, discarding, beyond the silence. Then Har rose a little stiffly, went to one of the books lying open and turned a page. "There is an old tale nagging at my mind that may not be worth considering: one out of Ymris, in Aloil's collection of legends, I think, with a suggestion of shape-changing in it . . ."

Raederle stood up, feeling the fraying tendrils of thought stir and eddy around her. The Masters' faces seemed remote, vaguely surprised as she moved. She said apologetically, "I'm half-asleep."

"I'm sorry," Master Tel said. He put a gentle hand on her arm, led her to the door. "One of the students had the forethought and kindness to go to the docks and tell your ship-master you were here; he brought your pack back with him. There will be a room prepared somewhere; I'm not sure—"

He opened the door, and a young student lounging beside the wall, reading, straightened abruptly and closed his book. He had a lean, dark, hook-nosed face, and a shy smile, with which he greeted Raederle. He still wore the robe of his rank: Beginning Mastery; the long sleeves were stained at the hems as though he had helped cook supper in it. He ducked his head after he gave her the smile and said diffidently to the floor, "We made a bed for you near the Masters' chambers. I brought your things."

"Thank you." She said good-night to Master Tel and followed the young student through the quiet halls. He said nothing more, his head still bent, the flush of shyness in his cheeks. He led her into one of the small, bare chambers. Her pack lay on the bed; pitchers of water and wine stood on a tiny table under a branch of burning candles. The windows, inset deeply in the rough stone, were open to the dark, salty air billowing up over the cliff's edge. She said, "Thank you," again and went to look out, though she could see nothing but the old moon with a lost star drifting between its horns. She heard the student take an uncertain step behind her.

"The sheets are rough . . ." Then he closed the door and said, "Raederle."

Her blood froze in her veins.

In the soft, shifting light of the candles, his face was a blur of spare lines and shadows. He was taller than she remembered; the stained white robe that had not changed with his shape-changing was puckered and strained across his shoulders. A wind shift stirred the candlelight, pulled the flames toward him and she saw his eyes. She put her hands to her mouth.

"Morgon?" Her voice jumped uncontrollably. Neither of them moved; a solid slab of air seemed wedged like stone between them. He looked at her out of eyes that had stared endlessly into the black, inner hollows of Erlenstar Mountain, into the rifts and hollows of a wizard's brain. Then she moved forward, through the stone, touched and held something that seemed ageless, like the wind or night, of every shape and no shape, as worn as a pebble runnelled with water, tossed for an eon at the bottom of a mountain. He moved slightly, and the knowledge of his own shape returned to her hands. She felt his hand, light as a breath, stir her hair. Then they were apart again, though she did not know which one of them had moved.

"I would have come to you at Anuin, but you were here." His voice sounded deep, harrowed, over-used. He moved finally, sat down on the bed. She stared at him wordlessly. He met her eyes, and his face, a stranger's face, lean, hard-boned, still, shaded into a sudden, haunting gentleness. "I didn't mean to frighten you."

"You didn't." Her own voice sounded remote in her ears, as though it were the wind beside her speaking. She sat down beside him. "I've been looking for you."

"I know. I heard."

"I didn't think . . . Har said you weren't coming here."

"I saw your father's ship off the coast of Ymris. I thought, since Tristan was with you, it might stop here. So I came."

"She might still be here; Cannon Master came for her, but—"

"They've gone to Hed."

The finality in his voice made her study him a moment. "You don't want to see her."

"Not yet."

"She asked me, if I saw you, to tell you this: be careful."

He was silent, still meeting her eyes. He had, she realized slowly, a gift for silence. When he chose, it seemed to ebb out of him, the worn silence of old trees or stones lying motionless for years. It was measured to his breathing, in his motionless, scarred hands. He moved abruptly, soundlessly, and it flowed with him as he turned, stood where she had been, gazing out the window. She wondered briefly if he could see Hed in the night.

"I heard tales of your journey," he said. "Tristan, Lyra and you together on Mathom's ship stealing by night out of Caithnard, blinding seven Ymris war-ships with a light like a small sun, taking a slow barge up the floodwaters of the Winter to the doorstep of the High One to ask him a question . . . And you tell me to be careful. What was that light that blinded even Astrin? It gave rise, among the traders, to marvellous speculation. Even I was curious."

She started to answer him, then stopped. "What conclusions did you come to?"

He turned, came back to her side again. "That it was something you did, probably. I remembered you could do small things . . ."

"Morgon—"

"Wait. I'll want to tell you now that—no matter what else has happened or will happen—it mattered to me that while I was coming down from Isig, you were making that journey. I heard your name, now and then, as I moved, Lyra's, Tristan's, like small, distant lights, unexpectedly."

"She wanted to see you so badly. Couldn't you have—"

"Not yet."

"Then when?" she said helplessly. "After you've killed Deth? Morgon, that will be one harpist too many."

His face did not change, but his eyes slid away from her, towards some memory. "Corrig?" He added after a moment, "I had forgotten him."

She swallowed, feeling as though the simple statement had set the slab of distance between them again. He assumed his stillness like a shield, impervious and impenetrable; she wondered if it hid a total stranger or someone as familiar to her as his name. He seemed, looking at her, to read her thoughts. He reached across the distance, touched her briefly. Then another memory, shapeless, terrible, welled through the stillness into his eyes; he turned his face slightly until it faded. He said softly, "I should have waited to see you, too. But I just—I wanted to look at something very beautiful. The legend of An. The great treasure of the Three Portions. To know that you still exist. I needed that."

His fingers brushed her again, as though she were something fragile as a moth wing. She closed her eyes, brought the heels of her hands against them and whispered, "Oh, Morgon. What in Hel's name do you think I'm doing in this College?" She let her hands fall and wondered if, behind the armor of his solitude, she had at last got his attention. "I would be that for you, if I could," she cried. "I would be mute, beautiful, changeless as the earth of An for you. I would be your memory, without age, always innocent, always waiting in the King's white house at Anuin—I would do that for you and for no other man in the realm. But it would be a lie, and I will do anything but lie to you—I swear that. A riddle is a tale so familiar you no longer see it; it's simply there, like the air you breathe, the ancient names of Kings echoing in the corners of your house, the sunlight in the corner of your eye; until one day you look at it and something shapeless, voiceless in you opens a third eye and sees it as you have never seen it before. Then you are left with the knowledge of the nameless question in you, and the tale that is no longer meaningless but the one thing in the world that has meaning any more." She stopped for breath; his hand had closed without gentleness, around her wrist. His face was familiar finally, questioning, uncertain.

"What riddle? You came here, to this place, with a riddle?"

"Where else could I go? My father was gone; I tried to find you and I couldn't. You should have known there was nothing in the world that would not change—"

"What riddle?"

"You're the Master here; do I have to tell even you?"

His hand tightened. "No," he said, and applied himself in silence to one final game within those walls. She waited, her own mind working the riddle with him, setting her name against her life, against the history of An, following strand after strand of thought that led nowhere, until at last he touched one possibility that built evenly onto another and onto another. She felt his fingers shift. Then his head lifted slowly, until he met her eyes again and she wished that the College would dissolve into the sea.

"Ylon." He let the word wear away into another silence. "I never saw it. It was always there . . ." He loosed her abruptly, rose and spat an ancient curse on a single tone into the shadows. It patterned the glass in the window with cracks like a spider's web. "They touched even you."

She stared numbly at the place where his hand had been. She rose to leave, not knowing where in the world she could go. He caught her in one step, turned her to face him.

"Do you think I care?" he demanded incredulously. "Do you think that? Who am I to judge you? I am so blind with hatred I can't even see my own land or the people I loved once. I'm hunting a man who never carried weapons in his life, to kill him while he stands facing me, against the advice of every land-ruler I have spoken to. What have you ever done in your life to make me have anything but respect for you?"

"I've never done anything in my life."

"You gave me truth."

She was silent, in the hard grip of his hands, seeing his face beyond its husk of stillness—bitter, vulnerable, lawless—the brand of stars on his forehead beneath his dishevelled hair. Her own hands lifted, closed on his arms. She whispered, "Morgon, be careful."

"Of what? For what? Do you know who was there in Erlenstar Mountain to meet me that day Deth brought me there?"

"Yes. I guessed."

"The Founder of Lungold has been sitting at the apex of the world for centuries, dispensing justice in the name of the High One. Where can I go to demand justice? That harpist is landless, bound to no King's law; the High One seems oblivious to both our fates. Will anyone care if I kill him? In Ymris, in An itself, no one would question it—"

"No one will ever question anything you do! You are your own law, your own justice! Danan, Har, Heureu, the Morgol—they will give you everything you ask for the sake of your name, and the truth you have borne alone; but Morgon, if you create your own law, where will any of us go, if we ever need to, to demand retribution from you?"

He gazed down at her; she saw the flick of uncertainty in his eyes. Then his head shook, slowly, stubbornly. "Just one thing. Just this one thing. Someone will kill him eventually—a wizard, perhaps Ghisteslwchlohm himself. And I have the right."

"Morgon—"

His hands tightened painfully. He was no longer seeing her but some black, private horror in his memory. She saw the sweat bead at his hairline, the muscles jump in his rigid face. He whispered, "While Ghisteslwchlohm was in my mind, nothing else existed. But at times when he . . . when he left me and I found myself still alive, lying in the dark, empty caverns of Erlenstar, I could hear Deth playing. Sometimes he played songs from Hed. He gave me something to live for."

She closed her eyes. The harpist's elusive face rose in her mind, blurred away; she felt the hard, twisted knot of Morgon's bewildered rage and the harpist's deceit like an unending, unanswerable riddle that no stricture could justify, and no Master in his quiet library could unravel. His torment ached in her; his loneliness seemed a vast hollow into which words would drop and disappear like pebbles. She understood then how his briefest word had closed court after court, kingdom after kingdom as he made his difficult, secret path through the realm. She whispered Har's words, "I would give you the scars off my hands." His hold loosened finally. He looked down at her a long time before he spoke.

"But you will not allow me that one right."

She shook her head; her voice came with effort. "You'll kill him, but even dead he'll eat at your heart until you understand him."

His hands dropped. He turned away from her, went again to the window. He touched the glass he had cracked, then turned again abruptly. She could barely see his face in the shadows; his voice sounded rough.

"I have to leave. I don't know when I will see you again."

"Where are you going?"

"Anuin. To speak to Duac. I'll be gone before you ever reach it. It's best that way, for both of us. If Ghisteslwchlohm ever realized how he could use you, I would be helpless; I would give him my heart with both my hands if he asked."

"And then where?"

"To find Deth. And then, I don't know—" He checked abruptly. The silence eddied about him again as he stood listening; he seemed to blur at the edge of the candlelight. She listened, heard nothing but the night wind among the shivering flames, the wordless riddling of the sea. She took a step toward him.

"Is it Ghisteslwchlohm?" Her voice was muted to his stillness. He did not answer, and she could not tell if he had heard her. A fear beat suddenly in the back of her throat; she whispered, "Morgon." His face turned towards her then. She heard the sudden, dry catch of his breath. But he did not move until she went to him. Then he gathered her slowly, wearily into his silence, his face dropping against her hair.

"I have to go. I'll come to you at Anuin. For judgment."

"No—"

He shook his head slightly, stilling her. She felt, as her hands slid away from him, the strange, almost formless tension of air where he might have slung a sword beneath his robe. He said something she could not hear, his voice matching the wind's murmur. She saw a flame-streaked shadow and then a memory.

She undressed, lay awake for a long time before she finally fell into a troubled sleep. She woke hours later, stared, startled, into the darkness. Thoughts were crowding into her mind, a tumultuous cross-weave of names, longings, memories, anger, a spattering cauldron of events, urges, inarticulate voices. She sat up, wondering what shape-changer's mind she had become embroiled in, but there was an odd recognition in her that had nothing to do with them, that turned her face unerringly towards An, as if she could see it through the blank stone walls and the night. She felt her heart begin to pound. Roots tugged at her; her heritage of grass-molded barrows, rotting towers, kings' names, wars and legends, pulling her towards a chaos the earth, left lawless too long, was slowly unleashing. She stood up, her hands sliding over her mouth, realizing two things at once. The whole of An was rousing at last. And the Star-Bearer's path would lead him straight into Hel.

SHE RODE OUT of Caithnard at dawn, stood a day and a half later in the vast oak forest bordering Hel, straining, as she had never done before, to unlock all the power and awareness in her mind. She had already sensed, as she came through the forest, the almost imperceptible movement of someone ahead of her, his need like a faint, indistinguishable scent, for swiftness, for secrecy. And at night, sleepless and aware, she had glimpsed for one terrifying moment, like the shape of some enormous beast rising against the moonlight, a relentless, powerful, enraged mind focussed to a single thought of destruction.

She wondered, as she stood looking over Hallard Blackdawn's lands, what shape Morgon was taking through them. The pastures, sloping gently towards the river that ran beside the Lord's house, looked quiet enough, but there was not an animal on them. She could hear hounds baying in the distance, wild, hoarse keening that never seemed to stop. There were no men working in the fields behind the house, and she was not surprised. That corner of Hel had been the last battlefield in the half-forgotten wars between Hel and An; it had held its own in an endless series of fierce, desperate battles until Oen of An, sweeping through Aum six centuries earlier, had almost contemptuously smashed the last stronghold of resistance and beheaded the last of the Kings of Hel, who had taken refuge there. The land had always been uneasy with legend; the turn of a plow could still unearth an ancient sword eaten to the core with age or the shaft of a broken spear banded with rings of gold. In so many centuries, King Farr of Hel, bereft of his head, had had much leisure to ponder his grievances, and, loosed at last from the earth, he would have wasted little time gathering himself out of Hallard's fields. The chaos of voices Raederle had heard two nights earlier had faded into a frightening stillness: the dead were unbound, aware, and plotting.

She saw as she rode across Hallard's upper pastures, a group of riders swing out of the woods into a meadow across her path. She reined, her heart pounding, then recognized the broad, black-haired figure of Hallard Blackdawn towering above his men. They were armed, but lightly; there was a suggestion of futility in their bare heads and the short swords at their sides. She sensed, unexpectedly, their exasperation and uncertainty. Hallard's head turned as she sat watching; she could not see his eyes, but she felt the startled leap in his mind of her name.

She lifted the reins in her hands hesitantly as he galloped up to her. She had no desire to argue with him, but she needed news. So she did not move, and he pulled up in front of her, big-boned, dark, sweating in the hot, silent afternoon. He groped for words a moment, then said explosively, "Someone should flay that ship-master. After taking you to Isig and back, he let you ride unescorted from Caithnard into this? Have you had news of your father?"

She shook her head. "Nothing. Is it bad?"

"Bad." He closed his eyes. "Those hounds have been at it for two solid days. Half my livestock is missing; my wheat fields look as though they've been harrowed by millwheels, and the ancient barrows in the south fields have been flattened to the ground by nothing human." He opened his eyes again; they were red-veined with lack of sleep. "I don't know what it's like in the rest of An. I sent a messenger to east Aum yesterday, to Cyn Croeg. He couldn't even get across the border. He came back babbling of whispering trees. I sent another to Anuin; I don't know if he'll make it. And if he does, what can Duac do? What can you do against the dead?" He waited, pleading for an answer, then shook his head. "Curse your father," he said bluntly. "He'll have to fight Oen's wars over again if he isn't careful. I'd wrest kingship from the land myself, if I could think how."

"Well," she said, "maybe that's what they want. The dead kings. Have you seen any of them?"

"No. But I know they're out there. Thinking." He brooded at the strip of woods along the pastures. "What in Hel's name would they want with my cattle? The teeth of these kings are scattered all over my fields. King Farr's skull has been grinning above the hearth in the great hall for centuries; what is he going to eat with?"

Her eyes slid from the unstirred woods back to his face. "His skull?" An idea flickered in the back of her mind. Hallard nodded tiredly.

"Supposedly. Some dauntless rebel stole his head from Oen, the tale goes, after Oen crowned it and stuck it on a spearhead in his kitchen-midden. Years later it found its way back here, with the crown cut and melded again to fit bare bone. Mag Blackdawn, whose father had died in that war, was still angry enough to nail it like a battle emblem, crown and all, above his hearthfire. After so many centuries the gold was worn into the bone; you can't keep one without the other. That's what I don't understand," he added at a tangent. "Why they're troubling my lands; they're my ancestors."

"There were lords of An killed here, too," she suggested. "Maybe they were the ones in your wheat fields. Hallard, I want that skull."

"You what?"

"Farr's skull. I want it."

He stared at her. She saw, gazing back at him, the faint struggle in him as he tried to shift her back to her place in his known world. "What for?"

"Just give it to me."

"In Hel's name, what for?" he shouted, then stopped and closed his eyes again. "I'm sorry. You're starting to sound like your father; he has a gift for making me shout. Now. Let's both try to be rational—"

"I was never less interested in being rational in my life. I want that skull. I want you to go into your great hall and take it off your wall without damaging it and wrap it in velvet and give it to me at your—"

"Velvet!" he exploded. "Are you mad?"

She thought about it for a split second and shouted back at him.

"Maybe! But not so I would care! Yes, velvet! Would you want to look at your own skull on a piece of sacking?"

His horse jerked, as though he had pulled it involuntarily back from her. His lips parted; she heard his quick breathing as he struggled for words. Then he reached out slowly, put his hand on her forearm. "Raederle." He spoke her name like a reminder to them both. "What are you going to do with it?"

She swallowed, her own mouth going dry as she contemplated her intentions. "Hallard, the Star-Bearer is crossing your land—"

His voice rose again incredulously. "Now?"

She nodded. "And behind him—behind me, following him, is something . . . maybe the Founder of Lungold. I can't protect Morgon from him, but maybe I can keep the dead of An from betraying his presence—"

"With a skull?"

"Will you keep your voice down!"

He rubbed his face with his hands. "Madir's bones. The Star-Bearer can take care of himself."

"Even he might be a little pressed by the Founder and the unbound forces of An all at once." Her voice steadied. "He is going to Anuin; I want to see that he gets there. If—"

"No."

"If you don't—"

"No." His head was shaking slowly back and forth. "No."

"Hallard." She held his eyes. "If you don't give me that skull now, I will lay a curse on your threshold that no friend will ever cross it, on the high gates and posterns and stable doors that they will never close again, on the torches in your house that they will never burn, on your hearth stones that no one standing under Farr's hollow eyes will ever feel warm. This I swear by my name. If you don't give me that skull I will rouse the dead of An, myself, on your land in the name of the King of An and ride with them into war on your fields against the ancient Kings of Hel. This I swear by my name. If you don't—"

"All right!"

His cry echoed, furious and desperate, across his lands. His face was patched white under his tan; he stared at her, breathing hard, while blackbirds startled up from the trees behind them and his men shifted their mounts uneasily in the distance. "All right," he whispered. "Why not? The whole of An is in chaos, why shouldn't you ride around with a dead king's skull in your hands? But, woman, I hope you know what you're doing. Because if you are harmed, you will lay a curse of grief and guilt across my threshold, and until I die no fire in my hearth will ever be great enough to warm me." He wheeled his horse without waiting for her to answer; she followed him down through his fields, across the river to his gates, feeling the frightened blood pounding in her ears like footsteps.

She waited, still mounted, while he went inside. She could see through the open gates the empty yard. Not even the forge fire was lit; there were no stray animals, no children shouting in the corners, only the incessant, invisible baying of hounds. Hallard reappeared shortly, a round object gathered in the folds of a length of rich, red velvet. He handed it to her wordlessly; she opened the velvet, caught a glimpse of white bone with gold melting into it and said, "There's one more thing I want."

"What if it's not his head?" He watched her. "Legends are spun around so many lies—"

"It had better be," she whispered. "I need a necklace of glass beads. Can you find one for me?"

"Glass beads." He covered his eyes with his fingers and groaned like the hounds. Then he flung up his hands and turned again. He was gone longer this time; the expression on his face when he came back was, if possible, more harassed. He dangled a small, sparkling circle of round, clear beads in front of her; a simple necklace that a trader might have given away to a young girl or a hard-worked farmer's wife. "They'll look fine rattling among Farr's bones." Then, as she reached down to take it, he grasped her wrist again. "Please," he whispered. "I gave you the skull. Now come into my house, out of danger. I can't let you ride through Hel. It's quiet now, but when night falls, there's not a man who will stir beyond his barred doors; you'll be alone out there in the darkness with the name you bear and all the twisted hatred of the old lords of Hel. All the small powers you have inherited will not be enough to help you. Please—"

She pulled loose of him, backed her horse. "Then I'll have to test the powers of another heritage. If I don't come back, it will not matter."

"Raederle!"

She felt the sound of her own name spin out over his lands, echo in the deep woods and places of secret gatherings. She rode swiftly away from his house before he could follow her. She went downriver to his southern fields, where the young wheat lay whipped and churned and the ancient graves of Hallard's ancestors, once smooth green swellings whose doors had sunk waist-deep in the earth, were smashed like eggs. She reined in front of them. Through the dark crumbled soil and the broken foundation stones she could see the pale glint of rich arms no living man dared touch. She lifted her head. The woods were motionless; the summer sky stretched endlessly over An, cloudless and peaceful, except toward the west where the blue gathered to a dark, intense line above the oak. She turned her horse again, looked out over the empty, whispering fields. She said softly into the wind, "Farr, I have your head. If you want it, to lie with your bones under the earth of Hel, then come and get it."

She spent the rest of the afternoon gathering wood on the edge of the trees above the barrows. As the sun went down she lit a fire and unwrapped the skull from its velvet coverings. It was discolored with age and soot; the gold banding its wide brow was riveted to the bone. The teeth, she noted, were intact in the tightly clenched jaws; the deep eyepits and wide, jutting cheekbone gave her a hint of the king whose head had stared, furious and unsubmissive, over Oen's midden. The firelight rippled the shadows in the eye sockets, and her mouth dried. She spread the bright cloth, laid the skull on top of it. Then she drew the necklace of glass beads out of her pocket, bound an image in her mind to them with her name. She dropped them into the fire. All around her, enclosing the skull, the firewood and her uneasy mount, rose a luminous circle of huge, fiery moons.

At moonrise, she heard the cattle in Hallard's barn begin to bawl. Dogs in the small farms beyond the trees set up a constant chorus of shrill, startled barking. Something that was not the wind sighed through the oak, and Raederle's shoulders hunched as it passed over her head. Her horse, lying beside her, scrambled to its feet, trembling. She tried to speak to it soothingly, but the words stuck in her throat. There was a great crashing in the distant trees; animals lying quiet until then, began to stir and flee before it. A stag running blind, reared and belled as it came suddenly upon the strange, fiery circle, wrenched itself around and shot towards the open fields. Small deer, foxes, weasels roused in the night, bounded silently, desperately past her, pursued by the rending of branches and underbrush, and a weird, unearthly bellow that shattered again and again through the trees. Raederle, shuddering, her hands icy, her thoughts scattering like blown chaff, added branch after branch to the fire until the beads swam red with flame. She stopped herself from burning all the wood at once by sheer will, and stood, her hands over her mouth to keep her heart from leaping free, waiting for the nightmare to emerge from the dark.

It came in the shape of the great White Bull of Aum. The enormous animal, whom Cyn Croeg loved as Raith of Hel loved his pig herds, loomed out of the night towards her flames, pricked and driven by riders whose mounts, yellow, rust, black, were lean, rangey, evil-eyed. Their heads snaking sideways, they nipped at the bull as they ran. The bull, flecked with blood and sweat, his flat, burly face maddened and terrified, swung past Raederle's circle so closely she could see his rimmed eyes and smell the musk of his fear. The riders swarmed about him as he turned, ignoring her, except the last who, turning a grinning face her direction, showed her the seam of the scar across his face that ended in a white, withered eye.

All sounds around her seemed to dwindle to one point inside her head; she wondered, dimly, if she was going to faint. The groan of the bull in the distance made her open her eyes again. She saw it, gigantic and ash-colored under the moonlight, blundering with its horns lowered across Hallard's fields. The riders, their arms flickering a bluish-silver like lightning, seemed mercilessly intent upon driving it into Hallard's closed gates. There they would leave it, she knew in a sudden, terrible flash of insight, like a gift at Hallard's doorway, a dead weight of bull for him to explain somehow to the Lord of Aum. She wondered, in that split second, how Raith's pigs were faring. Then her horse screamed behind her and she whirled, gasping, to face the wraith of King Farr of Hel.

He was, as she imagined him, a big, powerful man with a wide slab of a face hard as a slammed gate. His beard and long hair were copper; he wore rings of hard metal at every knuckle, and his sword, rising above one of the glass moons, was broad at the base as the length of his hand. He wasted no time with words; the sword, cutting down into the thin air of illusion, nearly wrenched him off his horse. He straightened, tried to ride his horse through it, but the animal balked with a squeal of pain and cast a furious eye at him. He reined it back to try to leap; Raederle, reaching for the skull, held it above the flames.

"I'll drop it," she warned breathlessly. "And then I will take it, black with ash, to Anuin and throw it back in the midden."

"You will not live," he said. The voice was in her mind; she saw then the ragged, scarlet weal at his throat. He cursed her in his hoarse, hollow voice, thoroughly and methodically, from head to foot, in language she had never heard any man use.

Her face was burning when he finished; she dangled the skull by one finger in an eye socket over the flames and said tersely, "Do you want this or not? Shall I use it for kindling?"

"You'll burn up your wood by dawn," the implacable voice said. "I'll take it then."

"You'll never take it." Her own voice, colored with anger, sounded with a dead certainty that she almost felt. "Believe that. Your bones lie rotting in the fields of a man whose allegiance is sworn to An, and only you remember what shinbones and snapped neckbone belong to you. If you had this crown, it might give you the dignity of remembrance, but you'll never take it from me. If I choose, I'll give it to you. For a price."

"I bargain with no man. I submit to no man. Least of all to a woman spawned out of the Kings of An."

"I am spawned out of worse than that. I will give you your skull for one price only. If you refuse me once, I will destroy it. I want an escort of Kings through Hel and into Anuin for one man—"

"Anuin!" The word reverberated painfully in her own skull and she winced. "I will never—"

"I will ask only once. The man is a stranger to An, a shape-changer. He is moving in fear of his life through An, and I want him hidden and protected. Following him is the greatest wizard of the realm; he'll try to stop you, but you will not submit. If the man is harmed on the way to Anuin by this wizard, your crowned skull is forfeit." She paused, added temperately, "Whatever else you do on your journey through An will be your own business, as long as he is protected. I'll give you the skull in the house of the Kings of An."

He was silent. She realized suddenly that the night had grown very quiet; even Haggard Blackdawn's hounds were still. She wondered if they were all dead. Then she wondered, almost idly, what Duac would say when he found the wraiths of the Kings of Hel in his house. Farr's voice seeped into her thoughts.

"And after?"

"After?"

"After we reach Anuin? What demands, what restrictions will you place on us in your own house?"

She drew a breath, and found no more courage left in her for demands. "If the man is safe, none. If you have kept him safe. But I want an escort of Kings of Hel only, not a gathering of the army of the dead."

There was another long silence. She dragged a branch onto the fire, saw the flick of calculation in his eyes. Then he said unexpectedly, "Who is this man?"

"If you don't know his name, no one can take it from you. You know the shapes of Hel: trees, animals, the earth; you are of them, rooted with them. Find the stranger whose outward shape is of An, whose core is of nothing of An."

"If he is nothing of An, then what is he to you?"

"What do you think?" she asked wearily. "When I'm sitting here alone for his sake in the roused night of Hel bargaining with a dead king over his skull?"

"You're a fool."

"Maybe. But you're bargaining, too."

"I do not bargain. An deprived me of my crown, and An will give it back to me. One way or another. I'll give you my answer at dawn. If your fire goes out before then, beware. I will show you no more mercy than Oen of An showed to me."

He settled himself to wait, his face, baleful and unblinking, rising out of the darkness above the fiery beads. She wanted to scream at him suddenly that she had nothing to do with his feuds or his death, that he had been dead for centuries and his vengeance was a matter insignificant in the turmoil of events beyond An. But his brain was alive only in the past, and the long centuries must have seemed to him the passing of a single night over Hel. She sat down in front of the fire, her mouth papery. She wondered if, when dawn came, he intended to kill her or to barter with Duac over her as she had bartered over his skull. Hallard Blackdawn's house, with all its windows lit at that hour, across two fields and the river, seemed as far away as a dream. As she gazed at it helplessly, the din began again in the fields, a new sound this time: the chilling clash of weapons in a night battle in Hallard's cow pasture. The hounds bayed the danger hoarsely, imperatively, like battle horns. The eyes of the King met hers over the illusion of the fire, relentless, assured. She looked down from him to the fire and saw the small, blazing circle, the core of the illusion, the glass beads cracking slowly in the tempering of the fire.

The cries faded to a corner of her mind. She heard the snap of wood, the sibilant language of the flames. She opened her hand, touched an angle of flame and watched the reflection of it in her mind. It groped for her shape as she held it in her mind and her hand; she kept her own thoughts mute, tapped a silence deeply within her mind which it slowly moved and gathered. She let it gather for a long time, sitting motionless as the ancient trees around her, her hand uplifted, open to the flame that traced constantly the twelve-sided figure on her palm. Then a shadow flowed over her mind, quenching the fire in it: another mind spanning the night, drawing into its vortex a comprehension of the living and dead of An. It passed like great, dark wings blocking the moon and brought her back, shivering and defenseless, into the night. She closed her hand quickly over the small flame and looked up to see the first hint of expression in Farr's eyes.

"What was that?" His voice rasped jarringly in her head.

She felt his mind unexpectedly and knew that she was beginning to startle him, too. She said, "That is what you will protect the Star—the stranger from."

"That?"

"That." She added after a moment, "He'll blot out your wraith like a candle if he realizes what you are doing and nothing will be left of you but your bones and a memory. Do you want your skull so badly now?"

"I want it," he said grimly. "Either here or at Anuin, Witch. Take your choice."

"I'm not a witch."

"What are you, then, with your eyes full of fire?"

She thought about it. Then she said simply, "I am nameless," while something too bitter for sorrow touched the back of her mouth. She turned again to the fire, added more wood to it, followed the wild flight of each spark to its vanishing point. She cupped the fire again, this time in both hands, and began slowly to shape it.

She was interrupted many times during the endless night: by the run of Hallard Blackdawn's stolen cattle, bawling in terror across his wheat fields; by the gathering of armed men around Farr as he waited, and his bellow of fury in her mind when they laughed at him; by the flurry of sword play that followed. She lifted her head once and saw only his bare bones on his horse, blurred with fire; another time, she saw his head like a helm in the crook of his arm, his expression changeless while her eyes groped for shape above the stump of his neck. Near dawn, when the moon set, she had forgotten him, forgotten everything. She had drawn the flames into a hundred varied shapes, flowers that opened then melted away, fiery birds that took wing from her hand. She had forgotten even her own shape; her hands, weaving in and out of the fire, seemed one more shape of it. Something undefined, unexpected, was happening in her mind. Glimpses of power, knowledge, elusive as the fire, passed before her mind's eye, as though she had wakened within her memories of her heritage. Faces, shadows stretching beyond her knowledge formed and vanished under her probing; strange plants, sea languages whispered just beyond her hearing. A void in the depth of the sea, or at the heart of the world, cut a hollow through her mind; she gazed into it fearlessly, curiously, too lost within her work to wonder whose black thought it was. She kindled a distant star of fire even in that barren waste. She felt then, as it stirred, that it was no void, but a tangle of memory and power on the verge of definition.

That knowledge sent her groping urgently for the simpler chaos of An. She came to rest like a weary traveller within herself. The dawn mists lay over Hallard's fields; the ash-colored morning hung amid the trees without a sound to welcome it. All that remained of her night fire was the charred stubble of branches. She stirred stiffly, sleepily, then saw the hand out of the corner of her eye, reaching for the skull.

She set it blazing with an illusion of fire from her mind; Farr flinched back. She picked up the skull and rose, stood facing him. He whispered, "You are made of fire . . ."

She felt it in her fingers, running beneath the skin, in the roots of her hair. She said, her voice cracking with tiredness, "Have you made up your mind? You'll never find Oen here; his bones lie in the Field of Kings outside of Anuin. If you can survive the journey, you can take your revenge there."

"Do you betray your own family?"

"Will you give me an answer?" she cried, stung; and he was silent, struggling. She felt his yielding before he spoke, and she whispered, "Swear by your name. Swear by the crown of the Kings of Hel. That neither you nor anyone else will touch me or this skull until you have crossed the threshold at Anuin."

"I swear it."

"That you will gather the kings as you journey across Hel, to find and protect the shape of the stranger travelling to Anuin, against all living, against all dead."

"I swear it."

"That you will tell no one but the Kings of Hel what you are sworn to do."

"I swear it. By my name, in the name of the Kings of Hel and by this crown."

He looked, dismounted in the dawn light with the taste of submission in his mouth, almost alive. She drew a soundless breath and loosed it. "All right. I swear in my father's name and in the name of the man you will escort, that when I see him in the King's house at Anuin, I will give you your skull and ask nothing further from you. All binding between us will end. The only other thing I ask is that you let me know when you find him."

He gave a brief nod. His eyes met the black, hollow, mocking gaze of the skull. Then he turned and mounted. He looked down at her a moment before he left, and she saw the disbelief in his eyes. Then he rode away, noiseless as a drift of leaves beneath the trees.

She met, as she herself rode out of the woods, Hallard Blackdawn and his men venturing out to count the dead cattle in the lower fields. He stared at her; his voice, when he found it finally, was strengthless.

"Oen's right hand. Is it you or a ghost?"

"I don't know. Is Cyn Croeg's bull dead?"

"They ran the life out of it . . . Come to the house." His eyes, the shock wearing away from them, held a strange expression: half-solicitous, half-awed. His hand rose hesitantly, touched her. "Come in. You look—you look—"

"I know. But I can't. I'm going to Anuin."

"Now? Wait, I'll give you an escort."

"I have one." She watched his eyes fall to the skull riding the pommel of her saddle; he swallowed.

"Did he come for it?"

She smiled slightly. "He came. We did some bargaining—"

"Oen's right—" He shuddered unashamedly. "No one ever bargained with Farr. For what? The safety of Anuin?"

She drew a breath. "Well, no. Not exactly." She took the necklace out of her pocket and gave it to him. "Thank you. I couldn't have survived without it."

Glancing back once, as she reached down to open a field gate, she saw him standing motionlessly beside a dead bullock, still staring at the worthless handful of cracked, fired beads.

She crossed the length of Hel as far as Raith's lands with a growing, invisible escort of Kings. She felt them around her, groped for their minds until they gave her their names: Acor, third King of Hel, who had brought through force and persuasion the last of the bickering lords under his control; Ohroe the Cursed, who had seen seven of his nine sons fall one after another in seven consecutive battles between Hel and An; Nemir of the Pigs, who had spoken the language of both men and pigs, who had bred the boar Hegdis-Noon and had as his pigherder the witch Madir; Evern the Falconer, who trained hawks for battle against men; and others, all Kings, as Farr had sworn, who joined him, the last of the Kings, in his journey to the stronghold of the Kings of An. She rarely saw them; she felt them range before and behind her, their minds joining in a network of thought, legend, plots, remembrances of Hel during their lives, after their deaths. They were still bound to the earth of An, more than even they realized; their minds slid easily in and out of different shapes that their bones had become entwined with: roots, leaves, insects, the small bodies of animals. It was through this deep, wordless knowledge of An, Raederle knew, that they recognized the Star-Bearer, the man whose shape would hold none of the essence of An.

They had found him swiftly. Farr broke his silence to tell her that; she did not ask what shape he had taken. The Kings surrounded him loosely as he moved: the hart, perhaps, that bounded in terror across a moonlit field at their presence; the bird startled into flight; the fieldmouse scuttling through broken shafts of hay. She guessed that he dared not keep one shape long, but she was surprised that the Kings never once lost track of him. They were a decoy to the powerful mind she glimpsed occasionally as it groped over the land. No man of An, and certainly no stranger, could have passed among them unnoticed; the wizard, she guessed, must search every man they did meet. She was surprised also that he did not threaten her as she rode alone through the troubled land; perhaps he thought, seeing the skull on her saddle, watching her sleep at night in the woods impervious to the tumult around her, that she was mad.

She avoided people, so she had no news of the extent of the trouble, but she saw, again and again, empty fields at midday, barns and stables locked and guarded, lords travelling with armed retinues towards Anuin. Their tempers, she knew, must be worn thin by the constant harassment; they would, in time, turn their houses into small, armed fortresses, draw into themselves and soon trust no man, living or dead. The mistrust and the anger against the absent King of An would fester into open war, a great battleground of living and dead, that not even Mathom would be able to control. And she, bringing the Kings of Hel into Anuin, might precipitate it.

She thought much about that, lying sleepless at night with the skull beside her. She tried to prepare for it, exploring her powers, but she had little experience to guide her. She was dimly aware of what she might be able to do, of powers intangible as shadows in her mind, powers she could not yet quite grasp and control. She would do what she could at Anuin; Morgon, if he could risk it, would help. Perhaps Mathom would return; perhaps the Kings would retreat from Anuin without an army behind them. Perhaps she could find something else to barter with. She hoped Duac, in some small measure, would understand. But she doubted it.

She reached Anuin nine days after she had left Hallard's land. The Kings had begun to appear before they entered the gates, riding in a grim, amazing escort about the man they guarded. The streets of the city seemed fairly untroubled; there were quite a few people out staring, uneasy and astonished, at the group of riders with their nervous, wicked mounts, their crowned heads, armbands and brooches of gold, their arms and rich clothes spanning nearly the entire history of the land. Among them, cloaked and hooded in the warm day, rode the man they had been guarding. He seemed resigned to his unearthly escort; he rode without a glance at it, slowly and steadily through the streets of Anuin, up the gentle slope to the house of the King. The gates were open; they rode unchallenged into the yard. They dismounted, to the confusion of the grooms, who had no intention, even under the weight of Farr's hot gaze, of taking their horses. Raederle, riding alone into the gates behind them, saw them follow the cloaked figure up the steps to the hall. The expression in the grooms' faces as they hesitated around her made her realize that they thought she, too, might be a wraith. Then one came forward uncertainly to hold her reins and stirrup as she dismounted. She took the skull from the pommel, carried it with her into the hall.

She found Duac alone in the hall, staring, speechless, at the collection of Kings. His mouth was open; as she entered, his eyes flicked to her and she heard it click closed. The blood ran out of his face, leaving it the color of Farr's skull. She wondered, as she went towards the hooded man, why he did not turn and speak to her. He turned then, as though he had felt her thoughts, and she found her own mouth dropped open. The man the Kings had followed and guarded through Hel had not been Morgon but Deth.

SHE STOPPED SHORT, staring at him in utter disbelief. The skin was strained taut, blanched against the bones of his face; he looked, haunted for nine days by the wraiths of Hel, as though he had not slept much. She breathed, "You." She looked at Farr, who was running a calculating eye over the beams and corners of the house. Duac, who had begun to move, finally, was coming towards her carefully through the assortment of Kings. They were standing silently, expectantly, their strange shields scrolled with nameless animals deflecting flat, burning fields of light from the windows. Her heart began to hammer suddenly. She found her voice again, and Farr's head turned sharply as she spoke, "What are you doing here? I left you in the backlands going to Lungold."

The familiar, even voice sounded frayed, almost tight. "I had no desire to meet the Morgol or her guards in the backlands. I sailed down the Cwill to Hlurle, and found passage on a ship to Caithnard. There are not many places in the realm left open to me."

"So you came here?"

"It is one last place."

"Here." She drew breath and shouted at him in sudden, furious despair, halting Duac mid-pace, "You came here, and because of you I have let all the Kings of Hel into their house!" She heard the hollow rasp of Farr's question in her brain, and she turned on him. "You brought the wrong man! He isn't even a shape-changer!"

"We found him in that shape, and he chose to keep it," Farr answered, in his surprise momentarily defensive. "He was the only stranger moving secretly through Hel."

"He couldn't have been! What kind of a poor bargain was it that you kept? You would have had to search all the back streets and docksides of the realm to find a man I wanted less to see."

"I kept the vows I swore." She could tell by Duac's expression that the harsh, unearthly voice was rebounding also in his mind. "The skull is mine. The binding is finished."

"No." She backed a step from him, her fingers locked tightly around the lidless gaze and grin of the skull. "You left the man you swore to guard somewhere in Hel, to be harried by the dead, to be discovered by—"

"There was no one else!" She saw even Deth wince slightly at his exasperated shout. He stepped towards her, his eyes dark smoldering. "Woman, you are bound by your name to your own vow, to the bargain that brought me across this threshold where Oen carried that skull and my last curse with it and throned me king of his midden. If you don't give me that skull, I swear by—"

"You will swear nothing." She gathered light from the shields, kindled it in her mind, and laid it like a yellow bar in front of him. "And you will not touch me."

"Can you control us all, Witch?" he asked grimly. "Try."

"Wait," Duac said abruptly. He held a hand, palm outward, in the air, as Farr's baleful gaze swung at him. "Wait." The authority of desperation in his voice held Farr momentarily at bay. Duac stepped cautiously past the light on the floor, reached Raederle and put his hands on her shoulders. She saw, looking up at him, Ylon's face briefly, the pale, angled brows, the eyes uneasy with color. Her shoulders flinched slightly at the sudden human touch, when she had spoken to nothing human for nine days, and she saw the anguish break into his eyes. He whispered, "What have you done to yourself? And to this house?"

She wanted, gazing back at him, to spread the whole tangled tale out for him, to make him understand why her hair hung lank and dirty to her waist, why she was arguing with a dead king over his skull and could seemingly shape pure air into flame. But in the face of Farr's anger she dared yield nothing. She said stiffly, "We made a bargain, Farr and I—"

"Farr." His lips shaped the word almost without sound, and she nodded, swallowing drily.

"I made Hallard Blackdawn give me his skull. I sat up all night during the rousing of Hel, circled by fire, working with fire, and by dawn I had the power to bargain. The Star-Bearer was coming through Hel to Anuin; Farr swore to gather Kings to protect him in exchange for the skull. He swore by his own name and the names of the Kings of Hel. But he didn't keep his part of the bargain. He didn't even try to find a shape-changer; he simply guarded the first stranger who he found travelling across Hel—"

"The stranger made no objection." The cold voice of Evern the Falconer cut across her words. "He was being hunted. He used our protection."

"Of course he was hunted! He—" Then the realization slapped at her, of the true extent of the danger she had brought into her house. She whispered, her fingers icy against the bone in her hands, "Duac—" But his eyes had flicked away from her face to the harpist.

"Why did you come here? The Star-Bearer has not reached Anuin yet, but you must have known the traders would bring his tale."

"I thought your father might have returned."

"What," Duac inquired more in wonder than anger, "in Hel's name would you expect my father to say to you?"

"Very little." He stood with a haunting, familiar quiescence, but there was a preoccupation in his face, as though he were listening for something beyond their hearing. Raederle touched Duac's arm.

"Duac." Her voice shook. "Duac. I am bringing more than the Kings of Hel into Anuin."

He closed his eyes, breathed something. "What now? You vanished two months ago from Caithnard, took our father's ship and left Rood to ride home alone without the faintest idea of where you were. Now you appear out of nowhere, with as much warning, accompanied by the Kings of Hel, an outlawed harpist and a crowned skull. The walls of this house could cave in on my head next and I doubt if I'd be surprised." He paused a moment; his hold tightened. "Are you all right?"

She shook her head, still whispering. "No. Oh, no. Duac, I was trying to guard Morgon against Ghisteslwchlohm."

"Ghisteslwchlohm?"

"He is—he followed Deth through Hel."

The expression died on his face. His eyes went beyond her to Deth, and then he lifted his hands carefully off her shoulders as though he were lifting stones. "All right." There was no hope in his voice. "Maybe we can—"

The harpist's voice, sprung taut, interrupted him. "The Founder is nowhere in An."

"I felt him!" Raederle cried. "He was behind you at the gates of Anuin. I felt his mind searching all the corners of Hel; he would break through my mind like a black wind, and I could feel his hatred, his rage—"

"That is not the Founder."

"Then who—" She stopped. The men, living and dead, seemed motionless as figures on a chessboard around her. She shook her head slowly, mute again, while the bone strained under her grip.

The harpist said with unexpected intensity, "I would never have chosen this place. But you didn't give me a choice."

"Morgon?" she whispered. She remembered then his quick, silent departure from Caithnard, the lawless mind that had found her, yet never threatened her. "I brought you here so he could kill you?" His face, hopeless, exhausted, gave her his answer. Something between a shout and a sob of grief and confusion welled through her. She stared at Deth, breathing tightly, feeling the hot swell of tears behind her eyes. "There are things not worth killing. Curse us all for this: you for making him what he has become; him for not seeing what he has become; and me for bringing you nearly face-to-face. You will destroy him even with your death. There's the door, open. Find a ship out of Anuin—"

"To where?"

"Anywhere! To the bottom of the sea, if nowhere else. Go harp with Ylon's bones, I don't care. Just go, so far he'll forget your name and your memory. Go—"

"It's too late." His voice was almost gentle. "You have brought me into your house."

She heard a step behind her and whirled. But it was Rood, flushed and dishevelled from riding, coming precipitously into the hall. He cast a crow-colored eye at the assembly of wraiths pulled out of their graves by a dream of revenge, armed as no King of An had armed himself for centuries. He stopped short; Raederle saw, even as his face whitened, the gleam of recognition in his eyes. Then Ohroe the Cursed, standing near him, whose face was seamed red from temple to jaw with his death wound, gripped the neck of Rood's tunic and wrenched him backward. His arm, heavy with chain mail, locked tightly around Rood's throat; a knife flashed in his other hand; the point of it pricked Rood's own temple. He said succinctly, "Now. Let us bargain again." Raederle's terrified, furious rill of thought blazed white-hot across the knife blade and leaped into Ohroe's eyes. He gasped, dropping the knife. Rood's elbow slamming into the mailed ribs seemed to have no effect, but the arm around his throat loosened as Ohroe lifted his hand to his head. Rood slipped free, pausing as he crossed the hall only to pull off the wall an ancient blade that had hung there since Hagis's death. He joined Duac who said tersely, "Will you put that sword down? The last thing I want is a pitched battle in this house."

The Kings seemed to be shifting together without sound. Among them, the harpist, his head lowered slightly as though his attention were focussed on nothing of the movement around him, was conspicuous in his stillness, and Rood made a sound in his throat. He took a firmer grip on the sword hilt and said, "Tell them that. At least when we're wraiths ourselves, we can fight on our own terms. Who brought them here? Deth?"

"Raederle."

Rood's head turned sharply. He saw Raederle, then, standing a little behind Duac. His eyes went from her worn face to the skull in her hands, and the sword tip struck the floor with a clink. She saw a shudder rack through him.

"Raederle? I saw you and I didn't even recognize you . . ." He flung the sword on the stones and went to her. He reached out to her as Duac had, but his hands dropped before he touched her. He gazed at her, and she saw that, deep in him, something dormant, unfamiliar to him, was struggling with the sense of her power. He whispered, "What happened to you? What happens to people who try to make that journey to Erlenstar Mountain?"

She swallowed, lifted one hand away from the skull to touch him. "Rood—"

"Where did you get such power? It's like nothing you ever had before."

"I always had it—"

"From what? I look at you now, and I don't even know who you are!"

"You know me," she whispered, her throat burning. "I am of An . . ."

"Rood," Duac said. His voice held an odd, flat tone of apprehension that pulled Rood's eyes from Raederle's face. Duac was staring at the doorway; he groped behind him for Rood. "Rood. That. Who is that? Tell me it's not who I think it is—"

Rood swung around. Crossing the threshold, soundless, shadowless, on a great black mount whose eyes were the color of the eyes of Farr's skull, rode a man with a single blood-red jewel on the circle of gold on his head. He was dark, sinewy, powerful; the hilts of his knife and sword were of braided gold; the rich coat over his mail was embroidered with the ancient emblem of An: an oak holding a bolt of black lightning in its green boughs. He left a following on the threshold that must have come out of the fields and orchards around Anuin. Beyond them, through the open doors, Raederle could see Duac's own guards and unarmed servants struggling to get through. They might as well have struggled against a stone wall. The effect of the crowned man on the wraiths in the hall was immediate: every sword in the room was drawn. Farr moved forward, his flat, expressionless face livid above the cut on his neck, the huge blade raised in his hand. The dead King's eyes, ignoring Farr, moving slowly over the gathering, touched Duac. The black horse stopped.

"Oen."

Rood's voice drew the King's attention to him briefly, then his gaze returned to Duac. His head bent slightly, he said, his voice temperless yet inflexible, "Peace be on the living in this house, and may no dishonor come into it. To those with honor." He paused, his eyes still on

Duac's face as he recognized the ageless instinct in him for land-law, together with something else. He gave a short laugh that held little amusement. "You have a face out of the sea. But your own father is more fortunate. You bear little more of my land-heir than his memory . . ."

Duac, looking harrowed, found his voice finally. "Peace—" The word shook, and he swallowed. "Will you bring peace with you into this house and leave it behind when you go?"

"I cannot. I have sworn a vow. Beyond death." Duac's eyes closed, his lips moving in a succinct, inaudible curse. Oen's face turned finally to Farr; their eyes met across the room for the first time outside of their dreams in six centuries. "I swore that as long as the Kings ruled Anuin, Farr of Hel would rule the king's midden."

"And I have sworn," Farr rasped, "that I would not close my eyes in my grave until those ruling Anuin were lying in theirs."

Oen's brow flicked upward. "You lost your head once before. I heard that a woman of Anuin carried your skull out of Hel, back to this house and to her shame opened the doors of this house to the dead of Hel. I have come to cleanse it of the smell of the midden." He glanced at Raederle. "Give me the skull."

She stood dumbfounded at the contempt in his voice, in his eyes, the dark, calculating eyes that had watched a tower with iron bars at its windows being built for his land-heir beside the sea. "You," she whispered, "bringing empty words into this house, what did you ever know of peace? You small-minded man, content in your battles, you left a riddle behind you in Anuin when you died that was far more than just a sea-colored face. You want to fight with Farr over this skull like dogs over a bone. You think I betrayed my house: what do you know of betrayal? You have roused yourself for revenge: what do you know of revenge? You think you saw the last of Ylon's strange powers when you walled him in his tower so efficiently with such little understanding, such little compassion. You should have known that you cannot bind a sorrow or an anger. You have waited six centuries for a battle with Farr. Well, before you raise your sword in this hall, you will have to fight me."

She stripped light from the shields, from the armbands and jewelled crowns, from the flagstones, blazed a circle on the stones around Oen.

She looked for a single source of fire in the room, but there was not even a candle lit. So she contented herself with drawing it out of her memory, the shapeless, flickering element she had mastered under Farr's ominous gaze. She laid the illusion of it around the illusions of the dead. She opened her hand and showed them how she could shape with it, drawing it high into the air, sending it spattering like waves breaking against her will. She circled them with it, as she had been forced by them to circle herself, watched them close together away from it. She burnished the shields with flame, saw them drop, soundless as flowers, to the floor. She ringed the crowns with it, watched the Kings send them spinning, wheels of flaming metal, into the air. She heard the voices, faraway, indistinct, birds' voices, the fragmented voice of the sea. Then she heard the sea itself.

The sound of it wove in and out of her shaping. She recognized the slow break and drag of it; the hollow wind moaning through broken iron bars. The harping was ended; the tower was empty. She drew her attention back to Oen; half-blind with the thought of fire, she saw him only as a shadow, hunched a little on his horse. And a fury that did not belong to her but to his roused land-heir began gathering in her like one enormous wave that might have torn the tower out of the rocks by its roots and flung it into the sea.

The fury gave her dark insight into odd powers. It whispered to her how to crack a solid flag-stone in two, how to turn the thin, black rift into a yawning illusion of emptiness that would drain the wraith of Oen, nameless, memoryless, into it. It showed her how to bind the windows and doors of her own house, lock the living and dead in it; how to create the illusion of one door in it opening constantly to an illusion of freedom. It showed her how to separate the hopeless essence of sorrow she felt from the sea, the wind, the memory of the harping, to work it into the stones and shadows of the house so that no one in it would ever laugh. She felt her own sorrow and anger stirred, as she had kindled the light, mixed with an older agony and rage against Oen until she could barely tell them apart; she could barely remember that Oen was to her simply a memory of An, and not the living, terrible, merciless figure of Ylon's memory.

She felt herself lost, drowning in the force of another's hatred. She struggled against it, blind, terrified, not knowing how to break free of the determined impulse to destruction aimed against Oen. Her terror gave way to a helpless anger; she was bound, as Oen had bound Ylon, by hatred, by compassionlessness, and by misunderstanding. She realized, before she destroyed Oen, before she loosed something alien to the very land-law of An into the house of its kings, that she had to force the wraith of Ylon, roused in her, to see clearly for the first time, the heritage they both shared, and the King who had been simply a man bound to its patterns.

One by one, with impossible effort, she drew the faces of the Kings out of the firelight. She wrested out of the dark void of rage and sorrow, names for them, histories, spoke their names as, weaponless, crownless, mute, they faced her again across the hall: Acor, Ohroe, cursed with sorrow for his sons, Nemir who spoke pig-language, Farr who had done her bidding for the sake of a six-hundred-year-old skull, Evern who had died with his falcons, defending his home. The fire dwindled away around them, became sunlight on the flagstones. She saw the High One's harpist again among the Kings. She saw Oen. He was no longer on his horse, but standing beside it. His face was bowed against its back. She saw then the black, jagged break from end to end in the flagstone at his feet.

She said his name. The naming seemed to shift him to perspective: the frightened wraith of a dead man who had once been, centuries ago, a King of An. The hatred in her roused only weakly against him, against the power of her seeing. It roused again, then drained away like a spent wave. It left her free, gazing at the broken stone, wondering what name she would bear for the rest of her life in that hall.

She found herself trembling so badly she could hardly stand. Rood, beside her, lifted his hand to hold her, but he seemed to have no strength either; he could not touch her. She saw Duac staring at the flagstone. He turned his head slowly, looked at her. A sob burned in her throat, for he had no name for her either. Her power had left her placeless, had left her nothing. Her eyes fell away from him to a strip of darkness at her feet between them. She realized slowly that the darkness was a shadow that stretched across the floor in a hall full of shadowless dead.

She turned. The Star-Bearer stood at the threshold. He was alone; Oen's following had vanished. He was watching her; she knew from the expression in his eyes, how much he had seen. As she gazed at him helplessly, he said softly, "Raederle." It was no warning, no judgment, simply her name, and she could have wept at the recognition in it.

He moved, finally, across the threshold. Plainly clothed, seemingly unarmed, he walked almost unobtrusively among the silent Kings, and yet one by one he drew their attention to him. The dark twisting of pain, hatred and power that had trailed them all into Anuin was no longer the awesome shadow of wizardry, but something they all recognized. Morgon's eyes, moving from face to face, found Deth's. He stopped; Raederle, her mind, open, vulnerable, felt the memories shock through him to his core. He began to walk again, slowly; the Kings shifted without sound, away from the harpist. Deth, his head bent, seemed to be listening to the final steps of the long journey that had begun for them both at Erlenstar Mountain. When Morgon reached him, he lifted his face, the lines on it etched mercilessly in the sunlight.

He said evenly, "What strictures of justice did you take at Erlenstar Mountain out of the brain of the High One?"

Morgon's hand lifted, cracked across the harpist's face in a furious, back-handed blow that made even Farr blink. The harpist recovered his balance with an effort.

Morgon said, his voice husked with pain, "I learned enough. From both of you. I am not interested in an argument over justice. I am interested in killing you. But because we are in a King's hall, and your blood will stain his floor, it would seem courteous to explain why I am spilling it. I got tired of your harping."

"It broke the silence."

"Is there nothing in this world that will break your silence?" His words bounced shapelessly back and forth in the high corners. "I must have done enough screaming in that mountain to shatter any silence but yours. You were well-trained by the Founder. There's nothing of you I can touch. Except your life. And even that I wonder if you value."

"Yes. I value it."

"You would never beg for it. I begged for death from Ghisteslwchlohm; he ignored me. That was his mistake. But he was wise enough to run. You should have started running that day you led me into that mountain. You aren't a fool. You might have known the Star-Bearer could survive what the Prince of Hed could not. Yet you stayed and played me songs of Hed until I wept in my dreams. I could have broken your harp strings with a thought."

"You did. Several times."

"And you did not have the sense to run."

There seemed, in the absolute silence of the hall, an odd illusion of privacy about them both. The Kings, their faces battle-weary and runnelled with bitterness, looked as engrossed as if they were watching a segment of their own lives. Duac, she could tell, was still struggling with the idea of the Founder in Erlenstar Mountain; Rood had stopped struggling. His face was drained of all expression. He watched, swallowing now and then the shout or the tears gathering in his throat.

The harpist, pausing a little before he spoke, said, "No. I am a fool. Perhaps I gambled that you might pursue the master and ignore the servant. Or that even then, you might have held, as you could not hold the land-rule, something of the tenets of riddle-mastery."

Morgon's hands closed, but he kept them still. "What have the sterile tenets of an empty College to do with either my life or your death?"

"Perhaps nothing. It was a passing thought. Like my harping. An abstract question that a man with a sword at his side rarely pauses to contemplate. The implications of action."

"Words."

"Perhaps."

"You're a Master—what stricture was strong enough to keep you adhering to the tenets of riddle-mastery? The first stricture of the Founder of Lungold: the language of truth is the language of power—truth of name, truth of essence. You found the essence of betrayal more to your taste. Who are you to judge me if I find the name of revenge, murder, justice—what name you want to put to it—more to my liking?"

"Who is anyone to judge you? You are the Star-Bearer. As you hounded me across Hel, Raederle mistook you for Ghisteslwchlohm."

She saw him flinch. Rood, the breath scraping in his throat, whispered, "Morgon, I swear, tenets or no tenets, if you don't kill him, I will."

"It is, as I said, an abstract question. Rood's idea of justice makes much more sense." Deth's voice sounded dry, tired, finished.

Morgon, an agony breaking into his face, screamed at him in a voice that must have reverberated through the black caverns of Erlenstar Mountain, "What is it you want of me?" He touched the air at his side, and the great starred sword startled into shape. It lifted, blurred in his hands. Raederle knew that she would see them locked forever that way: the harpist unarmed, unmoved, his head lifting to the rise of the sword as it cut upward through the sunlight, the powerful gathering of Morgon's muscles as he swung the blade in a double-handed stroke that brought it to balance at the apex of its ascent. Then the harpist's eyes fell to Morgon's face. He whispered, "They were promised a man of peace."

The sword, hovering oddly, knotted strands of light from the windows. The harpist stood under the raw edge of its shadow with a familiar stillness that seemed suddenly, to Raederle, in its implications, more terrible than anything she had seen either in herself or in Morgon. A sound broke out of her, a protest against the glimpse of that patience, and she felt Duac's hand pull at her. But she could not move. Light shivered abruptly down the blade. The sword fell, crashed with a spattering of blue sparks against the floor. The hilt, rebounding, came to rest with the stars face down on the stones.

There was not a sound in the room but Morgon's breathing, shuddering uncontrollably through him. He faced the harpist, his hands clenched at his sides; he did not move or speak. The harpist, gazing back at him, stirred a little. The blood came suddenly back into his face. His lips moved as though he were about to speak, but the word faltered against Morgon's unrelenting silence. He took a step backward, as in question. Then his head bowed. He turned, his own hands closed, walked swiftly and quietly through the motionless Kings, out of the hall, his head, unhooded, still bent under the weight of the sun.

Morgon stared, unseeing, at the assembly of living and dead. The unresolved, explosive turmoil in him hung like a dangerous spell over the room. Raederle, standing beside Rood and Duac, unable to move in the threat of it, wondered what word would bring Morgon's thoughts back from the black, inescapable caverns of stone, and the blind corner of truth into which the harpist had led him. He seemed, recognizing none of them, a stranger, dangerous with power; but as she waited for whatever shape that power would take, she realized slowly that it had just shaped itself, and that he had given them his name. She spoke it softly, almost hesitantly, knowing and not knowing the man to whom it belonged.

"Star-Bearer."

His eyes went to her; the silence ebbed away between his fingers as they loosened. The expression welling back into his face drew her toward him across the hall. She heard Rood start to speak behind her; his voice broke on a harsh, dry sob and Duac murmured something. She stood before the Star-Bearer, brought him with a touch out of the grip of his memories.

She whispered, "Who were promised a man of peace?"

He shuddered then, reached out to her. She put her arms around him, resting the skull on his shoulder like a warning against any interruption. "The children . . ."

She felt a tremor of awe run through her. "The Earth-Masters' children?"

"The children of stone, in that black cave . . ." His hold of her tightened. "He gave me that choice. And I thought he was defenseless. I should have—I should have remembered what deadly weapons he could forge out of words."

"Who is he? That harpist?"

"I don't know. But I do know this: I want him named." He was silent then, for a long while, his face hidden against her. He moved finally, said something she could not hear; she drew back a little. He felt the bone against his face. He reached up, took the skull. He traced an eye socket with his thumb, then looked at her. His voice, worn raw, was calmer.

"I watched you, that night on Hallard Blackdawn's lands. I was near you every night as you moved through An. No one, living or dead, would have touched you. But you never needed my help."

"I felt you near," she whispered. "But I thought—I thought you were—"

"I know."

"Well, then—well, then, what did you think I was trying to do?" Her voice rose. "Did you think I was trying to protect Deth?"

"That's exactly what you were doing."

She stared at him wordlessly, thinking of all she had done during those strange, interminable days. She burst out, "But you still stayed with me, to protect me?" He nodded. "Morgon, I told you what I am; you could see what dark power I was waking in me—you knew its origins. You knew I am kin to those shape-changers who tried to kill you, you thought I was helping the man who had betrayed you—why in Hel's name did you trust me?"

His hands, circling the gold crown on the skull, closed on the worn metal with sudden strength. "I don't know. Because I chose to. Then, and forever. Is that how long you intend to carry this skull around?"

She shook her head, mute again, and held out her hand for it, to give it back to Farr. The little, angular, blond-colored pattern on her palm shone clear in the light; Morgon's hand dropped abruptly to her wrist.

"What is that?"

She resisted the impulse to close her fingers over it. "It came—it came out the first time I held fire. I used a stone from King's Mouth Plain to elude the Ymris war-ships, with an illusion of light. While I was bound to it, looking into it, I saw a man holding it, as though I were looking into a memory. I almost—I was always just on the verge of knowing him. Then I felt one of the shape-changers in my mind, wanting his name, and the bidding was broken. The stone is lost, but . . . the pattern of it burned into my hand."

His hand loosened, lay with a curious gentleness on her wrist. She looked up at him; the fear in his face chilled her heart. He put his arms around her again with the same gentleness, as if she might drift away from him like a mist and only blind hope could keep her there.

The rasp of metal on the stones made them both turn. Duac, who had picked the starred sword up off the floor, said apprehensively to Morgon, "What is it? On her hand?"

He shook his head. "I don't know. I only know that for a year Ghisteslwchlohm searched my mind for a piece of knowledge, went again and again through every moment of my life looking for one certain face, one name. That might have been it."

"Whose name?" Duac asked. Raederle, horror shooting through her, dropped her face against Morgon's shoulder.

"He never bothered to tell me."

"If they want the stone, they can find it themselves," Raederle said numbly. He had not answered Duac's question, but he would answer her, later. "No one—the shape-changer could learn nothing from me. It's in the sea with Peven's crown . . ." She lifted her head suddenly, said to Duac, "I believe our father knew. About the High One. And about—probably about me."

"I wouldn't doubt it." Then he added wearily, "I think he was born knowing everything. Except how to find his way home."

"Is he in trouble?" Morgon asked. Duac looked at him surprisedly a moment. Then he shook his head.

"I don't—I don't think so. I don't feel it."

"Then I know where he might have gone. I'll find him."

Rood crossed the hall to join them. His face was tear-stained; it held the familiar, austere expression that he carried with him into his studies and his battles. He said softly to Morgon, "I'll help you."

"Rood—"

"He's my father. You are the greatest Master in this realm. And I am an Apprentice. And may I be buried next to Farr in Hel if I watch you walk out of this hall the same way you walked into it: alone."

"He won't," Raederle said.

Duac protested, his voice lowering. "You can't leave me alone with all these Kings, Rood. I don't even know half their names. Those in this hall may have been subdued for a little while, but for how long? Aum will rise, and west Hel; there are about five people in An who might not panic, and you and I are among them."

"I am?"

"No wraith," Morgon said shortly, "will enter this house again." He weighed the skull in his hand, as they watched him, then tossed it across the room to Farr. The King caught it soundlessly, vaguely startled, as if he had forgotten whose it was. Morgon surveyed the still, ghostly assembly. He said, to them, "Do you want a war? I'll give you one. A war of desperation, for the earth itself. If you lose it, you may drift like sorrow from one end of the realm to another without finding a place to rest. What honor—if the dead are concerned with honor—can you take running Cyn Croeg's bull to death?"

"There's revenge," Farr suggested pointedly.

"Yes. There's that. But I will seal this house against you stone by stone if I must. I will do what you force me to do. And I am not concerned with honor, either." He paused, then added slowly, "Or with the bindings and unbindings of the dead of An."

"You have no such power over the dead of An," Oen said abruptly. It was a question. Something hard as the ground floor of Erlenstar Mountain surfaced in Morgon's eyes.

"I learned," he said, "from a master. You can fight your private, meaningless battles into oblivion. Or you can fight those who gave Oen his land-heir, and who will destroy Anuin, Hel, the earth that binds you, if you let them. And that," he added, "should appeal to you both."

Even the Falconer asked, "How much choice do we have?"

"I don't know. Maybe none." His hands closed suddenly; he whispered, "I swear by my name that if I can, I will give you a choice."

There was silence again, from the living and the dead. Morgon turned almost reluctantly to Duac, a question in his eyes that Duac, his instincts channelled to the heartbeat of An, understood.

He said brusquely, "Do what you want in this land. Ask what you need from me. I'm no Master, but I can grasp the essentials of what you have said and done in this house. I can't begin to understand. I don't know how you could have any power over the land-law of An. You and my father, when you find him, can argue over that later. All I know is that there is an instinct in me to trust you blindly. Beyond reason, and beyond hope."

He lifted the sword in his hands, held it out to Morgon. The stars kindled the sunlight to an unexpected beauty. Morgon, staring at Duac, did not move. He started to speak, but no words came. He turned suddenly toward the empty threshold; Raederle, watching him, wondered what he was seeing beyond the courtyard, beyond the walls of Anuin. His hand closed finally on the stars; he took the sword from Duac.

"Thank you." They saw then in his face the faint, troubled dawning of curiosity, and a memory that seemed to hold no pain. He lifted his other hand, touched Raederle's face and she smiled. He said hesitantly, "I have nothing to offer you. Not even Peven's crown. Not even peace. But can you bear waiting for me a little longer? I wish I knew how long. I need to go to Hed awhile, and then to Lungold. I'll try to—I'll try—"

Her smile faded. "Morgon of Hed," she said evenly, "if you take one step across that threshold without me, I will lay a curse on your next step and your next until no matter where you go your path will lead you back to me."

"Raederle—"

"I can do it. Do you want to watch me?"

He was silent, struggling between his longing and his fear for her. He said abruptly, "No. All right. Will you wait for me in Hed? I think I can get us both safely that far."

"No."

"Then will you—"

"No."

"All right; then—"

"No."

"Then will you come with me?" he whispered. "Because I could not bear to leave you."

She put her arms around him, wondering, as she did so, what strange, perilous future she had bargained for. She said only, as his arms circled her, not in gentleness this time, but in a fierce and terrified determination, "That's good. Because I swear by Ylon's name you never will."

Harpist in the Wind

THE STAR-BEARER AND Raederle of An sat on the crown of the highest of the seven towers of Anuin. The white stone fell endlessly away from them, down to the summer-green slope the great house sat on. The city itself spilled away from the slope to the sea. The sky revolved above them, a bright, changeless blue, its expression broken only by the occasional spiral of a hawk. Morgon had not moved for hours. The morning sun had struck his profile on the side of the embrasure he sat in and shifted his shadow without his notice to the other side. He was aware of Raederle only as some portion of the land around him, of the light wind, and the crows sketching gleaming black lines through the green orchards in the distance: something peaceful and remote, whose beauty stirred every once in a while through his thoughts.

His mind was spinning endless threads of conjecture that snarled constantly around his ignorance. Stars, children with faces of stone, the fiery, broken shards of a bowl he had smashed in Astrin's hut, dead cities, a dark-haired shape-changer, a harpist, all resolved under his probing into answerless riddles. He gazed back at his own life, at the history of the realm, and picked at facts like potshards, trying to piece them together. Nothing fit; nothing held; he was cast constantly out of his memories into the soft summer air.

He moved finally, stiffly as a stone deciding to move, and slid his hands over his eyes. Flickering shapes like ancient beasts without names winged into light behind his eyelids. He cleared his mind again, let images drift and flow into thought until they floundered once again on the shoals of impossibility.

The vast blue sky broke into his vision, and the swirling maze of streets and houses below. He could think no longer; he leaned against his shadow. The silence within the slab of ancient stone eased through him; his thoughts, worn meaningless, became quiet again.

He saw a soft leather shoe then and a flicker of leaf-green cloth. He turned his head and found Raederle sitting cross-legged on the ledge beside him.

He leaned over precariously and drew her against him. He laid his face against her long windblown hair and saw the burning strands beneath his closed eyes. He was silent for a time, holding her tightly, as if he sensed a wind coming that might sweep them out of their high, dangerous resting place.

She stirred a little; her face lifting to kiss him, and his arms loosened reluctantly. "I didn't realize you were here," he said, when she let him speak.

"I guessed that, somehow, after the first hour or so. What were you thinking about?"

"Everything." He nudged a chip of mortar out of a crack and flicked it into the trees below. A handful of crows startled up, complaining. "I keep battering my brains against my past, and I always come to the same conclusion. I don't know what in Hel's name I am doing."

She shifted, drawing her knees up, and leaned back against the stone beside her to face him. Her eyes filled with light, like sea-polished amber, and his throat constricted suddenly, too full of words. "Answering riddles. You told me that that is the only thing you can keep doing, blind and deaf and dumb, and not knowing where you are going."

"I know." He searched more mortar out of the crack and threw it so hard he nearly lost his balance. "I know. But I have been here in Anuin with you for seven days, and I can't find one reason or one riddle to compel me out of this house. Except that if we stay here much longer, we will both die."

"That's one," she said soberly.

"I don't know why my life is in danger because of three stars on my face. I don't know where the High One is. I don't know what the shape-changers are, or how I can help a cairn of children who have turned into stone at the bottom of a mountain. I know of only one place to begin finding answers. And the prospect is hardly appealing."

"Where?"

"In Ghisteslwchlohm's mind."

She stared at him, swallowing, and then frowned down at the sun-warmed stone, "Well." Her voice shook almost imperceptibly. "I didn't think we could stay here forever. But, Morgon—"

"You could stay here."

Her head lifted. With the sun catching in her eyes again, he could not read their expression. But her voice was stiff. "I am not going to leave you. I refused even the wealth of Hel and all the pigs in it for your sake. You are going to have to learn to live with me."

"It's difficult enough just trying to live," he murmured, without thinking, then flushed. But her mouth twitched. He reached across to her, took her hand. "For one silver boar bristle, I would take you to Hed and spend the rest of my life raising plow horses in east Hed."

"I'll find you a boar bristle."

"How do I marry you, in this land?"

"You can't," she said calmly, and his hand slackened.

"What?"

"Only the king has the power to bind his heirs in marriage. And my father is not here. So we'll have to forget about that until he finds the time to return home."

"But, Raederle—"

She pitched a sliver of mortar across the trail feathers of a passing crow, causing it to veer with a squawk. "But what?" she said darkly.

"I can't . . . I can't walk into your father's land, trouble the dead as I have, nearly commit murder in his hall, then take you away with me to wander through the realm without even marrying you. What in Hel's name will your father think of me?"

"When he finally meets you, he'll let you know. What I think, which is more to the point, is that my father has meddled enough with my life. He may have foreseen our meeting, and maybe even our loving, but I don't think he should have his own way in everything. I'm not going to marry you just because he maybe foresaw that, too, in some dream."

"Do you think it was that, behind his strange vow about Peven's Tower?" he asked curiously. "Foreknowledge?"

"You are changing the subject."

He eyed her a moment, considering the subject and her flushed face. "Well," he said softly, casting their future to the winds over the dizzying face of the tower, "if you refuse to marry me, I don't see what I can do about it. And if you choose to come with me—if that is what you really want—I am not going to stop you. I want you too much. But I'm terrified. I think we would have more hope of survival falling head first off this tower. And at least, doing that, we'd know where we were going."

Her hand lay on the stones between them. She lifted it, touched his face. "You have a name and a destiny. I can only believe that sooner or later you will stumble across some hope."

"I haven't seen any so far. Only you. Will you marry me in Hed?"

"No."

He was silent a little, holding her eyes. "Why?"

She looked away from him quickly; he sensed a sudden, strange turmoil in her. "For many reasons."

"Raederle—"

"No. And don't ask me again. And stop looking at me like that."

"All right," he said after a moment. He added, "I don't remember that you were so stubborn."

"Pig-headed."

"Pig-headed."

She looked at him again. Her mouth crooked into a reluctant smile. She shifted close to him, put her arm around his shoulders, and swung her feet over the sheer edge of nothingness. "I love you, Morgon of Hed. When we finally leave this house, where will we go first? Hed?"

"Yes. Hed . . ." The name touched his heart suddenly, like the word of a spell. "I have no business going home. I simply want to. For a few hours, at night . . . that might be safe." He thought of the sea, between them and his home, and his heart chilled. "I can't take you across the sea."

"In Hel's name, why not?" she said.

"It's far too dangerous."

"That makes no sense. Lungold is dangerous, and I'm going with you there."

"That's different. For one thing, no one I loved ever died in Lungold. Yet. For another thing—"

"Morgon, I am not going to die in the sea. I can probably shape water as well as fire."

"You don't know that. Do you?" The thought of her caught in the water as it heaved itself into faces and wet, gleaming forms made his voice rough. "You wouldn't even have time to learn."

"Morgon—"

"Raederle, I have been on a ship breaking apart in the sea. I don't want to risk your life that way."

"It's not your risk. It's mine. For another thing, I have been on ships from Caithnard to Kyrth and back looking for you and nothing ever happened to me."

"You could stay at Caithnard. For only a few—"

"I am not going to stay at Caithnard," she said tersely. "I am going with you to Hed. I want to see the land you love. If you had your way, I would be sitting in a farmhouse in Hed shelling beans and waiting for you, just as I have waited for nearly two years."

"You don't shell beans."

"I don't. Not unless you are beside me helping."

He saw himself, a lean, shaggy-haired man with a worn, spare face, a great sword at his side and a starred harp at his back, sitting on the porch at Akren with a bowl of beans on his knees. He laughed suddenly. She smiled again, watching him, her argument forgotten.

"You haven't done that in seven days."

"No." He was still, his arm around her, and the smile died slowly in his eyes. He thought of Hed, gripped so defenselessly in the heart of the sea, with not even the illusion of the High One to protect it. He whispered, "I wish I could ring Hed with power, so that nothing of the turmoil of the mainland could touch it and it could stay innocent of fear."

"Ask Duac. He'll give you an army."

"I don't dare bring an army to Hed. That would be asking for disaster."

"Take a few wraiths," she suggested. "Duac would love to be rid of them."

"Wraiths." He lifted his eyes from the distant forests to stare at her. "In Hed."

"They're invisible. No one would see them to attack them." Then she shook her head a little at her own words. "What am I thinking? They would upset all the farmers in Hed."

"Not if the farmers didn't know they were there." His hands felt chilled, suddenly, linked around hers. He breathed, "What am I thinking?"

She drew back, searching his eyes. "Are you taking me seriously?"

"I think . . . I think so." He did not see her face then, but the faces of the dead, with all their frustrated power. "I could bind them. I understand them . . . their anger, their desire for revenge, their land-love. They can take that love to Hed and all their longing for war. . . . But your father . . . how can I wrest something out of the history of An and lead it to danger in Hed? I can't tamper with the land-law of An like that."

"Duac gave you permission. And for all my father is interested in land-law, he might as well be a wraith himself. But Morgon, what about Eliard?"

"Eliard?"

"I don't know him, but wouldn't he . . . wouldn't it disturb him maybe a little if you brought an army of the dead to Hed?"

He thought of the land-ruler of Hed, his brother, whose face he barely remembered. "A little," he said softly. "He must be used to being disturbed by me, even in his sleep, by now. I would bury my own heart under his feet if that would keep him and Hed safe. I would even face an argument with him over this—"

"What will he say?"

"I don't know . . . I don't even know him any more." The thought pained him, touching unhealed places within him. But he did not let her see that; he only moved reluctantly from their high place. "Come with me. I want to talk to Duac."

"Take them," Duac said. "All of them."

They had found him in the great hall, listening to complaints from farmers and messengers from Lords of An whose lands and lives were in turmoil over the restlessness and bickerings of the dead. When the hall finally cleared and Morgon could speak with him, he listened incredulously.

"You actually want them? But Morgon, they'll destroy the peace of Hed."

"No, they won't. I'll explain to them why they are there—"

"How? How do you explain anything to dead men who are fighting a centuries-old war in cow pastures and village market places?"

"I'll simply offer them what they want. Someone to fight. But, Duac, how will I explain to your father?"

"My father?" Duac glanced around the hall, then up at the rafters, and at each of the four corners. "I don't see him. Anywhere. And when I do see him, he will be so busy explaining himself to the living, he won't have time to count the heads of the dead. How many do you want?"

"As many as I can bind, of the kings and warriors who had some touch of compassion in them. They'll need that, to understand Hed. Rood would be able to help me—" He stopped suddenly and an unaccountable flush stained Duac's face. "Where is Rood? I haven't seen him for days."

"He hasn't been here for days." Duac cleared his throat. "You weren't noticing. So I waited until you asked. I sent him to find Deth."

Morgon was silent. The name flung him back seven days, as though he stood in the same pool of sunlight, his shadow splayed before him on the cracked stone floor. "Deth," he whispered, and the ambiguity of the name haunted him.

"I gave him instructions to bring the harpist back here; I sent fourteen armed men with him. You let him go, but he still has much to answer for to the land-rulers of the realm. I thought to imprison him here until the Masters at Caithnard could question him. That's not something I would attempt to do." He touched Morgon hesitantly. "You would never have known he was here. I'm only surprised Rood has not returned before this."

The color stirred back into Morgon's face. "I'm not surprised," he said. "I wouldn't want to be in Rood's boots, trying to bring Deth back to Anuin. That harpist makes his own choices."

"Maybe."

"Rood will never bring him back here. You sent him into the chaos of the Three Portions for nothing."

"Well," Duac said resignedly, "you know the harpist better than I do. And Rood would have gone after him with or without my asking. He wanted answers too."

"You don't question that riddler with a sword. Rood should have known that." He heard the harsh edge that had crept into his voice then. He turned a little abruptly, out of the light, and sat down at one of the tables.

Duac said helplessly, "I'm sorry. This was something you didn't need to know."

"I do need to know. I just didn't want to think. Not yet." He spread his hands on the rich gold grain of oak and thought again of Akren, with its sunlit oak walls. "I'm going home." The words opened his heart, filled him with a sharp, sweet urgency. "Home . . . Duac, I need ships. Trade-ships."

"You're going to take the dead by water?" Raederle said amazedly. "Will they go?"

"How else can they get to Hed?" he asked reasonably. Then he thought a little, staring back at his vague reflection in the polished wood. "I don't dare take you on the same ship with them. So . . . we'll ride together to Caithnard and meet them there. All right?"

"You want to ride back through Hel?"

"We could fly instead," he suggested, but she shook her head quickly.

"No. I'll ride."

He eyed her, struck by an odd note in her voice. "It would be simple for you to take the crow-shape."

"One crow in the family is enough," she said darkly. "Morgon, Bri Corbett could find ships for you. And men to sail them."

"It will cost a small fortune to persuade them," Morgon said, but Duac only shrugged.

"The dead have already cost a great fortune in the destruction of crops and animals. Morgon, how in Hel's name will you control them in Hed?"

"They will not want to fight me," he said simply, and Duac was silent, gazing at him out of clear, sea-colored eyes.

"I wonder," he said slowly, "what you are. Man of Hed, who can control the dead of An . . . Star-Bearer."

Morgon looked at him with a curious gratitude. "I might have hated my own name in this hall, but for you." He stood up, mulling over the problem at hand. "Duac, I need to know names. I could spend days searching the cairns with my mind, but I won't know who I am rousing. I know many of the names of the Kings of the Three Portions, but I don't know the lesser dead."

"I don't either," Duac said.

"Well, I know where you can find out," Raederle sighed. "The place I almost lived in when I was a child. Our father's library."

She and Morgon spent the rest of the day and the evening there, among ancient books and dusty parchments, while Duac sent to the docks for Bri Corbett. By midnight, Morgon had tamped down in the deep of his mind endless names of warrior-lords, their sons and far-flung families, and legends of love, blood feuds and land wars that spanned the history of An. He left the house then, walked alone through the still summer night into the fields behind the king's house, which were the charnel house for the many who had died battling over Anuin. There he began his calling.

He spoke name after name, with the fragments of legend or poetry that he could remember, with his voice and his mind. The dead roused to their names, came out of the orchards and woods, out of the earth itself. Some rode at him with wild, eerie cries, their armor aflame with moonlight over bare bones. Others came silently: dark, grim figures revealing terrible death wounds. They sought to frighten him, but he only watched them out of eyes that had already seen all he needed to fear. They tried to fight him, but he opened his own mind to them, showed them glimpses of his power. He held them through all their challenging, until they stood ranged before him across an entire field, their awe and curiosity forcing them out of their memories to glimpse something of the world they had been loosed into.

Then he explained what he wanted. He did not expect them to understand Hed, but they understood him, his anger and despair and his land-love. They gave him fealty in a ritual as old as An, their moldering blades flashing greyly in the moonlight. Then they seeped slowly back into the night, into the earth, until he summoned them again.

He stood once again in a quiet field, his eyes on one still, dark figure who did not leave. He watched it curiously; then, when it did not move, he touched its mind. His thoughts were filled instantly with the living land-law of An.

His heart pounded sharply against his ribs. The King of An walked slowly toward him, a tall man robed and cowled like a master or a wraith. As he neared, Morgon could see him dimly in the moonlight, his dark brows slashing a tired, bitter face over eyes that were like Rood's hauntingly familiar. The king stopped in front of him, stood silently surveying him.

He smiled unexpectedly, the bitterness in his eyes yielding to a strange wonder. "I've seen you," he said, "in my dreams. Star-Bearer."

"Mathom." His throat was very dry. He bent his head to the king he had summoned out of the night of An. "You must . . . you must be wondering what I'm doing."

"No. You made that very clear, as you explained it to the army you raised. You do astounding things so quietly in my land."

"I asked Duac's permission."

"I'm sure Duac was grateful for the suggestion. You're going to sail with them to Hed? Is that what I heard?"

"I don't . . . I was thinking of riding with Raederle to Caithnard and meeting the ships there, but I think perhaps I should sail with the dead. It would make the living men on the ships feel easier, if I am with them."

"You're taking Raederle to Hed?"

"She won't . . . she won't listen to reason."

The king grunted. "Strange woman." His eyes were as sharp and curious as birds' eyes, searching beneath Morgon's words.

Morgon asked him suddenly, "What have you seen of me, in your dreams?"

"Pieces. Fragments. Little that will help you, and much more than is good for me. Long ago, I dreamed that you came out of a tower with a crown in your hand and three stars on your face . . . but no name. I saw you with a beautiful young woman, whom I knew was my daughter, but still, I never knew who you were. I saw. . . ." He shook his head a little, drawing his gaze back out of some perplexing, dangerous vision.

"What?"

"I am not sure."

"Mathom." He felt cold suddenly in the warm summer night. "Be careful. There are things in your mind that could cost you your life."

"Or my land-law?" His lean hand closed on Morgon's shoulder. "Perhaps. That is why I rarely explain my thoughts. Come to the house. There will be a minor tempest when I reappear, but if you can sit patiently through that, we will have time to talk afterward." He took a step, but Morgon did not move. "What is it?"

He swallowed. "There is something I have to tell you. Before I walk into your hall with you. Seven days ago, I walked into it to kill a harpist."

He heard the king draw a swift breath. "Deth came here."

"I didn't kill him."

"Somehow I am not surprised." His voice sounded husky, like a voice out of a barrow. He drew Morgon forward toward the great moonlit house. "Tell me."

Morgon told him much more than that before they reached the hall. He found himself talking a little about even the past seven days, which were so precious to him he wondered if they had even existed. Mathom said little, only making a faint noise deep in his throat now and then, like a blackbird's mutter. As they entered the inner courtyard, they saw horses, trembling and sweating, being led to the stables. Their saddle-cloths were purple and blue, the colors of the king's household guard. Mathom cursed mildly.

"Rood must be back. Empty-handed, furious, wraithridden, and unwashed." They entered the hall, which was a blaze of torchlight, and Rood, slumped over a cup of wine, stared at his father. Duac and Raederle were beside him, their heads turning, but he got to his feet first, drowning their voices.

"Where in Hel's name have you been?"

"Don't shout at me," the king said testily. "If you had no more sense than to roam through this chaos searching for that harpist, I have no pity for you." He switched his gaze to Duac, as Rood, his mouth still open, dropped back into his chair. Duac eyed the king coldly, but his voice was controlled.

"Well. What brought you home? Dropping out of the sky like a bad spell. Surely not distress over the shambles you have made of your land-rule."

"No," Mathom said imperturbably, pouring wine. "You and Rood have done very well without me."

"We have done what very well without you?" Rood asked between his teeth. "Do you realize we are on the verge of war?"

"Yes. And An has armed itself for it in a remarkably short time. Even you have turned, in less than three months, from a scholar into a warrior."

Rood drew an audible breath to answer. Duac's hand clamped suddenly down on his wrist, silencing him. "War." His face had lost color. "With whom?"

"Who else is armed?"

"Ymris?" He repeated it incredulously, "Ymris?"

Mathom swallowed wine. His face looked older than it had under the moonlight, grim and worn with travel. He sat down beside Raederle. "I have seen the war in Ymris," he said softly. "The rebels hold half the coastal lands. It's a strange, bloody, merciless war, and it is going to exhaust Heureu Ymris' forces. He can never hope to contain it within his own borders once the people he is fighting decide to take it beyond the borders of Ymris. I suspected that before, but even I could not ask the Three Portions to arm themselves without reason. And to give reason might have precipitated attack."

"You did that deliberately?" Duac breathed. "You left us so that we would arm ourselves?"

"It was extreme," Mathom admitted, "but it was effective." He cast an eye at Rood again, as he opened his mouth and spoke in a subdued voice.

"Where have you been? And are you planning to stay home awhile?"

"Here and there, satisfying my curiosity. And yes, I think I will stay home now. If you can refrain from shouting at me."

"If you weren't so pig-headed, I wouldn't shout."

Mathom looked skeptical. "You even have a warrior's hard head.

What exactly were you planning to do with Deth if you had caught him?"

There was a short silence. Duac said simply, "I would have sent him to Caithnard eventually, on an armed ship, and let the Masters question him."

"The College at Caithnard is hardly a court of law."

Duac looked at him, a rare trace of temper in his eyes. "Then you tell me. What would you have done? If it had been you instead of me here, watching Morgon . . . watching Morgon forced to exact his own justice from a man bound to no law in the realm, who betrayed everyone in the realm, what would you have done?"

"Justice," Mathom said softly. Morgon looked at him, waiting for his answer. He saw in the dark, tired eyes a distant, curious pain. "He is the High One's Harpist. I would let the High One judge him."

"Mathom?" Morgon said, wondering suddenly, imperatively, what the king was seeing. But Mathom did not answer him. Raederle was watching him, too; the king touched her hair lightly, but neither of them spoke.

"The High One," Rood said. The warrior's harshness had left his voice; the words were a riddle, full of bitterness and despair, a plea for answer. His eyes touched Morgon's with a familiar twist of self-mockery. "You heard my father. I'm no longer even a riddler. You'll have to answer that one, Riddle-Master."

"I will," he said wearily. "I don't seem to have any choice."

"You," Mathom said, "have stayed here far too long."

"I know. I couldn't leave. I'll leave . . ." He glanced at Duac. "Tomorrow? Will the ships be ready?"

Duac nodded. "Bri Corbett said they'll sail on the midnight tide. Actually, he said a great deal more when I told him what you wanted. But he knows men who would sail even a cargo of the dead for gold."

"Tomorrow," Mathom murmured. He glanced at Morgon and then at Raederle, who was staring silently at the pooling candle, her face set as for an argument. He seemed to make his own surmises behind his black, fathomless gaze. She lifted her eyes slowly, sensing his thoughts.

"I am going with Morgon, and I am not asking you to marry us. Aren't you even going to argue?"

He shook his head, sighing. "Argue with Morgon. I'm too old and tired, and all I want from either of you is that somewhere in this troubled realm you find your peace."

She stared at him. Her face shook suddenly, and she reached out to him, tears burning down her face in the torchlight. "Oh, why were you gone so long?" she whispered, as he held her tightly. "I have needed you."

He talked with her and with Morgon until the candles buried themselves in their holders and the windows grew pale with dawn. They slept most of the next day, and then, late that evening, when the world was still again, Morgon summoned his army of the dead to the docks at Anuin.

Seven trade-ships were moored under the moonlight carrying light cargoes of fine cloth and spices. Morgon, his mind weltering with names, faces, memories out of the brains of the dead, watched the ranks slowly become half-visible on the shadowy docks. They were mounted, armed, silent, waiting to board. The city was dark behind them; the black fingers of masts in the harbor rose with the swell of the tide to touch the stars and withdrew. The gathering of the dead had been accomplished in a dreamlike silence, under the eyes of Duac and Bri Corbett and the fascinated, terrified skeleton crews on the ships. They were just ready to board when a horse thudded down the dock, breaking Morgon's concentration. He gazed at Raederle as she dismounted, wondering why she was not still asleep, his mind struggling with her presence as he was drawn back slowly into the night of the living. There was a single dock lamp lit near them; it gave her hair, slipping out of its jewelled pins, a luminous, fiery sheen. He could not see her face well.

"I'm coming with you to Hed," she said. His hand moved out of the vivid backwash of centuries to turn her face to the light. The annoyance in it cleared his mind.

"We discussed it," he said. "Not on these ships full of wraiths."

"You and my father discussed it. You forgot to tell me."

He ran his wrist across his forehead, realizing he was sweating. Bri Corbett was leaning over the side of the ship near them, an ear to their voices, one eye on the tide. "Lord," he called softly, "if we don't leave soon, there'll be seven ships full of the dead stuck in the harbor until morning."

"All right." He stretched to ease the burning knots of tension in his back. Raederle folded her arms; he caught a pin falling out of her hair. "It would be best if you ride up through Hel to meet me in Caithnard."

"You were going to ride with me. Not sail with wraiths of Hed."

"I can't lead an army of the dead by land to Caithnard and load them there at the docks under the eye of every trader—"

"That's not the point. The point is: However you are going to Hed, I'm going with you. The point is: You were going to sail straight to Hed and leave me waiting for you at Caithnard."

He stared at her. "I was not," he said indignantly.

"You would have thought of it," she said tersely, "halfway there, leaving me safe and foresworn at Caithnard. I have a pack on my horse; I'm ready to leave."

"No. Not a four day journey by sea with me and the dead of An."

"Yes."

"No."

"Yes."

"No." His hands were clenched; shadows wedged beneath the bones of his taut face as he gazed at her. The lamplight was exploring her face as he had explored it the past days. Light gathered in her eyes, and he remembered that she had stared into the eyes of a skull and had outfaced dead kings. "No," he repeated harshly. "I don't know what trail of power the dead will leave across the water. I don't know—"

"You don't know what you're doing. You don't know how safe you will be, even in Hed."

"Which is why I will not take you on these ships."

"Which is why I am going with you. At least I am born to understand the sea."

"And if it tears apart the wood beneath you and scatters planks and spice and the dead into the waves, what will you do? You'll drown, because no matter what shape I take, I won't be able to save you, and then what will I do?"

She was silent. The dead ranked behind her seemed to be looking at him with the same distant, implacable expression. He turned suddenly, his hands opening and closing again. He caught the mocking eyes of one of the kings and let his mind grow still. A name stirred shadows of memory behind the dead eyes. The wraith moved after a moment, blurring into air and darkness, and entered the ship.

He lost all sense of time again, as he filled the seven trade-ships with the last of their cargo. Centuries murmured through him, mingling with the slap of water and the sounds of Duac and Raederle talking in some far land. Finally, he reached the end of names and began to see.

The dark, silent vessels were growing restless in the tide. Shipmasters were giving subdued orders, as if they feared their voices might rouse the dead. Men moved as quietly across the decks, among the mooring cables. Raederle and Duac stood alone on the empty dock, silently, watching Morgon. He went to them, feeling a salt wind that had not been there before drying the sweat on his face.

He said to Duac, "Thank you. I don't know how grateful Eliard is going to be, but it's the best protection I can think of for Hed, and it will set my mind at ease. Tell Mathom . . . tell him—" He hesitated, groping. Duac dropped a hand on his shoulder.

"He knows. Just be careful."

"I will be." He turned his head, met Raederle's eyes. She did not move or speak, but she bound him wordless, lost again in memories. He broke their silence as if he were breaking a spell. "I'll meet you at Caithnard." He kissed her and turned quickly. He boarded the lead ship. The ramp slid up behind him; Bri Corbett stood beside an open hatch.

He said worriedly as Morgon climbed down the ladder into the lightless hold, "You'll be all right among the dead?"

Morgon nodded without speaking. Bri closed the hatch behind him. He stumbled a little around bolts of cloth and found a place to sit on sacks of spice. He felt the ship ease away from the dock, away from Anuin toward the open sea. He leaned against the side of the hull, heard water spray against the wood. The dead were silent, invisible around him, their minds growing quiescent as they sailed away from their past. Morgon found himself trying to trace their faces suddenly out of the total darkness. He drew his knees up, pushed his face against his arms and listened to the water. A few moments later, he heard the hatch open.

He drew a long, silent breath and loosed it. Lamplight flickered beyond his closed eyes. Someone climbed down the ladder, found a path through the cargo, and sat down beside him. Scents of pepper and ginger wafted up around him. The hatch dropped shut again.

He lifted his head, said to Raederle, who was no more than her breathing and faint smell of sea air, "Are you planning to argue with me for the rest of our lives?"

"Yes," she said stiffly.

He dropped his head back against his knees. After a while he drew one arm free, shaped her wrist in the dark, and then her fingers. He gazed back at the night, holding her scarred left hand in both his hands against his heart.

THEY ARRIVED IN Hed four nights later. Six of the trade-ships had turned westward in the channel to wait at Caithnard; Bri took his ship to Tol. Morgon, worn out from listening for disaster, was startled out of a catnap by the hull scudding a little against the dock. He sat up, tense, and heard Bri curse someone amiably. The hatch opened; lamplight blinded him. He smelled earth.

His heart began to pound suddenly. Beside him, Raederle, half-buried in furs, lifted her head sleepily.

"You're home," Bri said, smiling behind the light, and Morgon got to his feet, climbed up onto the deck. Tol was a handful of houses scattered beyond the moon-shadow flung by the dark cliffs. The warm, motionless air smelled familiarly of cows and grain.

He hardly realized he had spoken until Bri, dousing the light, answered, "On the lee side of midnight. We got here sooner than I expected."

A wave curled lazily onto the beach, spread a fret-work of silver as it withdrew. The shore road wound bone-white away from the dock to disappear into the cliff shadow. Morgon picked out the faint line above the cliff where it appeared again, to separate pastures and fields until it stopped at the doorstep of Akren. His hands tightened on the railing; he stared, blind, back at the twisted road that had brought him to Hed on a ship full of the dead, and the shore road to Akren seemed suddenly little more than one more twist into shadows.

Raederle said his name, and his hands loosened. He heard the ramp thud onto the dock. He said to Bri, "I'll be back before dawn." He touched the outline of the ship-master's shoulder. "Thank you."

He led Raederle off the dock, past the dreaming fisherman's houses and the worn, beached boats with gulls sleeping on them. He found his way by memory up the shadows to the top of the cliff. The fields flowed smoothly under the moonlight, swirled around hillocks and dips, to converge from every direction around Akren. The night was soundless; listening, he heard the slow, placid breathing of cows and the faint whimper of a dog dreaming. There was a light gleaming at Akren, Morgon thought from the porch, but as they drew closer, he realized it came from within the house. Raederle walked silently beside him, her eyes flickering over field walls, bean rows, half-ripe wheat. She broke her silence finally as they drew near enough to Akren to see the lines of the roof slanting against the stars.

"Such a small house," she said, surprised. He nodded.

"Smaller than I remember . . ." His throat was dry, tight. He saw a movement in one hall window, dim in the candlelight, and he wondered who was sitting up so late in the house, alone. Then the smell of damp earth and clinging roots caught at him unexpectedly; memory upon memory sent shoots and hair roots spreading through him of land-law until for one split second he no longer felt his body, and his mind branched dizzingly through the rootwork of Hed.

He stopped, his breath catching. The figure at the window moved. Blocking the light, it stared out at the night: broad-shouldered, faceless. It turned abruptly, flicking across the windows in the hall. The doors of Akren banged open; a dog barked, once. Morgon heard footsteps. They crossed the yard and stopped at the angled shadow of the roof.

"Morgon?" The name sounded in the still air like a question. Then it became a shout, setting all the dogs barking as it echoed across the fields. "Morgon!"

Eliard had reached him almost before he could move again. He got an impression of butter-colored hair, shoulders burled with muscles, and a face under moonlight that was startlingly like their father's. Then Eliard knocked the breath out of him, hugging him, his fists pounding against Morgon's shoulder blades. "You took your time coming home," he said. He was crying. Morgon tried to speak, but his throat was too dry; he dropped his burning eyes against Eliard's massive shoulder.

"You great mountain," he whispered. "Will you quiet down?"

Eliard pushed him away, started shaking him. "I felt your mind in mine just then, the way I felt it in my dreams when you were in that mountain." Tears were furrowing down his face. "Morgon, I'm sorry, I'm sorry, I'm sorry—"

"Eliard . . ."

"I knew you were in trouble, but I never did anything—I didn't know what to do—and then you died, and the land-rule came to me. And now you're back, and I have everything that belongs to you. Morgon, I swear if there was a way, I would take the land-rule out of myself and give it back to you—" Morgon's hands locked in a sudden, fierce grip on his arms and he stopped.

"Don't say that to me again. Ever." Eliard stared at him wordlessly, and Morgon felt, holding him, that he held all the strength and innocence of Hed. He said more quietly, his fingers tightening on the innocence, "You belong here. And I have needed you to be here taking care of Hed almost more than anything."

"But Morgon . . . you belong here. This is your home, you've come home—"

"Yes. Until dawn."

"No!" His fingers clamped on Morgon's shoulders again. "I don't know what you're running from, but I'm not watching you leave again. You stay here; we can fight for you, with pitchforks and harrow teeth. I'll borrow an army from somebody—"

"Eliard—"

"Shut up! You may have a grip like a bench vise, but you can't throw me into Tristan's rosebushes anymore. You're staying here, where you belong."

"Eliard, will you stop shouting!" He shook Eliard a little, astonishing him into silence. Then a small whirlwind of Tristan and dogs broke against them, shouting and barking. Tristan leaped at Morgon from a dead run, her arms clamped around his neck, her face buried at his collarbone. He kissed what he could find of it, then pushed her away, lifted her face between his hands. He barely recognized it. Something in his expression made her face crumple; she flung her arms around him again. Then she saw Raederle and reached out to her, and the dogs swarmed at Morgon. A couple of lights sparked in the windows of distant farmhouses. Morgon felt a moment's panic. Then he simply grew still, still as the motionless pour of the road under his feet, the moonlit air. The dogs dropped away from him; Tristan and Raederle stopped talking to look at him. Eliard stood quietly, bound unconsciously to his stillness.

"What's wrong?" he asked uneasily. Morgon moved after a moment to his side, dropped an arm wearily over his shoulders.

"So much," he said. "Eliard, I'm putting you in danger just standing here, talking to you. Let's go in the house at least."

"All right." But he did not move, his face turned away from Morgon to where Raederle stood, her face a blur of misty lines and shadows, jewelled pins here and there in her dishevelled hair flecking it with fire. She smiled, and Morgon heard Eliard swallow. "Raederle of An?" he said tentatively, and she nodded.

"Yes." She held out her hand, and Eliard took it as if it were made of chaff and might blow away. He seemed tongue-tied.

Tristan said proudly, "We sailed all the way to Isig and back, looking for Morgon. Where were you? Where did you—" Her voice faltered suddenly, oddly. "Where did you sail from?"

"Anuin," Morgon said. He caught the uncertain flicker of her dark eyes and read her thoughts. He said again, tiredly, "Let's go in the house; you can ask me."

She slid her hand into his free hand and walked with him, without speaking, to Akren.

She went down to the kitchens to find food for them, while Eliard lit torches and brushed a tangle of harness off the benches so they could sit.

He stood looking down at Morgon, kicking the bench moodily, then said abruptly, "Tell me so I can understand. Why you can't stay. Where do you have to get to so badly now?"

"I don't know. Nowhere. Anywhere but where I am. It's death to stand still."

Eliard scarred the bench with his boot. "Why?" he said explosively, and Morgon drew his hands over his face, murmuring.

"I'm trying to find out," he said. "Answer the unanswered—" He broke off at the expression on Eliard's face. "I know. If I had stayed home in the first place instead of going to Caithnard, I wouldn't be sitting here in the middle of the night wanting to hold dawn back with my hands and afraid to tell you what cargo I brought with me to Hed."

Eliard sat down slowly, blinking a little. "What?" Tristan came back up the stairs then with a huge tray full of beer, milk, fresh bread and fruit, the cold remains of a roast goose, butter and cheese. She balanced it on a stool between them. Morgon shifted; she sat down beside him and poured beer. She handed a cup to Raederle, who tasted it tentatively. Morgon watched her pour; her face had grown leaner, the graceful, sturdy bones more pronounced.

She was scowling at the head on the beer, waiting for it to subside before she finished pouring. Her eyes flicked at him, then dropped, and he said softly, "I found Deth at Anuin. I didn't kill him."

The breath went out of her soundlessly. She rested the beer pitcher on one knee, the cup on the other, and looked at Morgon finally. "I didn't want to ask."

He reached out, touched her face; he saw her eyes follow the white vesta-scars on his palm as he dropped his hand again. Eliard stirred.

"It's none of my business," he said huskily. "But you only tracked him clear across the realm." An odd hope touched his face. "Was he . . . did he explain—"

"He explained nothing." He took the beer from Tristan and drank; he felt blood ease back into his face. He added, more quietly, "I followed Deth through An and caught up with him at Anuin twelve days ago. I stood before him in the king's hall and explained to him that I was going to kill him. Then I raised my sword with both hands to do just that, while he stood without moving, watching it rise." He checked. Eliard's face was rigid.

"And then what?"

"Then . . ." He searched for words, pulled back into memory. "I didn't kill him. There's an ancient riddle from Ymris: Who were Belu and Bilo, and how were they bound? Two Ymris princes who were born at the same moment, and whose deaths, it was foretold, would occur at the same moment. They grew to hate each other, but they were so bound that one could not kill the other without destroying himself."

Eliard was eyeing him strangely. "A riddle did that? It kept you from killing him?"

Morgon sat back. For a moment he sipped beer without speaking, wondering if anything he had done in his life had ever made sense to Eliard. Then Eliard leaned forward, gripped his wrist gently.

"You told me once my brains were made of oak. Maybe so. But I'm glad you didn't kill him. I would have understood why, if you had. But I wouldn't have been certain, ever again, of what you might or might not do." He loosed Morgon and handed him a goose leg. "Eat."

Morgon looked at him. He said softly, "You have the makings of a fine riddler."

Eliard snorted, flushing. "You wouldn't catch me dead at Caithnard. Eat." He cut thin slices of bread and meat and cheese for Raederle and gave them to her. Meeting her eyes at last as she smiled, he found his tongue finally.

"Are you . . . are you married?"

She shook her head over a bite. "No."

"Then what—have you come to wait here?" He looked a little incredulous, but his voice was warm. "You would be very welcome."

"No." She was talking to Eliard, but she seemed, to Morgon, to be answering his own hopes. "I am doing no more waiting."

"Then what are you going to do?" Eliard said, bewildered. "Where will you live?" His eyes moved to Morgon. "What are you going to do? When you leave at dawn? Do you have any idea?"

He nodded. "A vague idea. I need help. And I need answers. According to rumor, the last of the wizards are gathering at Lungold to challenge Ghisteslwchlohm. From the wizards, I can get help. From the Founder, I can get some answers."

Eliard stared at him. He heaved himself to his feet suddenly. "Why didn't you just ask him while you were at Erlenstar Mountain? It would have saved you the bother of going to Lungold. You're going to ask him questions. Morgon, I swear a cork in a beer keg has more sense than you do. What's he going to do? Stand there politely and answer them?"

"What do you want me to do?" Morgon stood, unexpectedly, his voice fierce, anguished, wondering if he was arguing with Eliard or with the implacable obtuseness of the island that suddenly held no more place for him. "Sit here, let him come knocking at your door to find me?

Will you open your eyes and see me instead of the wraith of some memory you have of me? I am branded with stars on my face, with vesta-scars on my hands. I can take nearly any shape that has a word to name it. I have fought, I have killed, I intend to kill again. I have a name older than this realm, and I have no home except in memory. I asked a riddle two years ago, and now I am trapped in a maze of riddles, hardly knowing how to begin to find my way out. The heart of that maze is war. Look beyond Hed for once in your life. Try drinking some fear along with that beer. This realm is on the verge of war. There is no protection for Hed."

"War. What are you talking about? There's some fighting in Ymris, but Ymris is always at war."

"Do you have any idea who Heureu Ymris is fighting?"

"No."

"Neither does he. Eliard, I saw the rebel army as I passed through Ymris. There are men in it who have already died, who are still fighting, with their bodies possessed by nothing human. If they choose to attack Hed, what protection do you have against them?"

Eliard made a sound in his throat. "The High One," he said. Then the blood ran completely out of his face. "Morgon," he whispered, and Morgon's hands clenched.

"Yes. I have been called a man of peace by dead children, but I think I've brought nothing but chaos. Eliard, at Anuin I talked with Duac about some way to protect Hed. He offered to send men and warships."

"Is that what you brought?"

He said steadily, "The trade-ship at Tol that brought us carried, along with regular cargo, armed kings and lords, great warriors of the Three Portions—" Eliard's fingers closed slowly on his arm.

"Kings?"

"They understand land-love, and they understand war. They won't understand Hed, but they'll fight for it. They are—"

"You brought wraiths of An to Hed?" Eliard whispered. "They're at Tol?"

"There are six more ships at Caithnard, waiting—"

"Morgon of Hed, are you out of your mind!" His fingers bit to the bone of Morgon's arm, and Morgon tensed. But Eliard swung away from him abruptly. His fist fell like a mallet on the tray, sending food and crockery flying, except for the milk pitcher, which Tristan had just lifted. She sat hugging it against her, white, while Eliard shouted.

"Morgon, I've heard tales of the chaos in An! How animals are run to death at night and the crops rot in the fields because no one dares harvest. And you want me to take that into my land! How can you ask that of me?"

"Eliard, I don't have to ask!" Their eyes locked. Morgon continued relentlessly, watching himself change shape in Eliard's eyes, sensing something precious, elusive, slipping farther and farther away from him. "If I wanted the land-rule of Hed, I could take it back. When Ghisteslwchlohm took it from me, piece by piece, I realized that the power of land-law has structure and definition, and I know to the last hair root on a hop vine the structure of the land-law of Hed. If I wanted to force this on you, I could, just as I learned to force the ancient dead of the Three Portions to come here—"

Eliard, backed against the hearthstones, breathing through his mouth, shuddered suddenly. "What are you?"

"I don't know." His voice shook uncontrollably. "It's time you asked."

There was a moment's silence: the peaceful, unbroken voice of the night of Hed. Then Eliard shrugged himself away from the hearth, stepped past Morgon, kicking shards out of the way. He leaned over a table, his hands flat on it, his head bowed. He said, his voice muffled a little, "Morgon, they're dead."

Morgon dropped his forearm against the mantel, leaned his face on it. "Then they have that advantage over the living in a battle."

"Couldn't you have just brought a living army? It would have been simpler."

"The moment you bring armed men to this island, you'll ask for attack. And you'll get it."

"Are you sure? Are you so sure they'll dare attack Hed? You might be seeing things that aren't there."

"I might be." His words seemed lost against the worn stones. "I'm not sure, anymore, of anything. I'm just afraid for everything I love. Do you know the one simple, vital thing I could never learn from Ghisteslwchlohm in Erlenstar Mountain? How to see in the dark."

Eliard turned. He was crying again as he pulled Morgon away from the stones. "I'm sorry. Morgon, I may yell at you, but if you pulled the land-rule out of me by the roots, I would still trust you blindly. Will you stay here? Will you please stay? Let the wizards come to you. Let Ghisteslwchlohm come. You'll just be killed if you leave Hed again."

"No. I won't die." He crooked an arm around Eliard's neck, hugged him tightly. "I'm too curious. The dead won't trouble your farmers. I swear it. You will scarcely notice them. They are bound to me. I showed them something of the history and peace of Hed, and they are sworn to defend that peace."

"You bound them."

"Mathom loosed his own hold over them, otherwise I would never have considered it."

"How do you bind dead Kings of An?"

"I see out of their eyes. I understand them. Maybe too well."

Eliard eyed him. "You're a wizard," he said, but Morgon shook his head.

"No wizard but Ghisteslwchlohm ever touched land-law. I'm simply powerful and desperate." He looked down at Raederle. Inured as she was to the occasional uproar in her father's house, her eyes held a strained, haunted expression. Tristan was staring silently into the milk pitcher. Morgon touched her dark hair; her face lifted, colorless, frozen.

"I'm sorry," he whispered. "I'm sorry. I didn't mean to come home and start a battle."

"It's all right," she said after a moment. "At least that's one familiar thing you can still do." She put the milk pitcher down and got to her feet. "I'll get a broom."

"I will."

That brought the flash of a smile into her eyes. "All right. You can sweep. I'll get more food." She touched his scarred palm hesitantly. "Then tell me how you change shape."

He told them after he swept up the mess, and he watched Eliard's face fill with an incredulous wonder as he explained how it felt to become a tree. He racked his brain for other things to tell them that might help them forget for a moment the terrible side of his journey. He talked about racing across the northlands in vesta-shape, when the world was nothing but wind and snow and stars. He told them of the marvellous beauty of Isig Pass and of the wolf-king's court, with its wild animals wandering in and out, and of the mists and sudden stones and marshes of Herun. And for a little while, he forgot his own torment as he found in himself an unexpected love of the wild, harsh, and beautiful places of the realm. He forgot the time, too, until he saw the moon beginning its descent, peering into the top of one of the windows. He broke off abruptly, saw apprehension replace the smile in Eliard's eyes.

"I forgot about the dead."

Eliard controlled a reply visibly. "It's not dawn, yet. The moon hasn't even set."

"I know. But the ships will come to Tol one by one from Caithnard, when I give the word. I want them away from Hed completely before I leave. Don't worry. You won't see the dead, but you should be there when they enter Hed."

Eliard rose reluctantly. His face was chalky under his tan. "You'll be with me?"

"Yes."

They all went back down the road to Tol that lay bare as a blade between the dark fields of corn. Morgon, walking beside Raederle, his fingers linked in hers, felt the tension still in her and the weariness of the long, dangerous voyage. She sensed his thoughts and smiled at him as they neared Tol.

"I left one pig-headed family for another . . ."

The moon, three-quarters full, seemed angled, as if it were peering down at Tol. Across the black channel were two flaming, slitted eyes: the warning fires on the horns of the Caithnard harbor. Nets hung in silvery webs on the sand; water licked against the small moored boats as they walked down the dock.

Bri Corbett, hanging over the ship's railing, called down softly, "Now?"

"Now," Morgon said, and Eliard muttered between his teeth.

"I wish you knew what you were doing." Then the ramp slid down off the empty deck, and he stepped back, so close to the dock edge he nearly fell off. Morgon felt his mind again.

The stubbornness, the inflexibility that lay near the heart of Hed seemed to slam like a bar across the end of the ramp. It clenched around Morgon's thoughts; he eased through it, filling Eliard's mind with images, rich, brilliant, and erratic, that he had gleaned from the history of the Three Portions out of the minds of the dead. Slowly, as Eliard's mind opened, something emptied out of the ship, absorbed itself into Hed.

Eliard shivered suddenly.

"They're quiet," he said, surprised. Morgon's hand closed above his elbow.

"Bri will leave for Caithnard now and send the next ship. There are six more. Bri will bring the last one himself, and Raederle and I will leave on that one."

"No—"

"I'll come back."

Eliard was silent. From the ship came the groan of rope and wood, and Bri Corbett's low, precise orders. The ship eased away from the dockside, its dark canvas stretched full to catch the frail wind. It moved, huge, black, soundless through the moon-spangled water into the night, leaving a shimmering wake that curled away and slowly disappeared.

Eliard said, watching it, "You will never come back to stay."

Six more ships came as slowly, as silently through the night. Once, just before the moon set, Morgon saw shadows flung across the water of armed, crowned figures. The moon sank, shrivelled and weary, into the stars; the last ship moored at the dockside. Tristan was leaning against Morgon, shifting from one foot to another; he held her to keep her warm. Raederle was blurred against the starlit water; her face was a dark profile between the warning fires. Morgon's eyes moved to the ship. The dead were leaving it; the dark maw of its hold would remain open to take him away from Hed. His mind tangled suddenly with a thousand things he wanted to say to Eliard, but none of them had the power to dispel that ship. Finally, he realized, they were alone again on the dock; the dead were dispersed into Hed, and there was nothing left for him to do but leave.

He turned to Eliard. The sky was growing very dark in the final, interminable hour before dawn. A low wind moaned among the breakers. He could not see Eliard's face, only sense his massiveness and the vague mass of land behind him. He said softly, his heart aching, the image of the land drenched gold under the summer sun in his mind's eye, "I'll find a way back to Hed. Somehow. Somewhere."

Eliard, reaching into the darkness, touched his face with a gentleness that had been their father's. Tristan was still clinging to him; Morgon held her tightly, kissed the top of her hair. Then he stepped back, stood suddenly alone in the night feeling the wood shiver under his feet in the roiling water.

He turned, found his way blindly up the ship's ramp, back down into the black hull.

THE SHIP FOUND a quiet berth in the Caithnard harbor near dawn. Morgon heard the anchor splash in still water and saw through the lattice of the hatch cover squares of pearl-grey sky. Raederle was asleep. He looked at her a moment with an odd mixture of weariness and peace, as if he had brought some great treasure safely out of danger. Then he sagged down on the spice sacks and went to sleep. The clamor on the docks at midmorning, the stifling noon heat in the hold hardly troubled his dreams. He woke finally at late afternoon and found Raederle watching him, covered with floating spangles of sunlight.

He sat up slowly, trying to remember where he was. She said, "Caithnard." Her arms were crooked around her knees; her cheek was crosshatched with weave from the sacking. Her eyes held an odd expression he had to puzzle over, until he realized that it was simply fear. His throat made a dry, questioning sound. She answered him softly.

"Now what?"

He leaned back against the side, gripped her wrist lightly a moment, then rubbed his eyes. "Bri Corbett said he would find horses for us. You'll have to take the pins out of your hair."

"What? Morgon, are you still asleep?"

"No." His eyes fell to her feet. "And look at your shoes."

She looked. "What's the matter with them?"

"They're beautiful. So are you. Can you change shape?"

"Into what?" she asked bewilderedly. "A hoary old hag?"

"No. You have a shape-changer's blood in you; you should be able to—"

The expression in her eyes, of fear, torment, loathing, stopped him. She said distinctly, "No."

He drew breath, fully awake, cursing himself silently. The long road sweeping across the realm, straight towards the setting sun, touched him, too, then, with an edge of panic. He was silent, trying to think, but the stale air in the hold seemed to fill his brain with chaff. He said, "We'll be on the road to Lungold for a long time, if we ride. I thought to keep the horses just until I could teach you some shape."

"You change shape. I'll ride."

"Raederle, look at yourself," he said helplessly. "Traders from all over the realm will be on that road. They haven't seen me for over a year, but they'll recognize you, and they won't have to ask who the man beside you is."

"So." She kicked her shoes off, pulled the pins out of her hair and shook it down her back. "Find me another pair of shoes."

He looked at her wordlessly as she sat in a billow of wrinkled, richly embroidered cloth, the fine, dishevelled mass of her hair framing a high-boned face that, even tired and white, looked like something out of an ancient ballad. He sighed, pushing himself up.

"All right. Wait for me."

Her voice checked him briefly as he climbed the ladder. "This time."

He spoke to Bri Corbett, who had been waiting patiently all day for them to wake. The horses Bri had found were on the dock; there were some supplies packed on them. They were placid, heavy-hooved farmhorses, restless at being tethered so long. Bri, as the fact and implications of the long journey began filling his mind, gave Morgon varied, impassioned arguments, to which he responded patiently. Bri ended by offering to come with them.

Morgon said wearily, "Only if you can change shape."

Bri gave up. He left the ship, returned an hour later with a bundle of clothes, which he tossed down the hatch to Morgon. Raederle examined them expressionlessly, then put them on. There was a dark skirt, a linen shift, and a shapeless over-tunic that went to her knees. The boots were of soft leather, good but plain. She coiled her hair up under the crown of a broad-brimmed straw hat. She stood still resignedly for Morgon's inspection.

He said, "Pull the hat brim down."

She gave it a wrench. "Stop laughing at me."

"I'm not," he said soberly. "Wait till you see what you have to ride."

"You aren't exactly inconspicuous. You may be dressed like a poor farmer, but you walk like a land-ruler, and your eyes could quarry stone."

"Watch," he said. He let himself grow still, his thoughts shaping themselves to his surroundings: wood, pitch, the vague murmur of water and indistinct rumblings of the harbor. His name seemed to flow away from him into the heat. His face held no discernible expression; for a moment his eyes were vague, blank as the summer sky.

"If you aren't aware yourself, few people will be aware of you. That's one of a hundred ways I kept myself alive crossing the realm."

She looked startled. "I almost couldn't recognize you. Is it illusion?"

"Very little of it. It's survival."

She was silent. He saw the conflict of her thoughts in her face. She turned away without speaking and climbed up the ladder to the deck.

The sun was burning into night at the far edge of the realm as they bade farewell to Bri and began to ride. Great shadows from masts and piled cargo loomed in their path across the docks. The city, a haze of late light and shadow, seemed suddenly unfamiliar to Morgon, as if, on the verge of taking a strange road, he became a stranger to himself. He led Raederle through the twists of streets, past shops and taverns he had known once, toward the west edge of the city, down one cobbled street that widened as it left the city, wore out of its cobblestones, widened again, rutted with centuries of cartwheels, widened again and ran ahead of them through hundreds of miles of no-man's-land, until it angled northward at the edge of the known realm towards Lungold.

They stopped their horses, looking down it. Tangled shadows of oak faded as the sun set; the road lay tired, grey, and endless in the dusk. The oak fanned over their heads, branches nearly joined across the road. They looked weary, their leaves dulled with a patina of dust kicked up by the cartwheels. The evening was very quiet; the late traffic had already wound its way into the city. The forests blurred grey in the distance, and then dark. From the greyness an owl woke and sang a riddle.

They began to ride again. The sky turned black, and the moon rose, spilling a milky light through the forest. They rode the moon high, until their shadows rode beneath them on a tangle of black leaves. Then Morgon found the leaves blurring together into one vast darkness under his eyes. He reined; Raederle stopped beside him.

There was the sound of water not far away. Morgon, his face coated with a mask of dust, said tiredly, "I remember. I crossed a river, coming south out of Wind Plain. It must follow the road." He turned his horse off the road. "We can camp there."

They found it not far from the road, a shallow streak of silver in the moonlight. Raederle sank down at the foot of a tree while Morgon unsaddled the horses and let them drink. He brought their packs and blankets to a clear space among the fern. Then he sat down beside Raederle, dropped his head in his arms.

"I'm not used to riding, either," he said. She took her hat off, rested her head against him.

"A plow horse," she murmured. She fell asleep where she sat. Morgon put his arm around her. For a while he stayed awake, listening. But he heard only the secret noises of hunting animals, the breath of owl's wings, and as the moon set, his eyes closed.

They woke to the blaze of the summer sun and the tortured groan of cartwheels. By the time they had eaten, washed, and made their way back to the road, it was filled with carts, traders on horseback with their packs, farmers taking produce or animals from outlying farms into Caithnard, men and women with retinues and packhorses making the long journey, for indiscernible reasons, across the realm to Lungold. Morgon and Raederle eased their horses into the slow, rhythmic pace that would wear the monotonous, six-weeks journey to its ending. Riding in traffic varying between pigs and rich lords, they were not conspicuous. Morgon discouraged traders' idle conversation, responding grumpily to their overtures. Once he startled Raederle by cursing a rich merchant who commented on her face. The man looked angry a moment, his hand tightening on his riding crop; then, glancing at

Morgon's patched boots and the sweat beading his dusty face, he laughed, nodded to Raederle, and passed on. Raederle rode in silence, her head bowed, her reins bunched in one fist. Morgon, wondering what she was thinking, reached across and touched her lightly. She looked at him, her face filmed with dust and weariness.

He said softly, "This is your choice."

She met his eyes without answering. She sighed finally, and her grip on the reins loosened. "Do you know the ninety-nine curses the witch Madir set on a man for stealing one of her pigs?"

"No."

"I'll teach you. In six weeks you might run out of curses."

"Raederle—"

"Stop asking me to be reasonable."

"I didn't ask you!"

"You asked me with your eyes."

He swept a hand through his hair. "You are so unreasonable sometimes that you remind me of me. Teach me the ninety-nine curses. I'll have something to think about while I'm eating road dust all the way to Lungold."

She was silent again, her face hidden under the shadow of her hat brim. "I'm sorry," she said. "The merchant frightened me. He might have hurt you. I know I am a danger to you, but I didn't realize it before. But Morgon, I can't . . . I can't—"

"So. Run from your shadow. Maybe you'll succeed better than I did." Her face turned away from him. He rode without speaking, watching the sun burn across bands of metal on wine barrels ahead of them. He put a hand over his eyes finally, to shut out the hot flare of light. "Raederle," he said in the darkness, "I don't care. Not for myself. If there is a way to keep you safely with me, I'll find it. You are real, beside me. I can touch you. I can love you. For a year, in that mountain, I never touched anyone. There is nothing I can see ahead of me that I could love. Even the children who named me are dead. If you had chosen to wait for me in Anuin, I would be wondering what the wait would be worth for either of us. But you're with me, and you drag my thoughts out of a hopeless future always back to this moment, back to you—so that I can find some perverse contentment even in swallowing road dust." He looked at her. "Teach me the ninety-nine curses."

"I can't." He could barely hear her voice. "You made me forget how to curse."

But he coaxed them from her later, to while away the long afternoon. She taught him sixty-four curses before twilight fell, a varied, detailed list that covered the pig thief from hair to toenails, and eventually transformed him into a boar. They left the road then, found the river fifty yards from it. There were no inns or villages nearby, so the travellers moving at the same pace down the long road were camped all around them. The evening was full of distant laughter, music, the smell of wood burning, meat roasting. Morgon went upriver a way, caught fish with his hands. He cleaned them, stuffed them with wild onions, and brought them back to their camp. Raederle had bathed and started a fire; she sat beside it, combing her wet hair. Seeing her in the circle of her light, stepping into it himself and watching her lower her comb and smile, he felt ninety-nine curses at his own ungentleness march into his throat. She saw it in his face, her expression changing as he knelt beside her. He set the fish, wrapped in leaves, at her feet like an offering. Her fingers traced his cheekbone and his mouth.

He whispered, "I'm sorry."

"For what? Being right? What did you bring me?" She opened a leaf wonderingly. "Fish." He cursed himself again, silently. She lifted his face in her hands and kissed him again and again, until the dust and weariness of the day vanished from his mind, and the long road burned like a streak of light among his memories.

Later, after they had eaten, they lay watching the fire, and she taught him the rest of the curses. They had transformed the legendary thief into a boar, all but for his ears and eyeteeth and ankles, the last three curses, when a slow, tentative harping rippled across the night, mingling with the river's murmuring. Morgon, listening to it, did not realize Raederle was speaking to him until she put her hand on his shoulder. He jumped.

"Morgon."

He rose abruptly, stood at the edge of the firelight, staring into the night. His eyes grew accustomed to the moonlight; he saw random fires lighting the great, tormented faces of oak. The air was still, the voices and music frail in the silence. He quelled a sudden, imperative impulse to snap the harp strings with a thought, let peace fall again over the night.

Raederle said behind him, "You never harp."

He did not answer. The harping ceased after a while; he drew a slow breath and moved again. He turned to find Raederle sitting beside the fire, watching him. She said nothing until he dropped down beside her. Then she said again, "You never harp."

"I can't harp here. Not on this road."

"Not on the road, not on that ship when you did nothing for four days—"

"Someone might have heard it."

"Not in Hed, not in Anuin, where you were safe—"

"I'm never safe."

"Morgon," she breathed incredulously. "When are you going to learn to use that harp? It holds your name, maybe your destiny; it's the most beautiful harp in the realm, and you have never even shown it to me."

He looked at her finally. "I'll learn to play it again when you learn to change shape." He lay back. He did not see what she did to the fire, but it vanished abruptly, as if the night had dropped on it like a stone.

He slept uneasily, always aware of her turning beside him. He woke once, wanting to shake her awake, explain, argue with her, but her face, remote in the moonlight, stopped him. He turned, pushed one arm against his eyes, and fell asleep again. He woke again abruptly, for no reason, though something he had heard or sensed, a fragment of a dream before he woke, told him there was reason. He saw the moon drifting deeper into the night. Then something rose before him, blotting out the moon.

He shouted. A hand came down over his mouth. He kicked out and heard an anguished grunt. He rolled to his feet. Something smacked against his face, spun him jarringly into a tree trunk. He heard Raederle cry out in pain and fear, and he snapped a streak of fire into the embers.

The light flared over half a dozen burly figures dressed like traders. One of them held Raederle's wrists; she looked frightened, bewildered in the sudden light. The horses were stirring, nickering, shadows moving about them, untethering them. Morgon moved toward them quickly. An elbow slammed into his ribs; he hunched over himself, muttering the fifty-ninth curse with the last rag of his breath. The thief gripping him, wrenching him straight, shouted hoarsely in shock and shambled away in the trees. The man behind Raederle dropped her wrists with a sudden gasp. She whirled, touching him, and his beard flamed. Morgon got a glimpse of his face before he dove toward the river. The horses were beginning to panic. He caught at their minds, fed them a bond of moonlit stillness until they stood rock still, oblivious to the men pulling at them. They were cursing ineffectually. One of them mounted, kicked furiously at the horse, but it did not even quiver. Morgon flicked a silent shout through his mind, and the man fell backwards off the horse. The others scattered, then turned on him again, furious and uneasy. He cleared his mind for another shout, picked up threads of their thoughts. Then something came at him from behind, the man out of the river, drove into his back and knocked him to the ground. He twisted as he hit the earth, then froze.

The face was the same, yet not the same. The eyes he knew, but from another place, another struggle. Memory fought against his sight. The face was heavy, wet, the beard singed, but the eyes were too still, too calculating. A boot drove into Morgon's shoulder from behind. He rolled belatedly. Something ripped across the back of his skull, or across his mind, he was not sure which. Then a Great Shout broke like a thunderclap over them all. He put his face in the bracken and clung to a rocking earth, holding his binding over the horses like the one firm point in the world.

The shout echoed away slowly. He lifted his head. They were alone again; the horses stood placidly, undisturbed by the turmoil of voices and squealing animals in the darkness around them. Raederle dropped down beside him, her brows pinched in pain.

He said, "Did they hurt you?"

"No." She touched his cheek, and he winced. "That shout did. From a man of Hed, that was a marvellous shout."

He stared at her, frozen again. "You shouted."

"I didn't shout," she whispered. "You did."

"I didn't." He sat up, then settled his skull into place with his hands. "Who in Hel's name shouted?"

She shivered suddenly, her eyes moving through the night. "Someone watching, maybe still watching. . . . How strange. Morgon, were they only men wanting to steal our horses?"

"I don't know." He searched the back of his head with his fingers. "I don't know. They were men trying to steal our horses, yes, which was why it was so hard for me to fight them. There were too many to fight, but they were too harmless to kill. And I didn't want to use much power, to attract attention."

"You gave that one man boar bristles all over his body."

Morgon's hand slid to his ribs. "He earned it," he said dourly. "But that last man coming out of the water—"

"The one whose beard I set on fire."

"I don't know." He pushed his hands over his eyes, trying to remember. "That's what I don't know. If the man coming back out of the river was the same one who ran into it."

"Morgon," she whispered.

"He might have used power; I'm not sure. I don't know. Maybe I was just seeing what I expected to see."

"If it was a shape-changer, why didn't he try to kill you?"

"Maybe he was unsure of me. They haven't seen me since I disappeared into Erlenstar Mountain. I was that careful, crossing the realm. They wouldn't expect me to be riding a plow horse in broad daylight down Trader's Road."

"But if he suspected—Morgon, you were using power over the horses."

"It was a simple binding of silence, peace; he wouldn't have suspected that."

"He wouldn't have run from a Great Shout, either. Would he? Unless he left for help. Morgon—" She was trying suddenly to tug him to his feet. "What are we doing sitting here? Waiting for another attack, this time maybe from shape-changers?"

He pulled his arm away from her. "Don't do that; I'm sore."

"Would you rather be dead?"

"No." He brooded a moment, his eyes on the swift, shadowy flow of the river. A thought ran through his mind, chilling him. "Wind Plain. It lies just north of us . . . where Heureu Ymris is fighting his war against men and half-men . . . there might be an army of shape-changers across the river."

"Let's go. Now."

"We would only attract attention, riding in the middle of the night. We can move our camp. Then I want to look for whoever it was that shouted."

They shifted their horses and gear as quietly as they could, away from the river and closer to a cluster of traders' carts. Then Morgon left Raederle, to search the night for a stranger.

Raederle argued, not wanting him to go alone; he said patiently, "Can you walk across dry leaves so gently they don't stir? Can you stand so still animals pass you without noticing you? Besides, someone has to guard the horses."

"What if those men return?"

"What if they do? I've seen what you can do to a wraith."

She sat down under a tree, muttering something. He hesitated, for she looked powerless and vulnerable.

He shaped his sword, keeping the stars hidden under his hand, and laid it in front of her. It disappeared again; he told her softly, "It's there if you need it, bound under illusion. If you have to touch it, I'll know."

He turned, slipped soundlessly into the silence between the trees.

The forest had quieted again after the shout. He drifted from camp to camp around them, looking for someone still awake. But travellers were sleeping peacefully in carts or tents, or curled under blankets beside their firebeds. The moon cast a grey-black haze over the world; trees and bracken were fragmented oddly with chips and streaks of shadow. There was not a breath of wind. Single sprays of leaves, a coil of bramble etched black in the light seemed whittled out of silence. The oak stood as still. He put his hand on one, slid his mind beneath its bark, and sensed its ancient, gnarled dreaming. He moved towards the river, skirted their old camp. Nothing moved. Listening through the river's voice, his mind gathering its various tones, defining and discarding them one by one, he heard no human voices. He went farther down the river, making little more noise than his own controlled breathing. He eased into the surface he walked on, adjusting his thoughts to the frail weight of leaves, the tension in a dry twig. The sky darkened slowly, until he could scarcely see, and he knew he should turn back. But he lingered at the river's edge, facing Wind Plain, listening as if he could hear the shards of battle noises in the broken dreams of Heureu's army.

He turned finally, began to move back upriver. He took three soundless steps and stopped with an animal's fluid shift from movement into stillness. Someone was standing among the trees with no discernible face or coloring, a broad half-shadow, half-faded, as Morgon was, into the night. Morgon waited, but the shadow did not move. Eventually, as he hovered between decisions on the river bank, it simply merged into the night. Morgon, his mouth dry, and blood beating hollowly into his thoughts, formed himself around a curve of air and flew, with an owl's silence, a night hunter's vision, back through the trees to the camp.

He startled Raederle, changing shape in front of her. She reached for the sword; he stilled her, squatting down and taking her hand. He whispered, "Raederle."

"You're frightened," she breathed.

"I don't know. I still don't know. We'll have to be very careful." He settled beside her, shaped the sword, and held it loosely. He put his other arm around her. "You sleep. I'll watch."

"For what?"

"I don't know. I'll wake you before sunrise. We'll have to be careful."

"How?" she asked helplessly, "if they know where to find you: somewhere on Trader's Road, riding to Lungold?" He did not answer her. He shifted, holding her more closely; she leaned her head against him. He thought, listening to her breathing, that she had fallen asleep. But she spoke after a long silence, and he knew that she, too, had been staring into the night.

"All right," she said tightly. "Teach me to change shape."

4

HE TRIED TO teach her when she woke at dawn. The sun had not yet risen; the forest was cool, silent around them. She listened quietly while he explained the essential simplicity of it, while he woke and snared a falcon from the high trees. The falcon complained piercingly on his wrist; it was hungry and wanted to hunt. He quieted it patiently with his mind. Then he saw the dark, haunted expression that had crept into Raederle's eyes, and he tossed the falcon free.

"You can't shape-change unless you want to."

"I want to," she protested.

"No, you don't."

"Morgon . . ."

He turned, picked up a saddle and heaved it onto one of the horses. He said, pulling the cinch tight, "It's all right."

"It's not all right," she said angrily. "You didn't even try. I asked you to teach me, and you said you would. I'm trying to keep us safe." She moved to stand in front of him as he lifted the other saddle. "Morgon."

"It's all right," he said soothingly, trying to believe it. "I'll think of something."

She did not speak to him for hours. They rode quickly through the early morning, until the easier pace of the traffic made them conspicuous. The road seemed full of animals: sheep, pigs, young white bullocks being driven from isolated farms to Caithnard. They blocked traffic and made the horses skittish. Traders' carts were irritatingly slow; farmers' wagons full of turnips and cabbages careened at a slow, drunken pace in front of them at odd moments. The noon heat pounded the road into a dry powder that they breathed and swallowed. The noise and smell of animals seemed inescapable. Raederle's hair, limp with dust and sweat, kept sliding down, clinging to her face. She stopped her horse once, stuck her hat between her teeth, wound her hair into a knot in the plain view of an old woman driving a pig to market, and jammed her hat back on her head. Morgon, looking at her, checked a comment. Her silence began to wear at him subtly, like the heat and the constant interruptions of their pace. He searched back, wondering if he had been wrong, wondering if she wanted him to speak or keep quiet, wondering if she regretted ever setting foot out of Anuin. He envisioned the journey without her; he would have been halfway across Ymris, taking a crow's path to Lungold, a silent night flight across the backlands to a strange city, to face Ghisteslwchlohm again. Her silence began to build stone by stone around his memories, forming a night smelling of limestone, broken only by the faint, faroff trickle of water running away from him.

He blinked away the darkness, saw the world again, dust and bedraggled green, sun thumping rhythmically off brass kettles on a peddlar's cart. He wiped sweat off his face. Raederle chipped at the wall of her own silence stiffly.

"What did I do wrong? I was just listening to you."

He said wearily, "You said yes with your voice and no with your mind. Your mind does the work."

She was silent again, frowning at him. "What's wrong?"

"Nothing."

"You're sorry I came with you."

He wrenched at his reins. "Will you stop? You're twisting my heart. It's you who are sorry."

She stopped her own horse; he saw the sudden despair in her face. They looked at one another, bewildered, frustrated. A mule brayed behind them, and they were riding again, suddenly, in the familiar, sweltering silence, with no way out of it, seemingly, like a tower without a door.

Then Morgon stopped both their horses abruptly, led them off the road to drink. The noise dwindled; the air was clear and gentle with bird calls. He knelt at the river's edge and drank of the cold, swift water, then splashed it over his face and hair. Raederle stood beside him, her reflection stiff even in the rippling water. He sank back on his heels, gazing at its blurred lines and colors. He turned his head slowly, looked up at her face.

How long he gazed at her, he did not know, only that her face suddenly shook, and she knelt beside him, holding him. "How can you look at me like that?"

"I was just remembering," he said. Her hat fell off; he stroked her hair. "I thought about you so often in the past two years. Now all I have to do is turn my head to find you beside me. It still surprises me sometimes, like a piece of wizardry I'm not used to doing."

"Morgon, what are we going to do? I'm afraid—I'm so afraid of that power I have."

"Trust yourself."

"I can't. You saw what I did with it at Anuin. I was hardly even myself, then; I was the shadow of another heritage—one that is trying to destroy you."

He gathered her tightly. "You touched me into shape," he whispered. He held her quietly a long time. Then he said tentatively, "Can you stand it if I tell you a riddle?"

She shifted to look at him, smiling a little. "Maybe."

"There was a woman of Herun, a hill woman named Arya, who collected animals. One day she found a tiny black beast she couldn't name. She brought it into her house, fed it, cared for it. And it grew. And it grew. Until all her other animals fled from the house, and it lived alone with her, dark, enormous, nameless, stalking her from room to room while she lived in terror, unfree, not knowing what to do with it, not daring to challenge it—"

Her hand lifted, came down over his mouth. She dropped her head against him; he felt her heartbeat. She whispered finally, "All right. What did she do?"

"What will you do?"

He listened for her answer, but if she gave him one, the river carried it away before he heard it.

The road was quieter when they returned to it. Late shadows

striped it; the sun was hovering in the grip of oak boughs. The dust had settled; most of the carts were well ahead of them. Morgon felt a touch of uneasiness at their isolation. He said nothing to Raederle, but he was relieved when, an hour later, they caught up with most of the traders. Their carts and horses were outside of an inn, an ancient building big as a barn, with stables and a smithy attached to it. From the sound of the laughter rumbling from it, it was well-stocked and its business was good. Morgon led the horses to the trough outside the stable. He longed for beer, but he was wary of showing himself in the inn. The shadows faded on the road as they went back to it; dusk hung like a wraith ahead of them.

They rode into it. The birds stilled; their horses made the only noise on the empty road. A couple of times, Morgon passed gatherings of horse traders camped around vast fires, their livestock penned and guarded for the night. He might have been safe in their vicinity, but he was seized by a sudden reluctance to stop. The voices faded behind them; they pushed deeper into the twilight. Raederle was uneasy, he sensed, but he could not stop. She reached across, touched him finally, and he looked at her. Her face was turned back toward the road behind them, and he reined sharply.

A group of horsemen a mile or so behind them dipped down into a hollow of road. The twilight blurred them as they appeared again, riding no more quickly than the late hour justified. Morgon watched them for a moment, his lips parted. He shook his head wordlessly, answering a question in Raederle's mind.

"I don't know . . ." He turned his horse abruptly off the road into the trees.

They followed the river until it was almost too dark to see. Then they made a camp without a fire, eating bread and dried meat for supper. The river was deep and slow where they stopped, barely murmuring. Morgon could hear clearly through the night; the horsemen never passed them. His thoughts drifted back to the silent figure he had seen among the trees, to the mysterious shout that had come so aptly out of nowhere. He drew his sword then, soundlessly.

Raederle said, "Morgon, you were awake most of last night. I'll watch."

"I'm used to it," he said. But he gave her the sword and stretched out on a blanket. He did not sleep; he lay listening, watching patterns of stars slowly shift across the night. He heard again the faint, hesitant harping coming out of the blackness like a mockery of his memories.

He sat up incredulously. He could see no campfires among the trees; he heard no voices, only the awkward harping. The strings were finely tuned; the harp gave a gentle, mellow tone, but the harpist tripped continually over his notes. Morgon linked his fingers over his eyes.

"Who in Hel's name . . ." He rolled to his feet abruptly.

Raederle said softly, "Morgon, there are other harpists in the world."

"He's playing in the dark."

"How do you know it's a man? Maybe it's a woman, or a young boy with his first harp, travelling alone to Lungold. If you want to destroy all the harps in the world, you'd better start with the one at your back, because that's the one that will never give you peace." He did not answer. She added equivocally to his silence, "Can you bear it if I tell you a riddle?"

He turned, found the dim, moon-struck lines of her, the blade glittering faintly in her hands. "No," he said. He sat down beside her after a while, his mind worn from straining for the notes of a familiar Ymris ballad the harpist kept missing. "I wish," he muttered savagely, "I could be haunted by a better harpist." He took the sword from her. "I'll watch."

"Don't leave me," she pleaded, reading his mind. He sighed.

"All right." He angled the sword on his knees, stared down at it while the high moon tempered it to cold fire, until at last the harping stopped and he could think again.

The next night, and the next, and the next, Morgon heard the harping. It came at odd hours of the night, usually when he sat awake listening. He heard it at the far edges of his awareness; Raederle slept undisturbed by it. Sometimes he heard it in his dreams and it woke him, numb and sweating, blinking out of a dream of darkness into darkness, both haunted by the same inescapable harping. He searched for the harpist one night, but he only got lost among the trees. Returning wearily near dawn in the shape of a wolf, he scared the horses, and Raederle flung a circle of fire around them and herself that nearly singed his pelt. They discussed matters furiously for a few moments, until the sight of their weary, flushed, bedraggled faces made them both break into laughter.

The longer they rode, the longer the road seemed to stretch itself, mile after mile through changeless forest. Morgon's mind milled constantly through scraps of conversations, expressions on faces they passed, noises ahead and behind them, the occasional mute imagery behind the eyes of a bird flying overhead. He grew preoccupied, trying to see ahead and behind them at the same time, watching for harpists, for horse thieves, for shape-changers. He scarcely heard Raederle when she spoke. When she stopped speaking to him altogether once, he did not realize it for hours. As they grew farther from Caithnard, the traffic lessened; they had isolated miles, now and then, of silence. But the heat was constant, and every stranger appearing behind them after a quiet mile looked suspicious. Except for the harping, though, their nights were peaceful. On the day that Morgon finally began to feel secure, they lost their horses.

They had camped early that day, for they were both exhausted. Morgon left Raederle washing her hair in the river and walked half a mile to an inn they had passed to buy a few supplies and pick up news. The inn was crowded with travellers: traders exchanging gossip; impoverished musicians playing every instrument but a harp for the price of a meal; merchants; farmers; families who looked as if they had fled from their homes, carrying all their possessions on their backs.

The air was heavy with wine-whetted rumors. Morgon, picking a rich, heavy voice at random from a far table, followed it as though he were following an instrument's voice. "Twenty years," the man said. "For twenty years I lived across from it. I sold fine cloth and furs from all parts of the realm in my shop, and I never saw so much as a shadow out of place in the ruins of the ancient school. Then, late one night while I was checking my accounts, I saw lights here and there in the broken windows. No man ever walks across those grounds, not even for the wealth of it: the place reeks of disaster. So that was enough for me. I took every bolt of cloth out of that shop, left messages for my buyers to bring what they had for me to Caithnard, and I fled. If there is going to be another wizard's war in that city, I intend to be on the other side of the realm."

"In Caithnard?" another merchant answered incredulously. "With half the Ymris coastline to the north plagued with war? At least Lungold has wizards in it. Caithnard has nothing but fishwives and scholars. There's as much defense in a dead fish as in a book. I've left Caithnard. I'm heading for the backlands; I might come out again in fifty years."

Morgon let the voices fade back into the noise. He found the innkeeper hovering at his shoulder. "Lord?" he said briskly, and Morgon ordered beer. It was from Hed, and it washed a hundred miles of road dust down his throat. He dipped sporadically into other conversations; one word from a sour-looking trader caught his attention.

"It's that cursed war in Ymris. Half the farmers in Ruhn had their horses drafted into war—the descendants of Ruhn battle horses bred to the plow. The king is holding his own on Wind Plain, but he's paying a bloody price for stalemate. His warriors buy what horses they are offered—so do the farmers. No one asks any more where the horses come from. I've had an armed guard around my wagon teams every night since I left Caithnard."

Morgon set down an empty glass, worried suddenly about Raederle alone with their horses. A trader beside him asked a friendly question; he grunted a reply. He was about to leave when his own name caught his ear.

"Morgon of Hed? I heard a rumor that he was in Caithnard, disguised as a student. He vanished before the Masters even recognized him."

Morgon glanced around. A group of musicians had congregated around a jug of wine they were sharing. "He was in Anuin," a piper said, wiping spit out of his instrument. He looked at the silent faces around him. "You haven't heard that tale? He caught up with the High One's harpist finally in Anuin, in the king's own hall—"

"The High One's harpist," a gangling young man with a collection of small drums hanging about him said bitterly. "And what was the High One doing through all this? A man loses his land-rule, betrayed in the High One's name by a harpist who lied to every king in the realm, and the High One won't lift a finger—if he has one—to give him justice."

"If you ask me," a singer said abruptly, "the High One is nothing more than a lie. Invented by the Founder of Lungold."

There was a short silence. The singer blinked a little nervously at his own words, as if the High One might be standing at his shoulder sipping beer and listening. Another singer growled, "Nobody asked. Shut up, all of you. I want to hear what happened at Anuin."

Morgon turned abruptly. A hand stopped him. The trader who had spoken to him said slowly, perplexedly, "I know you. Your name hangs at the edge of my memory, I know it. . . . Something to do with rain . . ."

Morgon recognized him: the trader he had talked to long ago on a rainy autumn day in Hlurle, after he had ridden out of the Herun hills. He said brusquely, "I don't know what in Hel's name you're talking about. It hasn't rained for weeks. Do you want to keep your hand, or do I take it with me?"

"Lords, Lords," the innkeeper murmured. "No violence in my inn." The trader took two beers off his tray, set one down in front of Morgon.

"No offense." He was still puzzled, searching Morgon's face. "Talk with me a little. I haven't been home to Kraal in months, and I need some idle—"

Morgon jerked out of his hold. His elbow hit the beer, splashing it across the table into the lap of a horse trader, who rose, cursing. Something in Morgon's face, of power or despair, quelled his first impulse. "That's no way to treat fine beer," he said darkly. "Or the offer of it. How have you managed to live as long as you have, picking quarrels out of thin air?"

"I mind my own business," Morgon said curtly. He tossed a coin on the table and went back into the dusk. His own rudeness lay like a bad taste in his mouth. Memories stirred up by the singers hovered in the back of his mind: light gathering on his sword blade, the harpist's face turning upward to meet it. He walked quickly through the trees, cursing the length of the road, the dust on it, the stars on his face, and all the shadows of memory he could not outrun.

He nearly walked through their camp before he recognized it. He stopped, bewildered. Raederle and both the horses were gone. For a second he wondered if something he had done had offended her so badly that she decided to ride both horses back to Anuin. The packs and saddles lay where he had left them; there was no sign of a struggle, no flurries of dead leaves or singed oakroots. Then he heard her call him and saw her stumbling across a shallow section of the river.

There were tears on her face. "Morgon, I was beside the river getting water when two men rode past me. They nearly ran me down. I was so furious I didn't even realize they were riding our horses until they reached the far side. So I—"

"You ran after them?" he said incredulously.

"I thought they might slow down, through the trees. But they started to gallop. I'm sorry."

"They'll get a good price for them in Ymris," Morgon said grimly.

"Morgon, they're not a mile away. You could get them back easily."

He hesitated, looking at her angry, tired face. Then he turned away from her, picked up their food pack. "Heureu's army needs them more than we do."

He felt her sudden silence at his back like something tangible. He opened the pack and cursed himself again, realizing he had forgotten to buy their supplies.

She said softly, "Are you telling me we are going to walk all the way to Lungold?"

"If you want." His fingers were shaking slightly on the pack ties.

He heard her move finally. She went back down to the river to get their water skin. She said when she returned, her voice inflectionless, "Did you bring wine?"

"I forgot it. I forgot everything." He turned then, blazing into an argument before she could speak. "And I can't go back. Not without getting into a tavern brawl."

"Did I ask you to? I wasn't even going to ask." She dropped down beside the fire, tossed a twig in it. "I lost the horses, you forgot the food. You didn't blame me." She dropped her face suddenly against her knees. "Morgon," she whispered. "I'm sorry. I will crawl to Lungold before I change shape."

He stood gazing down at her. He turned, paced a half-circle around the fire, and stared into the gnarled, haggard eye of a tree bole. He tilted his face against it, felt it gazing into him, at all the twisted origins of his own power. For a moment doubt bit into him, that he was wrong to demand such a thing of her, that even his own power, wrested out of himself by such dark circumstances, was suspect. The uncertainty died slowly, leaving, as always, the one thing he grasped with any certainty: the fragile, imperative structure of riddlery.

"You can't run from yourself."

"You are running. Maybe not from yourself, but from the riddle at your back that you never face."

He lifted his head wearily, looked at her. He moved after a moment, stirred the lagging fire. "I'll catch some fish. Tomorrow morning, I'll go back to the inn, get what we need. Maybe I can sell the saddles there. We can use the money. It's a long walk to Lungold."

They scarcely spoke at all the next day. The summer heat poured down at them, even when they walked among the trees beside the road. Morgon carried both their packs. He had not realized until then how heavy they were. The straps wore at his shoulders as their quarrelling chafed at his mind. Raederle offered to carry one, but he refused with something kin to anger, and she did not suggest it again. At noon, they ate with their feet in the river. The cold water soothed them, and they spoke a little. The road in the afternoon was fairly quiet; they could hear the creak of cartwheels long before the carts came into view. But the heat was intense, almost unbearable. Finally they gave up, trudged along the rough river bank until twilight.

They found a place to camp, then. Morgon left Raederle sitting with her feet in the river and went hunting in falcon-shape. He killed a hare dreaming in the last rays of the sun on a meadow. Returning, he found Raederle where he had left her. He cleaned the hare, hung it on a spit of green wood above the fire. He watched Raederle; she sat staring down at the water, not moving. He said her name finally.

She got up, stumbling a little on the bank. She joined him slowly, sitting down close to the fire, drawing her damp skirt tightly under her feet. In the firelight, he took a good look at her, forgetting to turn the spit. Her face was very still; there were tiny lines of pain under her eyes. He drew a sudden breath; her eyes met his, holding a clear and definite warning. But the worry in him blazed out in spite of her.

"Why didn't you tell me you were in that much pain? Let me see your feet."

"Leave me alone!" The fierceness in her voice startled him. She was huddled over herself. "I told you I would walk to Lungold, and I will."

"How?" He stood up, anger at himself beating in his throat. "I'll find a horse for you."

"With what? We couldn't sell the saddles."

"I'll change into one. You can ride on my back."

"No." Her voice was shaken with the same, strange anger. "You will not. I'm not going to ride you all the way to Lungold. I said I will walk."

"You can hardly walk ten feet!"

"I'll do it anyway. If you don't turn the spit, you'll burn our supper."

He did not move; she leaned forward and turned it herself. Her hand was trembling. As the lights and shadows melted over her, he wondered suddenly if he knew her at all. He pleaded, "Raederle, what in Hel's name will you do? You can't walk like that. You won't ride; you won't change shape. Do you want to go back to Anuin?"

"No." Her voice flinched on the word, as if he had hurt her. "Maybe I'm no good with riddles, but I do keep vows."

"How much of your honor can you place in Ylon's name when you give him and his heritage nothing but hatred?"

She bent again, to turn the spit, he thought, but instead she grasped a handful of fire. "He was King of An, once. There is some honor in that." Her voice was shaking badly. She shaped a wedge of fire, spun thread-thin strings down from it through her fingers. "I swore in his name I would never let you leave me." He realized suddenly what she was making. She finished it, held it out to him: a harp made of fire, eating at the darkness around her hand. "You're the riddler. If you have such faith in riddles, you show me. You can't even face your own hatred, and you give me riddles to answer. There's a name for a man like you."

"Fool," he said without touching the harp. He watched the light leap soundlessly down the strings. "At least I know my name."

"You are the Star-Bearer. Why can't you leave me alone to make my own choices? What I am doesn't matter."

He stared at her over the flaming harp. Something he said or thought without realizing it snapped the harp to pieces in her hand. He reached across the fire, gripped her shoulders, and pulled her to her feet.

"How can you say that to me? What in Hel's name are you afraid of?"

"Morgon—"

"You're not going to change shape into something neither of us will recognize!"

"Morgon." She was shaking him suddenly, trying to make him see. "Do I have to say it? I'm not running from something I hate, but something I want. The power of that bastard heritage. I want it. The power eating across Ymris, trying to destroy the realm and you—I am drawn to it. Bound to it. And I love you. The riddler. The Master. The man who must fight everything of that heritage. You keep asking me for things you will only hate."

He whispered, "No."

"The land-rulers, the wizards at Lungold—how can I face them? How can I tell them I am kin to your enemies? How will they ever trust me? How can I trust myself, wanting such terrible power—"

"Raederle." He lifted one hand stiffly, touched her face, brushing at the fire and tears on it, trying to see clearly. But the uneasy shadows loomed across it, molding her out of flame and darkness, someone he had not quite seen before and could not quite see now. Something was eluding him, vanishing as he touched it. "I never asked anything from you but truth."

"You never knew what you were asking—"

"I never do know. I just ask." The fire was shaping itself between them into the answer his mind grasped at. He saw it suddenly, and he saw her again, at the same time, the woman men had died for in Peven's tower, who had shaped her mind to fire, who loved him and argued with him and was drawn to a power that might destroy him. For a moment pieces of the riddle struggled against each other in his mind. Then they slid together, and he saw the faces of shape-changers he knew: Eriel, the harpist Corrig, whom he had killed, the shape-changers in Isig he had killed. A chill of fear and wonder brushed through him. "If you see . . . if you see something of value in them," he whispered, "then what in Hel's name are they?"

She was silent, gripping him, her face gone still, fiery with tears. "I didn't say that."

"Yes, you did."

"No, I didn't. There's nothing of value in their power."

"Yes, there is. You sense it in you. That's what you want."

"Morgon—"

"Either you change shape in my mind, or they change shape. You, I know."

She let go of him slowly. She was uncertain. He held her, wondering what words would make her trust him. Slowly he realized what argument she would hear.

He loosed her and touched the harp into shape at his back. It filled his hands like a memory. He sat down while she watched him at the edge of the fire, not moving, not speaking. The stars on the harp's face, enigmatic, answerless, met his gaze. Then he turned it and began to play. For a while he thought of little but her, a shadowy figure at the edge of the light, drawn to his harping. His fingers remembered rhythms, patterns, drew hesitant fragments of song out of a year of silence. The ancient, flawless voice of the harp, responsive to his power, touched him again with unexpected wonder. She drew closer to him as he played, until step by step she had reached his side. She stood still again. With the fire behind her, he could not see her face.

A harpist echoed him in the shadows of his memory. The more he played to drown the memory, the more it haunted him: a distant, skilled, beautiful harping, coming from beyond blackness, beyond the smell of water that went nowhere and had gone nowhere for thousands of years. The fire beyond Raederle grew small, a point of light that went farther and farther away from him, until the blackness came down over his eyes like a hand. A voice startled him, echoing over stones, fading away into harsh cadences. He never saw the face. Reaching out in the darkness, he touched only stone. The voice was always unexpected, no matter how hard he listened for a footstep. He grew to listen constantly, lying on stone, his muscles tensed with waiting. With the voice came mind-work he could not fight, pain when he fought with his fists, endless questions he would not answer out of a desperate fury, until suddenly his fury turned to terror as he felt the fragile, complex instincts for land-law begin to die in him. He heard his own voice answering, rising a little, answering, rising, no longer able to answer. . . . He heard harping.

His hands had stopped. The bones of his face ached against the harpwood. Raederle sat close to him, her arm around his shoulders. The harping still sounded raggedly through his mind. He stirred stiffly away from it. It would not stop. Raederle's head turned; he realized, the blood shocking through him, that she was hearing it, too.

Then he recognized the familiar, hesitant harping. He stood up, his face white, frozen, and caught a brand out of the fire. Raederle said his name; he could not answer. She tried to follow him, barefoot, limping through the bracken, but he would not wait. He tracked the harpist through the trees, across the road to the other side, where he startled a trader sleeping under his cart; through brambles and underbrush, while the harping grew louder and seemed to circle him. The torch, flaring over dead leaves, lit a figure finally, sitting under a tree, bowed over his harp. Morgon stopped, breathing jerkily, words, questions, curses piling into his throat. The harpist lifted his face slowly to the light.

Morgon's breath stopped. There was not a sound anywhere in the black night beyond the torchlight. The harpist, staring back at Morgon, still played softly, awkwardly, his hands gnarled like oak root, twisted beyond all use.

5

MORGON WHISPERED, "DETH."

The harpist's hands stilled. His face was so worn and haggard there was little familiar in it but the fine cast of his bones and the expression in his eyes. He had no horse or pack, no possessions that Morgon could see besides a dark harp, adorned by nothing but its lean, elegant lines. His broken hands rested a moment on the strings, then slid down to tilt the harp to the ground beside him.

"Morgon." His voice was husky with weariness and surprise. He added, so gently that he left Morgon floundering wordlessly in his own turmoil, "I didn't mean to disturb you."

Morgon stood motionlessly, even the flame in his hand was drawn still in the windless night. The deadly, flawless harping that ran always in some dark place beneath his thoughts tangled suddenly with the hesitant, stumbling efforts he had heard the past nights. He hung at the edge of his own light, wanting to shout with fury, wanting to turn without speaking and go, wanting even more to take one step forward and ask a question. He did, finally, so noiselessly he scarcely realized he had moved.

"What happened to you?" His own voice sounded strange, flinching a little away from its calm. The harpist glanced down at his hands, lying at his sides like weights.

"I had an argument," he said, "with Ghisteslwchlohm."

"You never lose arguments." He had taken another step forward, still tense, soundless as an animal.

"I didn't lose this one. If I had, there would be one less harpist in the realm."

"You don't die easily."

"No." He watched Morgon move another step, and Morgon, sensing it, stilled. The harpist met his eyes clearly, acknowledging everything, asking nothing. Morgon shifted the brand in his hand. It was burning close to his skin; he dropped it, started a small blaze in the dead leaves. The change of light shadowed Deth's face; Morgon saw it as behind other fires, in earlier days. He was silent, hovering again within the harpist's silence. It drew him forward, as across a bridge, narrow as a blade, slung across the gulf of his anger and confusion. He squatted finally beside the fire, traced a circle around it, keeping it small with his mind in the warm night.

He asked, after a while, "Where are you going?"

"Back, to where I was born. Lungold. I have no place else to go."

"You're walking to Lungold?"

He shrugged slightly, his hands shifting. "I can't ride."

"What will you do in Lungold? You can't harp."

"I don't know. Beg."

Morgon was silent again, looking at him. His fingers, burrowing, found an acorn cap and flicked it into the fire. "You served Ghisteslwchlohm for six hundred years. You gave me to him. Is he that ungrateful?"

"No," Deth said dispassionately. "He was suspicious. You let me walk out of Anuin alive."

Morgon's hand froze among the dead leaves. Something ran through him, then, like a faint, wild scent of a wind that had burned across the northern wastes, across the realm, to bring only the hint of its existence to the still summer night. He let his hand move after a moment; a twig snapped between his fingers. He added the pieces to the fire and felt his way into his questioning, as if he were beginning a riddle-game with someone whose skill he did not know.

"Ghisteslwchlohm was in An?"

"He had been in the backlands, strengthening his power after you broke free of him. He did not know where you were, but since my mind is always open to him, he found me easily, in Hel."

Morgon's eyes rose. "Are your minds still linked?"

"I assume so. He no longer has any use for me, but you may be in danger."

"He didn't come to Anuin looking for me."

"He met me seven days after I left Anuin. It seemed unlikely that you would still be there."

"I was there." He added a handful of twigs to the fire, watched them turn bright then twist and curl away from the heat. His eyes slid suddenly to the harpist's twisted fingers. "What in Hel's name did he do to you?"

"He made a harp for me, since you destroyed mine, and I had none." A light flicked through the harpist's eyes, like a memory of pain, or a distant, cold amusement. The flame receded, and his head bent slightly, leaving his face in shadow. He continued dispassionately, "The harp was of black fire. Down the face of it were three burning, white-hot stars."

Morgon's throat closed. "You played it," he whispered.

"He instructed me to. While I was still conscious, I felt his mind drawing out of mine memories of the events at Anuin, of the months you and I travelled together, of the years and centuries I served him, and before. . . . The harp had a strange, tormented voice, like the voices I heard in the night as I rode through Hel."

"He let you live."

He leaned his head back against the tree, meeting Morgon's eyes. "He found no reason not to."

Morgon was silent. The flame snapped twigs like small bones in front of him. He felt cold suddenly, even in the warm air, and he shifted closer to the fire. Some animal drawn from the brush turned lucent, burning eyes toward him, then blinked and vanished. The silence around him was haunted with a thousand riddles he knew he should ask, and he knew the harpist would only answer them with other riddles. He rested a moment in the void of the silence, cupping light in his hands.

"Poor pay for six centuries," he said at last. "What did you expect from him when you entered his service in the first place?"

"I told him that I needed a master, and no king deluded by his lies would suffice. We suited one another. He created an illusion; I upheld it."

"That was a dangerous illusion. He was never afraid of the High One?"

"What cause has the High One given him to be afraid?"

Morgon moved a leaf in the fire with his fingers. "None." He let his hand lay flat, burning in the heart of the flame, while memories gathered in his mind. "None," he whispered. The fire roared suddenly, noiselessly under his hand as his awareness of it lapsed. He flinched away from it, tears springing into his eyes. Through the blur, he saw the harpist's hands, knotted, flame-ridden, clinging, even in torment, to his silence. He hunched over his own hand, swallowing curses. "That was careless."

"Morgon, I have no water—"

"I noticed." His voice was harsh with pain. "You have no food, you have no water, you have no power of law or wealth, or even enough wizardry to keep yourself from getting burned. You can hardly use the one thing you do possess. For a man who walked away from death twice in seven days, you create a great illusion of powerlessness." He drew his knees up, rested his face against them. For a while he was quiet, not expecting the harpist to speak, and no longer caring. The fire spoke between them, in an ancient language that needed no riddles. He thought of Raederle and knew he should leave, but he did not move. The harpist sat with an aged, worn stillness, the stillness of old roots or weathered stone. The fire, loosed from Morgon's control, was dying. He watched the light recede between the angles of his arms. He stirred finally, lifting his head. The flame drifted among its ashes; the harpist's face was dark.

He stood up, his burned fist cradled in his palm. He heard the faint, dry shift of the harpist's movement and knew, somehow, that if he had stayed all night beside that fire, the harpist would have been there, silent and sleepless, at dawn. He shook his head wordlessly over his own confusion of impulses.

"You drag me out of my dreams with your harping, and I come and crouch like a dog in your stillness. I wish I knew whether to trust you or kill you or run from you because you play a game more skillful and deadly than any riddler I have ever known. Do you need food? We can spare some."

It was a long time before Deth answered him; the answer itself was nearly inaudible. "No."

"All right." He lingered, both hands clenched, still hoping in spite of himself for one cracked, marrowless bone of truth. He turned finally, abruptly, smoke from the charred embers burning in his eyes. He walked three steps in the dark, and the fourth into a blue fire that snapped out of nothingness around him, grew brighter and brighter, twisting through him until he cried out, falling into light.

He woke at dawn, sprawled on the ground where he had fallen, his face gritty with dirt and broken leaves. Someone slid a foot under his shoulder, rolled him on his back. He saw the harpist again, still sitting beneath the tree, with a circle of ash in front of him. Then he saw who reached down to grip the throat of his tunic and pull him to his feet.

He drew breath to shout, in agony and fury; Ghisteslwchlohm's hand cut sharply across his mouth, silencing him. He saw the harpist's eyes then, night-dark, still as the black, motionless water at the bottom of Erlenstar Mountain, and something in them challenged him, checked the bitterness in his throat. The harpist rose with a stiff, awkward movement that told Morgon he had been sitting there all night. He laid his harp with a curious deliberateness across the ashes of their fire. Then he turned his head, and Morgon followed his gaze to where Raederle stood, white and silent in the eye of the rising sun.

A silent, despairing cry swelled and broke in Morgon's chest. She heard it; she stared back at him with the same despair. She looked dishevelled and very tired, but unharmed.

Ghisteslwchlohm said brusquely, "If you touch my mind, I will kill her. Do you understand?" He shook Morgon roughly, pulling his gaze away from her. "Do you understand?"

"Yes," Morgon said. He attacked the Founder promptly with his hands. A white fire slapped back at him, seared through his bones, and he slid across the ground, blinking away sweat, gripping at stones and twigs to keep sounds from breaking out of him. Raederle had moved; he felt her arm around him, helping him to his feet.

He shook his head, trying to push her out of the way of the wizard's fire, but she only held him more tightly, and said, "Stop it."

"Sound advice," the Founder said. "Take it." He looked weary in the sudden, hot light. Morgon saw hollows and sharp angles worn into the mask of serenity he had assumed for centuries. He was poorly dressed, in a rough, shapeless robe that gave his age an illusion of frailty. It was very dusty, as if he had been walking down Trader's Road himself.

Morgon, fighting to get words beyond the fury and pain in him, said, "Couldn't you hear your harpist's harping, that you had to guess where I was along this road?"

"You left a trail across the realm for a blind man to follow. I suspected you would go to Hed, and I even tracked you there, but—" His uplifted hand checked Morgon's sudden movement. "You had come and gone. I have no war with farmers and cows; I disturbed nothing while I was there." He regarded Morgon silently a moment. "You took the wraiths of An to Hed. How?"

"How do you think? You taught me something of land-law."

"Not that much." Morgon felt his mind suddenly, probing for the knowledge. The touch blinded him, brought back memories of terror and helplessness. He was helpless again, with Raederle beside him, and tears of despair and rage gripped at his throat. The wizard, exploring the mind-link he had formed at Anuin with the dead, grunted softly and loosed him. The morning light drenched the ground again; he saw the harpist's shadow lying across the charred leaves. He stared at it; its stillness dragged at him, wore even his bewilderment into numbness. Then Ghisteslwchlohm's words jarred in his mind and he lifted his eyes.

"What do you mean? Everything I know I learned from you."

The wizard gazed at him conjecturingly, as if he were a riddle on some dusty parchment. He did not answer; he said abruptly to Raederle, "Can you change shape?"

She eased a step closer to Morgon, shaking her head. "No."

"Half the kings in the history of An have taken the crow-shape at one time or another, and I learned from Deth that you have inherited a shape-changer's power. You'll learn fast."

The blood pushed up into her white face, but she did not look at the harpist. "I will not change shape," she said softly, and added with so little change of inflection it surprised both Morgon and the wizard, "I curse you, in my name and Madir's, with eyes small and fiery, to look no higher than a man's knee, and no lower than the mud beneath—" The wizard put his hand on her mouth and she stopped speaking. He blinked, as if his sight had blurred for a moment. His hand slid down her throat, and something began to tighten in Morgon to a fine, dangerous precision, like a harp string about to snap.

But the wizard said only, drily, "Spare me the next ninety-eight curses." He lifted his hand, and she cleared her throat. Morgon could feel her trembling.

She said again, "I am not going to change shape. I will die, first. I swear that, by my—" The wizard checked her again.

He contemplated her with mild interest, then said over his shoulder to Deth, "Take her across the backlands with you to Erlenstar Mountain. I don't have time for this. I will bind her mind; she won't attempt to escape. The Star-Bearer will come with me to Lungold and then to Erlenstar Mountain." He seemed to sense something in the stiff, black shadow across the bracken; he turned his head. "I'll find men to hunt for you and guard her."

"No."

The wizard swung around to one side of Morgon so that Morgon could not move without his knowledge. His brows were drawn; he held the harpist's eyes until Deth spoke again.

"I owe her. In Anuin, she would have let me walk away free before Morgon ever came. She protected me, unwittingly, from him with a small army of wraiths. I am no longer in your service, and you owe me for six hundred years of it. Let her go."

"I need her."

"You could take any one of the Lungold wizards and still hold Morgon powerless."

"The Lungold wizards are unpredictable and too powerful. Also, they are too apt to die for odd impulses. Suth proved that. I do owe you, if for nothing but your broken harping that brought the Star-Bearer to kneel at your feet. But ask something else of me."

"I want nothing else. Except a harp strung with wind, perhaps, for a man with no hands to play it."

Ghisteslwchlohm was silent. Morgon, the faint overtones of some riddle echoing through his memory, lifted his head slowly and looked at the harpist. His voice sounded dispassionate as always, but there was a hardness in his eyes Morgon had never seen before. Ghisteslwchlohm seemed to listen a moment to an ambiguity: some voice he did not quite catch beneath the voice of the morning wind.

He said finally, almost curiously, "So. Even your patience has its limits. I can heal your hands."

"No."

"Deth, you are being unreasonable. You know as well as I do what the stakes are in this game. Morgon is stumbling like a blind man into his power. I want him in Erlenstar Mountain, and I don't want to fight him to get him there."

"I'm not going back to Erlenstar Mountain," Morgon said involuntarily. The wizard ignored him; his eyes, intent, narrowed a little on Deth's face.

Deth said softly, "I am old and crippled and very tired. You left me little more than my life in Hel. Do you know what I did then? I walked my horse to Caithnard and found a trader who didn't spit when I spoke to him. I traded my horse to him for the last harp I will ever possess. And I tried to play it."

"I said I will—"

"There is not a court open to me in this realm to play in, even if you healed my hands."

"You accepted that risk six centuries ago," Ghisteslwchlohm said. His voice had thinned. "You could have chosen a lesser court than mine to harp in, some innocent, powerless place whose innocence will not survive this final struggle. You know that. You are too wise for recriminations, and you never had any lost innocence to regret. You can stay here and starve, or take Raederle of An to Erlenstar Mountain and help me finish this game. Then you can take what reward you want for your services, anywhere in this realm." He paused, then added roughly, "Or are you bound, in some hidden place I cannot reach, to the Star-Bearer?"

"I owe nothing to the Star-Bearer."

"That is not what I asked you."

"You asked me that question before. In Hel. Do you want another answer?" He checked, as if the sudden anger in his voice were unfamiliar even to himself, and he continued more quietly, "The Star-Bearer is the pivot point of a game. I did not know, any more than you, that he would be a young Prince of Hed, whom I might come dangerously close to loving. There is no more binding than that, and it is hardly important. I have betrayed him to you twice. But you will have to find someone else to betray Raederle of An. I am in her debt. Again, that is a small matter: she is no threat to you, and any land-ruler in the realm can serve in her place—"

"The Morgol?"

Deth was still, not breathing, not blinking, as if he were something honed into shape by wind and weather. Morgon, watching, brushed something off his face with the back of his hand; he realized in surprise that he was crying.

Deth said finally, very softly, "No."

"So." The wizard contemplated him, hair-thin lines of impatience and power deepening at the sides of his mouth. "There is something that is not such a small matter. I was beginning to wonder. If I can't hire you back into my service, perhaps I can persuade you. The Morgol of Herun is camped outside of Lungold with two hundred of her guard. The guard is there, I assume, to protect the city; the Morgol, out of some incomprehensible impulse, is waiting for you. I will give you a choice. If you choose to leave Raederle here, I will bring the Morgol with me to Erlenstar Mountain, after I have subdued, with Morgon's help, the last of the Lungold wizards. Choose."

He waited. The harpist was motionless again; even the crooked bones in his hands seemed brittle. The wizard's voice whipped at him and he flinched. "Choose!"

Raederle's hands slid over her mouth. "Deth, I'll go," she whispered. "I'll follow Morgon anyway, or I will be foresworn."

The harpist did not speak. He moved finally, very slowly toward them, his eyes on Ghisteslwchlohm's face. He stopped a pace away from him and drew breath to speak. Then, in a swift, fluid movement, the back of his crippled hand cracked across the Founder's face.

Ghisteslwchlohm stepped back, his fingers driving to the bone on Morgon's arm, but he could not have moved. The harpist slid to his knees, hunched over the newly broken bones in his hand. He lifted his face, white, bruised with agony, asking nothing. For a moment Ghisteslwchlohm looked down at him silently, and Morgon saw in his eyes what might have been the broken memories of many centuries.

Then his own hand rose. A lash of fire caught the harpist across the eyes, flung him backward across the bracken, where he lay still, staring blindly at the sun.

The wizard held Morgon with his hand and his eyes, until Morgon realized slowly that he was shaken with a dry, tearless sobbing and his muscles were locked to attack. The wizard touched his eyes briefly, as if the streak of fire torn out of his mind had given him a headache. "Why in Hel's name," he demanded, "are you wasting grief on him? Look at me. Look at me!"

"I don't know!" Morgon shouted back at him. He saw more fire snap through the air, across the harpist's body. It touched the dark harp and flamed. The air wailed with snapping strings. Raederle shimmered suddenly into sheer fire; the wizard pulled her relentlessly back into shape with his mind. She was still half-fire, and Morgon was struggling with an impulse of power that would have doomed her, when something in him froze. He whirled. Watching curiously among the trees were a dozen men. Their horses were the color of night, their garments all the wet, rippling colors of the sea.

"The world," one of them commented in the sudden silence, "is not a safe place for harpists." He bent his head to Morgon. "Star-Bearer." His pale, expressionless face seemed to flow a little with the breeze. From him came the smell of brine. "Ylon's child." His lucent eyes went to Ghisteslwchlohm. "High One."

Morgon stared at them. His mind, spinning through possibilities of action, went suddenly blank. They had no weapons; their black mounts were stone still, but any movement, he sensed, a shift of light, a bird call on the wrong note, could spring a merciless attack. They seemed suspended from motion, as on a breath of silence between two waves; whether by curiosity or simple uncertainty, he did not know. He felt Ghisteslwchlohm's hand grip his shoulder and was reassured oddly by the fact that the wizard wanted him alive.

The shape-changer who had spoken answered his question with a soft, equivocal mockery, "For thousands of years we have been waiting to meet the High One."

Morgon heard the wizard draw breath. "So. You are the spawn of the seas of Ymris and An—"

"No. We are not of the sea. We have shaped ourselves to its harping. You are careless of your harpist."

"The harpist is my business."

"He served you well. We watched him through the centuries, doing your bidding, wearing your mask, waiting . . . as we waited, long before you set foot on this earth of the High One's, Ghisteslwchlohm. Where is the High One?" His horse snaked forward soundlessly, like a shadow, stopped three paces from Morgon. He resisted an impulse to step backward. The Founder's voice, tired, impatient, made him marvel.

"I am not interested in riddle-games. Or in a fight. You take your shapes out of dead men and seaweed; you breathe, you harp and you die—that is all I know or care to know about you. Back your mount or you will be riding a pile of kelp."

The shape-changer backed it a step without a shift of muscle. His eyes caught light like water; for an instant they seemed to smile. "Master Ohm," he said, "do you know the riddle of the man who opened his door at midnight and found not the black sky filling his doorway but the black, black eye of some creature who stretched beyond him to measureless dimension? Look at us again. Then go, quietly, leaving the Star-Bearer and our kinswoman."

"You look," the Founder said brusquely. Morgon, still in his hold, was jolted by the strength that poured out of him: energy that slapped at the shape-changers, flattened an oak in its way and sent frightened birds screaming into the air. The silent thunder of the fire streaked towards their minds; Morgon felt it, but as at a distance, for the wizard had shielded his mind. When the trees had splintered and settled, the shape-changers slowly reappeared out of the flock of birds that had startled into the air. Their number had doubled, for half of them had been the motionless horses. They took their previous shapes leisurely, while Ghisteslwchlohm watched, puzzled, Morgon sensed, about the extent of their power. His grip had slackened. A twig in a bush rustled slightly, for no discernible reason, and the shape-changers attacked.

There was a wave of black pelt, soundless, shell-black hooves rolling toward them so fast that Morgon barely had time to react. He worked an illusion of nothingness over himself that he suspected only Raederle noticed; she gasped when he gripped her wrist. Something struck him: a horse's hoof, or the hilt of a shadowy blade, and he wavered an instant in and out of visibility. He felt his muscles tense for a death blow. But nothing touched him, only wind, for a few broken moments. He flung his mind forward, miles ahead along the road, where a trader driving a wagon-load of cloth was whistling away his boredom. He filled Raederle's mind with the same awareness and gripping her hard, pulled her forward into it.

A moment later he was lying with her at the bottom of the big covered cart, bleeding onto a bolt of embroidered linen.

RAEDERLE WAS SOBBING. He tried to quiet her, gathering her to him as he listened, but she could not stop. He heard beneath her weeping the grind of wheels in the dust and the driver's whistling, muffled by the bolts of cloth piled behind him and the canvas covering the wagon. The road was quiet; he heard no sounds of disturbance behind them. His head was aching; he leaned it against the linen. His eyes closed. A darkness thundered soundlessly toward him again. Then a cartwheel banged into a pothole, jarring him, and Raederle twisted out of his hold and sat up. She pushed her hair out of her eyes.

"Morgon, he came for me at night, and I was barefoot—I couldn't even run. I thought it was you. I don't even have shoes on. What in Hel's name was that harpist doing? I don't understand him. I don't—" She stopped suddenly, staring at him, as if he were a shape-changer she had found beside her. She put one hand over her mouth, and touched his face with the other. "Morgon . . ."

He put his hand to his forehead, looked at the blood on his fingers, and made a surprised sound. The side of his face, from temple to jaw, was burning. His shoulder hurt; his tunic fell apart when he touched it. A raw, wide gash, like the scrape of a sharp hoof, continued from his face to his shoulder and halfway down his chest.

He straightened slowly, looking at the bloodstains he had left on the floor of the wagon, on the trader's fine cloth. He shuddered suddenly, violently, and pushed his face against his knees.

"I walked straight into that one." He began to curse himself, vividly and methodically, until he heard her rise. He caught her wrist, pulled her down again. "No."

"Will you let go of me? I'm going to tell the trader to stop. If you don't let go, I'll shout."

"No. Raederle, listen. Will you listen! We are only a few miles west of where we were captured. The shape-changers will search for us. So will Ghisteslwchlohm, if he isn't dead. We have to outrun them."

"I don't even have shoes on! And if you tell me to change shape, I will curse you." Then she touched his cheek again, swallowing. "Morgon, can you stop crying?"

"Haven't I stopped?"

"No." Her own eyes filled again. "You look like a wraith out of Hel. Please let the trader help you."

"No." The wagon jerked to a stop suddenly, and he groaned. He got to his feet unsteadily, drew her up. The trader's startled face peered back at them between the falls of his canvas.

"What in the name of the wolf-king's eyes are you doing back there?" He shifted the curtains so the light fell on them. "Look at the mess you made on that embroidered cloth! Do you realize how much that costs? And that white velvet . . ."

Morgon heard Raederle draw breath to respond. He gripped her hand and sent his mind forward, like an anchor flung on its line across water, disappearing into the shallows to fall to a resting place. He found a quiet, sunlit portion of the road ahead of them, with only a musician on it singing to himself as he rode toward Lungold. Holding Raederle's mind, halting her in mid-sentence, Morgon stepped toward the singing.

They stood in the road only a minute, while the singer moved obliviously away from them. The unexpected light spun around Morgon dizzily. Raederle was struggling against his mind-hold with a startling intensity. She was angry, he sensed, and beneath that, panicked. She could break his hold, he knew suddenly as he glimpsed the vast resource of power in her, but she was too frightened to control her thoughts. His thoughts, shapeless, open, soared over the road again, touched the minds of horses, a hawk, crows feeding around a dead campfire. A farmer's son, leaving his heritage behind him, riding an ancient plow horse to seek his fortune in Lungold, anchored Morgon's mind again. He stepped forward. As they stood in the dust raised by the plow horse, Morgon heard his own harsh, exhausted breathing. Something slapped painfully across his mind, and he nearly fought back at it until he realized it was Raederle's mind-shout. He stilled both their minds and searched far down the road.

A smith who travelled from village to village along the road, shoeing horses and patching cauldrons, sat half-asleep in his cart, dreaming idly of beer. Morgon, dreaming his dream, followed him through the hot morning. Raederle was oddly still. He wanted to speak to her then, desperately, but he did not dare break his concentration. He threw his mind open again, until he heard traders laughing. He let his mind fill with their laughter until it was next to him among the trees. Then his sense of Raederle's mind drained out of him. He groped for it, startled, but touched only the vague thoughts of trees or animals. He could not find her with his mind. His concentration broken, he saw her standing in front of him.

She was breathing quickly, silently, staring at him, her body tensed to shout or strike or cry. He said, his face so stiff he could hardly speak, "Once more. Please. The river."

She nodded, after a moment. He touched her hand, and then her mind. He felt through the sunlight for cool minds: fish, water birds, river animals. The river appeared before them; they stood on the bank in a soft grassy clearing among the ferns.

He let go of Raederle, fell to his hands and knees and drank. The water's voice soothed the sear of the sun across his mind. He looked up at Raederle and tried to speak. He could not see her. He slumped down, laid his face in the river and fell asleep.

He woke again in the middle of the night, found Raederle sitting beside him, watching him by the gentle light of her fire. They gazed at one another for a long time without speaking, as if they were looking out of their memories. Then Raederle touched his face. Her face was drawn; there was an expression in her eyes that he had never seen before.

An odd sorrow caught at his throat. He whispered, "I'm sorry. I was desperate."

"It's all right." She checked the bandages across his chest; he recognized strips of her shift. "I found herbs the pig-woman—I mean Nun—taught me to use on wounded pigs. I hope they work on you."

He caught her hands, folded them between his fingers. "Please. Say it."

"I don't know what to say. No one ever controlled my mind before. I was so angry with you, all I wanted to do was break free of you and go back to Anuin. Then . . . I broke free. And I stayed with you because you understand . . . you understand power. So do the shape-changers who called me kinswoman, but you I trust." She was silent; he waited, seeing her oddly, feverishly in the firelight, the tangled mass of her hair like harvested kelp, her skin pale as shell, her expressions changing like light changing over the sea. Her face twisted away from him suddenly. "Stop seeing me like that!"

"I'm sorry," he said again. "You looked so beautiful. Do you realize what kind of power it takes to break one of my bindings?"

"Yes. A shape-changer's power. That's what I have."

He was silent, staring at her. A light, chill shudder ran through him. "They have that much power." He sat up abruptly, scarcely noticing the drag of pain down his shoulder. "Why don't they use it? They never use it. They should have killed me long ago. In Herun, the shape-changer Corrig could have killed me as I slept; instead he only harped. He challenged me to kill him. In Isig—three shape-changers could not kill one farmer-prince of Hed who had never used a sword in his life? What in Hel's name are they? What do they want of me? What does Ghisteslwchlohm want?"

"Do you think they killed him?"

"I don't know. He would have had sense enough to run. I'm surprised we didn't find him in the wagon with us."

"They'll look for you in Lungold."

"I know." He slid his palms over his face. "I know. Maybe with the wizards' help, I can draw them away from the city. I've got to get there quickly. I've got to—"

"I know." She drew a deep breath and loosed it wearily. "Morgon, teach me the crow-shape. At least it's a shape of the Kings of An. And it's faster than walking barefoot."

He lifted his head. He lay back down after a moment, drew her down with him, searching for some way to speak at once all the thoughts crowding into his head. He said finally, "I'll learn to harp," and he felt her smile against his breast. Then all his thoughts froze into a single memory of a halting harping out of the dark. He did not realize he was crying again until he lifted his hand to touch his eyes. Raederle was silent, holding him gently. He said, after a long time, when her fire had died down, "I sat with Deth in the night not because I was hoping to understand him, but because he drew me there, he wanted me there. And he didn't keep me there with his harping or his words, but something powerful enough to bind me across all my anger. I came because he wanted me. He wanted me, so I came. Do you understand that?"

"Morgon, you loved him," she whispered. "That was the binding."

He was silent again, thinking back to the still, shadowed face beyond the flame, listening to the harpist's silence until he could almost hear the sound of riddles spun like spider's web in the darkness in a vast, secret game that made his death itself a riddle. Finally some herb Raederle had laid against his cheek breathed across his mind and he slept again.

He taught her the crow-shape the next morning when they woke at dawn. He went into her mind, found deep in it crow-images, tales of them, memories she scarcely knew were there: her father's unreadable crow-black eyes, crows among the oak trees surrounding Raith's pigherds, crows flying through the history of An, carrion-eaters, message-bearers, cairn-guardians, their voices full of mockery, bitter warnings, poetry.

"Where did they all come from?" she murmured, amazed.

"They are of the land-law of An. The power and heart of An. Nothing more."

He called a sleepy crow out of one of the trees around them; it landed on his wrist. "Can you go into my mind? See behind my eyes, into my thoughts?"

"I don't know."

"Try. It won't be hard for you." He opened his mind to the

crow-mind, drew its brain-workings into his own, until he saw his blurred, nameless face out of its eyes. He heard movements, precise and isolated as flute notes, under dead leaves, under oak roots. He began to understand its language. It gave a squawk, more curious than impatient. His mind filled then with a sense of Raederle, as if she were within him, touching him gently, filling him like light. His throat ached with wonder. For a moment the three minds drew from one another, fearlessly, tentatively. Then the crow cried; its wings soared blackly over Morgon's vision. He was left alone in his mind, groping for something that had gone out of him. A crow fluttered up, landed on his shoulder. He looked into its eyes.

He smiled slowly. The crow, its wings beating awkwardly, swooped to a high branch. It missed its perch landing. Then it caught itself, and the fine balance of instinct and knowledge within it wavered. The crow became Raederle, dodging leaves as she changed shape.

She looked down at Morgon, breathless and astonished. "Stop laughing. Morgon, I flew. Now, how in Hel's name do I get down?"

"Fly."

"I've forgotten how!"

He flew up beside her, one wing stiff with his half-healed wound. He changed shape again. The branch creaked a warning under his weight, and she gasped. "We'll fall in the river! Morgon, it's breaking—" She fluttered up again with a squawk. Morgon joined her. They streaked the sunrise with black, soared high above the woods until they saw the hundreds of miles of endless forest and the great road hewn through it, crossing the realm. They rose until traders' wagons were only tiny lumbering insects crawling down a ribbon of dust. They dropped slowly, spiralling together, their wings beating the same slow rhythm, winding lesser and lesser rings through the sunlight until they traced one last black circle above the river. They landed among ferns on the bank, changed shape. They gazed at one another wordlessly in the morning. Raederle whispered,

"Your eyes are full of wings."

"Your eyes are full of the sun."

They flew in crow-shape for the next two weeks. The silent golden oak forest melted away at the edge of the backlands. The road turned, pushed northward through rich, dark forests of pine whose silence seemed undisturbed by the passage of centuries. It wound up dry rocky hills pounded the color of brass by the noon sun, bridged chasms through which silvery veins of water flowing down from the Lungold Lakes flashed and roared against sheer walls of stone. Trees blurred endlessly together in the crows' vision, ebbed toward a faint blue mist of mountains bordering the remote western edges of the backlands. By day the sun fired the sky a flawless, metallic blue. The night shook stars from one horizon to another, down to the rim of the world. The voices of the backlands, of land and stone and ancient untamed wind, were too loud for sound. Beneath them lay a silence implacable as granite. Morgon felt it as he flew; he breathed it into his bones, sensed its strange, cold touch in his heart. He would grope away from it at first, reach into Raederle's mind to share a vague, inarticulate language. Then the silence wore slowly into the rhythm of his flight and finally into a song. At last, when he scarcely remembered his own language and knew Raederle only as a dark, wind-sculpted shape, he saw the interminable trees part before them. In the distance, the great city founded by Ghisteslwchlohm sprawled against the shores of the first of the Lungold Lakes, glinting of copper and bronze and gold under the last rays of the sun.

The crows beat a final weary flight toward their destination. The forest had been pushed back for miles around the city to make room for fields, pastures, orchards. The cool scent of pine yielded to the smell of harrowed earth and crops that teased at Morgon's crow-instincts. Trader's Road, striped with shadow, ran its last scarred mile into the mouth of the city. The gateway was a fragile, soaring arch of dark polished timber and white stone. The city walls were immense, thick, buttressed with arms of timber and stone that rose high above the buildings scattered beyond the old bounds of the city. Newer streets had made inroads into the ancient walls; lesser gateways opened in it; houses and shops had grown against, and even on top of the walls, as if their builders had long forgotten the terror that had flung the walls up seven centuries before.

The crows reached the main gate, rested among the arches. The gates themselves looked as if they had not been closed for centuries. They were of thick slabs of oak, hinged and reinforced with bronze.

Birds were nesting on the hinges in the shadows. Within the walls, a maze of cobbled streets wandered away in all directions, lined by brightly painted inns, trade-halls, merchants' and craftsmen's shops, houses with tapestries and flowers trailing from the windows. Morgon, sifting through his crow-vision, saw across the rooftops and chimneys to the north edge of the city. The setting sun struck the lake with a full, broad battery, spangling it with fire, until the hundred fishing boats moored at the docks seemed to burn on the water.

He fluttered to the ground in the angle between the open gate and the wall and changed shape. Raederle followed him. They stood looking at one another, their faces thin, stamped with the wildness and silence of the backlands, half-unfamiliar. Then Morgon, remembering he had an arm, put it around Raederle's shoulders and kissed her almost tentatively. The expression began to come back into her face.

"What in Hel's name did we do?" she whispered. "Morgon, I feel as if I have been dreaming for a hundred years."

"Only a couple of weeks. We're in Lungold."

"Let's go home." Then a strange look came into her eyes. "What have we been eating?"

"Don't think about it." He listened. The traffic through the gate had almost stopped; he heard only one slow horseman preceding the twilight into the city. He took her hand. "Let's go."

"Where?"

"Can't you smell it? It's there, at the edge of my mind. A stench of power . . ."

It drew him through the twisting streets. The city was quiet, for it was supper hour; the succulent smells out of inns they passed made them both murmur. But they had no money, and with Morgon's torn clothing and Raederle's bare feet, they looked almost like beggars. The sense of decayed, misused power pulled Morgon toward the heart of the city, through wide streets full of fine shops and wealthy traders' houses. The streets sloped upward at the center of the city. The rich buildings dwindled away at the crown of the rising. The streets ended abruptly. On an immense, scarred stretch of land rose the shell of the ancient school, fashioned of the power and art of wizardry, its open, empty walls gleaming in the last of the light.

Morgon stopped. An odd longing ached in him, as at a glimpse of something he could never have and never knew before that he might have wanted. He said incredulously, "No wonder they came. He made it so beautiful . . ."

Huge rooms, broken open, half-destroyed, revealed the wealth of the realm. Shattered windows with jagged panes the colors of jewels were framed in gold. Inner walls blackened with fire held remnants of pale ash and ebony, of oak and cedar. Here and there, a scarred, fallen beam glinted with a joint work of copper and bronze. Long arched windows, through which prisms of refracted light passed, suggested the illusion of peace that had lulled the restless, driven minds drawn into the school. From across seven centuries Morgon felt its illusion and its promise: the gathering of the most powerful minds of the realm to share knowledge, to explore and discipline their powers. The obscure longing bruised his heart again; he could not put a name to it. He stood gazing at the silent, ruined school until Raederle touched him.

"What is it?"

"I don't know. I wish . . . I wish I could have studied here. The only power I have ever known is Ghisteslwchlohm's."

"The wizards will help you," she said, but he found no reassurance in that. He looked at her.

"Will you do something for me? Go back into crow-shape. I'll take you on my shoulder while I search for them. I don't know what traps or bindings might still linger here."

She nodded tiredly, without comment, and changed shape. She tucked herself under his ear, and he stepped onto the grounds of the school. No trees grew anywhere on them; the grass struggled only patchily around white furrows of scorched earth. Shattered stones lay where they had fallen, still burning deep within them with a memory of power. Nothing had been touched for centuries. Morgon felt it as he drew near the school itself. The terrible sense of destruction hung like a warning over the wealth. He moved quietly, his mind open, scenting, into the silent buildings.

The rooms stank with a familiar name. In most, he found bones crushed beneath a cairn of broken walls. Memories of hope or energy, of despair, collected about him like wraiths. He began to sweat lightly, struck by shadows, faint and fine as ancient dust, of a devastating, hopeless battle. As he entered a great circular hall in the center of the buildings, he felt the reverberations still beating within the walls of a terrible explosion of hatred and despair. He heard the crow mutter harshly in its throat; its claws were prickling his shoulder. He picked his way across the ceiling, which was lying in pieces on the floor, toward a door in the back of the room. The door, hanging in splinters on its hinges, opened into a vast library. A priceless treasure of books lay torn and charred on the floor. Fire had raged across the shelves, leaving little more than the backbones and skeletons of ancient books of wizardry. The smell of burned leather still hung in the room, as if nothing had moved through the air itself in seven centuries.

He moved through empty room after empty room. He found in one melted pools of gold and silver, precious metals and shattered jewels the students had worked with; in another, the broken bones of small animals. In another, he found beds. The bones of a child were crouched under the covers of one of them. At that point, he turned and groped through the torn wall back into the evening. But the air was filled with silent cries, and the earth beneath his feet was dead.

He sat down on a pile of stone blown out of the corner of the building. Down the barren crest of the hill, the maze of rooftops spilled toward the crumbling walls. They were all of timber. He saw vividly a sheet of fire spreading across the entire city, burning crops and orchards, billowing along the lake edge into the forests under the hot summer sky, with no hope of rain for months to quench it. He dropped his face against his fists, whispered, "What in Hel's name do I think I'm doing here? He destroyed Lungold once; now he and I will destroy it again. The wizards haven't come back here to challenge him; they've come back to die."

The crow murmured something. He stood up again, gazing at the huge, ruined mass looming darkly against the translucent wake of the sunset. Scenting with his mind, he touched only memories. Listening, he heard only the echoes of a name cursed silently for all centuries. His shoulders slumped. "If they're here, they've guarded themselves well . . . I don't know how to look for them."

Raederle's voice broke through the crow-mind with a brief, mental comment. He turned his head, met the black, probing eye. "All right. I know I can find them. I can see through their illusions and break their bindings. But, Raederle . . . they are great wizards. They came into their power through curiosity, discipline, integrity . . . maybe even joy. They did not get it screaming at the bottom of Erlenstar Mountain. They never meddled with land-law, or hunted a harpist from one end of the realm to the other to kill him. They may need me to fight for them here, but I wonder if they will trust me . . ." The crow was silent; he brushed a finger down its breast. "I know. There is only one way to find out."

He went back into the ruins. This time, he opened himself completely to all the torment of the destruction and the lingering memories of a forgotten peace. His mind, like a faceted jewel, reflected all the shades of lingering power—from cracked stones, from an untouched page out of a spell book, from various ancient instruments he found near the dead: rings, strangely carved staffs, crystals with light frozen in them, skeletons of winged animals he could not name. He sorted through all the various levels of power, found the source of each. Once, tracing a smoldering fire to its bed deep in a pool of melted iron, he detonated it accidentally and realized the iron itself had been some crucible of knowledge. The blast blew the crow six feet in the air and shook stones down from the ceiling. He had melted into the force automatically, not fighting it; the crow, squawking nervously, watched him shape himself back out of the solid stone he had blown himself into. He took it into his hands to soothe it, marvelling at the intricacies of ancient wizardry. Everything his mind touched—wood, glass, gold, parchment, bone—held within it an ember of power. He explored patiently, exhaustingly, lighting a sliver of roof beam when it grew too dark to see. Finally, near midnight, when the crow was dozing on his shoulder, his mind strayed across the face of a door that did not exist.

It was a powerful illusion; he had looked at the door before and not seen through it, or felt an urge to open it. It was of thick oak and iron, barred and bolted. He would have to pick his way over a pile of broken stone and charred timber to open it. The walls were crumbled almost to the ground around the door; it seemed bolted against nothing but the battle-seared ground between two ruined buildings. But it had been created out of a living power, for some purpose. He clambered over the rubble to reach it and laid his hand flat against it. Some mind barred his passage, gave him a feel of wood grain under his fingers. He paused before he broke it, disturbed once more by the ambiguity of his own great power. Then he walked forward, becoming, for a breath, worm-eaten oak, rusted locks, and encompassing the power that bound them there.

He stepped downward abruptly into darkness. Steps that lay hidden under an illusion of parched ground led down under the earth. His fire wavered, grew smaller and smaller until he realized what force was working against it. He held the flame clear, steady, burning out of fire deep in his mind.

The worn stone steps sloped sharply down a narrow passageway. Gradually they levelled, and a blank, empty face of darkness loomed beyond Morgon's shadow, smelling of rotting timbers and damp stone. He let his brand burn brighter; it probed feebly at the vastness. A chill, like a mountain chill, shivered through him. The crow made a harsh noise. He felt it begin to change shape, and he shook his head quickly. It subsided under his hair. As he drew the fire brighter and brighter, searching for some limit to the darkness, something began to seep into his thoughts. He sensed a power very near him that had nothing to do with a vast, underground chasm. Puzzling over it, he wondered if the chasm itself were an illusion.

He drew breath slowly and held it. Only one possibility suggested itself to him: a paradox of wizardry. He had no other choice, except to turn and leave. He dropped his torch on the ground, let it dwindle into blackness. How long he stood wrestling with the dark, he did not know. The more he strained to see, the more he realized his blindness. He lifted his hands finally, linked them across his eyes. He was shivering again; the darkness seemed to squat over his head like some immense, bulky creature. But he could not leave; he stood silently, stubbornly, hoping for help.

A voice said, almost next to him, "Night is not something to endure until dawn. It is an element, like wind or fire. Darkness is its own kingdom; it moves to its own laws and many living things dwell in it. You are trying to separate your mind from it. That is futile. Accept the strictures of darkness."

"I can't." His hands had dropped, clenched; he waited, very still.

"Try."

His hands tightened; sweat stung his eyes. "I can fight the Founder, but I never learned from him how to fight this."

"You broke through my illusion as if it scarcely existed." The voice was tranquil, yet sinewy. "I held it with all the power that I still possess. There are only two others who could have broken it. And you are more powerful than either. Star-Bearer, I am Iff." He pronounced his full name then, a series of harsh syllables with a flowing, musical inflection. "You freed me from the Founder's power, and I place myself in your service, to my life's end. Can you see me?"

"No," Morgon whispered. "I want to."

Stars of torch fire ringed him, upholding an arch of light. The sense of vastness melted away. The gentle, wordless awareness of something not quite real, like a memory haunting the edge of his mind, was very strong. Then he saw a death's head gazing at him quizzically, and another, amid a tangle of assorted bones. The chamber he stood in was circular; the damp walls of living earth were full of deep slits. The hair prickled on the nape of his neck. He was standing in a tomb, hidden beneath the great school, and he had interrupted the last living wizards of Lungold burying their dead.

7

He recognized Nun immediately: a tall, thin woman with long grey hair and a shrewd, angular face. She was smoking a little jewelled pipe; her eyes, studying him with an odd mixture of wonder and worry, were a shade darker than her smoke. Behind her, in the torchlight, stood a big, spare wizard whose broad, fine-boned face was carved and battered with battle like a king's. His dead hair was flecked with silver and gold; his eyes were vivid, smoldering with blue flame. He was gazing at Morgon out of the past, as if three stars had burned for a moment across his vision sometime in the darkness of forgotten centuries. Kneeling next to one of the crevices in the wall was a dark-eyed wizard with a spare face like a bird of prey. He seemed fierce, humorless, until Morgon met his eyes and saw a faint smile, as at some incongruity. Morgon turned a little to the tall, frail wizard beside him, with the voice of a Caithnard Master. His face was worn, ascetic, but Morgon, watching him step forward, sensed the unexpected strength in his lean body.

He said tentatively, "Iff?"

"Yes." His hand slid very gently up Morgon's shoulder, taking the crow, and Morgon thought suddenly of the books the Morgol of Herun had brought to Caithnard with drawings of wildflowers down their precise margins.

"You are the scholar who loves wild things."

The wizard glanced up from the crow, his still face surprised, suddenly vulnerable. The crow was staring at him darkly, not a feather moving. The hawk-faced wizard slid the skull he was holding into a crevice and crossed the room.

"We sent a crow much like that back to Anuin, not long ago." His spare, restless voice was like his eyes, at once fierce and patient.

Nun exclaimed, "Raederle!" Her voice slid pleasantly in and out of her pigherder's accent. "What in Hel's name are you doing here?"

Iff looked startled. He put the crow back on Morgon's shoulder and said to it, "I beg your pardon." He added to Morgon, "Your wife?"

"No. She won't marry me. She won't go home, either. But she is capable of taking care of herself."

"Against Ghisteslwchlohm?" A hawk's eyes met the crow's a full moment, then the crow shifted nervously back under Morgon's ear. He wanted suddenly to take the bird and hide it in his tunic next to his heart. The wizard's thin brows were puckered curiously. "I served the Kings of An and Aum for centuries. After the destruction of Lungold, I became a falcon, constantly caught, growing old and escaping to grow young again. I have worn jesses and bells and circled the wind to return to the hands of Kings of Anuin for centuries. None of them, not even Mathom of An, had the power even to see behind my eyes. There is great, restless power in her. . . . She reminds me of someone, a falcon-memory . . ."

Morgon touched the crow gently, uncertain in its silence. "She'll tell you," he said at last, and the expression on the aged, proud face changed.

"Is she afraid of us? For what conceivable reason? In falcon-shape, I took meat from her father's bare hand."

"You are Talies," Morgon said suddenly, and the wizard nodded. "The historian. At Caithnard, I read what you wrote about Hed."

"Well." The sharp eyes were almost smiling again. "I wrote that many centuries ago. No doubt Hed has changed since then, to produce the Star-Bearer along with plow horses and beer."

"No. If you went back, you would recognize it." He remembered the wraiths of An, then, and his voice caught slightly. He turned to the wizard built like a Ymris warrior. "And you are Aloil. The poet. You wrote love poems to—" His voice stuck again, this time in embarrassment. But Nun was smiling.

"Imagine anyone bothering to remember all that after a thousand years and more. You were well-educated at that College."

"The writings of the Lungold wizards—those that were not destroyed here—formed the base of riddlery." He added, sensing a sudden question in Aloil's mind, "Part of your work is at Caithnard, and the rest in the king's library at Caerweddin. Astrin Ymris had most of your poetry."

"Poetry." The wizard swept a knotted hand through his hair. "It should have been destroyed here. It was worth little more than that. You come bearing memories into this place, tales of a realm that we will not live to see again. We came here to kill Ghisteslwchlohm or die."

"I didn't," Morgon said softly. "I came to ask the Founder some questions."

The wizard's inward gaze seemed to pull itself out of memory, turn toward him. "Questions!"

"It's proper," Nun said soothingly. "He is a riddle-master."

"What has riddlery to do with this?"

"Well." Then her teeth clamped back down on her pipe, and she sent up a stream of little, perturbed puffs without answering.

Iff asked practically, "Do you have the strength?"

"To kill him? Yes. To hold his mind and get what knowledge I need . . . I must. I'll find the power. He is no use to me dead. But I can't fight shape-changers at the same time. And I am not sure how powerful they are."

"You do complicate matters," Nun murmured. "We came here for such a simple purpose . . ."

"I need you alive."

"Well. It's nice to be needed. Look around you." The firelight seemed to follow her hand as she gestured. "There were twenty-nine wizards and over two hundred men and women of talent studying here seven centuries ago. Of those, we are burying two hundred and twenty-four. Twenty-three, not counting Suth. And you know how he died. You have walked through this place. It is a great cairn of wizardry. There is power still in the ancient bones, which is why we are burying them, so centuries from now the small witches and sorcerers of the realm will not come hunting thighbones and fingerbones for their spells. The dead of Lungold deserve some peace. I know you broke Ghistesl-wchlohm's power to free us. But when you pursued that harpist instead of him, you gave him time to strengthen his powers. Are you so sure now that you can hold back a second destruction?"

"No. I am certain of nothing. Not even my own name, so I move from riddle to riddle. Ghisteslwchlohm built and destroyed Lungold because of these stars." He slid his hair back. "They drove me out of Hed into his hands—and I would have stayed in Hed forever, content to make beer and breed plow horses, never knowing you were alive, or that the High One in Erlenstar Mountain was a lie. I need to know what these stars are. Why Ghisteslwchlohm was not afraid of the High One. Why he wants me alive, powerful yet trapped. What power he is watching me stumble into. If I kill him, the realm will be rid of him, but I will still have questions no one will ever answer—like a starving man possessing gold in a land where gold has no value. Do you understand?" he asked Aloil suddenly, and saw in the burled shoulders, the hard, scrolled face, the great, twisted tree he had been for seven centuries on King's Mouth Plain.

"I understand," the wizard said softly, "where I have been for seven hundred years. Ask him your questions. Then, if you die, or if you let him escape, I will kill him or die. You understand revenge. As for the stars on your face . . . I do not know how to begin to place any hope in them. I don't understand all your actions. If we survive to walk out of Lungold alive, I will find a need to understand them . . . especially the power and impulse that made you tamper with the land-law of An. But for now . . . you freed us, you dredged our names out of memory, you found your way down here to stand with us among our dead . . . you are a young, tired prince of Hed, with a blood-stained tunic and a crow on your shoulder, and a power behind your eyes straight out of Ghisteslwchlohm's heart. Was it because of you that I spent seven centuries as an oak, staring into the sea wind? What freedom or doom have you brought us back to?"

"I don't know." His throat ached. "I'll find you an answer."

"You will." His voice changed then, wonderingly. "You will, Riddle-Master. You do not promise hope."

"No. Truth. If I can find it."

There was a silence. Nun's pipe had gone out. Her lips were parted a little, as if she were watching something blurred, uncertain begin to take shape before her. "Almost," she whispered, "you make me hope. But in Hel's name, for what?" Then she stirred out of her thoughts and touched the rent in Morgon's tunic, shifting it to examine the clean scar beneath. "You had some trouble along the road. You didn't get that in crow-shape."

"No." He stopped, reluctant to continue, but they were waiting for an answer. He said softly, bitterly, to the floor, "I followed Deth's harping one night and walked straight into another betrayal." There was not a sound around him. "Ghisteslwchlohm was looking for me along Trader's Road. And he found me. He trapped Raederle, so that I could not use power against him. He was going to take me back to Erlenstar Mountain. But the shape-changers found us all. I escaped from them"—he touched the scar on his face—"by that much. I hid under illusion and escaped. I haven't seen any of them since we began to fly. Maybe they all killed each other. Somehow I doubt it." He added, feeling their silence like a spell, compelling him, drawing words from him, "The High One killed his harpist." He shook his head a little, pulling back from their silence, unable to give them more. He heard Iff draw breath, felt the wizard's skilled, quieting touch.

Talies said abruptly, "Where was Yrth during all this?"

Morgon's eyes moved from a splinter of bone on the floor. "Yrth."

"He was with you on Trader's Road."

"No one was—" He stopped. A hint of night air found its way past illusion, shivered through the chamber; the light fluttered like something trapped. "No one was with us." Then he remembered the Great Shout out of nowhere, and the mysterious, motionless figure watching him in the night. He whispered incredulously, "Yrth?"

They looked at one another. Nun said, "He left Lungold to find you, give you what help he could. You never saw him?"

"Once—I might have, when I needed help. It must have been Yrth. He never told me. He may have lost me when we began to fly." He paused, thinking back. "There was one moment, after the horse struck me, when I could barely hold my own illusion. The shape-changers could have killed me then. They should have. I expected it. But nothing touched me. . . . He may have been there, to save my life in that moment. But if he stayed there after I escaped—"

"He would have let us know, surely," Nun said, "if he needed help." She passed the back of a workworn hand over her brow worriedly. "But where is he, I wonder. An old man wandering up and down Trader's Road looking for you no doubt, along with the Founder and shape-changers. . . ."

"He should have told me. If he needed help, I could have fought for him; that's what I came for."

"You could have lost your life for his sake, too. No." She seemed to be answering her own doubt. "He'll come in his own time. Maybe he stayed to bury the harpist. Yrth taught him harp songs once, here in this college." She was silent again, while Morgon watched two battered faces of the dead against the far wall shift closer and closer together. He closed his eyes before they merged. He heard the crow cry from a distance; a painful grip on his shoulder kept him from falling. He opened his eyes to meet the hawk's stare and felt the sudden, cold sweat that had broken out on his face.

"I'm tired," he said.

"With reason." Iff loosened his hold. His face was seamed with a network of hair-fine lines. "There is venison on a spit in the kitchens—the only room left with four walls and a roof. We have been sleeping down here, but there are pallets beside the hearth. There will be a guard outside the door, watching the grounds."

"A guard?"

"One of the Morgol's guards. They provide for us, out of the Morgol's courtesy."

"Is the Morgol still here?"

"No. She resisted every argument we gave her to go home, until suddenly about two weeks ago, without explanation she went back to Herun." He raised his hand, pulled a torch out of air and darkness. "Come, I'll show you the way."

Morgon followed him silently back through his illusion, through the broken rooms, down another winding flight of stone steps into the kitchens. The smell of meat cooling over the embers made even his bones feel hollow. He sat down at the long, half-charred table, while Iff found a knife and some chipped goblets.

"There is wine, bread, cheese, fruit—the guards keep us well-supplied." He paused, then smoothed a feather on the crow's wing. "Morgon," he said softly, "I have no idea what the dawn will bring. But if you had not chosen to come here, we would be facing certain death. Whatever blind hope kept us alive for seven centuries must have been rooted in you. You may be afraid to hope, but I am not." His hand rested briefly against Morgon's scarred cheek. "Thank you for coming." He straightened. "I'll leave you here; we work through the night and rarely sleep. If you need us, call."

He tossed his torch into the hearth and left. Morgon stared down at the table, at the still shadow of the crow on the wood. He stirred finally, said its name. It seemed about to change shape; its wings lifted to fly down from his shoulder. Then the outer door to the kitchens opened abruptly. The guard entered: a young, dark-haired woman so familiar yet unfamiliar that Morgon could only stare at her. She stopped dead, halfway across the room, staring at him without blinking. He saw her swallow.

"Morgon?"

He stood up. "Lyra." She had grown; her body was tall and supple in the short, dark tunic. Her face in the shadows was half the child's he remembered and half the Morgol's. She could not seem to move. So he went to her. As he neared, he saw her hand shift on her spear; he paused midstep and said, "It's me."

"I know." She swallowed again, her eyes still startled, very dark. "How did . . . how did you come into the city? No one saw you."

"You have a guard on the walls?"

She gave a little jerky nod. "There's no other defense in the city. The Morgol sent for us."

"You. Her land-heir."

Her chin came up slightly in a gesture he remembered. "There is something I stayed here to do." Then, slowly, she came toward him, her expression changing in the wash of the firelight. She put her arms around him, her face bowed hard against his shoulder. He heard her spear clatter to the floor behind him. He held her tightly; something of her clear, proud mind brushing like a good wind through his mind. She loosed him finally, stepping back to look at him again. Her dark brows puckered at his scars.

"You should have had a guard along Trader's Road. I went with Raederle, searching for you last spring, but you were always a step ahead of us."

"I know."

"No wonder the guards didn't recognize you. You look—you look like—" She seemed to see the crow for the first time, motionless, watching from under his hair. "That's—is that Mathom?"

"Is he here?"

"He was, for a while. So was Har, but the wizards sent them both home."

His hands tightened on her shoulders. "Har?" he said incredulously. "In Hel's name, why did he come?"

"To help you. He stayed with the Morgol in her camp outside of Lungold until the wizards persuaded him to leave."

"Are they so sure he went? Have they checked the mind of every blue-eyed wolf around Lungold?"

"I don't know."

"Lyra, there are shape-changers coming. They know they can find me here."

She was silent; he watched her calculate. "The Morgol had us bring a supply of weapons for the traders; there were very few in the city. But the traders—Morgon, they're not fighters. The wall will crumble like old bread under attack. There are two hundred guards . . ." Her brows creased again, helplessly, and she looked suddenly young. "Do you know what they are? The shape-changers?"

"No." Something unfamiliar was building behind her eyes: the first hint of fear he had ever seen in her. He said, more harshly than he intended to, "Why?"

"Have you heard the news from Ymris?"

"No."

She drew breath. "Heureu Ymris lost Wind Plain. In a single afternoon. For months he held the rebel army back, at the edge of the plain. The Lords of Umber and Marcher had gathered an army to push the rebels back into the sea. It would have reached Wind Plain within two days. But suddenly an army greater than anything anyone knew existed swarmed out of Meremont and Tor across Wind Plain. Men who survived said they found themselves fighting—fighting men they swore they had already killed. The king's army was devastated. A trader was caught in the battlefield selling horses. He fled with the survivors into Rhun, and then into Lungold. He said—he said the plain was a nightmare of unburied dead. And Heureu Ymris has not been seen anywhere in Ymris since that day."

Morgon's lips moved soundlessly. "Is he dead?"

"Astrin Ymris says no. But even he can't find the king. Morgon, if I must fight shape-changers with two hundred guards, I will. But if you could just tell me what we are fighting? . . ."

"I don't know." He felt the crow's claws through his tunic. "We'll take this battle out of the city. I didn't come here to destroy Lungold a second time. I'll give the shape-changers no reason to fight here."

"Where will you go?"

"Into the forest, up a mountain—anywhere, as long as it's not here."

"I'm coming," she said.

"No. Absolutely—"

"The guards can stay here in the city, in case they are needed. But I am coming with you. It's a matter of honor."

He looked at her silently, his eyes narrowed. She met them calmly. "What did you do?" he asked. "Did you take a vow?"

"No. I don't take vows. I make decisions. This one I made in Caerweddin, when I learned that you had lost the land-rule of Hed and you were still alive. I remembered, when you spoke of Hed in Herun, how much the land-rule meant to you. This time, you will have a guard."

"Lyra. I have a guard. Five wizards."

"And me."

"No. You are the land-heir of Herun. I have no intention of taking your body back to Crown City to give it to the Morgol."

She slipped out of his hold with a swift, light twist that left his hands gripping air. She swept her spear from the floor, held it upright beside her, standing at easy attention. "Morgon," she said softly, "I have made a decision. You fight with wizardry; I fight with a spear. It's the only way I know how. Either I fight here, or one day I will be forced to fight in Herun itself. When you meet Ghisteslwchlohm again, I will be there." She turned, then remembered what she had come in for. She took an ancient torch out of its socket and dipped it into the fire. "I'm going to check the grounds. Then I'll come back and guard you until dawn."

"Lyra," he said wearily, "please just go home."

"No, I'm simply doing what I am trained to do. And so," she added without a suspicion of irony, "are you." Then her eyes moved to the crow. "Is that something I should know to guard?"

He hesitated. The crow sat like a black thought on his shoulder, absolutely motionless. "No," he said finally. "Nothing will harm it. I swear that by my life."

Her dark eyes widened suddenly, going back to it. She said softly, puzzled, after a moment, "Once we were friends."

She left him. He went to the fire, but thoughts lay hard, knotted in his belly, and he could not eat. He stilled the fire, sent it back into the embers. Then he lay down on one of the pallets, his face on his forearm, turned to look at the crow. It rested beside him on the stones. He reached out with his free hand, smoothed its feathers again and again.

"I will never teach you another shape," he whispered. "Raederle, what happened on Wind Plain has nothing to do with you. Nothing." He stroked it, talking to it, arguing, pleading without response until his eyes closed and he melted finally into its darkness.

Dawn broke into his dreams as the door swung open and shut with a bang. He startled up, his heart pounding, and saw the young, surprised face of a strange guard. She bent her head courteously.

"I'm sorry, Lord." She heaved a bucket of water and an earthen jar of fresh milk onto the table. "I didn't see you sleeping there."

"Where is Lyra?"

"On the north wall, overlooking the lake. There is a small army of some kind coming across the backlands. Goh rode out to check it." He got to his feet, murmuring. She added, "Lyra told me to ask you if you could come."

"I'll come." Nun, in a cloud of pipe smoke, drifted into the corner of his eye, and he started again. She put a soothing hand on his shoulder.

"You'll go where?"

"Some kind of an army is coming; maybe help, maybe not." He scooped water onto his face from the bucket and poured milk into a cracked goblet and drained it. Then his head swung back to the pallet he had been sleeping on. "Where—?" He took a step toward it, his eyes running frantically over the iron and brass pots on the wall, over the smoky roof beams. "Where in Hel's name . . ." He dropped to his knees, searched the trestles under the table, then the wood-box, and even the ashes on the grate. He straightened, still on his knees, stared, white, up at Nun. "She left me."

"Raederle?"

"She's gone. She wouldn't even talk to me. She flew away and left me." He got to his feet, slumped against the chimney stones. "It was that news out of Ymris. About the shape-changers."

"Shape-changers." Her voice sounded flat. "That's what was troubling her then? Her own power?"

He nodded. "She's afraid . . ." His hand dropped soundlessly against the stones. "I've got to find her. She's foresworn—and the ghost of Ylon is already troubling her."

Nun cursed the dead king with a pigherder's fluency. Then she put her fingers to her eyes. "No," she said tiredly, "I'll find her. Maybe she will talk to me. She used to. You see what that army is. I wish Yrth would come; he worries me. But I don't dare call either him or Raederle; my call might find its way straight into the Founder's mind. Now. Let me think. If I were a princess of An with a shape-changer's power, flying around like a crow, where would I go—"

"I know where I would go," Morgon murmured. "But she hates beer."

He went on foot through the city toward the docks, looking for a crow as he walked. The fishing-boats were all out on the broad lake, but there were other small craft, mining barges and flat-bottomed trading-vessels nosing out of the docks full of cargo to peddle among the trappers and herdsmen around the lake. He saw no crows on any of the masts. He found Lyra, finally, standing at a piece of sagging parapet to one side of a gate. Much of the north wall seemed to be underwater, supporting the docks; the rest was little more than broad, arched gates, with fish stalls set up against the wall between them. Morgon, ignoring the glassy-eyed stare of a fishwife, vanished in front of her and appeared at Lyra's side. She only blinked a little when she saw him, as if she had grown used to the unpredictable movements of wizards. She pointed east of the lake, and he saw tiny flecks of light in the distant forest.

"Can you see what it is?" she asked.

"I'll try." He caught the mind of a hawk circling the trees outside of the city. The noise of the city rumbled away to the back of his mind until he heard only the lazy morning breeze and the piercing cry of another hawk in the distance who had missed its kill. The hawk's circles grew wider under his prodding; he had a slow, sweeping vision of pine, hot sunlight on dried needles that slipped into shadows, through underbrush, then out into the light again onto hot, bare rock, where lizards under the hawk-shadow startled into crevices. The hawk-brain sorted every sound, every vague slink of shadow through the bracken. He urged it farther east, making a broad spiral of its circles. Finally, it swung across a line of warriors picking their way through the trees. He made the hawk return to the line again and again, until finally a movement in the full light below snapped its attention, and as it flung itself eastward, he shirred himself from its mind.

He slid down against the parapet. The sun struck him at an odd angle, much higher than he expected.

"They look like Ymris warriors," he said tiredly, "who have spent days crossing the backlands. They were unshorn, and their horses were balky. They didn't smell of the sea. They smelled of sweat."

Lyra studied him, her hands at her hips. "Should I trust them?"

"I don't know."

"Maybe Goh can tell. I gave her orders to watch them and listen to them and then to speak to them if she thought it wise. She has good sense."

"I'm sorry." He pulled himself to his feet. "I think they're men, but I am in no mood to trust anyone."

"Are you going to leave the city?"

"I don't know. Yrth is still missing, and now Raederle is gone. If I leave, she won't know where I am. If you sight nothing more dangerous, we can wait a little. If they are Ymris warriors, they can deploy themselves around this travesty of a defense wall and everyone here will feel much easier."

She was silent a moment, searching the breeze, as for a shadow of dark wings. "She'll come back," she said softly. "She has great courage."

He dropped his arm around her shoulders, hugged her briefly. "So do you. I wish you would go home."

"The Morgol placed her guard in the service of the Lungold merchants, to watch over the welfare of the city."

"She didn't place her land-heir in the service of the merchants. Did she?"

"Oh, Morgon, stop arguing. Can't you do something about this wall? It's useless and dangerous and dropping apart under my feet."

"All right. I'm not doing anything else worthwhile."

She turned her head, kissed his cheekbone. "Raederle is probably somewhere thinking. She'll come back to you." He opened his mouth; she shrugged out of his hold, her face suddenly averted. "Go fix the wall."

He spent hours repairing it, trying not to think. Ignoring the traffic passing around him—the farmers and merchants eyeing him uneasily, the traders who recognized him—he stood with his hands and his face against the ancient stones. His mind melded into their ponderous silence until he sensed their sagging, their precarious balance against the buttresses. He built illusions of stone within the archways, buttressing them with his mind. The blocked gates snarled carts and horses, started fights, and sent crowds to the city council chambers to be warned of the impending dangers. The traffic leaving through the main gate increased enormously. Street urchins gathered around him as he circled the city. They watched him work, followed at his heels, delighted, marvelling as non-existent stones built under his hands. In the late afternoon, laying his sweating face against the stones in an archway, he felt the touch of another power. He closed his eyes and traversed a silence he had learned well. For a long time, his mind moving deep into the stones, he heard nothing but the occasional, minute shift of a particle of mortar. Finally, edging onto the sunwarmed surface of the outer wall, he felt wedged against it a buttress of raw power. He touched it tentatively with his thoughts. It was a force pulled from the earth itself, rammed against the weakest point of the stone. He withdrew slowly, awed.

Someone was standing at his shoulder, saying his name over and over. He turned questioningly, found one of the Morgol's guards with a red-haired man in leather and mail beside her. The guard's broad, browned face was sweating, and she looked as tired as Morgon felt. Her gruff voice was patient, oddly pleasant.

"Lord, my name is Goh. This is Teril Umber, son of the High Lord Rork Umber of Ymris. I took the responsibility of guiding him and his warriors into the city." There was a faint tension in her voice and in her calm eyes. Morgon looked at the man silently. He was young but battle-hardened and very tired. He bent his head courteously to Morgon, oblivious of his suspicions.

"Lord, Heureu Ymris sent us out one day before . . . the day before he lost Wind Plain, apparently. We just heard the news from the Morgol's land-heir."

"Was your father at Wind Plain?" Morgon asked suddenly. "I remember him."

Teril Umber nodded wearily. "Yes. I have no idea if he survived or not." Then beneath the drag of his dusty mail, his shoulders straightened. "Well, the king was concerned about the defenselessness of the traders here; he sailed on trade-ships once himself. And of course, he wanted to put as many men as he could spare at your disposal. There are a hundred and fifty of us, to aid the Morgol's guard in defending the city, if there's need."

Morgon nodded. The lean, sweating face with its uncomfortable fringe of beard seemed beyond suspicion. He said, "I hope there's no need. It was generous of the king to spare you."

"Yes. He did exactly that, sending us out of Wind Plain."

"I'm sorry about your father. He was kind to me."

"He talked about you. . . ." He shook his head, running his fingers through his flaming hair. "He's come out of worse," he said without hope. "Well, I'd better talk to Lyra, get men situated before nightfall."

Morgon looked at Goh. The relief in her face told him how worried she had been. He said softly, "Please tell Lyra I'm nearly finished with the wall."

"Yes, Lord."

"Thank you."

She gave him a brief, shy nod, smiling suddenly. "Yes, Lord."

As his work around the wall progressed and the day burned toward a fiery end, he began to feel enclosed by power. The wizard working with him silently on the other side of the wall strengthened stones before he touched them, sealed broken places with grey, grainy illusions, balanced cracked walls against a weight of power. The walls lost their look of having grown battered by sunlight and hunched under winter winds. They stood firm again, patched, buttressed, rolling without a break around the city, challenging entrance.

Morgon wove a force from stone to stone to seal one last crack in some ancient mortar, then leaned against the wall wearily, his face in his arms. He could smell the twilight riding over the fields. The stillness of the last moments of the sunset, the peaceful, sleepy bird songs made him think for a moment of Hed. A distant crow call kept him from falling asleep against the wall. He roused himself and stepped into one of the two front gates he had left open. A man stood in the archway at the other end, with a crow on his shoulder.

He was a tall old man, with short grey hair and a battered, craggy face. He was talking in crow-language to the crow; Morgon understood some of it. As the crow answered, a hard fist of worry around Morgon's heart eased until his heart seemed to rest on some warm place, on the hand of the ancient wizard, perhaps, scarred as it was with vesta-horns. He went towards them quietly, his mind lulled by the sense of the wizard's great power, and by his kindness to Raederle.

But before he reached them, he saw the wizard break off mid-sentence and toss the crow into the air. He cried something at it that Morgon did not understand. Then he vanished. Morgon, his breathing dry, quick, saw the twilight moving down Trader's Road, surely, soundlessly; a wave of horsemen the color of the evening sky. Before he could move, a light the color of molten gold lit the archway around him. The wall lurched; stones, murmuring, undulating, shrugged off a blast of power into the street that exploded the cobblestones and slammed Morgon to his knees. He pulled himself up and turned.

The heart of the city was in flames.

TWO OF THE Ymris warriors were already struggling to close the main gates as he slipped back into the city. The hinges groaned, flaking rust as the slabs of oak shuddered, rising out of the ruts they had rested in for centuries. Morgon slapped them shut with a thought that nearly cost him his life. A mind, familiar, deadly, groped at the flash of power, gripped him across the distance. The dark air in front of him tore apart with a blue-white seam, so quick and strangely beautiful that he could only stand and watch it. Then his bones seemed to fly piecemeal in all directions, while his brain burned like a star. He felt stone behind him, dimly, and let his mind flow into it, grow blank, motionless. The power slid away. He gathered his bones back out of the night and realized vaguely that he was still alive. One of the warriors, his face bleeding, pulled him off the ground. The other man was dead.

"Lord—"

"I'm all right." He flung his thoughts out of the fraction of time he stood in. When the next flare of energy raked across the night, he stepped away from it, into another moment near the burning school. People were running down the street toward the main gates: guards, armed Ymris warriors, traders, merchants, and fishermen carrying their swords with a fierce, clumsy determination. Children stood at the edge of the school grounds, transfixed in the play of light, their faces turning red, gold, purple. Then the wall of a house behind them shattered, swept an arc of fiery stones toward them. They scattered, screaming.

Morgon gathered a memory of the fabric of energy out of his thoughts, fed it with a power he had never tapped before. He let it build through him eating at all his thoughts and inner movements until it spat away from him, humming a high, dangerous language. It crackled luminously toward the source of power within the walls, disappeared within them, but it did not detonate. It reappeared before it struck, shooting back at Morgon with the same deadly intensity. He stared at it incredulously for a split second, then opened his mind to absorb it back. It imploded into darkness within him. It was followed, before he could even blink, by a blast of light and fire that jarred to the ground floor of his defenseless mind. It flung him flat on the cobblestones, blinded, gasping for air, while another surge of energy pounded into him. He let his awareness flow away from it, down into the cracks between the stones, into the dark, silent earth beneath them. A fragment of stone blasted to pieces near him, split his cheek, but he did not feel it. His body anchored to earth, he began to draw out of the mute, eyeless living things in it a silence that would shelter him. From moles and earthworms and tiny snakes, from the pale roots of grass, he wove a stillness into his mind. When he rose finally, the world seemed dark around him, flecked by minute, soundless flashes of light. He moved with an earthworm's blind instinct into darkness.

The mind-disguise took him safely across the grounds into the school. Fire had kindled the ancient power still locked within the stones; cold, brilliant flames swarmed across the broken walls, eating at the energy in the heart of them. Morgon, his mind still tapping the slow, languageless world beneath his feet, did not feel the dangerous wash of fire around him. A wall crumbled as he passed it; the stones scattered like coals across his shadow. He felt only a distant perturbation in the earth, as if it had shifted slightly in some point deep in its core. Then an odd, gentle touch in his mind brought his thoughts out of the earth to follow it curiously. He broke his own binding, stood blinking in the tumult of sound and fire. The unexpected touch turned imperative, and he realized that the room he had walked into was sliding into itself. He had no time to move; he shaped his mind to the fiery stones thundering toward him, became part of their bulky flow, broke with them and crashed into a fuming stillness. He dragged his shape out of them after a moment, pieced his thoughts back together. He saw Nun, then, elusive in the shimmering air, watching him. She said nothing, vanishing almost as he saw her, the fiery bowl of her pipe lingering a moment alone in the air.

The battle raging in the heart of the school was rocking the ground. He picked his way carefully toward it. From the flare of light through the jagged, beautiful windows, he knew that it was centered where it had begun: in the great circular hall that still echoed the cry of the Founder's name. He sensed suddenly, from the ease with which power was deflected away from the hall, that the battle was one-sided as yet. The Founder was toying with the wizards, using their lives as bait to lure Morgon to him. The next moment gave Morgon proof of that. He felt the Founder's mind sweep across the flames like a black beacon, searching. He touched Morgon's mind briefly: a familiar sense of dangerous, immense power yawned before him. But he did not try to hold Morgon. His mind withdrew, and Morgon heard a scream that made his blood run cold.

Aloil was being wrestled out of air into shape not far from him. He fought the dark pull over his mind with a desperate, furious intensity, but he could not free himself. His shape changed again, slowly. Great wind-twisted limbs pulled from his shoulders; his desperate face blurred behind oak bark, a dark hollow splitting the trunk where his mouth had been. Roots forked into the dead ground; his hair tangled into leafless twigs. A living oak stood on the grounds where nothing had grown for seven centuries. A lightning bolt of power seared toward it, to sunder it to the roots.

Morgon flung his mind open, encompassed it before it struck the tree. He threw it back at Ghistelwchlohm, heard one of the walls explode. Then, reaching ruthlessly into the Founder's stronghold, he joined their minds, as they had been joined before in the blackness of Erlenstar Mountain.

He absorbed the power that battered across his thoughts, letting it burn away at the bottom of his mind. Slowly his hold strengthened, until the Founder's mind was familiar to him once more, as if it lay behind his own eyes. He ignored experiences, impulses, the long mysterious history of the Founder's life, concentrating only on the source of his power, to drain it to exhaustion. He sensed the moment when Ghisteslwchlohm realized what he was doing, in the raw, frantic pulses of energy that nearly shook him loose again and again, until he forgot he possessed anything but a will and a mind at war with itself. The power-play stopped finally. He drew deeper, ferreting power and drawing it into himself, until the Founder yielded something to him unexpectedly: he found himself absorbing once more the knowledge of the land-law of Hed.

His hold faltered, broke in a wave of fury and revulsion at the irony. A chaotic flare of rage slapped him across the ground. He groped dizzily for shelter, but his mind could shape nothing but fire. The power broke through him again, sent him sprawling across burning rock. Someone pulled him off; the wizards, surrounding him, drew Ghisteslwchlohm's attention with a swift, fierce barrage that shook the inner buildings. Talies, beating at his smoldering tunic, said tersely, "Just kill him."

"No."

"You stubborn farmer from Hed, if I survive this battle I am going to study riddlery." His head turned suddenly. "There is fighting in the city. I hear death cries."

"There's an army of shape-changers. They came in the front gate while we were watching the back. I saw . . . I think I saw Yrth. Can he talk to crows?"

The wizard nodded. "Good. He must be fighting with the traders." He helped Morgon to his feet. The earth rocked beneath them, sent him sprawling to the ground on top of Morgon. He shifted to his knees. Morgon rolled wearily to his feet and stood gazing at the shell of the hall. "He's weakening in there."

"He is?"

"I'm going in."

"How?"

"I'll walk. But I have to distract his attention . . ." He thought a moment, rubbing a burn on his wrist. His mind, scanning the grounds carefully, came to rest in the ancient, ruined library, with its hundreds of books of wizardry. The half-charred pages were still charged with power: with bindings woven into their locks, with unspoken names, with the energy of the minds that had scrawled all their experiences of power onto the pages. He woke that dormant power, gathered threads of it into his mind. Its chaos nearly overwhelmed him for a moment. Speaking aloud, he spun a weird fabric of names, words, scraps of students' grotesque spells, a tumult of knowledge and power that formed strange shapes in the flaring lights. Shadows, stones that moved and spoke, eyeless birds with wings the colors of wizards' fire, shambling forms that built themselves out of the scorched earth, he sent marching toward Ghisteslwchlohm. He woke the wraiths of animals killed during the destruction: bats, crows, weasels, ferrets, foxes, shadowy white wolves; they swarmed through the night around him, seeking their lives from him until he sent them to the source of power. He had begun to work the roots of dead trees out of the earth when the vanguard of his army struck the Founder's stronghold. The onslaught of fragments of power, clumsy, nearly harmless, yet too complex to ignore, drew the Founder's attention. For a moment there was another lull, during which the wraith of a wolf whined an eerie death song. Morgon ran noiselessly toward the hall. He was nearly there when his own army fled back out of the hall, running around him and over him, scattering into the night toward the city.

Morgon flung his thoughts outward, herding the strange, misshapen creatures he had made back into oblivion before they terrorized Lungold. The effort of finding bats' wraiths and shapes made out of clods of earth drained all his attention. When he finished finally, his mind spun again with names and words he had had to take back into himself. He filled his mind with fire, dissolving the remnants of power in it, drawing from its strength and clarity. He realized then, his heart jumping, that he stood in near-darkness.

An eerie silence lay over the grounds. Piles of broken wall still blazed red-hot from within, but the night was undisturbed over the school, and he could see stars. He stood listening, but the only fighting he heard came from the streets. He moved again, soundlessly, entered the hall.

It was black and silent as the caves of Erlenstar Mountain. He made one futile attempt to batter against the darkness and gave up. On impulse, he shaped the sword at his side and drew it. He held it by the blade, turned the eye of the stars to the darkness. He drew fire out of the night behind him, kindled it in the stars. A red light split across the dark, showed him Ghisteslwchlohm.

They looked at one another silently. The Founder seemed gaunt under the strange light, the bones pushing out under his skin. His voice sounded tired, neither threatening nor defeated. He said curiously, "You still can't see in the dark."

"I'll learn."

"You must eat darkness. . . . You are a riddle, Morgon. You track a harpist all the way across the realm to kill him because you hated his harping, but you won't kill me. You could have, while you held my mind, but you didn't. You should try now. But you won't. Why?"

"You don't want me dead. Why?"

The wizard grunted. "A riddle-game . . . I might have known. How did you survive to escape from me that day on Trader's Road? I barely escaped, myself."

Morgon was silent. He lowered the sword, let the tip rest on the ground. "What are they? The shape-changers? You are the High One. You should know."

"They were a legend here and there, a fragment of poetry, a bit of wet kelp and broken shell . . . a strange accusation made by a Ymris prince, until you left your land to find me. Now . . . they are becoming a nightmare. What do you know about them?"

"They're ancient. They can be killed. They have enormous power, but they rarely use it. They're killing traders and warriors in the streets of Lungold. I don't know what in Hel's name they are."

"What do they see in you?"

"Whatever you see, I assume. You will answer that one for me."

"Undoubtedly. The wise man knows his own name."

"Don't taunt me." The light shivered a little between his hands. "You destroyed Lungold to keep my name from me. You hid all knowledge of it, you kept watch over the College at Caithnard—"

"Spare me the history of my life."

"That's what I want from you. Master Ohm. High One. Where did you find the courage to assume the name of the High One?"

"No one else claimed it."

"Why?"

The wizard was silent a moment. "You could force answers from me," he said at length. "I could reach out, bind the minds of the Lungold wizards again, so that you could not touch me. I could escape; you could pursue me. You could escape; I could pursue you. You could kill me, which would be exhausting work, and you would lose your most powerful protector."

"Protector." He dropped the syllables like three dry bones.

"I do want you alive. Do the shape-changers? Listen to me—"

"Don't," he said wearily, "even try. I'll break your power once and for all. Oddly enough I don't care if you live or die. At least you make sense to me, which is more than I can say for the shape-changers, or . . ." He stopped. The wizard took a step toward him.

"Morgon, you have looked at the world out of my eyes and you have my power. The more you touch land-law, the more men will remember that."

"I have no intention of meddling with land-law! What do you think I am?"

"You have already started."

Morgon stared at him. He said softly, "You are wrong. I have not even begun to see out of your eyes. What in Hel's name do you see when you look at me?"

"Morgon, I am the most powerful wizard in this realm. I could fight for you."

"Something frightened you that day on Trader's Road. You need me to fight for you. What happened? Did you see the limits of your power in the reflection of a sea-green eye? They want me, and you don't want to yield me to them. But you are not so sure anymore that you can fight an army of seaweed."

Ghisteslwchlohm was silent, his face hollowed with a scarlet wash of shadows. "Can you?" he asked softly. "Who will help you? The High One?" Then Morgon felt the sudden stirring of his mind, a wave of thought encompassing the hall, the grounds, seeking out the minds of the wizards, to shape itself to them, bind them once again. Morgon raised the sword; the stars kindled a blade of light in Ghisteslwchlohm's eyes. He winced away from it, his concentration broken. Then his hands rose, snarling threads of light between his fingers. The light swept back into the stars as if they had sucked it into themselves. Darkness crouched like a live thing within the hall, barring even the moonlight. The sword grew cold in Morgon's grip. The coldness welled up his hands, into his bones, behind his eyes: a binding numbing his movements, his thoughts. His own awareness of it only strengthened it; struggling to move only bound him still. So he yielded to it, standing motionless in the night, knowing it was illusion, and that the acceptance of it, like the acceptance of the impossible, was the only way beyond it. He became its stillness, its coldness, so that when the vast power that was gathering in some dim world struck him at last, his numb, dark mind blocked it like a lump of iron.

He heard Ghisteslwchlohm's furious, incredulous curse and shook himself free of the spell. He caught the wizard's mind an instant before he vanished. A last rake of power across his mind shook his hold a little, and he realized that he was close to the edge of his own endurance. But the wizard was exhausted; even his illusion of darkness was broken. Light blazed out of the stars once more; the broken walls around them were luminous with power. Ghisteslwchlohm raised a hand, as if to work something out of the burning stones, then dropped it wearily. Morgon bound him lightly, and spoke his name.

The name took root in his heart, his thoughts. He absorbed not power, but memories, looking at the world for a few unbroken moments out of Ghisteslwchlohm's mind.

He saw the great hall around them in all its first beauty, the windows burning as with the fires of wizardry, the newly panelled walls smelling of cedar. A hundred faces gazed at him that day, a thousand years before, as he spoke the nine strictures of wizardry. As he spoke, he harvested in secret, even from the mind of the most powerful of them, all knowledge and memory of three stars.

He sat in restless, uneasy power at Erlenstar Mountain. He held the minds of the land-rulers, not to control their actions, but to know them, to study the land-instincts he could never quite master. He watched a land-ruler of Herun riding alone through Isig Pass, coming closer and closer, to ask a riddle of three stars. He twisted the mind of the Morgol's horse; it reared, screaming, and the Morgol Dhairrhuwyth slid down a rocky cliff, catching desperately at boulders that spoke a deep, terrible warning as they thundered after him.

Long before that, he stood in wonder in the vast throne room at Erlenstar Mountain, where legend so old it had no beginning had placed the High One. It was empty. The raw jewels embedded in the stone walls were dim and weathered. Generations of bats clung to the ceiling. Spiders had woven webs frail as illusion around the throne. He had come to ask a question about a dreamer deep in Isig Mountain. But there was no one to ask. He brushed cobwebs from the throne and sat down to puzzle over the emptiness. And as the grey light faded between the rotting doors, he began to spin illusions. . . .

He stood in another silent, beautiful place in another mountain, his mind taking the shape of a strange white stone. It was dreaming a child's dream, and he could barely breathe as he watched the fragile images flow through him. A great city stood on a windy plain, a city that sang with winds in the child's memory. The child saw it from a distance. Its mind was touching leaves, light on tree bark, grass blades; it gazed back at itself from the stolid mind of a toad; its blurred face was refracted in a fish's eyes; its wind-blown hair teased the mind of a bird building a nest. A question beat beneath the dreaming, scoring his heart with fire, as the child reached out to absorb the essence of a single leaf. He asked it finally; the child seemed to turn at his voice, its eye dark and pure and vulnerable as a falcon's eye.

"What destroyed you?"

The sky went grey as stone above the plain; the light faded from the child's face. It stood tensely, listening. The winds snarled across the plain, roiling the long grass. A sound built, too vast for hearing, unendurable. A stone ripped loose from one of the shining walls in the city, sank deep into the ground. Another cracked against a street. The sound broke, then, a deep, shuddering bass roar that held at the heart of it something he recognized, though he could no longer see nor hear, and the fish floated like a white scar on the water, and the bird had been swept out of the tree. . . .

"What is it?" he whispered, reaching through Ghisteslwchlohm's mind, through the child's mind, for the end of the dream. But as he reached, it faded into the wild water, into the dark wind, and the child's eye turned white as stone. Its face became Ghisteslwchlohm's, his eyes sunken with weariness, washed with a light pale as foam.

Morgon, struggling, bewildered, to pick up the thread of his probing, saw something flash out of the corner of his eye. His head snapped around. Stars struck his face; reeling, he lost consciousness a moment. He wrestled back into shimmering light and found himself on the rubble, swallowing blood from a cut in his mouth. He raised his head. The blade of his own sword touched his heart.

The shape-changer who stood over him had eyes as white as the child's. He smiled a greeting and a fine-honed edge of fear rippled the surface of Morgon's thoughts. Ghisteslwchlohm was staring beyond him. He turned his head and saw a woman standing among the broken stones. Her face, quiet, beautiful, was illumined briefly by a red-gold sky. Morgon heard the battle that raged behind her: of swords and spears, wizardry and weapons made of human bone scoured clean in the depths of the sea.

The woman's head bowed. "Star-Bearer." There was no mockery in her voice. "You are beginning to see far too much."

"I'm still ignorant." He swallowed again. "What do you want from me? I still need to ask that. My life or my death?"

"Both. Neither." She looked across the room at Ghisteslwchlohm. "Master Ohm. What shall we do with you? You woke the Star-Bearer to power. The wise man does not forge the blade that will kill him."

"Who are you?" the Founder whispered. "I killed the embers of a dream of three stars a thousand years ago. Where were you then?"

"Waiting."

"What are you? You have no true shape, you have no name—"

"We are named." Her voice was still clear, quiet, but Morgon heard a tone in it that was not human: as if stone or fire had spoken in a soft, rational, ageless voice. The fear stirred through him again, a dead-winter wind, spun of silk and ice. He shaped his fear into a riddle, his own voice sounding numb.

"When—when the High One fled from Erlenstar Mountain, who was it he ran from?"

A flare of power turned half her face liquid gold. She did not answer him. Ghisteslwchlohm's lips parted; the long draw of his breath sounded clear in the turmoil, like the tide's withdrawal.

"No." He took a step back. "No."

Morgon did not realize he had moved until he felt the sudden pain over his heart. His hand reached out toward the wizard. "What is it?" he pleaded. "I can't see!" The cold metal forced him back. His need spat in fire out of the stars in the sword hilt, jolting the shape-changer's hold.

The sword clanged to the floor, lay smoldering. He tried to rise. The shape-changer twisted the throat of his tunic, his burned hand poised to strike. Morgon, staring into his expressionless eyes, sent a blaze of power like a cry into his mind. The cry was lost in a cold, heaving sea. The shape-changer's hand dropped. He pulled Morgon to his feet, left him standing free and bewildered by both the power and the restraint. He flung a last, desperate tendril of thought into the wizard's mind and heard only the echo of the sea.

The battle burst through the ruined walls. Shape-changers pushed traders, exhausted warriors, the Morgol's guards into the hall. Their blades of bone and iron from lost ships thrashed mercilessly through the chaos. Morgon saw two of the guards slain before he could even move. He reached for his sword, the breath pushing hard through his chest. The shape-changer's knee slammed into his heart as he bent. He sagged to his hands and knees, whimpering for one scrap of air. The room grew very quiet around him; he saw only the rubble under his fingers. The silence eddied dizzily about him, whirling to a center. As from a dream he heard at its core the clear, fragile sound of a single harp note.

The battle noises rolled over him again. He heard his voice, dragging harshly at the air. He lifted his head, looking for the sword, and saw Lyra dodging between traders in the doorway. Something stung the back of his throat. He wanted to call out, stop the battle until she left, but he had no strength. She worked her way closer to him. Her face was worn, drawn; there were half-circles like bruises under her eyes. There was dried blood on her tunic, in her hair. Scanning the battlefield, she saw him suddenly. The spear spun in her hand; she flung it toward him. He watched it come without moving, without breathing. It whistled past him, struck the shape-changer and dragged him away from Morgon's side. He grasped the sword and got to his feet unsteadily. Lyra bent, swept up the spear beneath one of the fallen guards. She balanced it, turning in a single swift, clean movement, and threw it.

It soared above the struggle, arched downward, ripping the air with a silver wake in a path to the Founder's heart. His eyes, the color of mist over the sea, could not even blink as he watched it come. Morgon's thoughts flew faster than its shadow. He saw Lyra's expression change into a stunned, weary horror as she realized the wizard was bound, helpless against her; there was no skill, no honor, not even choice in her death-giving. Morgon wanted to shout, snapping the spear with his voice to rescue a dream of truth hidden behind a child's eye, a wizard's eye. His hands moved instead, pulling the harp at his back out of the air. He played it as he shaped it: the last low string whose reverberations set his own sword belling in anguish and shattered every other weapon inside and out of the hall.

Silence settled like old dust over the room. Ymris warriors were staring in disbelief at the odd bits of metal in their hands. Lyra was still watching the air where the spear had splintered apart, two feet from Ghisteslwchlohm. She turned slowly, making the only movement in the hall. Morgon met her eyes; she seemed suddenly so tired she could barely stand. The handful of guard left alive were looking at Morgon, their faces haunted, desperate. The shape-changers were very still. Their shapes seemed uncertain, suddenly, as if at his next movement they would flow into a tide of nothingness. Even the woman he knew as Eriel was still, watching him, waiting.

He caught a glimpse then of the fearsome power they saw in him, lying in some misty region beyond his awareness. The depths of his ignorance appalled him. He turned the harp aimlessly in his hands, holding the shape-changers trapped and having absolutely no idea what to do with them. At the slight uncertain movement, the expression in Eriel's eyes turned to simple amazement.

She moved forward quickly; to take the harp, to kill him with his own sword, to turn his mind, like Ghisteslwchlohm's, vague as the sea, he could only guess. He picked up the sword and stepped back. A hand touched his shoulder, stopped him.

Raederle stood beside him. Her face was pure white within her fiery hair, as if it had been shaped, like the Earth-Masters' children, out of stone. She held him lightly, but she was not seeing him. She said softly to Eriel, "You will not touch him."

The dark eyes held hers curiously. "Ylon's child. Have you made your choice?" She moved again, and Morgon felt the vast, leashed power in Raederle's mind strain free. For one moment, he saw the shape that Eriel had taken begin to fray away from her, reveal something incredibly ancient, wild, like the dark heart of earth or fire. He stood gripped in wonder, his face ashen, knowing he could not move even if the thing Raederle was forcing into shape was his own death.

Then a shout slapped across his mind, jarred him out of his fascination. He stared dizzily across the room. The ancient wizard he had seen at the gates of the city caught his eyes, held them with his own strange light-seared gaze.

The silent shout snapped through him again: *Run!* He did not move. He would not leave Raederle, but he could not help her; he felt incapable even of thought. Then a power gripped his exhausted mind, wrenched him out of shape. He cried out, a fierce, piercing, hawk's protest. The power held him, flung him like a dark, wild wind out of the burning School of Wizards, out of the embattled city into the vast, pathless wasteland of night.

THE SHAPE-CHANGERS pursued him across the backlands. The first night, he bolted across the sky in hawk-shape, the fiery city behind him growing smaller and smaller in the darkness. He flew northward instinctively, away from the kingdoms, marking his path by the smell of water beneath him. By dawn he felt safe. He dropped downward toward the lake shore. Birds drifting to the gentle morning tide swarmed up at his approach. He felt strands of their minds like a network. He broke through it, arching back up in midair. They drove him across the lake into the trees, where he dropped again suddenly, plummeting through air and light like a dark fist, until he touched the ground and vanished. Miles away to the north, he appeared again, kneeling beside the channel of water between two lakes, retching with exhaustion. He sagged down on the bank beside the water. After a while he moved again, dropped his face in the current and drank.

They found him again at dusk. He had caught fish and eaten for the first time in two days. The changeless afternoon light, the river's monotonous voice had lulled him to sleep. He woke abruptly at a squirrel's chattering, and saw high in the blue-grey air a great flock of wheeling birds. Rolling into the water, he changed shape. The current flung him from one relentless sluice of water to another, spun him back downstream into still pools, where hungry water birds dove at him. He fought his way upstream, seeing nothing but a constant, darkening blur that shrugged him from side to side and roared whenever he broke the surface. Finally he foundered into still water. It deepened as he swam. He dove toward the bottom to rest, but the water grew dark and still, so deep he had to come up to breathe before he found the bottom. He swam slowly near the surface, watching moths flutter in the moonlight. He drifted until the lake bottom angled upward, and he found weeds to hide in. He did not move until morning.

Then a tiny fish dove into the sunlight near him, snapped at an insect. Rings of water broke above him. He rose out of the weeds; the water burned around him with the morning sun as he changed shape. He waded out of the lake, stood listening to the silence.

It seemed to roar soundlessly out of lands beyond the known world. The soft morning wind seemed alien, speaking a language he had never learned. He remembered the wild, ancient voices of Wind Plain that had echoed across Ymris with a thousand names and memories. But the voices of the backlands seemed even older, a rootwork of winds that held nothing he could comprehend except their emptiness. He stood for a long time, breathing their loneliness until he felt them begin to hollow him into something as nameless as themselves.

He whispered Raederle's name then. He turned blindly, his thoughts tangling into a hard knot of fear. He wondered if she were still alive, if anyone were left alive in Lungold. He wondered if he should return to the city. His fists pounded rhythmically against tree bark as he thought of her. The tree shivered with his uncertainty; a crow startled out of it, squawking. He raised his head suddenly, stood still as an animal, scenting. The placid lake waters began to stir, boil shapes out of their depths. The blood hammered through him. He opened his mind to the minds of the backland. Several miles away he joined a vast herd of elk moving northward toward the Thul.

He stayed with them as they grazed. He decided to break away at the Thul, follow it eastward until the shape-changers lost him, and then double back to Lungold. Two days later, when the slow herd began gathering at the river, he roamed away from it, eastward along the banks. But part of the herd followed him. He changed shape again, desperately, began flying south in the night. But shapes rose, swirling out of the darkness, beat him northward across the Thul, northward toward White Lady Lake, northward, he began to realize, toward Erlenstar Mountain.

The realization filled him with both fury and terror. On the shores of White Lady Lake, he turned to fight. He waited for them in his own shape, the stars in his sword-hilt flaring a blood-red signal to them across the backlands. But nothing answered his challenge. The hot afternoon was motionless; the waters of the huge lake lay still as beaten silver. Groping, he could not even touch their minds. Finally, as the waning sun drew shadows after it across the lake, he began to breathe a tentative freedom. He sheathed his sword, shrugged himself into wolf-shape. And then he saw them, motionless as air, ranged across his path, shaping themselves out of the blur of light and darkness.

He sparked a flame from the dying sun in his sword hilt, let it burn down the blade. Then he frayed himself into shadow, filled his mind with darkness. He attacked to kill, yet in his exhaustion and hopelessness, he knew he was half-goading them to kill him. He killed two shape-changers before he realized that in some terrible mockery, they had permitted it. They would not fight; they would not let him go south. He changed back into wolf-shape, ran northward along the lake shore into the trees. A great herd of wolves massed behind him. He turned again, flung himself at them. They grappled with him, snarling, snapping until he realized, as he rolled over and over on the bracken with a great wolf whose teeth were locked on his forearm, that it was real. He shook it away from him with a shudder of energy, burned a circle of light around himself. They milled around him restlessly in the dusk, not sure what he was, smelling blood from his torn shoulder. Looking at them, he wanted to laugh suddenly at his mistake. But something far more bitter than laughter spilled into his throat. For a while he could not think. He could only watch a starless night flowing across the wastes and smell the musk of a hundred wolves as they circled him. Then, with a vague idea of attacking the shape-changers, he squatted, holding wolves' eyes, drawing their minds under his control. But something broke his binding. The wolves faded away into the night, leaving him alone. He could not fly; his arm was stiffening, burning. The smell of loneliness from the cold, darkening water overwhelmed him. He let the fire around him go out. Trapped between the shape-changers and the black horror of Erlenstar Mountain, he could not move. He stood shivering in the dark wind, while the night built around him, memory by memory.

The light wing-brush of another mind touched his mind, and then his heart. He found he could move again, as though a spell had been broken. The voice of the wind changed; it filled the black night from every direction with the whisper of Raederle's name.

His awareness of her lasted only a moment. But he felt, reaching down to touch the bracken into flame, that she might be anywhere and everywhere around him, the great tree rising beside him, the fire sparking up from dead leaves to warm his face. He ripped the sleeves off his tunic, washed his arm and bound it. He lay beside the fire, gazing into the heart of it, trying to comprehend the shape-changers and their intentions. He realized suddenly that tears were burning down his face, because Raederle was alive, because she was with him. He reached out, buried the fire under a handful of earth. He hid himself within an illusion of darkness and began to move again, northward, following the vast shore of White Lady Lake.

He did not meet the shape-changers again until he reached the raging white waters of the Cwill River, as it broke away from the northernmost tip of the lake. From there, he could see the back of Isig Pass, the distant rolling foothills and bare peaks of Isig Mountain and Erlenstar Mountain. He made another desperate bid for freedom then. He dropped into the wild current of the Cwill, let it whirl him, now as a fish, now a dead branch, through deep, churning waters, down rapids and thundering falls until he lost all sense of time, direction, light. The current jarred him over endless rapids before it loosed him finally in a slow, green pool. He spun awhile, a piece of water-soaked wood, aware of nothing but a fibrous darkness. The gentle current edged him toward the shore into a snarl of dead leaves and branches. He pulled himself onto the snag finally, a wet, bedraggled muskrat, and picked his way across the branches onto the shore.

He changed shape again in the shadows. He had not gone as far east as he had thought. Erlenstar Mountain, flanked with evening shadows, stood enormous and still in the distance. But he was closer to Isig, he knew; if he could reach it safely, he could hide himself interminably in its maze of underground passages. He waited until nightfall to move again. Then, in the shape of a bear, he lumbered off into the dark toward the pattern of stars above Isig Mountain.

He followed the stars until they faded at dawn; and then, without realizing it, he began to alter his path. Trees thickened around him, hiding his view of the mountain; thick patches of scrub and bramble forced him to veer again and again. The land sloped downward sharply; he followed a dry stream bed through a ravine, thinking he was going north, until the stream bed rose up to level ground and he found himself facing Erlenstar Mountain. He angled eastward again. The trees clustered around him, murmuring in the wind; the underbrush thickened, crossing his path, imperceptibly changing his direction until, shambling across a shallow river, he saw Erlenstar Mountain again in a break between the trees ahead of him.

He stopped in the middle of the river. The sun hung suspended far to the west, crackling in the sky like a torch. He felt hot, dusty, and hungry within the shaggy bear pelt. He heard bees droning and scented the air for honey. A fish flickered past him in the shallow water; he slapped at it and missed. Then something rumbling beneath the bear-brain sharpened into language. He reared in the water, his head weaving from side to side, his muzzle wrinkled, as if he could smell the shapes that had been forming around him, pushing him away from Isig.

He felt something build in him and loosed it: a deep, grumbling roar that shattered the silence and bellowed back at him from hills and stone peaks. Then, in hawk-shape, he burned a golden path upward high into the sky until the backlands stretched endlessly beneath him, and he shot towards Isig Mountain.

The shape-changers melted out of the trees, flew after him. For a while he raced ahead of them in a blinding surge of speed toward the distant green mountain. But as the sun set, they began to catch up with him. They were of a nameless shape. Their wings gathered gold and red from the sunset; their eyes and talons were of flame. Their sharp beaks were bone-white. They surrounded him, dove at him, snapping and tearing, until his wings grew ragged and his breast was flecked with blood. He faltered in the air; they flung themselves at him, blinding him with their wings, until he gave one piercing, despairing cry and turned away from Isig.

All night he flew among their burning eyes. At dawn, he saw the face of Erlenstar Mountain rising up before him. He took his own shape then, in midair, and simply fell, the air battering out of him, the forests whirling up to meet him. Something cracked across his mind before he reached the ground. He spun into darkness.

He woke in total darkness. It smelled of wet stone. Far away, he could hear a faint perpetual trickle of water. He recognized it suddenly, and his hands clenched. He lay on his back, on cold, bare stone. Every bone in his body ached, and his skin was scored with claw marks. The mountain's silence sat like a nightmare on his chest. His muscles tensed; he listened, feverish, blind, expecting a voice that did not come, while memories like huge, bulky animals paced back and forth across him.

He began to breathe the darkness into his mind; his body seemed to fray into it. He sat up, panicked, his eyes wide, straining into nothing. From somewhere in the starless night of his thoughts, he pulled a memory of light and fire. He ignited it in his palm, nursed it until he could see the vast hollow of stone rising about him; the prison where he had spent the most unendurable year of his life.

His lips parted. A word stuck like a jewel in his throat. The flame glittered back at him endlessly, off walls of ice and fire, of gold, of sky-blue streaked with wind-swept silver like the night of the backlands rimed with a million stars. The inner mountain was of the stone of the Earth-Masters' cities, and he could see the frozen wrinkles where blocks of stone had been hewn free.

He stood up slowly. His face stared back at him out of wedges and facets of jewellike color. The chamber was enormous; he nursed the flame from its reflection until it shot higher than his head, but still he could see nothing but a vaulting of darkness, flickering vaguely with a network of pure gold.

The water, whose endless, changeless voice he had heard, had wept a diamond-white groove into a sheer wall of stone as it trickled downward into water. He shifted the flame; it billowed across a lake so still it seemed carved of darkness. The shores of the immense lake were of solid stone; the far wall curving around it was pure as hoarfrost.

He knelt, touched the water. Rings melted into rings slowly across its dark face. He thought suddenly of the spiralling circles of Wind Tower. His throat contracted, fiery with thirst, and he bent over the lake, scooping water with his free hand. He swallowed a mouthful and gagged. It was acrid with minerals.

"Morgon."

Every muscle in his body locked. He swung on his haunches, met Ghisteslwchlohm's eyes.

They were haunted, restless with a power not his own. That much Morgon saw before the darkness swallowed the flame in his hand, leaving him blind again.

"So," he whispered, "the Founder himself is bound." He stood up noiselessly, trying, in the same movement, to step into the fragment of dawn beyond the splintered doors in the High One's throne room. He stepped instead over the edge of a chasm. He lost his balance, crying out, and fell into nothingness. He landed on the lake shore, clinging to the stones at Ghisteslwchlohm's feet.

He dropped his face against his forearm, trying to think. He caught at the mind of a bat tucked in its secret corner, but the wizard gripped him before he could change shape.

"There is no escape." The voice had changed; it was slow, soft, as if he were listening beneath it for another voice, or a distant, uneasy rhythm of tides. "Star-Bearer, you will use no power. You will do nothing but wait."

"Wait," he whispered. "For what? For death?" He stopped, the word flickering back and forth between two meanings in his mind. "There is no harping this time to keep me alive." He lifted his head, his eyes straining again at the blackness. "Or are you expecting the High One? You can wait until I turn to stone here like the Earth-Masters' children before the High One shows any interest in me."

"I doubt that."

"You. You hardly exist. You no longer have the ability to doubt. Even the wraiths of An have more will than you do. I can't even tell if you're dead or alive still, deep in you, the way the wizards lived, somehow, beneath your power." His voice dropped a little. "I could fight for you. I would do even that for freedom."

The hand left his arm. He groped into the strange, sea-filled mind, to find the name it held. It eluded him. He struggled through swells and heaving tides, until the wizard's mind heaved him back on the shore of his own awareness. He was gasping, as if he had forgotten to breathe. He heard the wizard's voice finally, withdrawing into the dark.

"For you, there is no word for freedom."

He slept a little, then, trying to regain strength. He dreamed of water. His raging thirst woke him; he felt for the water, tried to drink it again. He spat it out before he swallowed it, knelt racked with coughing. He drifted finally back into a feverish sleep and dreamed again of water. He felt himself falling into it, drawing a cool darkness around himself, moving deeper and deeper into its stillness. He breathed in water and woke himself, panicked, drowning. Hands dragged him out of the lake, left him retching bitter water on the shore.

The water cleared his head a little. He lay quietly, staring into the darkness, wondering, if he let it fill his mind, whether it would drown him like water. He let it seep slowly into his thoughts until the memories of a long year's night overwhelmed him and he panicked again, igniting the air with fire. He saw Ghisteslwchlohm's face briefly; then the wizard's hand slapped at his flame and it broke into pieces like glass.

He whispered, "For every doorless tower there is a riddle to open the door. You taught me that."

"There is one door and one riddle here."

"Death. You don't believe that. Otherwise you would have let me drown. If the High One isn't interested in my life or my death, what will you do then?"

"Wait."

"Wait." He shifted restlessly, his thoughts speeding feverishly towards some answer. "The shape-changers have been waiting for thousands of years. You named them, the instant before they bound you. What did you see? What could be strong enough to empower an Earth-Master? Someone who takes the power and law of his existence from every living thing, from earth, fire, water, from wind. . . . The High One was driven out of Erlenstar Mountain by the shape-changers. And you came then and found an empty throne where legend had placed the High One. So you became the High One, playing a game of power while you waited for someone the stone children knew only as the Star-Bearer. You kept watch on places of knowledge and power, gathering the wizards at Lungold, teaching at Caithnard. And one day the son of a Prince of Hed came to Caithnard with the smell of cowdung on his boots and a question on his face. But that wasn't enough. You're still waiting. The shape-changers are still waiting. For the High One. You are using me for bait, but he could have found me in here long before this, if he had been interested."

"He will come."

"I doubt that. He allowed you to deceive the realm for centuries. He is not interested in the welfare of men or wizards in the realm. He let you strip me of the land-rule, for which I should have killed you. He is not interested in me . . ." He was silent again, his eyes on the expressionless face of darkness. He said, listening to the silence that gathered and froze in every drop of liquid stone, "What could be powerful enough to destroy the Earth-Masters' cities? To force the High One himself into hiding? What is as powerful as an Earth-Master?" He was silent again. Then an answer like a glint of fire burning itself into ash moved in the depths of his mind.

He sat up. The air seemed suddenly thin, fiery; he found it hard to breathe. "The shape-changers . . ." The blade of dryness was back in his throat. He raised his hands to his eyes, gathering darkness to stare into. Voices whispered out of his memory, out of the stones around him: *The war is not finished, only silenced for the regathering. . . . Those from the sea. Edolen. Sec. They destroyed us so we could not live on earth any more; we could not master it. . . .* The voices of the Earth-Masters' dead, the children. His hands dropped heavily on the stone floor, but still the darkness pushed against his eyes. He saw the child turn from the leaf it touched in its dreaming, look across a plain, its body tense, waiting. "They could touch a leaf, a mountain, a seed, and know it, become it. That's what Raederle saw, the power in them she loved. Yet they killed each other, buried their children beneath a mountain to die. They knew all the languages of the earth, all the laws of its shapes and movement. What happened to them? Did they stumble into the shape of something that had no law but power?" His voice was whispering away from him as if out of a dream. "What shape?"

He fell silent abruptly. He was shivering, yet sweating. The smell of water pulled at him mercilessly. He reached out to it again, his throat tormented with thirst. His hands halted before they broke the surface. Raederle's face, dreamlike in its beauty, looked back at him from the still water between his hands. Her long hair flowed away from her face like the sun's fire. He forgot his thirst. He knelt motionlessly for a long time, gazing down at it, not knowing if it was real or if he had fashioned it out of longing, and not caring. Then a hand struck at it, shattering the image, sending rings of movement shivering to the far edges of the lake.

A murderous, uncontrollable fury swept Morgon to his feet. He wanted to kill Ghisteslwchlohm with his hands, but he could not even see the wizard. A power battered him away again and again. He scarcely felt pain; shapes were reeling faster than language in his mind. He discarded them, searching for the one shape powerful enough to contain his rage. He felt his body fray into shapelessness; a sound filled his mind, deep, harsh, wild, the voices out of the farthest reaches of the backlands. But they were no longer empty. Something shuddered through him, flinging off a light snapping through the air. He felt thoughts groping into his mind, but his own thoughts held no language except a sound like a vibrant, untuned harp string. He felt the fury in him expand, shape itself to all the hollows and forms of the stone chamber. He flung the wizard across the cavern, held him like a leaf before the wind, splayed against the stones.

Then he realized what shape he had taken.

He fell back into his own shape, the wild energy in him suddenly gone. He knelt on the stones, trembling, half-sobbing in fear and amazement. He heard the wizard stumble away from the wall, breathing haltingly, as if his ribs were cracked. As he moved across the cavern, Morgon heard voices all around him, speaking various complex languages of the earth.

He heard the whispering of fire, the shiver of leaves, the howl of a wolf in the lonely, moonlit backlands, the dry riddling of corn leaves. Then, far away, he heard a sound, as if the mountain itself had sighed. He felt the stone shift slightly under him. A sea bird cried harshly. Someone with a hand of tree bark and light flung Morgon onto his back.

He whispered bitterly, feeling the starred sword wrenched from his side, "One riddle and one door."

But, though he waited in the eye of darkness for the sword to fall, nothing touched him. He was caught suddenly, breathless, in their tension of waiting. Then Raederle's voice, raised in a Great Shout, shook stones loose from the ceiling and jarred him out of his waiting. "Morgon!"

The sword hummed wildly with the aftermath of the shout. Morgon heard it bounce against the stones. He shouted Raederle's name involuntarily, in horror, and the floor lurched under him again, shrugging him toward the lake. The sword slid after him. It was still vibrating, a strange high note that stilled as Morgon caught it and sheathed it. There was a sound as if a crystal in one of the walls had cracked.

It sang as it broke: a low, tuned note that shattered its own core. Other crystals began to hum; the ground floor of the mountain rumbled. The great slabs of ceiling stone ground themselves together. Dust and rubble hissed down; half-formed crystals snapped and pounded to pieces on the floor. Languages of bats, dolphins, bees brushed through the chamber. A tension snaked through the air, and Morgon heard Raederle scream. Sobbing a curse, he pulled himself to his feet. The floor grumbled beneath him, then roared. One side of it lifted, fell ponderously onto the other. It flung him into the lake. The whole lake basin, a huge, round bowl carved into solid stone, began to tilt.

He was buried for a few moments in a wave of black water. When he surfaced again, he heard a sound as if the mountain itself, torn apart at its roots, had groaned.

A wind blasted into the stone chamber. It blinded Morgon, drove his own cry back into his throat. It whirled the lake into a black vortex that dragged him down into it. He heard, before he was engulfed, something that was either the ring of blood in his ears or a note like a fine-tuned string at the core of the deep wind's voice.

The water spat him back up. The basin had tilted farther, pouring him out with the water toward the sheer wall at the far side. He snatched a breath, dove under water, trying to swim against the wave. But it hurled him back, heaved him at solid stone. As he sensed the wall blur up before him, it split open. The wave poured through the crack, dragging him with it. Through the thunder of water, he heard the final reverberations of the mountain burying its own heart.

The lake water dragged him through the jagged split, poured over a lip of stone into a roiling stream. He tried to pull himself out, catching at ledges, at walls rough with jewels, but the wind was still with him, pushing him back into the water, driving the water before it. The stream flooded into another; a whirlpool dragged him under a ledge of stone into another river. The river cast him finally out of the mountain, dragged him down foaming rapids, and threw him, half-drowned, his veins full of bitter water, into the Ose.

He pulled himself ashore finally, lay hugging the sunlit ground. The wild winds still pounded at him; the great pines were groaning as they bent. He coughed up the bitter water he had swallowed. When he moved finally to drink the sweet waters of the Ose, the wind nearly flung him back in. He raised his head, looked at the mountain. A portion of its side had been sucked in; trees lay uprooted, splintered in the shift of stone and earth. All down the pass, as far as he could see, the wind raged, bending trees to their breaking point.

He tried to stand, but he had no strength left. The wind seemed to be hounding him out of his own shape. He reached out; his hands closed on huge roots. He felt, as the tree shivered in his hold, the core of its great strength.

Clinging to it, he pulled himself up by its knots and boles. Then he stepped away from it and lifted his arms as if to enclose the wind.

Branches grew from his hands, his hair. His thoughts tangled like roots in the ground. He strained upward. Pitch ran like tears down his bark. His name formed his core; ring upon ring of silence built around it. His face rose high above the forests. Gripped to earth, bending to the wind's fury, he disappeared within himself, behind the hard, wind-scrolled shield of his experiences.

10

HE DWINDLED BACK into his own shape on a rainy, blustery autumn day. He stood in the cold winds, blinking rain out of his eyes, trying to remember a long, wordless passage of time. The Ose, grey as a knife blade, shivered past him; the stone peaks of the pass were half-buried under heavy clouds. The trees around him clung deeply to the earth, engrossed in their own existences. They pulled at him again. His mind slid past their tough wet bark, back into a slow peace around which tree rings formed and hardened. But a wind vibrated through his memories, shook a mountain down around him, throwing him back into water, back into the rain. He moved reluctantly, breaking a binding with the earth, and turned toward Erlenstar Mountain. He saw the scar in its side under a blur of mist and the dark water still swirling out of it to join the Ose.

He gazed at it a long time, piecing together fragments of a dark, troubling dream. The implications of it woke him completely; he began to shiver in the driving rain. He scented through the afternoon with his mind. He found no one—trapper, wizard, shape-changer—in the pass. A windblown crow sailed past him on an updraft; he caught eagerly at its mind. But it did not know his language. He loosed it. The wild, sonorous winds boomed hollowly through the peaks; the trees roared around him, smelling of winter. He turned finally, hunched in the wind, to follow the flow of the Ose back into the world.

But he stood still after a step, watching the water rush away from him toward Isig and Osterland and the northern trade-ports of the realm. His own power held him motionless. There was no place anywhere in the realm for a man who unbound land-law and shaped wind. The river echoed the voices he had heard, speaking languages not even the wizards could understand. He thought of the dark, blank face of wind that was the High One, who would give him nothing except his life.

"For what?" he whispered. He wanted to shout the words suddenly at the battered, expressionless face of Erlenstar Mountain. The wind would simply swallow his cry. He took another step down the river toward Harte, where he would find shelter, warmth, comfort from Danan Isig. But the king could give him no answers. He was trapped by the past, the pawn of an ancient war he was finally beginning to understand. The vague longing in him to explore his own strange, unpredictable power frightened him. He stood at the river's edge for a long time, until the mists along the peaks began to darken and a shadow formed across the face of Erlenstar Mountain. Finally, he turned away from it, wandered through the rain and icy mists toward the mountains bordering the northern wastes.

He kept his own shape as he crossed them, though the rains in the high peaks turned to sleet sometimes and the rocks under his hands as he climbed were like ice. His life hung in a precarious balance the first few days, though he hardly realized it. He found himself eating without remembering how he had killed, or awake at dawn in a dry cave without remembering how he had found it. Gradually, as he realized his disinclination to use power, he gave some thought to survival. He killed wild mountain sheep, dragged them into a cave and skinned them, living on the meat while the pelts dried and weathered. He sharpened a rib, prodded holes in the pelts and laced them together with strips of cloth from his tunic. He made a great shaggy hooded cloak and lined his boots with fur. When they were finished, he put them on and moved again, down the north face of the pass into the wastes.

There was little rain in the wasteland, only the driving, biting winds, and frost that turned the flat, monotonous land into fire at sunrise. He moved like a wraith, killing when he was hungry, sleeping in the open, for he rarely felt the cold, as if his body frayed without his knowledge into the winds. One day he realized he was no longer moving across the arc of the sun; he had turned east, wandering toward the morning. In the distance, he could see a cluster of foothills, with Grim Mountain jutting out of them, a harsh, blue-grey peak. But it was so far away that he scarcely put a name to it. He walked into mid-autumn, hearing nothing but the winds. One night as he sat before his fire, vaguely feeling the winds urge against his shape, he looked down and saw the starred harp in his hands.

He could not remember reaching back for it. He gazed at it, watching the silent run of fire down the strings. He shifted after a while and positioned it. His fingers moved patternlessly, almost inaudibly over the strings, following the rough, wild singing of the winds.

He felt no more compulsion to move. He stayed at that isolated point in the wastes, which was no more than a few stones, a twisted shrub, a crack in the hard earth where a stream surfaced for a few feet, then vanished again underground. He left the place only to hunt; he always found his way back to it, as if to the echo of his own harping. He harped with the winds that blew from dawn until night, sometimes with only one high string, as he heard the lean, tense, wailing east wind; sometimes with all strings, the low note thrumming back at the boom of the north wind. Sometimes, looking up, he would see a snow hare listening or catch the startled glance of a white falcon's eyes. But as the autumn deepened, animals grew rare, seeking the mountains for food and shelter. So he harped alone, a strange, furred, nameless animal with no voice but the one strung between his hands. His body was honed to the wind's harshness; his mind lay dormant like the wastes. How long he would have stayed there, he never knew, for glancing up one night at a shift of wind across his fire, he found Raederle.

She was cloaked in rich silvery furs; her hair, blown out of her hood, streaked the dark like fire. He sat still, his hands stopped on the harp strings. She knelt down beside his fire, and he saw her face more clearly, weary, winter-pale, sculpted to a fine, changeless beauty. He wondered if she were a dream, like the face he had seen between his hands in the dark lake water. Then he saw that she was shivering badly. She took her gloves off, drew his windblown fire to a still bright blaze with her hands. Slowly he realized how long it had been since they had spoken.

"Lungold," he whispered. The word seemed meaningless in the tumult of the wastes. But she had journeyed out of the world to find him here. He reached through the fire, laid his hand against her face. She gazed at him mutely as he sat back again. She drew her knees up, huddled in her furs against the wind.

"I heard your harping," she said. He touched the strings soundlessly, remembering.

"I promised you I would harp." His voice was husky with disuse. He added curiously, "Where have you been? You followed me across the backlands; you were with me in Erlenstar Mountain. Then you vanished."

She stared at him again; he wondered if she were going to answer. "I didn't vanish. You did." Her voice was suddenly tremulous. "Off the face of the realm. The wizards have been searching everywhere for you. So have the shape—the shape-changers. So have I. I thought maybe you were dead. But here you are, harping in this wind that could kill and you aren't even cold."

He was silent. The harp that had sung with the winds felt suddenly chilled under his hands. He set it on the ground beside him. "How did you find me?"

"I searched. In every shape I could think of. I thought maybe you were with the vesta. So I went to Har and asked him to teach me the vesta-shape. He started to, but when he touched my mind, he stopped and told me he did not think he had to teach me. So, I had to explain that to him. Then he made me tell him everything that had happened in Erlenstar Mountain. He said nothing, except that you must be found. Finally, he took me across Grim Mountain to the vesta herds. And while I travelled with them, I began to hear your harping on the edge of my mind, on the edge of the winds. . . . Morgon, if I can find you, so can others. Did you come out here to learn to harp? Or did you just run?"

"I just ran."

"Well, are you—are you planning to come back?"

"For what?"

She was silent. The fire flickered wildly in front of her, weaving itself into the wind. She stilled it again, her eyes never leaving his face. She moved abruptly to his side and held him tightly, her face against the shaggy fur at his shoulder.

"I could learn to live in the wastes, I guess," she whispered. "It's so cold here, and nothing grows . . . but the winds and your harping are beautiful."

His head bowed. He put his arm around her, drawing her hood back so he could feel her cheek against his. Something touched his heart, an ache of cold that he finally felt, or a painful stirring of warmth.

"You heard the voices of the shape-changers in Erlenstar Mountain," he said haltingly. "You know what they are. They know all languages. They are Earth-Masters, still at war, after thousands of years, with the High One. And I am bait for their traps. That's why they never kill me. They want him. If they destroy him, they will destroy the realm. If they cannot find me, perhaps they will not find him." She started to speak, but he went on, his voice thawing, harsher, "You know what I did in that mountain. I was angry enough to murder, and I shaped myself into wind to do it. There is no place in the realm for anyone of such power. What will I do with it? I'm the Star-Bearer. A promise made by the dead to fight a war older than the names of the kingdoms. I was born with power that leaves me nameless in my own world . . . and with all the terrible longing to use it."

"So you came here to the wastes, where you would have no reason to use it."

"Yes."

She slid a hand beneath his hood, her fingers brushing his brow and his scarred cheekbone. "Morgon," she said softly, "I think if you wanted to use it, you would. If you found a reason. You gave me a reason to use my own power, at Lungold and across the backlands. I love you, and I will fight for you. Or sit here with you in the wastes until you drift into snow. If the need of the land-rulers, all those who love you, can't stir you from this place, what can? What hurt you in the dark at Erlenstar Mountain?"

He was silent. The winds roared out of the night, a vast chaos converging upon a single point of light. They had no faces, no language he could understand. He whispered, gazing at them, "The High One cannot speak my name, any more than a slab of granite can. We are bound in some way, I know. He values my life, but he does not even know what it is. I am the Star-Bearer. He will give me my life. But nothing else. No hope, no justice, no compassion. Those words belong to men. Here in the wastes, I am threatening no one. I am keeping myself safe, the High One safe, and the realm untroubled by a power too dangerous to use."

"The realm is troubled. The land-rulers put more hope in you than they do in the High One. You they can talk to."

"If I made myself into a weapon for Earth-Masters to battle with, not even you would recognize me."

"Maybe. You told me a riddle once, when I was afraid of my own power. About the Herun woman Arya, who brought a dark, frightening animal she could not name into her house. You never told me how it ended."

He stirred a little. "She died of fear."

"And the animal? What was it?"

"No one knew. It wailed for seven days and seven nights at her grave, in a voice so full of love and grief that no one who heard it could sleep or eat. And then it died, too."

She lifted her head, her lips parted, and he remembered a moment out of a dead past: he sat in a small stone chamber at Caithnard, studying riddles and feeling his heart twist with joy and terror and sorrow to their unexpected turnings. He added, "It has nothing to do with me."

"I suppose not. You would know."

He was silent again. He shifted so that her head lay in the crook of his shoulder, and his arms circled her. He laid his cheek against her hair. "I'm tired," he said simply. "I have answered too many riddles. The Earth-Masters began a war before history, a war that killed their own children. If I could fight them, I would, for the sake of the realm; but I think I would only kill myself and the High One. So I'm doing the only thing that makes any sense to me. Nothing."

She did not answer for a long time. He held her quietly, watching the fire spark a silvery wash across her cloak. She said slowly, "Morgon, there is one more riddle maybe you should answer. You stripped all illusions from Ghisteslwchlohm; you named the shape-changers; you woke the High One out of his silence. But there is one more thing you have not named, and it will not die . . ." Her voice shook into silence. He felt suddenly, through all the bulky fur between them, the beat of her heart.

"What?" The word was a whisper she could not have heard, but she answered him.

"In Lungold, I talked to Yrth in crow-shape. So I did not know then that he is blind. I went to Isig, searching for you, and I found him there. His eyes are the color of water burned by light. He told me that Ghisteslwchlohm had blinded him during the destruction of Lungold. And I didn't question that. He is a big, gentle, ancient man, and Danan's grandchildren followed him all over the mountain while he was searching for you among the stones and trees. One evening Bere brought a harp he had made to the hall and asked Yrth to play it. He laughed a little and said that though he had been known once as the Harpist of Lungold, he hadn't touched a harp for seven centuries. But he played a little. . . . And, Morgon, I knew that harping. It was the same awkward, tentative harping that haunted you down Trader's Road and drew you into Ghisteslwchlohm's power."

He lifted her face between his hands. He was feeling the wind suddenly, scoring all his bones with rime. "What are you telling me?"

"I don't know. But how many blind harpists who cannot harp can there be in the world?"

He took a breath of wind; it burned through him like cold fire. "He's dead."

"Then he's challenging you out of his grave. Yrth harped to me that night so that I would carry the riddle of his harping to you, wherever in the realm you were."

"Are you sure?"

"No. But I know that he wants to find you. And that if he was a harpist named Deth who travelled with you, as Yrth did, down Trader's Road, then he spun riddles so secretly, so skillfully, that he blinded even Ghisteslwchlohm. And even you—the Riddle-Master of Hed. I think maybe you should name him. Because he is playing his own silent, deadly game, and he may be the only one in this realm who knows exactly what he is doing."

"Who in Hel's name is he?" He was shivering suddenly, uncontrollably. "Deth took the Black of Mastery at Caithnard. He was a riddler.

He knew my name before I did. I suspected once that he might be a Lungold wizard. I asked him."

"What did he say?"

"He said he was the High One's harpist. So I asked him what he was doing in Isig while Yrth made my harp, a hundred years before he was born. He told me to trust him. Beyond logic, beyond reason, beyond hope. And then he betrayed me." He drew her against him, but the wind ran between them like a knife. "It's cold. It was never this cold before."

"What are you going to do?"

"What does he want? Is he an Earth-Master, playing his own solitary game for power? Does he want me alive or dead? Does he want the High One alive or dead?"

"I don't know. You're the riddler. He's challenging you. Ask him."

He was silent, remembering the harpist on Trader's Road who had drawn him without a word, with only a halting, crippled harping out of the night into Ghisteslwchlohm's hands. He whispered, "He knows me too well. I think whatever he wants, he will get." A gust struck them, smelling like snow, gnawing icily at his face and hands. It drove him to his feet, breathless, blinded, full of a sudden, helpless longing for hope. When he could see again, he found that Raederle had already changed shape. A vesta shod and crowned with gold gazed at him out of deep purple eyes. He caressed it; its warm breath nuzzled at his hands. He rested his brow against the bone between its eyes. "All right," he said with very little irony, "I will play a riddle-game with Deth. Which way is Isig?"

She led him there by sunlight and starlight, south across the wastes, and then eastward down the mountains of the pass until at the second dawn he saw the green face of Isig Mountain rising beyond the Ose. They reached the king's house at dusk, on a wild, grey autumn day. The high peaks were already capped with snow; the great pines around Harte sang in the north wind. The travellers changed out of vesta-shape when they reached Kyrth and walked the winding mountain road to Harte. The gates were barred and guarded, but the miners, armed with great broadswords tempered in Danan's forge fires, recognized them and let them in.

Danan and Vert and half a dozen children left their supper to meet them as they entered the house. Danan, robed in fur against the cold, gave them a bear's bulky embrace and sent children and servants alike scurrying to see to their comfort. But, gauging their weariness, he asked only one question.

"I was in the wastes," Morgon said. "Harping. Raederle found me." The strangeness of the answer did not occur to him then. He added, remembering, "Before that, I was a tree beside the Ose." He watched a smile break into the king's eyes.

"What did I tell you?" Danan murmured. "I told you no one would find you in that shape." He drew them toward the stairs leading up into the east tower. "I have a thousand questions, but I am a patient old tree, and they can wait until morning. Yrth is in this tower; you'll be safe near him."

A question nagged at Morgon as they wound up the stairs, until he realized what it was. "Danan, I have never seen your house guarded. Did the shape-changers come here looking for me?"

The king's hands knotted. "They came," he said grimly. "I lost a quarter of my miners. I would have lost more if Yrth had not been here to fight with us." Morgon had stopped. The king opened a hand, drew him forward. "We grieved enough for them. If we only knew what they are, what they want . . ." He sensed something in Morgon. His troubled eyes drew relentlessly at the truth. "You know."

Morgon did not answer. Danan did not press him, but the lines in his face ran suddenly deep.

He left them in a tower room whose walls and floor and furniture were draped with fur. The air was chilly, but Raederle lit a fire and servants came soon, bringing food, wine, more firewood, warm, rich clothes. Bere followed with a cauldron of steaming water. As he hoisted it onto a hook above the firebed, he smiled at Morgon, his eyes full of questions, but he swallowed them all with an effort. Morgon ridded himself of a well-worn tunic, matted sheepskin, and what dirt the harsh winds had not scoured from his body. Clean, fed, dressed in soft fur and velvet, he sat beside the fire and thought back with amazement on what he had done.

"I left you," he said to Raederle. "I can understand almost everything but that. I wandered out of the world and left you . . ."

"You were tired," she said drowsily. "You said so. Maybe you just needed to think." She was stretched out beside him on the ankle-deep skins; she sounded warmed by fire and wine, and almost asleep. "Or maybe you needed a place to begin to harp . . ."

Her voice trailed away into a dream; she left him behind. He drew blankets over her, sat for a while without moving, watching light and shadows pursue one another across her weary face. The winds boomed and broke against the tower like sea waves. They held the echo of a note that haunted his memories. He reached automatically for his harp, then remembered he could not play that note in the king's house without disrupting its fragile peace.

He played others softly, fragments of ballads wandering into patternless echoes of the winds. His fingers stopped after a while. He sat plucking one note over and over, soundlessly, while a face formed and vanished constantly in the flames. He stood up finally, listening. The house seemed still around him, with only a distant murmuring of voices here and there within its walls. He moved quietly past Raederle, past the guards outside the door, whom he made oblivious to his leaving. He went up the stairs to a doorway hung with white furs that yielded beneath him a strip of light. He parted them gently, walked into semi-darkness and stopped.

The wizard was napping, an old man nodding in a chair beside a fire, his scarred hands lying open on his knees. He looked taller than Morgon remembered, broad-shouldered yet lean beneath the long, dark robe he wore. As Morgon watched him, he woke, opening light, unstartled eyes. He bent down, sighing, groped for wood and positioned it carefully, feeling with his fingers through the lagging flames. They sprang up, lighting a rock-hard face, weathered like a tree stump with age. He seemed to realize suddenly that he was not alone; for an instant his body went motionless as stone. Morgon felt an almost imperceptible touch in his mind. The wizard stirred again, blinking.

"Morgon?" His voice was deep, resonant, yet husky, full of hidden things, like the voice of a deep well. "Come in. Or are you in?"

Morgon moved after a moment. "I didn't mean to disturb you," he said softly. Yrth shook his head.

"I heard your harping a while ago. But I didn't expect to talk to you until morning. Danan told me that Raederle found you in the northern wastes. Were you pursued? Is that why you hid there?"

"No. I simply went there, and stayed because I could think of no reason to come back. Then Raederle came and gave me a reason . . ."

The wizard contemplated the direction of his voice silently. "You are an amazing man," he said. "Will you sit down?"

"How do you know I'm not sitting?" Morgon asked curiously.

"I can see the chair in front of you. Can you feel the mind-link? I am seeing out of your eyes."

"I hardly notice it . . ."

"That's because I am not linked to your thoughts, only to your vision. I travelled Trader's Road through men's eyes. That night you were attacked by horse thieves, I knew one of them was a shape-changer because I saw through his eyes the stars you kept hidden from men. I searched for him, to kill him, but he eluded me."

"And the night I followed Deth's harping? Did you see beneath that illusion, also?"

The wizard was silent again. His head bowed, away from Morgon; the hard lines of his face shifted with such shame and bitterness that Morgon stepped toward him, appalled at his own question.

"Morgon, I am sorry. I am no match for Ghisteslwchlohm."

"You couldn't have done anything to help." His hands gripped the chair back. "Not without endangering Raederle."

"I did what little I could, reinforcing your illusion when you vanished, but . . . that was very little."

"You saved our lives." He had a sudden, jarring memory of the harpist's face, eyes seared pale with fire, staring at nothing until Morgon wavered out of existence in front of him. His hands loosed the wood, slid up over his eyes. He heard Yrth stir.

"I can't see."

His hands dropped. He sat down, in utter weariness. The winds wailed around the tower in a confusion of voices. Yrth was still, listening to his silence. He said gently, when Morgon did not break it, "Raederle told me what she could of the events in Erlenstar Mountain. I did not go into her mind. Will you let me see into your memories? Or do you prefer to tell me? Either way, I must know."

"Take it from my mind."

"Are you too tired now?"

He shook his head a little. "It doesn't matter. Take what you want."

The fire grew small in front of him, broke into bright fragments of memory. He endured once more his wild, lonely flight across the backlands, falling out of the sky into the depths of Erlenstar Mountain. The tower flooded with night; he swallowed bitterness like lake water. The fire beyond his vision whispered in languages he did not understand. A wind smashed through the voices, whirling them out of his mind. The tower stones shook around him, shattered by the deep, precise tuning of a wind. Then there was a long silence, during which he drowsed, warmed by a summer light. Then he woke again, a strange, wild figure in a sheepskin coat that hung open to the wind. He drifted deeper and deeper into the pure, deadly voices of winter.

He sat beside a fire, listening to the winds. But they were beyond a circle of stone; they touched neither him nor the fire. He stirred a little, blinking, puzzling night and fire and the wizard's face back into perspective. His thoughts centered once more in the tower. He slumped forward, murmuring, so tired he wanted to melt into the dying fire. The wizard rose, paced a moment, soundlessly, until a clothes chest stopped him.

"What did you do in the wastes?"

"I harped. I could play that low note there, the one that shatters stone . . ." He heard his voice from a distance, amazed that it was vaguely rational.

"How did you survive?"

"I don't know. Maybe I was part wind, for a while . . . I was afraid to come back. What will I do with such power?"

"Use it."

"I don't dare. I have power over land-law. I want it. I want to use it. But I have no right. Land-law is the heritage of kings, bound into them by the High One. I would destroy all law . . ."

"Perhaps. But land-law is also the greatest source of power in the realm. Who can help the High One but you?"

"He hasn't asked for help. Does a mountain ask for help? Or a river? They simply exist. If I touch his power, he may pay enough attention to me to destroy me, but—"

"Morgon, have you no hope whatsoever in those stars I made for you?"

"No." His eyes closed; he dragged them open again, wanting to weep with the effort. He whispered, "I don't speak the language of stone. To him, I simply exist. He sees nothing but three stars rising out of countless centuries of darkness, during which powerless shapes called men touched the earth a little, hardly enough to disturb him."

"He gave them land-law."

"I was a shape possessing land-law. Now, I am simply a shape with no destiny but in the past. I will not touch the power of another land-ruler again."

The wizard was silent, gazing down at a fire that kept blurring under Morgon's eyes. "Are you so angry with the High One?"

"How can I be angry with a stone?"

"The Earth-Masters have taken all shapes. What makes you so certain the High One has shaped himself to everything but the shape and language of men?"

"Why—" He stopped, staring down at the flames until they burned the shadows of sleep out of his mind and he could think again. "You want me to loose my own powers into the realm."

Yrth did not answer. Morgon looked up at him, giving him back the image of his own face, hard, ancient, powerful. The fire washed over his thoughts again. He saw suddenly, for the first time, not the slab of wind speaking the language of stone that he thought was the High One, but something pursued, vulnerable, in danger, whose silence was the single weapon he possessed. The thought held him still, wondering. Slowly he became aware of the silence that built moment by moment between his question and the answer to it.

He stopped breathing, listening to the silence that haunted him oddly, like a memory of something he had once cherished. The wizard's hands turned a little toward the light and then closed, hiding their scars. He said, "There are powers loosed all over the realm to find the High One. Yours will not be the worst. You are, after all, bound by a peculiar system of restraints. The best, and the least comprehensible of them, seems to be love. You could ask permission from the land-rulers. They trust you. And they were in great despair when neither you nor the High One seemed to be anywhere on the face of the realm."

Morgon's head bowed. "I didn't think of them." He did not hear Yrth move until the wizard's dark robe brushed the wood of his chair. The wizard's hand touched his shoulder, very gently, as he might have touched a wild thing that had moved fearfully, tentatively, toward him into his stillness.

Something drained out of Morgon at the touch: confusion, anger, arguments, even the strength and will to wrestle with all the wizard's subtlety. Only the silence was left, and a helpless, incomprehensible longing.

"I'll find the High One," he said. He added, in warning or in promise, "Nothing will destroy him. I swear it. Nothing."

11

HE SLEPT FOR two days in the king's house, waking only once to eat, and another time to see Raederle sitting beside him, waiting patiently for him to wake up. He linked his fingers into hers, smiling a little, then rolled over and went back to sleep. He woke finally, clear-headed, at evening. He was alone. From the faint chaos of voices and crockery that seeped into his listening, he knew that the household was at supper, and Raederle was probably with Danan. He washed and drank some wine, still listening. Beneath the noises of the house, he heard the vast, dark, ageless silence forming the hollows and mazes within Isig Mountain.

He stood linked to the silence until it formed channels in his mind. Then, impulsively, he left the tower, went unobtrusively to the hall, where only Raederle and Bere noticed him, falling quiet amid the noise to watch his passage. He followed the path of a dream then, through the empty upper shafts. He took a torch from the wall at the mouth of a dark tunnel; as he entered it, the walls blazed around him with fiery, uncut jewels. He moved unhesitantly through his memory, down a honeycomb of passageways, along the sides of streams and deep crevices, through unmined caves shimmering with gold, moving deeper and deeper into the immensity of darkness and stone until he seemed to breathe its stillness and age into his bones. At last he sensed something older, even, than the great mountain. The path he followed dwindled into crumbled stone. The torch fire washed over a deep green slab of a door that had opened once before to the sound of his name. There he stopped incredulously.

The ground floor was littered with the shards of broken rock. The door to the Earth-Masters' dead was split open; half of it had fallen ponderously back into the cave. The tomb itself was choked with great chunks of jewelled ceiling stone; the walls had shrugged themselves together, hiding whatever was left of the strange pale stones within.

He picked his way to the door, but he could not enter. He crooked one arm on the door, leaned his face against it. He let his thoughts flow into the stone, seep through marble, amethyst, and gold until he touched something like the remnant of a half-forgotten dream. He explored farther; he found no names, only a sense of something that had once lived.

He stood for a long time, leaning against the door without moving. After a while, he knew why he had come down into the mountain, and he felt the blood beat through him, quick, cold, as it had the first time he had brought himself to that threshold of his destiny. He became aware, as he had never been before, of the mountain settled over his head, and of the king within it, his ancient mind shaped to its mazes, holding all its peace and all its power. His thoughts moved once again, slowly into the door, until he touched at the core of the stone, the sense of Danan's mind, shaped to that tiny fragment of mountain, bound to it. He let his brain become stone, rich, worn, ponderous. He drew all knowledge of it into himself, of its great strength, its inmost colors, its most fragile point where he might have shattered it with a thought. The knowledge became a binding, a part of himself, deep in his own mind. Then, searching within the stone, he found once more the wordless awareness, the law that bound king to stone, land-ruler to every portion of his kingdom. He encompassed that awareness, broke it, and the stone held no name but his own.

He let his own awareness of the binding dwindle into some dark cave deep in his mind. He straightened slowly, sweating in the cool air. His torch was out; he touched it, lit it again. Turning, he found Danan in front of him, massive and still as Isig, his face expressionless as a rock.

Morgon's muscles tensed involuntarily. He wondered for a second if there was any language in him to explain what he was doing to a rock, before the slow, ponderous weight of Danan's anger roused stones from their sleep to bury him beside the children's tomb. Then he saw the king's broad fist unclench.

"Morgon." His voice was breathless with astonishment. "It was you who drew me down here. What are you doing?" He touched Morgon when he could not answer. "You're frightened. What are you doing that you need to fear me?"

Morgon moved after a moment. His body felt drained, cumbersome as stone. "Learning your land-law." He leaned back against the damp wall behind him, his face uplifted, vulnerable to Danan's searching.

"Where did you get such power? From Ghisteslwchlohm?"

"No." He repeated the word suddenly, passionately, "No. I would die before I did that to you. I will never go into your mind—"

"You are in it. Isig is my brain, my heart—"

"I won't break your bindings again. I swear it. I will simply form my own."

"But why? What do you want with such a knowledge of trees and stones?"

"Power. Danan, the shape-changers are Earth-Masters. I can't hope to fight them unless—"

The king's fingers wound like a tree root around his wrist. "No," he said, as Ghisteslwchlohm had said, faced with the same knowledge. "Morgon, that's not possible."

"Danan," he whispered, "I have heard their voices. The languages they spoke. I have seen the power locked behind their eyes. It is possible."

Danan's hand slipped away from him. The king sat down slowly, heavily, on a pile of rock shard. Morgon, looking down at him, wondered suddenly how old he was. His hands, calloused with centuries of work among stones, made a futile gesture. "What do they want?"

"The High One."

Danan stared at him. "They'll destroy us." He reached out to Morgon again. "And you. What do they want with you?"

"I'm their link to the High One. I don't know how I am bound to him, or why—I only know that because of him I have been driven out of my own land, harried, tormented into power, until now I am driving myself into power. The Earth-Masters' power seems bound, restrained by something . . . perhaps the High One, which is why they are desperate to find him. When they do, whatever power they unleash against him may destroy us all. He may stay bound forever in his silence; it's hard for me to risk my life and all your trust for someone who never speaks. But at least if I fight for him, I fight for you." He paused, his eyes on the flecks of fire catching in the rough, rich walls around him. "I can't ask you to trust me," he said softly. "Not when I don't even trust myself. All I know is where both logic and hunger lead me."

He heard the king's weary sigh in the shadows. "The ending of an age. . . . That's what you told me the last time you came to this place. Ymris is nearly destroyed. It seems only a matter of time before that war spills into An, into Herun, then north across the realm. I have an army of miners, the Morgol has her guard, the wolf-king . . . has his wolves. But what is that against an army of Earth-Masters coming back into their power? And how can one Prince of Hed, even with whatever knowledge of land-law you have the strength to acquire, fight that?"

"I'll find a way."

"How?"

"Danan, I'll find a way. It's either that or die, and I am too stubborn to die." He sat down beside the king, gazing at the rubble around them. "What happened to this place? I wanted to go into the minds of the dead children, to see into their memories, but there is nothing left of them."

Danan shook his head. "I felt it, near the end of summer: a turmoil somewhere in the center of my world. It happened shortly before the shape—the Earth-Masters came here looking for you. I don't know how this place was destroyed, or by whom . . ."

"I know," he whispered. "Wind. The deep wind that shatters stone. . . . The High One destroyed this place."

"But why? It was their one final place of peace."

"I don't know. Unless . . . unless he found another place for them, fearing for their peace even here. I don't know. Maybe somehow I will find him, hold him to some shape that I can understand, and ask him why."

"If you can do even that much—only that—you will repay the land-rulers for whatever power you take from the realm. At least we will die knowing why." He pushed himself up and dropped a hand on Morgon's shoulder. "I understand what you are doing. You need an Earth-Master's power to fight Earth-Masters. If you want to take a mountain onto your shoulders, I'll give you Isig. The High One gives us silence; you give us impossible hope."

The king left him alone. Morgon dropped the torch to the ground, watched it burn away into darkness. He stood up, not fighting his blindness, but breathing the mountain-blackness into himself until it seeped into his mind and hollowed all his bones. His thoughts groped into the stone around him, slid through stone passages, channels of air, sluices of slow, black water. He carved the mountain out of its endless night, shaped it to his thoughts. His mind pushed into solid rock, expanded outward through stone, hollows of silence, deep lakes, until earth crusted over the rock and he felt the snow, downward groping of tree roots. His awareness filled the base of the mountain, flowed slowly, relentlessly upward. He touched the minds of blind fish, strange insects living in a changeless world. He became the topaz locked in a stone that a miner was chiseling loose; he hung upside down, staring at nothing in the brain of a bat. His own shape was lost; his bones curved around an ancient silence, rose endlessly upward, heavy with metal and jewels. He could not find his heart. When he probed for it within masses of stone, he sensed another name, another's heart.

He did not disturb that name bound into every fragment of the mountain. Slowly, as hours he never measured passed, he touched every level of the mountain, groping steadily upward through mine-shafts, through granite, through caves, like Danan's secret thoughts, luminous with their own beauty. The hours turned into days he did not count. His mind, rooted to the ground floor of Isig, shaped to all its rifts and channels, broke through finally to peaks buried under the first winter snows.

He felt ponderous with mountain. His awareness spanned the length and bulk of it. In some minute corner of the darkness far beneath him, his body lay like a fragment of rock on the floor of the mountain.

He seemed to gaze down at it, not knowing how to draw the immensity of his thoughts back into it. Finally, wearily, something in him like an inner eye simply closed, and his mind melted into darkness.

He woke once more as hands came out of darkness, turned him over. He said, before he even opened his eyes, "All right. I learned the land-law of Isig. With one twist of thought I could hold the land-rule. Is that what you'll ask of me next?"

"Morgon."

He opened his eyes. At first he thought dawn had come into the mountain, for the walls around him and Yrth's worn, blind face seemed darkly luminous. Then he whispered, "I can see."

"You swallowed a mountain. Can you stand?" The big hands hauled him to his feet without waiting for his answer. "You might try trusting me a little. You've tried everything else. Take one step."

He started to speak, but the wizard's mind filled his with an image of a small firelit chamber in a tower. He stepped into it and saw Raederle rise, trail fire with her as she came to meet him. He reached out to her; she seemed to come endlessly toward him, dissolving into fire when he finally touched her.

He woke to hear her playing softly on a flute one of the craftsmen had given her. She stopped, smiling as he looked at her, but she looked weary and pale. He sat up, waited for a mountain to shift into place in his head. Then he kissed her.

"You must be tired of waiting for me to wake up."

"It would be nice to talk to you," she said wistfully. "Either you're asleep or you vanish. Yrth was here most of the day. I read to him out of old spell books."

"That was kind of you."

"Morgon, he asked me to. I wanted so badly to question him, but I couldn't. There seemed suddenly nothing to question . . . until he left. I think I'll study wizardry. They knew more odd, petty spells than even witches. Do you know what you're doing? Other than half-killing yourself?"

"I'm doing what you told me to do. I'm playing a riddle-game." He got to his feet, suddenly ravenously hungry, but found only wine. He gulped a cup, while she went to the door, spoke to one of the miners guarding them. He poured more wine and said when she came back, "I told you I would do whatever he wanted me to do. I always have." She looked at him silently. He added simply, "I don't know. Maybe I have already lost. I'll go to Osterland and request that same thing from Har. Knowledge of his land-law. And then to Herun, if I am still alive. And then to Ymris. . . ."

"There are Earth-Masters all over Ymris."

"By that time, I will begin to think like an Earth-Master. And maybe by then the High One will reach out of his silence and either doom me for touching his power, or explain to me what in Hel's name I'm doing." He finished the second cup of wine, then said to her suddenly, intensely, "There is nothing I can trust but the strictures of riddlery. The wise man knows his own name. My name is one of power. So I reach out to it. Does that seem wrong to you? It frightens me. But still I reach. . . ."

She seemed as uncertain as he felt, but she only said calmly, "If it ever seems wrong, I'll be there to tell you."

He spoke with Yrth and Danan in the king's hall late that night. Everyone had gone to bed. They sat close to the hearth; Morgon, watching the old, rugged faces of king and wizard as the fire washed over them, sensed the love of the great mountain in them both. He had shaped the harp at Yrth's request. The wizard's hands moved from string to string, listening to their tones. But he did not play it.

"I must leave for Osterland soon," Morgon said to Danan, "to ask of Har what I asked of you."

Danan looked at Yrth. "Are you going with him?"

The wizard nodded. His light eyes touched Morgon's as if by accident. "How are you planning to get there?" he asked.

"We'll fly, probably. You know the crow-shape."

"Three crows above the dead fields of Osterland . . ." He plucked a string softly. "Nun is in Yrye, with the wolf-king. She came here while you were sleeping, bringing news. She had been in the Three Portions, helping Talies search for you. Mathom of An is gathering a great army of the living and dead to help the Ymris forces. He says he is not going to sit waiting for the inevitable."

Danan straightened. "He is." He leaned forward, his blunt hands joined. "I'm thinking of arming the miners with sword, ax, pick—every weapon we possess—and taking them south. I have shiploads of arms and armor in Kyrth and Kraal bound for Ymris. I could bring an army with them."

"You . . ." Morgon said. His voice caught. "You can't leave Isig."

"I've never done it," the king admitted. "But I am not going to let you battle alone. And if Ymris falls, so will Isig, eventually. Ymris is the stronghold of the realm."

"But, Danan, you aren't a fighter."

"Neither are you," Danan said inarguably.

"How are you going to battle Earth-Masters with picks?"

"We did it here. We'll do it in Ymris. You have only one thing to do, it seems. Find the High One before they can."

"I'm trying. I touched every binding of land-law in Isig, and he didn't seem to care. It's as though I might be doing exactly what he wants." His words echoed oddly through his mind. But Yrth interrupted his thoughts, reaching a little randomly for his wine. Morgon handed it to him before he spilled it. "You aren't using our eyes."

"No. Sometimes I see more clearly in the dark. My mind reaches out to shape the world around me, but judging small distances is not so easy . . ." He gave the starred harp back to Morgon. "Even after all these years, I can still remember what mountain stream, what murmur of fire, what bird cry I pitched each note to . . ."

"I would like to hear you play it," Morgon said. The wizard shook his head imperturbably.

"No, you wouldn't. I play very badly these days, as Danan could tell you." He turned toward Danan. "If you leave at all for Ymris, you should leave soon. You'll be warring on the threshold of winter, and there may be no time when you will be needed more. Ymris warriors dislike battling in snow, but the Earth-Masters would not even notice it. They and the weather will be merciless adversaries."

"Well," Danan said after a silence, "either I fight them in the Ymris winter, or I fight them in my own house. I'll begin gathering men and ships tomorrow. I'll leave Ash here. He won't like it, but he is my land-heir, and it would be senseless to risk both our lives in Ymris."

"He'll want to go in your place," Yrth said.

"I know." His voice was calm, but Morgon sensed the strength in him, the obdurate power of stone that would thunder into movement perhaps once during its existence. "He'll stay. I'm old, and if I die . . . the great, weathered, ancient trees are the ones that do the most damage as they fall."

Morgon's hands closed tightly on the arms of his chair. "Danan," he pleaded, "don't go. There is no need for you to risk your life. You are rooted in our minds to the first years of the realm. If you die, something of hope in us all will die."

"There is need. I am fighting for all things precious to me. Isig. All the lives within it, bound to this mountain's life. You."

"All right," he whispered. "All right. I will find the High One if I have to shake power from his mind until he reaches out of his secret place to stop me."

He talked to Raederle for a long time that night after he left the king's hall. He lay at her side on the soft furs beside the fire. She listened silently while he told her of his intentions and Danan's war plans and the news that Nun had brought to Isig about her father. She said, twisting tufts of sheep pelt into knots, "I wonder if the roof of Anuin fell in with all the shouting there must have been over that decision."

"He wouldn't have made it unless he thought war was inevitable."

"No. He saw that war coming long ago, out of his crow's eyes . . ." She sighed, wrenching at the wool. "I suppose Rood will be at one side and Duac at the other, arguing all the way to Ymris." She stopped, her eyes on the fire, and he saw the sudden longing in her face. He touched her cheek.

"Raederle. Do you want to go home for a while and see them? You could be there in a few days, flying, and then meet me somewhere—Herun, perhaps."

"No."

"I dragged you down Trader's Road in the dust and heat; I harried you until you changed shape; I put you into Ghisteslwchlohm's hands; and then I left you facing Earth-Masters by yourself while I ran—"

"Morgon."

"And then, after you came into your own power and followed me all the way across the backlands into Erlenstar Mountain, I walked off into the wastes and left you without a word, so you had to search for me through half the northlands. Then you lead me home, and I hardly even talk to you. How in Hel's name can you stand me by this time?"

She smiled. "I don't know. I wonder sometimes, too. Then you touch my face with your scarred hand and read my mind. Your eyes know me. That's why I keep following you all over the realm, barefoot or half-frozen, cursing the sun or the wind, or myself because I have no more sense than to love a man who does not even possess a bed I can crawl into at night. And sometimes I curse you because you have spoken my name in a way that no other man in the realm will speak it, and I will listen for that until I die. So," she added, as he gazed down at her mutely, "how can I leave you?"

He dropped his face against hers, so that their brows and cheekbones touched, and he looked deeply into a single, amber eye. He watched it smile. She put her arms around him, kissed the hollow of his throat, and then his heart. Then she slid her hand between their mouths. He murmured a protest into her palm. She said, "I want to talk."

He sat up, breathing deeply, and tossed another log on the fire. "All right."

"Morgon, what will you do if that wizard with his harpist's hands betrays you again? If you find the High One for him, and then realize too late that he has a mind more devious than Ghisteslwchlohm's?"

"I already know he has." He was silent, brooding, his arms around his knees. "I've thought of that again and again. Did you see him use power in Lungold?"

"Yes. He was protecting the traders as they fought."

"Then he is not an Earth-Master; their power is bound."

"He is a wizard."

"Or something else we have no name for . . . that's what I'm afraid of." He stirred a little. "He didn't even try to dissuade Danan from bringing the miners to Ymris. They aren't warriors; they'll be slaughtered. And Danan has no business dying on the battlefield. He said once he wanted to become a tree, under the sun and stars, when it was time for him to die. Still, he and Yrth have known each other for many centuries. Maybe Yrth knew it was futile to argue with a stone."

"If it is Yrth. Are you even sure of that?"

"Yes. He made certain I knew that. He played my harp."

She was silent, her fingers trailing up and down his backbone. "Well," she said softly, "then maybe you can trust him."

"I have tried," he whispered. Her hand stilled. He lay back down beside her, listening to the pine keen as it burned. He put his wrist over his eyes. "I'm going to fail. I could never win an argument with him. I couldn't even kill him. All I can do is wait until he names himself, and by then it may be too late . . ."

She said something after a moment. What it was he did not hear, for something without definition in the dark of his mind had stirred. It felt at first like a mind-touch he could not stop. So he explored it, and it became a sound. His lips parted; the breath came quick, dry out of him. The sound heaved into a bellow, like the bellow of the sea smashing docks and beached boats and fishermen's houses, then riding high, piling up and over a cliff to tear at fields, topple trees, roar darkly through the night, drowning screams of men and animals. He was on his feet without knowing it, echoing the cry he heard in the mind of the land-ruler of Hed.

"No!"

He heard a tangle of voices. He could not see in the whirling black flood. His body seemed veined with land-law. He felt the terrible wave whirled back, sucking with it broken sacks of grain, sheep and pigs, beer barrels, the broken walls of barns and houses, fenceposts, soup cauldrons, harrows, children screaming in the dark. Someone gripped him, crying his name over and over. Fear, despair, helpless anger washed through him, his own and Eliard's. A mind caught at his mind, but he was bound to Hed, a thousand miles away. Then a hand snapped painfully across his face, rocking him back, out of his vision.

He found himself staring into Yrth's blind eyes. A hot, furious sense of the wizard's incomprehensible injustice swept through him so strongly he could not even speak. He doubled his fist and swung. Yrth was far heavier than he expected: the blow wrenched his bones from wrist to shoulder, and split his knuckles, as if he had struck stone or wood. Yrth, looking vaguely surprised, wavered in the air before he might have fallen and then vanished. He reappeared a moment later and sat down on the rim of the firebed, cupping a bleeding cheekbone.

The two guards in the doorway and Raederle all had the same expression on their faces. They seemed also to be bound motionless. Morgon, catching his breath, the sudden fury dissipated, said, "Hed is under attack. I'm going there."

"No."

"The sea came up over the cliffs. I heard—I heard their voices, Eliard's voice. If he's dead—I swear, if he is dead—if you hadn't hit me, I would know! I was in his mind. Tol—Tol was destroyed. Everything. Everyone." He looked at Raederle. "I'll be back as soon as I can."

"I'm coming," she whispered.

"No."

"Yes."

"Morgon," Yrth said. "You will be killed."

"Tristan." His hands clenched; he swallowed a painful, burning knot. "I don't know if she's alive or dead!" He closed his eyes, flinging his mind across the dark, rain-drenched night, across the vast forests, as far as he could reach. He stepped toward the edge of his awareness. But an image formed in his mind, drew him back as he moved, and he opened his eyes to the firelit walls of the tower.

"It's a trap," Yrth said. His voice sounded hollow with pain, but very patient. Morgon did not bother to answer. He drew the image of a falcon out of his mind, but swiftly, even before he had begun to change shape, the image changed to light, burned eyes that saw into his mind. They pulled him back into himself.

"Morgon, I'll go. They are expecting you; they hardly know me. I can travel swiftly; I'll be back very soon . . ." He stood up abruptly as Morgon filled his mind with illusions of fire and shadow and disappeared within them. He had nearly walked out of the room when the wizard's eyes pierced into his thoughts, breaking his concentration.

The anger flared in him again. He kept walking and brought himself up against an illusion of solid stone in the doorway. "Morgon," the wizard said, and Morgon whirled. He flung a shout into Yrth's mind that should have jarred the wizard's attention away from his illusion. But the shout echoed harmlessly into a mind like a vast chasm of darkness.

He stood still, then, his hands flat on the illusion, a fine sweat of fear and exhaustion forming on his face. The darkness was like a warning. But he let his mind touch it again, form around it, try to move through its illusion to the core of the wizard's thoughts. He only blundered deeper into darkness, with the sense of some vast power constantly retreating before his searching. He followed it until he could no longer find his way back. . . .

He came out of the darkness slowly, to find himself sitting motionless beside the fire. Raederle was beside him, her fingers locked to his limp hand. Yrth stood in front of them. His face looked almost grey with weariness; his eyes were bloodshot. His boots and the hem of his long robe were stained with dry mud and crusted salt. The cut on his cheek had closed.

Morgon started. Danan, on his other side, stooped to lay a hand on his shoulder. "Morgon," he said softly, "Yrth has just come back from Hed. It's mid-morning. He has been gone two nights and a day."

"What did you—" He stood up, too abruptly. Danan caught him, held him while the blood behind his eyes receded. "How did you do that to me?" he whispered.

"Morgon, forgive me." The strained, weary voice seemed haunted with overtones of another voice. "The Earth-Masters were waiting for you in Hed. If you had gone, you would have died there, and more lives would have been lost battling for you. They couldn't find you anywhere; they were trying to drive you out of your hiding."

"Eliard—"

"He's safe. I found him standing among the ruins of Akren. The wave destroyed Tol, Akren, most of the farms along the western coast. I spoke to the farmers; they saw some fighting between strange, armed men, they said, who did not belong in Hed. I questioned one of the wraiths; he said there was little to be done against the shape of water. I told Eliard who I am, where you are . . . he was stunned with the suddenness of it. He said that he knew you had sensed the destruction, but he was glad you had had sense enough not to come."

Morgon drew breath; it seemed to burn through him. "Tristan?"

"As far as Eliard knows, she's safe. Some feeble-minded trader told her you had disappeared. So she left Hed to look for you, but a sailor recognized her in Caithnard and stopped her. She is on her way home." Morgon put his hand over his eyes. The wizard's hand rose, went out to him, but he drew back. "Morgon." The wizard was dredging words from somewhere out of his exhaustion. "It was not a complex binding. You were not thinking clearly enough to break it."

"I was thinking clearly," he whispered. "I did not have the power to break it." He stopped, aware of Danan behind him, puzzled, yet trusting them both. The dark riddle of the wizard's power loomed again over his thoughts, over the whole of the realm, from Isig to Hed. There seemed no escape from it. He began to sob harshly, hopelessly, possessing no other answer. The wizard, his shoulders slumping as if the weight of the realm dragged at his back, gave him nothing but silence.

THEY LEFT ISIG the next day: three crows flying among the billowing smoke from Danan's forges. They crossed the Ose, flew over the docks at Kyrth; every ship moored there was being overhauled for a long journey down the river to the heavy autumn seas. The grey rains beat against them over the forests of Osterland; the miles of ancient pine were hunched and weary. Grim Mountain rose in the distance out of a ring of mist. The east and north winds swarmed around them; the crows dipped from current to current, their feathers alternately sleeked and billowed by the erratic winds. They stopped to rest frequently. By nightfall they were barely halfway to Yrye.

They stopped for the night under the broad eaves of an old tree whose thick branches sighed resignedly in the rain. They found nitches in it to protect themselves from the weather. Two crows huddled together on a branch; the third landed below them, a big, dark, windblown bird who had not spoken since they left Isig. For hours they slept, shielded by the weave of branches, lulled by the wind.

The winds died at midnight. The rains slowed to a whisper, then faded. The clouds parted, loosing the stars cluster by cluster against a dazzling blackness. The unexpected silence found its way into Morgon's crow-dreams. His eyes opened.

Raederle was motionless beside him, a little cloud of soft black plumage. The crow beneath him was still. His own shape pulled at him dimly, wanting to breathe the spices of the night, wanting to become moonlight. He spread his wings after a moment, dropped soundlessly to the ground, and changed shape.

He stood quietly, enfolded in the Osterland night. His mind opened to all its sounds and smells and shapes. He laid his hand against the wet, rough flank of the tree and felt it drowsing. He heard the pad of some night hunter across the soft, damp ground. He smelled the rich, tangled odors of wet pine, of dead bark and loam crumbled under his feet. His thoughts yearned to become part of the land, under the light, silvery touch of the moon. He let his mind drift finally into the vast, tideless night.

He shaped his mind to the roots of trees, to buried stones, to the brains of animals moving obliviously across the path of his awareness. He sensed in all things the ancient sleeping fire of Har's law, the faint, perpetual fire behind his eyes. He touched fragments of the dead within the earth, the bones and memories of men and animals. Unlike the wraiths of An, they were quiescent, at rest in the heart of the wild land. Quietly, unable to resist his own longings, he began weaving his bindings of awareness and knowledge into the law of Osterland.

Slowly he began to understand the roots of the land-law. The bindings of snow and sun had touched all life. The wild winds set the vesta's speed; the fierceness of seasons shaped the wolf's brain; the winter night seeped into the raven's eye. The more he understood, the deeper he drew himself into it: gazing at the moon out of a horned owl's eyes, melting with a wild cat through the bracken, twisting his thoughts even into the fragile angles of a spider's web, and into the endless, sinuous wind of ivy spiralling a tree trunk. He was so engrossed that he touched a vesta's mind without questioning it. A little later, he touched another. And then, suddenly, his mind could not move without finding vesta, as if they had shaped themselves out of the moonlight around him. They were running: a soundless white wind coming from all directions. Curiously, he explored their impulse. Some danger had sent them flowing across the night, he sensed, and wondered what would dare trouble the vesta in Har's domain. He probed deeper. Then he shook himself free of them; the swift, startled breath he drew of the icy air cleared his head.

It was nearly dawn. What he thought was moonlight was the first silver-grey haze of morning. The vesta were very close, a great herd wakened by Har, their minds drawn with a fine instinct towards whatever had brought the king out of his sleep and disturbed the ancient workings of his mind. Morgon stood still, considering various impulses: to take the crow-shape and escape into the tree; to take the vesta-shape; to try to reach Har's mind, and hope he was not too angry to listen. Before he could act, he found Yrth standing next to him.

"Be still," he said, and Morgon, furious at his own acquiescence, followed the unlikely advice.

He began to see the vesta all around them, through the trees. Their speed was incredible; the unwavering drive toward one isolated point in the forests was eerie. They were massed around him in a matter of moments, surrounding the tree. They did not threaten him; they simply stood in a tight, motionless circle, gazing at him out of alien purple eyes, their horns sketching gold circles against the trees and the pallid morning sky as far as he could see.

Raederle woke. She gave one faint, surprised squawk. Her mind reached into Morgon's; she said his name on a questioning note. He did not dare answer, and she was silent after that. The sun whitened a wall of cloud in the east, then disappeared. The rain began again, heavy, sullen drops that plumeted straight down from a windless sky.

An hour later, something began to ripple through the herd. Morgon, drenched from head to foot and cursing Yrth's advice, watched the movement with relief. One set of gold horns was moving through the herd; he watched the bright circles constantly fall apart before it and rejoin in its wake. He knew it must be Har. He wiped rain out of his eyes with a sodden sleeve and sneezed suddenly. Instantly, the vesta nearest him, standing so placidly until then, belled like a stag and reared. One gold hoof slashed the air apart inches from Morgon's face. His muscles turned to stone. The vesta subsided, dropping back to gaze at him again, peacefully.

Morgon stared back at it, his heartbeat sounding uncomfortably loud. The front circle broke again, shifting to admit the great vesta. It changed shape. The wolf-king stood before Morgon, the smile in his eyes boding no good to whoever had interrupted his sleep.

The smile died as he recognized Morgon. He turned his head, spoke one word sharply; the vesta faded like a dream. Morgon waited silently, tensely, for judgment. It did not come. The king reached out, pushed the wet hair back from the stars on his face, as if answering a doubt. Then he looked at Yrth.

"You should have warned him."

"I was asleep," Yrth said. Har grunted.

"I thought you never slept." He glanced up into the tree and his face gentled. He held up his hand. The crow dropped down onto his fingers, and he set it on his shoulder. Morgon stirred, then. Har looked at him, his eyes glinting, ice-blue, the color of wind across the sky above the wastes.

"You," he said, "stealing fire from my mind. Couldn't you have waited until morning?"

"Har . . ." Morgon whispered. He shook his head, not knowing where to begin. Then he stepped forward, his head bowed, into the wolf-king's embrace. "How can you trust me like this?" he demanded.

"Occasionally," Har admitted, "I am not rational." He loosed Morgon, held him back to look at him. "Where did Raederle find you?"

"In the wastes."

"You look like a man who has been listening to those deadly winds . . . Come to Yrye. A vesta can travel faster than a crow, and this deep into Osterland, vesta running together will not be noticed." He dropped his hand lightly onto the wizard's shoulder. "Ride on my back. Or on Morgon's."

"No," Morgon said abruptly, without thinking. Har's eyes went back to him.

Yrth said, before the king could speak, "I'll ride in crow-shape." His voice was tired. "There was a time when I would have chanced running blind for the sheer love of running, but no more . . . I must be getting old." He changed shape, fluttered from the ground to Har's other shoulder.

The wolf-king, frowning a little, his lined face shadowed by crows, seemed to hear something behind Morgon's silence. But he only said, "Let's get out of the rain."

They ran through the day until twilight: three vesta running north toward winter, one with a crow riding in the circle of its horns. They reached Yrye by nightfall. As they slowed and came to a halt in the yard, their sides heaving, the heavy doors of weathered oak and gold were thrown open. Aia appeared with wolves at her knees and Nun behind her, smiling out of her smoke.

Nun hugged Raederle in vesta-shape and again in her own shape. Aia, her smooth ivory hair unbraided, stared at Morgon a little, then kissed his cheek very gently. She patted Har's shoulder, and Yrth's, and said in her placid voice, "I sent everyone home. Nun told me who was coming."

"I told her," Yrth said, before Har had to ask. The king smiled a little. They went into the empty hall. The fire roared down the long bed; platters of hot meat, hot bread, hissing brass pots of spiced wine, steaming stews and vegetables lay on a table beside the hearth. They were eating almost before they sat down, quickly, hungrily. Then, as the edge wore off, they settled in front of the fire with wine and began to talk a little.

Har said to Morgon, who was half-drowsing on a bench with his arm around Raederle, "So. You came to Osterland to learn my land-law. I'll make a bargain with you."

That woke him. He eyed the king a moment, then said simply, "No. Whatever you want, I'll give you."

"That," Har said softly, "sounds like a fair exchange for land-law. You may wander freely through my mind, if I may wander freely through yours." He seemed to sense something in a vague turn of Yrth's head. "You have some objection?"

"Only that we have very little time," Yrth said. Morgon looked at him.

"Are you advising me to take the knowledge from the earth itself? That would take weeks."

"No."

"Then, are you advising me not to take it at all?"

The wizard sighed. "No."

"Then what do you advise me to do?" Raederle stirred in his hold, at the faint, challenging edge to his voice. Har was still in his great carved chair; the wolf at his knee opened its eyes suddenly to gaze at Morgon.

"Are you," Har said amazedly, "picking a quarrel with Yrth in my hall?"

The wizard shook his head. "It's my fault," he explained. "There is a mind-hold Morgon was not aware of. I used it to keep him in Isig a few days ago when Hed was attacked. It seemed better than to let him walk into a trap."

Morgon, his hands locking around the rim of his cup, checked a furious retort. Nun said, puzzled, "What hold?" Yrth looked toward her silently. Her face grew quiet for a moment, remote as if she were dreaming. Yrth loosed her, and her brows rose. "Where in Hel's name did you learn that?"

"I saw the possibility of it long ago, and I explored it into existence." He sounded apologetic. "I would never have used it except under extreme circumstances."

"Well, I would be upset, too. But I can certainly understand why you did it. If the Earth-Masters are searching for Morgon at the other end of the realm, there's no reason to distract them by giving them what they want."

Morgon's head bowed. He felt the touch of Har's gaze, like something physical, forcing his face up. He met the curious, ungentle eyes helplessly. The king loosed him abruptly.

"You need some sleep."

Morgon stared down into his wine. "I know." He felt Raederle's hand slide from his ribs to touch his cheek, and the weight of despair in him eased a little. He said haltingly, breaking the silence that had fallen over the hall, "But first, tell me how the vesta are bound like that into the defense of land-law. I was never aware of it as a vesta."

"I was hardly aware of it myself," the king admitted. "It's an ancient binding, I think; the vesta are extremely powerful, and I believe they rouse to the defense of the land, as well as land-law. But they have not fought anything but wolves for centuries, and the binding lay dormant at the bottom of my mind . . . I'll show you the binding, of course. Tomorrow." He looked across the fire at the wizard, who was refilling his cup slowly with hot spiced wine. "Yrth, did you go to Hed?"

"Yes." The pitch of liquid pouring into the cup changed as it neared the rim, and Yrth set the pot down.

"How did you cross Ymris?"

"Very carefully. I took no more time than necessary on my way to Hed, but returning, I stopped a few minutes to speak to Aloil. Our minds are linked; I was able to find him without using power. He was with Astrin Ymris, and what is left of the king's forces around Caerweddin."

There was another silence. A branch snapped in the fire and a shower of sparks fled towards the smoke hole in the roof. "What is left of the king's forces?" Har asked.

"Astrin was unsure. Half the men were pushed into Ruhn when Wind Plain was lost; the rest fled northward. The rebels—whatever they are: living men, dead men, Earth-Masters—have not attacked Caerweddin or any of the major cities in Ymris." He gazed thoughtfully through someone else's eyes at the fire. "They keep taking the ancient, ruined cities. There are many across Ruhn, one or two in east Umber, and King's Mouth Plain, near Caerweddin. Astrin and his generals are in dispute about what to do. The war lords contend that the rebels will not take King's Mouth Plain without attacking Caerweddin. Astrin does not want to waste lives warring over a dead city. He is beginning to think that the king's army and the rebel army are not fighting the same war . . ."

Har grunted. He rose, the wolf's head sliding from his knee. "A one-eyed man who can see. . . . Does he see an end to the war?"

"No. But he told me he is haunted by dreams of Wind Plain, as if some answer lies there. The tower on the plain is still bound by a living force of illusion."

"Wind Tower." The words came out of Morgon unexpectedly, some shard of a riddle the wizard's words unburied. "I had forgotten. . . ."

"I tried to climb it once," Nun said reminiscently.

Har took his cup to the table for more wine. "So did I." He asked, as Morgon glanced at him, "Have you?"

"No."

"Why not? It's a riddle. You're a riddler."

He thought back. "The first time I was on Wind Plain with Astrin I lost my memory. There was only one riddle I was interested in answering. The second time . . ." He shifted a little. "I passed through very quickly, at night. I was pursuing a harpist. Nothing could have stopped me."

"Then perhaps," Har said softly, "you should try."

"You're not thinking," Nun protested. "The plain must be full of Earth-Masters."

"I am always thinking," Har said. A thought startled through Morgon; he moved again without realizing it, and Raederle lifted her face, blinking.

"It's bound by illusion . . . no one can reach the top of it. No one works an illusion unless there is something to be hidden, unseen. . . . But what would be hidden for so long at the top of the tower?"

"The High One," Raederle suggested sleepily. They gazed at her, Nun with her pipe smoldering in her fingers, Har with his cup halfway to his mouth. "Well," she added, "that's the one thing everyone is looking for. And the one place maybe that no one has looked."

Har's eyes went to Morgon. He ran his hand through his hair, his face clearing, easing into wonder. "Maybe. Har, you know I will try. But I always thought the binding of that illusion was some forgotten work of dead Earth-Masters, not . . . not of a living Earth-Master. Wait." He sat straight, staring ahead of him. "Wind Tower. The name of it . . . the name . . . wind." They roused suddenly through his memories: the deep wind in Erlenstar Mountain, the tumultuous winds of the wastes, singing to all the notes of his harp. "Wind Tower."

"What do you see?"

"I don't know . . . a harp strung with wind." As the winds died in his mind, he realized that he did not know who had asked the question. The vision receded, leaving him with only words and the certainty that they somehow fit together. "The tower. The starred harp. Wind."

Har brushed a white weasel off his chair and sat down slowly. "Can you bind the winds as well as land-law?" he asked incredulously.

"I don't know."

"I see. You haven't tried, yet."

"I wouldn't know how to begin." He added, "Once I shaped wind. To kill. That's all I know I can do."

"Well—" He checked, shaking his head. The hall was very still; animals' eyes glowed among the rushes. Yrth set his cup down with a small, distracting clink as it hit the edge of a tray. Nun guided it for him.

"Small distances," he murmured ruefully.

"I think," the wolf-king said, "that if I start questioning you, it will be the longest riddle I have ever asked."

"You already asked the longest riddle," Morgon said. "Two years ago, when you saved my life in that blizzard and brought me into your house. I'm still trying to answer it for you."

"Two years ago, I gave you the knowledge of the vesta-shape. Now you have come back for knowledge of my land-law. What will you ask of me next?"

"I don't know." He drained his cup and slid his hands around the mouth of it. "Maybe trust." He set the cup down abruptly, traced the flawless rim with his fingertips. He was exhausted suddenly; he wanted to lay his head on the table among the plates and sleep. He heard the wolf-king rise.

"Ask me tomorrow."

Har touched him. As he dragged his eyes open and stood up to follow the king out of the hall, he found nothing strange in the answer.

He slept dreamlessly until dawn beside Raederle in the warm, rich chamber Aia had prepared for them. Then, as the sky lightened, vesta slowly crowded into his mind, forming a tight, perfect circle about him so that he could not move, and all their eyes were light, secret, blind. He woke abruptly, murmuring. Raederle groped for him, said something incoherent. He waited until she was quiet again. Then he got up soundlessly and dressed. He could smell one last sweet pine log burning into embers from the silent hall, and he knew, somehow, that Har was still there.

The king watched him as he came into the hall. He stepped quietly past small animals curled asleep beside the hearth and sat down beside Har. The king dropped a hand on his shoulder, held him a moment in a gentle, comfortable silence.

Then he said, "We'll need privacy or traders will spread rumors from here to Anuin. They have been flocking to my house lately, asking me questions, asking Nun . . ."

"There's the shed in the back," Morgon suggested, "where you taught me the vesta-shape."

"It seems appropriate . . . I'll wake Hugin; he can tend to our needs." He smiled a little. "For a while, I thought Hugin might return to the vesta; he became so shy among men. But since Nun came and told him everything she knew about Suth, I think he might turn into a wizard . . ." He was silent, sending a thought, Morgon suspected, through the quiet house. Hugin wandered in a few moments later, blinking sleepily and combing his white hair with his fingers. He stopped short when he saw Morgon. He was big-boned and graceful like the vesta, his deep eyes still shy. He stirred the rushes a little, flushing, looking like a vesta might if it were on the verge of smiling.

"We need your help," Har said. Hugin's head ducked an acquiescence. Then, gazing at Morgon, he found his tongue.

"Nun said you battled the wizard who killed Suth. That you saved the lives of the Lungold wizards. Did you kill the Founder?"

"No."

"Why not?"

"Hugin," Har murmured. Then he checked himself and looked at Morgon curiously. "Why not? Did you spend all your passion for revenge on that harpist?"

"Har . . ." His muscles had tensed under Har's hand. The king frowned suddenly.

"What is it? Are you wraith-driven? Yrth told me last night how the harpist died."

Morgon shook his head wordlessly. "You're a riddler," he said abruptly. "You tell me. I need help."

Har's mouth tightened. He rose, telling Hugin, "Bring food, wine, firewood to the shed. And pallets. When Raederle of An wakes, let her know where we are. Bring her." He added a little impatiently as the boy flushed scarlet, "You've talked to her before."

"I know." He was smiling suddenly. Under Har's quizzical eye, he sobered and began to move. "I'll bring her. And everything else."

They spent that day and the next nine nights together in the smokey, circular shed behind the king's house. Morgon slept by day. Har, seemingly inexhaustible, kept his court by day. Morgon, pulling out of Har's mind each dawn, found Raederle beside him, and Hugin, and sometimes Nun, knocking her ashes into the fire. He rarely spoke to them; waking or sleeping, his mind seemed linked to Har's, forming trees, ravens, snow-covered peaks, all the shapes deep in the wolf-king's mind that were bound to his awareness. Har gave him everything and demanded nothing during those days. Morgon explored Osterland through him, forming his own binding of awareness with every root, stone, wolf pup, white falcon and vesta in the land. The king was full of odd wizardry, Morgon discovered. He could speak to owls and wolves; he could speak to an iron knife or arrowtip and tell it where to strike. He knew the men and animals of his land as he knew his own family. His land-law extended even into the edges of the northern wastes, where he had raced vesta for miles across a desert of snow. He was shaped by his own law; the power in him tempered Morgon's heart with ice, and then with fire, until he seemed one more shape of Har's brain, or Har a reflection of his own power.

He broke loose from Har then, rolled onto a pallet, and fell asleep. Like a land-heir, he dreamed Har's memories. With a restless, furious intensity, his dreams spanned centuries of history, of rare battles, of riddle-games that lasted for days and years. He built Yrye, heard the wizard Suth give him five strange riddles for his keeping, lived among wolves, among the vesta, fathered heirs, dispensed judgment and grew so old he became ageless. Finally, the rich, feverish dreams came to an end; he drew deeply into himself, into a dreamless night. He slept without moving until a name drifted into his mind. Clinging to it, he brought himself back into the world. He blinked awake, found Raederle kneeling beside him.

She smiled down at him. "I wanted to find out if you were alive or dead." She touched his hand; his fingers closed around hers. "You can move."

He sat up slowly. The shed was empty; he could hear the winds outside trying to pick apart the roof. He tried to speak; his voice would not come for a moment. "How long—how long did I sleep?"

"Har said over two thousand years."

"Is he that old?" He stared at nothing a little, then leaned over to kiss her. "Is it day or night?"

"It's noon. You've slept nearly two days. I missed you. I only had Hugin to talk to most of the time."

"Who?"

Her smile deepened. "Do you remember my name?"

He nodded. "You are a two-thousand-year-old woman named Raederle." He sat quietly, holding her hand, putting the world into shape around him. He stood up finally; she slid an arm around him to steady him. The wind snatched the door out of his hand as he opened it. The first flakes of winter snow swirled and vanished in the winds.

They shattered the silence in his mind, whipped over him, persistent, icy, shaping him back out of his dreams. He ran across the yard with Raederle, into the warmth of the king's dark house.

Har came to him that evening as he lay beside the fire in his chamber. He was remembering and slowly absorbing the knowledge he had taken. Raederle had left him alone, deep in his thoughts. Har, entering, brought him out of himself. Their eyes met across the fire in a peaceful, wordless recognition. Then Har sat down, and Morgon straightened, shifting logs with his hands until the drowsing fire woke.

"I have come," Har said softly, "for what you owe me."

"I owe you everything." He waited. The fire slowly blurred in front of him; he was lost to himself again, this time among his own memories.

The king worked through them a little randomly, not sure what he would find. Very early in his exploring, he loosed Morgon in utter astonishment.

"You struck an old, blind wizard?"

"Yes. I couldn't kill him."

The king's eyes blazed with a glacial light. He seemed about to speak; instead he caught the thread of Morgon's memories again. He wove backwards and forwards, from Trader's Road to Lungold and Erlenstar Mountain, and the weeks Morgon had spent in the wastes, harping to the winds. He watched the harpist die; he listened to Yrth speaking to Morgon and to Danan in Isig; he listened to Raederle giving Morgon a riddle that drew him back out of the dead land, once again among the living. Then, he loosed Morgon abruptly and prowled the chamber like a wolf.

"Deth."

The name chilled Morgon unexpectedly, as though Har had turned the impossible into truth with a word. The king paced to his side and stopped moving finally. He stared down into the fire. Morgon dropped his face against his forearms wearily.

"I don't know what to do. He holds more power than anyone else in this realm. You felt that mind-hold—"

"He has always held your mind."

"I know. And I can't fight him. I can't. You saw how he drew me on Trader's Road . . . with nothing. With a harp he could barely play. I went to him. . . . At Anuin I couldn't kill him. I didn't even want to.

More than anything, I wanted a reason not to. He gave me one. I thought he had walked out of my life forever, since I left him no place in the realm to harp. I left him one place. He harped to me. He betrayed me again, and I saw him die. But he didn't die. He only replaced one mask with another. He made the sword I nearly killed him with. He threw me to Ghisteslwchlohm like a bone, and he rescued me from Earth-Masters on the same day. I don't understand him. I can't challenge him. I have no proof, and he would twist his way out of any accusation. His power frightens me. I don't know what he is. He gives me silence like the silence out of trees . . ." His voice trailed away. He found himself listening to Har's silence.

He raised his head. The king was still gazing into the fire, but it seemed to Morgon that he was watching it from the distance of many centuries. He was very still; he did not seem to be breathing. His face looked harsher than Morgon had ever seen it, as if the lines had been riven into it by the icy, merciless winds that scarred his land.

"Morgon," he whispered, "be careful." It was, Morgon realized slowly, not a warning but a plea. The king dropped to his haunches, held Morgon's shoulders very gently, as if he were grasping something elusive, intangible, that was beginning to shape itself under his hands.

"Har."

The king shook away his question. He held Morgon's eyes with an odd intensity, gazing through him into the heart of his confusion. "Let the harpist name himself . . ."

13

THE WOLF-KING GAVE him no more answers than that. Something else lay hidden behind Har's eyes that he would not speak of. Morgon sensed it in him and so did Yrth, who asked, the evening before they left Yrye, "Har, what are you thinking? I can hear something beneath all your words."

They were sitting beside the fire. The winds were whistling across the roof, dragging shreds of smoke up through the opening. Har looked at the wizard across the flames. His face was still honed hard, ancient, by whatever he had seen. But his voice, when he spoke to the wizard, held only its familiar, dry affection.

"It's nothing for you to concern yourself about."

"Why can't I believe that?" Yrth murmured. "Here in this hall, where you have riddled your way through centuries to truth?"

"Trust me," Har said. The wizard's eyes sought toward him through their private darkness.

"You're going to Ymris."

"No," Morgon said abruptly. He had stopped fighting Yrth; he trod warily in the wizard's presence, as in the presence of some powerful, unpredictable animal. But the wizard's words, which seemed to lie somewhere between a statement and a command, startled a protest out of him. "Har, what can you do in Ymris besides get yourself killed?"

"I have no intention," Har said, "of dying in Ymris." He opened a palm to the fire, revealing withered crescents of power; the wordless gesture haunted Morgon.

"Then what do you intend?"

"I'll give you one answer for another."

"Har, this is no game!"

"Isn't it? What lies at the top of a tower of winds?"

"I don't know. When I know, I'll come back here and tell you. If you'll be patient."

"I have no more patience," Har said. He got up, pacing restlessly; his steps brought him to the side of the wizard's chair. He picked up a couple of small logs and knelt to position them on the fire. "If you die," he said, "it will hardly matter where I am. Will it?"

Morgon was silent. Yrth leaned forward, resting one hand on Har's shoulder for balance, and caught a bit of flaming kindling as it rolled toward them. He tossed it back onto the fire. "It will be difficult to get through to Wind Tower. But I think Astrin's army will make it possible." He loosed Har, brushed ash from his hands, and the king rose. Morgon, watching his grim face, swallowed arguments until there was nothing left in his mind but a fierce, private resolve.

He bade Har farewell at dawn the next day; and three crows began the long journey south to Herun. The flight was dreary with rain. The wizard led them with astonishing accuracy across the level rangelands of Osterland and the forests bordering the Ose. They did not change shape again until they had crossed the Winter and the vast no-man's-land between Osterland and Ymris stretched before them. The rains stilled finally near dusk on the third day of their journey, and with a mutual, almost wordless consent, they dropped to the ground to rest in their own shapes.

"How," Morgon asked Yrth almost before the wizard had coaxed a tangle of soaked wood into flame, "in Hel's name are you guiding us? You led us straight to the Winter. And how did you get from Isig to Hed and back in two days?"

Yrth glanced toward his voice. The flame caught between his hands, engulfing the wood, and he drew back. "Instinct," he said. "You think too much while you fly."

"Maybe." He subsided beside the fire. Raederle, breathing deeply of the moist, pine-scented air, was eyeing the river wistfully.

"Morgon, would you catch a fish? I am so hungry, and I don't want to change back into a crow-shape to eat—whatever crows eat. If you do that, I'll look for mushrooms."

"I smell apples," Yrth said. He rose, wandering toward a scent. Morgon watched him a little incredulously.

"I don't smell apples," he murmured. "And I hardly think at all when I fly." He rose, then stooped again to kiss Raederle. "Do you smell apples?"

"I smell fish. And more rain. Morgon . . ." She put her arm on his shoulders suddenly, keeping him down. He watched her grope for words.

"What?"

"I don't know." She ran her free hand through her hair. Her eyes were perplexed. "He moves across the earth like a master . . ."

"I know."

"I keep wanting—I keep wanting to trust him. Until I remember how he hurt you. Then I become afraid of him, of where he is leading us, and how skillfully. . . . But I forget my fear again so easily." Her fingers tugged a little absently at his lank hair. "Morgon."

"What?"

"I don't know." She rose abruptly, impatient with herself. "I don't know what I'm thinking."

She crossed the clearing to explore a pallid cluster of mushrooms. Morgon went to the broad river, waded into the shallows, and stood silently as an old tree stump, watching for fish and trying not to think. He splashed himself twice, while trout skidded through his fingers. Finally, he made his mind a mirror of greyness to match the water and the sky and began to think like a fish.

He caught three trout and gutted them awkwardly, for lack of anything else, with his sword. He turned at last to bring them back to the fire and found Yrth and Raederle watching him. Raederle was smiling. The wizard's expression was unfathomable. Morgon joined them. He set the fish on a flat stone and cleaned his blade on the grass. He sheathed it once more within an illusion and squatted down by the fire.

"All right," he said. "Instinct." He took Raederle's mushrooms and began stuffing the fish. "But that doesn't explain your journey to Hed."

"How far can you travel in a day?"

"Maybe across Ymris. I don't know. I don't like moving from moment to moment across distances. It's exhausting, and I never know whose mind I might accidently touch."

"Well," the wizard said softly, "I was desperate. I didn't want you to fight your way out of that mind-hold before I returned."

"I couldn't have—"

"You have the power. You can see in the dark."

Morgon stared at him wordlessly. Something shivered across his skin. "Is that what it was?" he whispered. "A memory?"

"The darkness of Isig."

"Or of Erlenstar Mountain."

"Yes. It was that simple."

"Simple." He remembered Har's plea and breathed soundlessly until the ache and snarl of words in his chest loosened. He wrapped the fish in wet leaves, pushed the stone into the fire. "Nothing is simple."

The wizard's fingers traced the curve of a blade of grass to its tip. "Some things are. Night. Fire. A blade of grass. If you place your hand in a flame and think of your pain, you will burn yourself. But if you think only of the flame, or the night, accepting it, without remembering . . . it becomes very simple."

"I cannot forget."

The wizard was silent. By the time the fish began to spatter, the rains had started again. They ate hurriedly and changed shape, flew through the drenching rains to shelter among the trees.

They crossed the Ose a couple of days later and changed shape again on the bank of the swift, wild river. It was late afternoon. Light and shadow dazzled across their faces from the wet, bright sky. They gazed at one another a little bewilderedly, as if surprised by their shapes.

Raederle dropped with a sigh on a fallen log. "I can't move," she whispered. "I am so tired of being a crow. I am beginning to forget how to talk."

"I'll hunt," Morgon said. He stood still, intending to move, while weariness ran over him like water.

Yrth said, "I'll hunt." He changed shape again, before either of them could answer. A falcon mounted the air, higher and higher, in a fierce, blazing flight into the rain and sunlight, then he levelled finally, began circling.

"How?" Morgon whispered. "How can he hunt blind?" He quelled a sudden impulse to burn a path through the light to the falcon's side. As he watched, the falcon plummeted down, swift, deadly, into the shadows.

"He is like an Earth-Master," Raederle said, and an odd chill ran through Morgon. Her words sounded as if they hurt. "They all have that terrible beauty." They watched the bird lift from the ground, dark in the sudden fading of the light. Something dragged from its talons. She stood up slowly, began gathering wood. "He'll want a spit."

Morgon stripped a sapling bough and peeled it as the bird flew back. It left a dead hare beside Raederle's fire. Yrth stood before them again. For a moment, his eyes seemed unfamiliar, full of the clear, wild air, and the fierce precision of the falcon's kill. Then they became familiar again. Morgon asked his question in a voice that sounded timbreless, subdued.

"I scented its fear," the wizard said. He slid a knife from his boot before he sat down. "Will you skin it? That would be a problem for me."

Morgon set to work wordlessly. Raederle picked up the spit, finished peeling it. She said abruptly, almost shyly, "Can you speak a falcon's language?"

The blind, powerful face turned toward her. Its sudden gentleness at the sound of her voice stilled Morgon's knife. "A little of it."

"Can you teach me? Do we have to fly all the way to Herun as crows?"

"If you wish . . . I thought, being of An, you might be most comfortable as a crow."

"No," she said softly. "I am comfortable now as many things. But it was a kind thought."

"What have you shaped?"

"Oh . . . birds, a tree, a salmon, a badger, a deer, a bat, a vesta—I lost count long ago, searching for Morgon."

"You always found him."

"So did you."

Yrth sifted the ground around him absently, for twigs to hold the spit. "Yes . . ."

"I have shaped a hare, too."

"Hare is a hawk's prey. You shape yourself to the laws of earth."

Morgon tossed skin and offal into the bracken and reached for the spit. "And the laws of the realm?" he asked abruptly. "Are they meaningless to an Earth-Master?"

The wizard was very still. Something of the falcon's merciless power seemed to stir behind his gaze, until Morgon sensed the recklessness of his challenge. He looked away. Yrth said equivocally, "Not all of them." Morgon balanced the spit above the fire, turned the hare a couple of times to test it. Then the ambiguity of the wizard's words struck him. He slid back on his haunches, gazing at Yrth. But Raederle was speaking to him, and the clear note of pain in her voice held him silent.

"Then why, do you think, are my kinsmen on Wind Plain warring against the High One? If the power is a simple matter of the knowledge of rain and fire, and the laws they shape themselves to are the laws of the earth?"

Yrth was silent again. The sun had vanished, this time into deep clouds across the west. A haze of dusk and mist was beginning to close in upon them. He reached out, felt for the spit and turned it slowly. "I would think," he said, "that Morgon is correct in assuming the High One restrains the Earth-Masters' full power. Which is reason enough in itself for them to want to fight him . . . But many riddles seem to lie beneath that one. The stone children in Isig drew me down into their tomb centuries ago with the sense I felt of their sorrow. Their power had been stripped from them. Children are heirs to power; perhaps that was why they were destroyed."

"Wait," Morgon's voice shook on the word. "Are you saying—are you suggesting the High One's heir was buried in that tomb?"

"It seems possible, doesn't it?" Fat spattered in the blaze, and he turned the hare again. "Perhaps it was the young boy who told me of the stars I must put on a harp and a sword for someone who would come out of remote centuries to claim them . . ."

"But why?" Raederle whispered, still intent on her question. "Why?"

"You saw the falcon's flight . . . its beauty and its deadliness. If such power were bound to no law, that power and the lust for it would become so terrible—"

"I wanted it. That power."

The hard, ancient face melted again to its surprising gentleness. Yrth touched her, as he had touched the grass blade. "Then take it."

He let his hand fall. Raederle's head bent; Morgon could not see her face. He reached out to move her hair. She rose abruptly, turning away from him. He watched her walk through the trees, her hands gripping her arms as if she were chilled. His throat burned suddenly, for no coherent reason, except that the wizard had touched her, and she had left him.

"You left me nothing . . ." he whispered.

"Morgon—"

He stood up, followed Raederle into the gathering mists, leaving the falcon to its kill.

They flew through the next few days sometimes as crows, sometimes as falcons when the skies cleared. Two of the falcons cried to one another, in their piercing voices; the third, hearing them, was silent. They hunted in falcon-shape; slept and woke glaring at the pallid sun out of clear, wild eyes. When it rained, they flew as crows, plodding steadily through the drenched air. The trees flowed endlessly beneath them; they might have been flying again and again over the same point in space. But as the rains battered at them and vanished and the sun peered like a wraith through the clouds, a blur across the horizon ahead of them slowly hardened to a distant ring of hills breaking out of the forest.

The sun came out abruptly for a few moments before it drifted into night. Light glanced across the land, out of silver veins of rivers, and lakes dropped like small coin on the green earth. The falcons were flying wearily, in a staggered line that stretched over half a mile. The second one, bewitched, seemingly, by the light, shot suddenly ahead, in and out of sun and shadow, in a straight, exuberant flight towards their destination. Its excitement shook Morgon out of his monotonous rhythm. He picked up speed, soared past the lead falcon to catch up with the dark bolt hurtling through the sky. He had not realized Raederle could fly so fast. He streamed down currents of the north wind, but still the falcon kept its distance. He pushed toward it until he felt he had left his shape behind and was nothing more than a love of speed swept forward on the crest of light. He gained on the falcon slowly, until he saw its wingspan and the darkness of its underside and realized it was Yrth.

He kept his speed, wanting then, with all the energy in him, to overtake the falcon in the pride of its power and pass it. He sprinted toward it with all his strength, until the wind seemed to burn past him and through him. The forest heaved like a sea beneath him. Inch by inch, he closed the distance between them, until he was the falcon's shadow in the blazing sky. And then he was beside it, matching its speed, his wings moving to its rhythm. He could not pass it. He tore through air and light until he had to loose even his furious desire, like ballast, to keep his speed. It would not let him pass, but it lured him even faster, until all his thoughts and a shadow over his heart were ripped away and he felt if he went one heartbeat faster, he would burn into wind.

He gave a cry as he fell away from the falcon's side, down toward the gentle hills below. He could hardly move his wings; he let the air currents toss him from one to another until he touched the ground. He changed shape. The long grass spun up to meet him. He burrowed against the earth, his arms outstretched, clinging to it, until the terrible pounding in his heart eased and he began breathing air again instead of fire. He rolled slowly onto his back and stood up. The falcon was hovering above him. He watched it motionlessly, until the wild glimpse into his own power broke over him again. His hand rose in longing toward the falcon. It fell toward him like a stone. He let it come. It landed on his shoulder, clung there, its blind eyes hooded. He was still in its fierce grip, caught in its power and its pride.

Three falcons slept that night on the Herun hills. Three crows flew through the wet mists at dawn, above villages and rocky grazing land, where swirling winds revealed here and there a gnarled tree, or the sudden thrust of a monolith. The mists melted into rain that drizzled over them all the way to the City of Circles.

For once, the Morgol had not seen them coming. But the wizard Iff was waiting for them patiently in the courtyard, and the Morgol joined him there, looking curious, as the three black, wet birds lighted in front of her house. She stared at them, amazed, after they had changed shape.

"Morgon . . ." As she took his thin, worn face gently between her hands, he realized who it was that he had brought with him into her house.

Yrth was standing quietly; he seemed preoccupied, as though he had linked himself to all their eyes and had to sort through a confusion of images. The Morgol pushed Raederle's wet hair back from her face.

"You have become the great riddle of An," she said, and Raederle looked away from her quickly, down at the ground. But the Morgol lifted her face and kissed her, smiling. Then she turned to the wizards.

Iff put his hand on Yrth's shoulder, said in his tranquil voice, "El, this is Yrth; I don't think you have met."

"No." She bent her head. "You honor my house, Star-Maker. Come in, out of the rain. Usually I can see who is crossing my hills and prepare for my guests; but I did not pay any attention to three tired crows." She put her hand lightly on Yrth's arm to guide him. "Where have you come from?"

"Isig and Osterland," the wizard said. His voice sounded huskier than usual. Guards in the rich maze of corridors gazed without a change of stance at the visitors, but their eyes were startled, conjecturing. Morgon, watching Yrth's back as he walked beside the Morgol, his head angled toward her voice, realized slowly that Iff had dropped back and was speaking to him.

"The news of the attack on Hed reached us only a few days after it happened—word of it passed that swiftly through the realm. It caused great fear. Most of the people have left Caithnard, but where can they go? Ymris? An, which Mathom will leave nearly defenseless when he brings his army north? Lungold? That city is still recovering from its own terror. There is no place for anyone to go."

"Have the Masters left Caithnard?" Raederle asked.

The wizard shook his head. "No. They refuse to leave." He sounded mildly exasperated. "The Morgol asked me to go to them, see if they needed help, ships to move themselves and their books. They said that perhaps the strictures of wizardry held the secret of eluding death, but the strictures of riddlery hold that it is unwise to turn your back on death, since turning, you will only find it once more in front of you. I asked them to be practical. They suggested that answers, rather than ships, might help them most. I told them they might die there. They asked me if death is the most terrible thing. And at that point, I began to understand riddlery a little. But I had no skill to riddle with them."

"The wise man," Morgon said, "pursues a riddle inflexibly as a miser pursues a coin rolling towards a crack in a floorboard."

"Apparently. Can you do anything? They seemed to me something very fragile and very precious to the realm . . ."

The faint smile in his eyes died. "Only one thing. Give them what they want."

The Morgol stopped in front of a large, light room, with rugs and hangings of gold, ivory, and rich brown. She said to Morgon and Raederle, "My servants will bring what you need to make you comfortable. There will be guards stationed throughout the house. Join us when you're ready, in Iff's study. We can talk there."

"El," Morgon said softly. "I cannot stay. I did not come to talk."

She was silent, riddling, he suspected, though her expression changed very little. She put her hand on his arm. "I have taken all the guards out of the cities and borders; Goh is training them here, to go south, if that is what you need."

"No," he said passionately. "I saw enough of your guards die in Lungold."

"Morgon, we must use what strength we have."

"There is far more power in Herun than that." He saw her face change then. He was aware of the wizard behind her, still as a shadow, and he wondered then without hope of an answer whether he gathered power by choice or at the falcon's luring. "That is what I have come for. I need that."

Her fingers closed very tightly on his forearm. "The power of land-law?" she whispered incredulously. He nodded mutely, knowing that the first sign of mistrust in her would scar his heart forever. "You have that power? To take it?"

"Yes. I need the knowledge of it. I will not touch your mind. I swear it. I went into Har's mind, with his permission, but you—there are places in your mind where I do not belong."

Some thought was growing behind her eyes. Standing so quietly, still gripping him, she could not speak. He felt as if he were changing shape in front of her into something ancient as the world, around which riddles and legends and the colors of night and dawn clung like priceless, forgotten treasures. He wanted to go into her mind then, to find whatever lay in his harsh, confused past to make her see him like that. But she loosed him and said, "Take from my land, and from me, what you need."

He stood still, watching her move down the hall, her hand beneath Yrth's elbow. Servants came, breaking into his thoughts. While they roused the fire and set water and wine to heat, he spoke softly to Raederle.

"I'll leave you here. I don't know how long I'll be gone. Neither one of us will be very safe, but at least Yrth and Iff are here, and Yrth—he does want me alive. I know that much."

She slid her hand onto his shoulder. Her face was troubled. "Morgon, you bound yourself to him as you flew. I felt it."

"I know." He lifted her hand, held the back of it against his chest. "I know," he repeated. He could not meet her eyes. "He lures me with myself. I told you that if I played with him, I would lose."

"Maybe."

"Watch over the Morgol. I don't know what I have brought into her house."

"He would never hurt her."

"He lied to her and betrayed her once already. Once is enough. If you need me, ask the Morgol where I am. She'll know."

"All right. Morgon . . ."

"What?"

"I don't know . . ." she answered, as she had several times in the past days. "Only I remember, sometimes, what Yrth said about fire and night being such simple things when you see them clearly. I keep thinking that you don't know what Yrth is because you never see him, you see only dark memories . . ."

"What in Hel's name do you expect me to see? He's more than a harpist, more than a wizard. Raederle, I'm trying to see. I'm—"

She put her hand over his mouth as servants glanced at them. "I know." She held him suddenly, tightly, and he felt himself trembling. "I didn't mean to upset you. But—be quiet and listen. I'm trying to think. You don't understand fire until you forget yourself and become fire.

You learned to see in the dark when you became a great mountain whose heart was of darkness. You understood Ghisteslwchlohm by assuming his power. So, maybe the only way you will ever understand the harpist is to let him draw you into his power until you are part of his heart and you begin to see the world out of his eyes . . ."

"I may destroy the realm that way."

"Maybe. But if he is dangerous, how can you fight him without understanding him? And if he is not dangerous?"

"If he's not—" He stopped. The world seemed to shift slightly around him, all of Herun, the mountain kingdoms, the southern lands, the entire realm, adjusting into place under the falcon's eye. He saw the falcon's shadow spanning the realm in its powerful, silent flight, felt it fall across his back. The vision lasted a fraction of a moment. Then the shadow became a memory of night and his hands clenched. "He is dangerous," he whispered. "He always has been. Why am I so bound to him?"

He left the City of Circles that evening and spent days and nights he did not count, hidden from the world and almost from himself, within the land-law of Herun. He drifted shapelessly in the mists, seeped down into the still, dangerous marshlands, and felt the morning frost silver his face as it hardened over mud and reeds and tough marsh grasses. He cried a marsh bird's lonely cry and stared at the stars out of an expressionless slab of stone. He roamed through the low hills, linking his mind to rocks, trees, rivulets, searching into the rich mines of iron and copper and precious stones the hills kept enclosed within themselves. He spun tendrils of thought into a vast web across the dormant fields and lush, misty pastureland, linking himself to the stubble of dead roots, frozen furrows, and tangled grasses the sheep fed on. The gentleness of the land reminded him of Hed, but there was a dark, restless force in it that had reared up in the shapes of tors and monoliths. He drifted very close to the Morgol's mind, as he explored it; he sensed that her watchfulness and intelligence had been born out of need, the heritage of a land whose marshes and sudden mists made it very dangerous to those who had settled it. There was mystery in its strange stones, and richness within its hills; the minds of the Morgols had shaped themselves also to those things. As Morgon drew deep into its law, he felt his own mind grow almost peaceful, bound by necessity to a fine clarity of awareness and vision. Finally, when he began to see as the Morgol saw, into things and beyond them, he returned to the City of Circles.

He came back as he had left: as quietly as a piece of ground mist wandering in from the still, cold Herun night. He followed the sound of the Morgol's voice as he took his own shape once again. He found himself standing in firelight and shadow in her small, elegant hall. The Morgol was speaking to Yrth as he appeared; he felt still linked to the calmness of her mind. He made no effort to break the link, at rest in her peacefulness. Lyra was sitting beside her; Raederle had shifted closer to the fire. They had been at supper, but only their cups and flagons of wine remained of it.

Raederle turned her head and saw Morgon; she smiled at something in his eyes and left him undisturbed. Lyra caught his attention, then. She was dressed for supper in a light, flowing, fiery robe; her hair was braided and coiled under a net of gold thread. Her face had lost its familiar proud assurance; her eyes seemed older, vulnerable, haunted with the memory of watching guards under her command die at Lungold. She said something to the Morgol that Morgon did not hear. The Morgol answered her simply.

"No."

"I am going to Ymris." Her dark eyes held the Morgol's stubbornly, but her argument was quiet. "If not with the guard, then at your side."

"No."

"Mother, I am no longer in your guard. I resigned when I returned home from Lungold, so you can't expect me to obey you without thinking. Ymris is a terrible battlefield—more terrible than Lungold. I am going—"

"You are my land-heir," the Morgol said. Her face was still calm, but Morgon sensed the fear, relentless and chill as the Herun mists, deep in her mind. "I am taking the entire guard out of Herun down to Wind Plain. Goh will command it. You said that you never wanted to pick up another spear, and I was grateful you had made that decision. There is no need for you to fight in Ymris, and every need for you to stay here."

"In case you are killed," Lyra said flatly. "I don't understand why you are even going, but I will ride at your side—"

"Lyra—"

"Mother, this is my decision. Obeying you is no longer a matter of honor. I will do as I choose, and I choose to ride with you."

The Morgol's fingers edged slightly around her cup. She seemed surprised at her own movement. "Well," she said calmly, "if there is no honor in your actions in this matter, there will be none in mine. You will stay here. One way or another."

Lyra's eyes flickered a little. "Mother," she protested uncertainly, and the Morgol said:

"Yes. I am also the Morgol. Herun is in grave danger. If Ymris falls, I want you here to protect it in whatever way you can. If we both died in Ymris, it would be disastrous for Herun."

"But why are you going?"

"Because Har is going," the Morgol said softly, "and Danan, and Mathom—the land-rulers of the realm—impelled to Ymris to fight for the survival of the realm . . . or for some even more imperative reason. There is a tangle of riddles at the heart of the realm; I want to see its unraveling. Even at the risk of my life. I want answers."

Lyra was silent. Their faces in the soft light were almost indistinguishable in their fine, clean-lined beauty. But the Morgol's gold eyes hid her thoughts, while Lyra's were open to every flare of fire and pain.

"The harpist is dead," she whispered. "If that is what you are trying to answer."

The Morgol's eyes fell. She stirred after a moment, reached out swiftly to touch Lyra's cheek. "There are more unsolved questions than that in the realm," she said, "and nearly all, I think, more important." But her brows were constricted, as at a sudden, inexplicable pain. "Riddles without answers can be terrible," she added after a moment. "But some are possible to live with. Others. . . . What the Star-Bearer does at Wind Plain will be vital, Yrth thinks."

"Does he think you need to be there also? And if Wind Plain is so vital, where is the High One? Why is he ignoring the Star-Bearer and the entire realm?"

"I don't know. Perhaps Morgon can answer some of—" She lifted her head abruptly and saw him standing quietly in the shadows, his own thoughts waking again in his mind.

She smiled, holding out her hand in welcome. Yrth shifted a little, seeing, perhaps from her eyes, as Morgon came slowly to the table. Morgon saw him strangely for an instant, as something akin to the mists and monoliths of Herun that his mind could explore and comprehend. Then, as he sat down, the wizard's face seemed to avert itself from his eyes. He bent his head to the Morgol wordlessly. She said, "Did you find what you came for?"

"Yes. All I could bear. How long have I been gone?"

"Nearly two weeks."

"Two . . ." He shaped the word without sound. "So long? Has there been news?"

"Very little. Traders came from Hlurle for all the arms we could spare, to take them to Caerweddin. I have been watching a mist moving south from Osterland, and finally, today, I realized what it is."

"A mist?" He remembered Har's scarred palm, opening to the red wash of firelight. "Vesta? Is Har bringing the vesta to Ymris?"

"There are hundreds of them, moving across the forests."

"They are great fighters," Yrth said. He sounded weary, disinclined to face an argument, but his voice was patient. "And they will not fear the Ymris winter."

"You knew." His thoughts were jarred out of their calm. "You could have stopped him. The miners, the vesta, the Morgol's guard—why are you drawing such a vulnerable, unskilled army across the realm? You may be blind, but the rest of us will have to watch the slaughter of men and animals on that battlefield—"

"Morgon," the Morgol interrupted gently, "Yrth does not make my decisions for me."

"Yrth—" He stopped, sliding his hands over his face, trying to check a futile argument. Yrth rose, drawing Morgon's eyes again. The wizard moved a little awkwardly through the cushions to the fire. He stood in front of it, his head bowed. Morgon saw his scarred hands close suddenly, knotted with words he could not speak, and he thought of Deth's hands, twisted with pain in the firelight. He heard an echo, then, out of the still Herun night, of the strange brief peace he had found beside the harpist's fire, within his silence. All that bound him to the harpist, to the falcon, his longing and his incomprehensible love, overwhelmed him suddenly. As he watched light and shadow search the hard, blind face into shape, he realized he would yield anything: the vesta, the Morgol's guard, the land-rulers, the entire realm, into the scarred, tormented hands in return for a place in the falcon's shadow.

The knowledge brought him to a strange, uneasy calm. His head bowed; he stared down at his dark reflection in the polished stone until Lyra, looking at him, said suddenly, "You must be hungry." She poured him wine. "I'll bring you some hot food." The Morgol watched her cross the room with her lithe, graceful step. She looked tired, more tired than Morgon had ever seen her.

She said to Morgon, "Miners and vesta and my guard may seem useless in Ymris, but Morgon, the land-rulers are giving of all the strength they possess. There is nothing else we can do."

"I know." His eyes moved to her; he knew her own confused love for a memory. He said abruptly, wanting to give her something of peace in return for all she had given him, "Ghisteslwchlohm said that you had been waiting for Deth near Lungold. Is that true?"

She looked a little startled at his brusqueness, but she nodded. "I thought he might come to Lungold. It was the only place left for him to go, and I could ask him. . . . Morgon, you and I are both tired, and the harpist is dead. Perhaps we should—"

"He died—he died for you."

She stared at him across the table. "Morgon," she whispered, warning him, but he shook his head.

"It is true. Raederle could have told you. Or Yrth—he was there." The wizard turned light, burned eyes toward him, then, and his voice shook. But he went on, returning the riddle of the harpist's life to him unanswered, in exchange for nothing. "Ghisteslwchlohm gave Deth a choice between holding either Raederle or you as hostage while he forced me to Erlenstar Mountain. He chose to die instead. He forced Ghisteslwchlohm to kill him. He had no compassion for me . . . maybe because I could endure without it. But you and Raederle, he simply loved." He stopped, breathing a little painfully as she dropped her face into her hands. "Did I hurt you? I didn't mean to—"

"No." But she was crying, he could tell, and he cursed himself. Yrth was still watching him; he wondered how the wizard was seeing, since Raederle's face had disappeared behind her hair. The wizard made a strange gesture, throwing up one open hand to the light, as if he were yielding something to Morgon. He reached out, touched the air at

Morgon's back, and the starred harp leaped out of nothingness into his hands.

The Morgol's eyes went to Morgon as the first, sweet notes sounded, but his hands were empty. He was gazing at Yrth, words lumped like ice in his throat. The wizard's big hands moved with a flawless precision over the strings he had tuned; tones of wind and water answered him. It was the harping out of a long, black night in Erlenstar Mountain, with all its deadly beauty; the harping kings across the realm had heard for centuries. It was the harping of a great wizard who had once been called the Harpist of Lungold, and the Morgol, listening silently, seemed only awed and a little surprised. Then the harpist's song changed, and the blood ran completely out of her face.

It was a deep, lovely, wordless song that pulled out of the back of Morgon's memories a dark, misty evening above the Herun marshes, a fire ringed with faces of the Morgol's guard, Lyra appearing soundlessly out of the night, saying something. . . . He strained to hear her words. Then, looking at the Morgol's white, numb face as she stared at Yrth, he remembered the song Deth had composed only for her.

A shudder ran through Morgon. He wondered, as the beautiful harping drew to a close, how the harpist could possibly justify himself to her. His hands slowed, picked a final, gentle chord from the harp, then flattened on the strings to still them. He sat with his head bowed slightly over the harp, his hands resting above the stars. Firelight shivered over him, weaving patterns of light and shadows in the air. Morgon waited for him to speak. He said nothing; he did not move. Moments wore away; still he sat with the silence of trees or earth or the hard, battered face of granite; and Morgon, listening to it, realized that his silence was not the evasion of an answer, but the answer itself.

He closed his eyes. His heart beat suddenly, painfully, in his throat. He wanted to speak, but he could not. The harpist's silence circled him with the peace he had found deep in living things all over the realm. It eased through his thoughts, into his heart, so that he could not even think. He only knew that something he had searched for so long and so hopelessly had never, even in his most desperate moments, been far from his side.

The harpist rose then, his weary, ancient face the wind-swept face of a mountain, the scarred face of the realm. His eyes held the Morgol's for a long moment, until her face, so white it seemed translucent, shook, and she stared blindly down at the table. Then he moved to Morgon, slipped the harp back onto his shoulder. Morgon felt as from a dream the light, quick movements. He seemed to linger for a moment; his hand touched Morgon's face very gently. Then, walking toward the fire, he melted into its weave.

14

MORGON MOVED THEN, unbound from the silence. He cast with his mind into the night, but everywhere he searched he found only its stillness. He rose. Words seemed gripped in his chest and in his clenched hands, as if he dared not let them go. The Morgol seemed as reluctant to speak. She stirred a little, stiffly, then stilled again, gazing down at a star of candlelight reflected on the table. The blood came back into her face slowly. Watching her expression change, Morgon found his voice.

"Where did he go?" he whispered. "He spoke to you."

"He said—he said that he had just done the only foolish thing in his very long life." Her hands moved, linked themselves; she frowned down at them, concentrating with an effort. "That he had not intended for you to know him until you had gathered enough power to fight for yourself. He left because he is a danger to you now. He said—other things." She shook her head slightly, then spoke again. "He said that he had not realized there was a limit to his own endurance."

"Wind Plain. He'll be in Ymris."

She raised her eyes then, but she did not argue. "Find him, Morgon. No matter how dangerous it is for both of you. He has been alone long enough."

"I will." He turned, knelt beside Raederle. She was staring into the fire; he brushed at the reflection of a flame on her face. She looked at him. There was something ancient, fierce, only half-human in her eyes, as if she had seen into the High One's memories. He took her hand. "Come with me."

She stood up. He linked their minds, cast far into the Herun night until he touched a stone he remembered on the far side of the marshes. As Lyra entered the hall, bringing his supper, he took one step toward her and vanished.

They stood together in the mists, seeing nothing but a shadowy whiteness, like a gathering of wraiths. Morgon sent his awareness spiralling outward, out of the mists, through the low hills, far across them, farther than he had ever loosed his mind before. His thoughts anchored in the gnarled heart of a pine. He pulled himself toward it.

Standing beside it, in the wind-whipped forests between Herun and Ymris, he felt his overtaxed powers suddenly falter. He could barely concentrate; his thoughts seemed shredded by wind. His body, to which he had been paying only sporadic attention, was making imperative demands. He was shivering; he kept remembering the smell of hot meat Lyra had brought him. Pieces of the harpist's life kept flashing into his mind. He heard the fine, detached voice speaking to kings, to traders, to Ghisteslwchlohm, riddling always, not with his words, but with all he did not say. Then one memory seared through all Morgon's thoughts, shaking a sound from him. He felt the north wind whittle at his bones.

"I nearly killed him." He was almost awed at his own blundering. "I tracked the High One all the way across the realm to kill him." Then a sharp, familiar pain bore into his heart. "He left me in Ghisteslwchlohm's hands. He could have killed the Founder with half a word. Instead, he harped. No wonder I never recognized him."

"Morgon, it's cold." Raederle put her arm around him; even her hair felt chill against his face. He tried to clear his mind, but the winds wept into it, and he saw the harpist's face again, staring blindly at the sky.

"He was a Master . . ."

"Morgon." He felt his mind grope into his. He let it come, surprised. The sense of her quieted him; her own thoughts were very clear. He drew apart from her, looked through the darkness into her face.

"You were never that angry for my sake."

"Oh, Morgon." She held him again. "You said it yourself: you endure, like the hard things of the realm. He needed you that way, so he left you to Ghisteslwchlohm. I'm saying it badly . . ." she protested, as his muscles tensed. "You learned to survive. Do you think it was easy for him? Harping for centuries in Ghisteslwchlohm's service, waiting for the Star-Bearer?"

"No," he said after a moment, thinking of the harpist's broken hands. "He used himself as mercilessly as he used me. But for what?"

"Find him. Ask him."

"I can't even move," he whispered. Her mind touched his again; he let his thoughts rest finally in her tentative hold. He waited patiently while she worked, exploring across distances. She touched him finally. He moved without knowing where he was going, and he began to understand the patience and trust he had demanded of her. They did not go very far, he sensed, but he waited wearily, gratefully, while she found her way step by step across the forests. By dawn, they had reached the north border of Ymris. And there, as the red sun of storms and ill winds rose in the east, they rested.

They flew over Marcher as carrion crows. The rough, hilly borderland seemed quiet; but in the late afternoon, the crows spied a band of armed men guarding a line of trade-carts lumbering toward Caerweddin. Morgon veered down toward them. He caught one of the warriors' minds as he landed on the road, to avoid being attacked when he changed shape. He drew the sword out of its sheath of air, held the stars as the man stared at him. They flared uneasily in the grey light.

"Morgon of Hed," the warrior breathed. He was a grizzled, scarred veteran; his eyes, shadowed and bloodshot, had gazed across the dawn and deadly twilight of many fields. He halted the train of cars behind him and dismounted. The men behind were silent.

"I need to find Yrth," Morgon said. "Or Aloil. Or Astrin Ymris."

The man touched the stars on his upraised sword with a curious gesture, almost a ritual of fealty. Then he blinked as a gor-crow landed on Morgon's shoulder. He said, "I am Lien Marcher, cousin of the High Lord of Marcher. I don't know Yrth. Astrin Ymris is in Caerweddin; he could tell you where Aloil is. I'm taking arms and supplies to Caerweddin, for whatever good they'll do there. If I were you, Star-Lord, I would not show an eyelash in this doomed land. Let alone three stars."

"I've come to fight," Morgon said. The land whispered to him, then, of law, legends, the ancient dead beneath his feet, and his own body seemed to yearn toward the shape of it. The man's eyes ran over his lean face, the rich, worn tunic that seemed mildly absurd in those dangerous, wintry hills.

"Hed," he said. A sudden, amazed smile broke through the despair in his eyes. "Well. We've tried everything else. I would offer to take you with me, Lord, but I think you're safer on your own. There is only one man Astrin might want to see more than you, but I wouldn't want to lay any bets on that."

"Heureu. He's still missing."

The man nodded wearily. "Somewhere in the realm between the dead and the living. Not even the wizard can find him. I think—"

"I can find him," Morgon said abruptly. The man was silent, the smile in his eyes wiped away by a naked, unbearable hope.

"Can you? Not even Astrin can, and his dreams are full of Heureu's thoughts. Lord, what—what are you, that you can stand there shivering in the cold and have me believing in your power? I survived the carnage on Wind Plain. Some nights when I wake from my own dreams, I wish I had died there." He shook his head; his hand moved to Morgon again, then dropped without touching him. "Go, now. Take your stars out of eyesight. Find your way safely to Caerweddin. Lord, hurry."

The crows flew eastward. They passed other long convoys of supply-carts and strings of horses; they rested in the eaves of great houses, whose yards were choked with smoke and the din of forges. The brilliant colors of battle livery and the dark, sweating flanks of plow horses flickered through the smoke, as men gathered to march to Caerweddin. There were young boys among them, and the rough, weathered faces of shepherds, farmers, smiths, even traders, receiving a crude, desperate introduction to arms before they joined the forces at Caerweddin. The sight spurred the crows onward. They followed the Thul as it ran toward the sea, cutting a dark path through the dying fields.

They reached Caerweddin at sunset; the sky was shredded like a brilliant banner by the harsh winds. The whole of the city was ringed by a thousand fires, as if it were besieged by its own forces. But the harbor was clear; trade-ships from Isig and Anuin were homing toward it on the evening tide. The beautiful house of the Ymris kings, built of the shards of an Earth-Masters' city, burned like a jewel in the last light. The crows dropped down into the shadows just outside its closed gates. They changed shape in the empty street.

They did not speak as they looked at one another. Morgon drew Raederle against him, wondering if his own eyes were as stunned with weariness. He touched her mind; then, searching into the heart of the king's house, he found Astrin's mind.

He appeared in front of the Ymris land-heir as he sat alone in a small council chamber. He had been working; maps, messages, supply lists were strewn all over his desk. But the room was nearly in darkness, and he had not bothered to light candles. He was staring ahead of him into the fire, his face harrowed, colorless. Morgon and Raederle, stepping out of the street into the blur of light and shadow, did not even startle him. He gazed at them a moment as if they had no more substance than his hope. Then his expression changed; he stood up, his chair falling behind him with a crash. "Where have you been?"

There was a realm of relief, compassion, and exasperation in the question. Morgon, casting a glance at his past with an eye as probing as the single, wintry eye of the Ymris prince, said simply, "Answering riddles."

Astrin rounded his desk and eased Raederle into a chair. He gave her wine and the numbness began to wear out of her face. Astrin, half-kneeling beside her, looked up at Morgon incredulously.

"Where did you come from? I have been thinking about you and Heureu—you and Heureu. You're thin as an awl, but in one piece. You look—if ever I've seen a man who looks like a weapon, you do. There is a quiet thunder of power all over this room. Where did you get it?"

"All over the realm." He poured himself wine and sat.

"Can you save Ymris?"

"I don't know. Maybe. I don't know. I need to find Yrth."

"Yrth. I thought he was with you."

He shook his head. "He left me. I need to find him. I need him . . ." His voice had sunk to a whisper; he stared into the fire, the cup a hollow of gold in his hands. Astrin's voice startled through him, and he realized he was nearly asleep.

"I haven't seen him, Morgon."

"Is Aloil here? His mind is linked to Yrth's."

"No; he is with Mathom's army. It's massed in the forests near Trader's Road. Morgon." He leaned forward to grip Morgon, bringing him out of the sudden despair overwhelming him.

"He was there beside me, if only I had had enough sense to turn and face him, instead of pursuing his shadow all over the realm. I harped with him, I fought with him, I tried to kill him, and I loved him, and the moment I name him he vanishes, leaving me still pursuing . . ." Astrin's grip was suddenly painful.

"What are you saying?"

Morgon, realizing his own words, gazed back at him mutely. He saw once again the strange, colorless face that had been over him when he had wakened, voiceless, nameless, in a strange land. The warrior before him, with a dark, tight tunic buttoned haphazardly over a shift of mail, became the half-wizard once more in his hut by the sea, riddling over the bones of the city on Wind Plain.

"Wind Plain . . ." he whispered. "No. He can't have gone there without me. And I'm not ready."

Astrin's hand slackened. His face was expressionless, skull-white. "Exactly who is it you're looking for?" He spoke very carefully, fitting the words together like shards. The harpist's name shocked through Morgon then: the first dark riddle the harpist had given him long ago on a sunlit autumn day at the docks at Tol. He swallowed dryly, wondering suddenly what he was pursuing.

Raederle shifted in her chair, pillowing her face against a fur cloak draped over it. Her eyes were closed. "You've answered so many riddles," she murmured. "Where is there one last, unanswered riddle but on Wind Plain?"

She burrowed deeper into the fur as Morgon eyed her doubtfully. She did not move again; Astrin took her cup before it dropped from her fingers. Morgon rose abruptly, crossed the room. He leaned over Astrin's desk; the map of Ymris lay between his hands.

"Wind Plain . . ." The shaded areas of the map focussed under his gaze. He touched an island of darkness in west Ruhn. "What is this?"

Astrin, still hunched beside the fire, got to his feet. "An ancient city," he said. "They have taken nearly all the Earth-Masters' cities in Meremont and Tor, parts of Ruhn."

"Can you get through the Wind Plain?"

"Morgon, I would march there with no other army but my shadow if you want it. But can you give me a reason I can give to my war lords for taking the entire army away from Caerweddin and leaving the city unguarded to fight over a few broken stones?"

Morgon looked at him. "Can you get through?"

"Here." He drew a line down from Caerweddin, between Tor and the dark area in east Umber. "With some risk." He traced the southern border of Meremont. "Mathom's army will be here. If it were only men we were fighting, I would call them doomed, caught between two great armies. But Morgon, I can't calculate their strength, none of us can. They take what they want in their own time. They aren't pretending to fight us anymore; they simply overrun us whenever we happen to get in their way. The realm is their chessboard, and we are their pawns . . . and the game they are playing seems incomprehensible. Give me a reason to move the men south, to pick a fight in the bitter cold over land that no one has lived on for centuries."

Morgon touched a point on Wind Plain where a lonely tower might have stood. "Danan is coming south with his miners. And Har with the vesta. And the Morgol with her guard. Yrth wanted them there at Wind Plain. Astrin, is that enough reason? To protect the land-rulers of the realm?"

"Why?" His fist slammed down on the plain, but Raederle did not even stir. "Why?"

"I don't know."

"I'll stop them in Marcher."

"You won't stop them. They are drawn to Wind Plain, as I am, and if you want to see any of us alive next spring, then take your army south. I didn't choose the season. Or the army that is following me across the realm. Or the war itself. I am—" He stopped, as Astrin's hands closed on his shoulders. "Astrin. I have no time left to give you. I have seen too much. I have no choices left. No other seasons."

The single eye would have searched into his thoughts, if he had let it. "Then who is making your choices?"

"Come to Wind Plain."

The prince loosed him. "I'll be there," he whispered.

Morgon turned away from him after a moment, sat down again. "I have to leave," he said tiredly.

"Tonight?"

"Yes. I'll sleep a little and then leave. I need answers . . ." He gazed across at Raederle's face, hidden in the fur; only the line of her cheek and chin, brushed by light, showed beneath her hair. He said very softly, "I'll let her sleep. She might follow me when she wakes; tell her to be careful flying across Wind Plain."

"Where are you going?"

Raederle's hair blurred into fire; his eyes closed. "To find Aloil. . . . To find a wind."

He slept without dreaming and woke a few hours later. Astrin had covered Raederle; she was barely visible, huddled under fur-lined blankets. Astrin, lying between them on skins beside the fire, was guarding them. His sword was unsheathed; one hand rested on the bare blade. Morgon thought he had fallen asleep, but his good eye opened as Morgon stood. He said nothing. Morgon leaned down to touch his shoulder in a silent farewell. Then he caught at the night beyond the stones.

The night winds snarled in furious contention around him as he flew. He did not dare use power in the stretch between Caerweddin and Wind Plain. Dawn broke in sheets of cold, grey rain over hunched trees and lifeless fields. He flew through the day, fighting the winds. By twilight, he reached Wind Plain.

He flew low over it, a huge black carrion crow casting a bitter eye over the remains of the unburied warriors of Heureu's army. Nothing else moved on the plain; not even birds or small animals had come to scavenge in the fierce rain. A treasure of arms gleamed in the twilight all over the plain. The rain was hammering jewelled sword hilts, pieces of armor, horse's skulls and the bones of men alike down into the wet earth. The crow's eye saw nothing else as it winged slowly toward the ruined city; but beyond the shield of its instincts, Morgon sensed the silent, deadly warning ringing the entire plain.

The great tower rose above the city, spiralling into night as he winged past it. He kept his mind empty of all thought, aware only of the smells of the wet earth, and the slow, weary rhythm of his flight. He did not stop until he had crossed the plain and the south border of Ymris and finally saw the midnight fires of Mathom's army sprawled along the river near Trader's Road. He descended then and found shelter among the thick, leafless oak. He did not move until morning.

Dawn crusted the earth with frost and a chill like the bite of a blade. He felt it as he changed shape; his breath froze in a quick, startled flash in front of him. Shivering, he followed the smell of wood smoke and hot wine to the fires beside the river. Dead warriors of An were posted as sentries. They seemed to recognize something of An in him, for they gave him white, eyeless grins and let him pass among them unchallenged.

He found Aloil talking to Talies beside the fire outside the king's pavilion. He joined the wizards quietly, stood warming himself. Through the bare trees, he saw other fires, men rousing out of tents, stamping the blood awake in their bodies. Horses snorted the chill out of their lungs, pulling restively at their ropes. Tents, horse trappings, men's arms, and tunics all bore the battle colors of Anuin: blue and purple edged with the black of sorrow. The wraiths bore their own ancient colors when they bothered to clothe themselves with the memories of their bodies. They moved vividly and at will among the living, but the living, inured to many things at that point, took more interest in their breakfast than in the dead.

Morgon, finally warm, caught Aloil's attention as he began listening to their conversation. The big wizard broke off mid-sentence and turned his blue, burning gaze across the fire. The preoccupied frown in his eyes turned to amazement.

"Morgon . . ."

"I'm looking for Yrth," Morgon said. "Astrin told me he was with you." Talies, both thin brows raised, started to comment. Then he stepped to the king's pavilion and flung the flap open. He said something; Mathom followed him back out.

"He was here a moment ago," Talies said, and Morgon sighed. "He can't be far. How in Hel's name did you cross Wind Plain?"

"At night. I was a carrion crow." He met the black, searching eyes of the King of An. Mathom, pulling his cloak off, said crustily, "It's cold enough to freeze the bare bones of the dead." He threw it around Morgon's shoulders. "Where did you leave my daughter?"

"Asleep at Caerweddin. She'll follow me when she wakes."

"Across Wind Plain? Alone? You aren't easy on one another." He prodded the fire until it groped for the low boughs of the oak.

Morgon asked, pulling the cloak tight, "Was Yrth with you? Where did he go?"

"I don't know. I thought he came out for a cup of hot wine. This is no season for old men. Why? There are two great wizards here, both at your service." He did not wait for an answer; he cast a quizzical eye at Aloil. "You are linked to him. Where is he?"

Aloil, staring down at the fuming oak logs, shook his head. "Napping, perhaps. His mind is silent. He made a swift journey across Ymris."

"So did Morgon, by the look of it," Talies commented. "Why didn't Yrth travel with you?"

Morgon, caught without an answer, ran one hand through his hair vaguely. He saw a sudden glitter in the crow's eyes. "No doubt," Mathom said, "Yrth had his reasons. A man with no eyes sees marvels. You stopped at Caerweddin? Are Astrin and his war lords still at odds?"

"Possibly. But Astrin is bringing the entire army to Wind Plain."

"When?" Aloil demanded. "He said nothing of that to me, and I was with him three nights ago."

"Now." He added, "I asked him to."

There was a silence, during which one of the sentries, wearing nothing more than his bones under gold armor, rode soundlessly past the fire. Mathom's eyes followed the wraith's passage. "So. What does a man with one eye see?" He answered himself, with a blank shock of recognition in his voice, "Death."

"This is hardly a time," Aloil said restlessly, "for riddles. If the way is clear between Umber and Tor, it will take him four days to reach the plain. If it is not . . . you had better be prepared to march north to aid him. He could lose the entire strength of Ymris. Do you know what you're doing?" he asked Morgon. "You have gained awesome powers. But are you ready to use them alone?"

Talies dropped a hand on his shoulder. "You have the brain of an Ymris warrior," he said, "full of muscle and poetry. I'm no riddler, either, but living for centuries in the Three Portions taught me a little subtlety. Can you listen to what the Star-Bearer is saying? He is drawing the force of the realm to Wind Plain, and he is not intending to battle alone. Wind Plain. Astrin saw it. Yrth saw it. The final battleground . . ."

Aloil gazed silently at him. Something like a frail, reluctant hope struggled into his face. "The High One." He swung his gaze again to Morgon. "You think he is on Wind Plain?"

"I think," Morgon said softly, "that wherever he is, if I don't find him very soon, we are all dead. I have answered one riddle too many." He shook his head as both wizards began to speak. "Come to Wind Plain. I'll give you whatever answers I have there. That's where I should have gone in the first place, but I thought perhaps—" He broke off. Mathom finished his sentence.

"You thought Yrth was here. The Harpist of Lungold." He made a harsh, dry sound, like a crow's laugh. But he was staring into the fire as if he were watching it weave a dream to its ending. He turned away from it abruptly, but not before Morgon saw his eyes, black and expressionless as the eyes of his dead, who had been eaten to the bone by truth.

Morgon stood in the trees at the edge of Wind Plain at twilight, waiting as the night slowly drew the empty city and the long, whispering grasses into itself once again. He had been there for hours, motionless, waiting, so still he might have rooted himself to earth like a bare, twisted oak without realizing it. The sky spilled a starless black over the world, until even with his night-vision, the jewellike colors of the tower stones seemed permeated with the dark. He moved then, aware of his body again. As he took one final step toward the tower, clouds parted unexpectedly. A single star drifted through the unfathomable blackness above it.

He stood at the foot of the stairs, looking up at them as he had when he first saw them one wet autumn day two years before. Then, he remembered, he had turned away, uncurious, uncompelled. The stairs were gold, and according to all legend they wound away from the earth forever.

He bowed his head as if he were walking into a hard wind and began to climb. The walls around him were of the lustrous burning black between stars. The gold stairs ringed around the core of the tower, slanting gently upward. As he rounded it once and began the second spiral, the black gave way to a rich crimson. The winds, he realized, were no longer the thin, angry winds of the day; their voices were forceful, sinewy. The stairs beneath his feet seemed carved of ivory.

He heard the voices of the winds change again at the third spiral. They held tones he had harped to in the northern wastes, and his hands yearned to match their singing. But harping would be deadly, so he kept his hands still. At the fourth level the walls seemed of solid gold and the stairs carved out of star fire. They wound endlessly upward; the plain, the broken city grew farther and farther away from him. The winds grew colder as he climbed. At the ninth level he wondered if he were climbing a mountain. The winds, the stairs, and the walls around him were clear as melted snow. The spirals were getting smaller, and he thought he must be near the top. But the next level plunged him into an eerie darkness, as if the stairs were carved out of night wind. It seemed interminable, but when he came out of it again, the moon was exactly where he had seen it last. He continued upward. The walls turned a beautiful dawn-grey; the stairs were pale rose. The winds had a cutting edge, merciless and deadly. They were prodding him out of his own shape. He kept walking, half-man, half-wind, and the colors around him changed again and again, until he realized, as others had realized before him, that he could spiral through their changing forever.

He stopped. The city was so far beneath him he could no longer see it in the dark. Looking up, he could see the elusive top of the tower very near him. But it had been that near him, it seemed, for hours. He wondered if he were walking through a piece of a dream that had stood among the abandoned stones for thousands of years. Then he realized it was not a dream, but an illusion, an ancient riddle bound to someone's mind, and he had carried the answer to it with him all the way.

He said softly, "Death."

15

THE WALLS ROSE around him, circled him. Twelve windows opened through midnight blue stone to the restless, murmuring winds. He felt a touch and turned, startled back into his body.

The High One stood before him. He had the wizard's scarred hands, and the harpist's fine, worn face. But his eyes were neither the harpist's nor the wizard's. They were the falcon's eyes, fierce, vulnerable, frighteningly powerful. They held Morgon motionless, half-regretting that he had spoken the name that had turned in his mind after all that time to show its dark side. For the first time in his life he had no courage for questions; his mouth was too dry for speaking.

He whispered into the void of the High One's silence, "I had to find you . . . I have to understand."

"You still don't." His voice sounded shadowy with winds. Then he bound the awesomeness of his power somewhere within him and became the harpist, quiet, familiar, whom Morgon could question. The moment's transition bound Morgon's voice again, for it loosed a conflict of emotion. He tried to control them. But as the High One touched the stars at his side and his back, bringing them irrevocably into shape, his own hands rose, caught the harpist's arms and stilled him.

"Why?"

The falcon's eyes held him again; he could not look away. He saw, as if he were reading memories within the dark eyes, the silent, age-old game the High One had played, now with Earth-Masters, now with Ghisteslwchlohm, now with Morgon himself, a ceaseless tapestry of riddles with some threads as old as time and others spun at a step across the threshold into a wizard's chamber, at a change of expression on the Star-Bearer's face. His fingers tightened, feeling bone. An Earth-Master moved alone out of the shadows of some great, unfinished war . . . hid for thousands of years, now a leaf on a rich, matted forest floor of dead leaves, now the brush of sunlight down the flank of a pine. Then, for a thousand years, he took a wizard's face, and for another thousand, a harpist's still, secret face, gazing back at the twisted shape of power out of its own expressionless eyes. "Why?" he whispered again, and saw himself in Hed, sitting at the dock end, picking at a harp he could not play, with the shadow of the High One's harpist flung across him. The sea wind or the High One's hand bared the stars at his hairline. The harpist saw them, a promise out of a past so old it had buried his name. He could not speak; he spun his silence into riddles . . .

"But why?" Tears or sweat were burning in his eyes. He brushed at them; his hands locked once more on the High One's arms, as if to keep his shape. "You could have killed Ghisteslwchlohm with a thought. Instead you served him. You gave me to him. Were you his harpist so long you had forgotten your own name?"

The High One moved; Morgon's own arms were caught in an inflexible grip. "Think. You're the riddler."

"I played the game you challenged me to. But I don't know why—"

"Think. I found you in Hed, innocent, ignorant, oblivious of your own destiny. You couldn't even harp. Who in this realm was there to wake you to power?"

"The wizards," he said between his teeth. "You could have stopped the destruction of Lungold. You were there. The wizards could have survived in freedom, trained me for whatever protection you need—"

"No. If I had used power to stop that battle, I would have battled Earth-Masters long before I was ready. They would have destroyed me. Think of their faces. Remember them. The faces of the Earth-Masters you saw in Erlenstar Mountain, I am of them. The children they once loved were buried beneath Isig Mountain. How could you, with all your innocence, have understood them? Their longing and their lawlessness? In all the realm, who was there to teach you that? You wanted a choice. I gave it to you. You could have taken the shape of power you learned from Ghisteslwchlohm: lawless, destructive, loveless. Or you could have swallowed darkness until you shaped it, understood it, and still cried out for something more. When you broke free of Ghisteslwchlohm's power, why was it me you hunted, instead of him? He took the power of land-law from you. I took your trust, your love. You pursued what you valued most . . ."

Morgon's hands opened, closed again. His breath was beginning to rack through him. He caught it, stilled it long enough to shape one final question. "What is it you want of me?"

"Morgon, think." The even, familiar voice was suddenly gentle, almost inaudible. "You can shape the wild heart of Osterland, you can shape wind. You saw my son, dead and buried in Isig Mountain. You took the stars of your own destiny from him. And in all your power and anger, you found your way here, to name me. You are my land-heir."

Morgon was silent. He was gripping the High One as if the tower floor had suddenly vanished under him. He heard his own voice, oddly toneless, from a distance. "Your heir."

"You are the Star-Bearer, the heir foreseen by the dead of Isig, for whom I have been waiting for centuries beyond hope. Where did you think the power you have over land-law sprang from?"

"I didn't—I wasn't thinking." His voice had dropped to a whisper. He thought of Hed, then. "You are giving me—you are giving Hed back to me."

"I am giving you the entire realm when I die. You seem to love it, even all its wraiths and thick-skulled farmers and deadly winds—" He stopped, as a sound broke out of Morgon. His face was scored with tears, as riddles wove their pattern strand by gleaming strand around the heart of the tower. His hands loosened: he slid to the High One's feet and crouched there, his head bowed, his scarred hands closed, held against his heart. He could not speak; he did not know what language of light and darkness the falcon who had so ruthlessly fashioned his life would hear. He thought numbly of Hed; it seemed to lay where his heart lay, under his hands. Then the High One knelt in front of him, lifted Morgon's face between his hands. His eyes were the harpist's, night-dark, and no longer silent but full of pain.

"Morgon," he whispered, "I wish you had not been someone I loved so."

He put his arms around Morgon, held him as fiercely as the falcon had held him. He circled Morgon with his silence, until Morgon felt that his heart and the tower walls and the starred night sky beyond were built not of blood and stone and air, but of the harpist's stillness. He was still crying noiselessly, afraid to touch the harpist, as if he might somehow change shape again. Something hard and angled, like grief, was pushing into his chest, into his throat, but it was not grief. He said, above its pain, feeling the High One's pain as one thing he could comprehend, "What happened to your son?"

"He was destroyed in the war. The power was stripped from him. He could no longer live. . . . He gave you the starred sword."

"And you . . . you have been alone since then. Without an heir. With only a promise."

"Yes. I have lived in secret for thousands of years with nothing to hope in but a promise. A dead child's dream. And then you came. Morgon, I did anything I had to do to keep you alive. Anything. You were all my hope."

"You are giving me even the wastelands. I loved them. I loved them. And the mists of Herun, the vesta, the backlands . . . I was afraid, when I realized how much I loved them. I was drawn to every shape, and I couldn't stop myself from wanting—" The pain broke through his chest like a blade. He drew a harsh, terrible breath. "All I wanted from you was truth. I didn't know . . . I didn't know you would give me everything I have ever loved."

He could not speak any more. Sobbing wrenched him until he did not know if he could endure his own shape. But the High One held him to it, soothing him with his hands and his voice until Morgon quieted. He still could not speak; he listened to the winds whispering through the tower, to the occasional patter of rain on the stones. His face was bowed against the High One's shoulder. He was silent, resting in the High One's silence, until his voice came again, hoarse, weary, calmer.

"I never guessed. You never let me see that far beyond my anger."

"I didn't dare let you see too much. Your life was in such danger, and you were so precious to me. I kept you alive any way I could, using myself, using your ignorance, even your hatred. I did not know if you would ever forgive me, but all the hope of the realm lay in you, and I needed you powerful, confused, always searching for me, yet never finding me, though I was always near you . . ."

"I told . . . I told Raederle if I came back out of the wastes to play a riddle-game with you that I would lose."

"No. You startled the truth out of me in Herun. I lost to you, there. I could endure everything from you but your gentleness." His hand smoothed Morgon's hair, then dropped to hold him tightly again. "You and the Morgol kept my heart from turning into stone. I was forced to turn everything I had ever said to her into a lie. And you turned it back into truth. You were that generous with someone you hated."

"All I wanted, even when I hated you most, was some poor, barren, parched excuse to love you. But you only gave me riddles. . . . When I thought Ghisteslwchlohm had killed you, I grieved without knowing why. When I was in the northern wastes, harping to the winds, too tired even to think, it was you who drew me out. . . . You gave me a reason for living." His hands had opened slowly. He raised one, almost tentatively, to the High One's shoulder and shifted back a little. Something of his own weariness showed in his eyes, and the endless, terrible patience that had kept him alive in the world of men. Morgon's head bowed again after a moment.

"Even I tried to kill you."

The harpist's fingers touched his cheekbone, drew the hair back from his eyes. "You kept my enemies from suspecting me very effectively, but Morgon, if you had not stopped yourself that day in Anuin, I don't know what I would have done. If I had used power to stop you, neither of us would have lived too long afterward. If I had let you kill me, out of despair, because we had brought one another to such an impasse, the power passing into you would have destroyed you. So I gave you a riddle, hoping you would consider that instead."

"You knew me that well," he whispered.

"No. You constantly surprised me . . . from the very first. I am as old as the stones on this plain. The great cities of Earth-Masters built were shattered by a war that no man could have survived. It was born out of a kind of innocence. We held so much power, and yet we did not understand the implications of power. That's why, even if you hated me for it, I wanted you to understand Ghisteslwchlohm and how he destroyed himself. We lived so peacefully once, in these great cities. They were open to every change of wind. Our faces changed with every season; we took knowledge from all things: from the silence of the backlands to the burning ice sweeping across the northern wastes. We did not realize, until it was too late, that the power inherent in every stone, every movement of water, holds both existence and destruction." He paused, no longer seeing Morgon, tasting a bitter word. "The woman you know as Eriel was the first of us to begin to gather power. And I was the first to see the implications of power . . . that paradox that tempers wizardry and compelled the study of riddlery. So, I made a choice, and began binding all earth-shapes to me by their own laws, permitting nothing to disturb that law. But I had to fight to keep the land-law, and we learned what war is then. The realm as you know it would not have lasted two days in the force of those battles. We razed our own cities. We destroyed one another. We destroyed our children, drew the power even out of them. I had already learned to master the winds, which was the only thing that saved me. I was able to bind the power of the last of the Earth-Masters so they could use little beyond the power they were born to. I swept them into the sea while the earth slowly healed itself. I buried our children, then. The Earth-Masters broke out of the sea eventually, but they could not break free of my hold over them. And they could never find me, because the winds hid me, always . . .

"But I am very old, and I cannot hold them much longer. They know that. I was old even when I became a wizard named Yrth so that I could fashion the harp and the sword that my heir would need. Ghisteslwchlohm learned of the Star-Bearer from the dead of Isig, and he became one more enemy lured by the promise of enormous power. He thought that if he controlled the Star-Bearer, he could assimilate the power the Star-Bearer would inherit and become the High One in more than name. It would have killed him, but I did not bother explaining that to him. When I realized he was waiting for you, I watched him—in Lungold, and later in Erlenstar Mountain. I took the shape of a harpist who had died during the destruction and entered his service. I wanted no harm to come to you without my consent. When I found you at last, sitting on the dock at Tol, oblivious of your own destiny, content to rule Hed, with a harp in your hands you could barely play and the crown of the Kings of Aum under your bed, I realized that the last thing I had been expecting after all those endless, lonely centuries was someone I might love . . ." He paused again, his face blurred into pale, silvery lines by Morgon's tears. "Hed. No wonder that land shaped the Star-Bearer out of itself, a loving Prince of Hed, ruler of ignorant, stubborn farmers who believed in nothing but the High One . . ."

"I am hardly more than that now . . . ignorant and thick-skulled. Have I destroyed us both by coming here to find you?"

"No. This is the one place no one would expect us to be. But we have little time left. You crossed Ymris without touching the land-law."

Morgon dropped his hands. "I didn't dare," he said. "And all I could think of was you. I had to find you before the Earth-Masters found me."

"I know. I left you in a perilous situation. But you found me, and I hold the land-law of Ymris. You'll need it. Ymris is a seat of great power. I want you to take the knowledge from my mind. Don't worry," he added, at Morgon's expression. "I will only give you that knowledge, nothing that you cannot bear, yet. Sit down."

Morgon slid back slowly onto the stones. The rain had begun again, blown on the wind through the openings in the chamber, but he was not cold. The harpist's face was changing; his worn, troubled expression had eased into an ageless peace as he contemplated his realm. Morgon looked at him, drawing hungrily from his peace until he was enveloped in stillness and the High One's touch seemed to lay upon his heart. He heard the deep, shadowy voice again, the falcon's voice.

"Ymris . . . I was born here on Wind Plain. Listen to its power beneath the rain, beneath the cries of the dead. It is like you, a fierce and loving land. Be still and listen to it . . ."

He grew still, so still he could hear the grass bending beneath the weight of the rain and the ancient names from early centuries that had been spoken there. And then he became the grass.

He drew himself out of Ymris slowly, his heart thundering to its long and bloody history, his body shaped to its green fields, wild shores, strange, brooding forests. He felt old as the earliest stone hewn out of

Erlenstar Mountain to rest on the earth, and he knew far more than he had ever cared to know of the devastation the recent war had loosed across Ruhn. He sensed great untapped power in Ymris that he had winced away from, as if a sea or a mountain had loomed before him that his mind simply could not encompass. But it held odd moments of quiet; a still, secret lake mirroring many things; strange stones that had once been made to speak; forests haunted with pure black animals so shy they died if men looked upon them; acres of oak woods on the western borders whose trees remembered the first vague passage of men into Ymris. These, he treasured. The High One had given him no more of his mind than the awareness of Ymris; the power he had feared in the falcon's eyes was still leashed when he looked into them again.

It was dawn, of some day, and Raederle was beside him. He made a surprised noise. "How did you get up here?"

"I flew."

The answer was so simple it seemed meaningless for a moment. "So did I."

"You climbed the stairs. I flew to the top."

His face looked so blank with surprise that she smiled. "Morgon, the High One let me come in. Otherwise I would have flown around the tower squawking all night."

He grunted and linked his fingers into hers. She was very tired, he sensed, and her smile faded quickly, leaving something disturbing in her eyes. The High One was standing beside one of the windows. The blue-black stone was rimed with the first light; against the sky the harpist's face looked weary, the skin drawn taut, colorless against the bones. But the eyes were Yrth's, light-filled, secret. Morgon looked at him for a long time without moving, still enmeshed in his peace, until the changeless, familiar face seemed to meld with the pale silver of the morning. The High One turned then to meet his eyes.

He drew Morgon to his side without a gesture, only his simple wordless desire. Morgon loosed Raederle's hand and rose stiffly. He crossed the room. The High One put a hand on his shoulder.

Morgon said, "I couldn't take it all."

"Morgon, the power you sensed is in the Earth-Masters' dead: those who died fighting at my side on this plain. The power will be there when you need it."

Something in Morgon, deep beneath his peace, lifted its muzzle like a blind hound in the dark, scenting at the High One's words. "And the harp, and the sword?" He kept his voice tranquil. "I barely understand the power in them."

"They will find uses for themselves. Look."

There was a white mist of vesta along the plain, beneath the low, lumbering cloud. Morgon gazed down at them incredulously, then leaned his face against the cool stone. "When did they get here?"

"Last night."

"Where is Astrin's army?"

"Half of it was trapped between Tor and Umber, but the vanguard made it through, clearing a path for the vesta and the Morgol's guard and Danan's miners. They are behind the vesta." He read Morgon's thoughts; his hand tightened slightly. "I did not bring them here to fight."

"Then why?" he whispered.

"You will need them. You and I must end this war quickly. That is what you were born to do."

"How?"

The High One was silent. Behind his tranquil, indrawn gaze, Morgon sensed a weariness beyond belief, and a more familiar patience: the harpist's waiting for Morgon's understanding, perhaps, or for something beyond his understanding. He said finally, very gently, "The Prince of Hed and his farmers have gathered on the south border with Mathom's army. If you need to keep them alive, you'll find a way."

Morgon whirled. He crossed the chamber, hung out a south window, as if he could see among the leafless oaks a grim battery of farmers with rakes and hoes and scythes. His heart swelled with sudden pain and fear that sent tears to his eyes. "He left Hed. Eliard turned his farmers into warriors and left Hed. What is it? The end of the world?"

"He came to fight for you. And for his own land."

"No." He turned again, his hands clenched, but not in anger. "He came because you wanted him. That's why the Morgol came, and Har—you drew them, the way you draw me, with a touch of wind at the heart, a mystery. What is it? What is it that you aren't telling me?"

"I have given you my name."

Morgon was silent. It began to snow lightly, big, random flakes scattered on the wind. They caught on his hands, burned before they vanished. He shuddered suddenly and found that he had no inclination left for questions. Raederle had turned away from them both. She looked oddly isolated in the center of the small chamber. Morgon went to her side; her head lifted as he joined her, but her face turned away from him to the High One.

He came to her, as if she had drawn him, the way he drew Morgon. He smoothed a strand of her wind-blown hair away from her face. "Raederle, it is time for you to leave."

She shook her head. "No." Her voice was very quiet. "I am half Earth-Master. You will have at least one of your kind fighting for you after all these centuries. I will not leave either of you."

"You are in the eye of danger."

"I chose to come. To be with those I love."

He was silent; for a moment he was only the harpist, ageless, indrawn, lonely. "You," he said softly, "I never expected. So powerful, so beautiful, and so loving. You are like one of our children, growing into power before our war." He lifted her hand and kissed it, then opened it to the small angular scar on her palm. "There are twelve winds," he said to Morgon. "Bound, controlled, they are more precise and terrible than any weapon or wizard's power in the realm. Unbound, they could destroy the realm. They are also my eyes and ears, for they shape all things, hear all words and movements, and they are everywhere. . . . That jewel that Raederle held was cut and faceted by winds. I did that one day when I was playing with them, long before I ever used them in our war. The memory of that was mirrored in the stone."

"Why are you telling me?" His voice jerked a little. "I can't hold the winds."

"No. Not yet. Don't be concerned, yet." He put his arm around Morgon's shoulders, held him easily again within his stillness. "Listen. You can hear the voices of all the winds of the realm in this chamber. Listen to my mind."

Morgon opened his mind to the High One's silence. The vague, incoherent murmurings outside the walls were refracted through the High One's mind into all the pure, beautiful tones on the starred harp. The harping filled Morgon's heart with soft, light summer winds, and the deep, wild winds that he loved; the slow, rich measures matched the beat of his blood. He wanted suddenly to hold the harping and the harpist within that moment until the white winter sky broke apart once more to light.

The harping stilled. He could not speak; he did not want the High One to move. But the arm around his shoulders shifted; the High One gripped him gently, facing him.

"Now," he said, "we have a battle on our hands. I want you to find Heureu Ymris. This time, I'll warn you: when you touch his mind, you will spring a trap set for you. The Earth-Masters will know where you are and that the High One is with you. You will ignite war again on Wind Plain. They have little mind-power of their own—I keep that bound; but they hold Ghisteslwchlohm's mind, and they may use his powers of wizardry to try to hurt you. I'll break any bindings he forges."

Morgon turned his head, looked at Raederle. Her eyes told him what he already knew: that nothing he could say or do could make her leave them. He bent his head again, in silent acquiescence to her and to the High One. Then he let his awareness venture beyond the silence into the damp earth around the tower. He touched a single blade of grass, let his mind shape it from hair roots to tip. Rooted also within the structure of land-law in Heureu's mind, it became his link with the King of Ymris.

He sensed a constant, nagging pain, a turmoil of helpless anger and despair, and heard a distant, hollow drag and ebb of the sea. He had learned every shape of cliff and stone boring out of the shores, and he recognized the strip of Meremont coast. He smelled wet wood and ashes; the king lay in a half-burned fisher's hut on the beach, no more than a mile or two from Wind Plain.

He started to glance up, to speak. Then the sea flooded over him, spilled through all his thoughts. He seemed to stare down a long, dark passageway into Ghisteslwchlohm's alien, gold-flecked eyes.

He felt the startled recognition in the bound mind. Then a mind-hold raked at him, and the wizard's eyes burned into him, searching for him. The mind-hold was broken; he reeled back away from it. The High One gripped his shoulder, holding him still. He started to speak again, but the falcon's eyes stopped him.

He waited, shaken suddenly by the pounding of his heart. Raederle, bound to the same waiting, seemed remote again, belonging to another portion of the world. He wanted desperately to speak, to break the silence that held them all motionless as if they were carved of stone. But he seemed spellbound, choiceless, an extension of the High One's will. A movement streaked the air, and then another. The dark, delicately beautiful Earth-Master, whom Morgon knew as Eriel, stood before them, and beside her, Ghisteslwchlohm.

For a moment, the High One checked the power gathered against him. There was astonishment and awe in the woman's eyes as she recognized the harpist. The wizard, face to face with the High One, whom he had been searching for so long, nearly broke the hold over his mind. A faint smile touched the falcon's eyes, icy as the heart of the northern wastes.

"Even death, Master Ohm," he said, "is a riddle."

A rage blackened Ghisteslwchlohm's eyes. Something spun Morgon across the chamber. He struck the dark wall; it gave under him, and he fell into a luminous, blue-black mist of illusion. He heard Raederle's cry, and then a crow streaked across his vision. He caught at it, but it fluttered away between his hands. A mind gripped his mind. The binding was instantly broken. A power he did not feel flashed at him and was swallowed. He saw Ghisteslwchlohm's face again, blurred in the strange light. He felt a wrench at his side, and he cried out, though he did not know what had been taken from him. Then he turned on his back and saw the starred sword in Ghisteslwchlohm's hands, rising endlessly upward, gathering shadow and light, until the stars burst with fire and darkness above Morgon. He could not move; the stars drew his eyes, his thoughts. He watched them reach their apex and halt, then blur into their descent toward him. Then he saw the harpist again, standing beneath their fall, as quietly as he had stood in the king's hall at Anuin.

A cry tore through Morgon. The sword fell with a terrible speed, struck the High One. It drove into his heart, then snapped in Ghisteslwchlohm's hands. Morgon, freed to move at last, caught him as he fell. He could not breathe; a blade of grief was thrusting into his own heart. The High One gripped his arms; his hands were the harpist's crippled hands, the wizard's scarred hands. He struggled to speak; his face blurred from one shape to another under Morgon's tears. Morgon pulled him closer, feeling something build in him like a shout of fury and agony, but the High One was already beginning to vanish. He reached out with a hand shaped of red stone or fire, touched the stars on Morgon's face.

He whispered Morgon's name. His hand slid down over Morgon's heart. "Free the winds."

A SHOUT THAT was not a shout but a wind-voice came out of Morgon. The High One turned to flame in his hands, and then into a memory. The sound he had made reverberated through the tower: a low bass note that built and built until the stones around him began to shake. Winds were battering at the tower; he felt struck and struck again, like a harp string, by his grief. He did not know, out of all the wild, chaotic, beautiful voices around him, which was his own. He groped for his harp. The stars on it had turned night-black. He swept his hand, or the knife-edge of a wind, across it. The strings snapped. As the low string wailed and broke, stone and illusion of stone shocked apart around him and began to fall.

Winds the color of the stones: of fire, of gold, of night, spiralled around him, then broke away. The tower roared around him and collapsed into a gigantic cairn. Morgon was flung on his hands and knees on the grass beside it. He could sense Ghisteslwchlohm and Eriel's power nowhere, as if the High One had bound them, in that final moment, to his death. Snow whirled around him, melting almost as soon as it touched the ground. The sky was dead-white.

His mind was reeling with land-law. He heard the silence of grass roots under his hands; he stared at the broken mass of Wind Tower out of the unblinking eyes of a wraith of An at the edge of the plain. A great tree sagged in the rain on a wet hillside in the backlands; he felt its roots shift and loosen as it fell. A trumpeter in Astrin's army was lifting his long, golden instrument to his mouth. The thoughts of the land-rulers snarled in Morgon's mind, full of grief and fear, though they did not understand why. The entire realm seemed to form under his hands on the grass, pulling at him, stretching him from the cold, empty wastes to the elegant court at Anuin. He was stone, water, a dying field, a bird struggling against the wind, a king wounded and despairing on the beach below Wind Plain, vesta, wraiths, and a thousand fragile mysteries, shy witches, speaking pigs, and solitary towers that he had to find room for within his mind. The trumpeter set his lips to the horn and blew. At the same moment a Great Shout from the army of An blasted over the plain. The sounds, the urgent onslaught of knowledge, the loss that was boring into Morgon's heart overwhelmed him suddenly. He cried out again, dropping against the earth, his face buried in the wet grass.

Power ripped through his mind, blurring the bindings he had formed with the earth. He realized that the death of the High One had unbound all the power of the Earth-Masters. He felt their minds, ancient, wild, like fire and sea, beautiful and deadly, intent on destroying him. He did not know how to fight them. Without moving, he saw them in his mind's eye, fanning across Wind Plain from the sea, flowing like a wave in the shapes of men and animals, their minds riding before them, scenting. They touched him again and again, uprooting knowledge in his mind, breaking bindings he had inherited, until his awareness of trees in the oak forest, vesta, plow horses in Hed, farmers in Ruhn, tiny pieces of the realm began to disappear from his mind.

He felt it as another kind of loss, terrible and bewildering. He tried to fight it as he watched the wave draw closer, but it was as though he tried to stop the tide from pulling sand grains out of his hands. Astrin's army and Mathom's were thundering across the plain from north and south, their battle colors vivid as dying leaves against the winter sky. They would be destroyed, Morgon knew, even the dead; no living awareness or memory of the dead could survive the power that was feeding even on his own power. Mathom rode at the head of his force; in the trees, Har was preparing to loose the vesta onto the plain. Danan's miners, flanked by the Morgol's guard, were beginning to follow Astrin's warriors. He did not know how to help them. Then he realized that on the edge of the plain to the southeast, Eliard and the farmers of Hed, armed with little more than hammers and knives and their bare hands, were marching doggedly to his rescue.

He lifted his head; his awareness of them faltered suddenly as a mind blurred over his mind. The whole of the realm seemed to darken; portions of his life were slipping away from him. He gripped at it, his hands tangled in the grass, feeling that all the High One's hope in him had been for nothing. Then, in some misty corner of his mind, a door opened. He saw Tristan come out onto the porch at Akren, shivering a little in the cold wind, her eyes dark and fearful, staring toward the tumult in the mainland.

He got to his knees and then to his feet, with all the enduring stubbornness that small island had instilled in him. A wind lashed across his face; he could barely keep his balance in it. He was standing in the heart of chaos. The living and the dead and the Earth-Masters were just about to converge around him; the land-law of the realm was being torn away from him; he had freed the winds. They were belling across the realm, telling him of forests bent to the breaking point, villages picked apart, thatch and shingle whirled away into the air. The sea was rousing; it would kill Heureu Ymris, if he did not act. Eliard would die if Morgon could not stop him. He tried to reach Eliard's mind, but as he searched the plain, he only entangled himself in a web of other minds.

They tore knowledge, power from him like a wave eating at a cliff. There seemed no escape from them, no image of peace he could form in his mind to deflect them. Then he saw something glittering in front of him: his broken harp, lying on the grass, its strings flashing silently, played by the wind.

A strong, clean fury that was not his own washed through him suddenly, burning away all the holds over his mind. It left his mind clear as fire. He found Raederle beside him, freeing him for one brief moment with her anger, and he could have gone on his knees to her, because she was still alive, because she was with him. In the one moment she had given him, he realized what he must do. Then the forces of the realm shocked together in front of him. Bones of the dead, shimmering mail and bright shields of the living, vesta white as the falling snow, the

Morgol's guard with their slender spears of silver and ash closed with the merciless, inhuman power of the Earth-Masters.

He heard, for the first time, the sorrowing cry a vesta made as it died, calling plaintively to its own. He felt the names of the dead blotted out like blown flames in his mind. Men and women fought with spears and swords, picks and battle axes against an enemy that kept to no single shape, but a constant, fluid changing that mesmerized opponents to despair and to death. Morgon felt them die, parts of himself. Danan's miners fell like great, stolid trees; the farmers from Hed, viewing a foe beyond all their conceptions, nothing their placid history had ever suggested existed, seemed too confused even to defend themselves. Their lives were wrenched out of Morgon like rooted things. The plain was a living, snarling thing before his eyes, a piece of himself fighting for its life with no hope of survival against the dark, sinuous, sharp-toothed beast that determined the realm would die. In the few brief moments of battle, he felt the first of the land-rulers die.

He sensed the struggle in Heureu Ymris' mind as, wounded and unaided, he tried to comprehend the turmoil in his land. His body was not strong enough for such torment. He died alone, hearing the crashing sea and the cries of the dying across Wind Plain. Morgon felt the life-force in the king drain back to Ymris. And on the battlefield, Astrin, fighting for his life, wrestled suddenly with an overwhelming grief, and the sudden wakening in him of all land-instinct.

His grief woke Morgon's again, for the High One, for Heureu, for the realm itself, entrusted to his care and dying within him. His mind shook open on a harp note that was also a call to a south wind burning across the backlands. Note by note, all tuned to sorrow, he called the unbound winds back to Wind Plain.

They came to him out of the northern wastes, burning with cold; rain-soaked from the backlands; tasting of brine and snow from the sea; smelling of wet earth, from Hed. They were devastating. They flattened the grass from one end of the plain to the other. They wrenched his shape into air, uprooted oak at the edge of the plain. They moaned the darkness of his sorrow, tore the air with their shrill, furious keening. They flung apart the armies before them like chaff. Riderless horses ran before them; dead frayed back into memory; shields were tossed in the air like leaves; men and women sprawled on the ground, trying to crawl away from the winds. Even the Earth-Masters were checked; no shape they took could batter past the winds.

Morgon, his mind fragmented into harp notes, struggled to shape an order out of them. The bass, northern wind hummed its deep note through him; he let it fill his mind until he shuddered with sound like a harp string. It loosed him finally; he grasped at another voice, thin and fiery, out of the remote backlands. It burned through his mind with a sweet, terrible note. He flamed with it, absorbed it. Another wind, sweeping across the sea, shook a wild song through him. He sang its wildness back at it, changed the voice in him, in the winds, to a gentleness. The waves massed against the shores of Hed began to calm. A different wind sang into his mind, of the winter silence of Isig Pass and the harping still echoing through the darkness of Erlenstar Mountain. He shaped the silence and darkness into his own song.

He was scarcely aware of the Earth-Masters' minds as he battled for mastery over the winds. Their power was filling him, challenging him, yet defending him. No mind on the plain around him could have touched him, embroiled as it was with wind. A remote part of him watched the realm he was bound to. Warriors were fleeing into the border forests. They were forced to leave their arms; they could not even carry the wounded with them. As far as Caithnard, Caerweddin, and Hed the noises of his struggle with the winds were heard. The wizards had left the plain; he felt the passage of their power as they responded to bewilderment and fear. Twilight drifted over the plain, and then night, and he wrestled with the cold, sinewy, wolf-voiced winds of darkness.

He drew the power of the winds to a fine precision. He could have trained an east wind on the innermost point of the cairn beside him and sent the stones flying all over the plain. He could have picked a snowflake off the ground, or turned one of the fallen guards lightly buried under snow to see her face. All along both sides of the plain hundreds of fires had been lit all night, as men and women of the realm waited sleeplessly while he wrested their fates, moment by moment, out of the passing hours. They nursed their wounded and wondered if they would survive the passage of power from the High One to his heir. At last, he gave them dawn.

It came as a single eye staring at him through white mist. He drew back into himself, his hands full of winds. He was alone on a quiet plain. The Earth-Masters had shifted their battleground eastward, moving across Ruhn. He stood quietly a moment, wondering if he had lived through a single night or a century of them. Then he turned his mind away from the night to scent the path of the Earth-Masters.

They had fled across Ruhn. Towns and farms, lords' houses lay in ruins; fields, woods, and orchards had been harrowed and seared with power. Men, children, animals trapped in the range of their minds had been killed. As his awareness moved across the wasteland, he felt a harp song building through him. Winds in his control stirred to it, angry, dangerous, pulling him out of his shape until he was half-man, half-wind, a harpist playing a death song on a harp with no strings.

Then he roused all the power that lay buried under the great cities across Ymris. He had sensed it in the High One's mind, and he knew at last why the Earth-Masters had warred for possession of their cities. They were all cairns, broken monuments to their dead. The power had lain dormant under the earth for thousands of years. But, as with the wraiths of An, their minds could be roused with memory, and Morgon, his mind burrowing under the stones, shocked them awake with his grief. He did not see them. But on Wind Plain and King's Mouth Plain, in the ruins across Ruhn and east Umber, a power gathered, hung over the stones like the eerie, unbearable tension in the sky before a storm breaks. The tension was felt in Caerweddin and in towns still surviving around the ruins. No one spoke that dawn; they waited.

Morgon began to move across Wind Plain. An army of the Earth-Masters' dead moved with him, flowed across Ymris, searching out the living Earth-Masters to finish a war. Winds hounded the Earth-Masters out of the shape of stone and leaf they hid in; the dead forced them with a silent, relentless purpose out of the land they had once loved. They scattered across the backlands, through wet, dark forests, across bare hills, across the icy surfaces of the Lungold Lakes. Morgon, the winds running before him, the dead at his back, pursued them across the threshold of winter. He drove them as inflexibly as they had once driven him toward Erlenstar Mountain.

They tried to fight him one last time before he compelled them into the mountain. But the dead rose around him like stone, and the winds raged against them. He could have destroyed them, stripped them of their power, as they had tried to do to him. But something of their beauty lingered in Raederle, showing him what they might have been once; and he could not kill them. He did not even touch their power. He forced them into Erlenstar Mountain, where they fled from him into the shape of water and jewel. He sealed the entire Mountain—all shafts and hidden springs, the surface of the earth, and ground floor of rock—with his name. Among trees and stones, light and wind, around the mountain, he bound the dead once more, to guard the mountain. Then he loosed the winds from his song, and they drew winter down from the northlands across the whole of the realm.

He returned to Wind Plain, then, drawn by memory. There was snow all over the plain and on all the jagged, piled faces of the stones. There was smoke among the trees around the plain, for no one had left it. The gathering of men, women, animals was still there, waiting for his return. They had buried their dead and sent for supplies; they were settling for the winter, bound to the plain.

Morgon took his shape out of the winds, beside the ruined tower. He heard the Morgol talking to Goh; he saw Har checking the splint on a crippled vesta. He did not know if Eliard was still alive. Looking up at the huge cairn, he stepped forward into his sorrow. He laid his face against one of the cold, beautiful stones, stretched his arms across it, wanting to encompass the entire cairn, hold it in his heart. He felt bound, suddenly, as if he were a wraith, and all his past was buried in those stones. As he mourned, men began to move across the plain. He saw them without thinking about them in his mind's eye: tiny figures drawn across the blank, snow-covered plain. When he finally turned, he found them in a silent ring around him.

They had been drawn to him, he sensed, the way he had always been drawn to Deth: with no reason, no question, simply instinct. The land-rulers of the realm, the four wizards stood quietly with him. They did not know what to say to him as he stood there in his power and his grief; they were simply responding to something in him that had brought peace to the ancient plain.

He looked at the faces he knew so well. They were scarred with sorrow for the High One, for their own dead. Finding Eliard among them, he felt something quicken painfully in his heart. Eliard's face was as he had never seen it: colorless and hard as winter ground. A third of the farmers of Hed had been sent back to Hed, to be buried beneath the frozen ground. The winter would be hard for the living, and Morgon did not know how to comfort him. But as he looked at Morgon mutely, something else came into his eyes that had never been in the changeless, stolid heritage of the Princes of Hed: he had been touched by mystery.

Morgon's eyes moved to Astrin. He seemed still dazed by Heureu's death and the sudden, far-flung power he possessed. "I'm sorry," Morgon said. The words sounded as light and meaningless as the snow flecking the massive stones behind him. "I felt him die. But I couldn't—I couldn't help him. I felt so much death . . ."

The single white eye seemed to gaze into him at the word. "You're alive," he whispered. "High One. You survived to name yourself at last, and you brought peace to this morning."

"Peace." He felt the stones behind him, cold as ice.

"Morgon," Danan said softly, "when we saw that tower fall, none of us expected to see another dawn."

"So many didn't. So many of your miners died."

"So many didn't. I have a great mountain full of trees; you gave it back to us, our home to return to."

"We have lived to see the passage of power from the High One to his heir," Har said. "We paid a price for our seeing, but . . . we survived." His eyes were oddly gentle in the pure, cold light. He shifted the cloak over his shoulders: an old, gnarled king, with the first memories of the realm in his heart. "You played a wondrous game and won. Don't grieve for the High One. He was old and near the end of his power. He left you a realm at war, an almost impossible heritage, and all his hope. You did not fail him. Now we can return home in peace, without having to fear the stranger at our thresholds. When the door opens unexpectedly to the winter winds, and we look up from our warm hearths to find the High One in our house, it will be you. He left us that gift."

Morgon was silent. Sorrow touched him again, lightly, like a searching flame, in spite of all their words. Then he felt from one of them an answering sorrow that no words could comfort. He sought it, something of himself, and found it in Mathom, tired and shadowed by death.

Morgon took a step toward him. "Who?"

"Duac," the King said. He drew a dry breath, standing dark as a wraith against the snow. "He refused to stay in An . . . the only argument I have ever lost. My land-heir with his eyes of the sea . . ."

Morgon was mute again, wondering how many of his bindings had been broken, how many deaths he had not sensed. He said suddenly, remembering, "You knew the High One would die here."

"He named himself," Mathom said. "I did not need to dream that. Bury him here, where he chose to die. Let him rest."

"I can't," he whispered, "I was his death. He knew. All that time, he knew. I was his destiny, he was mine. Our lives were one constant, twisted riddle-game. . . . He forged the sword that would kill him, and I brought it here to him. If I had thought . . . if I had known—"

"What would you have done? He did not have the strength to win this war; he knew you would, if he gave you his power. That game, he won. Accept it."

"I can't . . . not yet." He put one hand on the stones before he left them. Then he lifted his head, searching the sky for something that he could not find in his mind. But its face was pale, motionless. "Where is Raederle?"

"She was with me for a while," the Morgol said. Her face was very quiet, like the winter morning that drew a stillness over the world. "She left, I thought, to look for you, but perhaps she needs a time to sorrow, also." He met her eyes. She smiled, touching his heart. "Morgon, he is dead. But for a little while, you gave him something to love."

"So did you," he whispered. He turned away then, to find his own comfort somewhere within his realm. He became snow or air or perhaps he stayed himself; he was not certain; he only knew he left no footprints in the snow for anyone to follow.

He wandered through the land, taking many shapes, reworking broken bindings, until there was not a tree or an insect or a man in the realm he was not aware of, except for one woman. The winds that touched everything in their boundless curiosity told him of lords and warriors without homes in Ymris taking refuge in Astrin's court, of traders battling the seas to carry grain from An and Herun and beer from Hed to the war-torn land. They told him when the vesta returned to Osterland, and how the King of An bound his dead once more into the earth of the Three Portions. They listened to the wizards at Caithnard discussing the restoration of the great school at Lungold, while the Masters quietly answered the last of the unanswered riddles on their lists. He felt Har's waiting for him, beside his winter fire, with the wolves watching at his knees. He felt the Morgol's eyes looking beyond her walls, beyond her hills, every now and then, watching for him, watching for Raederle, wondering.

He tried to put an end to his grieving, sitting for days on end in the wastes, like a tangle of old roots, piecing together the games the harpist had played, action by action, and understanding it. But understanding gave him no comfort. He tried harping, with a harp as vast as the night sky, its face full of stars, but even that brought him no peace. He moved restlessly from cold, barren peaks to quiet forests, and even the hearths of taverns and farmhouses, where he was greeted kindly as a stranger wandering in from the cold. He did not know what his heart wanted; why the wraith of the harpist roamed ceaselessly through his heart and would not rest.

He drew himself out from under a snowdrift in the northern wastes one day, impelled south without quite knowing why. He shifted shapes all across the realm; no shape gave him peace. He passed spring as it came northward; the restlessness in him sharpened. The winds coming out of the west and south smelled of plowed earth and sunlight. They strung his wind-harp with gentler voices. He did not feel gentle. He shambled in bear-shape through forests, flung himself in falcon-shape across the noon sun as it crossed his path. He rode the bow of a trade-ship three days as it scudded and boomed across the sea, until the sailors, wary of his sea bird's strange, still eyes, chased him away. He followed the Ymris coast, flying, crawling, galloping with wild horses until he reached the coast of Meremont. There he followed the scent of his memories to Wind Plain.

He found on the plain the shape of a prince of Hed, with scarred hands and three stars on his face. A battle echoed around him; stones fell soundlessly, vanished. The grass quivered like the broken strings of a harp. A blade of light from the setting sun burned in his eyes. He turned away from it and saw Raederle.

She was in Hed, on the beach above Tol. She was sitting on a rock, tossing bits of shell into the sea as the waves splashed around her. Something in her face, an odd mixture of restlessness and sadness, seemed to mirror what was in his heart. It drew him like a hand. He flew across the water, flickering in and out of the sunlight, and took his own shape on the rock in front of her.

She gazed up at him speechlessly, a shell poised in her hand. He found no words either; he wondered if he had forgotten all language in the northern wastes. He sat down beside her after a moment, wanting to be near her. He took the shell from her hand and tossed it into the waves.

"You drew me all the way down from the northern wastes," he said. "I was . . . I don't know what I was. Something cold."

She moved after a moment, drew a strand of his shaggy hair out of his eyes. "I wondered if you might come here. I thought you would come to me when you were ready." She sounded resigned to something beyond his comprehension.

"How could I have come? I didn't know where you were. You left Wind Plain."

She stared at him a moment. "I thought you knew everything. You are the High One. You even know what I am going to say next."

"I don't," he said. He picked a shell bit from a crevice, fed it to the waves. "You aren't bound to my mind. I would have been with you long ago, except I didn't know where in Hel's name to begin to look."

She was silent, watching him. He met her eyes finally, then sighed and put his arm around her shoulders. Her hair smelled of salt; her face was getting brown under the sun. "I'm wraith-driven," he said. "I think my heart was buried under that cairn."

"I know." She kissed him, then slid down until her head rested in the hollow of his shoulder. A wave rolled to their feet, withdrew. The dock at Tol was being rebuilt; pine logs brought down from the northlands lay on the beach. She gazed across the sea to Caithnard, half in shadow, half in fading light. "The College of Riddle-Masters has been reopened."

"I know."

"If you know everything, what will we have to talk about?"

"I don't know. I suppose nothing." He saw a ship cross the sea from Tol, carrying a Prince of Hed and a harpist. The ship docked at Caithnard; they both disembarked to begin their journey. . . . He stirred a little, wondering when it would end. He held Raederle more closely, his cheek against her hair. In that late light, he loved to harp, but the starred harp was broken, its strings snapped by grief. He touched a mussel clinging to the rock and realized he had never shaped one. The sea was still a moment, idling around the rock. And in that moment he almost heard something like a fragment of a song he had once loved.

"What did you do with the Earth-Masters?"

"I didn't kill them," he said softly. "I didn't even touch their power. I bound them in Erlenstar Mountain."

He felt the breath go out of her noiselessly. "I was afraid to ask," she whispered.

"I couldn't destroy them. How could I? They were a part of you, and of Deth. . . . They're bound until they die, or I die, whichever comes first. . . ." He considered the next few millenniums with a weary eye. "Riddlery. Is that the end of it? Do all riddles end in a tower with no door? I feel as if I built that tower stone by stone, riddle by riddle, and the last stone fitting into place destroyed it."

"I don't know. When Duac died, I was so hurt; I felt a place torn out of my heart. It seemed so unjust that he should die in that war, since he was the most clear-headed and patient of us. That healed. But the harpist . . . I keep listening for his harping beneath the flash of water, beneath the light . . . I don't know why we cannot let him rest."

Morgon drew her hair out of the wind's grasp and smoothed it. He tapped randomly into the continual stream of thoughts just beneath the surface of his awareness. He heard Tristan arguing placidly with Eliard as she set plates on the table at Akren. In Hel, Nun and Raith of Hel were watching a pig being born. In Lungold, Iff was salvaging books out of the burned wizards' library. In the City of Circles, Lyra was talking to a young Herun lord, telling him things she had not told anyone else about the battle in Lungold. On Wind Plain, the broken pieces of a sword were being slowly buried under grass roots.

He smelled twilight shadowing Hed, full of new grass, broken earth, sun-warmed leaves. The odd memory of a song that was no song caught at him again; straining, he almost heard it. Raederle seemed to hear it; she stirred against him, her face growing peaceful in the last warm light.

He said, "There's a speaking pig being born in Hel. Nun is there with the Lord of Hel."

She smiled suddenly. "That's the first in three centuries. I wonder what it was born to say? Morgon, while I was waiting for you, I had to do something, so I explored the sea. I found something that belongs to you. It's at Akren."

"What?"

"Don't you know?"

"No. Do you want me to read your mind?"

"No. Never. How could I argue with you, then?" His expression changed suddenly, and her smile deepened.

"Peven's crown?"

"Eliard said it was. I had never seen it. It was full of seaweed and barnacles, except for one great stone like a clear eye . . . I loved the sea. Maybe I'll live in it."

"I'll live in the wastes," he said. "Once every hundred years, you will shine out of the sea and I'll come to you, or I will draw you into the winds with my harping . . ." He heard it then, finally, between the drift of the waves, in the rock they sat on, old, warm, settled deep in the earth, deep in the sea. His heart began to open tentatively to something he had not felt for years.

"What is it?" She was still smiling, watching him, her eyes full of the last light. He was silent for a long time, listening. He took her hand and stood up. She walked with him to the shore road, up the cliff. The final rays of the sun poured down across the green fields; the road ahead of them seemed to run straight into light. He stood, his heart opened like a seedling, hearing all over Hed, all over the realm, a familiar stillness that came out of the heart of all things.

The silence drew deep into Morgon's mind and rested there. Whether it was a memory or part of his heritage or a riddle without an answer, he did not know. He drew Raederle close to him, content for once with not knowing. They walked down the road toward Akren. Raederle, her voice tranquil, began telling him about pearls and luminous fish and the singing of water deep in the sea. The sun set slowly; dusk wandered across the realm, walked behind them on the road, a silver-haired stranger with night at his back, his face always toward the dawn.

Peace, tremulous, unexpected, sent a taproot out of nowhere into Morgon's heart.

People and Places

ACOR OF HEL third King of Hel
AIA wife of Har of Osterland
AKER, JARL dead trader of Osterland
AKREN home of the land-rulers of Hed
ALOIL a Lungold wizard
AMORY, WYNDON farmer of Hed; Arin, his daughter
AN kingdom incorporating the Three Portions (An, Aum, Hel) ruled by Mathom
ANOTH physician at the court of Heureu of Ymris
ANUIN seaport in An; home of the Kings of An
ARYA a Herun woman subject of a riddle
ASH son and land-heir of Danan Isig
ASTRIN brother of Heureu; land-heir of Imris
ATHOL dead father of Morgon, Eliard and Tristan; a prince of Hed
AUBER OF AUM descendant of Peven of Aum
AUM ancient kingdom conquered by An
AWN OF AN ancient land-ruler of An; died because he deliberately destroyed part of An to keep it from an enemy

BERE grandson of Danan Isig; son of Vert
BLACKDAWN, HALLARD a lord of An, with lands in east Hel

CAERWEDDIN chief city of Ymris; seat of Heureu; a port city
CAITHNARD seaport and traders' city; site of the College of Riddle-Masters
CITY OF CIRCLES home of the Morgol of Herun
COL ancient lord of Hel
CORBETT, BRI ship-master of Mathom of An
CORRIG a shape-changer; ancester of Raederle
CROEG, CYN the Lord of Aum, with lands in east Aum; a descendant of the Kings of Aum
CROEG, MARA Cyn Croeg's wife; The Flower of An
CRON ancient Morgol of Herun; full name Ylcorcronlth. His harper was Tirunedeth
CROWN CITY chief city of Herun; ringed by seven circular walls; seat of the Morgol El of Herun
CYONE wife of Mathom of An; mother of Raederle and Rood

DANAN ISIG land-ruler and King of Isig
DETH a harpist
DHAIRRHUWYTH an early Morgol of Herun
DUAC Mathom's son; land-heir of An

EARTH-MASTERS ancient, mysterious inhabitants of the High One's realm
EDOLEN an Earth-Master
EL ELRHIARHODAN the land-ruler of Herun
ELIARD the Prince of Hed; Morgon's younger brother
ELIEU OF HEL the younger brother of Raith, Lord of Hel
ERIEL a shape-changer; a kinswoman of Corrig and Raederle
ERLENSTAR MOUNTAIN ancient home of the High One
EVERN "The Falconer"; a dead King of Hel

FARR the last of the Kings of Hel

GALIL ancient king of Ymris in the time of Aloil
GHISTESLWCHLOHM founder of the school of wizards at Lungold; also impersonator of the High One
GOH a member of the Herun guard

GRANIA dead wife of Danan Isig, mother of Sol
GRIM MOUNTAIN site of Yrye, home of Har of Osterland

HAGIS dead king of An, grandfather of Mathom
HAR the wolf-king; land-ruler of Osterland
HARTE mountain-home of Danan Isig
HED a small island ruled by the Princes of Hed
HEL one of the Three Portions of An
HERUN a kingdom ruled by the Morgol
HEUREU the King of Ymris
HIGH ONE sustainer of the land-law of the realm
HLURLE a small trade-port near Herun
HUGIN son of Suth the wizard
HWILLION, MAP a young lord with lands in south Aum

IFF a Lungold wizard
ILON ancient harper of Har of Osterland
IMER a guard in the Morgol's service
INGRIS OF OSTERLAND refused to take in the disguised Har of Osterland and died as a result
ISIG a mountain kingdom ruled by Danan Isig
ISIG PASS a mountain pass between Isig and Erlenstar Mountain

KALE first King of An, who won a desperate battle with a Great Shout
KERN OF HED ancient prince of Hed, subject of the only riddle to come from Hed
KIA a guard in the Morgol's service
KING'S MOUTH PLAIN site of a ruined city of the Earth-Masters
KOR, RUSTIN trader
KRAAL port-city at the mouth of the Winter River
KYRTH trade-city in Isig on the Ose River

LAERN Riddle-Master at Caithnard; lost his life in a riddle game with Pevin of Aum
LEIN kinsman of the High Lord of Marcher
LOOR fishing village in Ymris

LUNGOLD city founded by Ghisteslwchlohm; home of the School of Wizards

LYRA the land-heir of Herun; El's daughter

MADIR ancient witch of An

MARCHER territory in north Ymris governed by the High Lord of Marcher

MASTER, CANNON farmer of Hed

MATHOM King of An

MEREMONT coastal territory of Ymris

MEROC TOR high lord and ruler of Tor; subject of Heureu of Ymris

MORGON the Star-Bearer, at one time the Prince of Hed

NEMIR Nemir of the Pigs; a dead King of Hel

NUN a Lungold wizard

NUTT, SNOG pigherder of Hed

OAKLAND, GRIM overseer for Morgon of Hed

OEN OF AN conqueror of Aum; king of An; built a tower to trap the witch Madir

OHM a Riddle-Master of Caithnard

OHROE OF HEL a dead King of Hel; called "The Cursed"

OSTERLAND northern kingdom ruled by Har

PEVEN ancient lord of Aum

RAEDERLE daughter of Mathom of An

RAITH the lord of Hel

RE OF AUM offended an ancient lord of Hel, and in trying to insure his safety, allowed the lord of Hel to trap him on his own estate

RHU fourth morgol of Herun; built the seven walls surrounding Crown City; died seeking the answer to a riddle; full name Dhair-rhuwyth

ROOD Mathom's younger son; brother of Duac and Raederle

RORK high lord of Umber

RYE, TOBEC trader

Sec an Earth-Master
Seric the High One's watcher; trained by the wizards at Lungold
Sol of Isig dead son of Danan of Isig; died at the door of the cave of the Lost Ones at the bottom of Isig Mountain; cut the stones for the stars on the harp Yrth made
Spring Oakland dead mother of Morgon of Hed; wife of Athol
Stone, Harl farmer of Hed
Strag, Ash trader of Kraal
Suth an ancient wizard

Talies a Lungold wizard
Tel one of the Riddle-Masters of the college at Caithnard
Teril Son of Rork Umber
Thistin of Aum current lord of Aum, under Mathom
Tir Earth-Master; Master of Earth and Wind
Tirunedeth harper to the Morgol Cron, ancient ruler of Herun
Tol small fishing-town in Hed
Tor a territory in Imris
Trika a guard in the Morgol's service
Tristan Morgon's sister

Umber Midland territory of Ymris
Uon harpmaker of Hel, three centuries before
Ustin of Aum ancient king of Aum who died of sorrow over the conquering of Aum by An

Vert daughter of Danan Isig

Wind Plain the site in Ymris of Wind Tower and a ruined city of the Earth-Masters
Wind Tower only complete structure in the ruined city on Wind Plain; top of tower cannot be reached
Wold, Lathe great-grandfather of Morgon of Hed
Wold, Sil farmer of Hed

Xel wild cat belonging to Astrin, gift of Danan Isig

YLON an ancient King of An; son of a queen of An and the shape-changer Corrig
YMRIS a kingdom ruled by Heureu Ymris
YRTH a powerful, blind wizard at Lungold
YRYE home of Har of Osterland

ZEC OF HICON craftsman who did the inlay work on the harp with three stars

12.26.21
Given by Barbara Searle to Matthew Liddy, her son, at a moment of peril + confusion, connecting despair from 1989 to 2021.
Oven to ocean.